I0729141

ALSO BY WILLIAM COOK HAIGWOOD

Journeying the Sixties: A Counterculture Tarot

The Davenport Trilogy

A Time of Unsearchable Things

Songs of Surveillance:
Stories of Spying, Watching and Eavesdropping

ESCAPE
of the
ALIENATED WAR BABIES

ESCAPE
of the
ALIENATED
WAR BABIES

william cook haigwood

Printed in the United States of America

Published by Cooskie Creek Press

Library of Congress Cataloging-in-Publication Data

ISBN 978-1-7337262-2-1

For Claire Marie

INGER

I nger chatted up her seatmate, a lean, strong-jawed attorney who spoke for an hour about trade law. Inger could not grasp a word though it didn't matter since the attorney's forthright charm, penetrating hazel eyes and melodic tenor made her wet.

Yeah, I would, she thought halfway into their flight, as if returning home also returned her to the full bloom of a mutinous adolescence. Inger imagined him alone with her, his hands on her body. He would take her somewhere. She visualized a hotel room, an apartment, even the backseat of a car. She would ball him.

And as their plane began its final approach she had not changed her mind though it was clear, as the attorney hurriedly buckled his brief case and left to use the rest room, that sex with Inger was the farthest thing from his mind.

Inger squeezed her thighs together and closed her eyes. Since childhood it had been enough simply to imagine something both risky and also tender, enough to arouse her and, as she discovered in the first bumpy months of her puberty, also to comfort her. She was surprised then to know few other girls who shared her capacious sexual interest or her urgent response to it. Most seemed to consider sex too dangerous or serious even to guardedly abide, though many also thought falling in love would be the very best fun and said so. This was not the case in northern Europe where sex was fun and love was serious and Inger, blessed with a discreet Norwegian aunt who put her on the pill, could have her way with herself.

Inger's plane descended into the fog and she wondered which bus would take her from the airport and across the bay to Berkeley. Her brother, a fraternal twin and both ally and antagonist, would meet her. Once she checked the schedule and figured out a time and place of arrival, she phoned him.

"Karl?" Inger asked.

"Yeah, Inger…you here now?" the voice answered directly.

"A bus will drop me at the Hotel Shattuck," Inger reported. She gave an approximate time.

"OK," answered Karl. "Have you eaten?"

"Airplane food," said Inger. "I'm fine. Don't go to any trouble."

"OK," said Karl. "OK."

And that was it. Karl was cool but welcoming. It was their family way. Few in Inger's family spoke very much, probably because so few listened. Though she received occasional letters and cards from Karl in Norway, it was the first time in nearly five years she again heard his voice.

Inger had shown her passport in New York. Scenes of rioting in American cities filled the screens of the airport's television monitors, which she watched with no context for her interest. She passed quickly through customs. Oslo was one of the world's quieter capitals and her Nordic reddish blonde hair and green eyes seemed welcome everywhere. She had spent four years in Europe, four and half if she counted the first few months of 1968. But she was an American, and she was coming home.

In her senior year at Berkeley High School Inger fell into her first irresistible attraction engendered by a handsome, mellifluous English teacher named Fitz who swept her away and became her first lover. The risk was intensely satisfying and the sex astonishingly adept and delicious. And when he deserted her she had nothing with which to replace him. No mere boy would do. It was as if her identity, so enmeshed with the lust of her teacher, no longer existed. She would look in the mirror and not see anyone she resembled.

And then, and quickly, she realized she was pregnant.

Her father, Lars, a deeply religious man, could not understand the sexual needs that grew his 17-year-old daughter into a passionate victim or the vulnerabilities blooming from her subsequent loneliness and disillusion. She would not tell anyone the name of the father. A suicide attempt, likely more histrionic than intentional, brought her into therapy.

The consensus was that Inger needed both an abortion and a change of scenery and her father's native Norway offered both. Abortion had just been legalized in the country and an aunt's family included a physician who approved the procedure for Inger. The aunt supported Inger as she ended her pregnancy and then enrolled in a local art school. Inger loved Oslo and excelled at art, though her appetite for fun sometimes strained the limits of her host family's protestant values. Eventually she ended up in Copenhagen, and once as far south as Munich, while for two years she waitressed and modeled her way along the popular routes of a transient and continental bohemia. When her money ran out, she returned to Oslo with the realization she really wanted to go home.

Inger returned now as both fledgling artist and experienced outlaw though which would rule remained uncertain. Inger had her ideas but no plan other than to spend a first few weeks at her brother's new house among the eucalyptus and cedars in the Berkeley hills. From there her first steps likely would be down hill as she imagined walking into the city to look for work while combing the bayside flats for an affordable rental.

And the city of her childhood was at war, just as the country was at war. There were marches, protests and riots. Martin Luther King had been assassinated the previous month and what seemed a vicious national election was all over the papers. Would it be Nixon and Kennedy again? Another Kennedy? That much she had read.

"Berkeley's been at war for years," her brother told Inger when he picked her up at the hotel. "It started just about the time you left."

And the battles continued, students marching and organizing against war, against racism, against scab-picked grapes and increasing police violence.

"What are you going to do here?" Karl asked as he drove Inger north into the city's eastern hills. "You look older."

"Older than what?" Inger answered. "You look older, too, Karl. More than four years. Are you surprised?"

Karl was married now and his wife was pregnant. The new home, which he built himself, was not a year old. At the age of 19 he had foregone college to join his father's home-building business, *Lars Voll Construction*. All his life Karl had been the good son, which Inger interpreted to mean the good twin.

When their mother left Lars, the twins were ten years old. Mother drove to New York with her lover and Inger and Karl stayed with their father who alone raised them. Inger remembered the frustration of trying to live like a girl, and then a young woman, in what became an inter-generational bachelor pad. Lars demanded compliance, which Karl gave easily and Inger did not.

Visits with their mother were expensive and infrequent and ended altogether when the twins entered their restless, surly puberty. Mother phoned from time to time but said little and asked less, so distant was she from the facts of their lives. Letters and cards continued for a while, one birthday card each year addressed to both children, until they also stopped. The children did not respond and all communication ended. It seemed that in her mother's experience, Inger existed only as one-half of a litter—a child linked perpetually with her brother to a perilous and painful delivery and never regarded in her own right.

"You don't seem happy to see me," Inger announced flatly.

Her brother swallowed hard and backtracked. He worried more that his new wife would not like Inger more than Inger would overstay her welcome. His worries were specific and understood.

"How long will you be staying?" asked Karl. Inger thought she heard concern in his voice.

"I won't stay too long," she answered.

"Inger, that's not the goddamned point," Karl shouted.

"Then tell me what you're really feeling," shouted Inger. "You seem worried. Don't just stuff it."

"OK. We don't smoke in the house. If you want to smoke a cigarette you need to go outside."

And like that they again were brother and sister, intimately angry with each other while remaining viscerally distant and arguing over procedures of living that fed a lifelong battle for control. In better times they joked about a Scandinavian reticence to express emotions.

And through their entwined lives together they had perfected a thorough and mutual repression.

"What are you going to do here?"

It did not help that Karl's wife, Annalisa, asked Inger the same question her brother asked.

"Haven't decided yet," Inger answered briskly. "I've only been back for an hour."

Inger was accustomed to making herself welcome to strangers and for two days, while battling jet lag and a migraine, she did all the dishes, vacuumed the house and cleaned both bathrooms. She accompanied Annalisa to the food co-op, insisted on paying for a week's groceries and carried them to the car for her very pregnant sister-in-law who followed behind. And she went outside to smoke, usually wrapped in a parka against the cool May fog blowing off the bay.

By the third day, Inger was rested, her body's rhythms at last aligned with local time. She was ready to look for work. Her brother agreed to lend her his truck. She would drop him at his work site, a new home under construction in the Oakland hills, and pick him up in the evening.

"You know Larry?" Karl later asked.

Inger had jumped from the truck to run rashly onto the property and toward one of Karl's workers, a tall, young man with a deep chocolate complexion who was driving nails into recently erected four-by-fours. The worker saw Inger and greeted her with a smile before turning to see concern in the eyes of his young boss. Inger grabbed the man and swallowed his muscular frame in a swaddling hug.

"Larry...from high school. You don't remember?"

Karl did not. Larry had shared Inger's English class with Mr. Fitz. Inger asked for Larry's phone number, which he gave as if made naked by the witnessing of his employer. Inger told Larry she was staying with Karl, and that might have been the end of it had Larry not worried about dating the boss's sister. Inger made it clear with her intense, parting embrace that no such worry concerned her.

two

Inger's brother Karl and his wife Annalisa projected their attempted versions of the ideal marriage while each privately reckoned with the possible extent of its failure. A baby seemed to Inger the perfect postponement of reckoning and she was happy to help Annalisa as long as she was around.

After three months of Nordic celibacy during which she packed suitcases and arranged her trip home, Inger was eager for a date with Larry. When she phoned him the next evening he asked her to go with him for dinner. He picked her up and drove her to a pizza garden on the north side of the campus. It had been a high school favorite where a fake ID sometimes worked to get a beer.

Inger peered at Larry from within a harsh shadow thrown by the light of one of the garden's outdoor lanterns. He was more attractive than she remembered, his lean boyish frame now filled out. He appeared taller, if that were possible, and his eyes conveyed an electrifying focus sharper than that of the flummoxed teen she had known in high school. He seemed to shift self-consciously, his dark features an inventory of qualities Inger found attractive. He sat upright, framed by strong, broad shoulders. He wore a white turtleneck that softened his clear, brown eyes. He appeared shy but comfortably present.

"You been in Norway?" he asked uncertainly. "You gotta tell me about that."

Inger was ready to push through any door that opened between them. Her eyes widened, burnished and alert. She rambled on for at least five minutes.

"I left Berkeley a total wreck," she concluded. "I'm back now."

"Whatcha gonna do?" Larry asked simply.

It seemed the first or second question everyone asked her. What one "did" or planned to "do" seemed a defining question and, in Inger's recent experience, uniquely American.

"I'm an artist. We'll see what I can do with that."

Inger had taken control of her interest in Larry and regained her sense of the evening. She turned the question back to him, asking what he'd been doing since high school.

"This and that," he answered vaguely. "Went into the trades. Working for your brother."

More beers arrived while their words, at first cautious, began to flow and then accelerate. Thoughts turned into remembrances that became stories, opinions and, finally, jokes. Beer and pizza sustained their conversation while each examined the other with intent. Larry was drawn to Inger, unaware she already had made up her mind. As she climbed into Larry's GTO, Inger fell unsteadily into the driver's seat where Larry caught her and held her.

It was good sex though it had been long enough for Inger that anything might have felt good. Larry was sweet and his clean studio at the back of a triplex in a working class neighborhood on Ninth Street was spare but welcoming. He took her out to breakfast at a nearby seafood restaurant and drove her back to Karl's hillside home before noon. It was Saturday and Larry could see Karl through the kitchen window as he pulled up in front of the house on Hilldale.

"Your brother's not gonna fire me for fucking you, is he?" Larry asked Inger as she pulled herself together.

"He's not like that," she answered. "He's OK. He even smokes grass."

Larry gave her a suspicious look.

"I'll phone you tomorrow about the cottage," he said. "Gotta check with The Rev, but last I heard it was available."

More precious than Larry's body was Larry's link to a place where Inger could live alone. Larry's grandparents had a home in southwest Berkeley with a separate cottage in the back. They were old and frail but also the founders of the Wiggins feast. Grandpa Wiggins was one of the last Pullman porters to buy land in town. The Southern Pacific Railroad for decades used Oakland as a crew change point and black Pullman porters, enriched by generous tips and after a long labor battle that brought union salaries, began to buy homes in west Oakland and southwest Berkeley. Old Mr. Wiggins had a chance and took it. He bought one parcel near the bay and five years later bought another. Larry did not himself own anything but a candy red Ford truck but he was a Wiggins and thereby an always potential proprietor and heir.

The last cottage occupant was Larry's older brother, Sam, who a year before enlisted in the army.

"He's in Nam," Larry said. "He's doin' his last year."

Old Mr. Wiggins' son, Rev. Josiah Wiggins, was Larry's father and the one who handled his grandparents' affairs. He said Inger could rent the cottage month-to-month and pay part of the rent by providing a few hours of daily care for the elderly Wiggins. Inger was agreeable and by the end of the following week left her brother's spacious home in the hills to take up residence in the barely furnished cottage that, with her rent discount, cost $80 a month.

Larry helped to move her in and gifted her with a bottle of wine. After it was opened, he spent the night. In the morning Inger met Joe and Billie Wiggins who in their early eighties sat stolidly at a kitchen table and drank coffee while Larry fixed their breakfast.

"You need to poach the eggs…can you poach eggs?" Larry asked.

Inger nodded and borrowed a ballpoint from a shelf to take notes. She would fix the couple's breakfast on weekdays and then help them into the living room where they spent most of their day. She would help Joe with his walker and clean the bathroom twice a week. On weeknights she would spend an hour between 7 and 8 helping them get ready for bed. They were still able to dress themselves but falls were a worry. A hired aide arrived at noon to fix lunch and stayed with the couple through the dinner hour. Larry's family took care of them on the weekends.

"It's this or the old folks' home," Larry said jokingly.

"You stop it, Larry!" the old man shouted.

Larry smiled.

"See? Don't let him sass you, Inger. He won't hurt no one."

Inger was happy to leave her brother's house. She could smoke in the cottage. She could welcome whomever she wished and whenever she wished. A California spring's reliably clement mornings heated the land and as she lounged half-naked in her tiny backyard she felt happy at last to be home.

Within a week Inger had enrolled in a summer art class at Laney

College in Oakland and, with money running out, needed a job. Larry asked her what she could do and she said usually she waitressed but also modeled for art studios or photographers.

"Check out the Barb," said Larry.

It was a weekly tabloid that reported radical Berkeley politics and featured pages of want ads for models and more.

Inger bought a copy from a street vendor, the paper's black masthead a skeletal horse and rider charging into the darkness among scrawled cursive letters that spelled out *Berkeley Barb*. Inside, beyond stories and photos of a grape boycott, drug busts by "pigs," Vietnam protests, student strikes, and a long feature devoted to a peyote cultist named Charlie Brown who lived in a teepee on the front lawn of an Arch Street home, Inger found several pages of advertising, including four columns of job listings.

Several ads advertised for women or couples to model for photographers and filmmakers in San Francisco. Models were wanted for still photos and for movie work. She had done this. It paid well in Europe and she thought she could do it again. She wrote down an address on Powell Street and tucked the slip of paper into her purse.

In an embrace, Inger easily forgot the entire world. And as she lay under Larry in the crepuscular darkness of a forested meadow she was taken completely by the convulsions of her punctual come. Larry quickly followed and Inger held on tightly, exhaling an involuntary moan as his urgent lunges were transformed into lilting, light bounces. Eventually he fell over and beside her on the blanket they had spread for an afternoon picnic on a saddled bluff high in the ridges of Tilden Park. Inger was quiet for a moment until tears formed in her eyes and she rolled over to hunch into a protective ball.

"You OK?" asked Larry. "Whatsa matter?"

"Fitz brought me here," said Inger. "In high school."

Larry heard Inger's words as a confession and pressed her for more details. She told him.

"I went back to school to find him," she said. "He's not there anymore. Someone told me he's teaching art history at a junior college near Sacramento."

"What did you want from him?" Larry asked.

"Nothing," answered Inger. "Actually, I wanted to give him something."

"What?" asked Larry.

"I was thinking forgiveness," Inger answered.

Larry was quiet as they hiked back down the hill. It was nearly dark when they arrived at the trailhead and found his truck. It was nearly seven o'clock when they arrived at the cottage. Inger invited Larry to stay but he declined.

"You got my grandparents to get ready for bed," Larry said smiling. "Go on, get in there. I'll see you tomorrow."

Inger felt a chill from Larry and wondered if she hadn't said too much about Fitz. She walked to the main house where Joe and Billie were already in their pajamas and watching television.

"We're fine, darlin'" Billie said. "You go on and get yourself some rest."

Inger loved the body to which she was born. She loved to display it, to look at it, to touch it and to engage it with lovers. Larry returned the following evening. He brought a friend.

"Meet Raj," Larry said as he introduced a gaunt, rangy white male. His jeans hung low on his waist and bunched at his ankles over a pair of black loafers. Inger guessed him to be older than Larry.

"Raj Neville."

The man's large jutting jaw broke into a wide smile at the mention of his full name. He was not as tall as Larry and not as sturdy in the arms and chest. His lean frame and casual posture accentuated an intensity of gaze that made Inger think of a wan poet.

Raj was a self-described bohemian who lived south of the campus. He worked at a local bookstore.

"He digs art," said Larry. "I thought you'd like to meet him."

Raj searched her green eyes with an assertion Inger found connecting.

"Would love to see some of your work," he said.

It was the right question.

"I don't have a lot," Inger answered. "Left most of my paintings in Norway. Would you guys like some wine?"

Larry stayed for a glass and then left just as Inger found her box of sketches and watercolors and opened it on the kitchen table. Raj stayed for another glass of wine. And another. And then spent the night.

Inger enjoyed her new lover's lean, spare body that made his cock seem larger and harder. In her most open arousal she liked to feel its insistent thrusts against her cervix. And Raj took his time with her, teased her into a wet storm before entering her. Larry was sweet, passionate and vibrant but he was too fast. Raj was cool and in control. Each knew something about a woman but not everything and Inger wondered what men actually thought while they were fucking or if they thought anything at all.

three

In her dream Inger did all things from a single impulse. She made love in her dream with an obscure partner whose shadowy form both thrilled and frightened her. She awoke as the cause of all, and also aware she was in someone else's bed, a bed that belonged to Willy her art instructor. She recalled the evening that put her here. And though he was not here, she could hear him in the bathroom washing up.

"Oh...you're awake," he said coolly as he returned to the bedroom.

He was naked in the daylight and appeared different from how he felt in the darkness: his thin wiry arms like sticks thrust into a portly torso she had gripped in the night like a warm, firm egg and that now appeared slovenly and piggish with two brown, hairy nipples flaccid over a protruding white belly under which Willy's petite penis wriggled as he spoke.

"I guess..."

Inger spoke from a place of slumberous discontent. She was awake enough to feel her disappointment but still too tired to be angry. As she looked around Willy's bedroom, took in the paintings on his walls and the many books in a tall, room-length case against the opposite wall, she felt like a fragment barely within his sight. He was the artist she wished to be and so it seemed natural to follow him home after their friendly drinks at a tavern near the college and to revel in his trappings as if she could have what he had or be what he was.

And she was impressed. He was a good teacher. In a week in his class she had found a flow. Her drawings impressed him immediately, and she knew she could draw. He had given her a canvass and helped her to buy a few. Quickly she was applying acrylic in patterns simply to see what emerged before returning to the representational forms she found most rewarding even if they weren't contemporary.

But while the art and conversation were useful and even inspiring, and the drunken sex not anything very special but no worse than what she had known before, the morning after was becoming impossible. She felt like slime under his dirty sheets and his bobbing little dick was too much hair of the dog. She asked for a towel, which Willy grabbed from a shelf and threw to her. Inger wrapped it around her breasts and skipped out of the bed and past her naked, spindly host.

"Need to shower," she shouted without looking back and then closed and locked the bathroom door.

Willy would not drive Inger home and, instead, took her to a bus stop where she could catch the 51 to San Pablo Avenue. He would see her in class and may not have remembered he invited her to an art reception the next Thursday at a gallery on Shattuck Avenue.

"Sorry," said Willy, knowing in the cool morning he had not connected.

Inger thanked him and then confronted him.

"You aren't going to hurt me, are you?"

"Why no," Willy answered hesitantly. "What do you mean 'hurt you'?"

"Give me a bad grade because I won't fuck you anymore," Inger said directly.

Willy laughed nervously. He had wished to ask Inger not to tell anyone they had sex. Now he said nothing.

On the bus ride home she considered her new American sexuality, the most recent taste not even registering as an experience other than in an insincere horny-old-man sort of way. Still, she could count three men in three weeks and so far her favorite was Raj for sex and Larry for cuddles and she would not fuck Willy again.

Since adolescence Inger had been aware of a throbbing hum, a background noise of sexual assertion that was everywhere, in every step, turn, grip and shudder. She heard it in voices. Saw it in the streets. Felt it in the wind She recognized it in people's faces and in footsteps in front and behind her. It was a tectonic shove she could not ignore. Her resonance was pitch perfect and nothing could keep the sexual noise of human experience out of her ranging awareness. She had but to reach out and touch it, or to be touched, to fall into reliable syncopation with the pleasure of living. It would never be her need to manage a thrill that so conveniently and comfortably managed her. And it was pleasure, almost always, until it was not.

Until someone, anyone, like a cagey capitalist would try to own it in some way, as if sex were coal or gas or petrol that could be stored and priced and sold. She wrote these thoughts and feelings regularly into a journal.

I could physically and emotionally love and sleep with everyone. I could kiss them all; have sex with them all. I can't stop with one. Who can stop with one lover? Bodies exist to love and the body is the soul, bodies the only house a soul can live in. This is the touching of another. I was created for this. We all are created for the warmth of others.

God, I get so turned on just thinking about this. I have always or at least since I noticed I had a body. Nature is, otherwise, a dull affair: soundless, senseless, without color. What of seeing, hearing, taste, feeling and thought? What of wishing and loving? I suppose I'm a wild one to give myself up so easily.

No, I'm not easy. That's a mean thing to say and does not apply. I'm not even available. I choose to fuck, and with whom I fuck. Souls and bodies go fornicating everywhere so why not mine? It's the only life I have.

Larry took Inger to dinner at Brennan's, an Irish cafeteria and bar west of San Pablo Avenue.

"Great turkey legs," he said to her. "Great gravy."

He bought her an Irish whiskey, and another.

"You found work yet?" he asked as they started to drink.

"Some prospects," she answered. "Modeling. I used to model in Europe and it paid well. I have a few leads."

She didn't tell him that all her leads were culled from the *Barb* personals and that she would drive to the City soon and knock at a door on Powell Street.

"You gonna do porn?" Larry asked directly.

Inger was embarrassed. She watched herself speak the next words that came to mind.

"Some nudity, I suppose. What's the big deal?"

There were no footlights but she thought herself on stage and with Larry her audience. He seemed to be waiting for another act while she felt shy in an uncomfortable reckoning. The world of real work frightened her because she had so little to offer it.

"You are one beautiful woman," Larry responded. "Lots of jobs for pretty women," he said with authority. "Don't sell yourself short."

Larry's attention filled the rest of the evening as they munched gamey flavored turkey meat and each drank a glass of cheap red wine. Yes, she would screw him. Of course she would. He was a sweetheart and as they drove home he sang to her a chorus of *Ain't That Peculiar* by Marvin Gaye.

"You missed a lot a Motown," he told Inger. "Hear any of it in Norway?"

Inger remembered the Beatles and the hot, gushing passion of young girls giving up their unrequited sexual attention to four happy English musicians who wished only to hold their hands.

His singing filled the car until a bright white light, and then a red one flooded the rear view mirror and Larry pulled over.

"Shit. The pigs," he muttered.

He warned Inger to "just keep cool" while he handled the interaction. Larry jumped from the car and held his hands high.

"I got no gun!" he shouted in the direction of the Berkeley police car behind him.

An officer in a khaki uniform approached.

"Put you hands down," the officer instructed.

Larry dropped his arms and stood aside.

"I stopped you because you drove through a red light at the Gilman intersection," the officer said. "I need your license and registration."

"It wasn't red," Larry shouted. "Drove through a light? That's a new one."

"Who's in the car?" the officer asked.

"What's it to you?" Larry answered curtly. "She's a friend."

The officer ignored Larry and walked over to Inger's side of the car.

"Please get out, ma'm," he stated firmly.

Inger grabbed her purse.

"Leave that in the car and get out," the officer said again before taking Larry's license and registration back to the police car.

"What is this about?" Inger shouted at Larry across the hood of the car.

"It's bullshit," he said. "Don't move unless they tell you to. If they ask you anything, don't say shit. They can't make you talk."

The officer returned and said he would search the car.

"You not gonna even ask?" Larry said. "You gonna read me my Miranda rights?"

The officer waved and called his partner forward.

"This is starting to feel like resisting arrest," the officer said to Larry.

He instructed Larry to stand away from the car and told his partner to search the backseat. Under Larry's leather jacket the officer pulled out a black beret with a button on it.

"*Try the cops, not Huey*," the lead officer read as he handled the beret and the button.

"Sam, we got ourselves a Black Panther."

The cop told Larry he had the right to remain silent.

"I know my fucking rights," Larry shouted.

"Well, we'll let the judge sort that out," answered the cop as he pushed Larry against the car and told him to extend his arms behind him. In a moment Larry was handcuffed and walked slowly back to the police car.

"Call my dad," Larry shouted at Inger.

The second officer offered Inger a ride but she refused.

"What are you doing with this guy?" the officer asked her pointedly.

Inger ignored the question.

"I'll walk," she said. "Give me my purse."

four

Inger resisted the vassalage of her childhood and since returning had avoided seeing her father. Karl said their father had changed, had softened into his new wife's love and, while still very religious, was less judgmental.

"He asks about you," Karl said. "Wonders why you don't call."

Inger said she would.

And when she did she heard his familiar orotund voice though it was quieter and more tentative than when they last spoke. It had been at least a year and he asked after Inger with what she thought to be sincere interest.

"I'm good," she answered.

"Aunt Elle is good," she said. "She sends her love."

Inger wished to call her father by name, to say "Lars" instead of "Papa." Instead, she did not name him.

He hoped to see her soon. He wanted her to meet his wife.

"You will like her," he promised as he enunciated precisely each English syllable. "Pamela…"

But nothing followed after he mentioned her name, as if the name might be enough to engender his daughter's interest, if not affection.

Instead, Inger succumbed to a familiar futility and to the space made from her interminable dependency on the man who since her earliest memories had ruled her like a Titan. She could not let go and could not commit.

"I'll call again soon," she said at last. "I have to go now."

If Inger lacked anything, it was the blanching absence of a mother in her life. She was aware that what really frightened her was a dreaded meeting with Lars' new partner and seeing his affection for a woman other than her mother. Inger understood her mother ran out on Lars who therefore was entitled to his hurt then and his happiness now. But try as she might she could not experience her father as he might himself.

On a warm May morning Inger celebrated nearly a month in her new old country. She still did not have a job though she knew of an opening for a server at an Oakland bar near Alcatraz and Telegraph and named the Jug Handle. She had called but not gone by.

"I'm smart," she told Raj as they sat together at the Forum and she sipped a macchiato. "I just don't have a lot of skills. I can draw pictures and type in Norwegian. Know any openings?"

Raj smiled.

"I shelve books at Creed's and play guitar," he said. "Gets me a room to call my own and a couple of beers when I play at Freight and Salvage."

She had seen his room, located at the rear of a converted Craftsman fourplex on Haste Street and so small it must have been the original owner's laundry. Raj slept on a day bed, pushed under a window open to the constant wail of cars accelerating at the intersection below. Inger was immediately grateful for her cottage.

Raj sat tall at their table. Inger noticed he attracted the looks of other women, his curly blond hair and fuzzy three-day beard a textured frame for his open face and wide, brown eyes. He was cute, thought Inger. He was also poor, though his frank indifference to poverty embellished his charm. He had shown Inger his room and now waited with her for a friend.

"Here he comes," Raj said as another attractive man approached the table, a man who stepped sturdily forward and whose bulky leather boots shouted each step with a noisy crack. His name was Yitzhak.

"It means *he will laugh* in Yiddish," Raj announced. "Or something like that. Right, Raymond?"

Yitzhak frowned at Raj's use of his birth name.

"Sorry, man. Yitzhak, this is Inger."

Inger smiled and extended her hand, which Yitzhak ignored. He said nothing though his receded eyes widened as he examined Inger from her face to her ankles.

"Inger is celebrating her first month back in town. Let's get stoned."

Raj spoke abruptly and rose from the table. He picked up his rucksack before Yitzhak could sit down.

The three walked up Telegraph Avenue toward the university, Inger mildly aroused by the big men on each side of her. Together they strolled into a wide view of the campus campanile, a large, puncturing needle in a brilliant azure sky. The men led Inger east across a bridge and along a wooded creek that emerged below the college football stadium where a shortcut put them at the foot of a hillside smothered in brush and eucalyptus trees. A ten-minute climb and they were at the apex of one of a hundred Berkeley hills, one that provided an enwrapping view of the entire region, its buildings and bridges and bay spread out from the campus like the fields of Oz.

Raj found a fallen tree trunk where all three sat as he fumbled in his pack for a rolled joint and a lighter. In a moment Inger was sucking up a hit and passing the joint to Yitzhak who drew in deeply as the joint's tip flamed red hot. Inger felt immediately a flood of bodily relaxation as her mind raced wildly along a gantlet of wordless impressions. She liked Raj's dope. She had smoked others but his moved her deeply and whether it was the weed or Raj she could not yet say.

An hour passed in a churn of laughter, foolish words, and finally a vast, black hole of silence as Yitzhak wandered away and out of sight.

"Is he OK?" Inger asked.

"Most of the time," Raj answered. "Say, it's a warm night. I've got my sack and I'd like to spend the night up here. Are you cool with that?"

Inger was surprised and waited to answer.

"I'm cool, I guess," she answered. "But what about your friend?"

"He'll walk you back to town," said Raj. "Right, Yitzhak?"

Yitzhak turned and nodded.

As Raj plunged into the forest, Yitzhak led Inger back to the shortcut and guided her along the darkening creek and through the shadows in the woods. At the campus gate he waved her forward.

"Street's over there. You'll find the bus stop."

Yitzhak spoke quickly before turning west toward town and walking away.

The dope had made the hike back an affecting thrill and in her very active imagination Inger saw Yitzhak as a warrior, another Cuchulain crossing Strawberry Creek as Odysseus might the wine dark sea. It aroused her enormously. She found a phone booth at the student union building and called Larry's number.

"You remember me in high school?" Larry said as he sat up in Inger's bed and lit his cigarette and one for her.

"Pomade in my hair. That blue double-breasted jacket, the big collared white shirt and the fat kerchief around my neck? Damn! You'd think I wanted to look like Elvis. Maybe I did. Not anymore. Yeah, I'm a Panther. I'm one big black motha-fuckin' Panther."

Larry made a scary face at Inger, eyes wide and teeth broad and goofy. Inger laughed and then choked on the smoke of her first puff.

"Can't believe you never heard of us," Larry mused. "We need a Norwegian chapter."

"No damn black people in Norway, though," added Larry. "Right?"

Inger laughed again and rolled over on her side of the bed to drop ashes in an empty wine glass. Larry swiped at her naked bottom.

"Hard to think it was just five years ago we were in school together. Always thought you were cute, and so damned smart. Did you ever wonder if…never mind. Anyway, can you believe what's happened? They killed Martin. Now they killin' Panthers. You think being stopped by the police was an accident? Once they found out I'm a Panther I knew I was goin' to jail. A course, they didn't charge me. But they took my picture and made me take off my clothes and wrote a big, long report. They want us to know who's boss. You watch. I'm gonna get followed like every other Panther. Bobby and

Huey and Eldridge. We all criminals just for breathing. Those pigs won't stop. And we sure as hell ain't gonna stop. So what do you think's gonna happen?"

Inger froze, pulling the sheet up to cover her exposed breasts.

"Someone's going to get hurt?"

She posed her answer as a question and it was Larry's turn to laugh.

"Oh, hell yes, woman!" Larry shouted. "It might become a war. You ain't been here long enough to know what's goin' on. But we're black now, honey and, as we like to say, we ain't goin' back."

Larry's voice danced at the edge of a raucous rage that excited Inger. She pushed up against the crazy man who talked like a gang leader, though the only gang member was himself. She scooted down to snuggle into his angry, muscular thigh and then took his soft penis in her hand and then into her mouth, tasting what was left of them both from the night before.

"Damn, do you ever get enough?"

Larry let out a cheeky howl as he settled back on his pillow.

A crowd packed Willy's gallery opening, held in the back rooms of an art supply store on College Avenue that was popular with Laney art students. Willy had pulled together seven recent graduates for a summer show. Willy's minimalist rainbow paintings were prominent and filled two walls with large, mostly blank canvasses dabbed with lines of primary color.

Inger surprised Willy who did not expect her to attend. Inger herself was surprised to see Raj, who said one of his friends was an artist in the show.

"Check out Stan's work," Raj said to Inger.

He pointed toward a hallway.

Raj and Inger wandered through the gallery, brushing fractiously against others who drank and jabbered and stood for a few moments before the paintings of artists they knew. Inger recognized fellow students and a few members of the art faculty. She and Raj found a knot of viewers gathered around one artist, the only woman in the show whose name was Eva and who displayed at the very rear of the gallery a series of lithograph nudes rendered in uncanny detail. The work was striking as it floated in a sensual pool above the sea of lines, bars, and disjointed constructs of the other artists.

Inger heard a man call it "pussy art" before he walked up to a print to examine closely the discomposed ruby shades of an apparent opening, red like a slash of sunlight around which coalesced the springing legs and torso of an obvious and large breasted woman. Later as she inspected the frigid black strokes and intersecting rectangles of Stanley Slinger's *Big Black Motherfucker,* Inger was acutely aware of its many uses of lines and curves. They were oppositional in their expressions of urge and need, of response and rest, of aggression and retreat, of discovery and hiding, though the mechanically drawn and filled-in shapes were austere, cool and minimal. She preferred Eva's erratic searches to Stan's cool declarations, though Stan's large canvasses drew more attention and even more praise.

"This is Inger," Raj said as he approached the artist. "And Inger, this is Stan."

The artist, a slender man with a square chest, long black hair and peacock blue eyes that kindled Inger's unguarded attraction, asked what she did.

"Still life, sketches…I'm working with Willy on a larger canvass," she answered self-consciously. She was embarrassed to sum up years of work in such a trite and uninteresting phrase.

"I might be able to help you," Stan said.

He was full of himself, a co-star of the night's big show and eager to share his power with an attractive underling.

Inger sensed his aggravated attraction to her and knew how to use it.

"You'll need to see some of my work."

Her coy answer was intended to invite his interest without giving the appearance she even cared.

"Yeah. We'll make a time. When are you at Laney?"

Inger prepared another coy offering, a range of times when she thought Stan might be able to come to her cottage.

"Hello," a woman announced as she pushed between Inger and Stan.

"I'm Ginger," she said and, as if creating the artifice of an afterthought, added she was Stan's wife. She wore a one-piece knitted dress, simple in its design but bright with orange and red flavors, that hung at her thighs and ballooned at the shoulders giving her the look of a leggy butterfly.

"It's OK, hon. Inger's an artist," Stan interjected.

"Beautiful dress," Inger offered.

"From Anastasia's," answered Ginger. "Thanks."

Inger sensed Ginger's spousal vigilance. Even if Inger's regard for Stan were purely vocational, she knew immediately she would never sleep with him. Besides, Stan was merely the latest thing in this small regional art world. He would last a while but who knew how long? And Eva's paintings, despite their obscure gallery placement, were the show's secret hit and the only pieces not imitative of something older, larger and better known.

Two glasses of wine tipped Inger outside and into an alley with Raj, Stan and another man named Mack who took a joint from the breast pocket of his blue corduroy jacket, lit it and passed it around. Fog pushed up the alley and chilled Inger.

"Good shit," Stan choked as he passed the joint along to Inger.

"Don't thank me," said Mack who Inger noted was the shortest of the three men but who appeared in command.

"Raj scored this for me. It's from Oaxaca. Right, Raj?"

"So I'm told," Raj answered equivocally as he took the joint from Ingrid.

"What makes shit good?" Inger asked as she exhaled a protracted cloud of smoke.

"You serious?" Mack laughed until he could see that she was.

"It's flavorful, smooth and fast," Mack answered. "And it lasts."

Raj nodded.

"Mack knows his dope," he said to Inger. "He also knows his tequila and his bourbon."

"The burden of the writer's trade," Mack declared. "Drugs and booze. One opens the mind to its lovely demons and the other makes them tolerable while they speak."

"Mack's a reporter."

Stan spoke for the first time.

"Works for the Chronicle."

"I *write* for the Chronicle," Mack responded sarcastically. "Freelance. I'm a stringer and I cover the East Bay. Go places their suit-and-tie reporters can't or won't. They pay me by the inch."

"Man, they give you some heavy gigs," Stan said. "Huey Newton? The strike at Cal? I see your name on a lot of stories. What do they call you? A correspondent? *Mack Bellis, Chronicle correspondent.* That's it."

"Except when I'm writing about art, theater or film. Then I'm just Mack Bellis. Like tonight. "

"So why are you here?" Inger asked.

"I love art. And artists. Especially artists that are my friends."

Mack winked at Stan.

"He's our ticket to fame and fortune," Stan added.

"So where's Joan Brown? I heard she'd be here tonight," Mack asked sharply.

"Don't know. You'll have to check with Willy," said Stan.

"There you are!" a woman's voice shouted into the darkness.

All turned to see Ginger at the back door, her short dress caught by a consolidated breeze and blown up to briefly reveal her naked bottom. Ginger grabbed the hem of her dress like a wayward towel and pulled it down.

Inger retreated into the alley shadows.

"They need you in here, Stan," Ginger shouted.

Again, Ginger eyed Inger suspiciously with a look that inspired Inger's annoyance. She moved closer to Mack in a way she hoped would signal Ginger to leave her alone.

Stan left abruptly followed by Raj.

"What kind of art do you like?" Inger asked Mack.

Inger waited for Mack's answer to her question.

five

Mack praised Eva's lithographs. His words spread out and surrounded Inger like a soft glove. He sat up in her bed to continue their morning discourse on art.

Mack was literate and well read. After driving Inger home the previous evening Mack was invited in for a drink. He first noticed her small bookshelf and had read every book on it. Norman O. Brown, George Bataille, D.H. Lawrence, Anais Nin, Doris Lessing. He knew her books by the names of their authors and was the first male guest to tell her more about what she read than what she knew. He found a recent dog-eared copy of *Art Forum* in her bathroom. A friend of his had written the lead article about Diane Arbus. Mack's interest was impressive and arousing and, inevitably, the key to her heat if not her heart.

Sex was good for such a fresh and unexpected linkage of minds and feelings. Her body followed without hesitation, as it usually did but with more awareness than usual. She was kissing flowers and not toads. Mack did not know her heart but did understand her body and her arousal was substantiated by his kind, smart words that after a night of chimerical dreams picked up exactly where he had left off.

"It was a good show. I'll write about it," said Mack. "They are my friends and it's the least I can do, though minimalism often leaves me cold. There has to be something else coming. If this bleak geometry is the last word, then painting is on its last legs. Eva's stuff was revealing and beautiful. It's a new direction—not representational, exactly, but more like the Fauvists or the Surrealists. Expressive and also rooted in real life."

Inger offered to fix Mack breakfast and he accepted. He needed to be at the campus by 11 a.m. It was his day to check in at the university's public affairs office and to rummage among the daily press releases for story leads.

"Mostly boring stuff, but you never know. Ended up once at a press conference for a Nobel Prize winning physicist. Chron editors missed it completely. I saved their butts."

Inger resisted the agony of a likely infatuation by focusing on

Mack's deficiencies. He was short, shorter than all the men she knew save Willy, and his morning mouth reeked of garlic and the previous evening's cheap wine. But he was bright and, more importantly, interested in Inger's life as an artist. He asked to see her drawings and as she spread them across the bed, he described them in a way that pushed her insistently against his body. Breakfast never happened and Mack scrambled out the cottage door desperately late.

Was Inger a hippie?

In Norway she called herself a hippie or a *bohem*, a word more aligned with a free artistic life, though what others called her then didn't matter the way it seemed to matter now. The interviewer had asked if she were a hippie, as if that made any difference one way or another. She would still take off her clothes, still pose for a camera, but what Inger "was" dwelled in her consciousness. And to be conscious also was to be self-conscious, which she was in an environment already scary in its way: a spare room down a dim hall in a Powell Street walk-up, sitting on a lumpy, beige couch in front of a man she had known for moments and who offered her money to pose nude.

"That's it?" Inger asked. "I take off my clothes?"

"Well, sometimes sex can be involved," the man said. "But only if you want to, only if you consent, of course."

"Sex with who?" Inger asked.

"We're usually interviewing couples who give us permission to film them having, well…you know. Sex. Do you have a partner? We could find you a partner. No problem with that. It's just that the sex pays better than the nude stuff."

"Is it legal?" Inger asked.

"No….not yet, anyway," the man admitted. "But it still sells, which is why it pays well. It's kinda like dope. Not legal, but it sells."

The man was young, maybe younger than Inger and dressed in slick, brown polyester slacks, a yellow business shirt and a slender, black tie. And he appeared not at all comfortable as the gatekeeper for a porn studio.

"Tell me what it pays," Inger stated in her best business voice. She had done this before.

"You photograph my naked body. What does that pay?"

"OK, you're hip," the young man mumbled. "I asked if you were a hippie because, frankly, hippie chicks are usually as free as birds and it's a factor in what we anticipate can happen."

"Like if I'm a hippie chick I'm more likely to ball?" Inger asked impudently.

"Well, it does pay more," the young man answered.

"Let's start with just naked," Inger responded.

"Twenty-five dollars for the first session, then we'll see," the young man replied. "Would you get yourself off? Would you allow us to film you getting off?"

Inger absorbed the question for a half a minute before smiling.

"What does that pay?" she asked.

"A hundred," the young man answered.

Had she not already been hired by an Adeline Avenue dive bar to serve drinks Inger might have been more circumspect and reserved during her interview. But with a paycheck nearly in hand, she was emboldened to go for more. Yes, she could get herself "off" though what getting off had to do with what she thought as getting it "on" she could not fully fathom.

It was sex and while it was orchestrated for the benefit of those who would see her through the view of a camera, it could be done poorly or done well and if she were anything, she was confident of her delightful and primal sexuality. Nothing, or at least nothing she could imagine, frightened her about any of it. Unless a partner was involved, in which case other, deeper concerns took hold and would need to be tested and resolved. At least at this point, it wasn't necessary. It seemed that in this special arena she might have as much work as she wanted and would be paid relatively well for it.

She thought herself a very smart woman but also a woman with very few employable skills. Five years before she would have been housewife material: virginal, sexy, certifiably fertile, clever but not competitive and easily attracted to good men. Perhaps she still was a wife candidate, except for the virgin part. And she sometimes made poor choices with the easy men she met. And it was too easy, she thought sometimes, though she could smell a good man a mile away, smell all of them at once, which was more than many or most women could manage. Much more.

A warm Friday late in May was the last day Inger could play without thinking of work. She had let her savings fall under $200 and the Jug Handle's server job started just in time. Two dollars an hour plus tips. Three dollars if she worked topless. Her workday would begin at 9 p.m. and ended at 2 a.m. the next morning. Paid every Tuesday. She would earn nearly $100 a week just for showing up and taking off her blouse. She could put Larry's grandparents to bed before going to work.

And the following Wednesday she would have her first photo session at the DeResnay studio in the city. At least a hundred cash if she felt comfortable enough to masturbate.

She saw Raj at the Forum and told him of the first job but not the second.

"I'll come in sometime," Raj said.

"I'll buy you a coke," Inger offered with a laugh. "It's a dump but I met two of the other girls and they said everything's cool. No touching allowed."

"That's too bad," said Raj.

They walked together toward the campus where Raj suggested they share a joint under the taller Eucalyptus trees near the creek west of the biology building. They passed behind a crowd gathered for a rally at the steps of Sproul Hall. Inger heard the amplified voice of a woman who spoke ardently of a student revolution that would topple the "corrupt western centers of capitalist oppression."

"We can end this war!" the woman shouted. "We can end all wars. We can!"

Those in the crowd whistled and applauded as the woman left her place in front of a stand-up microphone and another speaker replaced her.

Inger searched the steps for a view of the woman, whose voice resonated with euphuistic defiance. She was surprisingly small and thin and dressed in black jeans and a white sleeveless top that exposed the soft, muscular curves of her upper arms. Straight black hair fell to the woman's shoulders from under an even blacker beret. Inger could not see her face.

"Who's that?" she asked Raj, who turned to squint in the

direction Inger pointed.

"Bronwyn?" Raj answered. "Bronwyn DeGroot. She's been around since the FSM. Activist and one hell of a speaker. I see her at the Forum from time to time. Helped her get the Bowditch Street commune on board with the grape boycott. She's one tough woman. Started out in '63 registering blacks to vote in Mississippi. Knew James Chaney before he was murdered."

"Who's James Chaney?" Inger asked.

Raj gave Inger a flummoxed look.

"You were in Europe. Long story," Raj answered. "Let's go get stoned."

Inger waited in a windowed studio, her naked body shrouded in a sheet. She tried to remember she was simply doing business though the terms produced a tumult of anxiety as she imagined how and if she would control her time before a camera. She was accustomed to posing, to being isolated among trivial delays while standing or sitting naked or while someone else told her what to do. In this instance, she was the one to decide. Would the photographer ask her to touch herself? Would she simply volunteer? A hundred dollars was guaranteed.

The door opened and a young, shorthaired man loped over to a tripod and attached a camera. He wore a dress shirt and slacks, much like the younger man who interviewed her.

"Let's get started," he said without looking up.

Inger waited. She would need eye contact before she could respond.

The man turned to her and said nothing until he filled the silence between them with his clear and curious eyes. He appeared older than Inger first imagined, though his interested eyes gave him a look of boyish eagerness.

"I'm sorry," he said in a melodic warble. "I'm Jeff and you are…."

"Inger," she answered.

"We're starting with some standard still poses?" Jeff stated as a question. A light meter hung from his neck and dangled near the crew bottom of a dark green sweatshirt.

Inger nodded.

"And then I'll film something extra if you're up to it?" he asked again.

"For a hundred, right?" answered Inger.

"Actually, $150," said Jeff. "I'd give you $200 if I could."

"We'll see," Inger answered, flattered by Jeff's apparent compliment.

"That's fine. You just get comfortable while I adjust the lights and the lens. Want a glass of wine?"

Inger hesitated.

"It's fine. Really. I'm having one. I'm nervous, too."

The wine lightened Inger's body and Jeff began to photograph her, asking first that she drape the sheet across her upper torso like a toga, that she turn and then whirl for an effect of motion. He complimented her generously, praising her delicate steps and intuitive responses. He asked her to remove the sheet as he removed his camera from the tripod. He followed behind her, again asking that she step and sweep and then turn to face him, to look deeply into his lens as she grew accustomed to the persistent snaps of his camera shutter.

Not so bad, Inger thought, as she followed an instruction to lie on a fluffy, faux fur rug. Jeff approached from a low position and asked Inger to assume a series of bending and crawling positions, then asked her to lie on her back and face upward as he stood slowly and backed away, as if understanding perfectly the exact perimeter of her private space. The night before she had spent her first time waitressing at a topless bar, pushing past loud patrons who would slide up next to her and bump her breasts while she balanced a tray of drinks. The tips were good. But so far this was easier. And it paid more.

"Let me put on some music," Jeff said and walked to the back of the studio, bathed now in an amber glow thrown by the sun's reflection in the wide windows of an adjacent building. The sound of a single piano seeped from a set of small speakers. Inger could not name the tune, though it was a familiar classical piece that further relaxed her into a reverie of indistinguishable memories.

Jeff's words were softer under the music and quite suddenly captivating, even ravishing, in their generous regard for Inger's responsive movements and, increasingly, the contours and features of what he described repeatedly as her lovely body. Words could have the equivalence of love or war and Inger succumbed to particular phrases and fragments that seemed to search her like touches for the source of her own pleasure. And she did feel pleasure in a way that surprised her so that when Jeff suggested a break and poured her another glass of wine he became a subject in her inevitable and idiosyncratic fantasy.

After a few minutes Jeff asked if Inger were ready to continue though he did not have to ask. He exchanged his still camera for a larger film camera sitting on a nearby shelf, which he mounted on the tripod. He took Inger's hand and helped her up onto a cream-colored chaise lounge. Jeff was the ravisher but Inger imagined he wanted nothing, that instead he was the object of her capture, the afternoon's true conquest. She touched herself teasingly, aware of Jeff's now silent and rapt attention and her own and immediate control. The whole idea had excited Inger with a suggestion of transgressing danger. She came within minutes, arching in a fervent, shaking spasm. Jeff waited and turned off the camera.

"That was beautiful," he said. "That was really something special."

Inger smiled, stood, found the sheet and wrapped herself in it.

She left with a check from DeResnay Studios for $150 and an appointment for another photo session the following week. Jeff wished to photograph her at a secluded beach location. There would be no sex but other women models would also be present for a group shoot. She was surprised at how comfortable and easily pleasurable it all had been. It just happened, she thought, which was exactly what her girlfriends in high school often said after their first sex. Though such a description seemed to Ingrid simply a way to assert that sex had happened without having to acknowledge their own role in it. Perhaps that was Inger's sense as well, though she admitted to being satisfied at being so comfortably used.

six

In recent weeks Inger had felt briefly uplifted. Her topless waitress job and photo sex work paid reasonably well. But they put her at the edge of America's ragged and forbidden sexual frontier that, similar to all of America's renowned frontiers, was lawless and unprotected. She wondered what it was about this nation that pushed her out of the enjoyment of her body and into a deeper and more lasting fear. How dangerous sex seemed here. It had been so easy in Europe to have a sex life on her own terms. She had returned to a culture where any open attitude about sex was treated as neurosis or, worse, as transgression.

And now she battled a bladder infection and menstrual cramps additionally irritated by scratchy crabs likely picked up from a tipsy back-seat encounter with an attractive bar patron who gave her a ride home. Her body now felt like more than she could manage. She was pushed out of its enjoyment by all the astringent noise coming from the primal opening that reliably actualized so much of her pleasure.

When anxiety prevailed, Inger smoked cigarettes. The last few weeks had brought her enough income to ignore the increasing sums she was spending to smoke, though she did feel the heaviness in her chest and tried to ignore the return of an uncomfortable cough. She waited for Raj one afternoon at a café on Telegraph Avenue and was surprised to see Yitzhak enter. She waved and drew him over to her table. He took a seat, squeezing his large and very muscular frame into a small wooden chair.

"You looking for Raj?" Inger asked. "He's coming."

Yitzhak looked toward her and through her, his gaze vaguely out of alignment with her eyes.

"Don't know," Yitzhak replied. "I'm dancing later. Can't stay long."

"You dance?" Inger asked.

Yitzhak turned away to search the room of crowded tables.

"Yeah," was his laconic reply as he continued to look away. "Flamenco. Spanish Flamenco."

He turned toward Inger, his eyes still unfocused as he now searched the wall, the windows, anything it seemed but her own face and eyes.

"Earth to Yitzhak," Inger announced jokingly. "Where do you dance?"

Yitzhak looked directly at Inger. His pupils appeared as two fierce brown beads that radiated either despair or anger. He had heard the joke. The disturbance behind Yitzhak's eyes thrilled Inger as much as it frightened her. But she tried to ignore it.

"Just kidding, Yitzhak," she responded with a futile sigh. "So is your name *really* Raymond?"

It was the wrong query. To question Yitzhak's name was to question his existence.

"OK, sorry about…"

Before she could finish her apology Yitzhak stood and walked out. It was a quick departure that left Inger both remorseful and peeved. She liked Yitzhak, thought him strong and silent and handsome and in the lack of details could easily build into him a substance of real beauty. And she wished to fuck him, even if he never said another word. She wished to fuck him and for as long as it would take to evoke the helpless grunting sigh of his assailable release.

Raj arrived and asked her if she would like to hear some blues.

"The Hoodoo Man's in town," Raj said. "Mack gave me his tickets."

They shared a cheese pizza at Pepe's before strolling the avenue to Bancroft where they boarded a bus to West Berkeley. At San Pablo Avenue they walked north to the New Orleans House where Junior Wells was to appear for one night only. Raj was a friend of one of the women in a Marin bluegrass band named *Diesel Ducks*, which opened for Wells who appeared late but rocked the full house into a frenzy. Inger bought beers until she was dizzy and Raj was drunk.

"See what you missed in Norway?" Raj chided as Inger walked with him back to her cottage.

"Soul and Blues. Damn, I miss Otis."

"Otis?" Inger asked.

"Otis Redding," said Raj. "*Dock of the Bay*. Heard it? His last hit. I saw him in June at Monterey Pops. He died this winter in a plane crash. The black Buddy Holly. Come over before work tomorrow. I'll put on his album."

Raj cuddled with Inger in her bed. She told him her vulva was a mess but that she would enjoy sucking his cock, which Raj gratefully accepted. Inger enjoyed giving oral sex. At times she liked to be the cool sexual operator who could with her mouth, tongue and hands watch, and also enjoy, the arrival of a partner's orgasmic convulsion. She noticed details unavailable when she was in the throes of her own passion. Later she would replay them to arouse herself.

"Say Raj," she coaxed before he turned over to fall asleep. "Could you ever ball in front of a camera?"

"Guess it would depend on who I was balling," he answered after a befuddled pause.

"What if it were me?" Inger asked again.

"Then I guess it would depend on who was filming," he replied. "Hey, are you serious?"

Inger told him about posing for DeResnay. She described being filmed while she made herself come.

"It was cool. Really. I got very turned on."

Raj sat up in bed.

"Really?" he asked.

"Yeah, and it pays a small fortune."

Raj stirred from his post-fellatio reverie.

"I'm flattered, babe," he answered. "But I wouldn't. Really, I don't know if I could, you know…perform."

"You'd be great," Inger replied encouragingly.

"No…not a chance," Raj concluded. "Sorry. Not in a million years."

He settled back on his pillow and turned toward the wall. After a moment he turned back and asked Inger how much it paid.

Through her art, Inger sought to abet creation. She was not religious like her father. She did not presume what creation was though it was an evident presence that appeared to fill all experience with motivating restlessness. It pushed her obsessive need to apply pen and pencil to paper and paint to canvass. She was helpless to resist it, as helpless as her body was to resist its own urges to eat, to pee, to shit, to sleep, to fuck.

You're not an artist until someone else calls you one she had heard Willy say in class. That made sense in an art gallery but not in a studio where urges to create grew like germs in a petri dish: fluid, prolific, and unrestrained. For now the studio experience meant more to Inger than the gallery. She wished to grow in art but, at least for a while, to grow alone.

As she painted on a Saturday morning in the college studio, she realized there was one exception. Stan arrived later in the morning to work on a painting. He stopped to speak with Inger. He looked at her canvass, an incomplete pastiche of abstract colors spread behind an emerging field of penciled detail that had the vague look of a small army of arms and faces. There was both a context and a story but Stan could not separate them.

"Well, I suppose that's my point," Inger said confidently. "I'm after something I can feel but can't yet see. You know what that's like."

Stan did know. He found Inger's succinct confidence attractive. Inger knew it immediately and wished she didn't. She fathomed Stan as she might herself and understood how an attraction could grow from a nest of shared interests. He was such an attraction to her, as she knew herself to be to him. It would take barely a nudge to move her into his orbit, his space, his arms.

"Am I interrupting something?"

It was a woman's voice. Inger and Stan turned to see Ginger standing at the studio door. Inger again heard in Ginger's tone a suspicion too vague to be identified but also too primal to be spoken.

"No," Stan answered quickly. "What would you be interrupting?"

Inger stood away as Ginger upped Stan's anxious ante.

"Art, I guess. Isn't it all about art?"

Ginger's tone was snide but still she asked a question, one that threw back to Stan a hot potato of apparent spousal resentment. Inger wondered what had happened between them that morning. It felt like the festering fall-out of an old quarrel.

A child ran into the room, a young girl Inger guessed to be about four years old, her brown hair thick and long and flying behind her as she ran. She charged Stan and hugged his thigh.

"Hello, little darling," Stan said as he cradled the child's head in his large, limber hands.

"Lila – meet Inger."

Stan spoke to the child and ignored Ginger who backed away several steps to create a wide space for Lila's excitement. Inger reached to touch the child's hand, which slipped unaware into her fingers and was as quickly withdrawn. Lila ran to hide behind Stan, holding tightly to his waist as she peered out from behind him.

"You're a sweetie, " Inger offered.

Lila ignored her.

"Stanny…would you like my mommy to be your mommy?"

Lila looked up at the man she held so tightly and tried to find his eyes. Stan looked at her clearly and directly, as if to hide. For a moment he had no desire for Ginger to be anything but gone.

"I already have a mommy," Stan answered. "We all have our own mommies. Inger has a mommy, don't you Inger?"

Somewhere between gentle despair and active resignation, Inger searched for words that could not be spoken. *Her mother.* The mother that bore her and decided not to love her. The flush of an endless mourning was suddenly stuck in her throat. Among love's innumerable catastrophes, the loss of a child was terrible but abandonment by a mother a catastrophe. Induced by a child's precious exposure, Inger retreated into wordless loss and moved away to avoid further questions.

"You OK?" Stan asked Inger who waved him back as she stepped urgently out of the studio.

Inger's mother left her but Inger never left her mother. It was a situation both of residue and ruin without any known potential for return and one that without warning induced a frightful panic. Even if the object of love leaves, love never does. Inger retained an unrequited bond with her very first link to love along with the wound left by each subsequent link that was lost. It was preferable to drown in love's wake than to be anchored anywhere without it.

Inger often wondered if her search for pleasure was a surrogate for a frightfully vague urgency. She could ignore this need up to a point and stayed away from children for the very reason she now fled. They reified for her the tender exposure of love's failure. It was a life-long burden that, like all her burdens she wanted no part. Until it re-entered her life at vulnerable times and reminded her she was essentially unhappy and not ever in love. She was still the lost child and might be always.

Sex in America was a system of amorous repression. The deferred urge, the furtive gaze, the unspoken desire were its principle features. Shame, embarrassment and opprobrious and hurtful exposure were its pertinent outcomes. Violence, too, was possible. And yet sex in America was so easy for Inger because it was so hard for everyone else.

It was nearly the end of May when Inger learned that nude photos of her had been appearing in local tabloids. The June edition of *Screw* featured a still photo of her exposed and touching herself on DeReznay's white rug. The *Berkeley Barb* ran a page of nude beach photos with Inger included in an image of three women splashing in the frigid waves at San Gregorio. From these, she imagined a loop of her masturbation scene likely was playing somewhere. Hundreds, thousands perhaps, were seeing her and the notoriety, however dubious, thrilled her with a cheeky hubris. She had become a regular in the DeReznay model rotation, scheduled for shoots each week. Jeff continued to work with her and urged her to consider a sex session.

"You could be in a group scene. Just hang in the background and jack someone off or give head," he suggested, which did nothing to interest Inger. Sex was fun for her but only in the context of relationship. She needed to care about someone, even just a little, before she could agreeably fuck. Anonymity, which Jeff thought would protect her, had no appeal.

"Topless?" Karl asked.

He shook his head and turned away.

There was no obscure way Inger could tell her brother she had a job and what it was. So she simply blurted it out. She said nothing about modeling.

"Really?" Inger mocked him. "You're going to judge *me*? When we were 13 you tried every trick you knew to see my tits."

Inger's comment shut down Karl's budding reprimand.

"How do you get away with it?" asked Karl.

"It's legal in the City," answered Inger. "It's not *illegal* in Oakland. At least not yet. The owner has a drawer full of pasties if or when there's a crackdown."

"And how do you get home? Don't tell me you hitchhike at two in the morning."

Inger wanted to assure Karl she always had a ride but it meant exposing herself to more of his custodial cross-examination and to reveal a boyfriend, and then perhaps another and another.

"No, of course not," Inger answered and left it at that.

Her tone said she was finished talking about her life.

"I have something for you," said Karl. He led Inger to the garage and lifted its door. Inside was a two-door 1964 Opel Kadett, its squat, square frame painted with a night blue top and a body the color of green vomit.

"Only 96,000 miles. Dad bought it after you left for Norway. Good car, if a little balky sometimes and not much acceleration. Anyway, he wants you to have it. Can you drive a stick? Can you drive?"

"Yeah…are you kidding me, Karl?"

"Yeah, I'm kidding you, you bugger. What do you think? Here are the keys."

He dangled a set of small keys in front of her eyes, took her hand and dropped the keys into her outstretched palm.

"You'll need a driver's license."

Her brother tried not to smile. He offered to drive Inger to the Department of Motor Vehicles for a driving test.

Annalisa appeared from the kitchen.

"Do you like the car?" she asked Inger.

Inger stared at the woman's midsection; swollen with a nearly full-formed baby she already used her arms to carry.

"When are you due?" Inger pointed at Annalisa's tummy.

Her question bounced off Annalisa like every similar query. There had been many.

"Weeks, if not days," Annalisa answered.

She perspired generously. Inger saw spreading wet blots below each shoulder. Annalisa watched Inger's search of her.

"Hot today," she said. "Hot in the kitchen."

Inger heard in Annalisa's voice a note of succinct resentment, that perhaps what had started as the fun of creation had become a pitched, sweaty battle with her body. And simply to make passage for a creature she knew existed but that she did not yet love. Annalisa stared at her husband's sister with what felt to Inger like an unacknowledged, if disquieting, envy.

"We'll drive over to Dad's," Karl answered. "He'd like that. You can thank him and then he'll leave you alone."

Inger's father looked much older than she thought he would. Family photos in the mail had prepared her for white hair and bushy eyebrows. Standing before him, she saw how his strong jaw appeared to draw its support from the symmetric rows of wrinkles that framed it. Though his eyes were clear and, surprising to Inger, appeared remarkably kind. His smile seemed inextinguishable where years before it had been non-existent.

"Thank you, Poppa," she said softly before giving him a vigorous hug.

It was more than he expected and more than she expected to give. She was grateful and for the first moment in a very long time wanted her father to hear and feel her gratitude. He did, but tipped into his own unexpected feelings he tried to deflect them by introducing his second wife.

"This is Pamela."

Lars took Inger's shoulders in his big hands and pushed her gently away.

The woman behind him smiled and came forward as if called on cue, drifting cautiously toward her new husband's only daughter. The woman was shorter than Inger and round in the places Inger was firm. The woman held out her arms. Bright light poured through the window behind her and masked Pamela's pupils in a flat, black shadow. She had long, brown hair laced with clusters of silver. Inger, seeing the woman approach, grabbed one of her hands with both of hers and held it with a patient, distancing rigidity. Like father, like daughter. Come close, but no closer.

Pamela seemed to understand and held her place just beyond the length of Inger's outstretched arm. *What do they look like fucking?* Inger thought. *Do they fuck?* It was a transgressing visualization that helped Inger neutralize Pamela's offer of affection. Inger defended herself, determined that no one would take the place of her mother. She did not know that, among Pamela's many good intentions, to be a mother to Inger was the very last.

Raj said Berkeley was at war. It had been at war for nearly five years. And as an ex-patriot for nearly all that time, Inger had managed to avoid it. She had left Berkeley before Vietnam protests, before students seized the campus, before radicals fought conservatives for control of the city's government, before the assertion of civil rights and, now, Black Power. She existed in the after-glow of the city's recent battles and at the edge of an emerging front against racism and war. Each time she strolled through the campus plaza, Inger walked among rallying crowds of student protesters.

The Free Speech Movement, the Vietnam Day Committee mobilizations, student strikes on campus, and a tumultuous attempt the previous October to stop the drafting of young soldiers by closing the Oakland Induction Center. Raj rattled off the history of Berkeley protest in a way to make it seem serious and romantic though it sounded to Inger like a bull fight she had seen once in Portugal: ten minutes of excitement and then a disorderly bore as the same bull, never killed, was used again and again.

Larry, too, talked to Inger about war in Berkeley. He cared about the war because blacks were being drafted into the army and the Berkeley draft board gave a pass to college kids who were almost always white. He asked Inger if she remembered he was the only black student in her English class. Inger did not. She had paid no attention to race, had few friends, and anyway was too busy falling into heedless love with their teacher whose attentions kept her obsessed and isolated for the entire year.

"Remember when all the black kids took over them pink boy club benches?" he asked.

Inger did not, but did recall the high school's exclusive white social clubs, about a dozen that acted as a prep version of fraternities and sororities. The clubs had mostly Greek names and members were legacy pledges whose parents usually lived in the affluent Berkeley hills, many themselves past club members.

Black students had never been asked to join any of the clubs. Club brothers and sisters, sporting pins and jackets, occupied specific benches adjacent to the high school's outdoor snack shack until a week into the spring of 1963 when a parade of black students led by a posse of star athletes arrived before lunch and took over the benches.

"No one bothered us," Larry said. "We were for real. They knew."

Shortly after the takeover, the principal banned club jackets and the benches were liberated.

"My dad went to BHS and he could never sit on any of those damn benches," Larry said bitterly. "We not doin' that," he said. "We Panthers now. We have power. We nobody's Negroes anymore."

He told her the Berkeley School Board was integrating its elementary schools by busing white children west into the flats and black children east into the hills.

"And what's your average liberal Berkeley Whitey doin'? Tryin' to recall the damned school board. And if they can't do that, they'll move to Albany or El Cerrito. You watch. You think things are gettin' better? Look what happened to Martin. He stood up. He got killed. Well, they can't kill us all. You know race isn't a part of this country's history. It *is* this country's history."

Larry's inverted anger with the past shortened Inger's distance from what she saw in the streets. She and Larry now shared space within the vortex of a social and political struggle too large for the local world.

In high school Larry was a model of the prevailing culture: his dark hair slick and combed and especially when he wore his red-letter sweater and smiled at everyone. He enjoyed his popularity with white students who, though they never said it to him, thought of Larry as a "friendly" Negro and a model of what Negroes might successfully become since most white classmates assumed all Negroes aspired to be white.

It was the first Tuesday in June when Inger fathomed the signs of an encroaching annulment by which something of her old Norwegian self would be forever abrogated. Larry returned to Inger's cottage after taking his grandparents to a nearby church to vote in the state's primary election.

"Did *you* vote?" Inger asked Larry.

"Yeah," he answered. "Did you?"

"I've never voted," Inger answered.

"Damn, woman. You gotta vote. November. Panthers are registering voters. I'll get you signed up. You gonna vote. You still a citizen, right?"

"Does it really change anything?" Inger asked.

"It might," Larry answered. "What can it hurt?"

He asked Inger to join him later while he and Raj and Mack sat at the Kip's Upstairs beer bar near the campus and watched election returns. Inger wanted to see Mack again. She offered to drive Larry in her Opel.

Kip's on Durant Avenue was packed with students though Mack and Raj had been drinking since seven and managed to get a table near a window. Inger walked into Mack's line of vision, which he directed at the rainbow glow radiating from a television cradled on a shelf above the bar. Inger turned to see numbers and names appear and a commentator also appear occasionally on the screen to say something no one could hear over the noisy crowd.

"It's close," Mack said pensively. He reached to pump Larry's fist and nodded toward Inger who found an empty chair and sat down.

"Kennedy's hanging on and LA hasn't come in yet," Mack said excitedly. "He could do this."

Inger had nothing to say as the men chattered their tough talk of numbers and candidates. There were jokes she didn't get and loud laughs she could not share. Mack nodded occasionally at Inger as if to give her an opening to speak. She simply shrugged and by her second beer was lost in a slight but effective inebriation. Around midnight a surge of noise rose from the crowd at the bar and Mack stood to see above them.

"LA's coming in big!" Mack shouted. "He's done it."

"All those blacks and Mexicans," Larry shouted at Mack. "Don't ever say we didn't do nothing for ya."

Inger turned again toward the TV screen. Numbers appeared and the number by Kennedy's name was the largest. Shortly after, she saw the winning candidate approach a podium. The upstairs bar rocked with cheers. She could make out the face of Robert Kennedy, a face so eerily similar to that of his late and famous brother. And like his brother, Kennedy looked up and brushed from his brow a curled, thick wave of his hair. Inger had no context for the political pleasure of this moment though Kennedy's appearance invigorated a visceral yearning, a reminder of another good and hopeful time observed obscurely now as if through a keyhole.

The senator first congratulated Dodgers' pitcher Don Drysdale for throwing his sixth straight shutout that night and, when supporters in the Ambassador Hotel ballroom ended their affiliating laughter, Kennedy thanked them. Inger listened as he ranged through a long tribute to friends whose names she did not recognize before thanking union workers, farm laborers and other vast swaths of the electorate and then stating with Bostonian inflection "my thanks to all of you, and on to Chicago, and let's win there."

Inger moved to stand near Mack who first clapped as Kennedy walked out of the TV frame. Seeing Inger beside him Mack grabbed her in a celebratory hug as the crowd in the bar began to break into small groups to search for empty tables and stools. Inger felt Mack's searching hands at the base of her back, felt enveloped and absorbed in a satisfaction that likely had nothing to do with her.

She felt warmth engendered by fondness, something Raj might have described as solidarity and that Inger felt as her place within a larger, more populated motion, the values of which were still comfortably vague. Annulled was the disinterest she had used to protect herself from vast and worldly wrongs. It was a moment of splendid, noisy serenity until Mack's hands relaxed, went limp and fell away.

"What's happening?" he asked without directing his question.

He stared at the television screen where the crowd milled in front of Kennedy's empty podium until a reporter emerged and was given a microphone. Mack pushed forward and tried to hear over the crowd.

"He's been shot. God, he's been shot!" a woman at the bar shouted.

"What?" someone else yelled.

A woman screamed. As Mack pushed toward the bar the crowd rapidly reassembled in front of him.

"No…it's not…no…" said someone beside Inger.

She looked back to see Raj and Larry turn toward others who were at the same time turning toward them.

"I don't know…" Raj said. "Where? When?"

Mack returned.

"Kennedy's been shot," he reported calmly. He didn't know anything other than the shooting had just occurred in the hotel kitchen and an ambulance was on the way. A suspected assailant was being held. The latest report indicated Kennedy was on the floor and likely unconscious.

"I've got to call the city desk," Mack said to Raj and Larry. "Need to work tonight, I'm sure."

He darted for the exit.

"Let's get stoned," Raj said to break a brooding silence.

Larry declined.

Inger offered to drive Larry home.

"No. I'll get myself back," Larry answered. "Need to check in with some friends. I'm fine. Really, man. It's cool."

Inger and Raj understood Larry needed to connect with the Panthers.

Raj lit a joint and passed it to Inger as they sat in her Opel. She had driven them into the hills behind the campus. They sat together in the front seat with a boundless night view of the campus, the city, the Bay and San Francisco in the distance, a glowing fire of light flushed through clouds of incoming fog. Inger's tinny car radio in fifteen minutes had confirmed Kennedy was seriously injured and unconscious, a suspect was in custody, and no one else had been hurt.

"Looks bad," Raj said.

Inger had no response. She was remote from it all in this quiet and innocuous seat somewhere in the last upper tier of a violent arena. Another annulment was underway, that of a fresh born optimism smothered in the agony of having no time even to be anxious over a loss already so complete. She was in America again, at home in her nation of desolate hope, astringent shame, afflictive sex and sudden and anonymous death.

eight

Inger knew her best features and dressed them with care. Looking into her mirror she highlighted her eyes with dark shadow that accentuated their large, green pupils. She slipped into a baggy long-sleeved garnet paisley top she could tie at the waist to reveal the suggested outline of her braless breasts.

She stepped into black, bell-bottom slacks that concealed what she thought her slightly too stocky calves. Blue string sandals displayed her high-arched feet. And her hair, washed and dried into a swirling mesh of burnished auburn, hung below her shoulders in such a way that if she tossed her head in a turn it would move like the trailing tail of a kite aloft.

This was not how she dressed in Norway. She reminded herself she was back in America where most everything was for sale. Here she was encouraged to offer herself as a product. Certainly her modeling work was just this. A certain kind of misrepresentation and, perhaps, even a lie. In America she was free to lie to others as long as she did not lie to herself.

Today she dressed for Mack. It was Friday and the third day Senator Kennedy was dead. Inger had accepted Larry's invitation to a meeting of local activists who would discuss responses to the assassination and ways to use Kennedy's death to mobilize resistance to the Vietnam War. The group met informally at the back of The Forum, though strategy meetings were held elsewhere, usually in someone's home or in the back room of an empty storefront on

Adeline not far from the Panthers' office.

It was part of Larry's affectionate campaign to involve Inger in politics. Inger's true interest was that Mack was likely to attend. She expected to see him and wanted to be certain he saw her.

She had arrived in Norway during the Christmas holiday of 1963. She was 17 and exactly a month had passed since the assassination of President Kennedy in Dallas. She returned to America on the first of May of 1968, three weeks after the murder of Martin Luther King and a month before the assassination of the late president's brother. So her nearly five years away were bookended by the killings of two Kennedys and she could, if she thought too much about it, hold herself responsible though it was only a coincidence and, really, what was her involvement other than as an unwilling witness to public events.

Inger had been gone from America long enough not to care. Her eyes, her face, her body, her life were without means and without love; her sexuality still ruled her like the cigarettes she also and always needed. They managed her responses, fed her various appetites and gave her relief. She was an artist but only after she was everything else.

"What is to be done?" Bronwyn asked.

Two tables at the rear of the Forum were pushed together to accommodate the seven people gathered around them. Five were men and Mack was not among them, though Raj and Larry were there. Three were women, if Inger counted herself, which she was reluctant to do. She sat quietly and sipped her espresso. She had met Bronwyn but not the other woman who was named Bette and who answered Bronwyn's question with another.

"To Lenin's query, why not respond with Lenin's answer?" Bette asked emphatically. She was a small woman who spoke with resonant, laconic assurance.

"We mobilize. We are the vanguard. Look at what's happening in Paris. We can do as much. We must."

Bette introduced a slender, dark man named Peter who proposed a rally on the Avenue in support of the French resistance in Paris.

"Communists, socialists, workers," Peter said. "They came together because French students led them. We can fight capitalism here—in the belly of this beast."

Peter introduced another man named Michael, a South Campus resident and merchant who owned a clothing store on Telegraph.

"The neighborhood is ripe," Michael said. "Look out there."

He pointed through an open door at the rear of the Forum where outside a noon sun illuminated a vast and dirty lot filled with automobiles, parked in disorderly clutches across an entire city block.

"The University spent all last year tearing down those homes and now what do we have? An ugly crater filled with cars."

"No shit," Raj added. "I lived in one of those houses. Beautiful old Victorian and it's just gone. I ended up in the Berkeley Inn for twice the rent before I found my room off Dwight."

Michael introduced Jorge, a member of the Brown Berets. He said the group was fighting for the rights of Mexicans in America and was aligned with the Black Panthers.

"And the Panthers?" Bronwyn asked Larry. "Will they show up?"

"Depends on where you are and what you do," Larry said cautiously. "We'll need to know more. And I'll have to talk to Bobby."

"And your friend?" Bronwyn asked. She looked at Inger directly. "Who are you?"

Inger skirmished momentarily with a sense of unreality about who she was and where she was. Bronwyn wore no make-up yet appeared inscrutable. Her long black hair today was held tight in a stringy ball of a bun. Inger wondered if she owned a mirror.

"I'm a friend of Larry and Raj," Inger said.

Bronwyn appeared to roll her eyes.

"Their friend or a girlfriend?" Bronwyn asked. "No girlfriends or boyfriends allowed. Larry, who is this woman? What's she doing here?"

Larry, who in just the previous moment had displayed his Panther authority, now retreated. He struggled for words that left a gaping, prolonged silence.

"She's cool," Raj spoke up. "She can help."

Bronwyn looked again at Inger.

"Are you a student? A socialist? What?" Bronwyn asked her directly.

Inger did not answer.

"Are you a spy?" Bronwyn persisted.

Inger felt a surge of blood fill her face and fists. She prepared to stand and run.

"Is this the meeting?" Mack asked as he strolled to the table. "You guys have something you can tell me? I need a story."

Inger caught Mack's eyes and he waved hello.

"You know her?" Bronwyn asked Mack.

An enveloping tension suggested that Mack's response would be the next potential point of its release. He looked around the table.

"It's Inger," he said. "She's from Norway. Been here a couple of months. Right Inger?"

Inger nodded. Bronwyn backed off. Three men at the table knew this woman and liked her. She might not be helpful but she was no threat.

"We could have something tomorrow," Peter said to Mack. "Support for the French and the French for us. It's time. It's god damned Berkeley. Phone me."

"I'd like to get the story before the Barb—just for once," Mack said.

"You do anyway," Peter answered. "Your paper, even if it is the pig press, comes out every day. The Barb can't beat you."

"Pig press?" Mack snorted. "My pig press endorsed Kennedy in the primary."

"Yeah, great," said Bronwyn. "It was his tool of a brother that got us into Vietnam."

"Too bad he didn't live long enough to get us out," Mack snapped. "He would have."

Lost in the straggling wake of Mack's appearance, Inger gazed downward and waited for a voice, any voice but not likely her own, to give direction.

"What can she do?"

Bronwyn did not speak directly to Inger. Instead she directed her question to Larry.

"Whatever…she's a good lady. She can help, right Inger?"

"Lady? I'm a lady?" Inger asked Larry.

Bronwyn laughed.

"That's a good one. She's a woman, Larry. We're women now.

You aren't Negroes anymore and we aren't ladies."

Bronwyn asked Inger how long she had been interested in joining the Movement.

"The what?" Inger asked.

Bronwyn shrugged and again turned to Larry.

"Maybe she can make some phone calls. Something. I have to go."

Bronwyn left hurriedly as others lingered to talk. Mack had crossed the café and was standing at a small window table occupied by a single woman writing in a notebook. He sat down with her and a conversation began.

"You coming?" Larry said to Inger as he stood up.

Inger said yes but first she needed to use the bathroom. Sitting in her stall Inger wondered how and why the words of revolution did nothing for her. War, race and rebellion were headlines that faded into yellow every day as the perpetual conditions of humankind. She was attracted to Bronwyn's grasp of her life as a woman but did not see how sensory experience would ever be improved by fighting in the streets.

Leaving the bathroom, Inger saw that both Mack and the woman at the small table were gone. Left on an adjacent chair was a notebook and a stack of folders the woman had been leafing through when Mack arrived. Inger asked Larry to wait while she went to the table and gathered them up in her arms. She would return them to Mack. It would be a reason to phone him.

Larry was quiet as they left the Forum while Inger wondered if it were reasonable to have expected more support from any of the three men at the meeting with whom she had shared a bed. She was not a revolutionary. She was not radical. She had her sympathies for those in need but the politics of struggle were an alien undertaking. She had neither the heart nor the vocabulary to enlist effectively in a local uprising.

Larry understood this without speaking to Inger. He carried his own resentment, grown from Bronwyn's brusque brush-off of his mention of the word "lady." She sounded like every woman schoolteacher he had ever known, all of them white and who could make him feel bitter and stupid. He could now presume they feared his black skin and his volatile and emerging self-respect.

Inger and Larry shared the afternoon walking in the hills above the city and ate dinner again at Brennan's before Larry stayed the night. Mack had slipped away and Raj left the Forum before she could get his attention. Larry was her third choice but enough for what was at hand. Inger was at least grateful for more than one lover; grateful her sexuality belonged only to her and was not an asset held by a man.

"How can I express my gratitude?" the woman said to Inger as they sat in a booth at King Pin Donuts. The woman turned again to shuffle through the folders, papers and notebook returned to her.

"It's all here. You can't know…thank you."

Inger sipped her coffee before taking a bite of greasy apple turnover. She watched curiously as the woman who said her name was Harriet set the papers aside and began quietly to cry.

Unknown to Inger, she had returned to Harriet the better part of a postgraduate thesis. It was a tedious two years worth of work on the life of the Italian poet Dante Alighieri during his 14th century exile from Florence.

"You can't know how much time I've put into this. To think I left it on a chair in a cafe…what's happening to me?"

Inger could not say, other than to acknowledge Harriet's anxiety and its roots in some kind of experience deeper and more pervasive than simply the temporary loss of her thesis. Being alone with any one person for more than an hour usually led Inger into feeling affection, if not outright love. Inger loved the moments of intimacy that grew from strangers. She actively sought them. It might make friendships or even ecstasies. Words were touches and for Inger touches were usually and most always soothing.

"So you're Mack's friend?"

Inger asked directly. She had first phoned Mack to tell him she found the papers. He didn't answer his phone. Inger found the woman's number in her notebook and phoned her.

"Mack?" Harriet appeared surprised. "You know Mack?"

"Friend of a friend," Inger answered vaguely. "How do you know him?"

If Harriet were Mack's lover, Inger may have already telegraphed too much information.

"Mack knows my dad," Harriet said. "Mack took his lit class while he was a student. He ended up spending a lot of time at our house, which you can imagine is not usual for an undergraduate. But it happened. He was a frequent dinner guest. Almost like family for a while. "

Harriet brushed away a shock of her hair, not quite blonde but also not brown, that hung straight down along the length of a prolonged, slender neck. Her eyes appeared alluringly wild as her pupils stirred like small, caged animals.

Harriet's father taught at the University. His academic specialty embraced the lives and works of medieval writers. He was the author of renowned books on the lives of Boccaccio and Chaucer. Dr. Harold Nash Alden was completing his 20th year of teaching and Harriet, who was too young to remember the family's move to Berkeley, had lived in the town most of her life.

"I'm only a TA," said Harriet. "But daddy has big plans for me."

Harriet rolled her lively eyes and made a face.

"So I owe you a dinner," Harriet said directly. "The least I can do."

By mid-June Inger had been home long enough to feel as if she were waiting for something. Barely seven weeks had passed since her return to America, yet it was all the time that mattered. Within a short period she had grown herself into an orbit of acquaintances, begun painting again, found a place to live and had two reliable lovers though it was the third just beyond her reliable two, the one who had offered a taste and nothing more, that she wanted most.

And she was working. Nearly a month at the Adeline bar and once a week for the DeReznay photographers where one afternoon's pay equaled what she made in five nights waiting tables though she was feeling more pressure from Jeff to have sex in front of the camera, to find a partner or to join a group. The pay was tempting but Inger resisted.

Inger let Raj drive her Opel. She wanted to enjoy the views and agreed to drive back.

"It's your dad's cabin?" Raj asked cautiously.

"Dad built it," she answered. "Bought two acres beside a creek north of town. Had the A-frame up in a summer. I wasn't even eight years old. He loved to go up for a snowy Christmas each year. Reminded him of Norway. And summers on the creek were hot and lazy. He doesn't visit as much as he used to. Must be a burden to care for. That's why he asks us to go up. He doesn't go anymore but he owns it and wants us to assure him it's still there."

Lars had offered the cabin to Karl for a summer vacation but his son and daughter-in-law were afraid to travel so close to the birth of their baby. Karl called Inger and offered it to her. She had a three-day window without work and asked Raj to join her though she would rather have taken Mack. She told Larry she needed to check on her father's house in the Sierras and he agreed to cover two nights with his grandparents. She did not tell him she was taking Raj.

The historic gold country foothills along Highway 49 opened to the steeper wilderness promised along Highway 4. After passing through the sputtering commercial villages of Angels Camp and Murphys the road meandered into the hamlet of Arnold and, beyond, to an old forest road that wound up a hill and back down into the tree-stuffed valley of San Antonio Creek.

"There! It's there!" Inger shouted and Raj drove down a buttressed incline to a small house shrouded in overgrown shrubs and trees.

The memory of the old summer home, which now appeared so small and hidden after her years away, contrasted with Inger's uncertain present, as if the home were her inanimate touchstone and Raj suddenly her very animate stranger.

Inside, she found her old bedroom—one of three if she counted the upstairs loft—and then visited the kitchen with its sweeping view of the creek, dammed by two neighbors to create an incidental swimming hole. Spring run-off still stirred in the creek, forging streaks of white foam as water rolled over a small stone bridge and toward a larger lake farther downstream.

It was mid-afternoon and the hot, dry air drove Raj immediately to the creek where he stripped off his clothes and plunged into the water.

"Yowweee!" he shouted, submerging quickly and rising again to throw his head back and wallow in the creek's frigid run-off. Inger resisted an urge to join him. She felt confined in an old house filled with new memories. The last Christmas with her mother was here. Inger walked to the corner of the dining room where a Christmas tree once stood and, after her mother left, never stood again.

While Raj swam in the creek, Inger swam in her own pool, a melancholy version of the part of her life that was without pleasure. She found the main bedroom and busied herself unpacking. When Raj returned for a towel, Inger was in the kitchen marinating salmon steaks for a barbeque.

After dinner Inger and Raj sat on the porch in the still warm evening air, Raj naked and Inger without her blouse. Her memories of loss faded. Two glasses of wine purified her of all regret, all diffidence. The creek's crickets quieted any other noise until Raj suggested they smoke some dope. He filled a corncob pipe bowl with two pinches of weed and then added a small pebble of hashish before incinerating it and sucking up a full cloud and passing the pipe to Inger.

"No joke, babe. This is excellent shit," Raj said through a choking gasp.

Inger inhaled easily as the smoker she was, holding the dope's hot brume in her lungs for nearly a minute. They finished the pipe in three more passes and fell each into a suddenly quiet hole with glittering, enhanced views of a billion stars. Later, they slipped into bed, their touches a comforting substitute for the prevailing scarcity of words. Inger handled Raj with purpose and took him deep into her mouth, loving his swelling erection and pleased with her power to induce it. Raj was familiar and gentle and Inger came twice before submitting as he held her ass while on his knees he thrust wildly until, in a yodel of excruciating pleasure, he pushed so hard her legs collapsed and he with them.

Raj suggested the next morning that they "get telepathic," which meant taking LSD. Inger wasn't sure until Raj said he would guide the trip and keep her safe. She had never taken the drug and had many questions, which he nimbly answered. It wasn't addicting. The trip lasted several hours but always ended. And Raj would guide her, hold her and protect her.

"Orange sunshine. It's cool," Raj said.

Raj had scored the acid from an Owsley link that lived on Berryman Street. Inger could begin with a small dose, less than a hundred micrograms. They would take a walk before the effects peaked and spend the rest of their time under the trees and safe in the house. Raj prepared ice water for the refrigerator and cut fruit and dished yogurt into bowls for later.

"You won't be hungry," Raj said. "You'll be telepathic."

The phrase said nothing to Inger but she was ready and after swallowing what appeared to be a miniature shred of paper, she laughed and waited. And waited.

A trail led from the house along the creek and into a wilderness area. They took a bottle of water and began a trek toward the granite ridge at the trail's eastern apex. A warm wind pushed up from the valley and also pushed them along, a push that for Inger began to feel like the touch of a hand. She laughed again as Raj stumbled in an effort to avoid stepping on a snail. Laughing continued as quite surprisingly they thought themselves lost, which they were not, but Raj was lost, even if Inger wasn't and the difference in their frames of reference became a great and luscious irony of the forest that swept both away.

Inger imagined herself an undigested morsel clinging to the shore of some larger creature's sunlit alimentary canal. She tried to describe this to Raj whose every query to her arrived like a punch line to some great cosmic joke. After an hour on the trail they had traveled barely 75 yards and were convulsed in laughter under a tree.

At some point Raj got out in front and beckoned Inger forward through a clearing she recognized as the final ascent to the ridge. A spirit of adventure seized her and she felt a luxuriant thrill as step-by-step she navigated a steep path through what appeared a vast assembly of friendly, helpful boulders. At the top she gazed with Raj at the wide view of the little valley occupied by Arnold. The thrill of elevation became quickly a fear of flying and both retreated below the rocks that now appeared to Inger as large, granite breasts, the cascading creek their nourishing milk.

Her fear of flying became for Inger a fear of walking and, too quickly to manage, a fear of moving at all. She cried to Raj for help. They were less than a quarter mile from the house but Inger thought they might as well be on another planet. She could not move her legs. Raj found shade and had Inger sit next to him while he whistled a Beatle's melody, gave her water to drink, and asked her to close her eyes. She did and felt the wind again. It was a wind that, instead of a pushing hand now felt more like the wave of a warm ocean.

She told this to Raj who suggested they hitch a ride on the wave and find their way home. With each step Inger sensed a vivid threat. Tall weeds reached for her ankles and knees. What kept her from dissolving into the earth? Why was she privileged to take steps and the fat, threatening trees unable to move at all? The barrier between her and the forest appeared non-existent and she feared that certainly she would never emerge from it.

As the house came into view, Raj cheered ecstatically while Inger, surprised by the size of the house and its immensity in her life, succumbed to a rush of remorse. The great house beckoned like a hungry beast, a beast that could chew away all her protection from the menacing ghosts within. She walked now but as if she carried heavy chains. Raj helped her up the steps until her foot touched the porch and she collapsed in sobs. He sat with her and held her, his hands rising and falling with each gasp and groan.

When there were no more tears to cry, Inger pictured her body as a dry desert, barren and no longer stalked by either life or death. If a reckoning were due she would face it. Instead, Raj presented her with a bowl of fruit and yogurt and another glass of water. The cold bowl landed in her hands like a summer rain and aroused a voracious thirst and hunger. From somewhere inside she watched in fascination as her hand lifted shaky scoops of a swimming curd into her mouth and her throat registered sensations of chewing and swallowing. *I am a creature*, she thought. *I am the earth and the animal. I am alive now, if not always.*

The food revived her and induced a calm surrender. She opened to acceptance of the terror still dancing at the back of her imagination and could now see Raj present before her. She watched him eat his yogurt and marveled at the process of his noisy mastication that, in an instant, seemed the only process of importance in the universe. It was strangely funny but she no longer felt like laughing.

Later Raj led her to a chaise lounge on the porch and made her comfortable as the red and golden sky brought an end to the day. In place of surrender, Inger now succumbed to simple silence, the day's urgencies also at an end. The trip was no longer fearful but still not a pleasure. Though within some quiet place she expressed an unusual gratitude for her experience of life and that without any illusion life was useful or meaningful or not important at all.

nine

Oak trees flew by outside the passenger window and Raj asked Inger if she were angry.

"Angry?" Inger asked and waited for Raj's response.

"You haven't said a word since we left the house and yesterday you said almost nothing. Are we cool?"

Inger released a sigh, which was not a signal of exasperation but rather intended to convey empathy. Since surfacing from her acid trip she was speaking only with herself. She assumed she was Inger but also someone else and from this dyad grew a dialogue she could not resist. It might be important, she thought. It might also mean she was crazy. Raj had said she would feel an ego death from acid. She would become telepathic. Far from dying, it felt that her ego had multiplied into many egos, all needing their own attention. And she did not feel telepathic.

"I can't describe it, Raj," Inger said after a long pause. "I can't say anything right now. I've never felt this way."

Raj told her she was going "inside," a common acid reaction. Acid "vibrations" were becoming acid "knowledge."

"Whatever you say," Inger answered vaguely as if to indicate she had nothing more to offer and might wish to be left alone.

"Well, you didn't take enough to hurt yourself so don't go all weird on me."

Inger heard Raj's fear for himself and impatience with her. She was surprised. Would acid kill their friendship? She pushed the Opel through Stockton and told Raj only that she would drop him off at

Haste Street near Telegraph before driving home.

The city lights at sunset formed a yellow-orange crescent in the dusty sky above the Oakland Hills. As Inger passed Livermore and climbed toward the ridge she felt as if she were passing into the atmosphere of another planet. Turning off Highway 24 at the Telegraph exit she was swallowed by lanes of cars and trucks vying for openings all around her. She drove to Haste Street and released Raj at the corner. There was no time for a hug and, besides, it was the last thing she needed. He jumped out and offered to... She was gone before he could finish speaking.

Her new old world of Berkeley was crowded, noisy and claustrophobic. Inger parked in the Wiggins' driveway and rushed with her bag into the cottage, closing and locking the door behind her. Was she still high? She was certainly stressed. She smoked three cigarettes one after the other. She made a sandwich and drank a glass of milk. There was a familiar knock at the door. It was Larry. She did not answer. He knocked twice more and then left. Inger took a long, hot shower, the water rolling over her like the mother's milk of the creek's granite breasts. She dried and fell onto her bed, naked, hot and weary.

She rested her body, feeling as never before the quiet rumbling hum of its autonomic mechanics: the swoosh of flowing blood, the rhythm of her pulse, the accretions growing in her bowels, bladder and uterus. Her period was due soon and she assessed the feeling of achy, turgid build-up that would advance finally into the release of the bloody nest of her unused egg and its nourishment. She had been having periods for 11 years and counted the months as a way to estimate the number of eggs she had so far flushed away. She then subtracted the three months of her brief pregnancy, the thought of which drew her back into the deep background of her unsocial and sexual adolescence.

She remembered that, just as her body bloomed and her awareness of its pleasure became apparent, she was told to hide both her body and her desire. The free-ranging outerwear of childhood: shorts, t-shirts, bare feet, bare skin and especially the lovely nakedness of summer swims, gave way to ponderous and imprisoning fashions:

binding bras and other girding under-armor intended for few other purposes than to be hard to remove. She was sold this wardrobe as the reward for maturity and her new adult life and, from what she could remember of the clothes and make-up worn by her mother, this was the path, the only obvious path into successful womanhood. She could joke about sex as long as she pretended that for her, and for all other girls, it did not really exist.

For so many of her school friends the consequences of sex with a boy could be devastating, which was probably why Inger chose a man. Fitz was kind, and thoughtfully present with her and made her first experience of sex a mysterious loveliness free of any inhibition. He insisted on nothing but her happiness and opened her with his words and touches like contingent footsteps opening a new trail.

In that time she thought she was in love, knowing so few words or ways to know. It was an experience much larger than her body's independent and reliable work to make more people, which was the ultimate and disrupting outcome. She would never tell anyone who had impregnated her and who thereafter deserted her.

She had returned to such a repressed and sex-obsessed nation where the sexual thoughts and experiences of everyone fed a great and universally antagonizing guilt. Surely the thrill of sex was a necessary feature of an urge to make babies. Yet this fact did not give to sex any useful or compelling regard.

Inger stayed in her cottage through the night and well into the next day. She took a brief trip to the house in her robe and fixed breakfast for Larry's grandparents. She returned to the cottage where she again fell asleep to strange dreams of blood and cavorting actors and warm nudity among a friendly, unspecified group of characters. She awoke compelled to masturbate, seized by a strong flush of urgent sexual energy.

Modeling her sexuality gave to Inger her first satisfying responses from men and a subsequent knowledge of the pleasure of her own body. It did nothing to build friendships with other women or create a secure stance in the world. The world was now her body and her body the loving source of all her pleasure. She made herself come again. She continued the dialogue that now existed between her and this body, this lovely, pleasing body that made her both angry and in love with herself.

Her first night back at the Jug Handle was not the chore Inger had anticipated while driving home from the mountains or while curled up in her bed for most of the previous night and day. She dressed carefully, uncertain if she would take off her blouse. No one insisted, but if she did she earned another dollar an hour and considerably more in tips. Her fellow server Kate showed off a pair of Birkenstock sandals.

"A dream. Like walking on a cloud," she said.

Inger tried them on and said she would buy some.

Kate asked about her time away.

"It was a trip," Inger answered.

And that was all she said for the next five hours as she removed her blouse and served drinks to the assembled men, a few of them regulars that on a Wednesday night left before closing time. She had served long enough to relax with the regulars, customers who knew her naked upper body as fully as her bathroom mirror.

She took care and wore a short, bright blue skirt that cut off high above her knees and exposed her strong, and newly tanned thighs. She felt the mountain blush of sun in her face and also her breasts that she carried like the firm, granite boulders at the river and that might themselves pour forth the mother's milk of alcohol sought by the Jug Handle's restless suppliants.

For a time she thought herself a mad Erinys and threw her shoulders back in the forward assertion of her breasts, bending and pushing and thinking herself an object of some kind of worship, some kind of temple pleasure that was the birthright and inheritance of an ancient time. She took home $53 in tips.

A really good painting looks as if it has happened only once.

Inger stood in the college studio before one of her large canvasses and recalled the observation of Helen Frankenthaler, an abstract expressionist of the Fifties whose work Inger had always admired. The artist's observation of Arcadian imperfection described for Inger her pleasure with imperfect awareness, since every view was imperfect and every perfect image incomplete.

Inger yearned for soft lines, jazzy colors, spumescent splashes of textured paint and figurative lines that suggested features rather than revealing them. All these approaches were either old or not yet available enough to be considered new. In any event, it was not Willy's art, not his idea of what was good, an idea developed out of criticism and one not really his own.

Inger was tempted constantly to feel a failure at the only work she considered her skill. Though there were other women in the art class, it was the men who seemed nearly always to prevail, with their giant, oversized canvasses layered sparingly, even tentatively, with hard, angular strokes that boasted indecision.

Inger wished to go deeper and yet could get no help from her instructor. She had considered the Art Institute in San Francisco but tuition was prohibitive. For the workshop's closing student show, Willy chose from Inger's work two small drawings and left her canvasses alone. It was just as well. The drawings were better: fluid, figurative and both of them bookends to a story of bodies enraptured even while apart. These were vaguely identifiable to Willy as "women's parts" inspired by Eva's vaginal portraits. Willy giggled nervously.

"Is this the new cunt art I've read about?" he asked boldly.

"I have no idea," Inger said, embarrassed by her teacher's crude assessment and disappointed with the confining limits of his perception.

Inger's affection for artistic experience produced a strange kind of invalidation. She was both artist and model, both object and subject. Her real life was spent creating imaginary impressions of experience. To be seen naked in public was not to be seen at all. Her paintings and drawings were the objects that represented her, which might have explained why she worried more about them than herself. Her body was expendable, available. Her creativity was holy and secret.

A week had passed since taking acid and Inger still lumbered in a secret garden of alteration where nothing grew easily and everything grew at once. Each moment was still a surprise and she had to work hard not to notice what no one else could see. After a week she accepted that nothing would look or feel the same again and she was ready for something else to move her.

She had returned from the mountains with no expectations. She had returned her newly emptied soul to a human center of engorging social and psychic gluttony. She was still Inger but the acid's lingering expansion of her mind made her aware that to grasp her existence she might have to navigate more than three dimensions. And as an artist, she was barely the master of two.

Inger tried for two days to connect with Mack. He did not answer his phone so she drifted up to Telegraph in the afternoons and nursed a coffee at the Forum. Yitzhak appeared the first afternoon and, before moving up to the bar to buy an espresso, gave Inger a stunned, frozen look, almost as if his mind needed time to gather her up in whatever was his reigning impression. Inger waved confidently but received nothing from him in return. After getting his coffee, Yitzhak scooted quickly out the back door. Bronwyn also came through and waved weakly at Inger as if to suggest she would have ignored her had Inger not seen her first.

Another meeting was taking place at the rear of the Forum at which neither Larry nor Mack were present, though the tall man with black hair named Peter stopped by her table and asked Inger if she would help with preparations for next week's rally in support of the Paris resistance. He invited her to a meeting of volunteers at the University Student Union the next weekend. Inger thanked him and said she would attend.

"I've always lived at home," said Harriet. "That is, if I don't count the trip to Florence daddy gave me last year."

She deftly scooped up a chunk of rice and set it on a thin slice of barbecued beef before poking it all into her mouth. Inger watched closely. Harriet had suggested a new Asian restaurant on San Pablo Avenue for dinner and had driven to Inger's cottage to pick her up.

"Thanks for feeding me," said Inger.

"Are you kidding? Do you know what I'd be doing right now if you hadn't phoned? I certainly wouldn't be eating."

Harriet's gratitude was effusive and Inger decided it was time to let go of her own.

"You teach Italian?"

Harriet wiped her mouth.

Not exactly. She did not teach Italian. She taught Italian literature with a particular emphasis on Dante Alighieri and the 13th Century's explosion of Italian poetry in the vernacular.

"The voice of modernity alive suddenly and immediately in the love and writing of Dante," Harriet extolled. "It was an extraordinary leap in human experience. I wish I'd lived it myself."

A scholar Harriet admired had written that the two greatest poets in the history of the world were Shakespeare and Dante.

"He said Shakespeare was better but I can't agree," she said. "Dante wrote less, but what he wrote...."

Harriet had no further words and, instead, lifted her hand to kiss her fingers.

The women finished their beers and Harriet ordered two more.

"You asked about Mack," Harriet said to Inger. "Do you like him?"

"He's a nice guy," Inger said without commitment. "He seems interesting. He saw my drawings and he liked them. But he's damned hard to reach. Does he ever answer his phone?"

"Never," Harriet said. "It's my dad's complaint, too. Now that Mack is a *journalist* (she made quote marks in the air), he's too busy to return calls. That won't last."

Inger asked why it wouldn't last.

"We'll all stop phoning him," Harriet said.

Their conversation relaxed into the banter of two people who had an acquaintance in common and then fell into the more intimate realm of two women with the same male friend before at last entering the zone of women in relationship. Inger noticed how their tentativeness abated in the way that their disclaimers, hedges and tag-on questions were subdued and ultimately ignored.

They were happy to learn that both experienced painful menstruation as teens and, while not unusual, were among the few of their friends willing to discuss it. First sexual touches for both occurred at age sixteen and were shared with girlfriends but for Harriet they were brief and unsatisfying. Inger did not elaborate. The lover's discourse grew from extreme solitude, which always made it a risky conversation for women in search of some affiliating equivalency. But risk it they would, especially after a nice dinner and a third drink.

Inger confessed her attraction to Mack even as she enumerated his apparent faults: he was short, he had bad breath, he wasn't responsive to her at all but for the one night they spent together. Harriet listened compassionately. Mack seemed always distracted by current events and by his own interests. Harriet assured Inger it was nothing personal.

Harriet then made her own confession.

"It's been a year. My best friend at the time. A librarian at the Bancroft. She was smart, beautiful and an enormous help to me. Then Mary met a crazy musician."

"Were you in love with her?" Inger asked.

"I was in a way," Harriet said. "But not like *that*. Though we did become deeply attached. The music guy was the object. And the problem."

Harriet described Mary as a sturdy, athletic woman with penetrating eyes and strong jaw who wore short dresses that advertised her sinewy body.

"A forward woman. Very smart. Very funny. I was surprised when she introduced me to her boyfriend and said she was moving in with him. That she was pregnant. It was spring of last year. She was someone I trusted so I thought I should have seen this coming."

Harriet said the lover was named Charlie and he was short, visceral and criminal.

"He's been in prison," she said.

Harriet visited Mary and there were always other women around. Charlie brought home strays from the Haight and two women began living with Charlie and Mary, which didn't bother Mary at all.

"Odd women and smart. Had this crazy repartee—the women and Charlie all going at it. They were always stoned and so was I when I visited so it didn't seem too weird at first. Yet something was off. I haven't been back."

Mary moved with Charlie and the other two women to Los Angeles where in March Mary had her baby.

"Truly a hippie chick now, whatever that really is beyond long hair, short dresses, no underwear and getting stoned," Harriet said.

Inger could listen as well as she spoke and with Harriet she located her new friend's softest spot and gave it all the comfortable room she would need to explore its vulnerable verities. Their intimate dinner grew for Inger and Harriet the green roots of a tender and potentially truthful relationship. Inger approached sex from the perspective of polymorphous perversity while Harriet wrestled with arousal stirred from a covetous virginal naiveté. The coherence of these opposite origins fed the attraction each woman held for the other.

ten

Inger stood with Raj at the corner of Telegraph and Dwight Way under a banner spread across three storefronts. It read *Support French Revolutionaries* in chunky, hand-printed lettering. Inger held her own sign that read *Under Heaven One Family*. She selected her sign at the volunteer meeting called by Peter, not because the sign said what she meant but because it was the only sign not to say what she did not know. She could not say the cops were pigs or that war was illegal or that, as Peter described through his microphone, "a revolution was needed, a revolution of the house slaves against the master."

Thousands lined the sidewalks and filled the street for three blocks north toward the campus. A chorus of anarchists chanted "Two, four, six, eight. Organize to smash the state!"

Inger knew nothing about the student resistance in Paris. She barely qualified as a student having just completed a short art workshop at Laney and not at all certain she would return. She wore a blue denim worker's cap provided by Raj as they looked together toward a speaker's platform improvised from two wooden boxes on the wide sidewalk in front of Cody's bookstore.

Larry waited in a line behind the microphone while Bronwyn paced anxiously and checked notes attached to a clipboard. Purple twilight faded faultlessly into a darkening grey overcast as a tide of fog flowed in from the bay and filled the western avenues.

The rally grew noisier as Peter, in a raging alto staccato, called for a "an independent revolution with no attachments to the establishment. A revolution to topple exploitation of one man by another."

Raj cheered, hooting like a TV Indian as he pounded his mouth with his palm. Inger saw Mack who stood near the speakers and spoke with Larry who still waited his turn at the microphone. She moved into the street in an effort to get closer to Mack, pulling Raj along with her. She was attentive to the smells, the noises, the colors fading in the nearly vanished daylight. She thought the acid might still be pulling her deliciously by her senses into the awareness of a creaking, turning wheel of time she could almost see moving.

Inger's hallucination ended quickly with the sound of a deeper, louder voice shouted through a bullhorn far above the crowd. A uniformed man standing on a rooftop identified himself as the chief of police. He announced that the rally on Telegraph was "an illegal assembly under Section 726 of the California Penal Code." He told people to clear the street or they would be arrested.

The crowd below booed as a chant of "Fuck You! Fuck You! Fuck You!" rose from the street. Two boys near the stage picked up rocks and hurled them uselessly at the roof. A tense expectation seemed to take hold as Inger saw the red lights of police cars move through the fog toward Telegraph. The crowd broke apart and Raj pushed Inger north along the avenue.

"We need to get to the campus," Raj shouted. "Stay with me."

Inger looked for Mack but he, the speakers, the microphone and boxes had vanished. Raj took Inger's hand and they ran forward past protesters building a barricade at Haste street by rolling a trash bin into the intersection and setting it on fire. Two tear gas canisters popped into the street and white smoke filled the air. Raj pushed Inger up Haste.

"They've blocked the avenue," he shouted. "This way!"

Inger turned and was nearly toppled by a young man fleeing past her, a cop behind him in furious pursuit. Inger saw a trash can at the side of the street. Without hesitating she pushed the can with her foot and into the path of the cop who collided with it instantly, his knees bouncing off the rolling spill of garbage as he slid along the street and dropped his baton in an effort to slow a helpless, scraping momentum.

"Shit!" Raj shouted. "Let's go!"

The cop rolled in pain, Inger catching his glance as he turned to see her.

"Come on!" Raj shouted.

He pulled Inger into an alley as another tear gas canister landed nearby. Within moments Raj had guided her through the backdoor of his building and upstairs to his small room. He pushed her in and closed the door.

"What's got into you?" he asked. "You a street fighter now?"

"I wasn't thinking," she answered. "It was just there. So I did it."

Raj made tea in the kitchen and brought it back to his room. They listened together as sirens grew louder and then retreated.

"Welcome to the war zone," said Raj. "How does it feel?"

Inger had no words to describe her curious sensations that oscillated between fear and thrill.

Raj invited her to stay the night, which she did. Raj was excited by Inger's aggression and wanted to fuck. She did not, but accommodated him with her lips and fingers, maintaining her own brilliant control throughout, Raj's noisy come similar in her mind to the stumbling collapse of the cop. She was in control. That was all that mattered. It was a sweet victory, though over what wasn't entirely clear.

Rallies and riots continued through the weekend, ending each night with pitched battles between cops and protesters. Fifty-five people were arrested but Inger was not among them. She worked both Saturday and Sunday at the Jug Handle and after closing time received eyewitness reports from Raj who wandered down to the bar and got a ride back in her Opel.

"It's all or nothing," he said. "The community is pissed. We're taking the street on the Fourth of July. The city council meets Monday and we're asking for a permit. If we don't get it, we could have a war on our hands."

Inger found the struggle invigorating. She bought a Chronicle Saturday and read Mack's story of the Friday riot. As the weekend violence continued, she arranged to get Thursday off work. She wanted to be on the Avenue on July Fourth when either war broke out or peace was declared. It was a wild time and she was caught in it, alive and furious with an anger activated by her clash with a cop but also grown from her life of submissive duplicities. After hearing Peter's speech to the crowd she remembered wondering what it would be like to fuck Peter. When he quoted Regis De Bray Inger wondered what it would be like to fuck Regis De Bray.

Work held no surprises. Her class was over and she spent Tuesday at the gallery again to see where Willy would hang her drawings. Stan was there.

"Love your lines," he said with noncommittal specificity.

On Thursday, Telegraph Avenue was closed from 12 noon to 10 p.m. Instead of declaring war, the City Council–following two meetings held in the Berkeley Community Theater and attended by hundreds–decided by one vote to open the Avenue to a Fourth of July party.

Inger met up with Raj and Larry. Together they milled in a crowd of thousands that jammed the Avenue to hear live music, watch the San Francisco Mime Troupe's latest political send-up, and hear the revolution broadcast from a larger, wider podium than the one used Friday night. The Mime Troupe threw foam bricks at the crowd that happily threw them back at the play's selfish, exploitative villain.

Eldridge Cleaver spoke for the Panthers and waved to Larry who chose to wear his Panther beret. Peter spoke again and called on the South Campus community to rally for political control of its neighborhood, and to fight capitalism in all its profit-earning modes, which seemed odd to Inger as she saw the Avenue's merchants open and doing good business. And did capitalistic exploitation extend to the drug dealers in the crowd selling joints and lids?

Inger walked with her two men toward the campus where Raj suggested they slip down a secluded bank of Strawberry Creek and smoke a joint. Yitzhak had recently given him some "really good shit." As they strolled together through the Student Union Plaza, Inger saw Mack sitting at a table with an old black man. Mack took notes as the man spoke from behind dark sunglasses. A guitar was settled firmly in his lap. Inger turned and approached the table.

"Blind Willie Davis," Mack told her. "Willie, this is Inger."

The old man stood and searched for what he could not see. Inger took his hand.

"Willie is one of the greats of folk blues," Mack said. "I'm interviewing him. Would you like to sit in?"

Raj heard Mack's invitation and he and Larry looked at each other with an expression of mutual helplessness.

"Sure," Inger said immediately. She turned toward her two companions who recognized they were an instant afterthought.

"I'll be fine," she said. "You guys go ahead. I'll find you later."

They knew they would and she wouldn't.

"She really likes that guy," Raj told Larry as they sat on the creek bank and toked. Both were her friends and also her lovers. And both knew this even if neither would say it.

Inger sat through the interview with Blind Willie, at one confident moment asking her own question. Your family? Did your family support your music?

Blind Willie loved the question and gave a long, extemporaneous answer that Mack scribbled wildly to record.

After the interview, Mack asked Inger to have dinner with him at La Val's and attend the evening performance that featured Sam Hinton and Shlomo Carlebach. They left the campus, Inger passing a line of police at the Sather entrance where she recognized the cop she tripped Friday night, his face bruised and bandaged. She turned away just as he sought eye contact. Inger knew he saw her and skipped ahead of Mack for a moment to move out of the officer's view.

Inger showed her desire, though there was no desire without a prohibition. Did she show too much? Mack spent the night in her cottage. She awoke with him, content for a moment with the feeling a child has when it plays while a mother quietly knits or reads. Mack slept while she weighed the seamless pleasure of a time that seemed again to be close to a peculiar induction that exposed so much of her own desire. How much had she shown Mack? Could she remember? And if so, would she ever say?

Mack left the cottage, creating a space for the return of Inger's mother grief. She thought it might be a residual association from her acid trip though at some point every emotional experience could not be attributed to a drug. Why had she not reached beyond her father to find her mother? Perhaps it was because the touch of her father was already too distant and her mother's even farther. She knew it would offend Lars for her to seek out a mother who left her, left them all.

Lars was her source of survival, even as she made so much trouble for him. For Inger the vast lack of a father's attention was filled with the comfort of sex. She was accustomed to using what she knew about the vulnerable exposures of intimacy to gain male approval. She interested men with little effort, which made Mack's friendly indifference an especially compelling challenge.

The first night Inger heard noise outside her cottage she thought it was Larry. But no one knocked and the sound—an oddly irregular scraping between her wall and the fence—continued until she turned out all her lights. Looking toward the house she thought she saw a hulky shadow disappear down the driveway. The next night she heard the same sound. She crawled toward the bathroom and locked herself in. As she stood to peek through the bathroom's slender window, she saw a large hand gripping the ledge and two flickering eyes reflected in the stray beam of a street lamp.

Inger screamed and waited. She heard running footsteps fade quickly away. She opened the door and ran to the house where she awakened Joe and Billie and phoned Larry who drove over. He found footprints in the flower boxes under the window, and more muddy prints in the driveway that turned onto the street and vanished at the curb.

"We should call the police," Billie said gruffly.

"No. No don't do that," Inger responded.

She turned to Larry.

"I'm going to have to move," she said. "It's my fault. Billie and Joe don't need this."

"Cops or no cops, we can protect you," Larry insisted. "You tell me…"

"No," Inger said emphatically. "No. No cops. No noise. Please."

What she knew and could not say was that the face she saw through her bathroom window belonged to a man she'd met at the

Jug Handle. It was a one-night-stand in the back of his car. He must have followed her home. But how could she explain all this to Larry, not to mention a cop? Whether it made any sense, Inger wanted nothing revealed. But she needed to leave Larry's family and Larry. It was time. And this was reason enough.

Larry's truck rumbled up College Avenue and just as he turned east into the evening darkness of a side street a police car pulled up behind him and flashed its red light.

"Where you going with all this stuff?" the officer asked after checking Larry's license and registration.

"Moving a friend," Larry said. "It's her furniture."

"Where does she live?" asked the cop.

"Three houses from here on the right. See?" Larry pointed.

"Let's go check it out," the cop said skeptically.

Inger appeared at the door and was surprised to see a police officer.

"Man here says he's bringing you your furniture," the officer said to her.

He was an older officer who asked his question with a tone of unsolicited caution.

"Hi Larry," Inger said, ignoring the cop. "You got my stuff?"

Larry smiled.

"OK," said the cop. "It's just that there have been robberies up here. It's a good neighborhood and…"

"Been a lot of robberies in my neighborhood," Larry countered. "But it's poor and I guess not so good. Cause you cops never come around to check on us. Hell, you don't even come when we call you."

"Listen, you…" the cop started toward Larry.

"It's OK, officer. He's my friend. It's fine. That's my stuff."

Saved again. Saved by the white woman, the authoritative witness who would be believed whatever she said in defense or accusation. He was glad Inger was still his friend. Larry stepped away and turned his back to the officer who strolled slowly to his car. The cop slipped into the driver's seat and waited while Larry began unloading bookcases.

"It's a big room," Inger said. "Bigger than I expected."

Larry was in Inger's new home, an upstairs flat in an old two-story craftsman on Garber converted into two rental flats by the venerable Berkeley family that owned it. Inger shared the upstairs with two other roommates, a man and a woman who were students at the university. A working couple lived downstairs. They were gone all day and kept normal hours though their sex was loud and their bedroom immediately below Inger's.

Her new roommate Freda had confided this to Inger when she appeared for the interview at which Inger described herself as an art student at Laney College. That Inger was unfazed was a winning point, as was the fact she had brought her deposit and first and last month's rent in cash. Sixty-five a month. The deal was sealed instantly, and Inger's name placed on the lease.

"It's a great neighborhood," Inger told Larry carelessly. "Store at the corner and ten minutes from the Avenue. And I can park the Opel in the driveway."

Except for the proximity of Telegraph, Larry's family cottage had all those amenities, and more. But the stop by the cop reminded Larry that by traveling a couple of miles east he had entered a foreign land, one at the edge of the wealthy Claremont district and closer to the hillside life of Inger's brother than the townie, lower-rent flatlands where the Wiggins had lived for decades.

It did not take a geographer to understand that a topographical map of Berkeley matched perfectly its socio-economic distribution with high, white wealth concentrated in the hills and low income common in the lowlands. And the lower the elevation the blacker the residents. It was no secret to anyone though Larry was just beginning to find his words to speak it. Just beginning to understand that to love Inger was to embrace the soul of a certain kind of enemy.

Larry was not a Christian like his parents and grandparents though he loved to tell them all he was baptized in dirty water, that he was a Panther because someone had to step forward and speak the offensive truths of a racist nation; had to announce the arrival of a revolution. It was the kind of talk that scared his parents who feared for Larry's life as a Panther.

How pleased they had been when he was elected to the high

school student council, his hair slick, his letter sweater an emblem of his acceptance and achievement among the school's popular students. That all changed quickly. Larry still worked. Still took care of himself. But his dream was for something his wise parents thought unobtainable. More than equality, Larry wished for respect. And the only respect he had ever known was fear.

After Larry moved Inger's mattress into the bedroom and helped her fill empty spaces with her bookcases and chairs, she hugged him closely and wished him well, which she knew instantly wasn't fair. It felt too final when she still wanted Larry for a friend. But she would no longer fuck him and needed some kind of closure, however vague, to assert her new sense of herself.

The stalker had frightened her with a reminder that men were interested only in her body and in ways that made nothing beautiful at all. That was fine at the Jug Handle where touching was not allowed, but terrible in her real life. Too many men assumed sexual freedom meant that women would fuck them whenever they wanted, not whenever women wanted to fuck them.

Inger needed more control of both herself and others. She was determined not to fuck Martin, the new man she was living with, a theater student with a mellifluous voice and attractive eyes and hands. She would not, she said to herself. She would not. There was art. There was life. There was revolution in the air and in the streets of her new old country. Two months as a returned citizen had at last gained for Inger the robust assurance she could do more than just survive.

LARRY

one

It was not a catastrophe. There was no violence, no doom. It was his own secret, his own frailty, and only he knew. He could not calculate the loss of Inger, which he might rationalize as more the loss of a fascination than a woman.

Since his first days in high school Larry had drawn the attention of white girls. He learned quickly he was thought to be "sexy" and not afraid of bodies, his or a woman's. He exuded a comfortable confidence that drew their attention to him. He was told, by a white woman teacher no less, that he carried a certain "liveliness" that was attractive.

What he could not tell her was that he was burdened also with a private proclivity for white women that, as his black pride grew, he carried with increasing shame. He had during his adolescence very satisfying and interesting relationships with the women he labeled *sisters*. He was a very black man and black women knew him well and in ways that at certain points of connection were almost always gratifying. One black classmate, in particular, a young woman who emerged as a campus leader for Civil Rights, inspired in Larry a deep and lasting regard some might even have described as a crush.

But Larry's interest in white women had some of the qualities of a compulsion. He tried once to trace its origin and landed finally at the age of five and the long year of his early life spent with a very lovely and very white kindergarten teacher who adopted him as if he were a son…or even a small, unintended lover. He was way too young at that time to articulate the feeling but her attention was a magical beatitude that swept him away, her touch that of an angelic protector so different from the sturdy, commanding grasp of his mother.

At its best, he thought his attitude a way to deal with his own objectification by white people; to look at white women and to see them all the same just as he was viewed by whites as a black "other" in their midst. Though the white object for him was now one of desire. He knew most white people viewed him with suspicion rooted in a nearly invisible privilege that was their benefit and his prison.

He might have dropped it all but for the effortless attraction he inspired in high school; a power that filled a discouraging gap deepened by his stunned realization he was not prepared for an academic life. He was not going to compete as a scholar, especially with white kids from the hills whose minds had been groomed and cultivated from birth. He might run circles around them on the basketball court or football field, but he would not, or could not, engage them in colloquy and in fact was discouraged from doing so as school counselors guided him and other black classmates into vocational tracks, shop classes, and sports.

He was told his best crack at college might come from playing basketball. And that worked well, until his senior year when he suffered a season-ending ankle injury that cost his team a championship. It was an injury that, after graduation, also kept him out of the army.

He exuded a comfortable confidence that appeared to warm others. And in high school this was enough. This, and a letter sweater, brought him regard as a sweet, lively boy. It also made him a seemingly irresistible object to a certain kind of Caucasian female.

This history did not explain Larry's melancholy as he drove away from Inger's new residence. He experienced a state of gentle despair coupled with active resignation. Unsullied by the festering provocations of race in America, Inger was the first white woman to embrace him, make love with him, as the man he thought himself to be. She had no expectations, no preconceptions, no projections, no imperative fantasies, and no fear. He was at ease in her arms, alive with her in what appeared to be a shared allure.

And the end had arrived without warning: no clear declaration or break-off, just a friendly separation as if there had only been friendliness from the beginning. As Larry was just realizing, there had been for him so much more than that.

"It's the Panther thing," Larry told Sylvia as he drove her south on Grove Street.

"My dad's a preacher. He says he hates violence. But he loves my brother who's off in Vietnam fightin' colored people. They're another color, for sure. But colored just the same."

Sylvia, close to Larry in age, had just joined the Oakland Black Panther chapter. Her black curly hair was combed out in an Afro style that seemed to create a cotton-like halo, which sprouted from her head like a newly trimmed shrub. Larry picked her up at her Richmond home where she lived with her parents and attended Contra Costa College. He was driving Sylvia to the Oakland Panther office for an orientation. Larry owned his truck and gladly offered it as a Panther asset. Transporting members was a high priority.

"He just don't understand," Sylvia sympathized. "My dad's the same. His life here's so different from his childhood in the South. Dirt poor. Father shot dead in a fight with a white sharecropper. He came out here with his brother to find work in the shipyards. He did. Even got into a union. Been working ever since and thinks sometimes he's died and gone to heaven. I should be so damned grateful, he says. I'm goin' to college, he says. Well, this ain't no heaven. Too many black boys still dyin'. And I mean boys. Like L'il Bobby. Seventeen years old and shot dead by an Oakland cop?"

"Two days after Martin," Larry added. "You think it's a damn coincidence they shoot an Oakland Panther dead two days after Martin?"

"You knew Bobby?" Sylvia asked.

Larry waited while the memory of Bobby's reckless life returned. He fended off a painful recollection of the young Panther's funeral three months before. Larry had waited in line with a hundred Panthers to walk past Bobby's open coffin and to view his pasty, very dead face. Larry nearly fainted at the sight. The burial was at Mountain View Cemetery—a plot right on the road donated by a Panther supporter—and Larry stood next to Bobby's mother as she sobbed uncontrollably, surrounded by a protective phalanx of young Panthers, their angry looks projected outward, though it felt to Larry like a wasted move, a defense of the community that was, as his father sometimes said, a dollar short and a day late.

"Daddy says it's better here than in Alabama."

"How much better?" she continued. "You ever sit in a restaurant and wait for someone to serve you and it takes just a little too long? You ever wonder, even for just a moment, that you might not get served? Even be asked to leave?"

"That happened once," Larry said. "Camped in the mountains and coming home dad stopped in Livermore so we could get some dinner. Went to a small diner that was nearly empty. We waited at a table and no one came to give us menus. We waited and waited. Dad went up to the counter to ask the cashier for some service. He came back without menus and said we needed to leave. Ended up at a Howard Johnson's. Dad never say a word but I could tell he was righteously pissed. Knew what happened but he was too proud to talk about it. That was five years ago."

"You like your classes?" Larry asked Sylvia.

"Junior college is OK," she said. "I was a good student in high school but turned out I wasn't good enough for the SAT. Couldn't get into a four-year. So Contra Costa will do for now."

"I was a good student in junior high," said Larry. "But when I got to high school I was tracked into shop and sports. The white kids wrote the school paper. I set the type. Basketball was about as close as I ever got to college. Then I broke my ankle in three places in my senior year. Crutches and pins for six months. Adios, college."

Sylvia was dressed in a white turtleneck that fell over the waist of a billowing green skirt with an aboriginal pattern of brown lines and splotches. She wore black leather sandals and Larry noticed a bracelet on her wrist comprising two intertwined wooden rings.

"Nice threads," Larry said.

"African," Sylvia answered. "My family has Geechee roots. Gullahs of North Carolina. Lots of African heritage passed on to us."

Sylvia appeared proud to have a tangible link to Africa.

"You?" she asked.

"Slaves," Larry answered with a frank brashness, purposely drawn down to mock Sylvia's claim to aristocracy with his family's earthen, unidentifiable roots.

"From where no one knows. Dad tells stories of what his granddaddy had to do to worship. Slaves sneakin' off at night to pray at the river. Even to Jesus. Whites didn't want niggers spending too much free time together. Might get some ideas. His daddy got a job as a Pullman waiter. The family name was Wiggins by then but no one knew why. Made good money. End of the line for the train was Oakland. He bought his home in the Twenties. The rest is in a photo album in my mom's closet."

"Africa or not, we still niggers, Larry," Sylvia said. "And this the only damned country in the world where we's niggers."

There was an awkward pause as Larry laughed nervously and did not respond.

"You workin'?" Sylvia asked in what appeared to be an attempt to change the subject.

"For the Panthers," Larry said. "Always, for the Panthers."

"Panthers don't pay much," Sylvia said sarcastically. "You have a real job?"

"Construction," Larry answered. "I build houses."

It sounded impressive the way Larry said it, as if he owned a business and employed a crew. And Karl had given Larry a $1500 bonus when the house was completed. Karl would hire Larry again for his next house. And what Larry most liked about Karl was that he brought him to work in the hills without asking neighbors for permission to have a Negro on the jobsite, which was common practice, even within the liberal canyons of Berkeley.

"You workin' now?" Sylvia asked again.

The inquiry had the feel of an assessment and Larry wondered if this were a way Sylvia had of expressing an interest in him.

"Takin' a break," Larry responded. "New house going up in the fall."

The second answer was a lie. Larry didn't know when he would work again but he didn't care. He wasn't interested in a deeper relationship with Sylvia.

"Do you work?" Larry asked.

"Not easy finding work," Sylvia answered. "Forget retail. I've applied to Capwell's, Macy's, JC Penney, and Sears. No one wants a black face out on the floor."

"Your face ain't hardly black," Larry responded. He had noticed how light-skinned Sylvia was, but then just about every black person was light-skinned next to Larry whose rich, lustrous color was notably dark chocolate.

"Yeah?" Sylvia huffed. "You sayin' I'm not black?"

Larry heard her angry, defensive response.

"Hell no, woman!" Larry shouted in embarrassment. "You just lighter than me. And who isn't?"

His self-effacement was unwelcome.

"Aren't we trying to lose all this color shit?" said Sylvia. "Aren't we trying to make black into something beautiful? Does anyone really care how black we look? No honkie I know seems to care. To them, even a little bit a black makes us black people. And I have a hell lot more than a little bit a black. I got Africa in my veins. What do you have? You don't even know."

Larry lost touch with the image of himself, as if his identity had vanished in a moving mirror that in every change of position also changed him. He wondered if he were even a black man or if he deserved to be a Panther. Why did Sylvia's lighter skin bare mentioning? Was there a fault in Larry's devotion to the cause? His infatuation with Inger returned as a factor in the sudden exposure of his comment about skin shade. It was a thoughtless interest that seemed to matter only to him, though Sylvia's fierce response suggested that any concern with the qualities of blackness posed the need for a deeper liberation.

Larry parked the truck and walked Sylvia into the Panther office, a modest storefront on Grove Street, its window covered with posters and photos, the largest an image of Panther founder Huey Newton as he sat regally in a rattan chair, wearing a leather jacket and his Panther beret while holding a rifle like a scepter. He stared affirmatively outward, his angry eyes the signal he was ready to defend himself, his people, his community and by any means necessary.

Larry introduced Sylvia to Captain Elgin, who was the officer of the day. Another woman sat nearby, her hair trimmed shorter but in the same Afro style as Sylvia's. Larry and Elmore air-punched a greeting with clenched fists, while the women air-kissed in a brief embrace. Sylvia had expressed an interest in community outreach and was told she'd be writing for the Panther newspaper. Larry remembered it was his week to peddle the paper, which sold for a quarter and, in just a few months, had expanded its circulation to more than 10,000. It brought in some revenue, as did the sale of Chairman Mao's renowned Little Red Book of revolutionary homilies, which the Panthers purchased for a quarter each in Chinatown and then sold on school campuses for a dollar.

"We heard from Sam!"

It was the first thing Larry's mother said when she opened the door. She and the Reverend occupied a small home behind the Community A.M.E. Church on Stuart Street where the Reverend was the pastor. His parents owned a home farther south on McGee but the congregation built the house on church property so the minister would be available to parishioners around the clock.

It was a small church but within Southwest Berkeley a prestigious one. It was supported by old money from established black families, most of them property owners. For the past seven years the Wiggins had lived in the small church bungalow and rented out their home. It was sometimes a hardship. There was only one small room in the bungalow for their sons. But it was free and by renting their home they greatly increased their income.

Larry's brother Sam was serving a tour of duty in Vietnam, one that had started in October of the previous year and that would end in September. Their mother, a small, slightly corpulent woman in her mid-forties, kept a calendar in the dining room. As each day passed, she crossed it out with an X. There were slightly more than two months left in Sam's tour.

"He says he's driving trucks now."

His mother told Larry the news.

"Thank dear Jesus! He's not even carrying a rifle anymore. He survived Khe Sanh. I know the Lord's lookin' out for him."

Larry's mother was a religious woman who met his father in

Divinity School. She was a clerical employee in the dean's office, having arrived at her job interview with a typing speed of 85 words per minute. She credited her high school typing class as her key to success. Despite her insistent pleas, neither son took a typing class.

She stood before Larry, her sturdy legs and weighty, obvious breasts encased in a full green dress with long sleeves, red lipstick applied like plaster to her large, brown lips. The combination of colors diminished the shade so that it looked garnet instead of rosy. And she loved the color rose, since Rose was her name and, within the tight community that was her congregation, she utilized her name as a moniker of authority. Rose was the minister's wife. Rose and Rev. Josiah Wiggins. She was a flower of faith. She was always present and available and always well dressed. She was a church asset, but one everyone clearly understood was on loan from her husband.

"Dad around?" Larry asked.

Rose shook her head no.

"Show me the letter," Larry asked.

Rose went to the refrigerator. A portrait of Sam in uniform was taped to the door, as was a letter commending Sam's service during the battle of Khe Sanh in February. *Pfc. Wiggins demonstrated extraordinary bravery. His successful effort to rescue three wounded soldiers occurred under a dangerous barrage of enemy fire.* The letter from his commanding officer mentioned Sam would be recommended for a bronze star.

Rose reached for Sam's latest letter and handed it to Larry.

Finally got some RnR in Saigon. Got a few minutes to write this. I'm good. Sure would love some of your fudge, mom. Driving trucks now. Convoys out of Saigon that go south. Boring but almost over. Can't wait to get home. Countin' the days. Love, Sam.

Larry read the brief letter, the first from Sam in nearly two months. Sam never wrote to Larry, just to their parents. And what he said was not very revealing or even very much. Until they received the commanding officer's letter, they did not know Sam was up for a medal. As Larry finished reading, the kitchen door opened and in walked the Reverend.

"Oh…excuse me. It's the mighty Black Panther. Is that right,

Rose? Is this the big scary Black Panther that's gonna win the war against white people?"

Prepared for a workday with the Party, Larry was dressed to work: black beret, black jacket, sky blue t-shirt imprinted with the emblem of a charging panther, and black jeans.

"Oh my god," his father said as he approached Larry and fingered the lapel of his jacket.

"Full uniform. Must be big doin's down at headquarters. 'Course your fearless leader is in jail and on trial for murder. You gonna fight a war against whites? Really? Are you goddamned crazy?"

Larry pulled back and set Sam's letter down.

"Reading Sam's letter?" his father continued to taunt. "That boy's a hero. A patriot. The other is…well…what are you son? A traitor? Just when things start turnin' around in this country you go and…"

"Turnin' round?" Larry shouted. "You think things are turnin' round? Wish you could ask Martin that question now. Oh yeah, and you could ask Malcolm X or Medgar or Lil Bobby. You tell me what's turnin' round."

"You need to find a real job," the Reverend scoffed and lumbered out of the kitchen, his tall, large frame completely filling the doorway as he moved toward the hall.

"A real job?" Larry shouted after him. "What's a real job?"

The Reverend returned.

"Your brother has a real job," he shouted back. "Hell yes. He's workin' for America. He's a hero. He's comin' home with a great life ahead a him. You just lookin' to get yourself killed."

"He's in the Army *there* 'cause he couldn't find a job *here*."

Larry's voice rose as he tried to speak over his father's.

"You know that's why. He was one of the boys on the block and he was headed for big trouble. Those weren't vitamins he was sellin' outta the trunk of his car. You know…"

"Get out!" the Reverend shouted. "Get the hell out of my house!"

"No, Josiah. You just calm down."

Rose at last entered the fray.

"And Larry, you stop this. This has got to stop between the two of you. I won't have it."

The Reverend shrugged his shoulders and walked briskly out of the kitchen.

"Goodbye, mom," Larry said to Rose as he handed her Sam's letter.

"He doesn't mean it," Rose said to Larry.

"He don't understand it," Larry responded. "He has a good job, don't he?"

"You stop it, Larry," she answered. "He worked hard for what we have. You could show some gratitude. And your brother…you don't mean that, do you?"

Larry waited a moment as he looked vaguely out the kitchen window; his heart pumping anger while his mind struggled for words.

"I love Sam," he said, for no reason other than that it was what his mother wanted to hear.

"But why does he have to go and fight a white man's war? Ain't no Vietnamese ever did anything to hurt *us*."

"Because he wanted to," his mom answered.

"Because he had to," Larry countered. "That or get back on the streets. No jobs. You remember Aunt Rema? She was the maid at the Hink's store on Shattuck. She musta been the only black person workin' downtown during daytime. Did you ever see anyone else? Not even a waitress. But plenty of janitors. Plenty of black people pushin' brooms after hours. And those were the good jobs."

"When he gets back, the Army is payin' for school," Rose answered. "That's gonna be worth the whole damned thing."

Larry was finished arguing. He hugged his mother again and turned to leave.

It was a stifling discourse, his father playing the role of tyrannical inquisitor. Against it, Larry could find no place for his own words, no place for the truth he so easily grasped and that his parents did not see. Perhaps it was simply the end of their effective time and the beginning of his, though his brother's happy soldiering suggested that within his own generation there was still no consensus.

In the morning Larry asked himself what he would do for the Panthers today. It was the first question he asked himself when he awoke. There was no easy answer. Usually he stopped by the Grove Street headquarters to consult with his section leader. Today that was Elgin again. Today Larry phoned.

"Papers gotta get mailed. Bennie's in LA and he can't cover it. Get over to the City and get the bundles out. Thousands of papers goin' to 49 goddamned cities. You know the drill."

In a year as a Panther Larry had risen through the ranks. He was smart and smooth and patient. The smoothness was especially welcome since the Panther core had a temper. It might be described as the temper of a raging 18-year-old on the corner, a temper that could start trouble, the kind of trouble that never ends. On one occasion, a white student at Merritt began heckling at a Panther rally. The word "nigger" was said and that was all it took. Three Panthers guarding rally speaker Bobby Seale went after the heckler, punched him the face, threw him to the ground and stomped on him. News crews filming the rally turned their cameras away from the speakers and toward the fight. Larry jumped in and pushed the Panthers back.

"Give him air," Larry said. "He's a fool."

That was enough. And that Larry's intervention made the news was a benefit even Bobby acknowledged. Larry became a liaison with white radical groups that supported the Panthers, and also a contact for the white press.

There was plenty to do. Panther founder Huey Newton was in jail and within weeks would go on trial for his life. He was accused of shooting and killing an Oakland cop the previous October while on one of the Party's community patrols during which armed Panthers followed police around as they drove through black neighborhoods.

The previous year Panthers showed up at the state capitol and walked with their unloaded rifles into a session of the state assembly. The incident, a misdemeanor, was charged as a felony of conspiracy; a conspiracy to commit a misdemeanor. Charges were eventually dropped. But now Panthers were constantly being harassed by the police, and stopped, arrested and searched.

"They know Panthers are a different animal," Larry told Mack as they drank coffee at the Café Med. "These are brothers who won't turn the other cheek."

Mack wanted an interview with Huey Newton.

"You don't ask much, do you?" Larry said.

"He's entitled," Mack responded. "If he wants to talk, I'd like to report his words. Might help. Lots of people think Panthers hate white people."

"Yeah, the cops want people to believe that. White people. Panthers don't hate white people. We hate pigs. We hate oppression. We hate authorities that want the black community suppressed and silenced."

"OK. OK. What do you think you can do?"

"I can ask," said Larry.

"Your dad's a preacher. What does he think of you being a Panther?"

Mack's question was like a slap. If Mack weren't his friend, Larry might have slapped back. Instead, he told the truth.

"Off the record," Larry said with emphasis, "he sure don't like it. He's a religious man. He's a disciple of Martin, the *late* Martin, that is—non-violence, polite engagement, respect. He don't understand self-defense. Probably 'cause he's never done it. He thinks black people are knockin' on the door, that we actually have permission to *knock* on the door, and that's progress. I try to show him that the door needs to be blown off its hinges. Until there's no door there's no justice."

Mack told Larry he, Raj and Yitzhak were going to Big Sur to camp for a few days. Would he like to come?

"You doin' drugs?" Larry asked.

"Do fish gotta swim?" answered Mack. "Pot and some beer. And acid. The acid is optional."

"Yeah. Sure."

Larry did not hesitate. The way his white friends used drugs differed notably from the substance abuse of his own community. Fortified wines in small bottles, opioids from discarded or stolen pill boxes, methamphetamine and heroin; these were the drugs of choice in his neighborhood. His uncle seemed always to have a fifth of Johnny Walker nearby. He liked to "let it run" when guests arrived until everyone was oblivious to the powerful pain that ran like an electric current through all of them.

White folks also could use drugs to numb deep, life-eviscerating pain. But Mack and Raj appeared to engage drugs for the achievement of some weird kind of enlightenment. And what was that about? What did they know he did not? What did they seek that he could not find? It was a reason to go to Big Sur. There was always a reason to run away from things as they are.

Larry added a query about an interview with Huey to his Panther work list. It included the Panther paper distribution, staffing a Panther informational table at a weekend rally, and a forced march practice for Panther recruits in DeFremery Park early Saturday morning. Panther boot camp also included training in the use of firearms but after a year Larry still did not own a gun. It was one part of being a Panther he could not abide. Self-defense sounded good and he would throw himself in front of anyone in his community who faced assault. But shooting to kill was not something he thought he could ever do, or at least not yet and especially after what had happened to Huey and Lil' Bobby.

He wondered again why Eldridge had sent Lil' Bobby out of the house during the shoot-out. Eldridge said he told the boy to strip naked but he was too embarrassed to take all his clothes off. Bobby took off his shirt but the minute he stepped outside he was shot dead by the cops.

As a soldier in the army, Sam likely had used a gun to kill another person. Larry wanted to ask his brother what that felt like, what it meant to kill someone he did not know.

"I ain't no race leader…does I look like I can race? Hah! Gotcha!" Murph shouted at Larry as he entered the Panther office.

"Where you gettin' your jive?" Larry asked Murph, a happy Panther with wide, funny eyes who moved with his laughter into any personal space like an ambulatory comic book. Willis Murphy, aka Murph, had joined the Panthers with Larry, marched with him at DeFremery and nearly lost both their memberships with his wild, funny eyes and irrepressible humor that broke up Larry and threatened to break ranks.

Murph read from Richard Wright.

Even when you's dead. They tell you where to go.

And then Murph riffed on a segregated graveyard where black ghosts were contained and unable to rape white ghosts.

"And why is Sunday morning the best time to drive in LA?"

Murph wasn't finished.

"OK, why?" Larry asked impatiently.

"The Catholics are in church, the blacks are in jail, and the Mexicans can't get their cars started."

Larry laughed. How could he not? Murph's deadpan delivery was his incomparable talent. Larry sometimes wondered if Murph alone could disarm the pigs, could tell his stories and leave them laughing so hard they would give up their hate and drop their guns and surrender to the fatal, funny truth.

Murph's humor and jive derived from several sources. Most came from his voracious consumption of black writing: especially the novels of Richard Wright, Chester Himes, Charles Wright and Ralph Ellison's *Invisible Man*. Murph hated school and dropped out at 16. But he loved to read, especially humor and satire and the darker the better. The rest was served up to him by a new generation of black comedians that included Godfrey Cambridge, Nipsey Russell, Dick Gregory, and a new young guy named Richard Pryor, who appeared recently at a club in North Beach. Murph helped Huey write his speeches and Bobby Seale, who himself had tried stand-up comedy, used Murph to develop his applause lines.

"It ain't all fun and games," Murph growled from time to time, halfway imitating Eldridge while the other half impersonated Huey. His capacity to mimic voices was a gift.

"If it takes a war to silence these monkeys, let's get it over with..."

Murph could sound just like Reagan—clipped, resonant words with widely enunciated syllables—and also make the governor's constipated grimace as he resurrected in a flat, open delivery the perfect insincerity of Reagan's attempt to sound both determined and alarmed. And then Murph's eyes fluttered knowingly while

Larry, and anyone else within range, cracked up.

Much of the time Larry felt as if he were in love's wrong place. The feeling returned to him as he drove Sylvia into Oakland for a meeting with Father Earl, the minister of a church that might become a site for the Panther's plan to serve free breakfasts to West Oakland children. The plan was barely an idea but Sylvia had taken it on and was told about Father Earl by two women Panthers who also were members of his congregation.

"This could work," Sylvia said to Larry after thanking him for the ride.

"Free breakfast for kids?" Larry asked. "Who pays?"

Sylvia smiled.

"That's your job," she answered. "Keep sellin' those papers."

Larry had two bundles of *The Black Panther* behind his seat and, after dropping Sylvia, would return to Telegraph Avenue and hawk them at the south entrance to the campus.

"Really," she continued. "It's an easy sell. Who wouldn't contribute to feeding kids a free breakfast? The Father says he'll give us his hall and kitchen for nothin'. We can get parents to cook. All we need is the food."

Sylvia's energy was contagious but Larry wasn't attracted to her. He admired her passion but in a way that left no room for desire. Larry wondered why his time was taken up with this woman and not another. It was the Party, of course. The essential and asexual work of the Party kept him contained. Though it seemed not to have that effect on other male Panthers. Some hustled every new woman who entered the Grove Street office.

The jolting truth of his misplacement in love arrived that afternoon when he took a break from selling papers and walked to the Forum for an iced coffee. From a block away he saw Inger and Harriet at an outside table. Inger's animated gestures suggested she was sharing big news and Larry considered walking away. But Inger saw him and waved.

"How ya' doin'?" he asked as Inger stood to hold him in a brief embrace through which she had complete control before quickly dropping her arms to let him go. Harriet remained seated and waved vigorously, as if her over grand gesture might serve as an apology for not standing.

"Not so good," Inger said calmly before looking again at Harriet in a seeming search for support.

"Karl and Annalisa lost their baby."

Larry took a moment to register his place in the context of Inger's statement. He had worked for Karl. Inger was Karl's twin sister. There was a baby somewhere and probably in the tummy of Karl's wife, whom he had never met. So there was no picture of anything but his time with Karl who, while he worked at the jobsite, said very little about his life at home. It was left for Larry to simultaneously learn more and to react.

"How?" Larry asked.

"Baby was born dead," Inger said directly. "Full term. No one knows why."

Her eyes assessed Larry who gathered he was being examined by Inger and searched for what feeling might still remain in their friendship. What could he say? How could he feel, other than strange and surprised?

"That's bad," Larry answered weakly. And after a cautious pause, spoke again.

"Damn, that's really bad."

He did not ask any more questions though Inger appeared to be waiting for at least one. When it was not forthcoming she looked back at Harriet before staring once again into the confusion rippling across Larry's face.

"I need to run," she said abruptly. She reached down to hug Harriet and then turned to walk away.

Larry looked at Harriet whose open eyes appeared to convey sympathy.

"It was a horrible surprise," Harriet said. "Can you imagine? You go to the hospital to have your baby and it comes out dead…I guess…"

Harriet searched for words she couldn't find.

"Well, it must have been awful."

She asked Larry if he would like to sit down.

He did.

"Inger's told me about you," Harriet blurted through the stream of awkwardness now rolling downhill toward the table.

"Yeah, what?" Larry asked with an urgency that appeared to frighten her.

"Just that you're a friend, a nice guy…"

Larry wanted nothing now, and so did nothing. Inger vanished around the corner, her legs swaying widely as if imminently she would take flight.

"Are you OK?" Harriet asked.

She appeared uncomfortable and Larry thought his presence was a factor.

"Oh…oh yeah…" he answered. "I mean, sorry. I'm Larry."

"I know," Harriet answered. "We were just introduced."

Larry managed to right himself and find some words to express his existence.

"I'm for real…don't worry," he suddenly blurted. "I'm Larry and I'm for real."

Harriet seemed to go along, as if pacing Larry's awkward governance of some weird ravishment.

"OK," Harriet answered. "Inger says you're a Panther."

The statement was perfect, leading Larry into a disorderly monologue of his time in the Panthers and his youth in Berkeley.

"And you?" Larry finally asked.

Harriet demurred, editing her academic life into barely a sentence and not even bothering to mention Dante. She went to high school around the corner. Larry had lived in Berkeley all his life and didn't know Anna Head School existed.

"I'd like to go back to school," Larry announced in response to Harriet's laconic description of herself as a student.

"What would you study?" she asked.

"I need credits for a contractor's license," he stated in a way to convey a life's purpose. "But I like to read. I liked English in high school. Read Huckleberry Finn. Wrote a paper about it."

"You might enjoy taking a college level class," Harriet offered cautiously. She asked if he would ever be interested in writing about his experiences as a Panther.

The suggestion and question locked Larry into an attentive gaze.

He assessed Harriet in a way he had not yet imagined seeing her. He awaited the arrival of a white woman's familiar sexual interest in his appearance, but it never came. Instead, he listened to Harriet's words of encouragement.

"You're living history," she announced. "You have a lot to say about what's true and what isn't."

Larry wrestled with the anxiety of waiting. He held the phone receiver tight to his ear as he hid in the hall of his grandparents. Karl's phone continued to ring, as it had for two days. No answer. But Larry, despite his reluctance, could not resist the commanding charge to speak with his most gainful employer and to offer condolences for what he knew to be a deeply personal loss.

The urge to do something right collided constantly with the right way to do it and speaking with Karl about a dead baby was not easily located in the resulting intersection. Something was right about it and also something wrong. He waited for Karl to answer the phone and also for the answer to a question he could never ask. Will you still need me to work for you? There is nothing I can do to help but I want to feel close to this man for his loss. He is a good man. He has been good to me in a way that, at last and for once, had nothing to do with race.

"This is Karl," the voice announced itself.

The formality of the response forced Larry to look up and down the hall to assure he was alone.

"It's Larry," he announced. "You doin' OK?"

It was what Larry wanted to ask but not the way he wished to ask it. White people were indirect and Larry didn't know how to wait or how to cut out a piece of time and sit on it until the arrival of the proper moment to let it go.

"Yeah. Why wouldn't I?" Karl asked.

It was the question that left Larry alone.

"Inger said you lost your baby," Larry blurted. He could tell immediately it was an unwelcome disclosure. A long silence followed.

"Inger told you?" Karl asked again.

It sounded as if he were taking names.

"She didn't say much. Anyway, I'm sorry, man. I'm real sorry."

Another long silence followed. Larry thought he could hear Karl struggle to catch his breath.

"Thanks, Larry. I need to go. Thanks for calling."

Karl hung up the phone without waiting for Larry's response.

It was impossible for Larry to hear Karl's few words as distraught and inadequate. Instead, he saw himself as the instigator of dissonance, the black man once again awkwardly engaged with a good master. Larry had hoped to connect with Karl as a colleague, though he knew his real relationship was that of a humble worker to a strong boss. And in this instance, race was a core concern. Larry tried to recall the first time he was aware of white people and his alienation from them; the first time he realized that two streets and two avenues circumscribed his comfortable universe: 22 square blocks of residential blackness wherein he lived with grace and self-respect.

Outside these neighborhood limits he was at first stunned to discover how threatening he was to those who did not know him; how in high school he was assessed for the limited qualities of his physical strength and attraction and then used as an athlete until he was completely used up. The championship photo of the basketball team in his junior year at Berkeley High said it all: it was exposed clearly for the faces of white players while his face, and those of his black teammates, melted into a glob of black, indistinguishable and shadowy tar. It was a horrible image but the white editor had no second thoughts about running it, as long as the white players were recognizable. Larry's parents were proud. Even if they couldn't identify him in the photo, they read his name in the caption. Larry was outraged and disappointed. His parents were used to it. He was back again between the odds and the ends.

three

"He said he had the people behind him and the people were his strength!"

Mack shouted from the backseat so Raj and Yitzhak could hear. Larry, who sat beside him, had already heard Mack's description of his jail interview with Huey Newton.

"He also has a pretty good attorney," Raj shouted back over the rumbling roar of the road as Yitzhak drove his bomber blue Chevy sedan south through Gilroy.

"That guy Garry, man, he knows the law."

"And how to beat it," added Larry. "He's a bad dude, for sure."

"Huey needs a bad dude," Mack added. "He's in big trouble and the cops and DA want him dead, stuffed and mounted for all to see."

The interview would run in the Chronicle the following week.

"When are we getting back? Four days?"

"Who cares?" Raj asked.

"When we run out of food," Mack said.

"And dope," Raj added. "Then it's time to go home."

Yitzhak was silent. It was late or early depending on whether one lived by night or awoke before dawn. The four comprised an uncommon troupe drawn to this journey by a sudden need to indulge the presumably enlightening magic of the southern coast. Yitzhak was their host and was taking them all to a stone house by the sea. It was a secret destination and he drove. Raj brought the dope and acid and Mack, the only fully employed member of the team, brought food and wine. Larry brought himself, which was enough. He was a good friend to all. A gas stop was needed in Monterey before the travelers slipped along the Carmel Highlands into the first expansive beaches and valleys of Big Sur.

"Should be some daylight by the time we cross at Bixby," Raj said. "Right Yitzhak?"

The stern Jew nodded affirmatively.

"And then a bath," Yitzhak said solemnly.

"And how far after that?" Raj asked.

Yitzhak shrugged his wide shoulders.

"Pacific Valley…maybe noon. It's south of there."

At a gas station in Seaside Larry left the car to use the bathroom, drawing the attention of a cop stopped at an adjacent intersection. Larry had offered to drive but declined after watching the cop pull his car into the station.

"Why attract trouble?" he said to his friends.

Instead, Mack took the wheel and waited for the cop to leave before starting the engine. They crossed the Bixby Bridge just as the grey shadows of nautical dawn formed over the ocean. After passing the Point they turned inland toward the hamlet of Big Sur and then climbed the mountains to hover a thousand feet above the water. As the sun rose, Yitzhak pointed to a sign-less pullout and directed Mack to turn and to drive slowly along a deepening driveway before parking at the side of a skinny trail.

"The Roman baths of Big Sur," Yitzhak announced as he led his three companions down a steep path that ran below an old house toward a shack without walls that faced the ocean. Inside, two couples lounged in the steaming waters of two large pools fed by a hot spring. Yitzhak stripped off his clothes and plunged into a pool. Mack and Raj followed slowly. Larry, whose caution was aroused by the small private property sign at the driveway's entrance, also undressed and slipped into the bracingly warm and soothing waters. The ocean, burnished by the day's first light, churned as if nearing a boil before colliding in thunderous splashes against the rocks below.

Larry allowed the water's heat to subdue him and to give relief from the familiar unease that was his waiting, that was his purest anxiety and one attached to both death and abandonment though he had no clear way to say this to himself. He was a Panther, of course, but here he was something or someone else. He breathed deeply as if pulled out of the ground, smelling new odors that might prophesize the flavors of a new life.

A half-hour passed in bliss as the day brightened over the sea and the couples, affectionate and unselfconscious, slipped naked from the water and away. In moments an older man arrived. He was thin and bearded and wrapped in a grey terry cloth robe.

"You guys have five minutes to get the hell out of here," he said directly.

"OK," said Yitzhak.

He climbed from the pool and began to dress. The others followed. Mack and Raj sauntered from the water like brash outlaws as if to advertise a weak, unauthorized defiance. Larry scrambled quickly, harnessed to a palpable fear he was trespassing dangerously in a white man's garden.

"The Roman baths are the Esalen baths," Mack said in the car as they left the driveway and turned south. "Private property."

"There's too damn much of that," Raj countered. "Why do they control access to the rivers and streams?"

"Because they can," Mack answered. "It's ownership: the foundation of a capitalist economy. Maybe we should have offered to pay."

"We will on the way back," Yitzhak suggested as if undaunted by their eviction.

No one responded as a silence settled in, all now held by Yitzhak in the orchestration of this journey. Was there a house? Yitzhak was a little crazy. But was he mad?

Past the bare hamlet of Lucia the road continued along a crumbling ledge until dropping beyond Kirk Creek into the open, green flatland of Pacific Valley. Spring run-off still filled flashing streams that flowed in profusion from tall mountains bursting up from the ocean. Past Plaskett the road began to climb until Yitzhak, like a dog searching for a buried bone, slowed the car and searched one pullout, and then another, for some clue or sign.

"Here," he finally announced. "This is it."

A climb began down a narrow path, Yitzhak running ahead to search switchbacks that led toward a rocky, shallow beach. The trail disappeared into a thicket of willows and poison oak before rising over a short ridge and down to the ocean.

"There."

Yitzhak pointed out an obvious structure built from the beach's rocks, a stone house comprising boulders assembled and cemented and covered with wooden slats and a wide sheet of corrugated tin that formed its roof. The house was perched securely on a single broad rim of earth that formed a solid saddle above the sea.

A ragged wind-ripped blanket served as a door. Inside were sleeping areas for everyone and a simple fireplace organized for warmth and cooking.

"No bathroom," Mack said sarcastically.

"Damn, this is so far out," Raj said as he shuffled off the remnants of his disbelief.

"And a stream right outside. Water and everything. We could stay here for weeks."

Larry absorbed the surprise long enough to miss claiming one of the two sleeping lofts installed at a window opened to a view of the beach. He settled for a corner near the fireplace and set down his pack.

"Let's get stoned," Raj shouted.

Larry passed the joint, his lungs full of chemicals that numbed the pain they created. He exhaled, his body calm and relieved of tension just as his mind entered a rat's maze of incalculable thoughts. *Need a job to get through the time of no Karl. Need to cover rent and insurance and…what is this muthah doin'? Dancin'. Yitzhak on the fuckin' beach in fat leather boots and he be dancin'. Raj claps and Yitzhak stares him down. Big boots, bell-bottom jeans and a red bandanna on his head. Boots look like they might come right off. He can't lift 'em. He's trying to tap his heels on the sand. It ain't workin'. I don't get it. Fuck, this is good shit. I'm really stoned. Need to cover rent and insurance. Need a job. What? Maybe Murph has somethin' at the machine shop. Panthers. No, can't take from the cadre. Not how it works. I am small. I am black. I am fuckin' black, man. Bobby, he's big and smart and says so much I can't even think to say. But something weird lives behind his eyes. These honkies…why has Mack read more Negro books than me? I don't fuckin' know, and just when I think I don't, I do. Hey…funny…I…*

"You diggin' this?," Raj shouted at Larry. "Flamenco."

"I need a beer," Larry answered. "I don't really get it, man. Looks like he's slippin' and slidin'. Where I live, that's not dancin'."

As Yitzak returned from the beach he was handed a can of beer by Raj, who pulled several from a case submerged in a pool of the cool stream that cascaded next to the stone house.

Talk drifted without much focus until Mack mentioned his interview with Huey and made a point of thanking Larry for the connection.

"You went into his cell?" asked Raj, chilled by the claustrophobic implications of imprisonment.

"We met in a visiting room. His attorney was there. Huey told me he lives in a cell ten feet long and five feet wide. It's the size of a fucking bathroom. The cops put him in 24-hour lock-up for two weeks just to show him who's boss. He has a bed and a toilet. A couple books. He seemed in pretty good shape. He's one smart man. He's certain he'll beat the murder rap."

"Yeah?" asked Raj. "Why is he so sure? The pigs are out to get him. The pigs and Reagan and the DA all want him dead. And why? He killed a white cop."

"He killed a white cop who was tryin' to kill him," said Larry. "It's slavery. It's black people who've been slaves for four centuries. Maybe somethin' worse in the world than slavery. But nothin' worse than being a black slave in white America. We ain't done with this. Free Huey!"

"Something worse than slavery?" Yitzhak asked. "How about the Holocaust?"

"How about it?" Larry asked. "For all those deaths, Jews still have a culture. Imagine a hundred years of Holocaust. Two hundred years. Four hundred years. No more Bar Mitzvahs. No more Hanukkah, no more Yom Kippur. After a dozen generations no Jews remember who they were. Yeah, you lost lots a your people. But you didn't lose no identity. You didn't lose who you were. And your skin ain't a color that gives you away, that makes you obvious and different from those who have held power over you for all the time your people was stomped on and destroyed."

"You guys…you don't know," Yitzhak responded. "I lost two uncles and an aunt in the camps."

"I don't know who I lost or how. Were they lynched? Shot?" Larry answered. "I don't even know where to begin lookin'. Before my grandfather's father the Wiggins, if that's who we actually are, were slaves. It don't matter they didn't die. It matters that we had nothing to call our own. Even our religion was white. Jesus…what the fuck? Africans worshipping Jesus? Why? My dad's a preacher and I will never understand why."

"But slavery's over," Mack said. "It's been over for a hundred years."

"And what came after slavery? Jim Crow. And lynchings."

Larry was on a roll.

"My granddaddy tole a story about working in a boarding house in St. Louis. Maybe 1912 or somethin'. Right before the first war. A black boy who worked in the kitchen was invited into bed by a white prostitute. Bunch of white guys came up from the bar, took him out back and cut off his nuts. He was 15 years old. 'He was lucky,' my grandpa said. Madam came and told the rest of the black help if that happened again, there would be a lynching. And she couldn't be responsible."

Larry took another swig of beer and let the alcohol do his talking.

"Grandpa just lived with it. That was all. Maybe slavery would have been better. If someone had owned him he might have been protected. As property, though. Not as a man. I got a friend, Murph. His great-grandma was born into slavery. She showed him her thumb before she died, all cut-up and scarred where her owner would take a knife and split it open when she didn't do something he asked."

"Black slaves outnumbered their white owners. Why didn't they rebel?" Mack asked.

"Why did Jews submit to the Holocaust?" Larry countered. "I've read everything I can find about it and I still wonder how and why it happened. They outnumbered by thousands the Nazi guards at every train station going to the camps. Why didn't they fight back? Why did they dig their graves, lie down and let themselves be shot? Why did they walk into the gas chambers?"

Larry paused a moment. He was stoned and knew he was rambling. This was a road trip and not a conference, though his last comment about the gas chambers once more aroused a glare from Yitzhak.

"Got a photo of a lynching," Larry continued. "There are hundreds of pictures because there were thousands of lynchings. Some are fucking postcards. They all look the same except for the faces. In my picture a crowd of white motherfuckers with big dogs stands next to a tree. From the top branch hangs the stiff body of a black boy younger than me. Probably about 1920. Dead arms hanging at his side and there's a hand-lettered sign tied to his feet that reads *Don't wake him up.* Well, we're woke now."

"It's history," said Mack. "It's the human experience and humans aren't particularly good at tolerating differences, especially when those differences assert the dominance of one group over another."

"No, it ain't history," said Larry. "Not for us. Still happenin' to us. You already forget about Martin? Not history yet. That's what the Panthers are about. To defend our own communities. To support our own people. To make our own god damned history."

Bodies have lives of their own. Larry's was a black body and while he sat with his white friends he felt himself outnumbered as he most often did outside the neighborhood. These were friends, but white boys and, however sympathetic, still distant from his fear and anger. They listened. He gave them that. But they couldn't really know or understand such a long and dismal history. Six million black slaves were taken during the 18th century alone and subjugated brutally: flogged, maimed, beaten, raped, decapitated, drawn and quartered, gibbeted or roasted alive on the whims of vicious white owners. Somehow a line from this terrorized past stretched precariously far enough to bring Larry into both life and awareness. He was here now and he was for real.

Huey knew this history and had studied it. But Huey also knew that going to war was crazy when you're outnumbered eight to one. Eldridge didn't seem to agree so now Lil' Bobby was dead. And Eldridge was in jail and probably headed back to prison. Larry thought it was stupid to go out and look for fights with cops. It was useless to start a fight you couldn't finish, much less win. That isn't self-defense. That isn't work on behalf of the black community.

It was a thoughtless provocation, though the Panthers continued to grow, and to pull in as many women as young men. Larry knew this really said something. The women, like Sylvia, wanted to start programs of community support. Huey called them survival programs. A food co-op was mentioned. So were free meals for children. Most of the boys just wanted to wear the party tam and jacket and carry a gun. The Party wasn't even two years old and it had more than fifty branches across the country and thousands of members. Could it hold itself together? Could it last? Would Larry last? The body was an animal. The body was more than simply its urges and wounds.

On his way back to the stone house, Yitzhak pressed Larry's shoulder with his palm. Perhaps it was a gesture of support though it felt more like a push. Dinner was wieners on sticks and buns toasted as they rested on rocks near the fire. A bottle of Red Mountain rouge loosened tongues while Raj pulled out his guitar and played a couple of Fred Neil tunes. Dessert was a watermelon, cut into chunks and followed by a happy smoke as two joints made the rounds of their foursquare circle. Larry had to pee and stood half-drunk at a rocky breast of the hillside as he watched the round orb of the sun, filtered safely through a bank of fog, fall like a gear into its place beyond the horizon.

The next day was set aside for the men's acid trip. At breakfast Larry said he would not take acid but would hang out to help and would prepare dinner for everyone.

"You don't want no stoned, angry niggah babbling up a bummer," he said. "I be cool. You white boys have your fun. I'm cool."

Raj brought out the tabs, small pieces of paper he said were as pure as orange sunshine though he could not name the source.

"Top secret," he said. "But at least as good as Stan's."

Raj always had a source and Mack and Yitzhak believed him.

The day passed in a fog that struggled to clear the coast. At first the effects of the drug were subtle, Raj and Mack giving themselves up within an hour to a bout of hysterical laughter as Mack tried to describe the convoluted plot of an action film. A brisk wind raked the beach as the two men sat on rocks, wrapped in heavy blankets and jackets like old women watching a sunset.

"Gay, madcap, thrill-seekers," Mack shouted to Larry and then collapsed again into a spasm of unmanageable giggles.

Yitzhak changed into black pantaloons and an embroidered white blouse. He pushed his feet into his heavy boots and wrapped a bandanna around his head, a process that took nearly an hour until he was able at last to stand and march decisively to the beach where he commenced a cumbersome, tireless dance.

Larry watched and waited. He watched as Raj and Mack talked and laughed and Yitzhak fell fully absorbed into a vigorous, futile and seemingly never-ending shimmy that had the look of a rough tango. Larry anticipated an acid trip would end like all drug trips which he knew first from observing his uncle after he let all the bourbon run and then would scream his slurred demands and offer to make trouble for anyone who would listen.

But this was different. By mid-afternoon Raj had left Mack to wander quizzically along the north beach as he searched for passage around a tide-swept point. Larry followed; concerned that Raj would misjudge the tide and be captured by an obvious undertow.

"So fucking beautiful," Raj kept shouting. "I have to see it."

Larry helped him over a rocky precipice and slipped with him onto another beach, wider than theirs. He followed Raj as he wandered aimlessly, searching tide pools for shells and sea life and oblivious to the roaring sea that appeared to move closer. After an hour, Larry saw the path across the precipice closing under the tide's surge. He pulled at Raj and marched him back.

"Come on, man!" Larry shouted. "We 'bout outta time."

"Time?" Raj answered. "Yes, we're running out of time. All of us. Out of time."

Larry pushed Raj over the rocks, just missing a wave that might have swept both away.

"Son of a fuckin' bitch," Larry shouted. "That was a close one."

"So fuckin' beautiful," Raj said again. "You are a prince. You are the people."

Larry guided Raj back to their beach where Mack stood talking to himself in a bank of high grass above the sand. Yitzhak still danced and Larry wondered if he had ever stopped.

"This is goddamned delicious," Mack said at last. "You are one good cook."

At some point in the late afternoon or early evening, Raj, Mack and Larry fell together into what appeared a bleary calm and sat motionless for an hour. They settled on towels aligned on the beach and Larry wondered again if, as with drunks or speed freaks, it was the calm before a drug-riled storm. Larry used the time to go through their food and found a package of noodles, two cans of beans, and a jar of tomatoes he boiled in a pot he found in the stone cabin. He added stream water, cheese and salt and boiled it all over a fire into a chunky gumbo. As the acid wore off, the white men—becalmed and chatty—returned to the stone house, each appearing in dazed, stoned wonderment as a humble suppliant drawn by the bubbles and smells of Larry's soup.

While his friends ate voraciously, Larry took slow and deliberate sips of the steamy broth. He was lost in a reflective paralysis, guessing at the intentions of companions he sometimes thought as strangers.

He knew Raj had slept with Inger and he wondered if he still did. Larry had waited for Raj to say something but nothing was said and Larry would not ask.

Instead, he lived impatiently in the evening's embracing darkness and with three white boys, each of whom had thrown away things Larry could not even dream to own. These might include a college education, an enriching family heritage, a privileged access to employment, the right to be anywhere without self-awareness, and even to decide which people were white and which were not. He knew his very high friends thought nothing of these things.

In the darkness and silence of the small cove, the ocean's ceaselessly loud moan grew into a vibrant thunder. A nearly full moon crested at the Santa Lucia ridge, throwing its glow onto the beach like a quavering spotlight through the wisps of a clearing fog. Yitzhak rose in the light and, still dressed in his pants and blouse, ran to the beach where he again commenced stomping on the sand. Raj and Mack laughed and sat back to watch while Larry's mind swam with impressions drawn from a vast array of bewilderments. He thought first of his attraction to white women and theirs to him. It was a bitter pill that extended instantly into a contemplation of slavery in America and how its pervasive horror still haunted the land.

Why did he hang out with white people? High school had something to do with it, though he had to rise through resentments and impersonal slights he did not—felt he could not—call out. Some were simply rude, like the curiosity of a classmate who without asking ran his hand over Larry's fuzzy, lightly pomaded scalp. Some were vicious, like the shouts of "Nigger!" and "Hey, Sambo" he heard from the bleachers as he scored in basketball, typically during away games in the valley. As much as his neighbors and even classmates welcomed him, he lived with the disquieting suspicion a larger world did not.

But these men were good to him and treated him fairly. They offered what he knew to be a genuine affection though was it even slightly the remnant of a master's alleged "love" for a slave? Was it at all fair if Larry could never own what these white boys could decide they did not want?

Larry met Raj in 1966 during a rally and march to protest the police killing of a sixteen-year-old black boy in Hunter's Point. The boy had stolen a car and ran away when police stopped him. He hopped a fence and was shot in the back as he raced across an empty field. Hunter's Point rioted and the community rallied in the streets. Both Raj and Larry were arrested and eventually released, Raj that afternoon and Larry four days later.

"So what do you think of when you think of soul?" Mack asked as he and Raj sat at the empty house window and watched Yitzhak dance in the moonlight.

"Is there one?"

"There's soul music," Raj answered. "Right, Larry?"

Larry first heard the question of soul as a play on his blackness. Was Raj pulling his leg?

"You askin' a black man 'bout soul?" Larry asked in mock incredulity. "When I think of soul I think of the blues."

A silence ensued which Larry felt compelled to fill.

"Soul is pain alive in your body. It's a hard edge. It's both funny and sad but the funny part says to me that it's alive and the sad part says to me that it lasts. Like a long time. Even after your body dies. "

"So being sad makes you feel alive?" Mack asked.

"Well, yeah, in a kind a way that comes through my body," Larry answered. "It also makes me feel like a part of somethin' we all have. Angry, funny, sad. We all have a voice for these things. We all live 'em. Do we all die? Sure. But what dies with us? Everything? There has to be some kinda meaning in a hard life."

"It becomes a matter of faith," Mack answered. "Do you believe or don't you? Does a hard life make it easier to believe?"

"I come from a long line of hard lived lives," Larry answered. "Gotta say the trick is to hate yourself and your bad luck but still be glad you're alive. Soul is the music. It's in the blues. And the blues lift you up. Lift me up. And why? They say our pain. They must come from a soul…the soul. And we know it. B.B. King…he said singin' the blues is like bein' black twice. And what makes me blue? Losin' my lady. Not getting' my due. Lettin' my family down. Slavery and hate. Lots a things and they sometimes bring such great suffering you gotta think it has to mean something. Sometimes it's all you have left."

Larry realized Mack and Raj were listening to him as if he were a spokesman, perhaps an inspirational speaker, or as if their dinner had been a sacrament and he their preacher. There was no comfort for Larry in the role of preacher. His father was a preacher and Larry wanted nothing to do with that.

"Hey, I'm tired. You guys going to sleep?"

Larry tried to change the subject.

"Heavy, man," Raj said gravely. "That is some heavy shit."

Mack nodded.

"I'm crashin'," Larry announced. "Someone tell that wild Hebe on the beach to get his ass to sleep."

Morning returned Larry's friends to themselves. Mack made coffee. Raj, who brought a camera, finally took it out and began making photos of the beach. Yitzhak walked down to the sand again to pound his feet into it as if his dance were a kind of running in place by which he searched for something the others seemed already to have found. The day passed as a subduing idyll of lounging, sleeping and exploring. Raj returned to the northern beach with Mack. Larry sat at the cabin's wide window, eager to return to his work as a Panther. *Need a part-time job,* he thought. *Need something to get by. Need to see Inger. Maybe just one more time.*

He weighed the worries of his father against the politics of anger. Taking up arms seemed the only way left for him to stand up as a black man. Yet the death of Lil' Bobby left him feeling cold and useless. His white friends knew better than to ask about his Panther life.

The ride home was subdued. Yitzhak occasionally muttered words with an oracular ring but no discernible substance. His proposal to stop again at Esalen to buy a bath was quickly and unanimously outvoted. Mack asked more questions than he answered. Raj at last mentioned he was not seeing Inger anymore and had a new old lady who lived on the north side of the campus. The news quickened Larry's breathing. By the time they reached Carmel, an irritating claustrophobia had taken over, all but Mack the driver looking out side windows to absorb any spacious, wide view.

Driving through Fort Ord, Raj noticed a soldier in uniform guarding an overpass. Raj threw his hand out the window and flashed a vigorous "V" for peace to the soldier who upon seeing it ran to the overpass barrier to lean over and return the V, his two fingers stretched as far as he could safely reach with a wild, rabid wave.

four

Larry loved his troops. He marched his Panthers across the tennis courts of DeFremery Park: one hundred and seven strong, wearing tams and leather jackets, shouting on every fourth step *Off the Pigs!* More came every week.

How did this happen? Panther leaders were on trial, in jail and on the run. Panthers were shot and killed by police. But more kept coming. Thousands enlisted, men and women from the black neighborhoods of more than fifty cities. Most were kids. And he wasn't much older. Yet here he was, running a Panther cadre and rehearsing it for an afternoon rally at the courthouse. *Free Huey. Ten point plan.* It was beautiful and also scary. Could it last? It would be so beautiful if it could last. Others in history might have asked the same question: any king with a glorious empire and half the world nearly and fully under his thumb and still a likelihood that in the end there would be nothing.

The cadre's shouts were a purgative for the sick and contaminated world in which the cadre lived. All its members, all black brothers, were always suspects first. The cops that patrolled their streets and corners created the unreality of suspicion that kept every resident on edge, and the dis-reality of fear that kept most everyone from talking about it.

All black men were suspects. Larry had a photo in his apartment taken at the previous year's Panther march on Sacramento when thirty black men carrying their rifles entered the chamber of the state assembly to protest a proposed law that would strip them of their guns. The photo showed a late-arriving deputy, his rifle out as he jacked a round into the barrel. Four Panthers also jacked their rifles though they had no shells in them. After the photo was taken the deputy dropped the rifle to his side, got back into his patrol car, and drove off. The pigs were on them. Now the Panthers were on the pigs, their own rifles not even loaded but enough to chase away an oppressor.

"It was in the eyes," Murph said later. "You could see the pig was fucked up because we weren't turning away like he expected. Instead, we stared right at him. It was the god damned fire in our eyes. We get it. He don't."

The Alameda County Courthouse stood like a white temple of Babylon on the shore of Lake Merritt. By late morning on a sunny Monday in mid-July the slender steps of its entrance were stacked with Panthers and supporters of Panther leader Huey Newton. A parade of protesters, white and black, crowded the sidewalk and marched back and forth. It was the first day of Huey's long-awaited trial.

The women went first. Some seventy of them. They lined up in front of the courthouse entrance, their hair glamorous balls of infinite afro curls and looking like dark atomic snowstorms. They blocked the doorway as they could, dancing in front as attorneys and litigants tried to enter. No one would go in today without knowing Huey's trial was beginning. And Huey would win. He had to win.

Larry's troops followed. Marching from around the corner. In formation. Fists up. *Off the pigs!* they shouted in unison in a call and response with the women who yelled *What you say?* in a rhythmic, syncopated shout.

Time for revolution has *come.*
Time to pick up the *gun.*

Off the pigs!

Black is beauty-*ful.*
Set our warrior *free.*

Off the pigs!

The nearly iambic rhythm of the shout was everything. It conveyed a strut of confidence. *We are a new people.* It was Larry's happy phrase for the change that was coming though it forced him to wonder what it might mean to become a new person. He had changed his identity many times in his life and none of these shifts, beyond those of his childhood, were characters he lived in comfortably. Now he was a leader. He was looked to as much as he looked. Everyone had their own idea of what it meant to defend the community. Everyone wanted to be told, though only a few could do the telling. All was in play. He thought of the time Big Gene thought it OK to rob a honky gas station attendant one night when they stopped for gas. He was gone. Bobby threw him out. It was a lesson Larry understood. Larry's father was a preacher. Larry knew right from wrong.

Murph stood beside Larry and smiled.

"You done it, my brother," he shouted. "You got 'em all lined up singin'. Damn!"

Murph laughed.

"Love the Panthers like a school boy loves his pie."

Larry didn't always understand Murph. But he was funny. And loyal. And he weathered oceanic changes. He floated on a deep blue sea. And he knew the blues.

"Springs are getting rusty, sleepin' single like I do…"

Murph, you got soul, Larry would say. And Murph would come back with something grand.

"Can't sleep at night, can't eat a bite, 'cause the woman I love don't treat me right…gonna go get some hop and get myself a gun and shoot myself a cop…"

Was there a blues lyric Murph did not know? When he wasn't doing a Dick Gregory riff, Murph spouted the blues. He did not sing them. He spoke them like an oracle, like a teller of tales and a harbinger of hard knocks.

The rally began to take its form as Larry found his place in front. He stood beside Kathleen, the wife of Eldridge Cleaver. She was Panther royalty and all eyes and cameras were on her as she puffed anxiously on a cigarette. The cameras were noteworthy and important. Larry was aware that much of what the Panthers did was intended for public consumption. Their tams, their afros, their leather jackets and guns, their women chanting on the steps, their fists raised in the air; these were all elements both iconic and theatrical and wisely necessary to grow a people's revolution within the belly of the world's largest beast.

Bobby called it *shock-a-buku* and it was an expression comprising all the Panthers did aggressively to draw attention. Larry saw Sylvia at the end of the women's line. She wore a vibrantly colored West African wrapper that covered her completely. She was wild within it, dancing excessively as the fabric's bright blue and green pattern of inter-stitched patches stretched against her wide, churning hips. A few other women had chosen African clothing, though most were in black skirts and leather jackets, some wearing small tams pinned into their hair.

Larry waved at Sylvia who did not see him. The women danced to the chants shared and exchanged with the troops. The only police presence was a fat-faced sheriff's deputy peeking out from inside the glass door of the courthouse. It was a good feeling, to have surrounded the citadel of so-called justice as if a castle of common fear was now under revolutionary siege.

There were few speeches and a bullhorn was all anyone could use. Panthers and supporters crowded the steps to a point that two deputies emerged from the building to clear a path up the stairs for the day's litigants racing to court. There was some shoving and two more deputies emerged, forcing the crowd back with their crossed batons. During a shout-out by Kathleen Cleaver, a bus pulled up to the corner and disgorged a parade of Peace and Freedom Party activists, most all of them white. Bronwyn appeared last, saw Larry and approached.

"Where do you want us?" she asked.

Photographers clamored toward the new arrivals. Cameras rolled. A newsman shoved a microphone at Bronwyn.

"Later," she dismissed.

"Steps are packed," Larry reported unnecessarily. Anyone could see that the narrow steps and sidewalk in front of the courthouse were filled to brimming.

"Get over to the side and form a line. You can all walk single file back and forth across the sidewalk. No one can bust you if you keep moving."

Bronwyn retreated to direct traffic and Larry held the center. The chanting continued as the new marchers began a slow walk and raised their fists in support of the Panthers and Huey.

Regardless its expressed defiance, Larry embraced the rally as a jubilant festivity. Beyond his attentive work as cadre coordinator, he reveled in the large Panther roar assembled to shout support to Huey and defiance to the pigs. Panther flags adorned with the Panther emblem hung from poles extended by his alert, serious troops.

So different from the somber rally that followed Lil' Bobby's funeral three months earlier at which every pain he shared with others was saturated for him by notions of personal guilt. Celebrities and leaders attended the funeral. Actor Marlon Brando spoke at a rally near the courthouse. He was humble and shaken.

"What if it had been my son?" the movie star shouted. "I can't begin to understand what you have experienced—and I need to. All of us need to."

There was no applause, only a common exhaustion and a fresh, nearly innocent, misery.

Today was different. Larry and everyone else were elevated above the notions of suffering by a cheerful commitment to the work of protest. There were no weakening notions of guilt, only a determination to shout and stomp and show up for Huey. And it was enough to sustain for hours the noise and obstreperous attendance of citizens united against injustice.

After a brief appearance by Huey's attorney Charles Garry, who waved to the crowd before speaking with reporters, the rally began a slow disintegration as people walked away from the courthouse steps in globs and clusters. Larry assembled his cadre for one last march back to the park. As he led his young Panthers past the Peace and Freedom Bus, Bronwyn pushed toward him.

"How about a debriefing?" she asked Larry.

"A what?" Larry answered, surprised.

"A powwow. A meeting."

"OK, I guess," Larry answered. "Where?"

"Let's meet at the Albatross," Bronwyn suggested. "We can get a beer."

"What time?" Larry asked, mindful of the cadre passing behind him.

"Couple of hours. How about five?"

"Yeah," Larry answered quickly and left to jump back in front of his marching Panthers.

He wondered who else would be at the meeting. He was the Panther contact with what Bobby described as their white collaborators. Should he first try to talk with Bobby or Big Man? He decided he didn't have time. His work and his devotion were evident though Larry frequently wondered to what was he truly devoted? What did he choose? What had he ever chosen? His race? His ethnicity? His home? His parents? His education? His friends? He was born to a glittering republic in which he had no real history and no assured place. He was one of a million details in a narrative without an author.

Larry entered the small pub on San Pablo Avenue. It was not far from where he lived. He saw Bronwyn before she saw him, her straight, black hair released from its bun. She had changed from her jeans and sweatshirt into a spare ensemble comprising an olive turtleneck and short denim skirt that revealed her stout, muscular legs. She had traded her boots for sandals. Larry drifted like a ghost ship toward her table. Bronwyn saw him and waved.

"A good day, don't you think?" Bronwyn offered as Larry ordered beers.

"Yeah," Larry answered cautiously.

He was nothing if not agreeable with Bronwyn whom he presumed was engaging him in a process of some kind, perhaps to test his authority or negotiate terms of an alliance. He was nervous, thinking he might have to speak for the Panthers, which he determined he would not do. He would make no promises and accept no offers.

"You looked great out there," Bronwyn said. "The people's man leading the cadre. You have a lot of class, Larry. And cameras everywhere. It will be all over the TV and radio tonight and all over the front pages tomorrow. Free Huey. Everyone will be shouting it."

Larry appeared confused. What were they debriefing?

"You got some business we need to do?"

Larry was direct in a way that at first startled Bronwyn. Her eyes widened. Larry noticed she had applied eye shadow.

"Why…no. I don't have any 'business' as you say," she answered. Her cheeks puffed in a mock pout.

"I just thought we could get acquainted. I've been organizing the last three years, trying to figure out how to involve people against the Vietnam War and racism. It takes a lot of time and a lot of knocking on doors. Sometimes I just need a break."

Purpose was gone and nuance immediately took its place. Larry now understood Bronwyn, knew her in the places she still might not know herself. She was attracted to him. He had been here before. He relaxed into that natural part of himself that like a metronome could keep a perdurable beat. He felt her pulse from across the table.

"Tell me about yourself, Bronwyn," Larry asked cordially.

He opened her mouth for her and her stories tumbled forth: her childhood in Queens, her dear Jewish friends, her mother the Communist housewife and her father the contractor who commuted to Staten Island, her adolescence and its dooming sexuality, her political awakening to Marx and Malcolm, her freshman year at NYU and her mad urge to attend Berkeley. She described her arrest in the Free Speech Movement, followed by the acronyms of groups and coalitions she had joined or led. She had helped to organize the Peace and Freedom Party's first state convention in Richmond.

"At last a progressive party will be on the ballot," said Bronwyn. "Ten states and counting. How does Eldridge Cleaver for President sound? It's either him or Dick Gregory."

Throughout Larry nodded with competent empathy. He ordered two more beers and asked her to continue.

"You been workin' hard, woman," he said as he reached across the table to take her hand briefly and then let go, as if to display an unassertive errantry. Bronwyn returned the gesture, which Larry understood clearly. He had lived a life in which amorous engagements resembled one another, had proceeded from the same hopes and errors. He was accustomed to the infinitely pursued dislocations of addictive infatuation. So often, and with white women particularly, he was the facilitator of buried and muted desires.

"Tell me, Bronwyn," Larry countered with what was meant to sound like ingenuous warmth. "Doing all this work for the people, have you ever fallen in love with anyone?"

A first consummation took place over more beers and bar snacks. Bronwyn was surprised by Larry's query though it opened her to something heartfelt and that produced at least some reflection. She couldn't say she had been in love. She had been attracted to others and at one time felt attractive to someone she didn't like. She enjoyed talking about love in a way Larry thought she would.

The two activists were woozy after an hour of drinking and discourse and as the bar filled with its evening regulars the noise level rose beyond their ability to either talk or hear.

"Let's go to my house," Bronwyn offered, a proposal fueled by alcohol but nevertheless inhibited by fretful risk. It was clear from her tentative delivery that Bronwyn's was a one-time-only offer and needed an immediate response to be fulfilled.

"Yeah," Larry answered, aware he was entering new territory where things might become either interesting or complicated.

He was still Bronwyn's colleague, though he could not shake a familiar feeling he was being pressed subtly into service. Would returning to her home, in which he had never been, widen or limit his choices? What use would they make of an intimacy on her terms? What use would she make of him? Decisions produced actions that led to outcomes. Already he felt the need for closure.

Larry rode in Bronwyn's Volkswagen as she lurched and jerked their way into the foothills north of the campus. Her basement apartment was off Virginia Street at Scenic and its plain, dark entrance confused him. He descended several steps and nearly tripped into his host as she searched her purse for keys. A ceiling light went on and Larry entered a cave-like room with only one wall of windows facing the street. The room was filled with political posters, including a large color print of two Soviet workers standing in front of a steel mill. They gazed synchronously toward a brightly rendered socialist sunrise.

"This is it," Bronwyn announced self-consciously. A loosely made single bed was pushed against one wall and a fat sofa against the opposite.

"Like some wine?" she asked.

Larry nodded and Bronwyn disappeared through a door into an adjacent, windowless kitchen and returned quickly with two water glasses nearly filled with a luminously pink rosé. She set the glasses on a small wooden table in front of the sofa and invited Larry to sit down. She switched on a table lamp and sat beside him.

"How'd you get involved with the Panthers?" she asked.

Larry wondered where to begin, wondered, too, if this were really the question that needed answering. He knew that relevant topics often were masked by irrelevant questions. If foreplay were required, there was no need to wait. He reached over and put his hand on Bronwyn's shoulder.

"You one sweet woman," Larry said with generous regard. "Why don't you move a little closer and I'll tell you all about it."

Bronwyn did as he asked and Larry wrapped her small shoulders under his long arm as she pressed against his chest, his words resonating against her ribs as he described his first high school foray into the civil rights movement.

"Tracy. Tracy Simms. She was a senior. She got me involved in the car dealer pickets and the Sheraton Hotel sit-in. It was quite a time. She went on to…"

Larry felt Bronwyn's breathing intensify and knew she wasn't listening. He continued to speak and also wait.

"How ya' doin'?" he asked. "You OK?"

Bronwyn buried her face in his chest and he kissed her quietly on the top of her head, catching strands of her straight black hair in his teeth. The rest was obvious. He knew what she wanted and what was expected. It was certainly lady's choice but Larry retained control until the moment when Bronwyn reached to unzip his pants, opening him as he thought he might open her, and exposed his swelling cock. She took it with her free hand and pulled at it vigorously.

"Whoa, baby," Larry shouted in surprise. "Let's take it easy. Let's move over to the bed."

Bronwyn followed his lead obediently, saying nothing as he spread her out on the mattress and lifted her turtleneck to kiss and fondle her breasts. They were small and lumpy, with slender black hairs sprouting from each areola. He sat up to remove her skirt and then her panties, exposing her short legs grown from meaty thighs that met at a thick, bushy crotch. A heaving belly protruded above her waist. For a moment he was frozen by her naked appearance, which was oddly asymmetrical and not initially interesting. He wondered what he was doing here.

"Let me turn off the light," Bronwyn announced self-consciously as she jumped naked from the bed and scurried toward the lamp, giving Larry a full view of her rumpy, squat and unfit body. She still had her glasses on.

The rest was easy, except when it wasn't. Bronwyn returned but Larry had lost his erection and they worked with collaborative embarrassment to arouse him again. Once recovered, Bronwyn handed Larry a condom taken from a small bedside table. As he fell into her body Larry become aware of an odor he could only think of as Bronwyn's smell. He could not say what it was but he knew it was something that stirred deeply within her and held her and that exuded a distinct and acrid aroma.

The odor then configured his experience; became its moderator of the moments as it might of his own life. He could not tune it out nor that their bodies were not at all coordinated: his large, lanky and muscular and hers short, squat and soft with a profusion of bony angles. They settled on a position, he prone and on his back and she on top, his cock inside her as she rocked too hard and vigorously against him.

They fucked this way until Larry, tired and distracted, suggested they turn over.

"Touch yourself," he commanded gently. "It would be hot. You can come with me. I'll help."

His frankness surprised and also excited Bronwyn in a way Larry knew it would. It was a technique he used with a woman when he came too fast and now seemed appropriate when he could not come at all. His experience of being a woman's interesting Negro allowed Bronwyn to feel her sexuality in a womanly way and without any of the guilt she might have with a white man and his conventional expectations. She could give up control, or take it, and in ways that were erotically interesting to her. She laughed self-consciously and then began to masturbate while Larry moved a finger, and then two, slowly inside her, careful to touch the soft tissue above and also to press against the spongy walls on either side. Within moments she convulsed in a splendid orgasm, Larry's inserted finger gripped by the spasms of her vulva.

"Oh my god," Bronwyn announced, still slightly drunk. "That was so far fucking out."

"No, far fucking *in*," Larry responded, laughing. "You come on down. Good girl!"

Bronwyn reached up to give Larry a hug. He leaned forward to receive it.

"I've never screwed a black man before," Bronwyn announced carelessly.

Larry was silent. He had been here with white women and did not want to be here again.

"You know…I need to split," he announced abruptly. "Need to work tomorrow."

He jumped up to dress.

"You need a ride?" Bronwyn asked from her inebriated, post-orgasmic haze.

"No, darlin'. You just stay in bed. I'll see you again soon."

Larry walked west on Delaware Street clinging to the shadows away from the street lamps. It was two in the morning and he was a roaming black man at risk of being stopped, searched and likely arrested for something. But he could not stay with Bronwyn, could not be another black man fucked and used by another white woman.

As he crossed San Pablo Avenue and found his block he realized Bronwyn was the first white woman he denied before she denied him. He thought again of Inger. That was the real thing and nothing of this evening seemed anything close to real.

five

Another day and Larry asked again what would he do for the Panthers. Where and with what would the Party strike next? Victims fed a city's appetites and victims who fed a city also needed feeding. Huey was smart to propose a free breakfast program for children. Ride-alongs to harass the cops only got Panthers arrested and killed, no matter how much Eldridge wanted to fight.

In a community linked by poverty and racial oppression, networks were everything. Most of the community's existing networks spread dope and cash and guns. It was time for one that connected children and families and what better connection than free breakfasts for kids?

Sylvia had no trouble getting the priest on board. St. Augustine's was a downtown Episcopal parish and Father Earl Neil was already a friend of the Party. He offered his hall and kitchen for morning breakfasts and Sylvia, who had been a Panther for barely a month, was put in charge. She asked Larry to help her.

"Free Breakfasts for Children. Five days a week," Sylvia announced. "Now we need money and volunteers."

"I got a cadre of volunteers," Larry said. "But what about the money?"

"We got to go out and ask for it," said Sylvia. "You know how to ask for money?"

Larry had sold the Panther newspaper and pictured himself on a street corner with a tin can and hand-lettered sign.

"No," Sylvia answered. "Hell no. We need big money. Where do you shop? Where do you mommy and daddy shop for groceries?"

"Safeway," Larry said. "But, shit…"

"No buts. We gonna ask Safeway for a donation. Least they can do. We gonna ask every business that takes money from the neighborhood. Damn, I'm up to askin' drug dealers and liquor stores if we have to. And every member of the Party needs to give it up. What they can, anyway. Even a buck or two."

"You be askin' money from a lot a white people," Larry answered.

"So what?" Sylvia shouted. "They take money from us every time we go in their stores. They don't hire us but they love to see us come shoppin'. Well, maybe if they can't help us give children a free breakfast we don't come shoppin'. Now I wouldn't put it that way at first. But I'd let 'em know how much their contribution will be appreciated by their customers."

"So how do we do all this asking?" asked Larry.

"We make a list," said Sylvia. "Start with our friends and work our way up. First I need to do a budget."

Larry was on a new trip. Where it would lead he couldn't say, only that it would mean he was no longer expected to play with guns. He might become like Emory, the artist for the newspaper, or like Murph who spent most of his time distributing the papers when he wasn't telling jokes or tuning into Lucky 13 for the latest soulful sounds. *Free Breakfasts for Children*. Sounded good and he would be working with Sylvia, though probably for her. She spoke earnestly as if her language were her skin.

Larry remained in thrall of her lemony complexion but knew better than to mention it again. Larry knew it was a sensitive issue, especially for colored girls whose looks were defined by white skinned fashion in which the shape of a nose, the curl and lustre of hair and the feel, smell and texture of touch were measured marks of beauty.

As a young child Larry overheard his mother say to a friend how lucky she was to have two sons and no daughters. Larry remembered her laughing as if it was a joke and he assumed it was because girls were emotional and argued a lot.

But it was no joke, as he learned in high school where imitating a white woman's appearance subsumed for many black girls all other fashion considerations. In his senior year a few brave young women came to school with natural Afros, the first to make an impression, as well as to endure flashes of ridicule from both black and white students, and whom Larry acknowledged instantly looked lovelier than he ever could have imagined.

Larry remembered the first time he faced up to the visibility of his color in a country in which all white people were invisible. He was a ninth grader in Berkeley's west side junior high. He played forward for the school's basketball team that was stumbling through a mediocre season and faced a home game against the streaking champions from an all-white junior high in north Berkeley. The visiting team entered a gym filled to the rafters with cheering black students and it clearly unsettled the white boys from across town.

Though it had not occurred to Larry that his fellow students were "black." Some had deep chocolate complexions but most ranged in shades from low brown and vaseline brown to coffee and cream and high yaller. There were dozens of words his classmates used to describe skin shades, though in a white culture it was never easy to evade the question of whether one was too black or not black enough. Pomades, straightening combs and skin whiteners still sold pretty well to Negroes. And the origin of skin shades raised the inevitable question of when and how a white taint entered the family line.

"You're not worried about me marrying your daughter," Murph quoted James Baldwin addressing a white Southern segregationist. "You're worried about me marrying your wife's daughter. I've been marrying your daughter ever since the days of slavery."

Still, Larry had taken for granted his life within a rainbow though to the white players everyone in the gym was black—black as coal and an intimidating presence since white was not a color but merely the absence of color and other than a flush of pink when they got sweaty, Larry's opponents had no color at all.

Larry and his team routed the intimidated champions and Larry never forgot how easily intimidated they were. Black was beautiful. Black was also powerful. And in his dreamier moments Larry imagined a black community, a black city, even a black state or a black country in which every person of color was invisible and every white person would live as Larry did now: with a hesitant, reverent self-consciousness but in a peaceful world without fear in which nobody is really white and nobody is really black and everyone is colored.

"Food for kids?" Mack asked Larry as they chowed on egg rolls in Robbie's Cafeteria.

"Really? Are you tripping? What happened to police patrols?" Larry smiled cautiously.

"Huey wants it. We got a church downtown that will do it. Free breakfasts for school kids every morning five days a week."

"You sure? You think the cops are going to be cool with that?"

"What can they do?" Larry asked.

"What can't they do?" asked Mack. "You need a permit? See how fast the city gives you one."

Larry fell quickly out of his depth. Mack was a news reporter and he knew city government.

"You need a friend on the council. You need about five friends on the council. Give me some time to get down with this and I might be able to help," Mack said. "But don't tell anyone I'm involved, especially the Panthers. You talking it up with families and neighbors?"

"We're going to ask for donations," Larry said. "I'm doin' it. It's happenin' right now. This is fresh and very real. You understand? It's revolution without the war."

Larry bragged a little to hold his own with Mack, whom he now imagined an ally.

"And what's in it for you?" Larry asked suspiciously.

"It's a great story. And I'll be the one who breaks it," Mack answered.

He munched his last bite of egg roll and jumped up to leave.

"Stan has a painting in a gallery in the City. Nice reception. Wanna come?"

The Vortex Gallery, located at the northwest edge of Hayes Valley, could be entered on Gough Street through the small side door of a warehouse. Once inside, the exhibit space opened to a cavern of large rooms and high ceilings and a vast wall of windows that faced southwest and through which a rosy twilight fought against drifting fog to briefly bathe the gallery in a shimmering orange glow.

Larry followed Mack who quickly found the buffet and got them glasses of wine. The gallery was crowded with people in suits and evening gowns. A rich crowd, Larry thought, as he felt self-consciously exposed in his blue sweatshirt and jeans. He caught the eyes of a well-dressed black couple that took notice and turned away.

A sign advertised the show as *Men and Women, Black and White* and featured both paintings and photographs. Mack found Stan holding court in front of his *Big Black Motherfucker*, the minimalist acrylic featuring one large black circle enclosing a small splash of red paint at its center. The painting filled a wall, though it appeared diminished by the other large paintings around it, many richly colored and representational of bodies, skies and landscapes.

"Hey man," Stan shouted at Mack, happy to see someone he recognized. Mack brought Larry over and introduced him.

"Cool show," said Larry as he pointed at Stan's painting. "That's one big…"

"Motherfucker," Stan interjected.

Stan wore a purple silk shirt with baggy sleeves, an exhibiting artist's privilege to wear whatever he wished. Perhaps guests would think Larry an artist.

Ginger stood nearby.

"Lot of women artists in this show," she said to Mack. "Lots of color and figure painting. Minimalists are significantly outnumbered here."

She sounded disappointed.

"Looks like you've made the big time," Mack said to Stan.

"Yes and no," Stan answered. "This gallery features a student artist in all its shows. The Merritt faculty recommended me and the owners went for it. And check out what they're asking for my painting."

Mack wandered up to the canvass, read the title card adjacent on the wall, and hurried back.

"Four hundred bucks," Mack announced and then whistled. "Wow."

"We'll see," Ginger responded cautiously. "It's a big show."

Ginger understood the cost of art was unrelated to the cost of living. She looked toward Larry.

"Have you seen the photos yet?" she asked.

Larry shook his head.

"Photos of Harlem from the Fifties. Go have a look."

Ginger pointed toward the arched entrance of another room.

Larry worked his way through the crowd and entered the room lined with mounted photographs that greeted him like friends. The images danced in a happy rotation of subjects: laughing children, eyes wide open; men smiling, appearing dignified in their walks through the frame. A mother's arm reached to touch a child's shoulder. A tall musician puffed hard into a saxophone. A couple embraced. Parents pushed a stroller through a park. And all were black.

It was the accumulated documentation of a life Larry only imagined, America as a great rainbow land where every face, every smile radiated the comfort of being within a colorful skin. He wandered twice through the room, counting some 30 photographs.

He found a poster with the name of the photographer and the book from which the images were taken. *The Sweet Flypaper of Life.* The photographer was named Roy and he had made photos for a book that featured the writing of Langston Hughes.

When the bicycle of the Lord bearing His messenger with a telegram for Sister Mary Bradley saying "Come Home" arrived at 113 West 134th Street, New York City, Sister Bradley said, "Boy, take that wire right on back to St. Peter because I am not prepared to go. I might be a little sick but as yet I ain't no ways tired."

And so it went, the words of Hughes spread across a reproduction of the book's cover on a poster highlighting the photography of Roy DeCarava of Harlem.

Larry was accustomed to Negro photos of prisoners, of lynchings, of civil rights protesters marching in oversized suits, of Panthers looking tough and angry, of ministers preaching and women crying; of thuggy young toughs mugging for the camera, of black athletes straining to win or of distant African cousins jiving and rumbling through incomparable rituals. Here before him was photographic evidence of another black world. And it was remarkable to *see* something he recognized and that was more than something he merely wanted. He saw it all plainly. It was clearer than a prophecy.

Larry could not leave the room. He walked again past every photograph, daring to touch one that was mounted and not covered in glass. The surface had a rough, slightly corrugated texture as if the print were alive within its wide range of tones. Larry forgot to find his friends who finally found him.

"Thought you'd left," Stan said as Ginger came up from behind.

"I wouldn't leave without saying goodbye. What time is it?"

"Closing time. For the gallery, anyway," Stan announced. "We're going to a bar across the street. Want to join us?"

Mack bought Larry a beer. Larry asked Stan if he'd ever studied photography.

"Tried it for a semester," he answered. "Pretty technical and not my thing. I still have the camera. Old Yashica twin-lens reflex. Easy to use. I did learn how to make slides of my paintings."

"Hard to use a camera?" Larry asked.

"Depends," said Stan. "Requires some patience. Want to borrow it? I'll show you the ropes."

Larry said yes. He was under the spell of a new kind of perception. He was caught between an obscurely known past and as yet unknowable future. Photos offered a new way to see but could he grasp what was involved? He would try. He was unaccustomed to expectation but now very much wished to approach the unexpected.

six

Until he saw the gallery's Harlem photos, Larry thought his skin to be another language, one of America's perpetually alien physical dialects that through DeCarava's eyes was made so immediately fluent and accessible. Larry's skin spoke a lingua franca and not merely a dialect.

He picked up Stan's camera the next day. Stan loaded a roll of film into the Yashica's back and demonstrated for Larry how to view subjects through a ground glass at the top and to focus and also set an aperture and shutter speed. He explained what he knew patiently and Larry listened, following along on the folded page of instructions that came with the film.

"A dozen frames on the roll," Stan said. "Shoot 'em and then take the camera to Palmer's Drugs on University. Ask for Zack in photo. He'll help you."

"Damn!" Larry said as he left Stan's studio.

He sat on a bench and opened the camera to explore again through the ground glass a vision of the world just in front of him. He focused the camera to bring into sharp relief the window on a nearby building, its glass reflecting the upper branches of a tree directly behind him. Would he have seen any of this beyond the camera's discriminating frame? A figure passed in front, a woman who looked at him through his lens, startling Larry with surprising embarrassment, as if he the intentional seer was now the one seen. He looked up as the woman winked, flipped him off, and strolled on past.

Larry asked his mother if she would sit for a photograph. At first she laughed, until Larry showed her his camera.

"My my my…that looks like a serious machine," she said

130

laughing. "Where'd you get that thing?"

"On loan from a friend," answered Larry, assuaging his mother's darker, barely guarded suspicions.

She consented to pose.

"You wanna take this picture in bright light," said Larry's mother. "And let's get my good side. Gotta fix my hair. I need a half-hour."

Delight was in her voice though how she would appear in a photograph alerted a larger, unspoken concern. It had been years since anyone had asked to photograph her. To become the subject of a photograph was in its way to receive an expenditure of affectionate interest and also a reminder that for so long she had not been seen. What would she see now in a picture of herself? What would others?

"If it turns out, I'll send it to Sam," his mother said as she sat in the shade in the backyard. "You sure there's enough light?"

His mother thought her skin had darkened over time and Larry knew she hadn't liked that. He remembered the beauty products that used to fill her bathroom, bottles and jars with names like Raveen and Nadinola that promised to lighten her complexion and give her longer, silkier hair. In other words, to look more like a white woman, though her skin wasn't dark. Her coffee color was as beautiful a shade as there was and she was lighter than Larry's father, whose dark chocolate skin Larry favored. Sam had gotten mama's lighter looks and, based on the color of their skins, no one would guess that Sam and Larry were brothers.

In recent years Larry's mother had thrown out her jars and cut her hair short though she still wore lipstick and the long and full-sleeved cotton dresses appropriate for a minister's wife. Larry rarely saw her in anything else.

"You ever thought a goin' Afro?" Larry asked as he circled with the camera, his face buried in the Yashica's viewfinder.

"Oh darlin', your mama's too old for that foolishness," she answered.

Larry signaled his intention and snapped the shutter. He signaled and snapped again. And again.

Larry needed a job. Karl had no work for him now. Larry applied to other contractors but the building season was nearly over and crews were full. He considered retail but knew from Sylvia's experience he likely would not be hired for a counter job. Instead, he agreed to meet Murph at his machine shop in downtown Oakland. The shop needed an additional janitor to work after hours.

"That's good," Murph said. "They don't want our black faces out front but they sure as hell want our black asses out back washing their benches and scrubbing their floors when no one's there. Wear a sweater and slacks and don't even mention the Panthers."

The shop manager that interviewed them was a friend of a Berkeley councilman who knew Larry's dad and the manager hired Larry on the spot. Four nights a week, Monday through Thursday. The shop and an attached office would be cleaned thoroughly each night. Murph would supervise. Larry would report for work at 6 p.m. and check himself out at 1 a.m. The pay was $60 a week. Larry was given checklists of cleaning chores that needed to be filled out each night and left in a mailbox in the lobby along with reports of any issues or problems.

"This gonna mess with my Panther work?" Larry asked Murph later.

"Naw, man," Murph answered. "Don't mess with mine. And we be safe inside after the sun go down and while the pigs are out lookin' for Panthers. The Eagle flies on Thursday and we got the weekends to get down."

"I be fagged after workin' all night," said Larry.

"Maybe," answered Murph. "Me…I'm gonna get my rest and get my pay, and then I'm out on the town to play, mothafuckah."

Larry noticed how easily his speech moved across the many idioms of English that included the dialects of his Negro life and also those of his black and white friends. He grew up in a home where English was read to him from books. His father was a preacher and words were his work. So Larry learned the syntax of a mother tongue even though he did not naturally speak it. In high school he demonstrated a capacity to conjugate verbs, even if it weren't the way he chose to speak. It was if he were a Visigoth who spoke Latin. Such a capacity might open doors but also leave him behind.

No longer in school, Larry had ceased to sustain a mastery of white English. That is, until he heard Malcolm and Martin and Bobby and Eldridge who spoke the conqueror's tongue mellifluously and who could sum up in a few phrases the terms of war and justice and with words comprehensible to everyone. It was a quality of public eloquence that moved him to join the Panthers. It was a wondrous weapon and with more impact than any number of guns.

It might be that Larry had something to say. But he would need to say it in a way others—all others from brothers to white boys—might understand it. The camera felt in his hands like some magical machine of translation: a way to state with an image all the feelings, ideas and experiences that words might otherwise say. Was there a grammar in photography? Was there a way to conjugate images or throw them down in a game of dozens? Words seemed to play no role. Though words were all he had to express his excitement that an image could show more than anyone might ever say.

That evening he sat at the Forum with his new camera. He drank a coffee and aimed the Yashica along the street; his face crouched over the viewfinder as he practiced focusing the lens. Since he was looking straight down into his lap, few people had any sense they were being watched. Larry snapped a frame of a young woman crossing at Haste Street, her granny skirt flying behind her as she ran. He saw Raj approach and waved.

"Hold it. Let me take your picture, man," Larry yelled.

Raj stood at the corner through an awkward wait while Larry rose from his chair, focused tediously and then snapped the shutter.

"Very cool," Larry said. "I'll buy you a coffee."

"I'd rather have a beer," said Raj. "Let's go up to Kip's."

Kips was full and as Raj and Larry sat at the bar with their pint schooners a raggy blast of *Jumpin' Jack Flash* by the Rolling Stones poured through the speakers.

"Well, he's not exactly black," Larry said to Raj who had slapped his knee joyfully when the song came on.

"He's English."

Raj thought Mick Jagger a soulful lead singer and loved the British Invasion for its rocked out sounds and re-orchestrated versions of old American rhythm and blues standards. Even the

Beatles impressed Raj. He especially liked *Eleanor Rigby*, which he described as a song of "wounded, learned white man blues."

"That's a new one on me," Larry answered. "White man's blues? Feels more like a minstrel show, sometimes, to hear a white man try to sing blues. All that's missin' is the blackface."

"Wow," Raj responded with surprise. "That's pretty heavy. Really? Whites don't do enough suffering?"

"Man, you got it all wrong," Larry moaned dismissively. "I ain't against anyone's music. But the Stones, the Animals, the Beatles, Spencer Davis, what are those other groups? They stealin' the core of rock n roll, which began in the 40s and 50s and which I'm sayin' was developed and invented by American blacks. Elvis was the first minstrel, though I admit he sounded blacker than some of the Negro groups who were, of course, doin' their best to sound white. Anyway, it fucks with my mind to think of Mick Jagger makin' millions off those black ballads the original writers couldn't make $5 from. Damn, in 1962 the Stones and Beatles *opened* for Little Richard during his wild European tour. You think Jagger can do a Marvin Gaye song better'n Marvin?"

"Ray Charles just released his cover of *Rigby*," Raj said defensively.

"Yeah, I heard it," Larry said. "He sounds like shit. Wrong goddamned blues for a black man to sing."

"Wrong blues. There's a wrong blues?" Raj was flummoxed.

"You damn right," Larry answered. "An what pisses me off is that the English who barged onto this continent and started importin' African slaves in 1619, who killed millions of Africans and built this country on our backs with a gun, a rope and a whip for hundreds of years, these English and their babies are taking our dollars to sing our music of suffering and hurt, *our* blues, back to *us*. "

Raj could hear Larry's Panther talking and backed off.

"Yeah, I see what you mean," he said wistfully.

"What about jazz?" Raj asked gingerly. "Can white people perform jazz?"

"White people can do any damned thing they want," Larry answered. "They do anyway. Jazz? At least white jazz players generally honor the music's source. And nobody makes the kind of money from jazz that's made from rock."

"Want to come over and listen to some Coltrane?" Raj asked. "I've got *A Love Supreme* and I can't stop playin' it. We can smoke a doob and…"

"I'm cool."

Larry shut off the invitation abruptly and the two sat silently and watched baseball on the television above the bar.

"You been to an A's game yet?" Raj asked. "First year in Oakland and they ain't half bad…"

Larry shrugged his shoulders.

"Sorry, man. Sorry I jumped down your throat."

Raj wiped his hand across the bar as if cleaning a slate.

"No big thang," he answered.

Another silence ensued before Larry asked his question.

"You still see Inger?"

Raj heard an interest greater than simple curiosity and took his time to answer.

"Not much," Raj responded cautiously. "I saw her new pad on the southside. It's nice but I don't go by, if that's what you mean. Haven't seen her in at least two weeks. I got a girlfriend."

The last reminder was intended to assure Larry they were not rivals.

Larry offered his thanks and drained his beer.

"Gots to move," he said to Raj. "Next time, my man."

The two men bumped fists and Larry turned down the stairs and left. He found his truck on Channing Way and pushed his camera under the seat before driving east to College Avenue where he turned on Inger's street. He found her flat. It was nearly seven and all the lights were out, though a car was parked in the driveway. Larry drove up to the end of the block, found a parking space and waited. Any pain in his life was a fiction in Inger's. It always had been.

Her apparent racial disinterest was a pleasure to him even if it were also a racial ignorance. Inger did not understand how, in her absence from the country, the stakes of black experience had grown from protest into war. Names were now taken as lives were now lost. It was reasonable to think that white pig cops were prepared to perpetrate another civil war.

"Don't tell me. You happened to be passing by and…"

Inger stood at her door; suspicious that Larry knocked moments after she returned home.

"Yeah…just a lucky shot," he answered. "I take the Warren from Oakland to get to Telly sometimes and it drops me out right here, so why not say hi?"

It was after nine when Larry saw Inger park her Opel and enter her flat. He assumed she would be alone and hoped she would be happy to see him.

"Are you going to Telegraph?" she asked as if to confirm the truth of his excuse.

"Wanna come? I'll buy you a beer."

His answer now put the choice to Inger who declined his offer, but as a consolation invited him in.

"The place is a mess," she half-apologized. "Martin and I are working on a show and…it's a long story."

Larry entered the living room he hadn't seen since moving Inger into the flat nearly a month before. Its furnishings were spare: a wooden-framed sofa, two easy chairs, and a long pine coffee table. All was covered with fabric and cardboard cut-outs. A roll of brown packaging paper spilled several feet across the floor, the exposed piece rich with stenciled sketches that had no meaning for Larry.

Inger offered Larry a glass of wine, which he accepted. She disappeared into the kitchen and returned with two glasses.

"How's work?" Inger asked indifferently.

"Got a new job," Larry answered. "Machine shop in Oakland. Trying something new since Karl isn't building now. How's Karl?"

"It's a bad scene," Inger stated neutrally, almost too neutral a tone to believe from Karl's twin sister.

"Yeah, that's too bad about the baby," Larry said. "I phoned him."

"Then you know about Annalisa?" Inger asked.

"His wife? No…something else happen?" Larry asked.

"Oh, hell yes something happened," said Inger. "Annalisa left Karl. She's moved back home with her parents and wants a divorce."

"Holy fuckin' shit," Larry answered. "That's messed up."

"Yeah. It is. It's not good," Inger again stated calmly.

"What's Karl gonna do?" Larry asked.

His self-interest was on his sleeve and Inger recognized it.

"No fears, Larry," she answered. "He'll need to build a bunch of new houses to pay for this divorce. He's working up plans now for a home in the East Oakland hills. Found a lot and bought it after Annalisa left."

"And you?" Larry asked the question he did not wish to ask and awaited the answer he did not want to hear.

"Damn, what a month!" Inger nearly shouted with her typically unrestrained exuberance. Something good was coming.

"I quit the Jug Handle and got a job waitressing at the Claremont Hotel. Better hours, better pay and I can keep my shirt on. But the big news is that Martin, he teaches drama at Cal, he's using me in one of his shows. I'm *acting*. Well, not exactly acting. I'm appearing. It's an experimental piece. And I'm also designing sets."

She opened her arms as if to scoop up all that was spread across the disheveled living room and to own it as the basis of a new life.

"Say more," Larry asked harmlessly as he waited in the path of Inger's cascading, changed fortune. She was doing a new kind of art. She loved where she lived. Martin was a genius and in the fall she was going to enroll in theater classes at Merritt.

Larry heard the door open downstairs and heavy footsteps make their complacent trudge up to the flat.

"And speak of the devil," Inger said to Larry.

At that moment a tall man entered carrying a large briefcase. He wore khaki pants and a blue, short sleeve Pendleton. He was fit, about 35 and greeted Larry with cool regard.

"This is Martin," Inger said to Larry. "Larry's an old friend, Martin."

Martin took large strides toward Inger and put his hands on her shoulders. He bent over her like a bear over a cub.

"Hi, darlin'" he said as Inger relaxed deeply into his chest.

It was enough. Larry learned what he came to know. He was still in love with Inger, which he knew before arriving. But the loved one need not wait for the lover and Larry grasped that Inger's polymorphous affections had taken her a quantum leap away. Was there danger? Had that ever bothered Inger?

"I better get goin'" Larry said sheepishly as he stood. Neither

Inger nor Martin objected.

"Nice to meet you," Martin said as he continued his long strides toward the kitchen.

"I'll see you out," Inger said directly.

At the door, she reached to give Larry an affiliating hug, one he accepted along with its tender, neutral assurance he would forever be nothing more than one of Inger's acquaintances. It could never be anything more than that. Waiting was a condition of his life as a black man, a Negro, a minister's son, a resident of a ghetto, a Panther. He returned to his truck. What can I do for the Panthers tomorrow? he asked himself. What must be done? He turned the ignition, goosed the gas pedal once, and drove away.

Sylvia was uncomfortable and Larry didn't care.

"I'm not used to posing. I don't like to pose," Sylvia said as she pushed her shoulders back against a desk chair in the Panther office and tried to relax her arms at her side.

"Where do you want me to look?"

Larry hadn't considered that as he shifted the Yashica in his lap to find Sylvia's face, which he did quickly and, again, as he brought her features into focus and nearly fell over from the impact of this deep and intimate view of his sister Panther.

"Look toward the window," Larry shouted without looking up.

Sylvia's lemony complexion glowed as the daylight struck her face, though shadows formed at her long neck and gave the brief appearance of a decapitated head. Larry stood to adjust the angle of the sun's repose in a way that embraced Sylvia completely in the summer morning brightness pouring in from the window.

"Is there enough light?" Sylvia asked, revealing the same concern Larry's mother expressed and also that she cared how she looked. A photograph was not inert. It risked telling Sylvia more than she wanted to know.

Larry made three exposures; moving closer for the final shot, which framed Sylvia's face in an exclusive rendering, along with her neck and hair and in a way that, without the evidence of clothing or accessories, might suggest Sylvia was naked. This did not occur to Larry until he saw the photo and, despite his first impression, showed it to her anyway.

"You about done?" Sylvia asked.

She had consented to the images that would finish Larry's first roll of film, the excuse he used to pose her, though he also said the photos might be good for promoting the Free Breakfast program. And while Sylvia had her doubts, she seemed flattered that Larry wished to take her picture.

The rest of the morning was spent going over a list of potential donors. Sylvia had identified more than two-dozen businesses and several individuals who might be approached for donations.

"Now we just have to go an' do it," she said.

What can I do today for the Panthers?

It was the question Larry substituted for the mourning queries of a remote delirium. He was not in love because he was unsuitable. His decision to give up an amorous condition was never his to make. Inger, who in her rejection of him had become a white goddess, an immolating catastrophe for his best version of himself, had no idea what had been done to him. Larry was clear. Inger had done nothing. But Larry also could do nothing and this was the impossible fact that suspended his future.

He looked again across the desk to see Sylvia's fingers pecking briskly at the keyboard of an old Olivetti. She was alive with the words of an urgent appeal. He struggled and dreamed and accused himself of nothing.

seven

Riots every year. Riots all his life. Larry thought too much about violence now. Rochester and Harlem '64. Watts '65. Hunter's Point '66. Newark, Detroit and Milwaukee '67. And this year, the biggest of all starting with the Orangeburg, South Carolina, massacre. The murder of Martin Luther King: 125 cities and still counting. Washington. New York. Detroit (again) the worst. Every riot started with the arrest or shooting of a black man and nearly all the riot victims were black. In Detroit a police sniper shot and killed a Negro child. Hundreds of deaths. Most all black people.

The death of black people at the hands of white people wasn't news. But it was new that blacks were fighting back. It was why Larry was a Panther.

And it was something his father could not understand. Rev. Wiggins was a man of God and at some holy remove he looked down on all the violence in his country and spoke fervently to the expansion of civil rights through peaceful means while Malcolm and Eldridge and Bobby spoke of Black Power and its achievement by any means necessary.

With a son fighting in the jungles of Vietnam, the Reverend understandably struggled with the difference between a black boy's fight in the streets against a racist nation and another black boy's fight in the jungles against an occupied colony's revolt. It was an alarming rationalization that required the Reverend to see evil in the streets of Detroit and Newark and solemn duty in the rice paddies outside Saigon.

For Larry, the risk of Sam's life in a white man's bad war as a down payment on the GI bill and a free pass through school was a devil's bargain. Sam had to come home alive to make it worthwhile and, while he likely would, the arrangement required his father, against all his righteous and religious beliefs, to support the war in Vietnam. Though it was curious to Larry that his father did not advertise his support. Did not clamor for his parishioners to grasp and rally around the good work of America abroad. He did not. He rarely mentioned the war and spoke broadly with the words of peace in ways intended to rationalize the pacification of violent protest at home and also to ignore the "complexities" of the wider, bigger world. But it was within those complexities that Reverend Wiggins lived with his most disturbing and unsettling visions.

History advanced, regardless, and as far as Larry was concerned history advanced in disguise. Sam had taken up arms and Larry, the loyal Black Panther, had not. The Panthers were a destabilized and destabilizing work in progress. Larry knew hundreds across the country joined the Panthers every week. There were too many and too fast for anyone, Bobby and Eldridge especially, to track. Though many suspected, and everyone knew, that some recruits were bound to be agents and infiltrators, funded spies for local police departments and the FBI. An armed resistance by black people had not happened for more than a hundred years and none had been successful.

"Non-violence is winnin' the day," Rev. Wiggins told his son. "Why you wanna go an screw it all up?"

This was said before the assassination of Martin that, despite the way it took the air out of the Rev's hopeful sermonizing, was a moment of truth for all Negroes, African-Americans, blacks, or whatever Larry's people were now called or called themselves. Larry understood that his was a culture still without a common name or communal understanding. There were as many versions of black as there were shades of any color. And each shade suggested a distinct engagement with the dominating white culture that had so much privilege it could not recognize how much it held and that for four centuries had forcefully polluted black progeny with the curse of its diluting, colorless genes.

Forcefully. That was the most important word for Larry who had learned how "black" became a word to describe anyone with even a drop of blackness in his blood. As if that were the problem. And not the many extra drops of whiteness, deposited forcefully and tyrannically into enslaved women, a dozen generations of them, by the white massas that served a white God.

Was God white? Not in the African church. Not in the green pastures occupied by Larry's assailable soul. To the degree that he drew from his childhood the only hopeful vision of a loving God, Larry connected with an old, dark man who sat on an eternal porch of evening, where the faithful gathered to hear stories and songs. That was it. Songs and stories and an evening free from fear within the protection of an invincible, immortal storyteller whose words generated both laughter and tears. In a dream, the old black man would walk everyone to a river for dance and conjuration.

There were tricks the whites did not know, tricks that might make any single moment into a flash of freedom. One had to live, no matter the shade of his or her blackness. One had to live and make the choices that would extend life long enough to remake itself into more life. More black life or, rather, more life that was not white. To be anything but white was to bear a meaning—and a knowing—no colorless conqueror could ever fathom. It was a power, to be certain.

It was a power with continuing application to the perpetual wars of survival.

Larry's cadre was causing trouble. Some of the new Panther boys he marched at DeFremery Park on Saturdays were still robbing neighbors and starting fights. Two were hitting hard on Panther women volunteers and had to be told by Elmo to stop. Larry was called into a meeting with Elmo and David and another Panther leader to discuss the problem of undisciplined Panther recruits.

"Some are just damned out a hand," Elmo said. "Bobby wants it to stop. Besides, some gotta be police plants. They spyin' on us or they actin' out all crazy shit to make the Panthers look bad. What you know, Wiggins?"

A few names came to Larry's mind. He said he hadn't seen anything too bad, but robbing neighbors or local businesses was going to hurt the Party big time.

"So we gonna clean house," David said to Elmo. "We want to do it before Bobby goes to Chicago."

Larry's requested participation at the leadership meeting was a signal he was trusted. But when was Bobby leaving and why?

"The Democratic Convention," David said. "Gotta be there for the people. A bunch of us goin'. You wanna go, Wiggins? We could use you."

"But right now we need to clean up the Panthers," Elmo shouted. "We need a united front for Huey's trial. We can't have no bunch a fools in the party fuckin' up our good name."

Larry agreed to investigate and get names of Panthers who were creating problems. Bobby and Eldridge would review them and determine who would stay and who needed to go. Larry also was reminded to look out for sabotage and to be alert for spies. All new recruits would have to enroll in political education classes and take them before they could wear Panther tams or shirts.

"Pigs are payin' brothers to spy on us. You know it. I know it. We just don't know who…" David said. "You hear about somethin', let us know."

Larry nodded agreeably. He now felt an additional weight of responsibility. And Chicago? Yeah, he might go. He wanted to go.

He'd never been anywhere.

Panther problems were for Larry the contagious symptoms of a broader culture infected by violence at nodal points of power, commerce and sex. Indeed, Larry could not think of a point of intersection anywhere in American life that was not blighted by encrusting decay. And if Panthers were Americans, and certainly black people were among the country's oldest and longest residents, they were not immune to the fallible failures of a reigning hypocrisy.

"Focus is sharp but exposure is a problem. What are you doing to figure your controls?"

Zack's question puzzled Larry as the two leaned over a contact sheet of Larry's first developed film roll. Zack was short and stocky with fuzzy white hair and though he still wore a pharmacist's smock he was Palmer's Drugs resident photo specialist. The roll featured three images of Larry's mother, three of Sylvia posing at the Panther office, a picture of Raj on Telegraph and a woman crossing Haste Street, a photo of trees in a park and three more photos of a crowd of old men sharing beers at a bus stop on San Pablo Avenue.

Photos of his mother were very light while the ones of Sylvia were surprisingly dark. The outdoor photos had good detail but the tones were washed out, especially his photos of the old men, which were made against a storefront brightly lit by the sun.

Larry asked about exposure and Zack gave Larry a light meter and showed him how to use it to determine shutter speed and aperture, which he also explained.

"That's cool," Larry said as he watched the meter's needle flutter across a scale as he pointed toward the light reflecting from various objects.

"How much for the meter?" Larry asked.

Zack offered to loan it to him for his next roll, which Larry purchased and loaded into his Yashica.

"And these pictures?" Larry said as he pointed to the images of his mother and Sylvia. "Can we save 'em?"

Zack had a photographer friend who made black and white prints.

"Cost you a dollar each. He'll fix the exposure. The large negative will give you some nice detail. Most people are shooting 35mm now. This is medium format. Slower to use but it makes better prints. You'll see."

Larry marked the images he wanted enlarged. Zack said they'd be ready in a week.

There were times Larry thought himself crazy. The week after police raided Panther Headquarters was one. Larry had started his job with Murph and missed the shift when cops arrived to search and trash the Panther offices on Grove Street.

"Of course it's a mess," said Sylvia. "That was the point. To hurt us. To stop us. They didn't find nothin' and didn't show no warrant. They fucked up the office and then they left. David got here late and missed it. They took some of Emory's drawings and a gun they found in the back. David phoned the lawyer."

Sylvia yelled at them until she was threatened with arrest.

"I told 'em to go ahead and shoot me. C'mon, shoot me. Goddamn, shoot me! They grabbed me, sat me down and handcuffed me to a chair. They dug around in my desk, threw stuff on the floor, and when they left they let me go."

As she spoke, Sylvia trembled.

Larry was wrecked by a breach of conviction. What was his faith and where was it safe? He had joined the Panthers but what were they? He stood on the ground with Sylvia, with Murph and with his cadre while above him swirled the moods and forces of a movement represented by a peculiarly evanescent leadership. Huey the founder was in jail and on trial for murder. Eldridge the warrior and writer faced felony charges and a trip back to prison. Bobby spoke at rallies and sustained the Party's flinty, if feckless, attempts at discipline, though he stayed mostly out of sight.

Could this last? The Party's ranks were growing beyond anyone's capacity to count. Leadership was taking hold in all the nation's large cities even if there were no way to gauge or measure or register its presence. Meanwhile Bobby and Eldridge negotiated with Stokely and SNCC, with Karenga's United Slaves, even with the Rangers gang in Oakland to enjoin a national syndicate of Black Power. Was it possible for so many diverse special interests to unite? And there was an enemy, known but not always seen. The pigs came and went while a lot of Panthers were getting shot and killed. It was no secret the FBI was out to destroy the Panthers, and probably could without it ever being known.

In two weeks Bobby was going to Chicago for the Democratic convention. Larry was invited. How could he not go? He talked with Murph about covering his shift on the Thursday of that week. He would leave in the morning and return Monday in time for work.

"You goin' where? To Chicago? With the Panthers? Didn't you just get a job?"

Larry's father flatly opposed his son's engagement with rebellion. In another time and with more years behind him, Larry might understand that his father knew enough to fear for his son's life. No black man could confidently confront injustice without fear.

Martin was the proof, a man whose father likely told him what all black boys heard from their fathers; that to have half of what a white man possessed you need to be twice as good. And if Martin could die, so could every other black man who raised his voice. And while the Reverend sympathized with his son's bitter grasp of their common reality, that of being a dishonored ancestor in a land where colored people had lived longer than most anyone else, he could not abide the dangerous exposure of his child to a possible, even likely, death. It was why the Reverend beat his sons with a belt when they were disobedient and why now, beyond the age he could ever think to lay a hand on him, the Reverend scoffed and threatened and complained against Larry's urge for insurrection.

"Decided I'm naturally curly, so why fight it?" Aunt Rhetta said laughing. "Really, aren't we all?"

The Reverend and then Rose approached her in what appeared to be a state of timid awe.

"That is somethin'," Rose said, her eyes fixed on the tight globe of curls bound tight to her sister's skull as if it were the black, swirling atmosphere of some small, new planet.

The Wiggins' wedding anniversary fell on a hot, muggy Saturday. It was a big day but not the biggest. Younger than her sister and still single, Larry's Aunt Rhetta wore a sleeveless dress with a flowery paisley print. Her new hairdo was a surprise.

"And you don't need a jell, I mean…how do you…?" Rose struggled with the question.

"Don't need a thing but a comb," Rhetta said as she strutted across the living room, her arms waving as if she were dancing the Watusi.

"Silver next year. That's the big one," the Reverend said as if to change the subject.

Reverend Wiggins had hired kitchen volunteers from his church to prepare a dinner, though Rose could not help herself and had thrown on an apron to roast the chicken and throw a dish of corn and greens together. A chocolate pie baked in the oven. Rose briefly stroked her own hair, combed straight—or as straight as she could manage—and returned to the kitchen.

Larry watched the awkward scene. Rhetta was the family cut-up and he loved her for it. Rhetta made him laugh; had always made him laugh. As a toddler in a somber house of faith, Rhetta rocked him with her funny faces and loquacious jokes. He wondered if the younger sibling were always the clown. Larry thought himself like Rhetta who appeared to be every unserious thing her sister wasn't.

Rhetta was in her late 30s and still unmarried, still without children. The family was all but finished waiting expectantly for her Mr. Right and the wrongs that would follow though it was clear to Larry that Rhetta wasn't waiting for anything. She was digging it now. She had her own apartment north of campus, had a job with the university as a data processor, had boyfriends, and also girlfriends, and a life she didn't say much about in front of Larry's parents.

Larry heard a knock and opened the door to welcome his cousin Dinah and her husband Jorel, a senior in economics at San Francisco State College. Walking up behind was Mary Louise, his brother Sam's girlfriend and also presumed fiancée. Mary Louise wore a flannel skirt, a preppy white blouse and saddle shoes that could have been her sophomore uniform. Larry wondered if she'd ever emotionally left the high school where she met Larry's brother.

"Not much," Mary Louise said when asked what she was doing. "I'm living with my mom now. Taking a class at Laney."

Everyone seemed to accept she was waiting for Sam to return, waiting for her boyfriend to come back with the expectation he would restart her life.

"Does Sam write to you?" Rose asked.

"Oh yeah," Mary Louise said. "Every week. He wants to come home. He's done with the Army and he's just countin' the days. Has big plans for school."

Rose sank back in her chair, submerged in either disappointment or jealousy. Had Sam written to her even twice in the last year?

"You still doin' work for the Panthers?" Jorel asked Larry who looked apprehensively toward the Reverend before even thinking to answer. His father's face had no expression.

"Free breakfasts for children," Larry answered. "We start the breakfasts soon at Father Neil's church downtown. We doin' it and he's helping us."

"Father Earl Neil?" the Reverend asked. "St. Augustine's Father Neil?"

Larry nodded.

"Know the Father," the Reverend answered curtly. "He's a good man."

"He knows you, too," Larry responded.

It was a lie. Larry had never spoken to Father Neil but his father smiled at the compliment and left Larry's Panther issue on the table.

"May be a strike at the college," Jorel continued. "Black Student Union wants a class in black history and admin says no. We'll see what happens next month when school starts."

Larry nodded knowingly, but let the subject drop.

"To mom and pop," Larry said as he lifted a glass of freshly poured champagne and offered his toast. The Reverend had splurged for a five-dollar bottle of Korbel Brut. The other guests joined in, except Mary Louise who did not drink alcohol and, instead, lifted her water glass. Then dinner was served amid a slightly inebriated chatter about Rose and Josiah's first date, their first year together, Sam's birth and their marriage, which surprisingly for the time occurred in that order. And while Josiah attended Divinity School, no less.

"We weren't the only ones…" said the Reverend defensively as the table erupted with laughter.

Chocolate pie was taken in the living room where Larry found on the coffee table the August edition of *Ebony* magazine, it's cover a color photo of Negro males dressed in a historical montage of military uniforms under a headline that read *The Black Soldier*. Thumbing from the back he found photos of James Brown performing at an air base in Vietnam. One photo showed the soul singer dancing in front of a faceless crowd of more than 7,000 soldiers.

"Read the story about Ft. Leonard Wood," Rose said. "It's where Sam did his basic training."

Larry held quietly to a moment of familial grace, fearful it might be the last he would ever experience. The magazine opened onto an array of troubling black military realities and basic training was the least of them.

As he thumbed forward he read first the story of a Negro soldier released as a prisoner of war through the intervention of anti-war activists that traveled to North Vietnam. Next he read about blacks that deserted the army and now lived in Sweden. Photos of their warm welcome to Stockholm by a group of young blonde women startled Larry into a miniature eruption of arousal.

He read that of nearly 1400 admirals and generals in the US military, only two were Negroes. He read excerpts from the diary of an enlisted black man named David who described how his white sergeant picked only Negroes and Puerto Ricans for the dangerous job of forward officer.

Every time he comes I get the feeling that I should have been born white. So now I'm on a mission and our platoon has to go after Charlie on foot. I'm carrying the phone with a big antenna, which makes a beautiful target. It's a sergeant's job but my sergeant's not going to promote me. Carrying a rifle in the Army is the same as pushing a broom in civilian life.

Larry read that 37,000 Negroes were drafted in 1967 accounting for more than 16 percent of all draftees. During the previous year, deaths of black soldiers increased by 25 percent. More than 300,000 Negroes were in the Army and 56,000 were serving in Vietnam.

It ain't luck, a black soldier said about surviving his tour of duty. *It's just that Charlie knows I don't want a damn thing from him but a ticket back to Bedford-Stuyvesant. Believe me, I don't give a good goddamn who takes over this place—I want to serve my time and make it.*

The stories confirmed what Larry already knew: that bigotry

at home and in school guaranteed the Negro soldier would get the larger share of dirty work in any American war. And, of course, for the white masters of war it was a problem no one could cure and for which no one should be blamed. Larry seethed quietly as he considered what he now beheld as the profile of his brother's own path: the limited choices that pushed him like a grain of sand to fall through the narrow of an hour glass and into the irresistible and only route left when, without money or work or hope, he at last chose the infantry.

Larry arrived at the magazine's ad-packed front pages to find several columns of letters to the editor. Rambling along a single column among full-page displays of cigarettes, vodka, hair-gels and beauty creams were the written words of nearly a dozen black soldiers.

Probably the most shocked and dumbfounded group of individuals over the tragic and wanton murder of Dr. Martin Luther King Jr. is the group of Negro servicemen serving 'freedom's' cause in Vietnam, wrote one soldier. *What the hell are we doing here? The greatest contribution that Uncle Sam is making to the Negro's freedom is teaching us how to kill.*

Another soldier told of seeing in a recent magazine a photo of an Armored Personnel Carrier sitting on a corner in riot-torn Detroit.

It stunned me because I know what one bullet from that gun can do to an individual. And you mean to tell me that whitey has a nerve to use something like this against us, the black people of America?

A sergeant at Fort Bragg asked for an editorial expressing *the discontent of all young black people in the service, because we are the ones manipulated to the glory and satisfaction of a history, which is not ours.*

The last letter described the experiences of a black sergeant who entered the service in 1965 and who would end his military obligation the following year.

I for one refuse to return to the same society of racism and discrimination.

Blacks are good enough to die for America in Vietnam, therefore, I am sure these same blacks are willing to die at home for a cause that is easier to understand. So I say now, America, get your own house in order because if you don't there won't BE any house to get in order.

Larry closed the magazine and reclined on the couch. His father was speaking, his resonant voice conveyed a vivid replay of the time he met Rose. Larry was still held in the restful and complacent embrace of family celebration even as he nearly burst with the disquieting realities of war. He wanted to shout, to sound an alarm, to ask pointedly if his mother or father had read any of this? It was a rich, nearly unbearable irony as Larry thought first to alert everyone, to be the messenger that would at last share the confirming and alarming truth, to say exactly why Sam was wrong and in danger. But who would listen? And on this day, the anniversary of the love that created Sam? How welcome was any warning no one could heed?

Sam was the older brother who both picked Larry apart and also and always had his back. Sam had taken another path and still, through it all, was the closest person Larry had ever known. He wagered a silent hope that some small sacrifice would allow Sam to return unharmed by anything he saw or experienced and that sacrifice would be Larry's restraint today. He would suppress every urgent desire to share the magazine's horrific truths, to rage about the conditions and concerns of soldiers like Sam or relate the deadening statistics that suggested clearly Sam was at far greater risk than anyone might imagine.

"What you thinkin' about?" Larry's mother asked him. "You haven't spoke in a half-hour."

Larry put down the magazine.

"There's a lot in here," he said vaguely. "Helps me understand what goin' on in Nam."

And that was it.

"Hate to go but I'm workin' tonight," Larry said as he stood.

Rose and the Reverend looked at him surprised.

"No…really?" his mother asked. His father said nothing. Larry wondered if the Reverend had also read the August Ebony.

Larry continued to make his excuses in a way he thought created the smallest disappointment for his father who seemed always to be disappointed in Larry's choices. Larry stood, gave Rhetta, Dinah and Mary Louise affable hugs, kissed his mom, shook his father's hand and made a restrained bolt for the door.

He would not imprison his family in a net of new tyrannies, his own or anyone else's and especially those already told to which there was little Larry could add. The journalists and photographers of Ebony had rendered real their full and staggering range.

Though it probably did not matter since these facts would never be real to his mother or father. Truth they could not create or control was no truth at all. His father was a preacher and Larry, bereft of any other capacity, would pray if necessary for the redemption of Sam's service and his safe return from a dangerous enrollment in the study of war.

"Charlie, Charlie, Charlie," Larry mumbled to himself as he walked toward his truck. "If it ain't honkey Mr. Charlie here, then it's killer Viet Cong Charlie over there…we all just dummies and you don't think we got enemies everywhere?

"I figure we got little more than a dozen square blocks we can move around in without worrying too much about being disturbed or bothered. But get out of our zones, our ghettos, we enter our own DMZ…and watch out!"

How could he absorb at a distance what was not distanced, what always would remain? His life might never move very far from its current darkness. Decades might pass and he would be as close to a deep hurt as he was now or perhaps even closer.

"I am a goddamned motherfucker. And it's already too late. Too late for us all."

The words had the sound of a lover's futile discourse by which one intolerant partner stifles the impossible dreams of the other. Larry realized he was speaking to his father.

eight

The Panthers needed allies and, as Malcolm said, allies weren't just the rich liberals in the hills or the leftist millionaires in Pacific Heights. *When we realize how large the earth is, and how many different people there are on it, how closely they all resemble us, then when we turn to them for some sort of aid, or to form alliances, then we'll make faster progress.*

Was anyone truly white? White people just thought they were white. Larry liked this idea and couldn't remember where it came from. White people who helped the Panthers certainly knew they weren't white. The genes of so many ancestors so many generations back polluted everyone. There was no pure race, which was important for Larry to remember in a country where race meant everything.

The Panthers needed allies. Black Power was control of neighborhoods, self-determination in the ghettos, maybe even a new country on the continent carved from the old slave states where Negros still formed vast, rural pluralities. Black Power was guns in the hands of self-defenders and communities under the control of black citizens. It was not integration, though as Bobby said, "we don't hate white people. We hate tyranny."

It was like a dream for Larry that such a movement had so much critical mass and so quickly and in such a critical time. But there were problems. Two Panthers had been shot and killed in Los Angeles, not in a battle with police but in an ambush staged by rival black militants. Rumors swirled that Eldridge would flee the country rather than face charges in the April shoot-out that killed Bobby Hutton. Huey's trial was reaching a climax and, while it seemed unlikely he would be sentenced to death, he might spend the rest of his life in prison. That left Bobby to lead a movement attracting thousands of members, and in a week he was going to Chicago for the Democratic National Convention.

US history leads us to the conclusion that our sufferance is basic to the functioning of the government. It was a quote from Huey on the wall at Panther headquarters and from what Larry had read in the August Ebony, it was true. The history of America was the history of race and centuries of abuse and injustice leveraged against the Negro by rulers who thought themselves white and who continued to accrue a large and overdue debt that needed to be paid.

"It's coming due, man. It's overdue," Murph said as Larry talked with him about the recent shooting deaths of the L.A. Panthers.

"We can't just stand by," Murph said, "but who do we attack? You know how that always turns out…"

Larry knew. Every man, woman and child with dark enough skin to prohibit them from pretending to be white also knew. If urban riots proved anything it was the futility of rage in the streets where you lived. And it was the great dilemma of a race and culture still without a common name, though "black" was taking hold, even if most blacks actually were chocolate or lemon or one of any infinite number of shades beyond or between.

"We worked four hundred years for free while they raped our people into a hundred different colors," Murph said again. "I figure we due back wages with overtime and interest and also damages plus the promised acreage and mules. One hell of a settlement, an they keep puttin' it off which only make it all worse."

Murph's fantasy was a national day of bank robberies during which black gangs would overwhelm cops with the robbing of every bank in every city of the nation and then meet in Mexico to divide the take.

"We become capitalists overnight," Murph laughed. "We be buyin' everything from Cadillacs to Congressmen."

A kiss was the beginning of the oldest idea, to ingest either the love of one's mate or the soul of one's enemy. As Larry handed Sylvia the large manila envelope containing her photograph, it felt momentarily like a kiss, like a searching touch that might have power to move her. And where? Closer to Larry who admitted to himself he did find Sylvia attractive, though he had little desire and few fantasies of what that might look like or become.

"That's the biggest damn photo of me I ever seen," she said, stunned by an 8x10 glossy black and white print that showed her sitting at her desk, her afro curling into the upper borders of the image, her smile caught on the fly, sweet and welcoming with little show of teeth though her posture, sturdy and upright, asserted her will either to help or to fight.

"My blouse is unbuttoned," Sylvia said again as she stared deeply into the image and looked back at Larry. Women noticed every detail and in such a large print from so sizable a negative there was nothing unrecorded. It was not so much the image but its size that impressed Sylvia. That Larry cared enough to take and print it and give it as a gift said a host of both confusing and lovely things to her.

"You good," she said at last. "You take a good picture. Thank you, Larry."

She spoke his name with uncharacteristic warmth, as if her gratitude were genuine and might carry hints of something more. Larry could not be certain and did not need to be.

"Goin' to Chicago with Bobby and David," Larry said, as if to move the conversation away from uncertainty.

"Well, take your damned camera," Sylvia nearly shouted.

How might Larry hide without lying? He had not seen Bronwyn in more than a week, not answered his phone or visited the Forum since spending the night with her. And he could have waited indefinitely for no meeting ever again until now when she stood in front of him, inadvertently blocking his path as he stumbled along a narrow sidewalk behind the Shattuck Avenue Co-op. He was looking for Raj who would get off work soon. Holding a bag of groceries, Bronwyn held her ground.

"Hello, Larry," she said with rehearsed formality. She must have seen him coming.

"Yah, Bronwyn!" Larry tried to appear both enthusiastic and impersonal, as if an improvised life might excuse, if not explain, his lingering inattention to her, the last woman with whom he had sex. Bad sex, but sex nonetheless, though it may not have been so bad for her. He had gambled and taken a risk, hoping it was possible Bronwyn simply would never bring it up when she again might see him.

Which was absurd, since Larry was a Panther and Larry was for real. And Bronwyn, a fixture in his political world, certainly would see him again, even as he tried to avoid her.

"Wait, Larry. We need to talk," Bronwyn said directly as if the request had been rehearsed and pigeonholed for just this moment.

Larry stopped and also stood his ground.

"Got time for a coffee?" he asked curtly.

Together they were silent through the three-block walk up Vine Street to Peet's on the corner, Bronwyn lugging her bag of groceries. At least she was walking toward home. Larry found a table and Bronwyn scooted into a chair while Larry sauntered to the bar to place an order and in so doing postponed an inevitable judgment against him. Attraction had enabled Bronwyn's suffering and, through his participation with it, Larry's guilt.

"You know, I get a lot of this," Bronwyn said after her first sip of latte. "I'm no fool, though after a few drinks I can sure act like one. I figured you weren't attracted to me and at the time I didn't really care. But you never called me. You stopped treating me like a friend. And that makes me feel like shit."

Larry shrunk from Bronwyn's directness as he envisioned what he could remember of their night and her specifically unattractive features. Her drunken libido was loud, demanding and had frightened him though he would never say this to her.

"I was in a haze and pretty drunk myself," Larry said without looking at Bronwyn. He wished he were wearing dark glasses to hide his distress.

"Bullshit," Bronwyn said. "You came home with me. That's what some dumb chick would say, that you had no control and ended up slipping along for the ride. You were the fucking man, Larry, and then you weren't."

Larry listened to his scolding as he might to one from his third grade teacher, also a woman and also unattractive to him. Larry imagined himself somewhere else, imagined Bronwyn's voice shrinking back into a short, squat body, imagined her face contorted now like a topographical map, anger poking from her brow as a forest of nose hair emerged subtly from a flaring nostril and her narrow eyes, squinting through bulky, black-rimmed glasses, searched him for evidence.

Head trip, Larry said to himself. *This woman is a fucking head trip.*

"I don't expect anything, Larry," Bronwyn began after a nervous pause. "You're a beautiful man. I'm not a beautiful woman. I know what's going on. I don't turn heads. Even if I wanted to I couldn't. I really enjoyed getting balled by you. I didn't expect it to mean anything. I never do. But you mean something. And I mean something. And that's what I don't get. Why you not liking sex with me means you can't still like *me.*"

Larry had no response. Bronwyn's words ran together in a blur of specific grievances. In some ways Bronwyn's resentment stated his own about Inger but it was too far and also too close to fully absorb.

"I wish men would wait around to find out what happened,"

Bronwyn said as if speaking to herself. "Women do it all the time. I wish we were able to talk about it. I wish you'd spent the night and had breakfast with me. That was the time to leave. After we talked about it."

Larry had never heard a woman express herself so clearly. He felt a surge of regret, that his disappearance that night had been like a death, that he had made an assumption about Bronwyn's dependence when, in fact, no one had any real need of him.

"Damn, I am so sorry," Larry said.

He waited for more words to emerge but none were forthcoming.

"What you want? What can I do now?" he asked finally.

Bronwyn was silent as she shifted in her chair and took another sip of her latte.

"Well, you could get me a bunch of Panthers for the Wallace rally Sunday at the Cow Palace."

Larry's head spun at the speed Bronwyn shifted from her revelation of tender feelings to a direct request for a political favor.

"We have a coalition going but we need reps from the black community, especially for this bigoted asshole. We want to make him squirm."

At first Larry thought her request a conniving resentment until he caught again the view of Bronwyn's tiny eyes behind her large glasses. They radiated an annulling judgment that left Larry naked on the table before them. She did judge him and this again aroused his guilt.

"Yeah, I can do that," Larry said quietly. "Yeah. We'll be there."

It was business again as Bronwyn relaxed into another coalition triumph by which Larry acknowledged the one partner that never disappointed her: the movement and all its coalescing and progressive forces. She was devoted to revolution and Larry was going to be its servant, by any means necessary.

George Wallace was a Southern segregationist. That he could make a serious run for the presidency, and in all fifty states, affirmed for Larry that race was the history of America and always would be.

"He want equality alright," Murph said on the bus to the Cow Palace. "Slavery made white men equal 'cause then they were all superior to black slaves. Segregation do the same thing, even if you take away the slave part—now, tomorrow and forever."

Murph mimicked the words from Wallace's 1962 inaugural address as Alabama governor when he praised the Confederacy and promised voters he would defend Jim Crow.

Four buses carried protesters to San Francisco.

"We got two maybe three hundred of us," Bronwyn said as the buses emptied and passengers gathered with their signs and flags.

"Yippies are coming so this could be fun."

The plan was to march into the Cow Palace through the rear entrance and take seats in the stands directly opposite the speaker's podium where the governor would clearly see them. Metal chairs were aligned in long rows across the Palace's broad ground floor and were a little more than half-filled by a crowd of white men, women and even some children. *Sacramento for Wallace*, read several signs. Larry assumed the state's conservative central valley would be well represented and as he entered the building he gazed curiously at the Wallace people.

Many wore straw hats printed with the words *Wallace for President*. Some were dressed in suits and long dresses as if they had come directly from church. All were people who thought themselves white and all he saw responded to Larry with cool glares before turning to greet their candidate who marched in from a side door and approached the podium.

"He one short dude," Murph said to Larry. "See how his head stick up from behind the podium? It's like a carved pumpkin on a window sill."

Several protesters stood up in the stands to wave Viet Cong flags. One held up a watermelon and waved it back and forth. Larry and the Panthers formed a line at the governor's eye level and stood at a kind of attention.

"Well, I see we have the anarchists with us today," Wallace announced.

"You don't know how grateful I am for you."

He pointed toward the protesters in a way that let Larry think Wallace was pointing at him.

"Every time you people show up at one of my rallies, I get

another million votes."

The Wallace crowd up front shouted and hooted their agreement while Bronwyn's protesters screamed "No More War!" in a squawking, imperative cadence.

It was only the first of Wallace's renowned zingers.

"You can take all the Democratic candidates for President and all the Republican candidates for President. Put them in a sack and shake them up. Take the first one that falls out, grab him by the nape of the neck, and put him right back in the sack. Because there is not a dime's worth of difference in any of them."

The Wallace crowd went wild, easily drowning out the voices of protest. Larry and his Panthers stood their ground but the space between them and the Wallace supporters was too wide to defend.

"And it's a sad day in the country when you can't talk about law and order unless they want to call you a racist. I tell you that's not true and I resent it and they gonna have to pay attention because people in this country, in the great majority, the Supreme Court of our country has made it almost impossible to convict a criminal. And if you walk out of this building today, and someone knocks you in the head, the person who knocked you in the head will be out of jail if you don't watch out."

The Wallace crowd roared again while Larry examined the short man's round face, seeing in his dark eyes the familiar and hateful gaze of those people who thought themselves white, those people who moved away from a café table where he was sitting, or those servers who waited those extra few minutes to take his order, fill his gas tank, even sell him a car. Larry thought of the angry glare of a sports dad in high school who shook his fist when Larry scored a basket against his pink-skinned son.

"And you…you people in the back…" Wallace spoke with a momentous confidence.

"You come up and I'll autograph your sandals for you. That is, if you got any on…"

The Wallace crowd laughed.

"You need a good haircut. That's all that's wrong with you… There are two four-letter words I bet you folks don't know—'work' and 'soap.'"

Larry's handful of Panthers stood their ground with the few hundred and vastly outnumbered protesters from Berkeley, but Wallace had the microphone and in the rallying misery of the governor's accusations there was no respite. Even in the Bay Area, presumed bigots who thought themselves white vastly outnumbered Larry and all bad ass Panthers.

"The working man cannot walk to work in safety, nor his wife ride the transit system nor go to the supermarket. Nor can you walk in the neighborhood because these anarchists threaten them everywhere."

Wallace might have been talking about Larry but Larry knew he was the target and not the constituent. He was even placed oddly in the balcony at the back of the hall like Negros at a white movie show. The color of his skin was enough to make him a criminal and he suppressed momentarily a secret feeling that Wallace had turned what was right—the national embrace of liberal values and civil rights—into a paradigm of cultural failure. And worse, that what was right had little or no support and, as always, it would be a mistake for a black man or woman ever to assume that in their case justice would necessarily or ever prevail.

"And you elect me president, and I come to California or go to Tennesee, if a group of anarchists lies down in front of my automobile, it's gonna be the last one they ever gonna want to lie down in front of."

Thousands of Wallace supporters jumped to their feet screaming, many turning to flip fingers at the protesters now swept up in their own lather of anger, even if vastly outnumbered, and vigorously waving flags and signs in a fraught effort to outshout a now formidable and entitled opposition.

A protester ran toward a Wallace supporter who pulled at his crotch to incite a fight. Bronwyn ran out and grabbed him. Larry followed to help.

"Don't start trouble," Bronwyn shouted at her defiant colleague while Larry held him in a bear hug.

"We're leaving. It's over."

The bus ride back to the East Bay was quiet and muffled by a deflated sense of defeat.

"That honkie sure made fools out a us," Murph said. "He had a microphone and we didn't."

The television coverage was more generous. The Panthers were prominently photographed and filmed and were thrust forward as equal adversaries of a segregationist white Southerner. Newspapers led with the protest and not with Wallace's punch lines. A photograph in the Chronicle featured Larry's face, his look forward and seemingly stern and determined. Only Larry knew that what appeared to be righteous anger was really an expression of unsettling fear.

Chicago surprised Larry. It was a big city and also a big black city. South Chicago was a new world and filled with countless welcoming faces. Larry walked anywhere from his crash pad near the park and saw only black and yellow and brown people, none of which ever looked at him. He was himself and at home in a city of many colors. In Berkeley his comfortable neighborhood of color comprised a few city blocks and barely a hundred thousand Negros lived on the flatlands of the Bay's surrounding cities. South Chicago alone held more than a million black residents.

The flight from Oakland took three hours. Supporters had paid for six Oakland Panthers to appear and protest at the Democratic National Convention and Larry was among them. Chicago Panther President Fred Hampton welcomed them to his apartment near the Amphitheater and booked them out to the homes of other Panthers, while offering Bobby and Larry the two couches in his living room. Fred's kind, open face engaged Larry immediately, reminding him of a childhood friend whom he loved and who loved him before the onset of knowledgeable defenses. Larry was also impressed with the tight organization of Hampton's Panthers, their obvious cohesion and discipline and loyalty to a competent and available leader.

Within a day Larry had visited the Maxwell Street Market, attended a performance of a local blues band, and stood with Bobby at a park near the Amphitheater. The place was alive and Larry with it.

"The TV stations report that Panthers hate white people," shouted Bobby through a handheld microphone. "And that's a bald face lie. We don't hate any people because of the color of their skin. We hate oppression."

A crowd of several thousand cheered.

"We hate that black men are being taken off to military service to fight for this decadent nation.

"One hundred and eight-six thousand black men fought in the Civil War and were promised their freedom and didn't get it.

"Two hundred and fifty thousand black men fought in World War I and were promised their freedom and didn't get it.

"Eight hundred and fifty thousand black men fought in World War II and were promised their freedom and didn't get it.

"Black men fought in Korea and were promised their freedom and didn't get it.

"Now thousands of black men are fighting in this damned Vietnam War. And we still ain't getting nothin'!"

Cheers went up again as Bobby relinquished the microphone to Yippie Leader Jerry Rubin who held in his arms a baby pig he had named Pigasus and that he nominated for President of the United States.

The Oakland Panthers gathered for a dinner given by the Chicago Panthers at a restaurant near Fred Hampton's place.

"There was a call for you," Fred told Larry.

"Said she was your aunt. Needs you to call."

Aunt Rhetta. Larry couldn't grasp why she would call him in Chicago. How did she have a phone number? It was late in Chicago but still early on the coast. He went back to Fred's apartment and dialed Rhetta's number.

"Rhetta…that you?" Larry said into the phone.

"Larry…oh god, Larry…" her voice shuddered with urgency.

"Larry I got some bad news."

"What?" Larry asked, his ears and eyes and heart quickly and helplessly open to something he wanted very much to be prepared for, and could not be.

"Sam…Sam is dead."

Larry flew home, his brother Sam a huge cargo bound to him by the innumerable tentacles of a life that reached deep around the mirror of Larry's own. That Sam was no longer a life, no longer living, had no meaning for Larry, or at least not yet. Larry could not deny life nor bow to death.

There had been some mistake. It was all just a horrible misunderstanding and Sam would appear as Larry landed in Oakland; would buy Larry a drink and drive him back to the house. *It's cool,* he'd say. *They got it all wrong. I'm OK. They just misplaced me.*

Larry was met by his father who pulled him from the line of departing passengers, embraced him and began to sob until Larry's chest also heaved with his first and irresistible convulsions of grief. Father and son then waddled together out of the airport; their quiet tears an awkward spectacle for those crowded around gates and stairwells and, finally, those also waiting for the baggage claim carousel.

"How mom doin'?" Larry asked during the awkward minutes before his suitcase appeared.

"Not good," said the Reverend. "Oh, damn, Larry, we jus can't..."

His father again wept as Larry grabbed his suitcase and guided the Reverend outside.

In the car, his father handed Larry a crumpled, yellow telegram.

The Secretary of the Army has asked me to express his deep regret that your son private first class Samuel H. Wiggins died in Vietnam on 25 August 1968 as a result of wounds received while his unit was under attack near the village of Ap Nhi south of Saigon. Please accept my deepest sympathy. This confirms personal notification made by a representative of the secretary of the army.

Kenneth J. Chatham
Major General USA

"You mom threw it away," said his father. "That's why it's all messed up. We just got a letter from Sam Monday. Said he was in Saigon last week for some RnR. That night a soldier comes to the house. He tells us Sam got it. We didn't believe him. Then Tuesday morning that telegram comes. And then we get a call from some Captain Poole at the Oakland Army Base. Say he gonna help with funeral arrangements. Mom fell apart. She can't…I mean…"

Larry's father attempted to start the car, his hand shaking as he tried to insert the key, which would not go. The Reverend dropped his key chain, sat up and began pounding the steering wheel as he wailed uncontrollably.

"Whoa, daddy, no…" Larry dropped the telegram and threw his arms around his father's shoulders.

"I gotcha, dad. OK dad…it's OK."

At the house Larry was surprised by his mother's relative composure. Aunt Rhetta strutted furiously and his father, weak from the drive, forced his large body onto the couch so he could catch his breath. But his mother welcomed Larry and had the presence to offer him food and some water. Larry hugged his mother and felt her small body crumble against his chest and stomach. He held her until she pushed him away.

"He's gone, Larry. Sam is gone," she said weakly and looked deeply into Larry's eyes as if to certify his existence. Photos of Sam, including his high school graduation photo, occupied the mantle along with the photo Larry made of his mother. She liked the photo. Though, just as Sylvia, his mother had noticed an imperfection, in this case the way her hair was combed more heavily to one side of her head and not the other.

"Another telegram arrived," Rhetta said to Larry.

"You mom can't read it. We been waitin' for you."

She handed Larry the yellow Western Union envelope. He tore it open and spread out the folded message, reading silently as everyone stood by in various states of reluctant acceptance. If death were real it would have to be experienced bit by bit. Larry's cargo of Sam was like everyone else's and all these cargos would need to sink however slowly to the bottom of an ocean before any of these people could get on with living.

This concerns your son PFC Samuel H. Wiggins. The Army will return your loved one to a port of the United States by first available airlift. At the port, remains will be placed in a metal casket and delivered (accompanied by a military escort) by most expeditious means to any funeral director designated by the next of kin or to any national cemetery where there is available grave space. You will be advised by the United States Port concerning the movement and the arrival time at destination.

The telegram went on to describe various sums ranging from $75 to $500 that the Army would pay the family for a designated variety of burial locations and funeral services. The family needed to reply with the name of the funeral director or national cemetery selected.

If additional information concerning return of remains is desired, you may include your inquiry in the reply to this message. Please do not set date of funeral until Port authorities notify you date and scheduled time of arrival destination.

"Next steps," Larry said. "They'll let us know. We need to tell them where to send him. Who doin' the funeral?"

The words were still new, the words of a real death of a real brother and they were not easily spoken or heard by anyone. Rhetta continued to pace, Larry's mother taking the only available comfort in these words of loss: that her still living son spoke them. Rose's eyes sparkled with a waxy redness as if something were becoming clear, as if after carrying the worry of Sam's death for so long, it might be almost a relief at last to have any outcome. Of course, it was not. Rhetta's anger stood in for her sister's despair.

"Death is evil," Rhetta later said quietly and only to Larry. "That is God's judgment. If death were good, then God would die."

"Maybe he already has," Larry answered and then moved past Rhetta to sit on the couch with his father.

Sam's remains arrived at Travis Air Force Base Sunday afternoon. The family was notified by a call from a Sergeant Robert Peterson who said he would accompany the casket to its delivery destination. The Reverend was not preaching that Sunday and for days had been taking condolence calls from members of the church who had heard of Sam's death, until at some point the Reverend could no longer bear it.

Rhetta and Larry then answered the phone and it was Larry who spoke to Sgt. Peterson. The soldier confirmed that Sam's coffin would be taken to the Harrison Funeral Home on San Pablo Avenue in Berkeley.

At 2 p.m. Larry, his parents, Aunt Rhetta and Mr. Harrison gathered in the funeral home's chapel. Mr. Harrison was one of the Reverend's old friends. They had gone to high school together in Oakland. The Reverend had preached numerous funerals for clients of Mr. Harrison.

A hearse arrived and a white man in uniform stepped toward the chapel's entrance and introduced himself as Sgt. Peterson. He asked for the funeral director and when Mr. Harrison appeared along with Sam's family the soldier handed him a letter. Mr. Harrison was a small man with a mustache and graying temples. His dark brown face had a jovial, portly appearance. His round belly pushed against a black Sunday suit coat as he opened the letter and read it.

A couple of minutes passed in silence.

"The coffin is sealed?" Mr. Harrison asked the sergeant.

"Yes, sir," the soldier answered quickly, eager to finish his task. "The deceased is unviewable."

"Unviewable?" Larry's mother cried out, incredulous. "What do you mean unviewable. I can't see my son?"

Mr. Harrison asked Sgt. Peterson to go with him inside.

"I'll be right back," Mr. Harrison told the family. "Just wait here. Please."

"What's he talkin' about?" Rose's voice rose in a surging crescendo of panic. "Unviewable? I need to see my boy…I can't…"

Larry walked toward the hearse. Inside he saw a metal casket covered by a large, bright American flag.

Mr. Harrison stepped out of the chapel and yelled.

"Josiah, Larry. Come in here. I need you."

Inside the chapel Mr. Harrison tried to hand the letter to the Reverend, but he refused it and pointed to Larry.

Larry took the letter and read it. He sighed a deep breath and turned to his father.

"Here's what the letter say, Daddy. *We are sorry that the circumstances of the deceased's death precluded restoring the remains to a viewable state.*"

While Sgt. Peterson shifted nervously, Rev. Wiggins covered his face, turned away and fell into a chair in the chapel lobby.

"What's this mean, Mr. Harrison?" Larry asked urgently.

Mr. Harrison drew him back to the rear of the chapel, away from the nervous soldier and inconsolable Reverend.

"This is the deal," Mr. Harrison began. "I been here before. The coffin is sealed and no one can open it. They got a mortuary in Saigon where bodies first arrive. Morticians there, they are good. They spend hours workin' on bodies to make them into something they can dress in a uniform and present to the family. Whatever happened to Sam, well there ain't enough a him left to make him look anything like he did before he died. And if they couldn't do anything to make him viewable, I know I can't."

"What's inside the coffin then?" Larry asked.

"Like I said, whatever they could find," said Mr. Harrison. "I hate to put it that way but it's the truth. What's left a Sam ain't pretty and it's sealed in an airtight bag. Believe me, what's inside that coffin no one would recognize as Sam. No one would want to look at."

"Shit," Larry said. "What am I gonna tell mom? She wanted an open casket."

Larry's mother could not grasp the reality of a sealed casket.

"It don't matter, Rose," the Reverend said as they left the funeral home.

"But how do I know it's him?" she asked again.

"It's him," said the Reverend.

"And why can't I see him?" she asked again.

"What you want to see him for, anyway? He's dead."

"Just one last time…"

"Please, Rose. Please stop talkin' about it."

And then everyone was silent as Larry drove the family home. The funeral was planned for Thursday with a service at the church, burial at Sunset View Cemetery, and a reception to follow at the large home of one of the church's prominent members. A core of church volunteers worked with Rhetta to manage all the details. Rev. John Jackson of a sister A.M.E. church in East Palo Alto would lead the funeral service.

Another letter arrived, this one from Army Commander General William Westmoreland.

Larry's father read the letter and began to crumple it into ball.

"No!" Rose yelled. "You give that to me right now!"

She took the letter, folded it gently and slipped it into her purse.

Sam's death suspended the forward motion of Larry's life, which was now smothered under the apprehension, anxiety and horror of his and his family's deeply painful loss. Larry, like everyone, now faced the question of how best to bury his own version of Sam, a memory that played much like a movie and that needed now to be reviewed, edited and transformed.

"He was a good brother," Murph said as he sat with Larry in the church.

Larry shrugged his shoulders. A good brother? A good brother wouldn't die and leave Larry all alone.

"Don't matter now," Larry answered. "He gone."

Larry pointed toward the chancel where Sam's flag-draped coffin rested on a church truck.

"Not enough a him in there to know if that even him."

More than a hundred people arrived at the church to shuffle into the pews and take their seats. Larry was given the task of helping his grandparents, who entered with him looking flummoxed and frightened. It was a large crowd for a Thursday service. Most were church members, though Larry saw Mary Louise enter through a side door just as his father's colleague and friend Rev. Jackson began to speak. Rhetta had phoned her to tell her of Sam's death, though Mary Louise never came to the house or contacted Rose or the Reverend. This was the first time Larry had seen Sam's sweetheart since returning from Chicago. She sat alone at the end of a vacant pew at the back of the church and left before the service was over.

Larry had mentioned Sam's death to Sylvia but told her not to share it with any Panthers. The last thing his father needed was to look out on a row of tams and black jackets while military honors were rendered to his deceased son.

The Reverend sat rigid in the front pew some space from Larry and with his arm around Rose while his own parents sat behind him. Larry's father was the living object of most interest to those in attendance, though it was the mother who bore openly the day's indelible sorrow, who had nurtured Sam's life and failed to forestall his death, at least until the occurrence of her own. It was one thing to accept that all who were born would die. It was another to outlive one's own child.

The crowd was smaller for Sam's burial and smaller still for the reception. Rose sat in a metal folding chair at the end of the hillside grave, tear streaks the only evidence of sorrow until the honor guard of uniformed pallbearers (five white soldiers and one black) stood back from the casket to fold its covering flag into a soft triangle of fabric. The last soldier to touch it handed the flag to Rose, whose face then collapsed into the flag's folded pleats as if it were a pillow of bereavement. Then Rev. Jackson pressed a button and Sam's coffin was lowered slowly into its backhoed grave.

"If only he hadn't gone to that damn war," Rhetta said as she poured another half glass of bourbon.

"That damn war—I hate it. We dyin' like flies over there."

The Reverend's younger brother, as small and thin as the Reverend was tall and thick, took the bottle back from Rhetta. They stood with Larry outside as a late afternoon fog encroached on the backyard of the generous church members hosting the reception.

"He coulda gone to jail," Rhetta said. "He coulda been one a those boys who ends up in jail 'cause they don't want no war."

"Sam was never that type," the uncle said as he let the bourbon run into his own glass.

"Yeah, but he'd be alive now."

Larry watched and listened as Rhetta let the alcohol do the talking.

"That's not how Sam was," the uncle said. "Sam a good boy. He always did what he was told."

"He never wanted to do no killin'," Rhetta responded, her voice rising. "He told the Army he wanted to learn a skill. He wanted a desk job."

"They told him he couldn't 'cause he didn't have experience," Larry interjected.

"Yeah, well he had no experience killin' either," Rhetta shouted.

"Didn't matter, I guess," said the younger uncle.

"What I don't understand," Larry said, "is if they could teach him to kill why couldn't they teach him to type?"

There were no more words. Rhetta took another swig from her glass and Larry walked back inside to look for Murph. He saw his father standing wearily, prominent in a circle of church members who touched his shoulders and held his arms while they spoke comforting words Larry could not hear.

The only comfort for Larry was the awareness he held within him an entire graveyard, a place where others who had lived in his life and had left, also were buried. Death entailed two departures. Sam had made his exit. It was now Larry's time to leave.

ten

For several days Larry drove his mother to the village of death where Sam's remains resided. Sunset Cemetery was a sylvan, hillside community with tall trees and old, full bushes spread among rows and rows of graves that, like the addresses of a subdivision, marked each loved one's final residence. A bronze plaque had been placed at the head of Sam's grave, screwed with steel bolts onto a block of concrete set and buried in the grass. The plaque identified the deceased resident as *Pfc. Samuel Wiggins, soldier and hero*. The dates of his birth and death were etched below his name.

The day after Sam's funeral Rose visited the grave. She asked the Reverend to join her. He dressed to go but could not pass the front door without collapsing in sobs. Larry drove instead and so became Rose's chauffeur whenever she wished to visit Sam, which at first was every day. Larry carried a metal folding chair from the church social hall and placed it beside Sam's grave where Rose could sit and see both the cropped grass covering Sam's coffin and the plaque that expressed with stark brevity the work of his short life. At first Larry tried to stand beside his mother, or sit on the grass nearby. But Rose said nothing so Larry retreated to the car and waited quietly in the driver's seat for the hour or so Rose bore her witness to Sam's death.

The village of graves was desirable real estate and relatively expensive. A collection by the Reverend's congregation contributed the down payment on Sam's plot. The rest would come over time though it was hard to imagine an eviction. The village also was a shrouded community, hidden off the main streets and visited only by those like Rose whose attachment to their dead loved ones was both incomplete and irresistible. Beyond the cemetery such sorrow might appear imposing or even repulsive to a living, breathing and working world, as if public mourning were bad manners and best done out of sight.

"You ready to leave, mom?" Larry asked when he saw his mother stand. He was careful not to rush her. How he approached depended entirely on her mood and what she seemed to presume was Sam's. She imagined his voice speaking to her, his warm eyes as he spoke. She heard his laugh. It was all still real and Larry, at first put off by his mother's lovingly morbid dance with Sam, came to see how helpful it was for her to imagine that something of her son might live on. He had been as a fetus merely a proposal offered by the mind of her God. Now she accessed her son through the secure belief Sam was still a sturdy figment of her God's eternal imagination.

"I guess I'll never know what happened," Rose said one afternoon as Larry drove her home.

"You wanna know?" Larry asked. "You think you wanna know how Sam got it?"

"Got it" was the awkward euphemism for Sam's moment of death and no; Rose did not actually wish to know. Every indication suggested it must have been horrible.

Larry knew. Following Sam's burial Larry had chased after the only brother on the honor escort and asked him how he could find out more about the battle in which Sam lost his life. The soldier told Larry to contact the chaplain at Letterman Hospital in San Francisco. He knew that a few wounded servicemen who survived the ambush at Ap Nhi were sent there. One might be willing to talk to Larry. And he was right.

The chaplain found a helicopter gunner who lost his foot and was done with war. Larry visited him at Letterman, a skinny white boy with dark hair and hollow eyes who hid his ruined limb under the blanket while he chain-smoked cigarettes. He didn't know Sam but he knew what had happened.

"It was an ambush," he said. "Bunch a charlies wearin' ARVN uniforms walking by as we drove in. Your brother was driving a truck. Right? Charlies waited until half the convoy passed and our troops were beyond the trucks. Then they opened fire and threw grenades into the trucks. Trucks exploded. Drivers killed instantly. Some trucks blown into a million pieces."

Larry guessed the drivers were, too. The soldier was on a helicopter called in from Saigon that crashed at the site, which was under heavy cloud cover.

"Lucky to be alive. I guess," said the pilot, inattentive to Larry's loss. "Never would have happened if the command had sent a helicopter escort to begin with."

Larry heard the irony in the last words spoken. Larry knew how Sam died and would never tell his mother.

Every week the gruesome truth of a soldier's death was dropped at hundreds of distinct doorsteps, all too far apart to turn into an aggregate of grief and rage that might produce a rebellious riot of parents, children, and sweethearts. Not like Detroit, or Watts, or Newark, where the injustice of assault and death slammed everyone in a community and all at once and quickly pulled an angry crowd into action.

Larry spent more time with his parents; time enough to gaze into the photo he took of his mother before the news of Sam's death, her eyes bright and alert while she smiled coyly. Now she was quiet and slow to respond to others, almost as if she refused to wake from a dream. She resisted her husband who shuffled helplessly around her as he tried to appear both assertive and pleasing. The two parents struggled to find useless answers and assess meaningless blame in a way that tied them more closely to their ancestors than to the future. Rose's only urgency appeared to grow from a new concern for Larry's safety.

The Chicago convention was televised and existed for Larry as a bleared, wordless mush of brief, inchoate scenes. He watched television without the volume, interpreting what he saw through the printed words of a daily newspaper. His family's home was a sanctuary of grief and Larry would not disturb it, though he saw enough to realize the Democrats had fallen into disarray, that protesters were being pummeled and beaten in Lincoln Park where he had heard Bobby give his first speech.

Calls for revolution sounded good in the streets but did not translate well to television. While the whole world might be watching, all it saw was chaos. Larry saw only a fateful failure and did not wish to succumb. He wanted a fate but not a fate to fall through like sand through an hourglass. He was not afraid of fate if it held a purpose. For a moment he was happy not to have joined the riots. It was the battle to have missed, and much like the battle his brother should have missed.

One morning Larry read a brief article about military prison rebellions led by black GIs in Army brigs in Long Binh and Da Nang. Ninety percent of the inmates in the Long Binh Jail, referred to by soldiers as "LBJ," were black. The rebellion had lasted nearly a week and the only soldier killed was a white prison guard.

Larry pictured Sam in jail in Vietnam, in big trouble with the Army but still alive.

That's where I would have been, Larry boasted to himself, suddenly furious with Sam for following orders.

"That be pretty bad shit," Murph said bleakly as he sat with Larry in the Argyle Lounge on Adeline Street. "Go on, you don't got no fight with no Vietnamese. Forget that charlie and remember Mr. Charlie—you fightin' him now. He the one that sent yo brother to Nam."

A second beer had induced Larry into the wishful thought he could avenge Sam's death. Larry mentioned to Murph he might enlist, though he knew his sports injury would likely keep him out of the army. But saying this lifted momentarily the infection of Larry's guilt that his brother had died and he had not.

"Naw—won't happen, Murph. I ain't goin' nowhere," Larry concluded.

The two friends waited for the night's performers, a quartet of soul singers known locally as *The Naturals*. Murph acted as their agent and said he was close to getting a record contract.

"Boola Boola Records up on Telegraph," he said. "They here tonight."

Larry searched the tables filling with arrivals. At the foyer he saw an old high school pal.

"There's Gilmore," Larry said to Murph. "Lamont Gilmore. Remember?"

Lamont's thick hair was straightened and combed in a waxy wave, a silk purple scarf tied around his neck. He wore a flashy black suit coat over a pair of dark jeans. His eyes were concealed behind thick blue-tinted sunglasses.

That funky dude, Larry thought as he ran his hand through his own thick, short-cropped hair. *Still dressed to kill. But to kill what?*

On his arm was Mary Louise in a strapless floral dress wrapped tightly at her breasts and thighs. The couple shuffled together toward the front, Larry catching a glance from Sam's former sweetheart. He waved but Mary Louise looked swiftly away as if not to acknowledge Larry or that she ever had known him. Sam was gone and so was Mary Louise.

The Naturals walked out, four tall men wearing color coordinated cardigans and dark corduroy slacks, their hair grown out in black cascades of symmetric, natural curliness. They approached four microphones at the front of the stage while the crowded room erupted with applause. Backed by a piano, a bass and two guitars, the Naturals opened with a soulful, doo-wop hit, "Love That Really Matters."

The lead singer poured out the song's tender lyrics through an exuberant tenor while his three mates spun through choreographies of bows and turns, arriving at their microphones to sing on the downbeat of each chorus. The effect was hypnotic and enriched the soulful song's supple, canorous harmony. Larry lost track of Lamont and Mary Louise, of the dark room and Murph and his drink in front of him. He lost his hold on Sam and the life of unwarranted penance his death had become for him. He wondered where Sylvia was tonight and when would he see her again.

News of Sam's death seeped out into Larry's world through a loosening chain of links and revelations. Mack was the first outside the family to find out. The city desk assigned him Sam's obituary, submitted by both the Army and the Harrison Funeral Home. It was a hard life to summarize. There were so few milestones. Mack steered clear of the specifics of Sam's death and used only the phrase "killed in action" which was standard. Mack later told Bronwyn, Raj and Yitzhak and, eventually Stan and Ginger. Bronwyn was the most moved by the news. She tried to phone Larry but he didn't answer.

On Sunday September 8th the jury in the Huey Newton trial reached its verdict. Newton was guilty of voluntary manslaughter. He would not die in the gas chamber. But neither would Newton go free. While people cheered, Larry wondered if the verdict might turn out to be a disappointment for the Panthers. Huey Newton was a martyr and his presumed sacrifice in the defense of his community had attracted thousands of members to the Black Panther Party.

"My life had to come to an end sometime," Newton had said. "But the people go on; in them lies the possibility for immortality. Since each man eventually gives up his life, death can only be controlled through the lives of the people."

The quote was pasted up at Panther headquarters and applied to the mirror in Larry's bathroom.

Following the death of Sam, the Newton verdict left Larry feeling empty and drained. It was good Huey would survive and also it wasn't. The end of this battle signaled the beginning of another and Larry worried about a loss of the Panther advantage against injustice when in Huey's case it could be argued justice was at least partially served. What Larry saw in Chicago had inspired him. And he wondered if the Panther Movement was too big to accommodate Huey's survival. Could he even imagine it would be better for Huey to die? Though it seemed likely Huey wanted to die, wanted to become in death something larger than his life.

That seemed bizarre and also strangely comprehensible. Was it also a buried motivation in Sam's enlistment? Or in any boy's urge for battle?

The question disappeared the next morning when Larry arrived at Panther Headquarters on Grove Street to find the front window shot full of holes, its glass shattered and posters ripped by gunfire. The unfolding story, that two Oakland cops had shared a few drinks the night of the verdict and then drove by in their patrol car to shoot up the Panther office, was beautifully victimizing. Justice was not served. The cops were still out of control and needed, in the words of Eldridge Cleaver who spoke into a dozen news microphones, "to be driven out of our community like the dogs they are."

Larry photographed the damaged windows and entered the office where Sylvia was picking up chards of glass while she swept the floor.

"Well, where *you* been?" Sylvia asked as she saw Larry walk through the door. "That was a long time in Chicago."

"Not Chicago," Larry answered abruptly. "Had to come back. My brother–well, he…"

Larry hesitated as if stranded on a ghost ship from which few directions were known or could be given.

"My brother Sam–he got killed in Vietnam."

Larry pushed the words forward as if each were a recalcitrant child that would not obey. The effort exhausted him.

Sylvia's face softened as she absorbed Larry's shy confession, her discourse unexpectedly constrained by a billowing sympathy with no words to support it.

"Larry…"

Sylvia propped the broom against a table and walked toward him. She reached with her arms to pull his face down toward hers and to hold him. Larry accepted Sylvia's embrace and lingered in its affectionate calm. She was a comfort and also an indulgence.

Larry cried his first tears of mourning. He felt his chest at last give up its throes of contained sorrow. Sylvia joined him, her eyes wet with their humane acceptance of him and his liberated grief. The embrace made Larry feel absolved and also infantile, as if he were held like a small child and, as such, easily aroused. He was now a boy baby and at last held protectively.

"We gonna get outta here," Sylvia whispered to him.

Larry, unaware of the strength of his grasp, released her quickly and nodded yes. Yes, yes…damn please, yes.

"I can't stop thinkin' about his dyin'—I can't stop."

Larry was again near tears. Sylvia had walked him to a small park near the Panther office and sat with him on a bench. Across a small lawn two young mothers pushed their toddler sons in swings.

"Maybe he felt nothin'. Maybe he was afraid. But he died alone without anyone to hold him."

Larry was excluded from the cruel images of war and his guilt about this was palpable.

"I know dad thinks I shoulda been there. Shoulda taken a bullet for Sam. I know that's crazy. But dad don't say nothin' anymore so I jus don't know."

"No, you can't," Sylvia said. "No one can know. I'm so sorry, Larry. I think your dad's grieving just like you are."

"Gotta go now," she said after a long, still silence. "Gotta see Father Neil about the breakfasts."

Sylvia apologized.

"Let's get lunch tomorrow. We'll meet at the office. My treat."

Larry said yes and Sylvia, after squeezing his forearm, stood and left Larry on the bench. He felt the confident touch of a woman who appeared to know him; a woman who did not pretend to be white and so had no spell over him. He felt the warmth of her empathy, drawn perhaps from the suffering both shared deep in their genes.

Larry realized that his father could not look clearly through his faith at the error that led Sam to his death. The steps toward Sam's enlistment were incremental, as was the government's entry into the war that took his life. It seemed at the time the last best choice for Sam who nearly 26 years old was already drifting into a somnambulistic street walk that might crush him.

And the uniform did it. Once Sam put it on he was conformed and aligned with every other soldier. And proud. Giddily proud to be a warrior. And for one critical moment the Reverend abandoned his faith in peace to justify war and raise his son up as a cherished and valued fighter. Though no one really expected Sam to fight. Or die. Now it seemed absurd that Sam could fight and survive through the Tet offensive and then get killed driving a truck 47 days before the end of his two-year tour of duty. It was an absurdity, and one that now ran like a vein of unreachable ore beneath the landscape of Larry's experience.

"She just lost," Larry said at last.

Sylvia sat at the table of a Grove Street diner and listened while Larry described his mother who since the return of Sam's remains was locked within an eerie beatitude of her own suffering.

"She sad all the time now but she won't talk about it."

Larry attempted to describe the wild, manic grieving Rose hid behind her calm, unfocused eyes.

"It's like she needs to hurt—hurt alone, and like it's a secret though it sure ain't no secret to me and dad and Aunt Rhetta."

"And you drive her to Sam's grave? How's that make you feel?"

Sylvia took a bite of her sandwich while Larry weighed her query.

"I been floatin' above it all," Larry at last answered.

"I been angry, too. Damn, I'd just be flyin' off at anything. At anything but mom. I hated the war. Then I hated my dad for helpin' Sam. Then I hated Sam for joinin' the army. Then I started hatin' white people again. Hated them for comin' here and startin' wars and then draggin' our asses outta Africa to be they goddamned slaves. And, well, you know the rest. My Aunt Rhetta's angry, too. She understand."

"She do and I do, too," Sylvia responded. "There's plenty to be mad about. Four centuries just about enough a this crap any people can take. We done. We don't need no more sorrow not of our making. Ol' Mr. Charlie wants each of us to apply for our rights. One at a time. He decides if we speak well enough, dress the right way, have enough money, think the right thoughts. He decide if we each qualified. That's what I like about black power. We gonna do it together and all at once, whether Mr. C likes it or not. We gonna insist. We cool. You know where cool come from don't you?"

Larry did not know, launching Sylvia into a developed discourse on the origins of the Yoruba concept of *itutu*, the idea that angry spirits might be calmed by a gentleness of character. Yoruba, she said, had lived in southwestern Nigeria since the middle ages, had at one time a highly developed civilization, elements of which were brought to America. Coolness, she said, was the open life, the offered gift, the real deal. It was Negro music, the black smile, the joyful celebration. It was bottle trees and Big John. It was vodun and jazz.

"White people got no idea how much their culture is rooted in ours. We been here a lot longer than most of 'em. You ever watch American Bandstand? Dick Clark? All those white teens dancing on the set and not a Negro in sight. Then the Supremes show up to lip-synch their hit *Baby Love*. And then Smokey. And Little Anthony. And Jimmy Jones. The only black faces on the screen. Each picked individually for the entertainment of a white audience. How could that not make us crazy? How is that not slavery?"

Larry's confessed anger had ignited Sylvia's, though it led her to speak over his grief. Her knowledge of cultural history was intimidating. She had told him her family traced its roots to the Gullah of South Carolina and their semi-autonomous antebellum coastal culture. Larry had only call and response and perhaps three generations of preachers and Pullman porters.

"You one good Panther," Larry said at last, jolting Sylvia back into his reality.

"I'm sorry, Larry," she said. "I been goin' on. I do that. I'm a big know-it-all. And I'm not a good Panther. You loved your brother, didn't you?"

Larry waited for an expected choke in his throat that did not come. He sat back and looked out the diner's window at all the people rushing along Grove Street, all with destinations not anywhere near his life, Sam's death, or even the war.

"He was my brother. A good brother. I can say that. We weren't close. We just far enough apart in age to have different schools and different friends. He was headed for trouble and my daddy wanted to stop him. That's all, really. I'm worried more about mom and daddy. Daddy havin' a real hard time. He's a preacher and right now he's at a loss for words. Not a good space for a preacher."

Sylvia reached over and touched Larry's hand.

"An what's this about you not bein' a good Panther?" Larry added. "Seems to me you do most a the work around here."

"And what's a good Panther?" asked Sylvia.

"You ever read Eldridge's book? *Soul on Ice?*"

Larry had not.

Sylvia confessed she had a lot of trouble with Eldridge and what he wrote about his reasons for raping black women, which he described as essentially "practice" for raping white women.

"He tries to make it sound like rape is a revolutionary act and it sure as hell aint'. And he likes white women more than black women. I don't like that at all. A lot a you Panther boys do. The women know. Hell a lot more women in that Panther office than boys. We be OK once the breakfasts get started. But we still got problems and I just don't know sometimes. We need power. We need community. But our community is gonna come together faster around breakfasts than around bullets."

Larry thought Sylvia should meet Bronwyn, though he cringed at her comment about Panther boys and white girls.

"Got a friend who says white people only think they white," Larry responded. "No one is really white."

Sylvia waited a moment and nodded.

"Suppose so," she answered, "but don't try to tell them that. You can be the darkest damn Mexican in America and still be white."

"That's one thing I liked about Chicago," Larry said. "Everybody black."

Sylvia gave Larry a disbelieving look.

"No, not everybody. But everybody southside. Must be more than a million black people in Chicago. Wherever I went that's all I saw. And the Panthers, they pretty cool, as you say. Freddie Hampton is their leader and one righteous dude. Everyone is a revolutionary. And the breakfasts, they got 'em goin'. I want to go back."

"When?" Sylvia asked.

"Don't know. When I can. Gotta tell you I liked livin' in an all black part of America. No one gave me a second look. We all just colored people walkin' around in rainbow town. Beautiful."

"Yeah," Sylvia said. "Maybe when you go you can take me."

Larry searched Sylvia's face for evidence of enticement, argument, perhaps impasse. Was she joking? Or was she really saying something? He was too shy to ask.

"Got somethin' to show ya," Larry said and pulled out a manila envelope. He reached in and grabbed a sheaf of photos that he spread out on the table. They were his photos of Panther headquarters after the police shoot-up. Sylvia picked out a striking image of the broken front window, a torn poster of Huey full of bullet holes hanging behind it.

"This damn good. Have you shown these to Emory? He'll wanna use 'em in the paper. I know he will."

The conversation was now a machine running all by itself, spinning out more thoughts than ever were contained in Larry's initial words of remorse. Sylvia liked him and he liked Sylvia. Out of their unanchored discourse he had woven both the fabric of a new way to live and the idea of a path that might lead him there.

"This sure good shit. You always have good shit," Larry said as he took another drag on the joint handed to him by Raj.

The two sat on a shoulder of a high ridge and looked out toward a sun seen through the condensing fog that poured into San Francisco and through the Golden Gate. For a moment the blinding ball of cosmic fire that created and fed them all fell into view like a bright orange marble, its violent brightness filtered by clouds and momentarily accessible.

"I guess it's God," Raj said. "What else? Nothing could exist without it."

Larry nodded. He, too, was subdued. After lunch with Sylvia he had dropped by the Forum where Raj asked him for a lift into the ridges of Tilden Park. He frequently spent the night there. Larry agreed and when they reached the trailhead, Raj asked Larry if he'd like to hike to the top and smoke a joint.

"You can see everything from here," Raj stated in stoned amazement. "Wow…"

Larry saw the Bay spread before him, a lake of towns where he had spent most of his young, Negro life. He traced the paths of his steps among the places below. He saw the grids of streets and the identifiable roofs and walls of buildings and landmarks. He could delineate the beginning and the end of his black neighborhood. He could see far into the distance across the bay the vacant shipyards of Hunter's Point where Negroes rioted in 1966 over the police shooting of an unarmed 17-year-old boy.

He identified the towers of wealth that formed a wall across the big city's financial district; a wall he imagined existed to keep him out. He followed Telegraph Avenue and then Grove Street south and east into the black neighborhoods of Oakland and West Berkeley to the point where they abutted the fully white communities of Elmwood and Piedmont. He imagined his steps across time as well as space. His was an interrupted geography; a matrix that had grown weeds and new blooms and that had recast the lives of its peoples along similar lines. He imagined a map of colors—the colors of people who by their shade of darkness were allowed to exist only along a particular axis.

"You just see the streets," Raj said as Larry described his view. "I see the mountains, the trees, the heights without human habitation. That's the best. That's where it's at."

Perhaps. But it was not where Larry was located. He was a city boy in need of another city. He had found one—or at least a substantial part of one—where color made no difference. And he admired Freddie, Chicago's head Panther. *Good work to be done for my people*, Larry thought. He was a person of color, a colored person of African heritage. He was an African-American. He recalled a poem Sylvia had given him to read, something about the "strong young, up of head, severe, not drowsy, not in-bitten, not outwitted by history..."

He was that young man. He would return to school. He would work and save his money. He would be a soldier for the Panthers and an army to himself. He had already acknowledged the unbearable. He could hear his own cry. He would renounce the old ways by any means necessary. He was Larry and he was for real.

RAJ

one

A hike and a bus ride and Raj Neville would be back, though in his heart there was no "back" to which he ever needed to return. He had spent another night in Tilden Park, a vast and forested ridge along the eastern hills of Berkeley that like a slow moving geologic wave straddled an active earthquake fault. He slept better on the ground than in a bed and a warm September night held him gently in the weeds. No fire was needed and he would never light one in the park. When nautical twilight at last faded, so did he. When dawn returned the morning shadows, Raj awoke.

An hour's walk brought him to the park exit at the mouth of Spruce Street. From there a city bus floated Raj downhill to the north side of the campus. The slow descent of the bus, rolling and jerking through its twisting route and many stops, felt like a rough re-entry from the trails and trees above to a jungle of people below. Outside he watched puffs of fog burn off the bay until the bus plunged below the fog line and the streets, increasingly dense with buildings, turned a sullen grey.

Raj had left heaven to return to earth, heaven over earth reminding him of a hexagram described in his Wilhelm *I Ching*. It was the sign of stagnation, of the month of September, of autumnal decay, of sod clinging to uprooted grass. Moon and man, nature and town were in play and Raj was lost and without use in his silence.

Poetry informed his time in the trees but in his walk across campus Raj was humming the lyrics of *Hey Jude*, rolling the song's blasting chorus through his mind to flood and drown senses opened under the stars. *I was telepathic*, he thought to himself. *Now I'm slipping into verbal. The head cop is taking over.* In the woods he could deal directly with the magical world. Words were needed in the urban jungle and singing was his natural way to hold them.

Raj waved at Harriet as she strolled into the Forum after noon. He had parked his pack and bought coffee and a roll. He had found the day's discarded front pages and shuffled past war and politics to read that singer Roy Orbison's two young sons were killed in a fire at his Tennessee home. Orbison was on tour in England, trying to revive his singing career following the death of his wife two years prior in a motorcycle accident. Raj liked Roy Orbison. He turned the ensuing apparitions of grief over to his head cop who began humming *Only the Lonely.*

"Where have you been?" Harriet asked Raj. "Sleeping in the woods again?"

Raj shrugged. The smell of his body was the smell of the forest. Harriet smelled like a bubble bath, her face clear and scrubbed, her long hair flagrantly curled, her skin lathered with lotion. She had just come from her home and Raj had not yet arrived at his, a very small room in a very large house two blocks east of Telegraph.

"Yeah, of course," Raj answered. "Where else? Peace and quiet in the trees. The view is spectacular. And it's free. You should try it sometime. Any news?"

"Jen was looking for you Friday," said Harriet. "And yesterday. Raj, do you ever tell your girlfriends where you're going?"

"Jen's not a girlfriend," Raj answered coarsely.

"That's not what she thinks," Harriet spoke again. "Haven't you guys been sleeping together for awhile?"

"Has it been awhile? I've forgotten," Raj replied.

"Don't tell Jen that," Harriet said. "That is, if you want to keep sleeping with her."

Raj preferred the news of the forest and his pipeline to plants and animals that shared with him the secrets of their seasons and never troubled him with questions. Perhaps it was why he hadn't told

Jen he was leaving to sleep in the forest. She would object or want to go. Women who liked him did that. Sleeping alone in the woods kept the natural order in his life and though he was a member of the community, a denizen in good standing on the wild streets south of the campus, he preferred the forest's news to the conduits and commitments of a city.

"Yeah, I'm a flake. I'll give you that," he said to Harriet. "No one would ever guess I'm the son of a banker."

"A banker?" Harriet asked. She was surprised. She knew Raj as a Telegraph habitué and could not imagine any previous life as a banker's son.

But Raj had grown up in Orinda as the child of a wealthy investment executive named Franklin Neville who spent his best years climbing through the food chain at Wells Fargo. Raj was tall like his father but not as tall, so he was characterized frequently as a diminutive version of the old man, "a little Frank," though his given name, Reginald, was bad enough. His Catholic mother had named him for an obscure French saint. By high school he had tired of being anyone's little anything and adopted the nickname Raj after a semester of bus rides to Berkeley and the City where he and a select group of pals drank espressos at cafés, listened to poetry and jazz, and decided to become beatniks. His friends thought he had taken an Indian name as a way to appear hip and cool. Raj didn't care what his friends thought. He liked the name and kept it.

As a 15-year-old sophomore Raj ended up at the Town Hall Theater on Shattuck one winter evening to hear a reading by Beat poets, among them Allen Ginsberg who for the second time read in public his poem *Howl*. It was a rich performance that connected Raj to peyote, cemetery dawns, wine drunks, ashcan rantings and, the line Raj remembered best, the *kind king light of mind*. Raj loved the words of the poet more than his own.

Shortly after, the not-as-tall son dropped off the high school basketball team, angering his father.

"He was always pissed about something," Raj said.

Raj's Beat proclivities made him a high school celebrity. He listened to Kerouac on LPs, Word Jazz records, and the hip "Naz" sermons of Lord Buckley. He wrote poems to his local girlfriend that *her* girlfriends read jealously. In his senior year he grew a goatee and was nearly expelled. But his grades were too good, he was too handsome, and his father too rich for that to happen.

When Raj was accepted at Berkeley his father hoped things would settle down until he saw his son on the TV news being bounced down the steps by cops during protests at the House Un-American Activities Committee hearings at San Francisco City Hall.

"That was it. Dad cut me off. I survived on the street and lasted another year at Cal. The classes were large and boring and what was happening was on the streets. I've served my time. Civil Rights. Free Speech. Filthy Speech. Stop the Draft Week. I've been here for it all."

"When did you start doing drugs?" Harriet asked.

"You mean grass? Acid? How about beer?"

"Whatever," Harriet said. "When?"

Raj was given a joint at the Café Trieste in North Beach on a summer afternoon in 1957. He remembered the day but not the date.

"So fucking mellow. I shared it with my high school main man Tom. We ended up at the top of Coit Tower really trippin'. It was fantastic to be so aware and so alive, to laugh so hard we thought someone would bust us. I finally understood what Beat was, what it meant to be hip and not square."

Raj was then 17 and his literary hero was Sal Paradise. And like Sal, Raj knew that *somewhere along the line there'd be girls, visions, everything.* Somewhere along the line he would be handed a pearl.

"And the university?" Harriet asked. "Why didn't you stay in school?"

Raj was grateful Harriet didn't ask about acid. He could not do it justice with his head cop in charge, could not talk about its entangling telepathy, its reproducible ego death in which cognition and vision are bathed in the same light, its exhausting hilarity and other profound and haunting emotional shades.

"I was reading the Beats," Raj said. "*Howl* and rock 'n' roll and Charlie Parker and Miles D were a whole new show. It's all I cared about and Tom Parkinson was the only professor who even talked about them. I took his Yeats class and a survey but I couldn't just take his classes. The rest was a waste. I got more out of reading the used books I shelved at Creed's. At least the good parts were already underlined. And when the professor was shot…"

"Wait," Harriet stopped him. "A gun? Parkinson was shot?"

"You didn't know? A former student, some crazy religious nut, shot him in the face. Must have been '61. Killed his TA. Bad scene. But he's still there, isn't he?"

Raj reveled in the historical gossip that gave him an odd and momentary seniority. Harriet was the scholar but Raj was the memory. Though Harriet was a graduate student, Raj had been on campus longer.

"When I quit school and stopped working my dad said I was wasting my time," he said. "I told him it was time I enjoyed wasting. And that's the last I heard from him. Damn, anyone with two arms and two legs can work. Living is the hard part. My dad thinks there's only one world—a real world. But there's another world where everything is magical, though even in the magic world some stuff is real and some stuff isn't."

"And your mom? Any other family?" Harriet asked.

"Mom sends the holiday and birthday cards and signs them. She comes over for lunch a couple times a year. We don't talk about dad. That's never good. And I don't go back to Orinda. Even if it's just over the hill, I haven't been there in eight years. My sister's a freshman at Wellesley and she writes. Her name is Stephanie. Made out better than I did in the name department. Grandparents are all dead. No cousins that I know of. That's me. That's my bloodline."

What Raj did not say was that he was a satyr that wanted his desire satisfied immediately, who had to hurl himself forward toward every promise of experience. His thoughts, some of which he wrote down, were like love letters that could not await a reply.

"You smell good, Harriet," Raj said glibly. "Makes me want to go take a shower."

Harriet grinned while Raj jumped up, grabbed his pack and sauntered away.

Raj liked Harriet, enough to look for her when he was on the Avenue where usually she sat at a chosen table at the Forum, her downcast eyes in a book, notes scattered, a half-sipped latte at her right, a bright slender moon of her lipstick pressed at the cup's rim.

He liked her and would love her but knew that would mean losing her so he put his head cop in charge and kept his ceremonial and vibratory distance. The vibes were good and he didn't have to get too close to enjoy them.

Raj had friends. He was not a hermit. Inger was still a friend, though she wasn't the same telepathic buddy he first met. The sex was good but their acid trip was unhinging and had put distance between them. Tripping out became too real and that was that. She would be acting in a play next month and he would go see her. He liked Brownyn though she was after him to help organize the neighborhood. Get down with the program. Vote. Fuck, so much head tripping. Too much.

And Ginger and Stan still invited him to their parties and art openings. That was cool. Mack was cool. News guy with lots of freebies (got Raj a press pass to Monterey Pop last year) and he bought pot and acid from Raj and was a regular. Mack knew literature and could talk William Carlos Williams and Gregory Corso and Ginsberg and Kerouac. Larry was Raj's black brother, though he never asked Larry about it. In Sal's words, Raj walked aching, wishing he were a Negro, feeling the white world didn't offer nearly enough ecstasy, joy, kicks, darkness or music.

And Larry also bought Raj's dope, though never his acid. Raj thought it would be a fair trade to offer Larry a telepathic experience in exchange for some soulful blues learnin'. But Larry had just lost his brother in the bad war.

And then there was Yitzhak. Some dangerous magic was at work with Yitzhak. It had been a year since his geeky college friend Raymond had taken the name Yitzhak, grown an abundant moustache and begun dressing in Flamenco pants and dancing boots. Over time Yitzhak was moving more and saying less and though he didn't buy his dope from Raj, he was doing something pretty heavy. Raj figured it was acid or DMT but whatever it was, Yitzhak wasn't saying. In fact there wasn't much he would say until the vibes became so unbearably heavy Raj would freak out and say something paranoid. And Yitzhak would look at him like *you are bringing me down, you are such a bummer* and nothing would go right for a while.

Yet there was deep magic between them. Raj felt it. Yitzhak

would follow him into the woods from time to time and was always good for a weekend in the Sur. And he drove. Raj hated to drive. There were no astral rewards sitting behind a wheel. There was no telepathy. No wondrous, trippy spell. Just a rushing, rattling roar.

All these friends Raj knew related as much or more to each other as they did to him. The stories and links were limitless and for a time in his shower Raj opened to an atomizing and inarticulate wonder. The head cop took his leave. The warm water washed away his flesh and bones until he flashed on a continually evolving web of relationships that extended beyond the streets, the city, the shoreline, the world, the planets, the stars, the galaxies. Was there anything in existence that did not respond to the motion of another?

two

Raj walked to the Garden Spot to buy bread and cheese. He also wanted a tomato. It was summer and Sunday on the Avenue and Raj was mellow though not quite telepathic. A few tokes after his shower and he was alert to a voracious hunger. He walked down the block, entering Telegraph at Dwight Way to pass Pepe's and its briny odor of broiling pepperoni, and then the leather shop and, again, The Forum. He passed women out in the hot sun wearing tie-dyed tank tops and no bras.

He found his groceries and added a bar of chocolate. The house kitchen was mostly empty on Sundays and he usually tried to eat at odd hours to avoid collisions with roommates, most of them students.

He was making his sandwich, having just liberated a scoop of mayonnaise from someone else's jar when he looked up to see Jen enter.

"You're home," she said coolly. "Where have you been?"

Raj put down the knife, acutely tuned to Jen's resentful tone. He waited for a vibration to find him that, like a tuning fork, might move him into Jen's flow, might allow him to throw something forward that could stone her into a quiet acceptance.

"Jen…" Raj was slow to respond. "Took some time in the woods. You know I do that."

Raj heard his defensiveness and recoiled. Jen was a small, thin-limbed woman but also a strong lady.

"Why not tell me?" Jen said.

The floor seemed to move vaguely as Jen took several steps into the kitchen.

Raj felt a surge of panic as the distance between them shrank. He waved off his head cop and tried again to contact Jen's radiant ego. Even if not fully telepathic, his mind could feel Jen's grave psychic vibe. It was serious. She stood with her long black hair spread out across her shoulders, her dark pupils like pellets aimed at his eyes. She wore an orange peasant blouse and a black granny skirt and Raj could see it was all she had on.

"Wanna get stoned?" he asked, twisting his mouth into a supplicating grin.

In his room, Raj rolled a joint from a stash he kept in a dresser while Jen sat on the bed. Jen loved to get stoned and Raj always had good dope. He had to. He sold it. Jen was young, seven years younger than Raj, and a senior and lived in a boarding house north of the campus. She and Raj met in Creed's while she browsed the fiction shelves. They had been spending time together for a month, and mostly at Raj's since the boarding house (which her parents were subsidizing) had strict rules about male guests. Jen took a drag on the joint and slipped back on Raj's bed, propping herself against his only two pillows.

"You're forgiven," Jen said as Raj again passed her the joint and she inhaled another hit. Raj felt their initially rigorous tension transformed into a curious and familiar alignment.

"It's good to see you, Jen," Raj said. "You are a magic woman."

He was sincere. Magic was real, even if fleeting.

Raj pulled his chair closer to the bed and placed his hand on Jen's small belly. She took his hand and moved it into the cleft of her breasts. The intelligence of telepathy was as much in its broadcast as its reception. Raj waited patiently to feel the first quickening of Jen's breathing and a long exhale that signaled a likely measure of astral contact. She was a Scorpio and he a Sagittarius. Raj had done their charts and visualized the sextiles reaching from his fifth house to her eighth, from his Jupiter to her Mars.

As her breathing quickened he moved his left hand from between her breasts and lifted her blouse. He then rolled his fingers gently over her bared nipples, dabbing each with a calm pinch before moving across her shoulders. Jen arched her back as Raj used his right hand to lift her skirt and tenderly spread her legs. For several minutes Raj stroked and touched Jen's prone body, at last slipping up the inside of a thigh to inquire gently at the lips of her vulva, pushing through a black pubic copse to find the convergence of her lips and the particularly moist points of her pleasure.

Raj then sat like a pianist at a keyboard, orchestrating with his two hands an arousal of the small, slender woman before him, one hand sweeping gently across her breasts and upper torso while the other probed and buffed her deepest, sparking source. One hand played a melody, the other kept the beat. Jen's body rose and fell in response, her legs finally stretched as two wobbling arcs in the air until a gasping shout and several quick, sturdy jerks signaled her come.

Raj was the older and wiser lover, which Jen happily acknowledged. He led her forward playfully and with assurance that was itself a turn-on. Raj encouraged Jen to play and to explore, to touch herself as well as him. Raj was not Jen's first lover but up until now her most interesting. He was an attractive animal and comfortable with uncertainty in a way no one else seemed to be. But while Raj's spontaneity was alluring, his poverty was a liability. To remain telepathic he avoided commitments, in fact worked hard not to work. But over time an attraction like Jen's graduated into desire and then into various forms of need that Raj knew he would never be able to meet.

Still, his years of flowering affiliation had acquired for Raj both a source for dealing grass and LSD as well as a stable of trusted clients. Each month he purchased a kilo of Mexican dope and fifty hits of orange sunshine. He broke the kilo into ounces and sold them for three times what he paid. Acid was cheaper and sometimes Raj just gave it away to build his relationships or turn on his friends.

For certain he was small-time and Raj wondered why Judson, who lived in Santa Cruz and was a high-end dealer, still bothered to sell to him. But Raj and Judson went back a ways and if the drug trade was about anything it was about loyalty.

"Say, can I borrow your car this week?" Raj asked Jen when she returned from the bathroom. "Have to run an errand Wednesday in San Jose. I'll fill the tank for you."

Jen was quiet in a way Raj interpreted as an aura of stubborn control, which he thought had been extinguished by all the flower power he had just thrown at her.

"It's my mom's car," Jen said. "Do you have a driver's license?"

Raj looked through Jen and could see the wall behind her. The vibes were tightening and he felt guilty after making her feel so free. The heaviest trips were those that rode the wave of personal need.

"Yeah," Raj said.

Jen asked to see it, which nearly brought Raj down. But he needed wheels to get his monthly dope and Jen had them to lend. He knew this. She rarely drove anywhere. He found his wallet and pulled out his license and gave it to her.

Jen stared at it as if to buy some time.

"And you're going to San Jose? Why do you need the car all day?"

Raj wrestled with the complications of psychic revelation. He could not tell Jen he was picking up his stash. And he could not ask her to drive.

"It's complicated," Raj finally said. "Family stuff. I'll throw in some dope and a dinner at the Hofbrau. OK?"

He sought with his telepathy to close some kind of cosmic sale. He took her hand and retrieved his license.

"I guess," Jen said with no enthusiasm.

"Really, Jen. It's cool."

Raj tried to send Jen a magic link of gratitude. But magic wasn't what was needed. He threw more flowers instead.

Raj drove south listening to the radio in Jen's VW. It did not receive FM stations so Raj tuned in drive-time rock on KYA and bounced with the beat of top 40 tunes until Larry Brownell broke in to bellow the news at the top of the hour. The Democratic Convention was over and Humphrey was the nominee, even though he had refused to run in a single primary. Raj wondered why he didn't care about Humphrey when so many others did. Larry, Mack and Bronwyn cared. It was politics and a kind of top tier corruption Raj scrupulously barred from touching his pure, natural soul.

Raj continued south on Highway 80 but did not stop in San Jose. Instead, he exited at Highway 101 and then found the slow lane of Highway 17. He climbed into the coastal mountains with all the juice he could pull from Jen's 36 horsepower VW. His destination was a cabin in rural Soquel, a small foothill town south of Santa Cruz. There he would find Judson and his wife Catherine and probably their toddling daughter whose name he could not recall.

Raj had smoked a doob before leaving and hallucinated briefly on an alternate universe in which his fantasies might have some connection to reality. *Heavens obdure, tho man'll Be man till heavens obdure or hells obscure*. A chorus by Kerouac inspired his choice of universes and also highway exits. He was on his way up that highway and then down again toward the oceanic coast where Judson had located his little farm of happiness, built it out of a small empire of dope sales.

Raj tripped through his suggestible high, imagining a life locked down on land, in business, keeping records, managing the flow of contraband. He was happy to be a small player. He was in that high place where the inside of the car felt like the inside of his head and he could watch with riveting attention his own passing. The hills, the trees, the swerving bends of the road were nothing but his own thoughts constructed to align him with the current plane of experience. It was a surprisingly strong stone he had on and he acknowledged it by slowing his speed and letting other cars go by.

A sign that read *Deep Water* signaled the entrance to Judson's property. It was placed there to alert drivers to a dangerous gully hidden by winter rains but instead had become the sign by which Judson's land was known. *And when you're in Soquel, be sure to stop at Deep Water.* Judson had chased away more vagrants and roadies than he could count.

Raj drove up the road and into a redwood forest that hid Judson's cabin from a long country road. In front of the house stood a platform bed framed under six tall redwoods where Judson and Catherine slept during the warm summers and where Judson's daughter was allegedly conceived.

Judson was one of Raj's old friends and he expected a warm welcome. Maybe share a joint and walk to a nearby river. Lots to catch up on. Judson sometimes was all business but could get telepathic quickly.

Raj parked the VW near the house and walked toward a front porch that extended out like a wide, shiny dance floor. He approached the steps as the door opened and a young man he did not recognize rushed out to confront him.

"What do you want?" the man shouted as he blocked Raj's path up the steps. He was muscular and imposing and used the porch's elevation to augment his height and strength over Raj.

"Who are *you*?" Raj asked. "Where's Judson?"

Raj saw something move behind a curtained window and then heard the voice of Catherine, Judson's wife.

"It's OK, Rocky," she called from inside the doorway. "It's Raj."

Catherine emerged holding her sleepy, naked toddler in her arms. She signaled Raj forward and the man named Rocky stood back and followed him into the house.

"Maybe I should have phoned," Raj said apologetically. "It's just my usual time to score. Where's Judson?"

"I…listen, Raj, there's been an accident. I…"

As Catherine struggled to speak, the toddler awakened and began to howl.

"She needs something," Catherine said. "I can't…"

She did not finish her sentence and turned quickly away form Raj.

"Rocky—you tell him. It's cool. I have to go."

Catherine scurried with her child to the back of the house. Raj turned to look quizzically at Rocky who flashed him an expression of converted neutrality, as if he believed Catherine but not necessarily Raj.

Raj could see that Rocky knew something he didn't want to say. That he would be the bearer of news.

"Judson's dead," Rocky said directly. "Plane accident in the desert a week ago Monday. He was flying some shit in. That damned plane. I was there to meet him and saw the crash. Everything in flames. Nothing left and I couldn't even get close. Judson, the pilot and 350 keys of Michoacán all gone. He could have brought that much over in two vans but he thought the plane would be safer, would make him rich fast. Bull-fucking-shit!"

Was this a joke? Raj waited for a reality that didn't come until at some point Rocky's words were translated into something he could feel. *Judson dead? A plane?* The world made crazy in an instant. And there was no place for grief that would be witnessed by a hostile stranger.

"Three hundred keys…" Raj mumbled, still tripping. "I'm just here to get one."

"Who are you?" Raj asked.

"Who wants to know?" Rocky answered menacingly.

Raj picked up Rocky's anxious vibe. He was tripping on something and Raj thought it might be speed. Raj knew the speed trip well, one usually fraught with paranoia and reckless urges. Rocky was anxious and probably loaded for action. Raj would guide Rocky, would make an infinite space for Rocky and not try to get into his head.

"You must be worried about all this," Raj said sympathetically. "I'm really sorry, man. Judson's one of my closest friends. I can't believe this is happening, has happened. Whatever happened. It's awful."

Rocky took a deep breath and sat down. Raj noticed he sat in an airplane seat, one of two likely removed from the crashed plane to make room for more dope and that Judson used in the living room as furniture. At the time the seats arrived, Judson thought them funny home accessories. Seatbelts hung from the seat arms and their buckles scraped the floor as Rocky squirmed in a skittish slouch.

Rocky shot Raj a suspicious stare that Raj caught with his open eyes and then returned on a stream of projected flower power.

"I'm a businessman," Rocky said, breaking an awkward silence. "Like you, right?"

Raj nodded meekly.

"Yeah. You got that…."

The phone in the kitchen rang.

"Have to get this," Rocky said and jumped to answer the phone.

Raj heard Rocky wait until he heard a voice. Then he spoke as if he were continuing a previous conversation, one already heard and exchanged but that for reasons of urgency needed to be heard and exchanged again.

Raj stood and wandered to the back of the house. He found Catherine sitting on the back porch nursing her baby.

Raj approached quietly, drawing looks from both Catherine and the baby. She had been crying though her face was now still and inscrutable. Raj sat on the porch rail across from the antique rocking chair that held the mother and her hungry, dependent child. It was a familiar view. Judson and Catherine had for years been Raj's model of the life he wanted: a house in the woods, a loving and beautiful woman, a child in her arms as Raj would write his poems and think his thoughts and love his life. Judson grew a garden of natural vegetables and Catherine cooked them. Dope paid the mortgage on their little property and Judson's taste for quality in everything was what inspired and attracted Raj. Raj paid more than other dealers for his weed. But he charged more, too, and never had trouble moving his product.

"Are you OK?"

It was a stupid question, Raj thought, not realizing that in Catherine's current state, no question was stupid.

"It's bad," she answered.

Catherine was furious Rocky could not save Judson. She was angry with Judson for risking and losing his life. She hated the loss of Judson but not as much as the loss of their life together, which was a greater loss of something more wondrous and harmonic than either of them alone. The baby was the symbol of this truth, which was never a truth but only and always a hope.

"This can't be happening. Morgan and I have to get out of here. Tonight won't be too soon."

"What about that guy?" Raj asked.

"Rocky? He was Judson's partner. He wants to take over now. So we're trying to work things out. I need cash to get to Oregon and also need to cover my trail. If they come looking for Judson I don't want them to find me."

"Oregon?" Raj asked.

"Don't ask," Catherine said, and then continued. "Why are you here and what do you want?"

Raj said he had come to see Judson and to pick up his monthly kilo.

"Can you take two?" Catherine asked him. "How about three?"

"I can only pay for one," Raj said regretfully.

Catherine stared out beyond the porch to the giant redwoods casting dark shadows into the chasm formed by the trickling creek left at summer's end. In another sixty days the creek would be a rushing torrent fed by storm clouds that each fall bumped against the mountains and dropped their showers along the steep ridges above Soquel.

"You can owe me," Catherine announced. "What was Judson asking?"

"$275 for the gold," Raj said.

"Gold is all that's left," Catherine answered. "We'll make it $250 each for three. Pay me for one now and owe me $500. We'll need to stay in touch. We'll figure it out."

Raj worked hard not to fall into a trip in a way that would loosen his attachment to the reality of Judson's death. He was still high and sensitive to the facts: that within Judson's inner circle Raj held a privileged place but that Judson's inner circle was barely Catherine's outer one. Her survival and that of her child was all she cared about now that Judson no longer existed as anything but a threatening trail to criminal prosecution. That Raj had scored three kilos of discounted dope with no timeframe for repayment was a benefit with which he would not argue.

Though when Rocky lifted the three bricks from a storeroom and set them on a table, Raj cut into each to touch them, smell them, visibly assess their color and, in a display of irritating aplomb, rolled a joint, took a toke and passed it to Rocky.

"Good shit," Raj said as he struggled to hold his chest full of smoke.

"You telling me?" Rocky answered in a tone of irritation. "You did OK. Now is a good time to go. We have a lot to do here."

Raj had thought of asking Rocky if he could remain a buyer but thought better after Rocky's dismissive injunction. The vibe was bad any way he fielded it. It would not work. Instead, Raj left his mailing address with Catherine and added his parents' address with the written admonition "only in an emergency."

He drove home in deep darkness, a night so dark it was illuminated only by small, blinking stars until, funneled at last from the mountains down into the south bay, Raj was nearly blinded by the sudden luminosity of eternal commerce. Enterprise had become sacrifice for Catherine and opportunity for Raj. He was late and Jen would be angry. He would cut her a chunk from a brick and give it to her. He would celebrate her reluctant trust with an offering. It was a night of great expenditure and also of subtle, nearly invisible profit.

three

Jen nudged Raj under the blanket. She had to pee. They shared Raj's day bed through the night but now it was morning. Raj awoke enough to fall out of the bed and release Jen who ran naked to the door, wrapped herself in a towel and rushed out of the room and down the hall.

Raj had returned late from Santa Cruz and Jen was waiting for him in front of his house. It was nearly midnight and she was furious. He said he would be back in time to take her to dinner. He listened patiently to Jen's accumulated grievances, making room for them in a way that drew her farther in. When he heard what he thought was her last or nearly last sputtering complaint Raj opened his pack.

"I'm sorry, Jen" he said with rehearsed remorse. "I brought you something."

Raj led Jen to his room. He found a knife from the kitchen and when he returned he thrust it into a corner of a tightly bound kilo and cut neatly from it a fat chunk. It was at least two ounces of Judson's primo gold. The gesture, not to mention the gift, silenced Jen immediately.

"That's your share," Raj said gratefully. "Let's roll a joint and see what we've got."

The affiliating invitation was all it took to soothe Jen who knew the value of Raj's gift. She would have her own stash of excellent weed, an asset for herself as well as one she could offer chosen others. Raj returned quickly to his role as the mystic mentor and Jen to her place as the entrusted novice. After a few tokes, it was easy for Raj to find and have his familiar way with her. It was easier still for Jen, who loved all properties of the quality high only Raj seemed able to provide.

As Jen lingered on the toilet, Raj considered the loss of his unusual friend and reliable dealer. Judson would be hard if not impossible to replace. He was that rare connection in an illegal trade who could be both known and trusted. For several years Judson's dope had been a given in Raj's equation of survival. The reliable delivery of great weed also brought Raj reliable customers who depended on him as he depended on Judson. Catherine's three kilos bought Raj some time but he would need a new supplier. And where? And who?

Raj rummaged his past for some forgotten dope connection, searched among flashes of sandalwood incense and scraggly beards, of Forum friends and Provo parties, of rock concerts and dealers, of friends who bragged about really good shit, of street brothers who fought for freedom, even of Larry who might know someone even though he bought from Raj what little grass he ever purchased.

Raj's political acquaintances were useless. Robyn, Peter, Mark, Michael--they rarely bought dope, though if someone had it they enjoyed getting stoned. He knew music people and they were always high but why would they ever help him score? He knew a bass player in the *Loading Zone* who was cool but to ask him the name of his dealer would not be cool.

Raj visualized the flow of marijuana through a vast network of communal veins and arteries and wondered how he might ever direct a drip of primo product toward his small and insignificant capillary. He wanted only great shit. It would cost him more but there was no other way. He had been a hip cat for more than a decade and would not stop now.

He even considered Yitzhak, who did not buy dope from Raj but who bought it from someone. He had imagined that Yitzhak's dope connection was dangerous based only on his friend's incipient symptoms of psychosis and his heavy use of acid and DMT. Perhaps not, Raj thought. Psychotic reactions were in the mind of the user and not the chemical in the leaves.

And besides, Raj only needed a source for grass. His friend

Skilly had provided LSD since before the Acid Tests, which Raj remembered fondly. Raj had been among the first to meet on Perry Lane with Skilly, Kesey and the pranksters. It was there he met Neal Cassady–the real man of trouble and speed–and decided to apply the core of his life to human blues and animal necessity.

Jen left for her class and Raj sauntered outside to the Avenue where he was chased for a moment by a pack of Hare Krishnas demanding alms. Raj held out his open hands to signal a state of useless poverty and then slipped into Creed's where he would work the afternoon sorting and shelving used books. Occasionally he sold some, though sales were slow since the arrival of Moe's Books two doors up.

Time passed slowly as Raj pawed through two boxes of estate sale hardbacks purchased by the owner. He hated the heft and old smell of these volumes, most outdated histories or yellowing first editions until he found a volume of cubist paintings in nearly perfect condition, its plates printed elegantly in full color and fitted individually onto each page. Raj admired the quality and workmanship of the prints and noted it was published in Amsterdam in 1938, a year before the war. Raj set it aside and looked up for a moment to see a familiar face.

"Holiday!" Raj shouted. "What the hell?"

The face swam toward Raj aboard a thick neck and a stout, muscular body adorned in a grey sweatshirt cut raggedly at the elbows and moving forward in scuffed denim jeans. A broad-rimmed straw hat topped the face that smiled at Raj with fat, plenteous warmth. The body's feet were bound in heavy leather boots that made a flat popping noise as they crossed the linoleum floor.

"Why I'm here to see you, you son a bitch," the face said. "Holiday's come to the city for provisions: a hundred pounds of brown rice, bandages and first-aid supplies."

"You still in Mt. Shasta?" Raj asked.

"In Mt. Shasta?" the man named Holiday answered. "No…I'm ON Mt. Shasta. I've been living on the mountain since May, in a meadow on the southwest flank of the mountain. Living rent-free. It's fucking amazing. You got a tour guide or a map in this god damned bookstore? I'll show you."

Holiday Johnson was a mountain man. Had always been as long

as Raj had known him. When Raj was a freshman at Cal, Holiday showed him the trails in the Berkeley hills and where he could sleep on the weekends. Later he showed him where to hide in the regional ridges and mountains and, finally, more secret trails in the Sierras that Raj could never again find without him. Holiday, a moniker taken from his habit of saying every day was a holiday, loved the outdoors and lived as if he were completely a piece of it. Like Raj, Holiday worked hard not to work and thus was wealthier in time than money.

"There it is—Squaw Meadow."

Raj had found an atlas of California and opened it to a map of the northeastern counties. Holiday pointed to the white-rendered peaks of Mt. Shasta and then toward a confluence of trails adjacent to an altitude wrinkle Holiday identified as Red Butte, elevation 8,377 feet.

"Nine of us up there right now. It's been a glorious and beautiful summer. A creek runs through it and it's just below the tree line. "

"Rent free?" Raj asked.

Holiday scratched his scraggly jet-black beard and nodded vigorously.

"It's national forest," said Holiday as he sat in Raj's room. "Rangers leave us alone most of the time. There's only one for the whole mountain and he's cool. People in town can be a little uptight when hippies stroll through and, sure, we get hassled by the straights. But no one bothers us in the meadow."

"Sounds like a semi-paradise," Raj said to Holiday.

"Yeah, my friend. Prettiest damned spot on earth. You gotta see it. Say—why don't you come back with me? Weather's fairly good now but in a couple of weeks we'll all be looking for a place to winter. Night temps are starting to cool but the days are still hot. You've got a bag. You'll be fine."

"How do I get home?" Raj asked.

"Someone's always comin' this way," said Holiday. "Man, give yourself a break. I don't know how you stand this place, panhandlers on every corner, crowds pouring down the sidewalks, and cops everywhere. I mean…just come up and have a look. Won't cost you a dime, not even gas."

Life for Raj was love and love was an amorous system that operated continuously through his body and gaze. He needed only one look at an old map of mountain trails to feel and see himself walking in wild backcountry. Holiday's friendly temptation was impossible to resist and as he rode with his friend north along the big highway to Sacramento he ran through his checklist.

He'd left Jen a note taped to the locked door of his room. He arranged with the manager at Creed's to be gone until the following week. He locked his kilos in his secured closet. He had his sleeping bag, guitar and rucksack and a warm jacket and wore his best boots. He had thirty dollars just in case. And he had some primo weed to smoke on the mountain.

Raj was coursing along what the poet described as that old night Highway *99*, the river of asphalt that passed from Seattle to Los Angeles but that in Raj's lifetime was transmogrifying into a ferocious interstate–big, broad Highway 5. Beyond Sacramento the highway opened into the morning shadows flowing down from the eastern foothills. A few clouds hugged a distant peak. Cars whizzed by Holiday's pokey '63 Mercury, which hugged the slow lane all the way up.

Holiday switched on the radio and found a Redding station with headlines on the hour: Denny McClain won his 30th game for the Tigers. Russia's Zond Five rocket with turtles aboard was hurtling toward the moon where it would spend one orbit and return to earth. Music followed. *Born to Be Wild* by Steppenwolf got Holiday to rock in rhythm and briefly hit the brake lights on the downbeats. The two travelers waited for the next hit single and weren't disappointed with *Piece of My Heart* by Janis Joplin, which pushed Raj to watch himself in the side mirror as he lip-synched the bluesy lyrics.

A corny car ad interrupted the flow of rock and Holiday switched off the radio while Raj sat back to attach his poetic mind to the dark shadows of passing hills and pastures. The two had left Berkeley after midnight and were nearing a truck stop about twenty miles south of Dunsmuir. Both fell back into a tripping isolation and Holiday stopped for gas.

At various turns in the road Raj glimpsed the dawn spectacle of the mountain, its snow-covered apex a shadowy, looming fact of the landscape. As Holiday pulled into town the mountain rose like a monolith to dominate the eastern view in high relief and nearly fill the available sky with its white snowy ridges. Beautiful disorder was the essence of life for Raj who in his first glimpse of the mountain succumbed to a juicy surge of telepathy.

"Out of fucking control, man," he murmured to Holiday. "You live on that thing? How the hell do you do that?"

"Just watch me," Holiday answered and then turned off Mt. Shasta boulevard and goosed his gas pedal for a surprisingly straight drive up the west side of the mountain. It gave Raj the feeling they were headed directly into the snow until Holiday turned again on an unpaved switchback road that appeared to wind along a flank of the mountain. At the end of the narrow, dirt artery, Holiday stopped the car and turned off the engine.

"It's all walking from here," Holiday said as he unloaded his pack, bag and bottle and Raj gathered up his gear.

"About an hour and half in. We'll leave the rice in the trunk for now. There's no hurry. We'll have breakfast at my camp."

Raj was high on the snow-capped mountain of his dreams, its farther peak stony and barren with a few alpine trees. Words of a poet arose again in Raj, his fluid steps pressed against an array of irregularities as climbing the trail led him from a forest as thick as any on the coast into a rocky bleakness near tree line that appeared in the distance as barren as the moon.

He was strung along the edge of two valleys, one lush and the other austere. The trail proceeded around the so-named Red Butte and descended again through trees and shrubs into a small valley filled with Manzanita and covered by a bright green shrubbery fed from a sloshing creek that at the end of the short valley formed a small, tumbling waterfall.

"My camp's over here," Holiday said and crossed the creek.

Raj followed, aware others were living here. He saw a couple of tents, barely visible through the trees and, at the top of the meadow, saw a woman hovering over the creek with a water bottle.

Holiday's camp, pushed up against a large rock, had no tent. Instead, Holiday had made a pile of dead branches that allowed him to drape a plastic tarp from the rock to the wood and thereby create a spacious lean-to.

"I'll get a fire started. How's pancakes?" Holiday asked. "I even brought butter and I can borrow some honey from James over there."

Raj said yes and asked if he could help.

"Plenty to do, but not now," said Holiday who pulled out a plastic bowl and frying pan and went to work.

"Living here isn't hard at all," Holiday said as he shaved a chunk from the butter cube and melted it in his frying pan.

"The hardest thing about living here is leaving. They don't like us much in town. Think we're all crazy hippies. They just don't know, do they?"

After breakfast, Raj followed Holiday as he made the rounds of the meadow to catch up on news and bring news of his own.

Raj first met Jasper, the meadow resident who had been on the mountain the longest. A student at Oberlin College, Jasper had done a year in jail for resisting the draft.

"He spent last winter up here," Holiday said.

Jasper nodded.

"Ranger said to tell him where Jasper was camping so he'd know where to go to find the body. Right, Jas?"

Jasper nodded again.

"Be sure to teach him how to shit in the woods," Jasper said before turning to Raj.

"You staying here long?" he asked Raj.

"About a week, I guess. I'm from Berkeley."

Jasper said that was cool.

"We'll talk later. I'm on my way down the hill today. Have something in town."

"Going to the Inn to see Mother Mary?" asked Holiday.

"Oh yeah," said Jasper.

As Holiday paraded him through the meadow, Raj was introduced to Mark, a tall, lanky fellow who had attended Oberlin with Jasper. He also met James, a short man with a hoary beard and wide, searching eyes and his wife, Mia, who peeked out from inside the tent where she played with their toddler Moon, pulling at her mother's long dark hair and screaming for attention. Two women named Loren and Sonia occupied the next camp, both with athletic builds and a cautious presence that suggested they might prefer to be left alone. It was their second summer on the mountain. A young hiker from Sacramento had taken a small clearing at the ridge of the meadow. He had been there for two weeks and was leaving soon to return to college.

"The mountain is filled with people like us," Holiday said as he and Raj made their way back to his site.

The meadow was indeed a neighborhood and Raj marveled in his faded morning high that such a cozy human intimacy could exist within the vast majesty of the mountain. Was it really so easy, so simple? Raj wished to think such a life in the wilderness might be possible.

Raj found a flat space near Holiday's rock, set down his guitar and rolled out his bag. He unpacked his rucksack and put his food into a covered bucket Holiday used to keep it safe from critters. They spent the afternoon roaming trails that led from the meadow, eventually climbing above the butte where a view of the valley extended west toward more mountains and a few visible lakes. The air was clean and dry and the sun hot on Raj's shoulders.

Evening brought the valley's residents together at Holiday's fire pit for a communal meal. Onions and carrots sliced into a big pot formed the base of a substantial rice stew supplemented with slices of dense, fried bread. Holiday used up the rest of his butter while Mark and James tended the fire and stirred the soup.

"What do you do in Berkeley?" Mia asked Raj as she watched Moon scramble in the dirt.

"I was a student for awhile. Work in a bookstore now," he answered.

Dealing wasn't something he thought wise to advertise.

As the soup bubbled, Sonia and Loren arrived with apples and a melon and a long knife they used to slice the fruit on a wrinkled grey stone. As the sun teetered at the horizon, Jasper appeared from the trail. Voices welcomed him in unison as if he were a returning chieftain. Raj retreated from the chatter to watch the little community come alive in the twilight and to stare into the fire that had been humanity's first colonizing technology, scaring bears from their caves and replacing them with humans. Later, he sat with his guitar to sing a few songs by his favorite folk artist, Fred Neil. Raj's version of *Blues On the Ceiling* raised calls for an encore from his newest audience.

On this small island of people on the side of a great mountain, Raj identified an intertwining simplicity of a life lived in nature. All was relationship and his immediate task was simply to locate his welcome place within a small circle of new friends self-cast into a wider sphere of earth and air. He was clearing his mind and slipping into a newly created space. A web of water streamed over rocks. Raj again recalled the poet's words for the feeling of a life lived at the extremes of pure solidarity and also pure solitude. It was community and also place and everything between.

four

Raj spent his second morning on the mountain stirring restlessly in a sleeping bag as he waited for the sun to rise high enough to warm the meadow's frigid shadows. Holiday had started a fire and Raj emerged wearing his rimless glasses. These and his blue khaki coat gave him the look of an exiled rebel who might have arrived at the end of a long march to take refuge in the high country.

As a new visitor he drew more attention from the meadow's residents. The reclusive women living at the top of the mountain walked down to borrow sugar from Holiday and lingered to talk with Raj.

"I'm not much of a city boy even though I live in Berkeley," Raj said. "I sleep in the woods but you guys live in them. What's that like?"

"It's cheap," said Sonia whose identity emerged as Raj watched her: a compact woman with an oval face whose eyes appeared to him as burnished blue pearls: shiny, moist and searching. A crop of blonde hair stuck out from under her tightly wrapped headscarf.

"Loren brought me here last year. Now it's home. Right Loren?"

The other woman, tall and gaunt, nodded without looking at Raj. She stuffed her fists into a worn leather jacket and sat near

Holiday's fire.

"And winter? What then?" Raj asked the women.

Only Sonia answered.

"Last year we went back to Sacramento. Not this year. We're staying. Loren's found a cabin at the north end of town. It's a seasonal rental that would be empty anyway. We offered forty a month and the owner said OK."

"And why here?" Raj asked.

"And why not?" Loren shouted before Sonia could answer. "Look around. It's all we need. And it's free."

Raj nodded and turned back to Sonia.

"Maybe you could show me around," he asked. "Take a hike… or something."

The something wasn't anything intended, though its mention seemed to alert Loren who looked peevishly at Raj as if to assess a clear and present danger.

"Yeah…that would be cool," Sonia said. "We're going to town today. Maybe tomorrow. I know some trails you'd never find."

Loren stood.

"Let's go, Sonia. We need to catch a ride."

Loren walked away and Sonia fell in behind her.

Raj rejoiced silently in his arrival at a source of all good things. The mountain was beautiful and big and rode the planet's orbit like a separate world though under the same sky and sun of its host. As a younger man he had reveled in the poetic epiphanies of visionary Beat writers, envying the journeys of Dharma bums into the mountains and forests, his feet crushing a hundred flowers with every step. He heard again the words of a poet, words that framed the meadow as its life rose with him in the steadying light of morning.

He ate one of Holiday's pancakes with an appetite diminished by excitement and what he thought might be the altitude. Raj offered Holiday a joint that he declined.

"No, man," said the older camper as he shook his head. "Not here. Not now. Not ever."

Raj stood away from Holiday to inhale a few tokes and then extinguished the joint as a soothing transition settled him into another kind of awareness; the familiar stoned feeling resonating so hard that every small thing within his vision grew into its own formidable, haunting strength. Rocks tumbled under foot, birds shouted in his ears. The noisy wind blew hard into his nose and mouth, which he opened to welcome and swallow. He lay on the ground to trip out in the dirt and shrubbery. He rolled into a ball and played possum to the robustly imminent landscape.

His rapture was out of proportion to his high that, in normal circumstances, would keep him calm and cool. Here he was at an edge of an experience and one that cried to him for something more, that would make him telepathic and allow his mind to fathom all the secrets and pleasures of this mountain all at once and without hesitation.

"Want to drop some acid?" Raj asked Holiday as he prepared a lunch of bread, cheese and olives.

"No, Raj," Holiday said. "Not here...not here."

"Sure, man," Raj responded meekly from the shimmering *terroir* that supported his mild hallucination.

Holiday sat back against his rock to read and nap while Raj wandered a ways downstream to fill his canteen beneath the creek's abridged waterfall.

"Think I'll walk up to the ridge," he said to Holiday who gave him a drowsy nod.

"Great view of the sunset from up there. But watch your step," Holiday cautioned.

Raj searched his sack for a t-shirt and a small matchbox that held six 300-mic hits of orange sunshine. He popped one into his mouth and took a swig from his canteen. It would be good for a trip he calculated would peak in the late afternoon and float him back down to camp in time to help Holiday with dinner.

He trekked slowly through the meadow and in a half-hour reached the apex of a short ridge. By this time the acid was coming on quickly. Raj felt at first a thrilling burst of fear as he straddled a small saddle on the ridge and stared back at the lush green meadow that appeared now as a chimeric refuge. He could make out a smudge of neon yellow he presumed was the flap of a tent.

He was hot under the late summer's mid-day sun and removed

his shirt; happy he had worn shorts and also a baseball cap. Its long brim shadowed his face though he still could not look very far without squinting. He stuffed the shirt into his waistband and turned toward the mountain. At the lower end of a steep rocky valley above him, he spied a shiny, wide snowfield and was struck immediately by the desire to touch it, walk onto it, to feel its soothing coolness and report back all of this to his new friends.

A rush of acid juice pushed him forward and he clawed his way carefully down the far side of the ridge, but not without examining the minute details of small rocks and pebbles or stopping to follow the path of a spider or an ant and imagining his own crawling journey as that of an insect through a vast and endless space.

Insects barely feel the pull of gravity. Elephants need stout legs to resist it. Raj walked over fields of rocks infinitely sized and shaped by the granular realities of their atomic structures he would never be able to see.

He could not experience anything in this natural world that exceeded a certain power of ten. He was drawn to powers of ten as a way to measure his distance between what was infinitely small and what was infinitely large. He himself was a bubbling, churning factory of a trillion cells, each outnumbered ten to one by bacterial parasites. A momentary thrill arrived at the vector of this biologic awareness and his geologic position. He sat on the ground and gave his mind permission to resist the first tremulous tugs of a bummer. Doors opened that he knew well – the doors of perception that could lead him higher or the trap doors of ego that might burn him up in desolation.

He made himself walk. He put one foot in front of the other and tried to resist the entrapping magic of his motion. He thought himself analytical and worked through the juice of this trip to simply experience the simple flow of motion while keeping his squinty eyes trained on the snow ahead of him.

Far fucking out, he thought to himself as his feet felt the distinct flattening of the ridge's incline and he stood on the far valley's floor. He needed now to look up to see the snowfield that appeared to hover like a cloud caught in the vortex of two small, grey peaks. His range of vision felt to him like a sphere and he like a satellite that could levitate through its orbit to touch down on the snow.

The snowfield appeared larger, which meant it was closer. He let himself flow into the mountain. He had the power and the imagination. A thousand ghosts pointed the way and he heard their voices in the shrieks of a hawk, in the wind flying past his ears, in the crunch his ephemeral feet made as they displaced rocks that had been undisturbed for millennia.

At last he arrived at the lip of the field. At first he stepped gently onto its edge and finding it a crusty mush he plunged farther toward its center where the snow deepened to reach his lower calves while his boots sunk below the surface. Raj roared with delight, picking up fistfuls of snow to rub all over his sweaty chest producing a cool, stinging ecstasy. He stopped for a moment to sort through a handful of slushy melt in a futile search for snowflakes born from the chaos of a winter storm but now lost forever in their diffusion from order into disorder.

He laughed again at the fractal qualities of experience, powerful and also immeasurable. He was wildly high on acid and knew it. He tried to pop up through the levels of telepathy he carried like a stack of books but could not see over them. Instead, he gave into an urge to lie down and stare upwards toward the sky, nestling into the snow that was now not so bitterly cold and that held him in a steadying, sweet chill.

He sat up to see a black shape held in the grip of two large rocks jutting out of the snow. He stood and walked over to explore it, recognizing immediately the carcass of a large mammal, its dark fur falling away from its skeletal remains like the withering peel from a rotten piece of fruit. Raj examined the bones and saw their arrangement—the vertebrae, the ribs, the angular, white pelvis—all lying where they fell. His heart raced with a queer curiosity until he saw the skull, its large eyeholes open to him like the sorrowful gaze of a begging child. It was too much for his telepathic mind and he fell back to the ground to sob helplessly over life's embryonic mystery and its predictable end in suffering. Images of a thousand deaths, perhaps a million, flooded into his illuminated consciousness.

He considered nature's indifference to such suffering and this brought up the question of human indifference. He thought of Auschwitz and photos he had seen of Nazi death camp prisoners, lined up and naked–mothers with their bare babies–to be shot or gassed and later buried in trenches. Death made anonymous, death robbed of human meaning, deaths of individuals who were no longer individuals, who even in death belonged to no one or themselves, who were intended to die as if they had never existed. Was this also Nature's nature?

Raj's tripping mind focused on a vision of Nature moving ceaselessly through the universe as its multitude of forces fostered new growth only later to crush and to destroy it. Again Raj sat and sobbed in the snow, full and heaving sobs that flushed out his eyes and nose in streams of soft, warm mucus.

I am nothing, he thought. *I am and am always nothing.*

As his vision subsided, the cold snow alerted Raj to the cooling air. He worked to slip on his soggy t-shirt and then looked toward the sun, which appeared to rest at the crest of the ridge behind him. He knew where he was but could not say exactly from where he came. He was past the peak of his acid trip and knowing what he knew about such things he resisted the urge to panic though an assessment of his situation included the realization he was feeling colder just as the sky was growing darker.

As the sun fell from sight, Raj marched quickly away from the snow and toward what he thought was the ridge he left and which now appeared hours in the distance. He had thought to fill his canteen with snow and so had water even as in his unmanageable fear he drank too much of it. He could not adequately gauge his appetites or his thirst. He felt the air chill and, in turn, chill him. And then it was dark and he could see nothing.

He felt for a rock and sat on it, pulling his hat down over his ears. He wrapped his arms into himself and waited at a familiar junction where he could imagine the acid as a train that was at last leaving the station. The platform was cleared of distractions and he could move now since the acid was moving on. But where was he? Left with the potential for hallucination he wondered if an animal might eat him. He had brought nothing, not even a match to make light or fire or to show him a way home.

And he was cold, now perilously cold. He was still high and shivered violently. He did not know how late it was but it had been dark for a long time. Should I stay? Should I walk? A waning moon rose that told Raj it might be very late in the evening. It was not much light, but the only light, and it gave him a view ahead and a vague outline of a ridge, though now there were ridges in every direction. His shivering intensified.

He used the moon to find which ridge was most to the west. He took anxious steps over the rocks that rattled underfoot. He was succumbing. He would die. He would open his telepathic mind and accept whatever happened. He drew on his past and expressed both his gratitude and regrets. He lifted himself above his tripping worries. It was acid and what was left should free him from worry. He might feel the pain of dying, but it simply wouldn't be that important.

He kept walking and eventually watched himself climb a subtle but persistent incline. He was rising toward the ridge. He stopped to look ahead and saw a flash of light explode above him. It was dark again until light reappeared, this time sweeping in an arc that illuminated the valley he was leaving behind. Raj scrambled up the ridge toward the light, his bare legs and arms slashed by shrubs and branches that told him he was near the meadow. The light became brighter and Raj yelled and called for it until, breaching the ridge's last, denying ledge of boulders, the light was on him, blinding him, and bathing him in a stark radiance.

"He'll be OK."

Holiday spoke as Raj shivered in his sleeping bag, the older camper's hands and Sonia's rubbing him in a tentacular syncopation. Raj wanted to speak his telepathic gratitude to them, for the mountain, for his rescue from a shivering brush with disappearance. He could not find the words.

"It's OK. Just rest now. Rest."

In the fading, and last, blush of hallucination, Raj saw himself as an embryo in the darkness of a cold womb birthed back into existence by the deliberate intention of a watchful midwife. Otherwise, there was nothing to life but a shout of despair at the lip of an open grave.

Sonia's voice was melodic and also assertive. She had held the flashlight that brought Raj back. She had agreed to stay up all night if necessary and hold the ridge for him, hold a light that might guide his return. Holiday, unaware Raj had taken acid, assumed his friend's experience in the wilderness would serve him and so did not worry when he did not return for dinner. Sonia met Raj and soothed his delirium by wrapping him in her sweater before leading him down the meadow to Holiday's camp where the two warmed his frozen body with incessant touches while Raj babbled wildly the few coherent phrases of his telepathic epiphany. The merciful demise into sleep was not the shadow of death because the dreams came and came until at some point under a brilliant, warming sun Holiday shook Raj awake.

"Really? You dropped acid?" Holiday asked.

"You don't take that here. If you need acid *here*, you don't belong here. All you ever need is already here."

Raj chewed vigorously as he consumed another of Holiday's buckwheat pancakes. He was too hungry to respond with anything but a repentant nod.

"You rest today," Holiday said. "Don't leave the meadow."

Later Sonia walked down to check on Raj.

"I'm OK," Raj said. "I was OK most of the time...until the end."

Sonia heard his defensiveness.

"I don't know how to thank you," he said after a protracted silence through which Sonia quietly regarded him.

"I wasn't going to let you go," Sonia said directly and in a way Raj could acknowledge and also regard.

five

Death might be the ultimate corrosion and while Raj at last realized he was in little danger of dying on the mountain, his search within found the evidence of someone deceased. Holiday's words froze him with their harsh assessment of some quality of carelessness Raj had mistaken for insight.

For a decade Raj applied psychedelics to the agendas of his days. Reliably, grass and acid had awakened diverting enhancements that reordered the maintenance of common survival into something seemingly relevant and also entertaining.

But as euphoria was nearly always followed by depression, Raj's crisis on the mountain contained the elements of a condensed and incomplete odyssey among his emotions. Wherever he had been in all his years, he still had not arrived at a home. Until this day when the sun and the mountain and the snow and the lush Manzanita filling the meadow opened him like no drug ever had.

"Simplicity," Holiday said to Raj as they sat together.

"A robe and a bowl. What else does the monk need? A pack and a trail. What else do we need, the bums that we are?"

Bums was Holiday's acerbic moniker for the beats and hippies that had preceded him on the road toward a certain kind of outlaw enlightenment to which Holiday religiously subscribed. The scripture was in the words of Kerouac, Ginsberg and Snyder. The truth was in the living and Holiday, a loner in his late-thirties, was a true believer. The mountains gave him space enough to exercise a full command over himself and asked only for his alert, conscious presence.

"I've wondered what's real and what isn't," Raj said vaguely.

"That's a question drugs can never answer," said Holiday. "Drugs illuminate every possible irregularity. But do nothing to sort them or to comprehend them. What's real is right here and right now."

Holiday picked up a rock and smashed it against the large boulder that supported his tarp, pounding the rock until it shattered.

"Forms are formless. We are music, my friend. We are frozen light."

It took a sandwich at The Inn in town for Raj to understand he was a living cemetery for all that within him was suddenly dead.

"You hold such a small heart inside such a large man," Mother Mary said as she described her first impression of Raj, which she did with everyone she met.

"You are responsible for your life."

Mother Mary was the proprietor of The Inn, a restaurant in town where food was served with a portion of Mary's Eastern wisdom whether or not it was requested. The old woman, wrapped usually in a saffron sari, offered her nuggets like complimentary mints.

Jasper was one of Mary's devotees and because he suggested the Inn for dinner, Raj and Holiday, Sonia and Loren, and James and Mia and Moon were present to hear her.

"Nothing good is ever lost," Mary said as she wandered among the tables occupied by dwellers of the meadow that had caravanned to town to buy staples, to do their laundry and to eat food not cooked over an open fire. After a life of pilgrimages to India and studies with several gurus, in the spring of 1957 Mother Mary moved to Mt. Shasta. Following the death of her husband, she purchased The Inn where daily meals became a way of luring the spiritually minded to her versions of enlightenment.

"She believes in the Brotherhood," Holiday said skeptically as he drove back to the meadow trailhead.

"The what?" asked Raj.

"The Spiritual Brotherhood that lives inside Mt. Shasta," Holiday said.

"They're a tribe of extraterrestrial beings that come out from time to time to wander the mountain. And since her arrival here, Mary is about the only one who has seen them."

"Right…" Raj offered through a skeptical slow motion.

"Careful what you say to Jasper," Holiday added. "He believes it, too."

Brotherhood notwithstanding, Raj was moved enough by Mary's words to go to the bathroom and flush his last five tabs of acid down a toilet. The next morning he handed Holiday his small bag of pot and rolling papers.

"All yours," Raj said. "I'm done."

"For good?" Holiday asked.

"At least for a while," Raj answered.

Raj fixed breakfast and told Holiday he was going to take a hike.

Holiday gave him a look of concern.

"I won't be alone," said Raj.

Sonia met Raj at the crest of the small ridge where she had found him two nights before. Her hair remained fastened under a blue headscarf, a few blonde shocks sprouting forth at her ears and neck. She carried a canteen and wore a green long john top and no bra.

"This OK?" Raj asked her.

"OK with me," answered Sonia.

Loren was not mentioned.

Sonia had proposed a walk back to Raj's snowfield. She mentioned the walk to Raj while Loren was away with Holiday to fill their cans from the hundred pound bag of brown rice Holiday purchased in Chinatown. Brown rice was the staple of the mountain clan and The City the closest place to buy it in quantities large enough to make the trip worthwhile.

Raj described his Catholic childhood, his estranged family and nearly a decade living in Berkeley, amplifying on his studies and his employment at Creed's and saying little about drugs.

Sonia had nothing to spin. Her adolescence was spent in a bleak suburb of Sacramento as an only child, her junior year in high school marked by the divorce of her parents. Loren had been her best friend and Sonia spent her last year in school living at Loren's house as the separation of her parents passed through its increasingly high conflict and ultimately angry conclusion. After graduation, the two pals entered a local junior college together to prepare for a transfer to Sacramento State College. Then Loren found Shasta the previous summer and invited Sonia to join her.

"We took to the outdoor life, and pretty fast," Sonia told Raj. "People on the mountain welcomed us. We loved having nothing to do but survive. It made a certain kind of sense."

"Does it still?" Raj asked.

The question was personal, perhaps too personal, and Sonia shrugged in response. Thereafter there were few words though Sonia seemed interested in what Raj remembered of his life until they arrived at the snowfield where Raj splashed again into the slush of the field, inviting Sonia to join him, which she did, hesitant at first. Raj took her sweaty hand and pulled her down with him. The chill surprised her.

For Sonia, the snow was nothing new but Raj was new. So was the bewitched exhaustion that made her struggle to stand as Raj stood first and pulled her up by her arms and into his. He felt Sonia resting against him as his mind recalled his recent drug delirium and the feeling of being hopelessly lost while less than an hour from the meadow. It was a capsule characterization of his incidental life. *I am always lost. I am always too far from the things in front of me.*

Was he changing too quickly? Was today the refutation of yesterday? Was a new awareness simply another soft wrinkle of an abiding disorder? He released Sonia who did not immediately release him.

On their hike back to the meadow Sonia spoke cautiously about the discomfort of her life, her feeling of hanging on and staying under the spell of Loren whom she thanked for "saving" her from an abusive family but, as Raj silently concluded, had taken deepening control of Sonia's milestones. Sonia was twenty years old and Raj eight years older though he felt surprisingly humbled in her presence as he did also in the presence of the mountain.

Raj listened to Sonia's words as if he were a container for some vast, pelagic wave of new awareness. As they parted at the ridge, he was surprised again by the fulfilling qualities of this connection with Sonia and in ways that were not presumptive or expected. She was not an object of desire. Yet she felt closer in many ways than he could say. Without his drug filter there appeared to be no illusions and, therefore, no temptation for a familiar kind of failure.

Raj's last day on the mountain was defined by his imminent departure. A camper from Sand Flat was returning to Half Moon Bay and could drop Raj in Berkeley. Raj woke up early and did not wait for the cooling shadows to clear. He bounded outward for a last morning hike into the rocky valley beyond the Meadow, its austerity a welcome cleansing before his return to the city and all its immersing ways with him. He met again with Sonia and gave her his address and phone number in Berkeley. He invited her to visit him in a way that evoked a shy but evident interest.

"I've never been to Berkeley," she told Raj.

"Let me know when you and Loren move off the mountain," he said. "I'll write and we'll figure it out."

"Where will I stay?" Sonia asked.

"With me," Raj said without hesitating.

The ride back was quiet, Raj's thoughts dwelling throughout on the nature of a thoughtful life that might replace his high times. He would be clean but also empty, at least at first. He still experienced flashbacks of his fearful night on the mountain, apparitions of his body dissolving and of an immediate, stupid death. Apparitions were his familiar touchstones and now, as the silent driver in the noisy Volkswagen microbus pushed through Sacramento, Raj addressed a life without them.

He would have to sell his kilos. He would start with his acid connection, a chemist named Skillikorn who lived on Hopkins. He might then buy a car and drive back to the mountain, as he wanted. He would need income to replace his grass trade. He would ask Creed's for more hours or apply to Moe's and Cody's. He was a bookseller and knew the trade.

The mountain taught him he didn't need much. But what was enough? The city was not the mountain though he hoped and expected that mountain wisdom would simplify the terms of a likely new and discordant survival. What he thought he knew was now formless. What he hoped to understand was barely visible. Raj was left to scrutinize, and to no longer dismiss, the cluttered morphology of an amorphous life.

"I wish I could help you," Skilly said.

The small, balding man in a black sweater rubbed his chin and pushed back in his chair at the kitchen table. As one of the region's primary dealers in psychedelics, Skilly was shy, soft-voiced and unimposing.

"I sell acid, Raj," he added. "Hell, I give acid away. I really don't need any grass and certainly not three kilos. And, no, I don't know anyone who does. I'm sorry."

Skilly's home on Hopkins Street was a small bungalow with two bedrooms and from the airy kitchen, elevated like a porch above the small living room, Raj could look out at the wide avenue and its intersection with busy Grove Street.

Raj had been back from the mountains less than twelve hours and did not waste time. It was a mid-morning meeting and Skilly was happy to see him. But business was not possible and Raj should have known. Skilly wasn't an acid dealer as much as he was an acid prophet. He and a partner named Charles believed LSD to be a sacrament of enlightenment and that if there were a way for the whole world to trip on acid, humans immediately would stop all hostilities and become one huge loving family.

For two years Charles had been living in a suburb of the North Bay making batches of acid while Skilly quietly moved it through the Bay Area drug pipeline. Their cover was this middle class home in North Berkeley where Skilly lived with his wife, a high school chemistry teacher in the neighboring town of Albany.

"Well, there might be someone," Skilly said.

"It's probably a long shot but I'll see him Saturday. I'll ask and get back to you."

Raj was grateful for anything Skilly might do. He looked back out the window and noticed two white sedans pull up together in front of the house.

"You expecting visitors?" Raj asked.

Skilly looked outside to see two men in suits climb out of the front seat of the first car, speak to others in the second car, and then walk across his lawn to the cement path leading to his front door. The solid knock at his door was unfamiliar to Skilly.

"This might not be good news," he said calmly.

Skilly told Raj to move toward the rear of the kitchen where a small hallway led to a utility room and a back door.

"Be ready to bail," he said. "Go over the back fence and down the side yard to Grove."

There was another, louder knock.

"Who is it?" Skilly shouted as he approached the door.

"Berkeley Police. Open the door. We have a warrant."

Raj heard the police. He scurried like a hungry cat down the hall, pushed open the backdoor and saw the fence ahead. He charged it with athletic momentum, expecting to leap high enough to grab firmly at the top and pull himself up and over. Instead he was tackled around the ankles and waist and brought to the ground.

"Look what we have here," one of two uniformed police officers said as he rolled Raj into a flower bed and over onto his stomach, pulled his arms behind him and slipped his wrists into handcuffs. Pulled up by his arms, Raj yelled in pain as he was thrown against the fence. He had not yet seen the faces of his attackers, his view limited to black gun belts, khaki pants etched with blue stripes, and hard brown shoes that straddled his own as he was positioned, patted and searched, the pockets of his jeans turned out and his wallet taken.

"He's not carrying," one officer said to the other.

"Let's put him in the car and get back inside."

Raj was led through the house, passing Skilly sitting in a chair, also handcuffed and guarded while one of the men in suits stood before him and asked questions. Skilly met Raj's eyes briefly with a look of pitiful resignation before the suited man passed between them to sever any contact.

Raj heard the heavy sound of footsteps in the back of the house and then banging sounds as if furniture were being overturned and drawers were hitting the floor. Outside, he was led to one of three police cars parked farther down the block. He looked back to see a half dozen officers swarming the property as neighbors emerged from their homes to see what was happening. Raj was thrown into one of the car's back seats to sit behind a caged separator. He was read his rights. Pushed up against the upholstery, his hands and wrists ached and he could not move them.

At the station, Raj was stripped of his belt and shoes and placed in a holding cell. He sat on a metal bench; aware he was being watched but unable to see by whom. An hour passed until the cell was opened and an officer led him to a room furnished only with a table and three chairs. Raj was directed to sit. A uniformed officer and the suited man he saw at Skilly's home then joined him at the table.

"I'm Inspector Mattioli," the suited man said. "And this is Officer Linden."

The inspector was tall and corpulent and held his hands in his pockets in a way that opened his suit jacket to reveal a holstered handgun. He took a seat opposite Raj while the officer sat adjacent to him and just out of his line of sight.

"Mr. Neville, we have some questions we'd like to ask and hope you'll cooperate with us so we can get you on your way."

The inspector attempted an avuncular tone, and Raj noted the oblique offer of his freedom, no doubt if he told the inspector what he wished to hear. Raj fixed on the small, neatly trimmed black mustache that moved with the inspector's mouth.

"I don't know how I can help," Raj said. "I've done nothing wrong."

"Why were you at Mr. Skillikorn's home today?" the inspector asked.

Raj sensed he was being set up to expose Skilly who might or might not be in any trouble right now.

"He's a friend," Raj answered.

"Good friend? Long time friend?" the inspector asked.

"What's that got to do with anything?"

Raj turned the question back to the inspector.

"Your so-called friend is being held for felony possession of LSD to sell, and a rather large quantity of the drug was found and taken from his home."

The inspector leaned threateningly toward Raj.

"We have reason to think you're dealing for Mr. Skillikorn. Are you?" he asked.

Raj waited for his mind to catch up with the events at hand, hoping it could not be seen or heard by the inspector. He returned to the mountain and waited several moments there.

"I don't know anything about any LSD. I don't do drugs," Raj at last responded. "Am I being charged with something?"

The inspector paused and excused himself. Raj waited with the officer through a barren silence until the inspector returned.

"You can pick up your things at the desk downstairs," the inspector said roughly.

"You're free to go."

Raj stood and walked slowly toward the hallway.

"Hope you're on the level," the inspector shouted after Raj. "If we get you in here again, it's not going to be fun."

"This is fun?" Raj squawked sarcastically.

Raj left the station and walked briskly up Center Street, alert like a small, endangered mammal to the threat of a predator. And Skilly?

What would become of him? What could he know without drawing more attention to himself?

Have I dodged a bullet or am I still caught in a web?

Raj had to unload his kilos, and fast. He tried to suppress a panic. He would phone Yitzhak. He might take the kilos and stash them in his room at his mother's house on Thousand Oaks. No one would find them there. No one would even look. Raj stopped at a phone in the campus student union after breaking a bill in the bookstore.

"You vant who?"

Yitzhak's mother answered the phone.

"You mean Raymond? His name is Raymond."

Raj heard her shout *Raymond* in a loud, gravelly squeal that hurt his ear. He waited. He heard steps.

"Yeah?"

It was Yitzhak.

"I'm in a jam, man," Raj said quickly while his eyes searched the student quad for any face or movement that might suggest he was being followed.

"Can you drive downtown and meet me? I'll explain."

Raj told Yitzhak to pick him up at the north campus gate.

"Yeah, sure…" Yitzhak answered, his voice neutral and disengaged as it had increasingly become during recent weeks. It caused Raj to worry again that his friend was slipping off course.

"Oh, and you got a backpack?" Raj asked.

"It's pretty beat up," Yitzhak answered.

"Bring it."

Raj walked across the campus in time to see Yitzhak's bomber blue Chevy rumble up Hearst Street. He stood at the gate and as the car slowed, Raj jumped in.

As Yitzhak climbed the hill Raj told the quick version of his panic, his bust, his apparent close call, and his current predicament.

"I got three kilos in my room that can't stay there. Can you take them? It won't be long. I just need to…"

"Sure," said Yitzhak without looking over.

Raj released a long shiver of a sigh, as if he were finally turning a corner on a day with barely any room for error. Whether Yitzhak fully understood what was being asked was another question. For now, though, Raj offered Yitzhak what he thought was a simple plan: to go with Raj to his room, load the kilos in the backpack and then have Yitzhak leave the big rooming house through a back door.

But as Yitzhak drove up Dwight Way, Raj saw a white sedan parked at the corner three doors from his house. It was identical to the cars that pulled up in front of Skilly's's home and Raj dropped down in the front seat so as not to be seen.

"Anybody in the car?" Raj asked.

"Two guys wearing suits," Yitzhak answered.

"Shit!" Raj shouted. "They're waiting for me."

Raj instructed Yitzhak to drive up to College Avenue and find a side street they could park on.

"You don't have to do this," Raj said, "Those are the cops who busted me this morning and they're waiting for me to come home. They don't know you. You can walk into the house, check the car from the lobby and if no one gets out, you go to my room, get the kilos and walk out the side door that leads up an alley to College. Can you do that?"

Yitzhak nodded, but not vigorously, though the plan made sense. The cops couldn't know Yitzhak or suspect him of anything.

Yitzhak left with his pack and walked back toward the house. Raj noticed his friend was wearing dance pants and boots and a tight black vest over a blousy white shirt. His long sideburns grew almost to his chin. He looked a little crazy, but not abnormally so for the neighborhood. If Yitzhak were busted Raj knew he would have to come forward.

A half-hour passed. Raj resisted an urge to creep down the block for a better view of his street. He turned to get back into the car and saw Yitzhak turn the corner behind him, a clear sign he had left the house through the alley.

"All done, man," Yitzhak announced sharply as he slipped the backpack off his shoulders, opened the rear passenger door of the Chevy and dropped the pack on the seat. He returned the room key to Raj.

Raj looked anxiously up and down the street while reaching into the pack to nervously finger what he could determine were three distinct blocks, one sliced open at the corner he had cut off for Jen.

Raj put his face into the bag to smell the pungent, sweet aroma of pot and then suspended the bag from the seat to gauge its weight, which he determined to be about six or so pounds and what would be expected of three kilos.

"They'll be in my closet whenever you want 'em," Yitzhak said.

"Smoke whatever you like," Raj offered with ebullient gratitude.

Yitzhak gave Raj a strange look of puzzlement and shook his head.

"Don't smoke anymore," he said. "Need a ride back?"

"Hell, no!" Raj responded. "You get going. I'll walk back and take it from here. You one hip brother, my friend."

Yitzhak slipped into the driver's seat and started the car. The engine shouted a loud, barely muffled roar of combustion and then settled into a steady growl as Yitzhak checked his mirror, pulled out, turned on Telegraph and disappeared.

Raj found his street and approached the white sedan from behind. He could see the two suited detectives, one of them Inspector Mattioli. He ignored them as he passed and slowly entered his house. He raced to his room and unlocked his closet. Of course, the kilos were gone. He left his room door ajar, sat on his bed and waited for a knock, which came quickly.

"Mr. Neville?"

Raj heard the inspector's voice.

"Who is it?" Raj asked.

"It's Inspector Mattioli. I'm here with an officer. May we come in?"

"Sure," said Raj. "What do you want?"

Since Raj had said he didn't use drugs or deal, perhaps he wouldn't mind if the inspector searched his room.

"And if I mind?" Raj asked.

The inspector said his partner would remain in the hall until a search warrant was issued. If Raj allowed them to look now, and no drugs were found, they would leave and not come back.

"OK," Raj said confidently. "Have at it."

The two men in suits went in opposite directions. The inspector walked directly to Raj's closet and searched the shelf where Raj had stored his kilos. *Did he know?* Raj thought. *Why there?*

The inspector continued to search the closet, sweeping his hand over objects and clothing as if seeking any speck of weed. The inspector's partner walked to an alcove where he lifted books, a potted ficus, and a stack of records, and also swept his hand along flat horizontal surfaces.

Raj felt uneasy, even violated, but confident they would find nothing.

"May I?"

The inspector pointed at the chest of drawers across from the day bed.

Raj nodded affirmatively.

The inspector reached into the top drawer and pulled out a locked metal box commonly used to store index cards. He shook it.

"What's in here?" the inspector asked.

"My money," answered Raj.

"Let's have a look," said the inspector.

Raj unlocked the box, opened it and held it up to show the green bills inside.

"Let's see how much," said the inspector as he took the box from Raj, pulled a wad of bills out and began to count them.

"Wow, Mr. Neville. More than six hundred dollars," the inspector said with faux surprise.

"I've got a job," Raj responded warily.

The inspector asked him how often he was paid and did his employer pay him in cash and, if so, was he always paid in five and ten dollar denominations?

Raj swallowed hard.

"It's my money. No law against having money," Raj said nervously.

The inspector smiled and nodded in agreement.

The search of the drawers continued, the inspector lingering at each of the four remaining drawers as he pushed his hands along the sides, gently lifted clothing and underwear and again swept his hand over every inch of surface.

At the last drawer the inspector's hands appeared impatient and eager to finish when they momentarily froze while the inspector turned toward Raj.

"Can you tell me about this?"

The inspector slowly lifted his arms from the drawer; his hands cradling a small, plastic bag that bulged with pale green weed, a bag Jen had left there a month before and that Raj had forgotten existed.

I am not here, Raj thought, drawn back inside his child self and into memories that could not be adequately remembered. He embraced a new fact of his life with complete abandonment as he was transported slowly back to the tyrannies of time and place. *The world does everything wrong on purpose. Why then give it any further consideration?*

six

A night in jail was a test of endurance, not very different from his last acid trip on the mountain but without the experience of shivering cold. He had made his one phone call to Mack who gratefully answered for once and to whom he now owed a hundred dollars. It was the cost of a bail bond that freed Raj from custody, though he was charged with a significant felony: possession of marijuana for sale. His own cash, kept in a metal box, had been confiscated as evidence along with what Raj thought was an ounce or less of grass.

"It's not what they have on you that's the problem," Mack said to Raj as they shared a late breakfast at Buddy's café.

"They've known for a long time you deal dope on the Avenue. They aren't busting you for an ounce. They're busting you for years of dealing they know about but couldn't ever prove."

"Then what the fuck do I do?" Raj asked.

"You get an attorney," Mack said. "Today. Don't wait. It's like getting busted in Mexico. The more you put it off, the more people you have to pay off. An attorney can talk to the cops and the court. Can enter your plea. Can negotiate."

"But attorneys cost a fortune," Raj said.

"And can save your fucking ass," Mack said. "It's time or money. Pay now and get your life back. What you don't spend in money will come back to you as time you spend in jail."

225

Mack said an attorney would never have allowed the cops to search Raj's room.

"You're a righteous cat," Mack said. "But you didn't know your rights. You still don't."

Raj was not accustomed to martialing his civil wits or worldly resources. Decision. Action. Outcome. A life lived among the inspirations of his mind's intoxication had made little room for effective action, though Raj was now impatient for a result that would absolve and free him from the clutch of criminal justice. Bronwyn might help him. Certainly she knew attorneys. She had been arrested at least twice. And Mack was right. He had nothing and so, as the song went, he had nothing to lose. *It is so diffuse being alive. Suddenly one is aware that nobody really gives a damn.*

"I know someone," Bronwyn said as she pulled an address book from her bag and fluttered through its small pages.

Raj raised the issue of money. At the moment, he was broke.

"He'll work with you," she said. "Half of us in the Movement are still paying off attorneys."

She scribbled a name and number on a sheet of notepaper and handed it to him.

"Phone him. Today. The cops will fuck with you but not with your lawyer."

Peter, one of Bronwyn's colleagues in struggle, arrived along with Larry who brought a colleague of his own. Carlos was a Mexican-American activist and officer in the Brown Berets.

"Raj is in trouble with The Man," Bronwyn said to Peter. "Busted for selling pot."

"That's what they say," Raj added.

Larry's surprised look caught Raj off guard.

"That where you been?" Larry asked. "In jail?"

"No. I was busted yesterday. It's bullshit."

"In other local news…" Bronwyn spoke sarcastically. "Really, I'm sorry for Raj here but we have some work to do. Right, Larry?"

"You mean Eldridge and his class?" he asked.

"That, too," Bronwyn responded. "You all know that yesterday thousands of Mexican students were shot at by the army in Mexico

City. How many killed? Hundreds? No one knows. It's outrageous. We're all in this together. Our world is in revolt and how do we respond to this?"

"By bringing it all back home," said Peter. "We need a rally speaker tomorrow on the Mexican riot. What can you do, Carlos? And Larry, this is connected to Eldridge. Students and faculty want him to teach a sociology class on racism. Reagan and the Regents want to stop him. We have a fight brewing three blocks away that is central to the issue of cultural nationalism. Do we get Black studies? Do we get Chicano studies? And what do we do if we don't? This has been brewing at San Francisco State for the last six months. It might be time to strike."

"Can't believe the Mexicans are going ahead with the Olympics," Bronwyn said. "When do they start? Next week?"

"Why not?" Peter responded. "It's the bread and the circus that will keep citizens docile. That and the threat of getting shot. We do it here, too. If the Mexicans can shoot students dead, are we next?"

"Maybe, if that ofay Nixon wins the election," Larry said. "You can bet on it if Wallace wins."

"That can't happen, right?" Raj said in response to weak laughter from everyone else.

Raj retreated into his unwoven world. He sought recovery and not solution. In what he imagined was a time of emerging clarity after his mountain adventure, he felt dropped from a dangerous height or thrown against a wall. The elements supporting this entrapment were either invisible servants or discomforting powers and he did not know which. Water filled spaces, air filled his lungs, fire consumed his best intentions and earth was all he could see. He begged secretly for a path back, a reset of the last days so he might learn from the future what should have been his past. He thought during one memorable acid trip that time appeared to move both forward and backward. He could see now it did not.

Harriet entered the Forum and Raj excused himself, thanking Bronwyn for her referral.

"For selling dope?" Harriet asked as if an arrest were the last thing she thought could happen to Raj.

"I don't sell it anymore," Raj answered, trying to make a joke.

He gave Harriet a brief summary of his past week but not the details of his Mt. Shasta flash, saying merely he had taken a hike on a beautiful mountain and come down refreshed and determined to take a new turn with his life. He tried to present the drug bust as a distraction, an embarrassing slip-up along the way to a confident and fully satisfying enlightenment, though he knew nothing was assured.

"I'm closing doors," he said. "This is one of them. I don't know what I'll find. But at least I'm looking."

Raj looked to acknowledge Harriet for her concern and, instead, saw Jen approach the table.

"Is this your new girlfriend?" Jen shouted at Raj without looking at Harriet.

"Girlfriend? No…" Raj struggled with his surprise.

"You seem to spend a lot more time with her than me."

"I'm nobody's girlfriend," Harriet said testily to Jen.

"Jen, I just got back, I…" Raj struggled for his words.

"Why didn't you come to see me?" Jen said. "Why is it always me looking for you?"

Jen's passion was overwrought and embarrassing for Raj, especially in front of Harriet.

Raj stood and took Jen's hand to lead her to an outside table. She pulled away at first, but followed Raj out.

"I can't do this anymore, Jen," Raj said directly.

He told her of his arrest and the trouble he saw ahead. He was not good for her now. He would only be a risk as the police closed in around him. He dramatized his poorest attributes: forgetfulness, self-absorption, and irresponsibility. His feet moved under the table as if he were already dancing away.

"You're better off without me fucking up your life," Raj said.

Jen was offended by Raj's self-inflicted derogation and heard through it to the terms of a brush-off. Her hippie lover, the man who made her happy and high, who held her tenderly and made her come, was dumping her. She began to cry.

"You don't understand," Jen spoke through her tears.

And then she turned hostile.

"You're just another bastard, aren't you? Just another tripped-out stoner. I should know. Damn, I should know!"

Raj sat through Jen's painful rage, as he had done with other women who were better off without him. He wanted to withdraw quickly, to run away, to sequester himself, even for a fleeting moment to kill himself if that would relieve Jen of her excruciating disappointment.

Raj faced, as he knew he would, the variable standards of failure that defined his history of incomplete coupling. *Done for again,* he said silently to himself. *Trapped again in my own insincere system because I cannot stop doing it. Even if I am good, good itself inflicts the harm.*

Jen stood and left, her sobs drawing the attention of those seated nearby who turned to look at Raj as if he were giving off an offensive smell. Raj saw Harriet at her table inside the Forum. She made a gesture that appeared to invite him back. Raj shook his head and left.

The prospect of going to prison allowed Raj to consider what he might ever do with his freedom. No acid vision was necessary to grasp that freedom was the origin of all his possibilities. But there was no act without a cause and where he now stood appeared precipitous as he thought himself teetering at a dangerous apex dividing him between fear and choice.

"At least you didn't say the pot was yours," said the attorney, a small, congenial man in his forties who sat behind a desk covered in a sea of books and documents spread around as if work were actually happening though only the attorney would know what it was.

"It wasn't, sir," responded Raj as he sat and rocked in his chair.

"Call me Rick," the attorney said. His name was etched into the wooden door of his office on the third floor of the downtown bank building. It read Richard F. Bosworth, Esq. but the man's name was Rick. Bronwyn had called him Rick when she made the referral. Raj made no presumptions.

"Did you tell them anything else?" Rick asked.

"Nothing. They cuffed me, read me my rights and took me back to the station."

"Yeah," Rick added. "The acid dealer bust. Surprised they didn't keep you as an accessory. Your friend is doing his part. Hasn't said a word to implicate you. And they're trying, believe me."

"They're what?" Raj asked.

The attorney sat forward. He had done his homework.

"Here's what I know. They've been trying to get inside the big acid trade for a while and knew a lot was coming through town. Students and all, right? They've suspected for at least a year that you're a major South Campus dealer. Just haven't found any way to bust you because you don't leave a trail and you have no enemies.

But then they found you with the Acid Man. What's his name, Skillicain?"

"Skillikorn," Raj interjected.

"Yeah, you won't believe your bad luck. The day you go visit the Acid Guy his partner is busted at the Napa Airport with more than 60,000 hits of orange sunshine. The drug cops find the Acid Guy's name in his address book and call the Berkeley PD. Bingo! So they bust Acid Guy, who has another 80,000 hits of acid in his bedroom. And they find you, someone who has already been on their drug radar. The cops are in fat city. They know you deal. They just have to get you. Instant Trifecta."

"So what do we do?" Raj asked.

"Don't worry yet," Rick said. "I've spoken with the DA. They don't want to send you to prison. But they do want to make life hard for dope dealers in the South Campus. They're trying to clean it up and that means getting rid of the hippies. Why do you think they're bulldozing all those houses between Haste and Dwight?

Clean it up or clear it out. Who was the soldier in Vietnam who said they had to destroy the village in order to save it?"

"I don't deal anymore. I don't use drugs anymore," Raj said.

"When did you stop?" Rick asked.

"Last week," Raj answered.

"Well, one day at a time, I suppose."

Rick did not disguise his sarcasm. His phone rang.

"Yeah…yeah…yeah…no…no,no,no! Listen, I'll call you back."

Rick hung up the phone.

"Here's the deal," said Rick, rushing to end the meeting. "You're charged with felony possession to sell. They don't have enough to prove it at trial. They don't want to go to trial and you don't want to go to trial. They'll settle if you plead guilty to misdemeanor possession of less than an ounce. You'll get informal probation for two years, a $50 fine and no jail time. If you ever again get caught selling dope you'll go to prison."

"But it wasn't my grass," Raj pleaded.

"They don't care," Rick said.

Raj envisioned his three secret kilos dropping ounce by ounce into Yitzhak's toilet.

"How much is this going to cost?" Raj asked.

"Couple hundred, if we don't go to trial. We'll work it out. I do a lot of work with your friends."

Raj stood. He knew it was time to leave.

"Your court date is Wednesday, October 30th at 10 a.m. Phone me the day before and I'll meet you there. We'll plead and it will be over. Except for the probation, of course. But it's informal. You won't have to report to anyone."

"Thanks, I guess," Raj said as he opened the office door to leave.

"Cheerfully accepted," Rick said through a wide, tooth-baring smile.

Raj stayed home for several days. His once accessible world had become monstrously claustrophobic. He could not step outside his house without seeing a cop or a detective, or constantly thinking he saw one. Every face he passed could see through him to his oppressive guilt and naked fear. At least his roommates were absent during his arrest, save one who passed him in the hall as the man in a suit escorted Raj out. The student roomer said "Hi" as Raj was marched past him, and did not see that Raj was handcuffed. Did his landlord know about his arrest?

Raj waited and worried while he shut all apertures and closed all doors, even calling in sick to Creed's, spending most of his time on his day bed listening to John Fahey's intimate, supple strumming from *The Transfiguration of Blind Joe Death*.

When he grew weary of Fahey's sonorous messaging, he put on Blue Cheer and rocked out to the metallic battering of *Summertime Blues*. He slept into the afternoons and stayed awake all night, using headphones to dissolve himself into the chords and beats of his music. He waited until dark to shop at the Garden Spot, occasionally buying a beer or a half-bottle of cheap white to smother his wickedly tenacious angst. He looked everywhere within and could find nothing.

But he wanted relief and did not want to get high. Eventually his drawn-out solitude drew a few friends in. Larry was the first to find Raj in his room.

"That's fucked up," Larry said. "Guess you done dealin'."

"Done usin'," Raj responded. "Done droppin', done smokin', done trippin'."

"Yeah, I'd be pissed off, too," said Larry. "How long you been cooped up in here?"

Raj thought it might have been a week. He asked Larry if he knew anyone who would make him a fake ID.

"Aw man," Larry moaned. "Why you dudes always think a brother can break the law for you?"

Raj backed off.

"Sorry, man," said Raj. "I'm desperate."

Raj asked Larry how he and his family were coping with Sam's death.

"Each day different," Larry said stiffly. "Dad's strugglin' now but mom, she never gettin' over it. Holidays gonna be tough this year. Sam was due home at Thanksgiving. I can feel trouble brewin' cause they fight a lot now, though they like Sylvia."

"Sylvia?" Raj asked.

"Kind a my girlfriend. Joined the Panthers two months ago. We been workin' together and, well…what do they say? Familiarity breeds attempt."

Raj asked Larry to tell him more.

"Lotsa women joinin' the Panthers. Maybe more sisters than brothers. This breakfast thing is gonna happen, probably first of next year. Free breakfasts for the community's children. Sylvia's on it. She's on lotsa stuff. Black English, African history, and she fierce, man. She a fierce lady and no one pushes her buttons 'cause she pushes right back. I learned that fast."

"And she likes you?" asked Raj.

"That's what she says. She hung in there during Sam's death.

She helped me a lot. Her family lives in Richmond and she's a student at CCC. Good folks. My dad loves her. Thinks she's good for me. But then, he's not the preacher he used to be. Sam's death wrecked him."

Raj absorbed the new details of Larry's life. He imagined the scope of links that held him to his family, to his culture, to his people. Raj had nothing so tight, so close and personal. Larry's life as a Panther forced Raj to consider Holiday's life on Mt. Shasta, supported also by a community committed to mutual welfare and survival. Raj, however, had nothing. Nothing but three kilos of grass he might have to sell, and soon, to cover the cost of a deep and disturbingly singular trouble. Those kilos were the last friends he had.

Raj walked out into the afternoon's fading daylight. He had put on a pair of slacks and a blue, long-sleeved shirt. He had checked himself in a mirror.

"Look like a graduate student," he said to himself as he pushed his hair back and knotted it into a ponytail. "Hope it helps."

Outside he did not see bulldozers or hear their loud, monotonous cacophony. For many months the sound had filled his ears while the university's work crews tore down residences and rooming houses along the city block just east of Telegraph. The block was purchased by the state through a bill offered in the legislature by the city's Republican assemblyman. A university spokesman said the plan was to build a medical school but no such plan existed. Instead, the destruction of thirty historical residences and the displacement of some three hundred residents were understood to be actions intended to rid the South Campus of hippies and vagrants.

Raj crossed the dusty block where numerous cars parked among the ruts of what was once a residential community and was now a muddy, barren lot. Only two empty buildings were left at the far end of Haste, their shingled exteriors evidence of an architectural esthetic dating to the Twenties but now useless and doomed. Two bulldozers stood nearby, silent and driverless but positioned to gut and to eradicate at some undetermined but assured time the old structures, beautiful to anyone who looked at them and memorably valued by most all who had been their occupants.

It was an ugly death. Raj was resentful; having himself lost a lovely room to the bulldozers earlier in the year. But resentment was an impotent response to this kind of death and, like so many of his friends, Raj could not yet imagine any way to acquire justice or to impose a righteous vengeance.

"Nothing right now," said the young manager as he sat at a desk and fumbled through a file drawer to pull out an application for employment that he handed to Raj.

"Fred and Pat won't be back until next week," he said. "Check in from time to time. Timing is everything."

The young manager of Cody's Books was impressed with Raj's retail book experience, enough to give him a private interview. He had seen Raj at Creed's but seemed more interested in Creeds than Raj.

"Is he going out of business?" the manager asked.

Raj shrugged.

"Don't think so," Raj said.

"So many bookstores just on this block," the manager said. "It's a damned book ghetto. Somethin's gotta give."

Raj made a second stop at Moe's next door and found the owner, Moe Moskowitz, a stocky, balding man wearing a tattered tweed jacket. Moe stood at the counter sorting books while he chewed on the stub of an unlit cigar.

"I know you," Moe said. "You used to hang around at my Shattuck store. And you wanna work here?"

"I'm looking for better hours," Raj said.

"Better than what?" asked Moe.

"I'm only working ten a week for Simon at Creed's. I need more, like about thirty."

Moe nodded.

"You know music? Ever bought or sold records?"

"I know music," Raj answered boldly. "Jazz, rock, classical. I know books and music. I read, write and listen. I'm a fucking sponge. And I live just up the street."

Moe dropped a stack of books on the counter.

"OK. OK. I got an idea. Give me your phone number. Better

yet, check back with me next Monday."

Raj took out a pen and wrote his house phone on a bookmark and handed it back to Moe.

"Hey," Moe asked quietly. "Is Creed's folding?"

"Don't think so, Moe," Raj said. "It's an institution…like you."

Moe recoiled from Raj's obsequious compliment but laughed appreciatively.

Raj bore his wariness to the Garden Spot where he bought a night's groceries and then returned to his room. Life was no longer beatific but neither was it boring or simply a diversion. The mountain still loomed as his most significant milestone and the birthplace of an experience that, despite his dangerous and sudden fall, clothed him in all varieties of light and dark. He saw both his ignorance and his method and the new world he had made was also the world through which, for the very first time, he might see himself. A journey was taking shape, perhaps a real odyssey. He would throw coins or shuffle cards and thereby map his new directions.

seven

Raj heard himself the narrator of his life. Immediately he was displeased with the narration's deficient first draft. For many years he lived with what he thought was self-awareness. It appeared now to be something closer to self-absorption. His fascination with the details precluded any deeper relationship.

He had been happy not to be jealous or vengeful, happy simply to be happy without any need or ambition. This embedded him with a quality the poet might have described as *suchness*, a pleasant state by which all experience could be grasped without assessment and lived without value.

It's cool. How many times had he said that in response to broken hearts, bad dreams, or otherwise insufferable discomfort? He was above conflict and cooler than all those ordinary souls separated and also touching, seeing and also unseen, in love and also in despair. Acid provided a glimpse of unsullied truth but left him the only subject of its insight. Was it any different than watching television?

Certainly it was a thrill, a grey and sometimes colorful glow, but a relationship that existed only within and for himself. And he knew himself well. In truth, since his scare on the mountain he was his only friend.

"You think you want to help?" said Bronwyn.

She was surprised by Raj's sudden interest in the whirlwinds of war, injustice and oppression. He had arrived at the Forum's informal back table meeting in time to catch her alone.

"Is this because of your bust?" she asked, searching for the source of Raj's new and urgent interest.

"You might want to think about that. Cops won't go easy if they arrest you again."

"It's cool," Raj heard himself say and in a way he hoped would be the very last time.

"I don't like cops. Do you?"

Bronwyn flashed a sardonic smile.

"It's a busy week," she told him. "Catonsville Nine trial starts today. Eldridge speaks at the X139 class Wednesday. The Mexican students are in full revolt on the eve of the Mexico City Olympics. And there's word that DA Coakley wants to prosecute the organizers of last year's Stop the Draft Week. Mike, Frank, Bob and Peter have been mentioned as likely targets."

Raj shrugged his acknowledgment.

"You can get some posters up for the Cleaver class. A rally will follow. Come back at four. We'll all be here and I'll have something for you."

She handed Raj a dozen posters.

Raj nodded.

"And thanks," Bronwyn added. "If you're for real, it will be a huge help."

Raj returned at four, all his posters placed on campus, his presence a surprise to the others convened for a meeting.

"You all know Raj," Bronwyn said. "His participation goes back to the HUAC protests of 1960. Remember? They bounced you down the wet stairs just like everyone else, right Raj?"

Raj nodded.

"Raj wants to help the Movement."

Raj nodded again, hoping his documented protest at the beginning of the decade, his first youthful social investment of righteous anger, and one that preceded those of the others, would win him acceptance even as many at the table knew him as a habitué and drug dealer, had in fact purchased from him.

"You still dealin'?" someone at the table asked Raj directly.

Raj shook his head.

"Done with that," Raj answered. "Other things are more important now. I'm sure you'd agree."

Everyone nodded.

Raj dove into a week of scrub work for the ever present and always over-extended Movement. Fighting injustice was a Sisyphean project and, for now, he did not care. He awoke early to distribute leaflets, make phone calls, march across campus, staff rallies and attend a dozen meetings. He slipped into his room at night and locked the door. He avoided cops as best he could and sauntered behind other pedestrians if he crossed in front of patrol cars.

The work was lonely even in solidarity with others and from within a smothering desolation he once thought to contact Jen again, to apologize for his bad behavior and to enlist her as well in a fight for the people, before realizing it likely was his dope and not affection that had held her interest in him.

Within a few days Raj was well schooled on the issues closest at hand: the rise of Black Power represented both in Eldridge's appearance on campus and the surge of student protest on behalf of a college curriculum of Third World Studies that could serve Black, Mexican and Asian students. Protests continued against the War in Vietnam, with agitprop stunts by Jerry Rubin's Yippies that included Rubin appearing in Washington before a HUAC committee meeting dressed as a Viet Cong and cradling a plastic toy machine gun. And there was the national election and its grotesque choices for president.

As usual, the world was a mess. The future of everyone existed no farther than a twenty-minute window, the time it took Raj to walk from his room to the campus and also the time it would take for launched ICBMs to destroy its thousands of targets, as missiles surely would in the ultimate holocaust of a final World War. And what reason was there to think such a war would not happen? What indeed, if thousands could die daily and with unremarkable anonymity in the jungles of Southeast Asia?

Raj checked his post office box every Thursday and this week scooped out all his junk mail and found within it a hand-lettered envelope from Sonia. He hadn't recognized the handwriting but saw the firmly penned letters of her first name and her last. *Sonia Bogle.* He had not known her last name, only where he might once again find her. Raj opened the envelope and pulled out a letter written on two lined pages torn from a hand-sized spiral notebook. Her handwriting had the literate curl of an attentive schoolgirl.

How are you doing? My turn for the rice run. I'm driving to San Francisco the last week of the month. Will you be around? I can come to see you. It's already raining here and we're in the cabin now. It's small and close quarters, for sure. But a wood stove keeps us warm. Tell me where you are and how to reach you. I will be in San Francisco on the 25th. Write to me care of General Delivery Mt. Shasta, CA.
Warmly,
Sonia

Raj hiked home, cutting across the campus under the lush, late shadows of eucalyptus trees and down the swarming incline of the Avenue to his street and his house and his room. Inside he locked the door, found an extra Eldridge leaflet and on its blank side wrote his response. He would go to the City and meet her. He wrote the address of a café in North Beach. *Easy to find. I'll be there the afternoon you arrive. Let me get you dinner.*
Raj appropriated an envelope from his next-door roomie, addressed it and hustled back to the post office where he bought a stamp. He slipped his letter into the outgoing mail slot, flipping its drawer open and closed a few times to be certain the letter was on its way.

At home he pulled a record from his long shelf of LPs and put it on the turntable, stoked through his earphones by the voice of Jim Morrison caressing the soundtrack of The Doors' first album.

Morrison's lyrics, his words about unconsciousness and kisses and a fleeting chance at bliss were driven from behind by the primitive tensions of an electric keyboard. They filled whatever remained of Raj's psychedelic mind with a desperate and fibrillating hunger as if he were a child in the night, his stomach aching for the flavors of a flourishing survival. It did occur to Raj he never had left his childhood, had remained at the very most an adolescent in stubborn emotional rebellion. And he extended this uprising for all its important purposes, the most important being its use as a mortar in which were ground up and resolved all the social and natural tensions of his wrecked, Catholic youth.

The city itself was a fractal wilderness like any outlying forest or valley or mountain he ever had visited. As the music played, Raj imagined himself in the same place a million years hence as males and females of a derivative hominid species, returned to the treetops, sat on branches to comment on the outsized rodents passing below. His fantasy arrived unaided by dope and in a jumble of awareness and intensity almost too much to manage. And he could not leave it yet. He heard the first strains of *The End* as Morrison sang the phrases and praises of annihilation and the wait of insane children for the rains of an unspecific summer.

Raj could not leave it, this vortex where fervor confronted caution, where desire fought with necessity, where young truths could be twisted into elaborate adult rationalizations. He lacked a luminous sense of identity and so was more intently aware of everyone else's. But his arrest had entered him into the world. He was a documented suspect, a bona fide enemy of the state. Having no identity, he was therefore given one. It was time now to live up to his fate. It was time to ride the snake.

Raj arrived at the Forum on a Sunday to see Harriet again at her favorite table, books and journals spread about as she wrote copious notes in a binder. She held her own court, the written words of classical authors her consorts and committee members. The late morning light illuminated her red, round cheeks and lit cool sparkles in her yellow hair that fell forward with her face as she tried to read.

"You're deep into it," Raj observed as he passed her.

Harriet looked up.

"Yes. Always," she answered. "I suppose it's my fate. Never enough time to read all I should. Not a week goes by that someone doesn't have something else to say about Dante. Most of it isn't great, but I need to know it. I need to know all of it. That's the life of a scholar."

"If that's the life you want," Raj said skeptically.

"It's the life I know," Harriet responded firmly. "And I really know it."

The life Raj knew best had no basis in fact, unless he counted his status as an accused offender, which was his most organized and documented existence. The police knew him and everything about him. He lived under a legal cloud and wished only to have the time back before his arrest, before his unlucky outreach to Skilly, before his purchase of three kilos of grass he could do nothing with. He had the panicky idea he might contact Catherine and give her back the kilos and no longer owe her money. But how?

"You seen Jen?" Raj asked.

Harriet looked at Raj somberly.

"You serious?"

Raj wasn't and he shook his head as Bronwyn entered the Forum and passed behind him.

"You're early for a change," Bronwyn said to Raj. She proceeded to a back table and pushed it together with another to make space for a meeting.

"Rallies all week," Bronwyn said to those eventually assembled to do the heavy lifting of revolution. The Catonsville Nine had been convicted and faced years in prison. The carnage of the Mexican student revolt had been erased by cheery sports coverage of the Mexico City Olympics. Eldridge was supposed to teach again at Dwinelle Hall but what if the university refused to let him? The war was still killing thousands of Vietnamese and American soldiers and, while he wouldn't be executed, Huey faced up to 15 years in prison and might be killed before he was freed. And there was the movement to create Third World Studies. Student strikes were planned for the next month if demands weren't met.

"And those demands are non-negotiable," Peter shouted from his end of the table.

Mack arrived late and was allowed to sit in as long as everything he heard was off the record.

"I'm here to cover the news, not to make it," Mack said.

"Well, get ready for a busy week," said Bronwyn. "We're in full mobilization."

Larry wasn't present and another Panther named David arrived late to discuss the next steps in the Eldridge battle on campus. A consensus developed around occupying the administration building and, if that didn't succeed, taking over another building and holding it until demands were met. Raj watched as phone calls were assigned, meetings were organized and a cadre formed to connect the dots of resistance up the Avenue and across the campus.

"It's starting to feel like a war," Raj said.

"It's been a war for eight years," a woman shouted from the rear table. Her brown leather jacket and stern, aquiline profile gave her the appearance of a sturdy, battle-worn veteran.

"Look what's happened to our community. Look outside at that flooded vacant lot where more than three hundred people used to live. See the cops still patrolling our streets? Busting our brothers and sisters, knocking the heads of those who protest. We will lose this war if we don't take it to the streets. And we will lose this war if we don't commit to winning by any means necessary."

"Thank you, Tracy," Brownyn shouted back in a voice intended to preserve order and to keep everyone focused. She gave Raj a list of local communes, student boarding houses, and campus clubs he would need to contact about the week's events.

"We expect a fight," she said to him. "We expect the cops to show up and try to stop us. These people hate the cops, almost as much as you do."

Yes, Raj thought, he hated cops. That was as far as he could think politically and Bronwyn knew that a political consciousness grew from someone's first trouble with authority. Raj's first was with his father at a childish time when he had no words to understand the man's savage assertion of family rule and, later, his father's love of a God that danced fecklessly around him in a holy ether and never answered his prayers.

After the meeting Raj caught up with Mack to request a favor.

"Can you check on a plane crash last month in the desert near Bishop?" he asked, describing what he knew of the incident and giving him an approximate date.

"A four-seat Cessna," Raj said. "At least two dead. It was flying in from Mexico."

Mack nodded and said he'd check the AP wire and, if necessary, phone the Bishop paper.

"A friend?" Mack asked.

"Maybe," Raj answered.

Living in his new way was becoming for Raj a great study of death. Since he was no longer high, he was no longer concerned with any perception of eternal contact, any telepathic cue that might divert or entertain him. His feet were on the ground in a way he could not remember, even if he stumbled badly. Yet it was a pleasure not to feel transcendent, not to hide from the discriminating mind, not to see anymore through the solidity and firmness of his obstacles. He was finished with his life as a microscopic insect only able to wander among the encroachments of a fluid and infirm existence.

eight

Raj sat at Kip's bar and sipped a black coffee. If he were to have a role in the undoing of a mean world he needed at least to see it. His new habit was to arrive at Kip's in time for the noonday news, which he watched on the bar's color television.

On this day the screen was filled with the image of two black American Olympians, one the winner and the other the third place finisher in the two hundred yard dash. They stood on the victors' platform beside the second place finisher from Australia and lowered their heads while raising black-gloved clinched fists during the playing of the national anthem.

A camera panned the Mexico City stadium while the two athletes held a pose of protest unmistakably supportive of Black Power. A smattering of cheers and boos could be heard from the surprised crowd, many of them Americans. The athletes were identified as Tommie "Jet" Smith and John Carlos and their unprecedented action was being widely condemned as ungrateful and unpatriotic by politicians, athletes, celebrities and all three presidential candidates.

The news was that International Olympic Committee President Avery Brundage demanded that the two black athletes be stripped of their medals and kicked out of the Olympics or the entire US team would be sent home.

"What's this damned country coming to?"

The shouted lament came from one of the bar's older regulars who hunched over his pint as he might have a decade or more before. *Wonder which frat he joined* thought Raj. *Wonder if he graduated.*

"Those two punks should be tried for treason and locked up."

"Easy for you to say," came another shout from a nearby table. "You're an old white cracker who probably can't walk fifty yards, much less run two-hundred. Stick it up your tight, bigoted ass."

The older man turned and jumped from his stool as if to confront the unseen voice. He saw a lanky, muscular boy push his chair back to stand.

"You lookin' for me?" the student said. "I run track for Cal. Wanna race? Loser has to shut his fucking mouth."

The older man, an acquired gut slumbering over the belt of his baggy pants, mentally measured the terms, made a face and then sat back down as the bartender raced on to the floor to get between a man and a boy poised either at the brink of patricide or filicide.

Raj watched the showdown and saw Mack enter the bar. He waved him over.

"Hot story," Mack said as he slipped into a stool next to Raj. "I'm supposed to find some black students to talk to. I'd rather interview some Panthers. Where's Larry these days?"

"Try Panther Headquarters," Raj said. "If you find him, tell him to call me."

Mack ordered a beer.

"It doesn't show in the film, but Smith and Carlos also stood without their shoes on. They had on black socks. Something about black poverty. They haven't said much yet, other than that their message was meant for the world and not just America."

"Might help with organizing," Raj responded. "The whole Eldridge class thing is about to blow up."

Mack nodded.

"I have some other news for you," said Mack. "I made some calls this week and, as far as I can determine, there was no plane crash last month near Bishop."

"What?" Raj asked. "No crash?"

"The Bishop paper has no report of a plane going down anywhere, especially in an area accessed by roads. Authorities also have nothing. Someone would have seen the crash you describe. Unless you have more details or are willing to say what you know, no one I spoke with wants to go searching for a phantom."

Raj cast a vacant stare at nothing in particular.

"You look surprised," Mack said.

"Yeah. I am…I mean, I have no reason not to believe…"

"Believe who?" asked Mack, getting no response from Raj.

"The desert hides nothing. Anyone flying over the area would have seen the smoke or at least the wreckage. It's not like a plane that crashes in the Sierras and isn't found until the snows melt. The noise alone would have carried for miles."

Everyone running around to sell their piles of shit. Why would Catherine lie to him? What was she offering: gold or shit? If there were no plane crash, if Judson were not dead, if the kilos were either a gift or a temptation, Raj might be the last to know. He weighed an inexplicable mistruth that would never be grasped or understood. Time was done with it, and with him. Answers would never be forthcoming until he was the one to be questioned.

Among all the things he pretended to be, Raj was actually and officially an accused drug dealer. An appearance before a judge was two weeks away and his attorney said if he pleaded to possession that would be the end of it. But what if he were arrested again prior to his court date? Had he been set up some way? It made no sense. If Judson were alive, what were he and Catherine running from? If Raj could see everything, then everything would uncomfortably crowd his mind and he would still know nothing.

And how would he ever unload his kilos? He was $250 in the hole and needed cash now. Two weeks had passed since he sold anyone dope and rent was due in a week. He barely had enough to feed himself peanut butter and occasionally buy a cup of coffee. At this rate he might end up on the corner of Dwight and Telegraph selling the weekly Barb.

On the following Saturday Raj walked down to Civic Center Park where the Provos passed out free food and two bands drew crowds of students and hippies for an afternoon concert. He carried a ream of leaflets announcing a rally and protest the following week. They featured a photo of Smith and Carlos, their gloved fists held high on the Olympic podium. Among the hundreds gathered on the lawn he saw Stan and Ginger and little Lila who played naked with other children in the park's dry, dirty fountain.

"You free next weekend?" Ginger asked. "We're going to Inger's theater piece at the Moving Space on Bancroft. Invitation only. And you're invited."

"Inger's show?" Raj asked. "I wondered if it would ever happen."

"It's gonna happen," Stan affirmed. "It's an experimental play. Something written by Picasso but never performed. Anyway, there's a party after the show."

Raj said he would be there.

Raj roamed the park with his leaflets while he watched motleys of dancers sway to the punchy rhythms of two conga drummers. A chocolate-skinned flautist wearing a straw hat blew a daedal melody that sustained the throbbing lurches of the crowd, led by a tall, slender black man in a suit and tie known as WherethepartyPercy. The name derived from Percy's habit of asking *Where's the party?* as park crowds later broke into scattering clutches that moved like small surging worms toward private homes or venues where it was safer to let it all run. If anyone existed wholly for himself it was Percy, who might appear anywhere and everywhere, smiling and laughing like that of a prowling Cheshire cat.

Percy also shared his dope. He was discreet but bold, and lit joints in the park even as cops patrolled the perimeter or sat in their cars to watch the lurching, emboldened festivities. Dressed like a Sunday preacher in a black suit and tie, Percy both stood out and melted away. He was not a hippie. He was not a Panther. He was WheresthepartyPercy.

Later Raj could not explain why he approached Percy to offer him his kilos. It wasn't intended. He lived in fear of being arrested again but also lived in fear of starving.

"You looking for a good deal on weed?" Raj asked as Percy finished dancing and stepped behind a tree to toke on a joint.

"Who's dealin'?" Percy asked directly.

"A friend," Raj said.

"It's always a goddamned friend," Percy answered. "So how much is your friend selling and is it any good? And why?"

Raj heard Percy's sarcasm. He did not believe Raj and found it easy to put him on.

"My friend got busted by the cops but they didn't find his stash and now he has to unload it. Three keys and it's Gold. Genuine."

Raj's answer shook Percy into a quieter, more serious alertness.

"You ain't bullshittin' are you?"

"Swear to god, man," Raj answered.

"Meet me tomorrow," Percy answered. "Bring me a joint. This better be for real."

Raj nodded and agreed to meet Percy near the basketball courts at Live Oak Park though as he walked away he immediately regretted his risky offer. Percy was familiar and present but how reliable was he? Raj outlined to himself the terms of a sale. Cash only. A quick exchange at some neutral location, but where would that be?

And only Percy. No one else, even if others were involved, he would sell only to Percy. He considered the full contingency of his foolish situation. A confessed drug dealer awaiting sentencing makes a felony-level sale before going to court. He did not have to do this, and yet he did. He would ask a thousand for the kilos. It was good shit. The best. If he were to break it into ounces and sell it himself, he would make five times that amount. But that wasn't going to happen. Unloading the kilos would be his very last sale.

"So here's the deal. You work thirty hours. Friday through Monday. Six hours at the register and two after closing or before opening when you'll sort and shelve books, except Sunday when we close early. You want it?"

Moe's words were all business: succinct and to the point. Raj stared intently at Moe, a middle-aged man with a wave of diminishing dark hairs that spread across his uncombed balding head. He spoke through a square jaw while his brown corduroy sport jacket and baggy jeans gave him the look of an aging beatnik.

"Oh…and stay with us three months and you get benefits."

"Benefits?" asked Raj.

"You know. Medical and retirement. Even a vacation. Blah, blah, blah. I'll give you the paperwork later."

Moe turned to ring up a customer's sale.

"And the wage?" asked Raj.

"Two-twenty-five an hour to start. You could work out in the used records department. It's taking off. So, you want it?"

Raj said yes. He didn't even do the math.

"You start two weeks from Friday. Can you do that?"

Raj nodded again. He thought ahead quickly. His court date was on a Wednesday. It would work. He thanked Moe who appeared unmoved as he turned to ring up another sale.

It was nearly noon as Raj tacked north along the Avenue, pushing against the mid-day tide of students flowing down toward him under a hot October sun, all flashing past him in their committed search for food and coffee and places to lean or sit. Raj caught their indirect gazes, alert just enough to avoid collisions but not enough to make contact.

All was preoccupation and errand even if the minds were lost in reflection. The cascade of fleeting bodies was washed at Channing Way into a lazy eddy of Avenue regulars who lounged on the curbs and begged for spare change or discreetly offered joints and matchboxes for sale while bulldozers continued to chug above them, clearing the large eastern block of its every structure.

Two Hare Krishnas wobbled together in front of the bakery, their saffron robes and long tangled hair giving them the look of plainly dressed Hindu fakirs. A few musicians huddled on the wider sidewalk outside Cody's Books. One played a saxophone and another a drum. Raj swam through them all. He needed to cross the campus and hike the several blocks to Live Oak Park where Percy would be waiting. On the way Raj calculated his new income from Moe's and wondered momentarily why he needed to sell his kilos. He was in enough trouble so why risk more than enough?

Percy sat on a bench near the basketball courts. He was watching a pick-up game of three-on-three and cheering for a friend who spun out toward the court's corner to release a hook shot just as he flew out of bounds. The ball rose in a lazy arc before falling within the rim where it bounced viciously before sinking through the net.

"You got junk, Birdie man. You got the junk!"

Percy stood and whistled as the ball was picked up by a humbled defender and thrown back toward half-court.

Raj waved at Percy who walked over to him.

"So what you got?"

Raj took two joints from his pocket and handed them to Percy.

"If you want it, I'll be at the Forum tomorrow at two. Come by and we'll figure it out. If not, don't bother. If you don't show up I'll find someone else."

"Well, OK...." Percy said, aware of some shift in Raj's initial eagerness.

"Thanks for the sample."

"De Nada," Raj said and left the park.

The next morning ended with a rally on the Plaza where a thousand students assembled to hear Eldridge speak.

"Martin said a riot is the language of the unheard," Eldridge shouted in his soothing, elongated drawl. "We need to tell these campus pigs—PEE-IGS—we will resist. We will be heard."

The demand to have Eldridge as an instructor on campus was non-negotiable, though it was hard for Raj to imagine what would not be negotiated. He was new to the struggle or movement or revolution or whatever was the operative word for the fight ahead.

After the rally, Raj walked down to the Forum. He found Percy sitting at a table waiting for him.

"Hey, my man," Percy shouted at Raj. He stood and grabbed Raj's hand, held it high and pumped his fist twice before letting go.

"Your friend still dealin'?" Percy asked.

Raj nodded cautiously.

"What does your friend want?"

Raj at first felt his freedom extend only as far as Percy could see him. His instinct was to hide his true desire. He was both frightened and excited by what he assumed was an easy deal in the making.

"He wants a thousand dollars," Raj said and bit his lip before saying more.

"Holy shit!" shouted Percy and then laughed, his wide mouth open to the view of his pink tongue and beautifully white teeth..

"I ain't sayin' your shit—I mean, you friend's shit—ain't good, 'cause it is. But you askin' more than $300 a key and my friends won't likely go for that. Wanna try again?"

It was Raj's turn to laugh. The sale was too big a risk to settle for less. And who were Percy's friends? Probably the same as Raj's friend. The whole contrived deal still existed only between Raj and Percy.

"My friend will need to think about it," Raj said. "I've given you a price. Maybe you need to talk with your friends and bring back an offer."

Raj thought of the sale of his dope as something like a kite in the wind. He would let its string out slowly and deliberately to keep it aloft and climbing. He would hold it and not let go and watch for turbulence so that he could always reel it back, though the farther away it flew the less important it appeared.

"Can you wait?" Percy asked.

"I can wait a week," Raj answered, feeling in full control. "I can wait a week," he repeated.

"Maybe not that long. Where do I find you?" asked Percy.

"Right here," Raj answered.

Madness was in Raj's heart and he enjoyed his command of the deal. He knew he could be arrogant because he did not care. For now, the pleasure of living had nothing to do with results.

An accident might help Raj remember what he was doing. Opportunities to fail were everywhere and as he lifted chairs onto a desk he heard someone scream at him.

"Columbia!"

It was a rallying cry Raj did not completely understand. It likely belonged to another college's uprising at another place and time perhaps not very far from the revolution he supported now. He had not slept in two nights. The previous day's campus rally on behalf of Cleaver's class had turned into a mass occupation of Sproul Hall by more than a hundred students. They refused to leave at closing time and by midnight were under arrest and pushed onto three buses that took them to the county prison farm in Santa Rita.

A crowd of two thousand watched from outside and cheered, threw rocks at the buses and let the air out of several tires. A leaderless mob gathered around a bonfire set at the campus' south entrance while packs roamed down Telegraph to smash the windows of a local bank. Police stood on the roof and photographed them.

Another dawn rolled seamlessly into another rally of thousands who rambled through the campus to occupy first the Chancellor's office in one hall and then the campus administration center in another, settling finally on Moses Hall, an administration hub entered at first by some five hundred protesters who chased out the staff and settled in to occupy halls, lobbies and offices. A thousand more stood outside, squeezed between old South Hall and the Campanile Plaza where Raj also stood until Peter waved him into the building.

"These are our demands," Peter said as he handed Raj a single page from the office mimeograph machine. "We aren't leaving until they're met."

"We aren't?" Raj asked. "Didn't we just do this last night?"

"*We* didn't," said Peter. "*We* were outside. Tonight it's our turn."

The demands included university credit for SA 139X, Eldridge's sociology class, and amnesty for everyone arrested the previous night or who would be arrested tonight.

A few more people standing outside entered the building. Raj saw Larry, who ran forward carrying a camera and nearly knocked

Raj over before seeing him.

"Whoa, man," Raj said as he caught Larry with his arms.

Larry jumped away.

"Is that a new camera?"

"This? Nikon F, man. Yeah, it's mine. I bought it."

"Must have set you back," said Raj. "Looks brand new."

"My life savings," answered Larry.

"Why are you here?" Raj asked as if nothing but time had passed between them.

"Eldridge," Larry answered. "What do you think? I'm shootin' for The Panther's next edition."

"I have something to show you," Raj said and led Larry down a hall. A banner hung at the entrance to the building's largest office. It read "Cleaver Hall."

Larry lifted his camera and snapped off several frames.

"This pretty cool," he said to Raj who smiled, looked toward the ground and flashed Larry the upright Olympian's fisted salute.

Hours flew by until there was no more sunlight. Larry wandered the building with his camera while Raj waited. The police would arrive but no one knew when. By mid-evening the hall's occupancy force was down to less than a hundred.

"Columbia!"

Raj heard the cry again as he helped to barricade the building's front entrance from within. To arrest the hall's new occupants, the police would first have to enter. And it was Raj's current assignment to make entry as difficult as possible.

By midnight an army of cops had pushed back the crowd outside and taken up positions in front of the building. Raj walked toward the exit to leave.

"You're not going now," Peter said to him. "Too late. Every door is blocked and they have us surrounded."

Peter called everyone together to describe the arrest protocol. He read off a phone number all were to call after they were jailed.

"Arraignment will be in two days. Don't resist arrest. Resisting arrest is a felony."

"Haven't we already resisted arrest?" Raj asked. "Look at this place. We've blocked the doorways and torn the offices apart. How is this not a felony?"

"Misdemeanor or felony. They're coming," Peter told the assembled occupants.

In the dizzying pace of the past 48 hours, Raj had lost track of his place in time. He had not intended to risk arrest. He hated the cops but knew he would not be helped by another arrest just weeks before a hearing for dealing drugs. And in two days Sonia was arriving in the City.

"What the fuck?" Larry whispered to Raj. "I can't get busted. I'm a goddamned Panther. They'll whip my fuckin' ass. They'll take my camera. They could break it. Shit, I gotta get out a here."

Raj took Larry's arm and guided him to a back stairway that descended to a row of small offices on a lower floor.

"This way," Raj instructed. "These windows open onto the creek."

Raj turned off the lights in one office, pushed open a window and searched the darkness outside.

He told Larry the creek was just a few yards below.

"Drop down and you can follow the creek back into the faculty grove. From there you walk out. Go! Now! I'm right behind you."

Larry shimmied through the window's flat narrow opening, fell to the ground and was gone. Raj pushed his head and shoulders through the opening and grabbed the outside window frame to pull himself out. A bright beacon momentarily blinded him.

"There's one!" a voice yelled.

Raj looked up to see two cops charging down from a hill above the creek. He pulled himself back into the dark room and slithered across the floor and through the office doorway as the cops' searching flashlight beams spun across the walls. Raj hurried toward a rear door blocked by a desk and several chairs. Upstairs he heard a cluster of successive crashes at the building's entrance while Peter led the occupants in a version of an old civil rights song. *We will, we will not be moved. Like a tree planted by the water, we will not budge an inch.*

Raj searched the hall for another exit and found instead a windowless closet, its door half-open. He walked inside where brooms and buckets shared the small space with a short filing cabinet. Floor-to-ceiling shelves were loaded with paper towels, cleaners and what appeared to be a hundred rolls of toilet paper.

He looked at the door handle and saw that it locked from inside. He pressed the lock button, closed the door behind him and turned off the light. He waited.

He could hear the muffled shouts of the protesters as police entered the building and surrounded them. He heard cops march down the stairs and roam the basement halls looking for protesters. One tried the closet door handle and Raj watched the door shake against the thin outline of hall light seeping under the crack. The cop used a flashlight to look through the slanted bars of an air vent but could see nothing.

"Utility closet," he heard the cop say to another cop.

The voices moved away and into adjacent offices. Raj stood silently, exhausted by two days of revolution and desperate to close his eyes in the darkened room. He heard the cops ascend the stairs. He peed into one of the mop buckets and dropped to sit on the floor. He waited. Why had he done this? Because he believed in the Movement though there was still much of its history he did not know and too many of its tactics he did not fully grasp. Every belief was a belief that fell short and he wondered if he already knew too much to continue believing. Raj pulled rolls of toilet paper from the shelf, assembled them as a pillow in a tight corner of the closet, stretched out as best he could and fell asleep.

In a dream someone sang to Raj from the middle of the universe and he struggled to hear, his arms and legs locked in a confining stillness. He ached. He still heard words but they no longer sang.

"What a fucking mess. Did this really happen?"

It was a woman's voice. He opened his eyes in the darkness. His arms and legs ached from sleeping weirdly on the floor. The words came from outside the closet, which Raj reminded himself still hid him from a curious and dangerous world. He waited for more words and more women spoke.

"Do we get any help with this?" one asked.

"Admin is supposed to have a crew here this afternoon to get the furniture moved back and figure the damage."

It was the voice of a younger male.

"We need to find what's left. What were these kids thinking?"

Raj waited for a period of sustained quiet before creeping to the door and opening it barely enough to blind him with the corridor's indirect daylight. He was able to peek in one direction to see the empty hall and hear voices in adjacent offices. He opened the door another inch and saw that his path to the stairs was clear. Raj slipped out of the closet, closed the door quietly and walked rapidly down the hall, trying very hard not to run.

A middle-aged woman in a wool suit walked out of an office and collided with him.

"Who are you?" she asked while searching his face. "I don't think I know you."

Raj saw in her eyes the incipient trauma of an incident that would color every subsequent encounter with sinister conclusions.

"I'm looking for Dean Reynolds," said Raj.

"Dean who?" the woman asked, thrown off by Raj's mention of a dean.

"I don't know a Dean Reynolds. How did you get in here?"

Raj ignored the question.

"Maybe I'm in the wrong building," he said and walked toward the hall's outdoor exit where two men were pushing a large desk away from the door.

"Let me help you," Raj said to the men and without waiting grasped a corner of the desk and shoved it hard to clear a path to the outside door, which he immediately pushed open.

"There. Open for business," he said as he glanced back at the mistrustful woman and then stepped outside and walked casually away along a path that passed a campus police car parked at what appeared to be one of the building's checkpoints. An officer emerged from the car and saw Raj who smiled and waved and continued toward the bridge that crossed into the faculty grove.

Raj did not look back until, at the crest of a hill, he merged with a clique of students entering the anthropology building. He stood at a lobby window to assure himself he was not followed, that he was not a doomed loser who, whenever he died, would also lose whatever was lost.

Raj sat at a table in the Café Trieste. Curtis Mayfield's *Darker than Blue* played on the café hi-fi. Raj felt futile, unsure, even pathetic. He wanted to smoke a joint. He had for two days since his escape from Moses Hall. Now he waited in North Beach to meet Sonia whom he assumed was at that moment somewhere down Grant Avenue in Chinatown buying a hundred pounds of rice. He had offered to help her but she never responded. His presence in the café was itself an assumption she would know to walk north on Grant Avenue from wherever she was and thereby arrive at the café where he waited.

From the anxiety that grew his unconfirmed assumptions, Raj rehearsed responses to a variety of outcomes. Sonia would enter the café and apologize for being late, whatever late was. He would smile and obsequiously forgive her. She would phone the café to say she was late or needed directions. She would ask for him but would the woman at the counter recognize him from Sonia's description? He would go to the counter and introduce himself. Or Sonia wouldn't show up at all and tomorrow he would find a letter from her in his mailbox canceling her trip. He would write to her again. Or there would be no Sonia, no letter, nothing. He searched his mind again for the facts of a proposed experience-in-waiting, acutely aware he had no confirmation it was intended to happen.

Was the woman he waited for real? He still wanted a joint. He didn't miss taking acid but being mildly stoned would be welcome now. He was still addicted to weed and to the ritual of smelling, rolling and smoking as much as to the buzz it gave him. Enough time had passed for him to understand how he wasn't served by the dope's provision of faulty attention to the facts of his life, though the details became more colorful and riveting while also meaningless to anyone but himself.

Was she late? He might have arrived late but there was no late. There was no set time but afternoon, a word that vaguely defined the hours between noon and six, which he was barely halfway into occupying. Raj went to the counter to order another coffee and looked out the window across Vallejo Street.

He saw her. She had crossed at the corner and passed the café. He might have missed her but for her long, yellow hair and large-rimmed glasses. She wore a dress, granny style in a deep blue print that fell to her ankles and fluttered as she took long steps through the intersection. He had never before seen her in a dress.

"Sonia!"

Raj yelled from the café's entrance.

Sonia turned, smiled and waved.

"Am I late?" Sonia asked as Raj escorted her to his table. Her few words quashed all his anxious theories. He was glad he wasn't stoned.

"No," Raj answered. "Did you get your rice?"

Sonia had her rice. Short grain brown rice. The merchant's son loaded the 100-pound bag into her VW. She parked in the garage at Portsmouth Square and walked back to Grant.

"So here I am," she said.

"That's a beautiful fabric," Raj said. "The dress. It brings out the blue color in your eyes."

It was a prerogative of attraction to make someone wait. Raj willingly complied by being attracted. Sonia was real. He had wondered for some time and now he knew.

Was she hungry? Was she tired? Would she like to have dinner? See a movie?

Sonia said she did not care. Her work was finished; she had the night ahead and was staying with a high school friend who lived on Clayton in the Haight and didn't care when she returned.

"Have you seen *2001*?" Raj asked.

Sonia had not, but heard it was a brilliant, mysterious film.

A plan took shape. They would go to a theater on Market to see the movie, hike back to North Beach for dinner and then walk to Portsmouth to get her car.

"Is that too much walking?" Raj asked solicitously.

"I'm a mountain woman," Sonia said. "Are you serious?"

They were among a handful attending the late afternoon matinee. The film had been out for months and Raj saw it in the spring while stoned on acid. Its opening scenes of a screaming monolith appearing before pre-hominid primates, a 2001 space journey to Jupiter, the rebellion of HAL the spaceship computer, and the concluding scenes of mysteriously compressed time, death and rebirth—all orchestrated with classical themes by Johann and Richard Strauss—had left Raj frightened, thrilled and annoyingly flummoxed. Sonia watched the film while Raj watched her. Would she like it? Her eyes roamed the screen, searching out clues to the film's enigmatic and suggestive themes.

"It was an odd story and I don't think I fully get it," she told Raj over dinner. "I guess that's why it's called an odyssey. It's a personal journey so it will always be open to anyone's interpretation."

She shouted over the din of the tavern where they shared a calzone and drank glasses of red wine.

While walking with her and viewing the film, Raj had seen Sonia almost exclusively from the side. Now she faced him with her rosy cheeks and bright, inquiring eyes. Her voice rose and fell mellifluously and her hair was longer and thicker than Raj remembered. Her large glasses drew his attention to her aqua eyes, creating the appearance of an assessing intellect. Her arms were smooth though muscular and she moved them as she spoke with an elegant, athletic grace.

"We can describe the universe," she said after Raj proposed the idea that the movie contained a suggestion that time did not really exist.

"But all our descriptions are just ignorant guesses. I don't know what Kubrick is trying to do, but the meanings we give to the stars are loaded with human purpose and intention. The cosmos is really just a bunch of bubbles. Some create life and some don't."

Raj heard her thought and shared his own.

"What I wondered after seeing this movie was whether a universe that produces self-awareness is itself aware of anything. Is the rebirth a fantasy or a reincarnation? Weird."

"Yeah," agreed Sonia. "Very weird."

Words built a bridge of the spoken and unspoken and returned them to their peculiar dance of hope and expectation.

Walking back to the square, Sonia reached to hold and squeeze Raj's hand. It was nearly a lover's question that asked his skin to reply. He reacted quickly with his own subtle and clandestine touch, and threw his arm briefly over her shoulders. In a festival of corroborating words they stammered their way into a weekend plan. She would come over Saturday to visit for the day and stay for

Inger's performance and Ginger and Stan's party. They would have Sunday together before Sonia drove back to Mt. Shasta on Monday.

"I am so happy to see you again," Sonia said as she drove up to the East Bay bus terminal to drop Raj off. He leaned over to give her a kiss, which she deftly deflected with a huge, locking embrace.

"Tomorrow," she said, as if making a promise.

It was enough. Any touch, any word, anything like a promise whether real or imagined was all Raj needed to believe in the future. He slipped out of the car seat and waved again as Sonia's VW chugged through its shifting gears up Mission Street.

"We agreed it wasn't going to work out," Sonia said as she walked the trail's single track behind Raj.

Sonia had moved out of Loren's cabin. It was news Raj expected but not in this way. As they approached Grizzly Peak he pointed toward the small meadow where he spent his nights in the park.

"Where are you living now?" Raj asked.

"Mother Mary gave me a room in the Inn," said Sonia. "I help out in the dining room. I can stay until the tourist season starts. Late April. Then it will be warm enough to sleep on the mountain."

They reached the summit as Sonia looked in all directions and extolled the view.

"So much woodland so close to a big city. I didn't believe this was possible."

They sat aligned on a boulder to again look outward though as in the theater Raj watched Sonia's gaze from the side, her eyes sprinting from the hills to the bay to the bridges beyond and toward the mountains of clouds moving across the City's rising architecture.

"Rain tomorrow," Raj said.

He took her for dinner to an Italian beer garden on the north side of campus where one glass and then another loosened torrents of words. Each rubbed their language against the other with no end in sight. He was a Sagittarius and she a Taurus for which he knew the signs and she knew the meanings. He told her about his new attention to the Movement and his new job at Moe's. He did not mention his arrest or upcoming day in court.

She described her autumn on the mountain and the end of what she called her friendship with Loren. Raj heard a loss deeper than Sonia would fully reveal. She was open to thinking about a new direction but wanted at least another few seasons on the mountain.

"No other place has ever given me such freedom to live within myself."

She said this with a solemnity and assertion that was beyond mere commentary and more like a prayer.

Sonia stifled a laugh when the naked actor wearing a wig and horns stormed onto the stage holding a fat four-foot long cardboard penis, it's tip the bulb of an inflated red balloon. He waved it as if it were his own and staggered menacingly toward the invited audience of less than thirty gathered to view a play that was bawdy, raucous, and utterly unintelligible. The tall, muscular satyr huffed and roared until Inger walked onto the stage, completely nude but for threads of shiny tinsel running through her hair.

A chase ensued with the phallus-burdened satyr pursuing Inger as other characters emerged, one in a police uniform and others in white robes that, too, were eventually removed. Inger ended up at the middle of the stage and spoke a phrase in German before collapsing forward to the floor where others gathered around her as the satyr dropped his phallus and also fell.

The one-act piece had more the feeling and short length of a Fluxus happening than a theatrical production and, as Inger said later, Picasso had never intended the play to be performed.

"Martin always wanted to direct it," she said later at Stan and Ginger's party when Raj introduced her to Sonia.

"Inger lives with Martin," Raj told Sonia.

"We share a house," Inger clarified emphatically. "We're roommates."

Stan had painted the play's expressionist set and built the phallus that, with all the laughing it produced, might have been the play's real star. It was the weekend before Halloween and several party guests wore costumes. Ginger dressed as a flapper in a short, fringed dress while Lila followed wearing a cape and fairy wings as her mother served drinks. Sonia appeared relaxed among Raj's friends, including Larry who arrived in a George Wallace mask and Mack, who promised Inger he would write a review.

"You have nice friends," Sonia told Raj as the need for introductions faded. "There are so many of them."

They left the party and walked back to Raj's room where Sonia had changed her clothes for the show. There was an accidental touch that did not feel like an accident. How quickly things happened was a surprise to them both, or at least Sonia said she was surprised when they finally caught their breaths and realized they hadn't closed the door. Raj understood how bodies find their ways but presumed nothing until soft, warm, downy Sonia was against him and, in a lovely and practical way, expressed her desire.

"We can't screw," she said.

She was ovulating and did not take birth control pills. She had not been with a man since high school. Raj understood as Sonia suspected he would. Their interests coalesced around touch and not insertion. The pleasure was deep, intense and, at one affiliating juncture of openings, momentarily whimsical.

Sunday began with a breakfast at the Forum where plans formed, even if they seemed fantastic and premature. Raj wanted Sonia and wished to go with her. They would need to see each other again and soon.

"I want this to last," she said as they took a final walk through the campus.

Raj knew their bond in the mountains was now the central fact of his life in a city. He believed in a certain kind of fate. She said she was ready to have what was in front of her now. He said goodbye in the rain, her car chugging off again to leave him waiting for the next point of tender entry, the streets shiny and prismatic as a dry and hard old world melted away.

ten

"We've had a problem on Telegraph for a long time, your honor," said the assistant district attorney. "We believe the accused is a major drug dealer and the people argue for a large fine now and a jail sentence should he violate the terms of

260

parole. It is his first arrest and we want it to be his last."

Raj stood before the judge as directed by his attorney who led him to believe it would be a routine pleading that would at last set him free. As the courtroom filled behind him, Raj began to have second thoughts. *Don't' say anything,* his attorney told him. *No matter what happens, don't say anything.*

"Your honor," Rick responded. "The DA has expressed a willingness to resolve this case fairly. My client is prepared to plead to misdemeanor possession of a controlled substance, even though the marijuana found at his residence was not his. He is not a dealer and is gainfully employed. He wishes to get on with his life."

"Where do you work?" the judge asked Raj who looked at Rick for some clue.

"He is employed in the book trade and recently accepted a full-time position with a local book seller."

"What fine are you considering?" the judge asked the assistant DA.

"The people would accept a fine of $600," he responded.

"Your honor, that's what they took from my client when they arrested him," Rick shouted. "He keeps his income in his home because he doesn't have a bank account. That hardly seems fair or even warranted, under the circumstances."

The judge leaned forward and looked into Raj's eyes.

"Put your earnings in the bank," she said. "It's safer and you'll earn some interest."

"Yes, your honor," Raj answered.

The judge looked out at the crowded courtroom. She appeared dauntingly tired. Her black robe accentuated the dark bags under her eyes, a striking contrast with the brilliant highlights she had washed that morning into her long, tawny hair.

"Already 10:30?" she said to the assistant DA. "Let's get moving. The court accepts the plea by the accused and imposes a $150 fine for misdemeanor possession of a controlled substance. The accused will serve two years of summary probation."

She dropped her gavel hard against the bench.

"Next case," she shouted as the courtroom broke into a babbling river of voices while benches emptied, people shuffled about, and

Raj was grabbed by his attorney and pulled from the courtroom.

Without his birth there would have been no error and as his attorney led Raj to the ground floor of the courthouse Raj accepted his life as something purely contingent. He was no longer in himself as much as he was for himself. He had been held and punitively identified. But he was still free and always free, even if he were to be sentenced to confinement in a six by eight foot cell. Things in his life were either hostile or useful and, despite his fear of capture or confinement, he was separated from nothing. Acceptance was a tool and adversity the chore.

"Sign here twice," the court clerk said through a window as he handed Raj a form describing his conviction and listing the terms of his sentence. The clerk prepared to return Raj's moneybox to him and asked conveniently if he wished to pay his fine now or make arrangements.

"Pay it," Rick said.

As they left the courthouse, Rick asked Raj to pay him.

"Two-fifty," he said. "You're a free man."

Raj sorted through his box, counting again the money he had left.

"Well, sort of," he answered. "I'm free. But I'm still a convict."

Rick stood by as Raj counted out the bills.

"Technically," Rick said. "In five years you can have the arrest expunged. That is, if you don't get arrested again. I don't advise it."

The attorney laughed while Raj handed him cash.

The world was misleading though as one of its products Raj had no room to complain about being misled. He tried to understand what room was left for him to move about. What had changed? He wasn't taking acid anymore. His feet were on the ground, even if they were for the moment uncomfortably shackled. His brush with an enemy was the right fight for the wrong reason. Cops were in his sights but not in his way. Not yet.

He hoped to break their hold on his community without again breaking the law. He hoped also eventually and inevitably to run to Sonia and the mountain. He was prepared to fight, even as he planned his escape.

Raj thought himself diminished by his conviction as he delved into the condition of human existence. No one else at Bronwyn's table appeared to share his sentiment. Peter and the others arrested the previous week spoke with defiant pride, as if their capture and confinement by a tyrannizing force was actually a crucial victory. The next step would be a strike.

"We have them where we want them," Peter said. "Students are on our side, not to mention the faculty. It is time. A strike is starting at State. Why not here?"

"Well, not so fast," said Larry. "We got the ASUC board but do we really have the students? And the faculty? Moses Hall is gettin' some bad press. Y'all trashed the joint. How do the professors support that? Columbia just don't resonate with these guys. They support resistance but not vandalism, especially when it's their offices being vandalized."

"The proletariat will rise," Peter said again. "Workers have had enough."

"Yeah, workers," Larry said. "You mean students? Rich ass students whose parents can afford both bail and tuition? You fuckin' with me? Show me the goddamned Berkeley proletariat. Most are black and they sure as hell aren't UC students. Hell, even Tom Hayden snuck outta Moses Hall."

"It's working at State," Peter shouted. "Third World Studies or the campus shuts down. "

"And we'll be there," Bronwyn interjected, using her parliamentary experience to seize back the table.

"We do need to mobilize. We're up against Reagan and the cops and who knows, maybe the FBI. Soldiers could be next. No, we're not fighting from a position of strength. But that doesn't mean we shouldn't fight."

Small, vigorous Bronwyn held her own, a woman of her word who thought all human experience was a political choice in the making. She let the men rant and rage until at some point of exasperation she took control with a mindful, deft touch, repeating again and again the goals of revolution and the principles needed to achieve them. Her father, a respected scholar and communist, articulated a glorious Hegelian synthesis that had yet to occur. It was offered on the menu of revolutionary objectives as a tasty and promising steak. And Bronwyn had been raised and trained to sell the sizzle.

"So you got out OK."

Raj nodded.

Larry was half way through a schooner that Raj had bought him at Kip's.

"Y'know, this sposed to be about blacks and chicanos and minorities," said Larry. "American minorities, which is everybody that ain't white. And yet a bunch a white people makes all the choices right now. Even Eldridge thinks that's cool. He's runnin' for President on the Peace and Freedom ticket. Why we doin' this?"

"Yeah," Raj said through the haze of his mild drunk, his schooner nearly empty. "Yeah, that's weird and yeah, I got out OK after spending the night in a broom closet."

He told Larry about his close call in Moses Hall and then moved on to Sonia and the mountain and his desire to leave the city and live in the green meadows near tree line.

"You can do that?" Larry asked.

"Maybe. I need more money, more time, more freedom. I've been reading the poets. Even threw the I Ching. I'm stuck between some kind of stagnation and the promise of progress. Winter and spring. Art and fear. One line I read said it all—the great depart and the petty arrive."

"You white folks always have the freedom and the time and the money," Larry said. "And when you white guys get weird, I gotta tell ya', it scares the hell out of us black folks 'cause we never know why and don't have time to get out a the way. Whoever departs and whoever arrives? Don't matter much to us. We usually don't get a say."

Raj sat on his day bed and counted his money. He had less than $200 left in his moneybox. Were he to sell the kilos, he might have as much as $1200, more than enough to get to Mt. Shasta and live for a year. Selling the kilos was crucial if he wanted the freedom to leave. Yet he was to start a job on Friday that would pay him more than $60 a week, that appeared secure, and that would allow him to continue to live in the snug, uproarious bohemia that had been his home for a decade. Two choices, each burdened with equal amounts of progress or stagnation. He wanted to see Sonia again and had built his escape around their quick and immediate attraction.

She did not expect him. She was for now devoted to living on a mountain. How could she abide his uncertainties and hopes? He needed more time. He wished for the immediate passing of a year in a way that would allow him to awaken another day to the certainty of Sonia. Progress without stagnation, even as he registered the moments, days, weeks, months and years that would be needed to accumulate and describe the terms of any lasting intimacy. In a certain way, to run toward Sonia was to flee the pain of his new and modern life. To successfully flee himself.

"Your people still interested?" Raj asked.

"Fuck yeah," answered Percy, who looked like a student in his blue jeans and grey sweatshirt. He sipped his coffee.

"So how does this happen?" asked Raj as he reflexively searched the Forum's tables for suspicious eavesdroppers.

"An empty warehouse on south Sixth. You and I meet. I bring the money and you bring the keys. They're offering $800."

"Shit. Not enough," answered Raj.

"Really? What else your busted friend gonna do with this shit? My people are good for it. Cash, man. They trust me, which is more than I can say about you."

Raj recalled another line from his I Ching reading. *No worry about gain or loss. Have faith in ultimate success.*

"Give me a couple of days. I need to set this up. Just the two of us, right? No one else involved? I give you the dope and you give me the money."

"Hell, yes," Percy said eagerly. "Hell, yes."

"I think I can unload my kilos," Raj said to Yitzhak who walked with him across a large meadow adjacent to Tilden Park's snug swimming lake. The weather was warm but the lake was empty.

"I'd like your help, if you think you can do it."

Yitzhak nodded in stoic silence.

"I need you to drive me to a warehouse in West Berkeley. You won't have to go in. Just wait for me."

Yitzhak nodded again.

"You OK?" Raj asked. "You haven't said shit."

"Yeah," Yitzhak said. "Just trippin'. Going to Hawaii in a few weeks. Navy business. There's work to be done."

"Navy?" asked Raj. "Whose navy?"

"It's a secret," Yitzhak answered. "I can't talk about it."

"Really?" Raj asked again.

Raj could see Yitzhak's discomfort; as if his friend had revealed a perplexity about himself he wanted no one to know.

"I'll phone when I have the time and place," Raj said. "Later in the week."

"Sure," said Yitzhak as he stared vacantly into a copse of trees.

Raj arose the next morning from a dream of conspiring terrors that left him choking on an occlusive scream. He had been sentenced to wipe and sweep the floor of a jail before his scheduled hanging. His panicked strategy in the dream was to keep finding stains and particles of dirt as a way to prolong his life while he planned an impossible escape. He argued with his jailers over the miniscule size of tiny blemishes and the presence of barely existent dirt.

The liberating loophole arrived with an abrupt awakening. As he trolled his memory for meaning, his mind wandered into an acid flashback. Every thought was a draining omen. He could draw lines in space and open doors with his telepathy. He recalled a tree in the forest that suddenly began to move, sporting a living face and eyes formed from the creases of its bark that sparkled with an expression of both kindness and ridicule.

He was separated and linked in a kind of psychic karate. He could see inside and outside simultaneously. In the mirror he saw flames shooting up from the top of his head. He sat back on his bed and attempted to calm the fluent, saturating energy of psychedelic perception. *A dream already ended*, wrote the poet. *The world cannot deny the truth with its intuitive mind.*

"She'll be here for a while," Harriet said while nodding over the dinner table toward Inger who responded with a tight smile.

"Dad's met her and he's fine with it. And whatever suits Dad suits mom. Larry loaded his truck and moved Inger's stuff up here yesterday."

Harriet's parents were out for the evening and the women and Raj ate in the kitchen rather than the dining room. The kitchen's bright, austere interior advertised an expensively acquired modernity of white walls and subtle shelving built along clean lines of utility and sight. A window at the kitchen's farthest wall opened to a view of trees and stars.

"It's generous of Harriet," Inger acknowledged gratefully though Raj sensed something else at work behind her wild, glaring eyes.

"What happened with the place on Garber?" Raj asked.

It was an impudent question. Raj was an invited dinner guest. He had seen Harriet and Inger at the Forum. Harriet asked him to come to her family home for supper. He had climbed the paths through Codornices Park, walked along La Loma and taken the steps to Campus Drive where Harriet lived in the house she had occupied for most of her life. Raj had his own good news but was not invited to share. Instead, he heard over dinner the latest about Inger and her new and not surprising transience.

"Martin's cool," answered Inger. "It just wasn't working out to live together."

She fucked him, Raj thought. *She fucks everybody.*

It was not judgmental but his visualization of Inger and her legs spread wide under the humping thrusts of her landlord helped Raj to understand the resolution of Inger's latest crisis. Few men who fucked Inger could live with her freewheeling attitude. She loved sex but loathed the sexual pressure most men applied in an effort to pin her to the fulfillment of their perpetual and puerile dependencies. Raj was a puer. He had never grown up but he never asked anyone for obedience. He was his own fool, as Inger was hers. It was their common experience and why they were still friends.

Harriet had her own hang-ups, but they weren't Inger's. Harriet appeared inexperienced and guarded, a sensitive intellectual who engaged analysis as her primary life filter, though Raj thought her unusually emotional for a scholar or what he thought a scholar should be. The two women could have been sisters, each the mirror opposite of the other but in a way that united them. Little wonder to Raj that Harriet's father would welcome sexy Inger.

"Still working?" Raj asked Inger.

"Good hours and big tips," Inger replied. "But I'd like to do more theater, even though it doesn't pay jack shit. Always the problem. Porn and posing nude pay big money but art pays nothing."

Raj looked at Harriet, as if the revelation of Inger's secret life as a nude model and topless waitress might get her evicted from her proper new home in the hills.

"It's OK," Inger said. "Not much Harriet doesn't know about me. And not much I don't know about Harriet."

Inger winked and Harriet blushed.

"Pasta was excellent," Raj said as Inger jumped up to clear the table.

Though she made the dinner, Harriet had barely touched the food on her plate.

"Not hungry?" asked Raj.

"I snack a lot while I cook."

Harriet's answer had the tone of a rebuttal.

Inger offered to do the dishes. Taking quick charge of the chores of others made Inger a welcome guest.

"I'm making a move myself," Raj said to Harriet. "I'm going away."

"Where?" she asked. "When?"

Raj skipped from La Loma down the short flight of Rose Steps, a hill path that brought him to Vine Lane and then to the path across Hearst Street and finally into the tree-shrouded groves of the north campus. He had said too much. He wasn't prepared for the questions that would fly once he confessed his plan to run away. Harriet could not understand how someone lived on a mountain. Inger quizzed him skeptically, as if to titrate from his spoken dreams the ounce or two of truth that might survive.

"Does she know you're coming?" Inger asked.

"No," Raj said. "It doesn't matter."

"It might matter to her," Inger cautioned in a way that framed an unconsidered and fearful wrinkle but without any tone of personal concern. Inger expressed little interest in Raj's plan, other than to locate its flaws. She had her own fearful wrinkles to navigate.

Of course, he would surprise Sonia. It was essential to the brilliant magic of his journey. It was the poetry that drove all other considerations, which included the sale of his kilos, finding a ride north, packing what he could take while leaving the rest in his room (paid up through November), and how he would arrange for Yitzhak to bring him those things later. He would tell Bronwyn on Wednesday that he was leaving, and then stop by Moe's to say he could not take the job. The prospect of a new life was a dream but certainly not a delusion. *Abandon pride of life and you will be as free as water to flow to the dream.* The poet spoke to him again. He was confident of his power and certain of his good intentions.

It was Election Day. Raj took the trouble to appear at his precinct and vote before selling his kilos. The deal would go down at noon. Percy would meet him at the abandoned warehouse west of Sixth and near the train tracks. Yitzhak drove his bomber down Hopkins Street while Raj sat in the passenger seat, hiding between his legs a green backpack containing more than six pounds of primo Mexican weed.

Why was the warehouse abandoned? It was a question that emerged subliminally as Yitzhak approached the block where the building stood like a shabby, grey fortress of neglect. We could have done this at a café.

"A side door is supposed to be open," Raj said. He asked Yitzhak to park around the corner at the end of the block.

"When you see me come out, start the car," Raj said.

It would be a quick exchange and Raj anticipated holding a fistful of bills and being rid forever of the burden of dope. What could go wrong? Anything and nothing. Raj had never done a deal like this and had only Percy's word that the terms of their negotiation would also be the terms of their mutual survival.

Raj walked toward the warehouse carrying the backpack. The side door opened for him, extended by Percy who had arrived early.

"Over here," Percy said to Raj as he walked him to a large

storage space furnished with a card table and two chairs. Within minutes the transaction began with Percy smelling a slice from one of the bricks, feeling it with his fingers, and spreading it out to gauge the proportions of seeds and stems to dry leaf.

"You got the cash?" Raj asked nervously.

"Hell yes, mothafuckah," said Percy, his obscenity intended as a respectful, if hostile, attribution appropriate to the business at hand. However a deal was made, its dealers were in all ways adversaries and connected only by mutual greed.

Percy pulled a wad of bills from his coat. It took less than a minute for him to count the bills out into a short stack at a corner of the table. Raj's last view of the balance of this transaction, the terms of a briefly secured equal footing, were in front of him: a pile of cash, the now settled market value of the three kilos, and the kilos themselves assembled in an impressive stack next to the money. It was for a moment a sublimely structured equivalence.

Until the door burst open and three men wearing ski masks entered to point handguns at Percy and Raj.

"What the fuck?" Percy shouted. "That you, Jackson? What the fuck you doin'?"

The largest man approached the table while his two companions stood near the door.

"Looks like a deal right here in the one empty warehouse on Sixth Street. What a fuckin' coincidence."

"C'mon. That you Jackson?" Percy asked again. "What the goddamned fuck you doin'? This ain't your shit. This ain't your money. This ain't none of you goddamned business."

"Well, it is now," the large man answered as he picked up the bills and swept up a pinch from Percy's weed sample and held it briefly under his nose.

"Percy, you disappoint me," the large man said through his black ski mask. "You should know better. You know nothin' happens down here without me knowin' bout it."

He ordered Percy and Raj to the floor.

"Lie the fuck down," the large man ordered.

"Better do it," Percy whispered to Raj.

Percy and Raj dropped to the floor and spread out on their

bellies, arms extended and legs spread apart.

"Percy, we're takin' this stuff—but we got a problem," the large man said again.

"You think you know me. That sure as hell ain't good. No one knows me. I'm afraid we're not going to able to let you leave."

"What you talkin' about?" Percy shouted frantically. "You gonna shoot us?"

Percy tried to stand but was pushed back down by one of the large man's accomplices who took a rope from his pocket and began to tie Percy's hands behind his back.

"Goddamn you!" Percy shouted. "You can't kill us…an for what? Less than a grand and six pounds of fuckin' pot?"

"People 'round here have died for less," said the large man.

Raj strained from his prone surrender on the floor to see that the side door was open some twenty feet in front of him and that the large man's accomplices had abandoned it to tie up him and Percy.

"Go for it!" Percy yelled at Raj.

Raj rolled forward, crawled frantically to his feet and charged the open door. In a moment he was outside, the sound of two gunshots immediately behind him.

He ran the length of the block and dove into the front seat of Yitzhak's waiting bomber.

"Drive!" Raj shouted while he curled into a protective fetal posture in which he experienced a realization already ended before it began. Illusion was a universal phantom and he a mere mendicant. But Raj was still alive and farther from death the faster Yitzhak drove.

eleven

Raj thought himself and all people to be inconsequential and degraded. The trauma of his busted deal, the threat of death and the uncertainty of Percy's fate, reduced Raj to a whimper of feckless defiance. He was lost now. No money or kilos to leverage a new life. No capacity and no justice. Raj spent all day Wednesday in his room, waiting for the drop of another shoe though there were no shoes left to fall. Was Percy dead? Should Raj call the police? And why? To report the theft of his kilos?

Raj ventured out in the evening. He walked into Kips and ordered a beer. He saw on the bar's TV that Nixon was the president-elect. It was a close election but only because Wallace took the South. The election was his country's profound and disgusting distraction and Raj might have picked a thousand pockets and disappeared from view without anyone even noticing.

Instead, he fell into line. He would work for Moe. He would write to Sonia and not surprise here. He would pay his rent and live in Berkeley, at least into spring or until he had enough money and courage to try again to leave. Would Sonia ever come to Berkeley to be with him? He wanted to know but understood it was too soon to ask.

Raj's first day working at Moe's was a revelation. He needed to learn a new system for shelving books, which was a challenge since Creed's had no system. He could operate the register and found the newly opened used records section a haven of glorious sound. Vintage folk, old blues, rock 'n' roll of all kinds, classics from Vanguard and Nonesuch, and the smattering of collector's jewels, including 78s from the eras of ragtime through swing. Moe and the management noted quickly Raj's acuity and interest in music and six of his hours were assigned to sorting and pricing albums.

Raj looked through every newspaper for some report of the presumed violence of his aborted deal on Sixth Street. He searched for days and found nothing. He thought to ask Mack again but decided against raising another suspicious flag, even with a good friend.

His second afternoon after work Raj walked to Civic Center Park to support an evening rally against the war. The Provos served free soup and bread. Country Joe and the Fish appeared for a half-hour set. The usual speakers: Peter, Mario, Bronwyn and Michael shouted their epithets of opposition to war while a festive and much more laid back crowd listened, cheered and partied.

As the sun fell behind city hall it cast seasonally steep shadows across the park lawn and toward the empty fountain where Raj saw Percy, dressed in his slick, tidy suit. Percy was engaged in some kind of transaction. Raj watched Percy pull from his checkered coat's inside pocket a plastic bag filled with yellow-green weed. Percy handed the bag furtively to a young man from whom he took a wad of bills that he then stuffed into the side pocket of his coat.

"You dealin'?" Raj asked as he approached Percy from behind.

The nappy dealer swiveled on his hips before dropping into a defensive crouch.

"What the hell you afraid of?" Raj shouted. "Bet you have some good dope. Would you sell me some? Where's it from? Don't tell me—it's pure gold from the Sierra Madre."

"I thought you were leavin' town," Percy growled at Raj.

"Well, I can't leave now," Raj said. "Someone ripped me off. Do you know who'd do somethin' like that?"

"Sorry, man," said Percy as he feigned a withering helplessness. "I didn't know we'd get hustled."

"You don't look hustled to me," said Raj. "You look more like a hustler."

"Well, what you gonna do, you dumb Ofay?" Percy asked at last and with a rawness that implied the outcome of the kilo sale should never have been a surprise.

"What the hell you gonna do? Call the cops?"

Raj tried to look through Percy with some purposeful hope he might become suddenly transparent and collapse in shame. Instead, Percy glared while Raj succumbed to his own illusions. A sad vision of the truthful world would take millennia to change.

Raj was not destroyed. Instead he had been rendered a reject, his dream of a liberating escape shelved for lack of resourceful caution. He blamed himself as he stood beside Moe's cash register, thinking his naive mistakes apparent to everyone he saw.

"I thought you were leaving."

Raj heard Harriet's voice and turned to see her at the end of the counter. Raj shuffled down to where she stood. He felt from her an expectation he would not be able to satisfy, even with the truth.

"Long story," Raj said.

Harriet looked briefly askance.

"Is there a problem?" Harriet asked. "You in some trouble?"

Raj noticed a police car parked outside on the Avenue. He recognized the detective climbing out on the passenger side as one of the investigators in his case. He was dressed in a business jacket and black slacks. A uniformed officer remained at the wheel. The detective entered the store and approached Raj.

So this is it, Raj thought. *The final humiliation. I lose my kilos and still get busted.*

He nearly thrust his arms out to be handcuffed and led away.

The detective approached him.

"I'm here to get snatch," the officer said to Raj.

Raj froze. He looked over at Harriet and back at the detective.

"You want what?" Raj asked.

"Snatch," the man said again. "Where is it?"

The detective did not seem to recognize Raj and spoke only at him.

Raj tried to process the detective's request.

Is this guy joking? Is this some fucking test? Like he's looking for what? For pussy?

"Snatch?" Raj asked vacantly.

"Yeah," the suited man said again. "The comic. Snatch. Where is it?"

Raj got it. The detective wanted to buy the latest R. Crumb comic book.

"All the way to the back," Raj said. "Comics are in a small hall on the right."

Raj watched him carefully while Harriet stood by.

The detective returned with a copy of *Snatch* and purchased it. Raj rang up the sale.

"Is that all?" Raj asked.

"No," said the detective. "Is the owner here?"

"Just a minute," Raj answered and walked back into the bookstore office where Moe was unpacking periodicals.

"Someone to see you," Raj said. "He just bought a copy of *Snatch*. He's not in a uniform but I think he's a cop."

Moe looked up.

"*Snatch*, eh? OK, I'm coming."

Moe walked out to the counter where the officer from the car had joined the detective.

"What do you want?" Moe asked.

The detective reached into his pocket and drew out a badge.

"I'm detective James Kelly of the Berkeley Police Department. I'm arresting you for the sale of an obscene publication. "

"Obscene what?" Moe asked angrily. "This is pretty obscene. Have you guys read the First Amendment?"

The detective ignored Moe's question as two more officers entered the bookstore. Moe was handcuffed and led out to the car while the detective and officers walked past the counter. Raj watched as they scooped up stacks of comic books, and then searched shelves for other books or periodicals they determined were obscene.

"Have Lou phone my attorney," Moe shouted at Raj as he was pushed out the front door and led to a waiting police car.

"Can they do that?" Harriet asked.

"They just did," said Raj who reached for the phone to call Lou.

"Would you ever consider going back to school?" Harriet asked Raj as he took a bite of Egg Foo Yung.

Robbie's was nearly empty but it was the only open Avenue cafeteria after Raj got off work. Harriet offered to meet him and get him dinner, though she ordered nothing for herself.

"Ate earlier," she said.

"It might be nice if I weren't involved in something else," Raj said after chewing his bite. He had been a dilettante all his adult life and college was a particularly wicked gantlet for his easily distracted attention.

I'd be gone by now if I hadn't made a foolish mistake," he said.

"What was that?" asked Harriet.

"I squandered a chance to run away," he said. "I was made blind by a deep desire. I should have known that there is no desire without prohibition."

"You've lost me," Harriet said. "I thought you were in love. That you had a plan."

"I'm still in love," Raj said. "I just don't have a plan right now. What I have is a plan to make a plan and that's as far as I've gotten."

It was easier for Raj to say this than to admit that every plan he might make grew from a potential hallucination. Ideas swarmed in a way that reminded him of his experiences with acid. Withdrawal, travel, sacrifice, battle, appetite, and ultimately separation and even suicide loomed equally as potential outcomes. He was still gripped by the tenacious tendrils of a psychogenic imagination that teased him with too many extreme and theatrical possibilities. Would he ever win? Could he even survive? Perhaps his goal was already realized in a dream already ended.

It was not the living earth or the wheel of time that hurt him; it was his inescapable link to a species with such a pompous and collective consciousness that he was all but lost in its jungle of futile absurdities. Raj could identify little that was human and that also held meaning and merit. Love, perhaps. But love was more than human. Love was, reliably and always, a long walk in the woods.

HARRIET

one

Harriet sat with her breakfast of fruit and black coffee while her mother made motions in the kitchen.

"Eggs? Sweetie, don't you want eggs?" her mother asked.

"No mom. I told you. I'm fine," answered Harriet.

"Protein, you know, and you have a busy–"

"She said no, Pamela."

Harriet's father spoke firmly to his wife as if enforcing the terms of a pre-existing agreement.

"She's an adult, dear," he added as if pointing out the obvious, however demeaning, was still necessary. His tone was instructional but he was a professor and Harriet had heard his lectures, those he gave in the classroom and nearly all he gave at home.

Harriet was silent.

Food was an old battle and she had nothing more to say after years of struggle over the terms of her appetite. As a young child she ate quickly and voraciously everything she took or was given and with a hunger that never appeared satisfied. Her mother's battle then was to limit her only child's persistent compulsion to constantly stuff herself until at age eight a notably chunky Harriet was enrolled in a ballet class.

After a year Harriet's fleshy, stout body began to strengthen and lengthen into its pre-pubertal growth spurt and in a way remarkably and esthetically coordinated with the hopeful expectation of her ballet instructor. By age ten, Harriet had a slightly tall and very lean look and an offer for advanced classes from an academy in the City.

Harriet loved to dance and learned early that to own a dancer's pleasing lightness of being, she would have to weigh less than ninety-one pounds. By age eleven Harriet had nearly extinguished her appetite, starting a new food war with a mother that now hounded her daughter to please, please eat. Thus ensued another mother-daughter battle of indomitable willfulness over the terms of Harriet's eating, which continued into her adolescence as the mother cooked, shopped, harped and raged to keep her child nourished while the daughter stood her ground. Harriet was beautiful, envied, and regarded and fed more love in mirrors than food could ever provision.

As Harriet's resistance collided with her mother's elaborate, persistent meal prep, a war of words escalated into pouting, outbursts and hysterics until the professor stepped into the fray. Outwardly, the professor saw no problem. His daughter was an excellent student, well behaved, and beautiful. Her classmates and dance mates, all young women, loved her and admired her.

Inwardly, the mother worried her daughter was starving herself and when at age sixteen Harriet still had not started her period, a doctor was consulted.

"I don't need to have a period," Harriet snorted at the physician.

She didn't want to bleed and of those friends and dancers who did, none reported enjoying it. A compromise was agreed to and Harriet began drinking a protein supplement until the year she started both college and her period and the demands of scholarship inexorably pushed dance to the sidelines of a new life. Still, the fasting habit was ingrained, as was the indelibly mirrored image of herself as a lithesome sylph. At a naked weight of 104 pounds, it was still difficult for Harriet not to think herself fat.

"Where's Inger?" her father asked.

"Still sleeping," said Harriet. "She works a late shift on Thursdays."

"Is she settling in?" her father asked again. "She's such a help around here already."

"It's her way of saying thank you," said Harriet. "She's generous to a fault."

Harriet enjoyed her father's appreciation of her new friend; though she worried at a still subliminal level that Inger could, of all things, replace her in her own family of origin. Inger had swaggered into Harriet's life with the oozing sexual presence she knew might interest her father and likely frighten her mother, while it also aroused in Harriet a viral curiosity. Harriet wondered if she would ever be able to step away from her home, seeing how easily Inger stepped into it.

The life Harriet had always lived with her parents on a verdant Berkeley hillside was the set point of an impregnably secure existence. And at some time it would need to change. She was nearly 25 and would have to leave. But not yet, though her father's interest in Harriet's future at times bordered on the planning of her life. He was the founder of her scholarly career and the author of her post-graduate studies.

Her mother, once again a student herself, was ten years younger than her father. She had been the student of a then Adjunct Professor Alden in the late Forties when he taught at a small Midwestern college. Harriet's mother was also her professor's lover and when she became pregnant with Harriet, Alden immediately married her and took the first opening at a California state college to move far away from any breath of scandal. Devoted scholarship led the professor to his tenure-track post at Berkeley where for nearly a decade he had reigned as a renowned scholar of medieval literature.

Harriet's mother, recently aroused by a pre-menopausal urgency and the threat of an imminent empty nest, decided she should go back to school and earn a degree in library science. So all three family members, father, mother and daughter, drove dutifully and separately each week to the same campus and returned, each of them, to the house on Campus Drive where Inger now occupied the rambling craftsman's only guest bedroom.

Harriet was still a virgin and that did create for her a stirring impatience though she could not say entirely why. Inger might have had something to do with it. Her sensuality and sexual life were a constant fragrance. For most of Harriet's adolescence she had missed out on the estrogens that seemed to fuel the arousal of her friends.

Now that she was hormonal, an urge of some kind was there and notable in her attraction to the looks and smells of the assembled virility in the undergraduate sections she supervised. One boy in particular, tall, strong and bright-eyed and who spoke in a husky tenor as he recited cantos in Italian was too often a seductive distraction.

"Coming out," Inger shouted from inside the bathroom. "Give me another minute."

Harriet was not used to sharing her bathroom with guests and paced while Inger pissed, flushed and ran naked back to her room.

Harriet loved her long, spacious bathroom which from her time as a young ballerina she accepted as a royal privilege and her own private studio, one with a wall solid in mirrors from floor to ceiling and before which she danced elaborate, fantastic performances. She would tie on her point shoes and spin naked before her beloved reflection, admiring her childish breasts, her thin hips, strong legs and elegantly long arms that opened and closed in the classical motions of clear, clean and memorized rhythms.

"I dream in Italian now," she told Inger one evening.

It was the beautiful language that opened her to the otherwise imposing structures of her father's academic specialty. She had chosen Dante probably because her father first suggested she study Shakespeare who, she admitted and her father insisted, was the greater genius. It didn't matter. Both literary giants had been taught and commented on for centuries, which meant for Harriet that there was even more she had to read and more authors she needed to know. From childhood she had planned to follow her parents into the academy and herself become a scholar. It would have been daunting were she not her father's daughter, or rather the professor's daughter and thereby assured affiliation and academic entrée as long as her labors were diligent and her insights robust.

Harriet's small office barely held her and her books as she searched through the texts and commentaries of the *Inferno*. Volumes were spread across her small desk, tipping in their piles and held open at certain marked sections by paperweights and pencils. She was one of Professor Andretti's four teaching assistants that led weekly sections of fifteen students in his undergraduate lecture class, *The Divine Comedy* in translation. She was to lead a discussion of Cantos V and XIX, poems of love and power she thought would best illustrate two of Dante's most apparent themes.

"The word Dante uses for the bleeding darkness of the second circle is *perso*," Harriet told her students. "It conveys a color of dried blood, both red and black. And doves? Why are doves flying around in the darkness of hell?"

Silence prevailed until an older woman at the back of the classroom raised her hand.

"Because this is the part of hell where lovers live," said the woman.

"Well, to say they live in hell isn't quite accurate, but, yes, what kind of lovers?" asked Harriet. "What's wrong with love?"

There was silence.

"What about Paolo and Francesca?" Harriet asked. "Why are they floating around in hell?"

"And are they floating around?" the cute male student asked in his mellifluous tenor. "And how are they connected? It reads as if they are stuck together forever, like they're—well—maybe having sex for eternity. What's so bad about that?"

There were titters.

"Well, what if it isn't good sex?" asked another woman.

More titters.

"Not good sex?" the young man asked.

"Oh yeah," the woman spoke again. "Is there any sex that for a man isn't good sex?"

More laughter.

Harriet waited. She couldn't say what was so bad about eternal sex since she had never had sex.

"Good or not, both are weeping."

Harriet spoke.

"Paolo has no words for his despair. Do you notice how souls in Dante's hell are condemned to do forever and with constant suffering what they did in their lives? And what was the sin of Francesca and Paolo?

More silence until another woman in the back again raised her hand.

"Adultery," she said.

"But they were in love," another student shouted. "They read the love story of Guinevere and Lancelot together and couldn't resist. Besides, Francesca's husband was an ugly old cripple who tricked her into marrying him."

"And he killed them both," another student interjected. "What's worse: adultery or murder? Where's his place in hell?"

"It's coming," answered Harriet. "Read ahead. But first, what does Francesca say about falling in love with Paolo?"

"She couldn't help it," said the woman in the back. "It was romantic. He kissed her. It was too much to resist."

"Then why does Dante put them in hell?"

More silence.

Once again, the woman in the back raised her hand.

"In Dante's view, sin is a choice. And a Christian would know what choice to make. Forgiveness was a choice, but if you didn't ask for it and didn't do your required penance, you were condemned to hell."

"And where is the devil?" asked Harriet.

"At the bottom of hell. Frozen in ice," answered another.

"So the devil is in no position to make anyone do anything," said Harriet. "It would appear Dante is saying the choice to sin is our own, and the choice to ask for forgiveness and to do penance is our own and that therefore the fate of our souls is our own to choose. There is something in this view that is very modern. And a reason we still find Dante so compelling. What is Dante's response to hearing Francesca?"

"He passes out," answered the woman in the back.

"Yes, he's overcome," said Harriet. "Why?"

"Because, even though he hasn't committed adultery, he's had the same feeling of love, the same urge as Francesca though he hasn't done anything about it," another student answered.

"Though maybe he has," the student said again. "Did he commit adultery?"

Harriet smiled.

"Keep reading," she said. "Next week we'll look at the simoniacs and how they are punished. A quick preview: popes are involved."

The campanile bell struck two and her students picked up their books to push their way out of the classroom.

Harriet returned to her office where she forced herself to devote two more hours to the draft of her dissertation. She sought to make her own case for Dante's modern outlook by citing the specifics of his political exile from Florence. It was not a new idea but Harriet thought there were parallels not fully expressed by the hundreds of commentators who had gone before.

Was there even an inch of Dante's life or language that had not been thoroughly addressed by someone? Boccaccio, Keats, Eliot, Bigi, Dragonetti, Fumagalli, Rahner, Singer, Singleton, even Sayers and Ciardi whose popular translations were still in circulation, had all touched in some way on Dante's political troubles though Harriet hoped at least to reinterpret the poet's life with a view toward understanding better how the violence of his world and his alienating wanderings created such a broad and, to her mind, nearly existential philosophy.

And women. There were as yet no prominent women Dante scholars and certainly none who wrote about the way any woman beyond Beatrice might have influenced the creation of his rich and complex poem.

Harriet wanted for herself what she wanted for her students: the courage to see beyond the "great thing" of the Commedia to her own perceptions of the smaller thing that was hers. Dante's truth, like anyone's, was only what a reader might grasp. Harriet suspected many of her students knew much more about love and power than she had yet to even consider.

two

The avaricious and the prodigal, the angry and the sullen and among all qualities of Canto VII, Harriet could find no answer to the question of line 20. Why does our own guilt destroy us? *E perche nostra colpa si ne scipa?*

The author offered no answer. Not in all one hundred cantos of the great Comedy could Harriet find any link to her own guilt, her own wearying habit of recrimination. Self-loathing had been her strength for years. She had loved her body by punishing it. She had cultivated her mind by deriding its thoughts.

"I'm a high achiever," she told Inger as they sat on the hillside near her home. The vast bay, the distant city and towering bridges were spread out before them.

Inger asked what she meant by achieving.

"Being really good at something," Harriet answered. "I was a good dancer. I've always been a great student."

"Are you happy?" asked Inger.

Harriet stopped to think. And took a while.

"That's not a good sign," Inger said. "You have to think about it? Have you ever been in love?"

Harriet continued to think.

"Haven't had time," she answered. "I'm perfectly organized so that if something goes wrong I'm always prepared to manage it. There is a logical reason for everything in my life, even down to the food I eat or don't eat. And love? Maybe someday. It sounds interesting but it just hasn't happened."

"God, do you ever get horny?" Inger asked directly.

"You mean sex," said Harriet. "I have desire. Sure. I am attracted to certain bodies, certain looks. But I wouldn't want to make a mistake. I'd feel bad about that. I just haven't had a reason to say yes to anyone."

Inger laughed.

"I can rarely think of a reason to say no," she said.

From her table at The Forum, Harriet could see and hear the revolution that wasn't televised. She had arrived early, an hour before lunch, to spread out her books, notes and papers at her usual place near the window. She ordered a coffee, lit a cigarette and sank into her work, oblivious to the loud conversations all around her while also animated by the voices that created them.

By noon the Forum's back tables were arranged for the current cast of rebels. Included were Harriet's familiars. Raj and Larry each stopped at her table to greet her. Larry brought Sylvia who was a new member of the cast and attended for the first time.

"You teach English?" Sylvia asked when she was introduced.

"Actually, I teach literature," Harriet answered. "Italian. Dante."

"I'm workin' with children," said Sylvia. "Giving them a start with Black English. It's time."

"What's Black English?" Harriet asked.

"Like Italian," Sylvia answered. "One culture speaks it and other cultures don't understand it. They need to learn. You ever read poetry?"

Harriet said yes. That she taught poetry.

"Whose?" asked Sylvia. "Ever teach the Black Arts?"

Harriet looked puzzled.

"How about Imamu Amiri Baraka? Ahmed Alhamisi? Raymond Patterson? "

Harriet did not know them.

"Unless they were born before 1450," Harriet answered, "I'm not the one to ask. I teach medieval poetry and a lot of it was written in Latin, a language no one even speaks anymore."

"If I bring some black poetry would you read it?" Sylvia asked forcefully.

Harriet nodded.

"Yeah. I'd be really interested."

Harriet could feel Sylvia's suspicion she was being patronized.

"No, really. Here comes Raj. He works at Moe's. He could find something for me. I'm serious."

Harriet hovered over the 19th line of Canto XIV. The poet described naked souls of many flocks, all weeping, and how different laws governed them. It seemed oddly appropriate to the revolutionary upheavals in her midst. Harriet sat daily at the Forum and among the constituents of history's current conflicts, Raj, Larry, Bronwyn,

Peter, Mack and Sylvia, all souls that sought to legislate from the street the new laws of a new order. There was no choice in Dante's hell, though as an intellectual she grasped that a modern hell had been described as simply the existence of other people. Would we ever get along? It seemed unlikely, until everyone passed beyond the gate and was broken by creation.

Harriet's father was not a sports fan. But the Big Game was a ritual he had cultivated since his first fall at Berkeley. Stanford versus Cal was a football rivalry with little impact on the larger world but for three generations the locus of annual cross-bay hostilities between the region's two great universities. And it was the fall Saturday Harriet hated most, had hated all her young and maturing life. It was a family affair and Professor Alden started early with a breakfast at the faculty club that Harriet's mother and Harriet were commanded to attend.

The men drank beer and chardonnay and the women their mimosas while a full breakfast was served to those lucky enough to secure reservations, often years in advance. As a tenured instructor the professor had first right of refusal and he never refused.

The breakfast, the game, the lavish dinner afterward in a banquet room at a nice restaurant, these were the trappings of her father's perverse version of school spirit. It was a daylong drunken feast through which she would have to mindfully refuse course after course of greasy, ugly food or take spare bites and spread the rest around on the many plates set before her. She was grateful for the game, despite the uncomfortable seats and usually cold weather, when she would be offered nothing to eat.

She also was grateful her father attended only the home games. One year they boarded a faculty bus to eat breakfast in the City before riding down to Stanford for the game. After another dismal Cal loss, a dinner followed in Palo Alto that smothered everyone in a mood so oppressive the professor and her mother agreed never to do it again.

"Plunkett's good," her father said over breakfast as if he knew anything about sports. "Hell of a quarterback. Nearly beat O.J. and USC. We have our work cut out for us."

"Plunkett's Mexican and O.J. is black," a colleague said to Harriet's father. "Maybe there's something to this Third World Studies thing. Certainly enough to make the sports page."

The colleague laughed while Harriet's father shook his head.

"As if we don't have enough to do to save Western civilization," he said. "It's frightful how little my new students know of the canon. And someone wants to start a campus strike so we teach Black studies? Mexican studies? What the hell is that? It isn't scholarship. It's politics."

"Not politics, daddy," Harriet interrupted. "It's political science. You don't think the experiences of blacks or Mexicans in America are worth studying?"

"It's phony scholarship," said Professor Alden. "Come on, dear. You don't believe Eldridge Cleaver has a place in the canon. A man who writes about raping white women for fun."

"Really father?" Harriet asked pointedly. "I don't think a place in the canon matters much to blacks and Mexicans. Which is why we should pay more attention to their experiences."

"The past has much to teach them. And everyone," the professor pontificated.

"You mean *our* past," said Harriet. "And what can their past teach us?"

"Damn little if you ask me," the colleague interrupted. "Who is the black Shakespeare? Who is the Mexican Dante? Where do their cultures stand in the hierarchy of history? It's bullshit."

"Maybe the hierarchy is bullshit," Harriet replied.

A glass of champagne on an empty stomach had seized control.

"My daughter is an idealist," the professor, a small man, said as he threw his arm up over his tall daughter's high, strong shoulders. For a moment he appeared like the friendly elf of a statuesque princess.

"I'm a scholar," she countered while pulling away from her father's patronizing embrace.

"You were one once," she said to her father. "What happened to the spirit of inquiry you used to talk so much about?"

Harriet walked away while her father mumbled something to his colleague. She heard her father's snide tone but none of his words.

"Saw your essay on Chaucer in the new Spectrum collection," said the colleague to Harriet's father. "Damned robust."

The game was awful. Cal lost to Stanford 20-0 with the Indians' Mexican sophomore throwing bombs to a brilliant black receiver. Dinner at the Hotel Durant had all the joy of a subdued post-mortem. When she wasn't refusing food, Harriet found an art history professor to speak with about famous painters that had depicted scenes from the *Commedia*. Professor Alden sunk into his cups while Harriet's mother attempted to bridge barely sustainable social links that existed for only a single meal and only once every other fall.

"Next year," her father said as he tried to stand and to leave.

"I don't think so," said a departing dean. "We'd need a miracle."

Harriet later imagined meeting her father in Purgatory and wondered on what ledge she would find him. He would be waiting in line behind others while he climbed the steps of his venial offenses. Had he lived before the 14th century, her father might have been one of Dante's sinners. He was in desperate need of purgation. Pride, avarice, envy were all possibilities. She knew him but did not love him.

Harriet thought she might love her mother but only from dutiful habit. She did not know love, at least if Dante was to be believed. There was no intellect of love, no thrilling and private mythology of grace she ever had uncovered in regard for another. Friendship made sense as a colloquy or conversation.

Inger was a friend, as were Mack and Raj. But love was different and from a place of disciplined study she could write rigorously about how it was different and still not understand why.

Eldridge Cleaver had vanished. It was Monday's main topic of discussion at the Forum. Harriet had read a report in Sunday's paper, a story headlined *Black Panther jumps bail, flees country* though no one could say exactly where Cleaver was and his wife Kathleen would not say anything at all. Harriet's interest in the issue of Third World Studies had begun obliquely and, to some uncomfortable degree, in response to what she thought her father's useless opinions.

Cleaver had been a main player and Harriet had attended his one and only campus lecture the previous month where he spoke about race and sex and the "systemic" incarceration of black men. His street-smart confidence and muscular voicing of the issues impressed her. She would say later, when she understood better what was meant, that his strong presence had turned her on.

It was grapes, though, that had sparked Harriet's germinal interest in campus politics. The United Farmworkers Union had called for a boycott of table grapes to support the unionization of farm workers. A dozen Mexican-American student leaders tried to meet with the university's president to seek support for the boycott. Instead, they were all arrested while Governor Reagan ordered scab-picked grapes served in the university's dormitories. Until then, injustice was for Harriet a quality of sin found in one of the ditches of Dante's hell. Now it was something to be considered among the events of her current and modern life.

It was a surprise to Harriet that her graduate teaching job came with membership in union local 1570 of the American Federation of Teachers.

"You're a TA," Raj said to Harriet as he passed her table. "Do you ever go to the meetings?"

Harriet shook her head.

"Would you go?" Raj asked again. "Strike talk is brewing. Look at what's happening at SF State."

Harriet was aware that a strike by students and graduate teaching assistants at San Francisco State had closed the campus. She was sympathetic to the call for black and chicano studies but reluctant to get involved.

"You could do something," Raj said. "If you want black studies, you can help us. Want to sit in with us?"

Harriet did not. She was a fearful introvert. She loved to work among the chatter and noise of a café and could rule a classroom from behind a detailed curriculum. But she loathed meeting strangers. She would rather walk through hell, probably because she knew the way.

"They aren't strangers," Raj said. "You see them and they see you practically every day. Come on, no one's going to bite."

In this way Harriet began to move her books, her notes, her coffee, her mind, her body, her resentments and worries, her fear of engagement and her anger with her father. She moved all of her and all she possessed toward a chair at the long table near the back of the Forum, the new beachhead of a new battle with the errors of her civilization.

three

Harriet awoke early on Thanksgiving. She swore to herself after the previous year's holiday she would never again spend it with her family. But Raj was visiting his parents for the first time in a decade and Inger was with her father and brother for her first family Thanksgiving in five years, so unless Harriet wished to sling dressing at the St. Vincent's Dining Room she was stuck again at home.

Her grandparents were coming to dinner. Joe and Barbara were the parents of her mother who two decades earlier had followed their daughter from Omaha to Fresno after her quick courtship and marriage to the professor. Joe took a plumbing job and within a year the parents purchased a home in the foothills east of town.

Pamela was her parents' only child, making Harriet their only granddaughter, a one-child legacy that pushed Harriet into accepting the obsessive attentions of two old and infrequent caregivers that frightened her, bored her and, later in her adolescence, enraged her with their inbred ignorance and bigotry. It had been more than a decade since the death of Jeanette, her grandmother on her father's side. Harriet loved Jeanette, a small and literate woman who honored Harriet's teenage misgivings and made her laugh. Jeanette lived in Pittsburgh and began traveling west for the holidays after her husband died.

Harriet's was a family that groomed its resentments with dysfunctional expertise. Joe never forgave the professor for impregnating his only child before he married her. It was a sin, thought Joe. Nevertheless, he moved himself and Barbara west to be close to Pamela. Joe assumed his daughter would some day take care of him and did not want to be far from her. Joe loved to flaunt what he called his "redneck roots" and found ample support among his central valley neighbors.

Joe adopted an emblematic wardrobe that included Stetson hats, bola ties and cowboy boots that he wore everywhere, and once very aggressively to a special department reception celebrating the professor's appointment to tenure. Harriet knew Joe would time his arrival for their Thanksgiving dinner to match the kick-off of a football game and the TV would blare while Barbara sat and drank a Manhattan and Harriet's mother prepared enormous quantities of food Harriet would not eat.

Harriet threw on her terry cloth robe and stepped reluctantly into the kitchen where her mother struggled to push a pale turkey carcass into the oven.

"I wondered when you'd get up."

Her mother's mouth was a pursed, impatient sneer.

"I could really use some help in here. Gramps and gramma are coming in three hours and we're not anywhere near ready."

Harriet gathered into her view the kitchen's accumulating clutter: dirty pots, greasy bowls, cooking spoons, sharp knives, a cleaver, and measuring cups stacked and spread around like a miscellany of worn-out tools on a mechanic's bench. An open, half-empty bottle of white wine stood on the stovetop.

Harriet checked the clock.

Mom's starting early this year. It's not even noon.

"Someone run the vacuum," Pamela shouted as the professor entered the kitchen.

"I will," said Harriet. "Let me get dressed first."

Her father saw the wine bottle and, like Harriet, looked at the clock.

With everyone playing their parts, the morning ran like a self-starting machine and produced its expected product: a house made warm and clean by a family that dreaded the arrival of holiday guests. Harriet put on a plaid wool skirt over her panty house and slipped into a bulky, spacious blue sweater so she wouldn't need a bra. She wore flat shoes to shrink her height.

Just past one o'clock, all was ready: food, drinks, a sumptuously set table and fresh towels in the downstairs bathroom. Every one was dressed well and variously committed to the presentation of an exhaustively conceived household hospitality.

The doorbell rang and Joe entered first, carrying a bag of groceries. He hugged Pamela briefly, brushed by the professor and scooted into the kitchen where he threw the bag onto a counter.

"Traffic was god awful," he shouted.

He pulled a small half bottle of bourbon from the grocery bag and set it discreetly on top of the refrigerator. Barbara followed him in, lingering to hug her daughter and also the professor. She waited for Harriet to come down the hall and reached up to hold her by the shoulders at arms length.

"Well, just look at you," she said to Harriet. "You look more beautiful each time I see you. Whoever makes you his wife will be one lucky young man."

Harriet ignored her grandmother's controlling compliment and went into the kitchen to greet Grandpa Joe.

"You little cutie," he oozed affectionately and wrapped her aggressively in his fat stubby arms. His hands climbed down her back to her waist and up again. It felt to Harriet as if Joe were searching for something.

"Hey! You aren't wearing a bra," he said as Harriet pushed him away. "You goin' hippie on us, honey?"

Joe laughed.

"Look, you're blushing," Joe shouted and laughed again with a hoarse, gargling snort.

"Hey, Gene, your daughter's goin' hippie. Did you know that?"

Here we go, thought Harriet who knew better than to bite at Joe's bait.

Harriet looked to her parents for help, but her father said nothing while her mother opened a second bottle of chardonnay.

"I'll fill the water glasses," Harriet said and left the kitchen.

Joe asked Pamela for a glass and poured whiskey from his personal bottle. He would have offered some to anyone who asked. But he knew no one would ask. He walked into the living room and turned on the television.

"Who is it this year?" the professor called out.

"Big Raiders game," Joe shouted. "Hell of a team this season.

They're goin' all the way."

As with the bourbon, no one would join with Joe to watch football. But no one would ask the reigning patriarch to turn it off. Joe insisted on keeping the volume turned up so he could hear the play-by-play from the dining room table. Harriet wondered how all this got started; how Joe's obnoxious behavior had become a Thanksgiving norm. Her grandparents weren't guests. They were invaders that swept into her home like Saracens.

"And how about those teddy bears, Gene?" Joe shouted to his son-in-law who was opening a bottle of pinot noir.

"What the hell's wrong with your football program? Stanford whipped your goddamned ass. Your boys play like they they're wearing petticoats and don't want to get them dirty."

The professor stiffened.

"We're working on it, Joe," he responded bleakly.

During dinner Harriet's sobriety was neither a power nor a consolation. While football play-by-play boomed from the TV, her family members drowned the noise and themselves in alcohol. At first it was some relief that each was drunk or getting drunker. Joe drank more bourbon, while Barbara and Harriet's father drank wine. The professor was on his second glass. But her mother was on her second bottle and Harriet could hear festering notes of icy sarcasm as Pamela let the alcohol do her talking. She mentioned that Harriet would be studying in Florence the following year.

"Good Italian food," said Joe. "That'll fatten her up. She's as thin as a rail. Looks like that English model. What's her name? Twiggy? What husband wants a skinny wife? Little wonder she doesn't wear a bra."

"Who says I want a husband?" said Harriet.

"Damn, you aren't one of those lezzie man-haters are you?"

Joe's question sounded like an accusation.

"Of course not," Barbara interjected. "She's a sweetheart. But honey, you sure don't eat much. You're really skinny. Look at your plate. You haven't touched a thing."

"No, I haven't," answered Harriet.

Her plate had been served by Barbara, which apparently entitled her to a proprietary interest in her granddaughter's appetite. Harriet stared at the vast and oleaginous servings before her and began to eat. She scooped up fat slices of turkey breast smothered in gravy. She stuffed her mouth with spoonfuls of mashed potatoes and forkfuls of soggy, mixed vegetables. She reached for a corn muffin and wolfed it. Then she grabbed another and did the same. She took two scoops of cranberry sauce and mashed them into a mountain of dressing which she lifted to her lips in a series of swift, steam-shoveling sweeps. The family watched in silence while Harriet ate with industrial efficiency, pushing bite after bite into her mouth, sometimes not waiting to swallow. In a few minutes her plate was empty.

"There," she said boldly. "Now, if you'll excuse me…."

Harriet leaped from the table and walked brusquely upstairs. In her bathroom she closed the door, forked two fingers of her right hand and shoved them vigorously down her throat. She bit her knuckles and waited over the toilet until the familiar and relieving spasms took hold. She then removed her hand to release a gushing, muddy river of barely digested dinner.

Purge. Purgation. She had climbed the mountain with the poet and found her empyrean. She put the lid down and sat on the toilet. She reached for a towel and smothered her hot, wet face in it.

As her stomach settled Harriet stood to catch her breath. It had been nearly a year since she last made herself vomit. She remembered her Monday weigh-ins at the dance studio and how she and other girls would line-up before noon to grab a stall in the women's bathroom where they would throw-up their breakfasts. She needed to get her place early before the bathroom smelled so bad no one could use it.

Though she had broken the habit of throwing up her meals, it still gave her some relief from stress, and especially that created by her grandmother's provocation at the dinner table. Vomiting still made Harriet dizzy and could induce exhaustion, but it also gave her a pleasurable feeling of control.

Harriet splashed water on her face, rinsed her mouth and dried it before combing her hair. She straightened her sweater in the mirror and left to descend the stairs to the table's suety, vinous ruin.

Grandpa Joe continued to hold his intemperate court

"How do you put up with all those bums running around your campus? All those monkeys marching for their so-called rights? One of your own professors has proved that Negroes have lower IQs. I read about it."

"Proved what?" Harriet asked as she sat down. "You're talking about Jensen. He hasn't proved anything."

"No," said her father, reluctant to say much that would keep Joe fired up. "It's a very debatable hypothesis."

"Hypothesis, my ass," Joe continued. "We should draft them all into the army and send them off to Nam. That's about all they're good for."

"C'mon, Daddy, you don't mean that," Pamela slurred. "Stop talking like a stupid bigot."

"Your father is not a bigot," Barbara spoke up. "You shouldn't be so disrespectful. He knows what he's talking about. So do most people. Why do you think we elected Reagan governor?"

"And Nixon," Joe chimed in. "You'll see. We're the silent majority and we're sick of this crap at the colleges."

"What does that make me?" Harriet spoke up. "I'm part of that crap."

"No you aren't honey," Pamela said. "You're just a student."

"No. I'm a teaching assistant and, as it turns out, I belong to a union. We may vote next month to go on strike if the university won't create a Black Studies department."

"A what?" Joe shouted. "What does a black person study? Dancin'? Stealin'? Drug-dealin'? I heard that guy Cleaver once. He calls all the cops pigs. A lotta nerve for someone who spent years in prison for rape."

"So how would you vote, dear?" Harriet's father interrupted.

"Yes," said Harriet as she looked directly at him. "Yes. I support Black Studies. I'd go on strike."

A loud cheer blasted from the television.

"Damn," shouted Joe. "Just a minute."

"But, sweetie, what if you were to get arrested? What about your career?" the professor asked.

Harriet could hear the tension in his voice.

"What about it?" answered Harriet.

Her mother's elbow slipped from the table as she tried to balance her glass to pour more wine. The glass hit the floor and shattered.

Joe yelled and hooted from the living room and bounded back to the table. "Lamonica to Belitnikoff. Classic. That's the game! Go Raiders!"

It was the professor's turn to jump up and go into the living room. He turned off the television. On the way back he stepped on shards of Pamela's glass, driving them deeper into the floor's linoleum tiles.

"Shit," the professor muttered.

"Get me a broom, Pamela," he yelled.

"Don't talk to me like that," Pamela shouted back with woozy abandon. "Get it yourself."

"I'll get dessert," shouted Barbara. "Joe, come and help me."

The grandparents vanished into the kitchen. Harriet waited and gauged the room's emerging moral topography. Who would prevail? She had watched her parents argue many times and knew the dynamic, especially when her mother was drunk and capable of anything. Her father pretended to be the reasonable one and sought with his cool tone to neutralize Pamela's hysterics, which only made Pamela more upset and more determined to control the outcome by whatever means necessary.

Dessert was strawberry shortcake, served and picked at in near silence until Joe announced they would have to leave to beat the traffic home. Harriet helped them with their bags and prepared a dish of leftovers. She slipped away from Joe's attempt at another embrace, while her mother drank another glass of wine in preparation for the next explosion. The professor watched his in-laws toddle down the driveway and then closed the door.

"This was crazy," he shouted at Pamela. "Your parents never make this easy. It's the worst day of the year. And all you do is get drunk. You need to get control of yourself."

Within 15 minutes a screaming, tearful Pamela had both her husband and her daughter on the floor, searching tiles for every last tiny piece of glass while, barely able to stand, she directed them. The professor's rational ways were no match for a wife who was her own theater and who could endlessly escalate a din of difficult feelings.

At some point Inger returned from her own father's dinner and had to pass through an awkward war zone to get to her room.

"Can I help?" Inger asked.

"No help needed," said the embarrassed professor.

"We're way beyond help," added Harriet as Inger turned toward the stairs to move up and away.

"We are dealing with high levels of hate," Bronwyn said from the head of the table.

"We can argue about what this election means, but there is no way to avoid the fact we are outnumbered. We are outnumbered in California. We are way outnumbered in the nation. If you polled all the college students across the country, I guarantee that a majority of them still support the war and certainly don't support Black Studies."

"That's not true at State," said Peter. "The campus is closed because students support the strike. You saw how many turned out for that meeting with the president. And the teachers' union is ready to vote on a strike as early as next week."

"The parents of these students aren't so happy about the strike." Bronwyn spoke again.

"Have you forgotten Reagan won in a landslide? He's been a popular governor for two years and wants the campus opened. He wants scab grapes in our dormitories. He wants student protesters expelled. He would fire striking teachers."

"Then what can we do?" asked Raj.

Harriet listened. She was Raj's silent guest at the table and welcomed first because theoretically the revolution welcomed anyone interested and also because her friend Raj was trusted. Her status as a campus TA and voting teachers' union member gave her extra value in the current mobilization.

"It's always a Mobe," said Bronwyn. "Local or national, we have a chance to win if we're mobilized. It doesn't take a majority. But we have to be organized."

"Nixon didn't win a majority," Peter said.

"Yeah, but Reagan did—like big time," said Larry. "Look, you talkin' about a majority of voters that are white. It's their vote that scares me 'cause white folks aren't naturally inclined to support black folks. I don't care what you say. And it's gettin' violent out there. Martin, Bobby…who's next? I don't think Reagan cares if we get shot. I know Nixon don't."

Harriet followed the conversation. She was still assembling a political identity. Was she a supporter? An activist? Where would she make sense as a member of a mobilization?

What she heard made her think of a canto of Purgatorio in which the medieval politician Provenzan Salvani is punished for his attempted grip to master all of Siena. Pride was his sin. Was it also Bronwyn's? Peter's? Was there anything inherently wrong with a desire for political leverage?

And what was her reason to join and to help? Weren't all political desires essentially selfish? She thought of her father and the fathers and mothers of those at the table. Then she visualized her students, her classmates, her colleagues and those her age beyond the halls and pathways of the university. And she imagined their fathers and mothers, those who voted for Reagan or Nixon or Wallace or McCarthy.

The alleged innocence of youth provided no moral leverage. Like young people of any era, most children of the Sixties were still very much like their parents. And politics? In Dante's hell the corruption of power was punished as the mockery of Fortune whose wheel of worldly outcomes could turn on nothing more than a roll of the dice.

four

Harriet worried about her mother. At least, that's what she told Inger as they again sat together on the hillside beyond her home. It was an unusually warm December day and the late season's encroaching shadows pushed across the tall trees as if they were marking a sundial.

Inger lit a cigarette and passed it to Harriet.

"Gauloises? Where do you find those?" Harriet asked.

"There's a smoke shop downtown," said Inger. "He carries them and if he doesn't have Gauloises he always has Gitanes."

Inger developed her French cigarette habit while living in Europe. Harriet began smoking in college as another way to manage her weight after realizing she would never become a ballerina.

"I love these," said Harriet as she took a long, deep drag.

The cigarettes were made with dark tobaccos from Syria and Turkey that imparted a harsh, full flavor.

"They aren't cheap," said Inger.

"I know," said Harriet. "I usually smoke Camels. But not at home. Nobody smokes at home."

Inger knew the house rules and was a good guest. She said she was trying to quit smoking, though she always had cigarettes.

"So what is it about your mom?" Inger asked as she blew a puff of smoke into the breeze.

"She's drinking more," said Harriet. "She's pissed off most of the time. I really shouldn't have to deal with it. But then I shouldn't be living at home. I'm too old for this."

"Have you looked for a place?" Inger asked. "Even a room somewhere?"

"It's been easy to stay at home…at least until now. Dad would be disappointed if I left, but mom would fall apart. She thinks she still needs to feed me meals and buy my tampons or neither would happen. I think sometimes I'm all that holds them together. I'm twenty-five but I'm still their daughter and they can focus a lot of attention on me they don't have to give to each other."

"What do you want?" asked Inger.

"Love, I guess. That is, if I knew anything about love. I have a graduate education in love and I'm working on a PhD in love. But it's medieval love, courtly love, Godly love. I've taught Dante for two years. And most of my students know more than I do about falling in love. I really don't know how love feels, or even how it's supposed to feel. I have never loved anyone."

"Has anyone loved you?" asked Inger.

"My parents love me," she said. "Either that or they just want to control me."

"A lot of people will say they love you when they only want to control you," said Inger.

"Have you ever had a boyfriend?"

"No," said Harriet.

"And you've never had a lover?" Inger asked again.

"If you mean sex, no," answered Harriet.

"There was my best friend in high school. We spent some sleepovers making out with each other and pretending we were with a boy. It was instructive and one of our 'best friend' secrets but we never told anyone and stopped at the end of ninth grade and never spoke of it again. I told you my friend Mary was attracted to me and I spent an afternoon with her and her old man Charlie in the City last year. They wanted me to get it on with them. I just couldn't, though I hung around for the party."

"The party?" Inger asked.

"Charlie brought two other women. It was pretty far out. Mary seemed to like it. After I turned down an invitation to join in, no one paid attention to me. They were really stoned. All naked and moving around from partner to partner and room to room. I was embarrassed and no one saw me leave."

"You are sexual, though," said Inger. "You've told me. You get off. So you must have fantasies."

"Yeah…" Harriet's voice trailed away as she considered the truth of Inger's observation.

"I am attracted to people, a few men I know. But I wouldn't know how to begin. One is a student, so I know he's off limits. Another drifts in and out of my life in a mysterious way. I see him at the Forum but I can't seem to attract his attention. And he's weird. He may do a lot of drugs. But he's physically a very attractive man. I was a dancer for many years and he's strong like a dancer. Strong and slender. And tall. Being held and spun by a strong dancer was my first big thrill. I think about it all the time."

"Tell me more about Charlie," said Inger.

Harriet sat with her lesson plan. She pushed herself to find a simpler way to explain the difference between an allegory of poets and one of theologians, an explanation simpler and clearer than the one given her. She read and reread the Inferno's 10th Canto in which Epicureans who believed death was all that followed life spent eternity standing erect in their graves.

Yes, she thought. This was the outcome of a certain kind of will. Did it negate the pleasure of a life lived for pleasure? She had recently begun to question the place of pleasure in her life. What did she truly enjoy beyond coffee, cigarettes, sleep and occasional masturbation?

Scholarship seemed to her its own reward though she found Dante as challenging as he was rewarding. She did not enjoy food though she struggled with wanting to eat. She could not recall when she did not struggle. She needed the power of will to deny her appetite, a denial that did not distinguish between nutrition and indulgence. To dance successfully she had economized the nutritional needs of her body by grinding vegetables in a blender, drinking protein or, when succumbing to a flavorful temptation, throwing up.

Love interested her now. It was everywhere around her. In her music, her books, her friends, her deeper readings of literature, even in the headlines. She had lived through an entire Summer of Love and not grasped at all what it meant other than a generalized peace and affiliation of people young like herself though unlike her in their emotional and sexual freedom. She was not free and wasn't certain she would ever have sex. Harriet could not decide how to love and whom to love because she was not yet sure if she were her father's daughter or her mother's.

It was almost as if her parents were happy to keep her in a sexless state, to suppress and restrain her growth in the way a gardener trains a bush or a vine to the needs of a garden. A desire was growing in her, but was it hers or another's?

I am the parent in this family. I am in control of them through the control they have extended over my desires. I am the safe ground between them. I exist as the arbiter of their conflicts. I can't imagine them as a sexual couple. I cannot bear the thought for reasons I do not understand. Perhaps for so long I have been incurious about the drives that move within me.

These thoughts made her aware of a question deeper than sex as an act. It was the idea of sex as an inclination and, despite her biology, a way of attraction that made the most sense. She was a woman. That wasn't in question. But what kind of loving woman was she? She had only recently emerged from the puerile biology of a postponed adolescence. What erotic life she had was deeply private and personal and grown from her conversations with other women who shared with her a critical appreciation of the womanly form in motion and with a specificity of detail greater than any boy or man could manage.

Harriet sat at her table at the Forum and when at last she spoke up she was like a bird, a newcomer in an old tree. She had seen Raymond enter and called him to her table. She knew from Raj that his name was Raymond, though for several months he had taken the name Yitzhak. And it was Yitzhak she called over, Yitzhak the one who laughs though he seemed rarely to laugh or even smile. Raj first introduced him to Harriet as Raymond. Now it was Yitzhak who approached. It was apparent he was looking for Raj.

"You seen him?"

Yitzhak spoke.

Harriet had not seen Raj. She invited Yitzhak to sit and wait with her. He hesitated long enough for Harriet to take the full measure of him. He was strong, tall, his face that of one distracted or preoccupied as if he were twisted perpetually among a confusion of choices.

"Would you like a coffee?" she asked as she extinguished her cigarette. "Please, sit down."

Yitzhak looked around cautiously as one not used to an invitation. He took the chair opposite Harriet.

"What do you take? Cream, sugar?"

Yitzhak nodded.

"I'll be right back," said Harriet and went to order his drink.

She watched him from the counter. He fingered one of her books and picked it up. He opened it and turned its pages. He stopped somewhere and lingered as if reading.

"What did you find?" Harriet asked when she returned.

"What's in every book in the world," he answered as Harriet handed him his cup.

"And what's that?" asked Harriet.

"Words."

It was an old joke but Harriet laughed and Yitzhak at last smiled.

Somewhere under his cool exterior Yitzhak nurtured a sense of humor, one made funnier by Harriet's surprise at finding it. As she was learning, humor was an intelligent touch point on a path toward intimacy. Yitzhak's joke drew Harriet closer on a trajectory she had only vaguely plotted.

Harriet looked up to see Raj rushing across the street from Moe's.

"Here he comes," Harriet said, aware her tenuous link with Yitzhak would imminently dissolve. She was sorry to lose him now. It would not be easy to begin again though she imagined how she might.

Raj bounded into The Forum and saw Yitzhak with Harriet.

"Hey man, I'm really sorry," Raj said to Yitzhak while nodding toward Harriet. "Can we do this in an hour? They have me on the register through lunch."

"Yeah, that's cool," Yitzhak said. "Meet you here?"

"Yeah," Raj answered. "And I have some good news."

Raj bolted back out the door and across the street.

"Sounds important," said Harriet.

"Raj used to work at the Co-op," said Yitzhak. "I applied for a job. Raj is my reference."

"You hungry?" asked Harriet. "Can I get you a snack?"

Yitzhak stared aridly at Harriet. For a moment she worried he had lost the thread of their conversation, had fallen into a lost, secret ditch.

"OK," he answered.

Harriet was full, so full. She ignored the tension in her thighs and the pressure against her bladder, alert only to the feeling inside her and the hard and insistent presence of a cock. For a moment she drifted from the otherwise riveting sensation of the new and yet also familiar motility of genital warmth to look at herself from outside, to try to see the experience she could feel so deeply and not at all describe.

Since she was a child, she had touched and handled her vulva, inserted objects as part of her self-play and exploration. But this excitement was a surprise and, aligned as it was with the carefully constructed and mindfully managed intention to fuck Yitzhak, an odd kind of fulfillment. Were she to be asked later, and she was, she would say the pleasure was negligible even as her body opened to touch, to penetration, and to the flow of her own moisture.

But there was also too much to think about as she straddled Yitzhak's bare thighs in the back seat of his old model Chevrolet, paper sacks, wrappers and rags pushed away to make room for their sex. Harriet had asked Yitzhak to pick her up at the campus after dinner. This way she avoided an awkward scene at the front door of her home and also the chore of having to choose—and eat—food. They drank beers at a tavern on Solano Avenue and then saw a movie before driving consensually and together to the apex of Grizzly Peak Boulevard to find a view of the Bay that would also hide them in shadows. Both lived at home with their parents, so the backseat of Yitzhak's car was the only room available.

This is so retarded, Harriet at first thought, until she remembered she was a virgin who still lived at home and, if nothing else, that embarrassing fact would no longer haunt her, however she felt afterward. And it was not painful. She had for years been friendly with her vulva and did not worry about an obstacle.

Yitzhak was quiet, but not inept. His silence had housed the evening's mood under a canopy of cool composure that others might have found distancing on a first date, but for which Harriet was prepared. She had her own agenda. She had decided before dinner she would have her first intercourse with him.

He was distant, but kind. He would not hurt her. Despite his silence, the mood was comfortable and the movie, a stupid comedy about hippies starring Peter Sellers as a straight elder who discovers the Counterculture by mistakenly eating from a batch of pot-laced brownies, kept both of them united in their laughter. In addition to surprising her with a gift of Gauloises, Inger also gave Harriet a package of condoms.

"Just in case," Inger said coyly, which was another way of saying it was time to get laid.

Harriet might have hoped her first fuck would be with a voluble and romantic man, a poet, who would walk her through a cemetery on a warm summer night and make thoughtful love to her on a sarcophagus, all the while reciting the words of Keats, Shelley or Byron. She had rehearsed for years her sexual response to such a lover.

Instead, she was joined and fitted, vagina to penis, in the back seat of a dirty car with a large, lean and strong figure of mystery. There was nothing soft about Yitzhak's body or his touch. But his strength was firm and reassuring. And there were few words, though as she expressed her excitement with cushioned moans, he was fully present. He held her close. She could feel the affection for which he had no words. He was a mystery to her but the kind of mystery that permitted her to be safely mystified.

Later, after Yitzhak took her home and she spent an hour in her bathroom searching her face and lean, naked body for some physical evidence of new capacity, Harriet settled for the benefits of knowledge. Her sex with Yitzhak had been both an intense arousal and an unsettling distraction. But it had been a passage and, despite its abashing imperfection, she was wise to have made it.

Harriet sat again with her mother to watch television. And again *Laugh-In* was on with its running and building cavalcade of gags that carried over from week to week. A cast of ingénues performed all the stock parts. The most enjoyable for Pamela were those of Ruth Buzzi as a hair-netted spinster who sat on a park bench and Arte Johnson as the dirty old man Tyrone in an overcoat and derby who harassed her with racy double entendres until Buzzi would whack him viciously with her handbag.

Harriet felt an odd kind of solidarity with her mother, despite what she still considered to be her mother's chiding tone and propensity to anger, her drinking to excess and deep anxieties that had infected Harriet with all her own worries. Still, they were both women and, as Harriet thought now, both women who had taken into themselves a penis.

five

Dante spoke from hell and said that art was God's grandchild. Because Harriet was a scholar and not an artist, her human toil was not applied to nature but to the art produced from it. This allowed her to think of her developing dissertation as a cousin of God's grandchildren, perhaps even a second cousin. It was a silly idea but it entertained her and for a week kept her focused on the tedious deadlines she set for herself to finish her research and to write.

Before she could do that she needed to finish her teaching semester. She would score papers and post grades for her dozen undergraduates that had struggled to walk alongside Dante as he descended an inverted mountain of terror that was also the poet's geography of human choice. She did not expect insights from her students but hoped for more than rewritten Cliff Notes, lifted citations, insipidly derived theses or, worst of all, plagiarism.

The last she would have to report, and she hated being responsible not simply for an undergraduate's failure but also for their suspension or expulsion. For many the journey toward a college degree could also be a journey through hell though Harriet hoped Dante's poetry might persuade a few to take possession of their fates.

It was close. Harriet thought it was so close. She felt Yitzhak's deep thrusts in a way that for a moment amplified this curious sensation into a nearly full arousal. Again, she was in the back seat of the Chevrolet bomb and also returned to the hidden pullout in the hills. There was no movie to create the excuse of a date. They had beers again and at her prompting drove directly up the Arlington to the woodsy overlooks of Grizzly Peak.

Harriet's anticipation of their first date also was arousing. She took days to absorb the revived facts of her first coitus and its exhilarating commotion of strain, heat and smell. And she wanted it again with some thought she could be more attentive, more immediately aroused, and more satisfied.

She had examined her memory of their previous sex as if she were searching the stitches of a piece of embroidery. Yitzhak's cock was an important feature though this new sexual experience was still mostly about her.

They took longer this time, Harriet desiring to touch and look at Yitzhak's hard erection to which he comfortably submitted. Her curiosity extended to the position they took and she had two or three others in mind, which he accommodated also with gracious silence. She wanted him to touch her. To use his fingers in a particular way that was familiar and exciting to her from her own touches. He made an effort that was sloppy and not successful but he smiled throughout and things got silly and in way that allowed Harriet to relax into her own experience.

Later she was surprised by the idea that sex could be so raw and also delicious and with a man she likely would never choose for a partner. This time she ran her hands over his bare shoulders as if she were framing the shapes of mountains. Again, she was anchored by his sturdy long limbs and, at the end, as she bounced vigorously against his thighs, Harriet quietly howled at the revelation of so many hungers.

Harriet's campus life, sequestered for so long within the college's tall brick towers of learning, had enforced another kind of virginity. She had missed the Free Speech Movement battles of 1964 and barely registered the winter strike of 1966 when students and faculty protested campus military recruitment.

"These university actions seem to skip years," Bronwyn said.

Harriet thought her tone whimsical. No one at the table laughed. A campus strike was already underway at the state college across the Bay in support of a Department of Third World Studies. It was becoming an issue on the Berkeley campus and would likely grow the next student-driven battle for social justice.

"Get out your raincoats," Bronwyn said. "It's winter 1968. Is anyone surprised after the year we've had that we're heading into another storm?"

"Where would you like to start?" Mack asked Harriet as they later sat together for coffee.

Harriet entered the university in the fall of 1962 and was embarrassed to ask Mack for a history of protest at a school where she had spent so many years studying.

"How did you miss all this?" he asked her.

"I haven't missed it," she answered. "To tell the truth, I've ignored it."

She remembered Mario, the FSM, the arrests and the negotiations and the large and amplified rallies in the plaza she passed daily on her way to class. She could name some leaders: Mario, of course, and Jack Weinberg "the guy in the car" as well as Mike Rossman, Bettina Apthecker, Jerry Rubin, Tom Hayden and the SDS. Bob Avakian was her anthropology TA in an undergraduate anthropology class. She heard Martin Luther King speak on campus. She attended a Charter Day ceremony in 1962 with her father when President Kennedy spoke to a packed football stadium. But none of this had motivated her to engage.

"My father was against the whole Free Speech thing at first, but my anthro professor was a friend of his. He told my dad the faculty needed 'a good kick in the ass from the students' to remind them what a university is supposed to do."

"And what's that?" asked Mack.

"To promote free inquiry," answered Harriet.

"And advocacy," Mack added. "The issue wasn't about what a student could study. It was about what a student could do. Could students raise money, organize protests, and in other ways mobilize? Mario, for instance. He'd spent his summer teaching black kids in Mississippi and registering Negro voters. He was risking his life to do these things, only to come back to Berkeley to be told by a dean he couldn't solicit money to support civil rights?

"In October last year, more than 15,000 marched from the campus to the Oakland Army base but were stopped by the Hells Angels at the Oakland city limits. A later march made it through after Ken Kesey turned the Angels on to acid. Like they say, acid doesn't kill the pain but it can certainly make the pain seem unimportant."

"I've never taken LSD," said Harriet.

"If you're ever tempted," replied Mack, "talk to me first."

"So where are we now?" asked Harriet.

"Spring was relatively calm until the King and Kennedy assassinations" Mack continued. "Then we had the Telegraph riots supporting the students of Paris. Bronwyn and Peter pulled that off. They've been trying for years to develop a socialist vanguard out of student protest. Meanwhile, all summer the pressure was building at SF State for a showdown over Third World Studies. You could say we're back to the civil rights issues again. But it's not civil rights anymore."

"What is it?" asked Harriet.

"It's Black Power and Chicano Power and Native American Power. Take the Panthers. They're the most innovative revolutionary movement going right now and they aren't talking about integration. They're talking about nationalism. Black nationalism, which means they are no longer seeking equality. The Panthers see blacks as a separate people under the colonial thumb of American oppression. They don't want equality. They want independence."

"Well, I see their point," answered Harriet. "I know a few women who feel the same way about men."

Mack appeared thrown by Harriet's observation.

"I don't know about that," he said. "But what I can say is that the future belongs to those who control real power. And so far, we don't. It was four brave black kids in Greensboro, North Carolina, who started all this nearly eight years ago. They were students at a local college and had the temerity—hell, the stone-cold courage—to sit-in at a segregated dime store lunch counter and ask politely for coffee. They were refused, of course. But they kept coming back even though whites showed up to harass them; squirted mustard and ketchup onto their jackets and shirts and in their faces. And none of them even flinched. Just kept showing up in their good clothes, their suits and ties, until the TV news made their ordeal a national spectacle…and a national shame."

"And now we have Black Power?" Harriet asked.

"What we have are angry black kids who want power," answered Mack. "They don't have it yet. That's what the strike at state and all this noise about Black Studies is about. The Sproul Hall sit-in and the Moses Hall riot—those were actions to support Cleaver's appearance in the sociology department's class. What they want is their own department dedicated to Black Studies."

"Can they get it?" asked Harriet.

"The chancellor is considering a proposal now," answered Mack. "And a committee of deans is meeting to discuss what might be possible. We'll know soon. They're putting it all off until after Christmas and can you blame them? It's a loaded issue and the students are bringing a lot of heat. Unfortunately, there's an angry governor on the other side who has the support of their parents to spank them hard if they resist."

"So what can I do?" Harriet asked. "Bronwyn seems to think I have some influence. I want to help. I support Black Studies."

"You're a member of AFT local 1570," said Mack. "You not only have a voice, you have a vote. The union's support could certainly influence the faculty. And if the faculty supports a Black Studies Department, it will be hard for the administration to say no."

"And if they say no?" asked Harriet.

"Here's where it gets interesting," Mack answered.

"This isn't just a university issue. It's a community issue. Blacks are a much larger political presence in Berkeley and the East Bay than they are on a state college campus. Reagan and the Regents can slap down Black Studies but they can't do much about local politics. Though they're trying. Look at what the university did to the block behind us."

Mack pointed toward the vacant lot beyond the Forum's back door.

"The university knocked down more than two dozen handsome old homes and displaced about 400 residents. And for what? A medical center? A dormitory? Neither is included in any UC budget I've seen. Really, it was to crush the South Campus community, which the Regents see as the garden that grows all the troubles on campus."

"But that's bullshit," said Harriet. "The so-called troublemakers are students and they live everywhere."

"Yeah, but they all hang around here and, of course, there are lot of drugs in this neighborhood and the cops would love to clean it out. But getting back to the local scene, last year Ron Dellums was elected to the Berkeley City Council. A black leftist now sits on the same council as a white Republican mayor. Radical communist Bob Avakian got 10,000 votes and Jerry Rubin, pixie king of the Yippies, got almost 8,000. So while there's a lot of action on campus, the real political fight is downtown. And the next city election could be a turning point."

When he finished, Mack sat back in his chair and gathered up another thought.

"The Panthers are famous for saying that political power derives from the barrel of gun. And they were certainly impressive when they carried their rifles into the state capitol last year.

"But Huey's in jail and Eldridge is who-knows-where but not in the country, I'll bet you anything. After being such a big star, he's not going back to prison for a parole violation. No, if power comes from guns we are shit out of luck because we don't have any guns. You saw what happened this year across the world. You saw the firepower that was blasted at protesting students from Tokyo to Paris. Remember Dubcek and this year's Prague spring? The Russians put a stop to that. And Mexico City? We'll never know how many students were killed in September. Really, it wouldn't take much to push our revolution completely off the map and out of historical memory. Maybe Reagan saying 'Enough!' and Nixon backing him up with troops."

"You don't sound very hopeful about change," Harriet said.

"I say fasten your seatbelt," Mack answered. "This is either the end of a beginning or the beginning of an end. Will we see a revolution or a counter-revolution? The recent election wasn't promising."

Mack had brought Harriet some books, which he set before her on the table. They included *The Berkeley Student Revolt: Facts and Interpretations*, an anthology of news coverage and analysis of the Free Speech Movement; a collection of short stories by Richard Brautigan; *Revolution for the Hell of It* by Abbie Hoffman; an early Beat anthology edited by Seymour Krim; an anthology of contemporary poetry entitled *A Controversy of Poets*; a recent edition of *The Realist*; and a dog-eared copy of a Pocket Poets Series edition of Allen Ginsberg's *Howl*.

"Literature and commentary for our time," Mack said. "Not one of these authors or poets was born before 1500. And if you want to get a bead on what the struggle is all about, after you read *The*

Berkeley Student Revolt, read Ginsberg's *America*."

Harriet thanked Mack for his time and his books.

"Nada," Mack said. "Tell your dad I said hello and ask him to forgive me for corrupting you with literature by still-living authors."

Mack left Harriet to the words and thoughts of her imagination by which every new world still existed only as its own separate shadow. Strange roots were taking hold that opened her under a limitless and starry sky, a sky that might at any time drop a rain of prolific, instructive pains.

A third date with Yitzhak was not going well and Harriet wondered what had happened. Preliminaries to their previous sex had little importance but now had a mood of foreboding. Sitting with their beers, Yitzhak shared some of his life with her.

"I live at home most of the time," said Yitzhak.

He had just taken a job as a courtesy clerk at the Berkeley Co-op. His father, a renowned mathematician at the university, had suffered a severe stroke two years before.

"Had to drop out of school," he added. "Need to take care of him while mom works. My sister comes straight home from school and cares for him when I go to the co-op".

"How do you manage all that?" asked Harriet. "It must be so hard for you and your family."

Yitzhak looked at Harriet as if her words had passed right through him.

"Dancing," he said vaguely. "There is always something spoken in the dance."

He began snapping his fingers to a non-existent beat and turned away as if he were locking himself inside an invisible closet.

"Yitzhak," Harriet called after a long few minutes of his continued and oblivious snapping. "Yitzhak, can you hear me?"

She reached for his shoulder and shook him gently.

"Yitzhak?"

The finger snapping stopped while Yitzhak, as if dropped out of dream, returned to her, his eyes probing her eyes with welcome intent.

"Thought I'd lost you there," Harriet said.

"I'm not lost," answered Yitzhak. "I can't get lost. I'm on call."

"On call?" asked Harriet. "For work? For your dad?"

"For the people. The people are the water, and the soldiers must live among them as fish," he answered. "I can't tell you anything more."

A pool of distance formed on the table between them. Perhaps it had always been there and simply ignored by Harriet who had another, more primal objective with Yitzhak. The distance traveled with them to the Grizzly Peak viewpoint that had become the hill station of Harriet's blooming libido.

Determined to have her body's way with herself, she pushed forward with sex. Yitzhak was the quiet and accommodating partner and apparently happy with their arrangement until, as Harriet pushed hard against him and felt at last the exhilarating and irresistible wave, he grabbed her by the waist and pushed her up.

"What's that?" he asked.

"What's what?"

"It's wet down there. Everywhere."

They looked together to see on their thighs and clothes and the car seat another pool of distance between them, formed now from the bloody gush of Harriet's sudden menstrual flow.

"Oh shit," Harriet shouted. "I'm so sorry."

Though why was she sorry? It was her period. It was evidence of her health and fertility and while she had spent most of her lean, dancing adolescence without it she now enjoyed getting her period. It was evidence of something real within her, a process that identified not only her existence as a woman but also its potential. She had mistreated it. She knew that. She had starved herself, still starved herself in certain ways that made the appearance of her period hard to predict. Her bleeding was like a friend and she felt guilty only because she believed she had mistreated her friend, and therefore herself and, while she had lived her youth for the syncopated movements of dance, had not paid enough attention to the rhythms of her life.

"Fuck," Yitzhak blurted. "It's everywhere."

"I have some tissue," said Harriet. "Just a minute."

Harriet grabbed her purse and jumped from the car. Outside she

searched for a tampon and inserted it under her skirt before pulling
out a pack of tissues and throwing it to Yitzhak who remained inside,
kneeling barelegged over the backseat as if held suspended over the
fires of hell.

"Relax, for heaven's sake," Harriet said impatiently. "It's just a
little blood. Probably not even a teaspoon."

"It stinks," shouted Yitzhak. "I don't want to touch it."

Before Yitzhak dropped Harriet at her home, she knew this
was their last date. She thanked him but had no idea why, though
it didn't matter. Yitzhak was silent and nothing seemed to register.
Harriet searched herself for some evidence of truth. Her body was
a conception in the air—a concrete idea streaming through the
atmosphere. Every created thing is a ripple, a wave. Though Harriet
had never seen a wave. She had only felt one.

six

"The Soviet Union isn't what we talk about when we talk
about socialism," Bronwyn told Harriet.

"But that's what a lot of people think," said Harriet.
"What do you say to people who bring that up?"

"That we're Americans. That we support the Constitution and
the Bill of Rights and that what we want is an American government
that protects all its citizens, that defends the rights of everyone, that
supports peace and justice everywhere in the world."

"That sounds lovely," said Harriet. "But it sounds like something
Reagan would say."

"Yes, but we mean it," said Bronwyn. "And Reagan doesn't."

"So what do we do?" asked Harriet. "Judging from the election
there are a lot more of them than there are of us."

"One way is to confine the debate and decision-making process
to the university," said Bronwyn. "Let the students and faculty vote
and decide. It's a constituency we can influence. And if the governor
overturns the university, then we have an injustice that can be more
widely identified and targeted."

"Another way is to threaten them," said Larry. "Panthers have

314

been threatened by the government since we first started organizing. Some of our brothers have been killed. At a certain point we got nothin' to lose by fighting. Look at France. The students nearly brought down the government."

"Nearly," said Bronwyn. "Nearly is not enough."

"It's a process," said Peter. "The administration has a decision to make right now, not us. We can wait but if what's happening at State is any clue, we might be able to close down the university."

Harriet was given an assignment: to use her union membership to contact other members and work with other TA supporters of Third World Studies to determine what support existed for a campus strike.

"If it's needed," Bronwyn said firmly.

"Oh, it gonna be needed," said Larry. "It the least that's gonna be needed."

After the meeting Harriet searched for another table where she could work for an hour grading papers. A cool first Monday of December had closed off the Forum's outdoor seating and pushed everyone inside. She at last found one table, recently abandoned and piled with cups and dishes that she pushed away to clear a space for her work.

Harriet began to take notes when Yitzhak appeared, dressed in a dark overcoat with a red scarf around his neck, the cultivated look of an *Aristide Bruant* poster as painted by Toulouse-Lautrec but for the gypsy scarf around his head and his high, black flamenco boots. Yitzhak approached Harriet with a flourish and presented Harriet with a rose in a way that drew unsettling attention from others in the café. A few began to clap but others saw the tension in Harriet's eyes and the flicker of applause died away.

"It's not necessary," Harriet said tersely.

Yitzhak appeared puzzled, as if he were expecting the rose to open a door.

"Really, it's not necessary," Harriet said again with emphasis. "It's better if we're just friends now. Can we do that? Can we just be friends?"

Yitzhak's eyes opened wide, his puzzled look transformed by

an emerging awareness. He heard Harriet and after a moment he looked down at his feet. Harriet could see he was rattled and unable to speak.

"Would you like a coffee?" Harriet offered, hoping Yitzhak would not accept.

Yitzhak shook his head.

"Gotta work," he answered. "There are people who need me."

"Yes," Harriet said, uncertain how to respond but thinking it best to leverage whatever might be taking shape in Yitzhak's mind.

"You go do that, Yitzhak. You're a strong, good man."

Yitzhak turned quickly and left. Harriet set the rose on the table. When the busser arrived to clear the dishes, she set the rose on a dirty plate and watched for a moment as it was born away.

Her semester complete, Harriet entered the winter break with a social life; the first since high school and its ballerina days when she and her girlfriends converged to giggle and scream, to maraud through streets and malls, to stay up late and steal secret sips of their parents' alcohol until, giddy and unbridled, they could rage as the leads in their own one-acts. It was a hiatus of pleasure, but one not greater than what was now set before her.

Larry had invited her to attend a benefit performance of the San Francisco Mime Troupe. The Panthers had organized a fundraiser for the Panther Free Breakfast program set to begin after the holidays. Larry's girlfriend Sylvia had reserved the Finnish American Hall in Berkeley for both the show and a reception. Proceeds would help kick-off the serving of free breakfasts to schoolchildren at St. Augustine's Church in Oakland.

Harriet gave Inger a ride to the hall.

"If they had an opening, I'd audition," Inger said of the Mime Troupe. "Have you ever seen them?"

Harriet had not.

"Revolution with theatrical wit," said Inger. "Revolution without gravitas. The rebels of Berkeley seem so serious most of the time. Honestly, if you can make someone laugh, you know you've really made your point with them."

The small hall was packed. Inger and Harriet knew no one until

Mack approached.

"Big turn-out and the black community is well-represented," Mack said. "There's your progressive black councilman holding court near the stage."

Mack pointed toward a tall man with a long face and moustache wearing a tweed coat and plain navy blue tie who stood in a group near the hall's modest stage. A woman standing near him was notably animated, her arms flying up and out, as the councilman remained still and appeared to listen.

Harriet offered to buy Mack and Inger drinks at the event's no-host bar. As she stood in line she watched others in the hall, some watching Inger who stood out in a one-piece sequined peacock blue mini-dress that displayed her sleek legs up to her mid-thighs. *She is such a provocation,* thought Harriet. *She knows. Every living thing ripples. She is a wave.*

David Hilliard of the Panthers introduced Father Earl Neil of St. Augustine's who thanked everyone for their support of the food program.

"Beginning next month we'll be feeding free breakfasts to as many as fifty children each day. We owe it all to the Panthers."

Father Neil named names, Sylvia among them.

"This woman is brilliant. What she's done in six months to make this idea a reality is beyond anything we could have imagined. Contacting businesses, organizing neighbors, coordinating with the schools. There isn't a thing she hasn't thought of."

Sylvia stood as the audience applauded.

The show began with a march down the aisle by the Troupe's Gorilla Marching Band and their rendition of "I Got Fucked in Vietnam" sung to the tune of the *Ballad of the Green Berets.* The Gutter Puppets followed, a company of small agitprop effigies given voice by their manipulators and who performed three short pieces.

The first, *Meter Maid,* suggested to the audience they protest local ordinances by stuffing soda can tabs into parking meters. The second, *Meat and Eagle Fuck,* featured larger puppets adorned in black with bone-white skulls as heads and carrying smaller puppet babies. They were Vietnamese mothers quickly attacked by a large American Eagle puppet with a fabric-stuffed pink penis used to rape the women puppets before killing them.

Its five minutes of pure puppet terror received muted applause before the last puppet skit entitled *Telephone or Ripping Off Ma Bell* that comically instructed the audience how to charge long distance phone calls to major corporations.

"It's like some deadly flood of comedy," Harriet said to Inger and Mack at intermission. "Horrific in some ways because it is just so raw. Yet how can you not laugh? They're such skilled performers."

"Something like that," said Mack. "The puppet stuff feels so much larger inside. They usually perform in the parks."

"I'm starving," said Inger. "Is there a buffet?"

The three stepped together toward the back of the hall where a long table held a spread of plates and bowls covered and filled with meats, cheeses, soupy dips, crackers, breads and salads. Inger seized a paper plate and a fork and pushed into the crowd as if burrowing for her place at a trough.

Harriet held back. For her, eating was a necessity that was also a kind of suffering. And public eating was the worst for however pleasant it might be to taste and digest, it was not at all pleasurable to see in process the rampant hunger of others. In such displays Harriet saw nothing but dirty, bloated death sucked into the mouths and bellies of fellow beasts.

The second act began with a ten-minute short film titled *O Dem Watermelons*, a grainy 16mm color production in which watermelons appeared everywhere: exploding watermelons, crushed watermelons, eviscerated watermelons giving up their animal guts, and a watermelon chased down a hill by frenzied young men who, in turn, were chased back up the hill by the watermelon.

Following this was *A Minstrel Show or Civil Rights in a Cracker Barrel*, more agit-prop that used minstrelsy to poke vicious fun at white racist hypocrisy. Though the cast was half white and half black, all performers wore black face and blue satin minstrel suits, except one white performer who appeared as a straight man named the "Interlocutor."

Nothing was sacred. In a spoof entitled *Negro History Month*, Crispus Attucks, the first African-American to die in the revolutionary war, was shot by Redcoats while he pushed a broom. In another skit, black soldiers were ordered to kill yellow men in Asia by a zealous and addled white commander.

Harriet found some of the action hard to follow; particularly a scene that seemed to mimic sex between a white woman and black man in a way intended to highlight prejudicial racial myths of sexual prowess and desire. It was very dark humor that tested constantly the limits of brutishness and raunch.

After a final blackout and a round of applause, the Troupe's director appeared on stage.

"An imperialist war has one healthy effect," he told the audience. "It exposes the foundations of the imperialist society. We must change those foundations."

The audience stood, clapped and whistled.

Larry joined Inger, Harriet and Mack for a drink after the show.

"Looks like you did well tonight," Mack said.

"You writin' a story?" Larry asked Mack. "You gonna write about the Panther breakfast program?"

"I'm writing a feature with photos," said Mack. "My editor says he'll publish it. You guys are sure busy."

"And we have more new members than we know what to do with," said Larry. "More members and fewer leaders."

"Do you know where Eldridge went?" Mack asked.

Larry shook his head.

"Some say Cuba. But whoever knows, ain't tellin'."

Harriet went to pee. When she returned, she found Larry and Sylvia but not Inger.

"Read any of those poets I told you about?" Sylvia asked Harriet.

"No. Not yet," said Harriet. "School's out now so I have some time. Have you seen Mack or Inger?"

"Here she comes," said Larry.

Inger approached and pulled Harriet aside.

"I'm leaving with Mack now. I hope that's OK with you."

It would have to be OK. Harriet's first response was to retreat from the wide outward sweep of Inger's will and to give her friend an even wider berth for her wild ways. Though to be half as wild would have given Harriet pleasure and, while she was still a babe in the arms of her own desires, Harriet stared with her healthy eyes into the vast open spaces she had yet to own.

Three nights later Inger drove Harriet to a gallery opening on Haight Street.

"How's Mack?" Harriet asked.

"A dream, of course," said Inger. "He's funny. He's bright. He's sexy, even if he's shorter than I'd like."

"Does it bother you to sleep with so many men?" Harriet asked.

Inger smiled while her eyes watched the road.

"We don't sleep very much. I'm pretty free, I know. Isn't that what being a woman means now? That we choose the men we want to fuck? Or the women, for that matter."

Inger described herself as polymorphous.

"What does that mean?" asked Harriet.

"That sex is just another way of connecting. It's usually fun and thrilling but otherwise no big thing."

"It can make babies," responded Harriet. "That seems like a pretty big thing."

"Be thankful for the pill," said Inger.

The small gallery a half-block from Ashbury Street was actually the foyer and lobby of a performing arts space named *The Zoetrope* that featured live music, experimental theater and independent films. Mack had told Inger about the art show. Stan was one of the exhibiting artists.

"Stan!" Inger shouted as she left Harriet at the door and ran down the hall.

"Your friend?" said a woman standing beside Harriet.

"My friend and my ride," Harriet answered. "Who's Stan?"

"My husband," said the woman. She wore a long winter wool coat over what appeared underneath to be a winter green party dress.

"I'm Ginger, and you are…?"

Harriet learned that Ginger was Stan's wife of two years, that she was the mother of a pre-school daughter named Lila by a previous marriage, and that Ginger worked as a legal secretary for a local law firm while Stan made his life as an artist.

"And you know the joke about the difference between an artist and a 12-inch pizza?" asked Ginger.

"No," answered Harriet.

"A 12-inch pizza can feed a family of four."

The punch line was voiced as if Ginger bore a vague and seeping resentment for her mate that had not yet found its words.

"Do you like art?" Harriet asked.

"Stan's art," she answered. "I'm more interested in dance."

That was all Harriet needed to hear to ignite an exploration of two women's lives lived as teenage ballerinas and, in Ginger's case, as a modern dancer who, when she wasn't at work all week or at home caring for Lila, took a few hours to dance.

"A Japanese dancer. She has a performing group. She lets me practice with her."

The women exchanged phone numbers before walking together down the hall. They agreed to meet soon and share their stories.

"The Big Black Motherfucker has a home," Inger announced to Harriet.

"Hello Ginger," Inger said, nearly as an afterthought.

All stood with Stan to admire his large canvass of concentric black rings that dominated the wall at the end of the hall.

"Yeah," said Stan. "It looks great. Even I'm impressed."

Later as she climbed the stairs to her room, Harriet heard from their bedroom the rising, angry voices of her parents. Her mother was drunk again and her father, both bitter and enabling, engaged her rage. What they fought about didn't matter. That they fought was the abiding exercise of their last unbroken wedding vow: to remain partners in both sickness and health.

Harriet drove herself to her last party before Christmas. It was a Solstice Celebration held at the Spaulding Avenue home of a Berkeley activist. Bronwyn had invited her. Bronwyn might have considered it a coup that the daughter of a prominent and conservative UC professor had been enlisted into the miasmic student mobilization against war and racism. Perhaps Bronwyn wished to show her off. It didn't matter to Harriet who enjoyed her sudden popularity among strangers.

It was another caucus of rebellious friends that, even if they weren't friends of Harriet, were friends with each other. That was enough for Harriet who arrived at the party, found the bar, got a drink, and waited for Bronwyn as she might for a telephone call. A new double album by the Beatles was playing through two large speakers mounted over the home's open, brick fireplace. *Helter Skelter* shook the room and stimulated among the party's guests a collective and rhythmic stir.

"This music is fucked up," said someone behind Harriet.

"What were the Beatles thinking? This album is a bunch of schlock."

It didn't take long for someone to argue the point.

"You aren't hearing what I'm hearing," said a roundish, older man who wore a white jacket and a red tie.

"It's not only the most creative album the Beatles have made, it's also damned humorous. So many of the songs are such clever, parodic covers. My god, they take on just about every form of contemporary music. And I'm saying everything, including country music, blues, bluegrass and jazz. I hear the Beach Boys, Dylan, and heavy rock. I hear a lullaby and even muzak. What do they care about breaking boundaries? For me, this is an exploration of the history of music in the West. And what's really striking is that the Beatles' put-ons of all these forms are better than the fucking originals. They created a parody of modern musical forms and improved on every one of them."

Before the man finished speaking, a clutch of party guests surrounded him as if drawn to the fount of a pleasurable controversy. Among them was Bronwyn who saw Harriet and waved her over.

"Come here, you," Bronwyn shouted. "I want you to meet some people."

The first person she introduced was the current center of attention.

"Al, this is Harriet," she said to the man in the white jacket who smiled.

"Al is a music critic in New York," said Bronwyn.

"We went to high school together. Right, Al?"

The small chubby man smiled and retreated into a smaller group interested in a continuing colloquy. Harriet followed Bronwyn who imposed herself into clusters of guests to introduce Harriet with energy fully out of the range of the guests' interest.

Harriet was "the daughter of Professor Alden" or "a member of the teaching assistants union" or simply "one of us." Bronwyn was enthusiastic but without the sisterly intimacy Harriet recalled from their earlier time at the Forum. In any of Bronwyn's invasive introductions Harriet was never just Harriet, which began to irritate her until she realized Bronwyn was drunk.

"I see someone I need to talk to," said Bronwyn before snaking away from Harriet through the crowded living room.

Harriet refilled her wine glass and sat in a corner where she could remain self-contained and also observant. She watched Bronwyn chatter at a young and awkwardly quiet member of the UC African American Students Union. She looked up to see Larry pass in front of her. She called to him. How are you?

"I guess we doin' OK," Larry said. "Sylvia and I are doin' well and my parents just love her. Who wouldn't?"

It had been a hard holiday. If Sam had not died in Vietnam, he would have been home for Christmas. He would have started a new life built from a hope that his investment in the Army would return as the Army's investment in him. But Sam's life had been taken, a loss the Army had not insured him against.

"Mom is better, but she'll never be good again. It's like she waitin' for another shoe to drop. She always askin' 'bout me. She hates the Panthers more than the Army now. Looks to her sometimes like just another way for a black boy to get hisself killed."

"That has to be hard," Harriet said.

She did not know how hard and struggled to grasp Larry's deep and abiding grief.

"It's cool," said Larry, sensing Harriet's challenge. "We'll get through this."

He cast her an empathic grin, as if to say, *I know you don't know and that you want to know and in a helpful way but I can't tell you what you don't know.*

Harriet waited out the rest of the party. As she was about to leave, a young man she had seen earlier approached her. Brownyn introduced them during her first whirlwind tour of the party.

"I was hoping to talk with you again," he said directly.

He was a teaching assistant and they shared a common and topical interest in the politics of the university and a mutual identity with the responsibilities of teaching. He was interesting but Harriet was tired and needed to leave. She exchanged phone numbers with the man, who was named Michael.

Driving home she held in mind the voice and gestures of the Michael man who made such an effort to speak with her. Had she left too soon? Her awareness that she might be attracted to him was like a lingering double take. He was a colleague, of course, and he had left her with a link, and so the interest he showed in her was now growing into an interest of her own. She imagined vaguely a meeting, coffee perhaps, and some more words and then a choice. That would be fine. She was still cautious and understood there would be no choice without a decision and no decision without a desire.

seven

Harriet sat with her mother on Christmas Eve while together they watched television coverage of Apollo Eight's arrival at the moon. Three American astronauts were tucked into a space capsule the size of a second bathroom and during the previous day had become the first humans ever caught entirely by the gravity of another world. As the small ship disappeared into a lunar sunset the tiny crew took turns reading from the Book of Genesis. It might have been the expression of a hope that God, or some god not yet grasped or known, was on their side. It was for Harriet the modern version of an old journey toward the stars that began for her and her species, as it had for Dante, in a dark wood.

Harriet's mother followed on television this first manned flight from the earth to the moon as she followed all momentous news of human grief and commerce. The space mission was scheduled to last little more than a hundred hours; nearly the duration of the televised coverage of President Kennedy's assassination, a president that six years before had launched the country's ambitious space program. Harriet had spent the current and dying year with two other such incidents that also were assassinations.

The first was the murder of the nation's most prominent civil rights leader, Martin Luther King, on a motel balcony in Memphis where he had gone to lead a labor strike. The other was of Kennedy's younger brother Bobby, himself a candidate for president and moments after his victory in the California primary.

The coverage of those explosive murders and of the riots that followed also lasted for about a hundred hours; little more than four days while the violent acts were examined, reprised and riotously repudiated. Once the prominent victims' bodies were in the ground, the rioting ceased as more dead were gathered and buried. It stunned Harriet to hear one of the astronauts say, from his distant remove in the vast vacuum of space, "a good night to that good Earth." Was consciousness a folly of creation or was it a further furnishing of the universe?

Harriet was tired and wished to sleep. Her mother said good night. But a critical blast of the capsule's rockets was scheduled after midnight. And if it failed, the astronauts would be trapped in perpetual lunar orbit and lost forever. Her mother wished to stay up until she could hear that the boys were coming home. No, she said to Harriet's sarcastic query, the boys in space, not the boys in Vietnam.

"It's the Baby Express," Mary shouted over the phone. "Little human critters everywhere. We're one big family. Come over and see us!"

"Is Charlie with you?" Harriet asked.

Mary was a former campus librarian and Harriet's dear friend before becoming a fugitive from the Summer of Love. Harriet had witnessed Mary's rash attraction to a short, black-bearded guitarist named Charlie who prowled the Haight/Ashbury in the spring of the previous year. Mary and Charlie lived together in an apartment in Berkeley and then on Cole Street in the City where the baby was conceived while Charlie wrote songs and played his guitar and looked for other women he could interest in creating a new family with him.

Harriet visited a few times, at first struck by Charlie's intensity and self-assurance though perplexed by her friend's infatuation with him and her acceptance of other young women into her home and her bed. After an evening during which Charlie, with Mary's apparent blessing, tried to seduce Harriet, she stopped visiting.

In the fall, Charlie, his pregnant Mary, and a few other women who had joined the family, drove to Los Angeles. Mary stayed in touch with Harriet, phoning and occasionally writing. In April she sent Harriet a letter describing the birth of her son in a cabin on a Topanga Canyon ranch where the family, now numbering more than twenty, made its home.

Mary was visiting old friends at a crash pad in the Haight. She drove up with another member of her polygamous family, a woman named Sadie who Harriet knew from the Summer of Love days and who had just had her own baby.

"No, Charlie couldn't come. He's got a gig," Mary said. "He sold a song to the Beach Boys and it's been recorded. He's playing this week in Venice and writing all the time. And two more babies this year. We're a big family now. Charlie says the moment is all that matters. Charlie says there is no time. There was no time until man made it. You should come see us. It's a paradise. It's our own world. Charlie says it's not worth adjusting to the free, 'out there' world. He's made up his own world so we don't have to adjust or get into the race anymore."

Harriet asked if she could bring a friend for her visit.

"It's cool but call first," said Mary.

Harriet knocked on the door of a large, weathered Victorian half-way up the hill on Ashbury. Mary answered the door and threw her arms around Harriet and squeezed her hard. Once disentangled, Harriet introduced Inger.

"Get in here!" Mary shouted jovially and showed her and Inger the way down a long hall and down again a flight of stairs to a vast, carpeted basement.

Two wooden chairs, a low table and three double mattresses were strewn randomly around the room. Sadie sat on one mattress, wrapped in a crumpled cotton blanket while she nursed her baby. Sadie was tall, even as she sat to nurse. She appeared tired, her dark hair in need of a wash. Sadie's brown eyes probed Harriet and

Inger as women who were not yet mothers and who either might be encouraged to join her in motherhood or be vigorously warned off.

Mary's boy struggled in his mother's arms. Mary set him down on the carpet where he crawled toward a pull toy shoved under a folding chair. Stacked in a corner were two large bags filled with disposable diapers. A nearly full garbage can stood at the stairway.

"No, I'm not working now," Mary said in response to Harriet's question. "This little guy keeps me so fucking busy. Nursing, diapers, keeping him off the stairs and out of trouble. Right, Sadie?"

Sadie smiled.

"Yeah, Sadie knows what I mean. Was it a year ago you were dancing topless in North Beach? Those boobs look a lot different now, don't they?"

Sadie stopped smiling.

"You danced in North Beach?" Inger asked Sadie. "What was that like?"

"Why do you want to know?" Sadie asked.

Inger said she had worked at a topless bar and needed to make more money. She was thinking of trying out in North Beach.

"It's a trip," said Sadie. "Helps to be stoned, though. You're up there in front of a bunch of real creeps. You gotta love your body if you want 'em to like you. But if they do, they tip big. I made a lot a cash for not very much work. But do you wear a bra?"

"Not usually," said Inger. "Why?"

"If you're not big enough to wear a bra, you probably aren't big enough for North Beach. But there's a modeling scene in the City that pays good, too."

"Yeah, I know," said Inger. "It can be pretty rough, though. Usually you have to like having sex in front of the camera to make decent money."

"Shit, yes," Sadie answered with what sounded to Harriet like avid endorsement.

"What's it like to live on this ranch of yours?" Harriet asked Mary.

"It's an old ranch," Mary answered.

"Used for years as a movie set, mostly for old cowboy westerns. It's like living in a Wild West ghost town. Owned by a guy named

George. He's at least eighty years old. We take good care of him and he lets us have the run of the place. A couple of his ranch hands joined the family."

Harriet asked how they survived.

"Don't need to work," said Mary. "Working is for straights. We have all the food and money we need. We don't pay rent. A deal comes through, like Charlie selling a song. Or we score some dope and sell it. Whatever we need. We sometimes just take things we need. We'll dumpster dive. You'd be amazed how much good food the markets toss. Or we'll take stuff. Charlie calls it 'appropriating' and says the rich pigs all have enough and owe us. We only take from the rich. It may not make sense to you but Charlie says no sense makes sense. We live in the moment. You should come down and see for yourself."

"It feels like you've really changed," Harriet said, attempting a neutral tone to introduce her concern for an old friend's welfare.

"What you have to understand," Mary answered sharply, "is that the past is over. There is no past. It is dead. Gone. There is no past and no future. As Charlie says, there is no time. Really, it's a beautiful scene. We do a lot of acid. We are happy as hell. All of us. Thanks to Charlie. Living with Charlie is like living in group therapy all the time."

Harriet offered to take the women and their children out for dinner.

"No way," said Mary. "The little guy can't sit still for five minutes and Sadie will have to nurse. These kids are used to being on a giant ranch where no one cares what they do. This is the big old city. Let's order out."

Over pizza and cokes, Mary continued to extoll the ranch and its freedoms, the beautiful weather of Los Angeles, the closeness of a very large family and most of them women, and always and at last Charlie, the brilliant founder of their new and free feast.

Throughout the meal, Mary's baby screamed, pushing away the bites of pizza offered by his mother.

"Do you have something else to give him?" asked Harriet.

Mary put the child down, rummaged through a grocery bag and came back with a torn-open box of baby crackers.

"He'll eat these," she said.

After dinner, Mary asked Harriet and Inger if they would like to get stoned.

Harriet declined, but Inger took a few tokes while Sadie told Inger more stories of her topless days in North Beach. On one occasion she was paid to dance nude for the coven of a local Satanist. Sadie gave Inger the phone number at the ranch.

"Two hundred for one hour," said Sadie. "Most I've ever made."

"I'm on track for a doctorate," said Harriet in response to a question from Mary. "I'm active in campus politics; trying to get a black studies department on campus. And no, no boyfriend. Not yet."

"It's too late for black studies," said Mary, ignoring the boyfriend comment. "Too late for civil rights. There's going to be a war. A race war."

"Really? Who says?" asked Harriet.

"Charlie," answered Mary.

"Charlie says a race war is coming and we're going to hide out at the ranch until it's over. When it's safe to come out, a lot of people will be gone. A lot of white people will die."

After eating a slice of pizza, Harriet stood quickly and said she would need to get back to Berkeley, though Inger—who was connecting with Sadie—said she wanted to stay awhile and would catch a bus back.

"You sure?" Harriet said quietly to Inger. "You feel comfortable here?"

"I wouldn't say comfortable, exactly," said Inger. "I'm curious."

Harriet drove home alone, disillusioned by a hundred unspoken details of her visit: Mary's dirty appearance, her greasy and wrinkled denim skirt and smelly pee-stained blouse, the spare crash pad with its own patina of filth, syringes in the bathroom trash and frantic children wearing soaked diapers and little else. And Charlie. Who was this guy? Harriet knew him as a short, dark man with a booming voice, enormous energy and a look behind his piercing eyes that gave Harriet the feeling he might be capable of anything. She remembered feeling repulsed and also attracted. Mary said Charlie had spent time in jail but wouldn't elaborate.

And dinner. Harriet could barely eat. There were no plates or forks. Sadie went to the bathroom and brought back a roll of toilet paper for napkins. Harriet credited the dirty house as the trigger for her lost appetite though she knew something deeper was at work. An old feeling was returning, one that divided Harriet from her body in a way that mimicked deeper divisions between her and her parents or between her and her existence within a life that demanded more than she received, that trapped her within its gelid and scholarly trappings.

Or she might be agitated by her first experience of sex with another person and its awkward and rude passage. Her Thanksgiving purge in the bathroom did not help, paving as it did a return path to the lightening joys of a fruitful emptiness.

All this had pushed Harriet back in front of her bathroom mirror and onto her scales. She again served the perfected body, a vessel that surely would lead her to the perfect life.

Harriet suffered because she was at fault. When she spoke with her father at his campus office, she was the aspiring and perpetual student barely able to master her material. In her seventh year of study at the university, she approached her chosen work with hesitancy. So many Dante litterateurs had preceded her, centuries of them, that to create original insights was a daunting challenge.

Though she loved Dante and his poetry and had learned to read and write fluently in the peculiar Italian vernacular of the 14th century. She felt herself falling into a perpetually narrowing range of expertise. To win her doctorate she eventually would know only one very specific thing, but know it very well.

And it was a lonely life that she spent competing with fellow scribes, all of them in their quiet and private pursuits of that one infinitesimally dimensioned topic each would come to know better than everything else. It was in her father's campus office that Harriet regularly reckoned with her academic duties and failures. She was her own worse critic, but no worse than her father.

At home, Harriet was accustomed to sitting with him in his study as he rendered judgments of her life. From an early age she had sat shrunken in a large chair, staring at the diplomas and artwork on his walls, at his tall and threatening bookcases full of volumes of literary work and commentary, a small amount his own. He would speak from behind his desk to command her at first confused and, ultimately, resentful attention. On the first Sunday of the New Year, he called Harriet into his study.

"Are you really going to get involved with this Black Studies thing?" he asked her.

He reported that an associate professor in the department had seen her passing out leaflets supporting a campus strike.

"We all hope it doesn't come to that," said Harriet.

"We? Who's we?" her father asked.

"Lots of us," said Harriet.

"Students, mostly. And some faculty. It's time, Daddy. Why shouldn't students who don't claim European ancestors, why shouldn't they be able study their own cultures and origins? Why shouldn't they be able to explore their own literature and art?"

"If you could call it literature and art," said her father.

"I mean, Eldridge Cleaver of all people? Why should the academy support a program without any recognized content?"

"Recognized by whom?" asked Harriet. "It's not recognized because it isn't seen."

Her father sensed the beginning of an argument without end. And he wished to say only one thing.

"There is an indisputable fact here. And that is, if you continue to participate in actions against the university, it will seriously impact your academic career. And you've invested so much. I urge you strongly to quit this fight and get back to finishing your doctorate. You are already attracting the wrong kind of attention. You are my daughter. If you can't do this for yourself, consider what your actions reflect about me. Please quit, before you get involved in a riot."

Harriet stood to leave. She was at fault again but had a new idea whom to blame.

"Martin Luther King said that a riot is the language of the unheard," Harriet said. "You are grasping, Daddy. You are defending something indefensible. What I do has no relation to you. I love you but you are not my master."

Harriet left, hearing her father chuckle nervously in a way that sounded defensive and also fearful.

"Don't say I didn't warn you," he called after her.

"That's something I will never say, Daddy," Harriet answered without turning to look at him. "You've been warning me all my life."

Did knowing someone precisely include knowing his desire?

It was the question raised by Ginger as she stood in her kitchen and poured tea for Harriet. It was Saturday and Stan had taken Ginger's daughter Lila to the studio to finish a painting while Ginger took her weekly morning of rest, the one she now shared with her guest.

"He's an artist," said Ginger. "And he loves Lila. Takes her to the studio where she paints and colors while he works on a canvass. He's good. I never worry about him with her though I know he worries that I do. When money's short, as it is this month, I can get cranky. He hasn't sold anything in four months. I think I know what he wants. I just don't think he knows what he can honestly do."

Ginger moved toward the table with what Harriet imagined as lilting grace, her square face dominated by a strong, narrow nose. She was at least thirty but younger than Stan. Her body was strong, if slightly paunchy at the waistline, which Harriet guessed had been stretched irreversibly during her pregnancy.

"Where did you dance?" Harriet asked.

"In school, at first. Ballet was a P.E. elective in junior high thanks to a former balletomane who also taught English. He actually interested some boys in ballet because he was such a cool teacher. I took to it. By ninth grade I was dancing with a junior company downtown. I was fourteen and already too old and too fat. No, I wasn't fat. But you know how that goes in ballet."

"So no crash diets?" Harriet asked.

"Oh hell yes," said Ginger. "I lost twenty pounds by not eating anything but celery and chocolate for a month. Then I got dizzy and sick at practice and had to step down. It was just as well. I looked too much like a woman already. Full-on boobs and a big butt no amount of dieting could shrink. See?"

Ginger did a turn that raised her skirt and flashed enough of her bottom to make her point.

"But you still dance?" asked Harriet.

"You could call it that," answered Ginger. "I dance with Ichiko. Her husband owns a restaurant in Oakland. She's a fan of Merce Cunningham and has formed a company. I practice with them two evenings a week. Sometimes I perform. It keeps me alive. My secretarial job with a law firm doesn't do shit for me. But it pays the rent. Speaking of which, do you know a student who needs a room for the spring semester? We're looking to rent out a room."

"How much?" asked Harriet.

"Forty-five a month. It's the sun porch, but it's completely windowed and we have a space heater that warms it up fast. Furnished, too. A good bed, a desk and a coffee table with a couple of chairs. And right off the kitchen. And we live five blocks from the campus. Let me show you."

"Why rent it only for the semester?" asked Harriet.

"Stan and I may want to leave town," said Ginger.

"For the summer?" asked Harriet.

"Forever," said Ginger.

eight

Students returned to campus in a slow post-holiday wave. They waited in lines to enroll and bought their books. Professors and teaching assistants arrived to finalize their curricula, mimeograph handouts and renew their reading lists at the library. Political activists set up their tables on the plaza to pitch and enlist those returning for the spring. The following week all would rush together into the yawning jaws of a new semester.

Harriet walked through a cool winter fog to the Forum where she took her place at the big table in the back before anyone else arrived. There would be news, but whose? Along with Bronwyn, Peter, Larry and the regulars, new faces appeared. Harriet saw Michael arrive, the TA she met at the holiday party on Spaulding.

"So I have some good news and some bad news," Bronwyn said

to open the first meeting of the year. "The professor charged with studying the issue of a Black Studies Department recommended its creation to the Chancellor. However, the College of Letters and Science Committee, meeting without the professor or any student representatives, has eliminated key elements of the proposal, including community involvement and student participation. And it won't say whether Black Studies should be a program or a department."

"That sounds like bullshit," said Larry.

"More than bullshit," said Peter. "They're hoping the process will make us all tired and we'll just go away."

"They've tried it before," said Bronwyn. "It never works for them."

"Reagan works for them," said Larry. "Reagan won the election by running against Berkeley."

"We need a plan," said Bronwyn. She rattled off the acronyms of several campus organizations: AASU, MASC, AAPA, the CPE and an entity described simply as "the coordinating council."

"We work together or nothing gets done. I remember when Bettina got up on the police car the day the Free Speech movement started. She quoted Frederick Douglas: *Power concedes nothing without a demand*. It brought the loudest cheer of the afternoon. I'll never forget that. It was true then. It's true now. We'll need to prepare for a strike. And we'll need campus support for a strike. We need the TAs and the faculty."

Brownyn spoke to Michael.

"How about the AFT? Will the union support a strike? It did at State."

At last Harriet heard an acronym she recognized.

"I'm pretty certain the TAs will support a strike. A few might need persuading," he reported

"Can you and Harriet get on that for us?" asked Bronwyn.

Harriet and Michael made eye contact and nodded together as Michael gestured with his finger, pointing first at himself and then at Harriet. Again, they nodded as if the end of the meeting conveniently marked a curious new beginning.

Like the astronauts, Dante had returned to earth. It was Harriet's way of introducing students to the poet's passage from the Inferno to the Purgatorio, from a timeless, eternal horror to a place where the sun rose and set, where night gave way to day and souls existed once more in time. Of the three parts of the Commedia, Purgatorio was the only to offer its penitent arrivals a measure of the hours, days and seasons. Those who climbed the mountain could count the years spent at each of its seven ledges of vice and sin. Finally, having been purged through their weary and time-bound labor; the humbled souls were welcomed to Paradise, free of sin and at last off the clock.

"Virgil again leads the way, but beyond the mountain's peak he can go no farther. Why?"

Harriet waited through the new year's first muddling student silence until she saw at last a raised hand at the back of the classroom.

"Because he isn't a Christian," the woman said. "Only Christians can enter heaven. God takes care of Virgil in other ways."

"That's a start," said Harriet.

She asked her favorite young male student to read a few lines from Purgatorio's first canto. He stood and cleared his throat.

Dolce color d'oriental zaffiro,
che s'accoglieva nel sereno aspetto
del mezzo, puro infino al primo giro,
a li occhi miei ricommincio diletto…

The color of a sapphire growing deeper in the cloudless air might describe an earthly sunset though Harriet's first thought was of the astronauts, those modern pilgrims that had approached an empyrean and also returned to earth. What would they see now as far as the horizon? A colorful sky diminished in meaning by their extraterrestrial insights or an assuring return of the warm, brilliant sunsets of home? And would it all still delight their eyes?

Inger had news for Harriet. She sat with her in her parents' quiet kitchen to tell her she was moving back to her brother's house. Inger's hours at the hotel had been cut and she was going to need to find other work.

"But you're a guest here," said Harriet. "You don't need to move."

Inger thanked Harriet.

"You're kind to me," Inger said. "I'm grateful. But I need to have control of my own life in all ways. When I go too long without control, I lose perspective and make bad choices. My brother isn't great, but he'll store my stuff at no cost."

Inger's second disclosure was that she intended to visit Sadie and Mary later in the month at their ranch commune in Topanga Canyon.

"A couple of days…maybe a week," Inger said to minimize her apparent interest in what she knew Harriet considered a bizarre living situation.

"That's all."

"What's there for you?" asked Harriet.

"If I knew, I might not be going," Inger answered. "It's LA…If I want to be an actress I need to go there and at least look around. But even if their scene sounds crazy, Mary and Sadie are smart women and maybe they know something we don't."

Harriet could feel her chest tighten. She thought of her friend Mary now as anything but smart and wondered what had happened to the bright and thoughtful librarian she had known just a year before.

"I'm worried about her," said Harriet. "I've met Charlie. I know Mary loves him, that she thinks he's the smartest and greatest man she's ever met. Me, I'm scared of him."

"It's a new time," said Inger. "We're all looking for new ways to live. New ways to make love happen. Everything can seem scary, even if it's just another way to do things. Sadie invited me to come stay with her and I need, at least, to have a look."

"If you ever need to come back here…" Harriet didn't finish her sentence.

Inger's faced reddened. Harriet thought she might cry.

"Are you OK?" asked Harriet.

"Never better," Inger answered. "Never."

Michael met Harriet at a table in the Student Union cafeteria.

"I have a roster," he said. "Let's have a look."

Harriet sat across from him, watching his eyes scan a list of AFT members of local #1570. He checked the names of university teaching assistants. His eyes were a bright and riveting blue and, Harriet thought, moved in tandem with his mind. She found both his eyes and mind attractive and based this on little else but a wanton projection. Though it was enough. Without fully realizing it, she was interested in much more than Michael's eyes and mind.

"You teach in anthropology? What professor?"

Harriet intended her question to be professionally affiliating though she felt self-conscious asking even this.

"Yeah," answered Michael. "Washburn. I have two sections of his Intro to Physical Anthropology. He's everything they say about him."

"And what's that?" asked Harriet. "I don't know the field. I teach Medieval Lit."

"He put Berkeley on the map," said Michael. "His work is legendary. He was the first to suggest that tool use, hunting and gender division in labor were critical to human evolution. Forty years ago he was the first anthropologist to link homo sapiens with an ancestor that walked on its knuckles, a now extinct creature that must have looked something like today's great ape."

For several moments Michael's voice was all Harriet heard. His voice and eyes and ingenuous smile intrigued her and alerted her to some flickering though indescribable possibility impossible to categorize.

"Would you like to get dinner?" he asked her.

He had noticed something. She knew from the way his attention moved from their common task and his scholarship and towards her. His eyes were on her and she had more than her fill of them.

"OK," she said, not thinking now of food or the meals it comprised. She would eat with him. Eat for him. She would address the challenging choices presented by food for more of his voice and his eyes and the pleasure these gave her.

They walked to the Hofbrau and passed through the buffet line. Harriet picked out a muffin and a bowl of cucumber salad. Michael ordered a French dip with fried potatoes. They shared a half-carafe of white wine.

Harriet relaxed into Michael's generosity. He was interested in her. He asked questions, which helped Harriet pace her bites so he might not notice how little she ate.

"Your doctorate, what are you doing?" he asked.

He sat attentively as Harriet spoke about her dissertation. She tried to describe the perverse imagery of the lower circles of Dante's Inferno and her goal to decipher why Dante portrayed the sins of malice as those committed by the most potentially noble people in his world.

"It's a long poem, of course," said Harriet. "I've focused on a particular section, perhaps a thousand lines, that appears surprisingly modern. Dante knew the politics of his time. Those punished for malice in the lower circles of hell are politicians, warriors and kings.

"One is a poet that for selfish reasons advised a king to fight a needless war. He walks holding his decapitated head by the hair as the head's mouth protests the injustice of his punishment. It's the fate of those who sought to divide people in conflict to be divided themselves, even cut up and cut off from others. It's a curious fate for the fraudulent, those that complicate in order to deceive."

"Modern, indeed," said Michael. "You make me think of our last election. Deceit and division? Needless war? Fraud? What would Dante have to say about all this?"

"Plenty," said Harriet. "Though if one reads him closely, I think he's already said it."

Michael spoke about fossils and hominids and how his aptitude for biology grew into an obsessive interest in the origin of the human species. His enthusiasm drew her in as if she were being allowed to walk inside his head, to touch his interests and experience them. Her own academic life had been an essentially visual search, had held her in a hunt among incalculable words in countless books and from which she, like a gleaner in an abandoned French garden, took few morsels she could call her own. Michael's studies were different. His work was empirical, scientific, and rigorous in its application.

"My apartment isn't far from here. Would you like to come over?" he asked.

"I don't even know your last name," Harriet said.

"Yeah," said Michael. "It's Hassler. Michael Hassler. I didn't mean to appear forward. Could I have your phone number? And may I walk you to your car?"

Harriet consented to both.

Gratefully, Harriet arrived early at the university to teach her Dante section. She had driven her father's Karmann Ghia, which she used occasionally when he stayed home to write. With his faculty pass, she was allowed to park on campus. She was grateful because she had forgotten her syllabus and would drive home to get it and still return in time to teach.

She entered her home through the kitchen and heard sounds upstairs, a soft murmuring and garrulous laughter that seemed to be coming from her parents' bedroom. She might have thought her parents were having sex, revealed usually in a furtive but compelled symphony of groans and bounces from which Harriet would hurriedly flee. But her mother was gone, had left for her classes just after breakfast. Harriet climbed the stairs quietly. The sounds were louder and unmistakable. A woman was in the bedroom with her father and it was not her mother. Harriet entered her room and closed the door. She searched quietly for her syllabus, found it and prepared to leave.

As Harriet left her room to sneak back downstairs, the door of her parents' bedroom opened. Out stepped Inger, naked and flush as she staggered toward Harriet's bathroom down the hall.

"What?" shouted Harriet.

Inger turned to see her.

"Oh shit," Inger mumbled, as if suddenly and sadly resigned to a thousand jeopardous consequences that would flow from the moment forming before her and her friend.

Later Harriet tried to recall the blur that followed: how she ran back into her room as Inger ran back into her parents' bedroom; how she tried to imagine another man with Inger, that her friend might have decided to use the house to meet another lover however improbably rude and thoughtless this might seem, how she listened at her door for the voices that were unmistakable and then confronted in the hall both her father, sweaty and also flush in his black terrycloth robe, and Inger, quickly dressed and desperate to leave.

There were words, but she couldn't remember them, only that her father said something like *I can explain* and Inger said nothing as she ran downstairs and out the front door. Harriet remembered saying something like "How could you do this?" and "Where's mom?" before rushing out herself to face her students.

At noon she left the section meeting and saw her father waiting for her outside her classroom. She left through another door and ended up at the student union where she phoned Ginger who, gratefully, answered.

"Your sun porch still available?" Harriet asked.

"Yeah, you got someone who's interested?"

"Yes," answered Harriet. "Me."

The rest of Harriet's day was spent acknowledging the unbearable. By mid-afternoon she had reconciled herself to the facts of her new life and the deep chasm of all things for so long unknown. When she returned to her office for a conference with one of her students she found, instead, her father. He had sent her student away and now sat in Harriet's chair.

"It's really not what you think," her father said.

"And what do I think?" Harriet answered.

"That Inger is my lover," her father answered.

"Well, isn't she?" said Harriet. "How long have you been fucking her?"

Harriet's directness surprised her and seemed to frighten her father.

"It's complicated," he said evasively.

"I don't suppose mother knows," said Harriet.

"Oh god," he said. "Please don't tell her. Another one of these will kill her."

"Another?" Harriet shouted. "There are others?"

"Really, it's not what you think," he said again. "I've got this, well...."

A confession seemed to be forming before Harriet cut him off.

"It's treachery," said Harriet. "It is a deep betrayal and it severs all ties."

Her father slumped deeper into her chair as if he were the one being wronged.

"It's not your friend's fault," he offered.

"I suppose it's no one's fault," said Harriet. "But I hold you responsible."

"I have a new place to live," she added. "If you don't want me to tell mother, here's what you do. You will pay my rent. You will bring me some clothes and bedding tonight. I will give you the address. Tell mom I'll phone her tomorrow."

"What do I say about you moving out?" her father asked, now a minion to his daughter's wishes.

"It's time," Harriet shouted. "It's just fucking time."

To acknowledge what was unbearable was one thing. To act on it was another. Stan and Ginger accepted Harriet's hasty decision and asked no questions. Harriet arrived after their dinner and while Stan was putting Lila to bed. Harriet's father came in the early evening bearing Harriet's requested items and a check for the first two months rent. Harriet arranged to return home on another day for the rest of her things. She would do it only at a time both her mother and father were away.

"It's just so sudden," said Harriet's mother on the phone. "What are you doing? Are you OK?"

Harriet said an opportunity to live with friends had come up suddenly and she took it.

"I've been thinking about it for awhile," she said to her mother. "Nothing's wrong. I'm going to be 26 this year and it's time for me to live on my own."

Uncertainty still surrounded the hoped-for creation of a Department of Black Studies on campus. The African-American Students Union demanded the immediate creation of such a department while groups representing students of Asian and Mexican descent joined with the campus student union to form the Third World Liberation Front.

A Strike Support Committee was formed to mobilize white student and faculty support and within a week student picket lines went up at all major entrances to the campus. On the same day, the teaching assistants voted for a work stoppage that would support the Front's strike.

"We have something to celebrate," Michael said to Harriet after the union vote.

He asked her to have dinner with him. He knew an Asian restaurant on San Pablo Avenue that specialized in Indonesian cuisine. Harriet said yes. She felt engulfed by both the woe and well being of her week of upheaval and its resulting and embryonic independence. Harriet could not decide whether she had been softened or dismantled. She was in a swoon and did not know if she would again find a place to land.

Dinner was fun and delicious. She approached her food without fear and it rewarded her courage with its delicate textures and fragrant flavors. She asked for a second glass of wine and took the unprecedented step of ordering a dessert.

"You seem distracted," said Michael as Harriet's eyes strayed occasionally away from him as if she were forming thoughts she could not say.

"I'm sorry," Harriet answered, embarrassed by her inattention but grateful Michael was sensitive enough to notice.

"Tell me more about your studies. I really enjoy listening to you."

Michael spoke while Harriet floated along on his kind and intelligent words.

"Shall I take you home?" Michael asked as they left the restaurant.

"Not my home," Harriet said directly. "Yours."

She was engulfed. She might assert or succumb. She might experience fear or joy. But she would not dissolve nor melt nor cease to exist.

nine

Harriet awoke in Michael's bed. Morning light painted the far wall much as the light did in her room at home. It was the only touchstone. Everything else was fresh, including the body under the covers that was not hers and that she had touched and held and finally grasped desperately in a cave of vague, dark and memorable pleasure. The body stirred.

"How long have you been awake?" Michael asked.

He turned toward her, his hair a wild black spray of curls.

"Not long," she said.

She found his eyes, which squinted in the light. She was desperate for a view of him or a touch from him that would assure her something deeply known in the night was not forgotten.

Michael reached out in his morning blindness to find Harriet's arms and shoulders. He pulled her toward him. She fell into his chest, her thighs curled against his legs while his arm encircled her shoulders and breasts.

"How are you?" he asked.

"Good," Harriet said cautiously. "And you?"

"Happy you're here. Happy you stayed."

"I'm happy, too," said Harriet, though it was more a wish than the truth. In fact, she felt odd and displaced.

There was some comfort in his tone and timbre and the moist warmth of his breath on her neck as he pulled her closer and kissed her shoulder.

"Let me make you breakfast," he said. "What would you like?"

Food again. Her stomach felt as if it were rolling away from her. She had eaten a big dinner and wasn't used to keeping so much down. Would she throw up if she ate again? She felt anxious, though also anchored by Michael's resolute hold of her.

"Coffee and toast," she answered.

Bad news greeted Harriet and Michael at the Forum. An arson fire the night before had gutted Wheeler Auditorium, a venerable campus landmark and its largest lecture hall.

"No suspects," said Bronwyn. "But we all know who they

suspect."

"Weathermen?" asked Raj.

"Too out west for those freaks," answered Bronwyn. "Besides, Berkeley has enough independent crazies. Someone who loves Che Guevara more than building a community."

"Does it change our plans?" said Michael. "Pickets are up and we could have TAs marching as early as next week."

"We can't stop now," said Larry. "Damn, we won't be made scapegoats again."

As Harriet listened, she looked up to see Inger standing at the doorway and staring at her. Harriet looked away and crouched down in her seat in a useless effort not to be seen. When she looked up again, Inger was inside and approaching the table.

"Excuse me," said Harriet.

She stood and advanced steadily toward Inger. She pointed at the door, as if to say to Inger that whatever must happen would happen outside.

Inger retreated. Harriet approached her on the sidewalk.

"What do you want?" Harriet asked.

"To say I'm sorry," Inger spoke directly. "I know it's not enough. Nothing can be enough. I didn't want this to happen."

"There's no comfort for me in that," Harriet said sharply.

"No," said Inger. "No comfort for either of us. We're women, you know."

"And what does that mean?" said Harriet.

"That, whether we like it or not, we still answer to the needs of men."

Harriet thought for a minute. *Men?*

"You mean my father?" said Harriet. "My father made you do this? Are you saying he had control of you?"

"Why should that be a surprise?" Inger asked. "He's had control of you. And for quite a long time."

Harriet searched for words but there were none.

"I wanted to apologize for making a mess and to thank you for what you've done to help me. I'm leaving. Going south like I said. So I won't cause you any more pain."

Inger looked sharply at Harriet who absorbed the labored

remorse reflected in her one-time friend's moist, luminous eyes.

"Goodbye."

Inger turned and walked fast toward Dwight Way where she turned the corner and disappeared.

Harriet remained standing until Michael approached her.

"You OK?" he asked. "That looked serious."

"It's fine," she said, knowing she could not conceal that it wasn't. "I need to get to my class."

"When can we…?" Michael let the question hang.

"I need some time to move into my new place," Harriet said.

"How about a movie this weekend?" Michael asked. "There's a great Truffaut film at the Cinema. *The 400 Blows*. Have you seen it?"

"I'll phone you," said Harriet.

She reached to touch Michael with a gawky thrust that landed at his elbow and not, as intended, his neck or shoulder. Embarrassed, Harriet pulled back and walked quickly into the Forum to gather her coat and books.

"Put your food here," Ginger said as she pointed to a lower shelf of the refrigerator.

"Use our pots and dishes. Just wash them when you're done. And if there's not enough heat on the porch, let us know. We have a larger heater in the garage. And, by all means, make yourself at home. The den next to the kitchen is a great place to work and we do our thing each evening in the living room. You're welcome to join us. That is, unless we're fighting."

Ginger gave Harriet a key to the house and also the porch and left the kitchen. Harriet spent the evening setting up a work area on a small desk. Her father had delivered her portable Olivetti along with her clothes and books and she placed the small typewriter at the desk's center. She would need a pillow to comfortably type. She unpacked her essential books and made the bed. By ten o'clock the house was quiet and Harriet slipped under the covers and turned out the bedside lamp.

She rummaged among her recollections of the previous night. She thought of Michael. He was a sweet guy and satisfying lover though Yitzhak was all she had for comparison. Michael had approached her with a warm and cordial patience along with the light touch of his very sensitive fingers, which surprised and impressed Harriet. They ended up giggling in a sticky embrace before falling asleep.

Harriet replayed the feeling and touch of Michael while pondering her sudden and impetuous sex life. In two weeks she had fucked two men, after nearly a quarter century of virginity. It both tickled and flummoxed her and seemed, in conjunction with her flight from home, a mighty and profound undertaking. She wondered also about her fullness after their dinner, which gave her an unusual satisfaction she normally would have tried immediately to be rid of, to throw up and out of her and so return herself to a state of light-headed hunger.

In a brief and restless sleep Harriet dreamed that a member of her doctorate committee stood and forced her into a hole deep in the earth where she would need to finish her dissertation. Other doctoral candidates also were shoved into holes to complete their work. All remained frozen and buried like condemned souls in the deep circles of Dante's hell, and the closer they were to completing their studies the more frozen and immobile they became until Harriet awoke moaning against a wave of terrifying claustrophobia. Later, she would question the dream's meaning and wonder if a pursuit of scholarship, so important to her father, might be disconnected from the pursuit of her happiness.

The thought that such a risk might be necessary brought on the familiar symptoms of a panic attack. She might fall. She might fail. Alone in her first house away from home Harriet thought herself ready to claim a new life and there were hundreds from which to choose.

Harriet phoned Michael on Friday. She thanked him for the movie invitation but said she needed the weekend to unpack and to get settled.

"Another time," she heard herself say. "And soon…really…"

She could hear the disappointment in his voice but resisted an urge to please him. She retreated to the fully windowed sun porch and pulled away the curtains, flooding the room with winter light. Deep shadows spread across her bed. She sank into them and waited. For what, she couldn't say. Evening arrived and she remained on the bed through the descent of an enveloping, almost caressing darkness. On Saturday morning, Ginger knocked on the door.

"Are you OK?" she asked.

"Oh yes," Harriet answered. "I was sleeping."

She wasn't. She had not slept, or had slept very little, and knew from the phantasm that was her memory she might for a while not sleep very much at all.

She left the room Saturday afternoon to phone her mother but her father answered and Harriet hung up. She walked to the corner market for food. Overwhelmed by the stocked shelves and freezer, she bought two chocolate bars and a bottle of Tab and hurried back to her porch. She fell on her bed to watch the whirl of flat, straight clouds against a grey sky until, again, the evening arrived. She thought she might be waiting for something but couldn't think what. She felt dizzy and closed her eyes. If she slept, it was fitful and interrupted constantly by a surging, irresistible anxiety.

On Sunday morning Ginger again knocked.

"We're having breakfast. Would you like to join us?" she asked.

Harriet knew Ginger was likely worried about her new tenant.

"I'm fine. Really," Harriet shouted. "I have a draft due Monday and I'm working."

Ginger retreated and Harriet fell back on her bed.

Harriet thought herself a witness to the laws of planetary motion. She pictured the earth turning on its axis and also its elliptical orbit around the sun. She could almost feel the motions of the heavens, wondering if like Dante the little ship of her wit had hoisted its sails to leave behind a sea so cruel.

Harriet emerged from the porch on Monday morning, tired but still sleepless. And while she had not eaten in days, she was not hungry.

"No, thank you," she said to Ginger, who was scrambling eggs in a cast iron pan.

"I'm teaching a section at eleven."

Harriet walked toward the campus and bought a black coffee at the donut shop on Telegraph. She arrived at her classroom prepared, she thought, to explore the contrasts of Purgatorio with the Inferno, the mountain of purgation rising high under the sun whereas the circles of hell plunged into a deepening, eternal darkness. She had notes on Dante's many parallels and references and searched for them as students arrived, some staring at her as they entered.

"Are you OK?" one student asked.

"Fine. Why?" said Harriet.

The student shrugged and took his seat.

Harriet turned to face the class and became instantly enchanted with all the faces before her. They appeared to her as a constellation of miniature moons, all eyes eager and interested in her, in what she had to say, in the life of Dante and her life which was ever more like that of a pilgrim and poet. She walked from behind her podium to begin her lecture. She heard her few first words and that was all.

"Food seems to have a big impact on you," said Dr. Wheat. "Why is that, do you think?"

Harriet waited to answer. It was more than a week since she had fainted in front of her class, fallen forward and luckily into the arms of a student in the front row who said later he had worried about her, had noticed her pale face and shaking hands and asked her if she were OK.

"I may have no place inside where I can put the world," said Harriet. "I have no room inside for food. I feel much better when I'm empty. I guess I feel I have more control of what's going on around me."

"Even as you starve yourself?" asked the therapist. "Why do you do that?"

Harriet did not answer.

It was Harriet's second meeting with a therapist at the student health center to whom she was referred after an ambulance ride to Alta Bates Hospital where she was kept overnight for observation. Harriet thought Wheat a funny name for a therapist, who asked her new patient to call her by her first name, Malvina. At least the therapist was a woman.

"Who have you told about what happened?" asked Malvina.

"No one," answered Harriet.

"Not even the professor who found a substitute TA for you this week?"

"I told him I was ill. Had a flu."

"And your family?" Malvina asked.

"You mean my parents? Never!" Harriet nearly shouted.

"Deep feelings there," said Malvina. "What's going on at home?"

"I don't live there anymore," said Harriet.

"How long have you lived away from home?" Malvina asked.

"About two weeks," said Harriet.

"Do you miss your parents?"

"No," said Harriet. "I hate them. I have hated them for a long time. I didn't know how much until I moved out."

"It sounds as if there is much in your life you find hard to take in, to digest," said the doctor. "Do you have friends you can talk to? Do you have a boyfriend?"

"A few weeks ago I had sex with a man for the first time," said Harriet. "He was perfect. I had no feeling for him other than arousal. He could not get into me. I could hold him away and finally get myself fucked."

"Did you enjoy it?" the therapist asked without any apparent reaction.

"Yes," said Harriet.

"Did you have an orgasm?" Malvina asked.

"No," said Harriet.

"Have you ever had an orgasm with a partner?"

"Yes," said Harriet. "Another man I met recently. I guess he's kind of a boyfriend."

Harriet had phoned Michael the day she was released from the hospital and told him she had been sick and would call him again when she was feeling better. He seemed fine with that. She remembered going back to her office later in the week to find a bouquet of wilting roses in a vase on her desk. She still had not opened Michael's card.

"How did that make you feel?" asked Malvina.

Harriet hesitated as if she lacked any space to mediate between her body's experience of a stimulus and the stimulus itself.

"I felt good at first. Then I felt scared, almost as if something had slipped out of me that would expose me to danger."

"And your friends? Do you talk to friends?"

"I had what I thought was a good friend. But while she was staying with me this month she had sex with my father. She's gone now."

"That sounds like a deep betrayal," said Malvina. "By both your friend and your father."

"It was treachery," said Harriet. "I hate them both. I've always had trouble trusting people. Now I wonder if I'll ever trust anyone again."

Malvina wrote notes as Harriet spoke.

"I must have been really unhappy when I was a child," said Harriet.

"Let's talk about that next time," said Malvina who concluded the session by giving Harriet a prescription for birth control pills.

She also asked her to keep a diary of her eating and the feelings that came up when she ate. She asked Harriet to promise she would eat three meals each day and to eat only what she knew she could keep down. How much she ate mattered much less than that she made a regular time to eat. Malvina's instructions were oddly reassuring to Harriet who for the first time in her life was given authoritative permission to feel a deep hurt and also to supervise her own hungers.

Harriet phoned Michael but he didn't answer. She had at last read his card included with the flowers and on which he wrote a sentiment of affection obviously intended to express warmth and not pressure. *I like you, Harriet. You are a beautiful woman. Sincerely, Michael.* That was all but it was more than enough.

Harriet returned to the Forum but the rear table was vacant. She had missed a week of student protests, cops on campus, and violent clashes and arrests. She walked to Michael's apartment and knocked and when there was no answer she pulled out a spiral notebook and penned a note. *Finally feeling better. Thank you for the flowers. They are lovely. Please phone soon.* She added Ginger's phone number and pushed the note into a slender crevice between the door and doorway.

Harriet walked back to Ginger and Stan's house, stopping first at the corner market to buy a bag of real groceries.

"Feeling better?" Stan asked as she entered the kitchen.

"Much better. Thanks," said Harriet.

That evening Harriet joined Stan and Ginger in the living room and played Old Maid with Lila. Stan had sold a painting and a new gallery in Oakland wanted him in a group show. The couple was planning a spring trip north to visit a ranch in the mountains.

"Think I'm finally my old self," Harriet said; aware it was a new self she coveted.

ten

It had been two weeks since Harriet last saw her mother, the longest time she could remember them being apart. Harriet returned none of her mother's calls, determined not to collude again as the scorned object of her mother's despair and regret. It was a shaming that for all of Harriet's childhood was presented by her mother as her great personal sacrifice for a disappointing and imperfect daughter. It was a hopeless collusion, leaving Harriet without anywhere to turn for a nourishing life.

And it was not a mother's love. So Harriet had, through her theft of food and subsequent purges, her desperate management of her weight and appetites, her distancing of friends and the reclusive pursuit of dance, refused to accept it. A real mother's love was different. But until Harriet could have some practice receiving love, she would be unable to give it.

"I hope you're keeping up with your school work," her mother said before taking a swift sip from her glass of rosé.

"It's not school work, mother," answered Harriet. "It's scholarship. It's what Daddy does."

The constant calls to Ginger's phone had embarrassed Harriet into meeting her mother for lunch. They agreed to eat at Larry Blake's on Telegraph where Pamela would be able to order something stronger than a beer.

"Whatever. You say you've been sick. I just hope it hasn't hurt your chances."

"Chances for what?" Harriet snapped.

"Don't get strange with me now," her mother snapped. "I'm just concerned, that's all. I'm your mother."

"How are your library studies going?" Harriet asked, avoiding the withering tone of her mother's probing.

It was not a subject Harriet liked to discuss, that her mother was an older woman student at the university, and one some faculty members, mostly men, enjoyed ridiculing: another returning menopausal co-ed trying to pick-up where her real life stopped some twenty years before. Such women stood out in classes and in the quads and were not mistaken for faculty members since they carried their books in bags or packs just like the students. Harriet's embarrassment suggested she still colluded with her mother in some mutual theft of self-esteem.

Her mother responded guardedly. Classes were fine. She had another year but might be able to finish in the fall. She was looking forward to working again, though when had she ever worked? Harriet listened as the food arrived and her mother ordered another glass of wine.

Harriet took a bite of her shrimp salad. Her mother poked at a grilled chicken breast, sliced and spread on an open bun. Her wine arrived and she took a deep gulp before cutting into the meat.

"You seem to be gaining weight," Pamela said without looking up.

Caught in her first bite, Harriet resisted an urge to spit it out, perhaps into her mother's wine glass.

"I feel good," said Harriet. "What do you mean?"

"I'm just saying…" her mother reached for her wine glass without finishing her sentence.

"So you are not the only one in the family with something wrong with you?"

Malvina's question caught Harriet by surprise.

"What do you need?" asked Malvina.

"Love, I think," said Harriet. "I've worried about my place in the home. I didn't realize it but Daddy fucking Inger brought up my worst fear. I have lived a long time worried I could be replaced easily. I have no more illusions. I have no place there anymore."

"Your mother seems to want something from you. Is that possible?" asked Malvina.

"She's always saying she wants things *for* me. But I don't believe her. It feels as if I've been an object at the heart of my parents' hunger, some kind of mutual hunger for love, regard and compliance they cannot seem to satisfy with each other."

Malvina nodded.

"I used to shut myself off from other people," Harriet said. "I would stuff everything in and wait, and then throw it all up again. I was naked. No protection. No defenses against my mother's constant correcting of me, or my father's demands on my future. My future, not his."

Harriet began to cry.

"I wanted to believe they loved me. Whatever it really was, I don't think it was love."

Malvina waited in silence as Harriet let go and convulsed in a loud, extended wail. If starvation were a death wish, Harriet was at least aware of it. If relationships in her family paralleled Harriet's lifelong relationship with food, then a deeper nature might be emerging, one that could better tolerate experience and find its truths more digestible.

On a cold, overcast morning Harriet crossed at Bancroft Way and entered the campus past a line of students picketing on the sidewalk and, later, past another line of students and TAs that blocked the entrance to Sather Gate. Because there was a strike, she did not have a class section to convene. She had planned to visit her office but saw Michael on the picket line and walked over to him.

"Where have you been?" he asked. "I'd hoped to hear from you."

Harriet was about to answer when Michael grabbed her and pushed her away from the gate. She turned to see a phalanx of cops in yellow raincoats waving wooden clubs. They charged the line of pickets.

"What the fuck?" Michael shouted at the cops as he continued to push Harriet down a path next to Strawberry Creek.

"Get down over here!" he shouted to Harriet as they descended to a hill above the creek bed behind and beneath the gate. From there they watched a pitched battle between pickets and cops, the cops getting the better of it. Officers grabbed protesters and pulled them back toward a circle made by other cops. Those captured were handcuffed and led away.

"Welcome to the strike," said Michael. "This happened last week, too."

"How can they do this?" asked Harriet. "Isn't it legal to picket?"

"You'd think," answered Michael. "But not with this governor."

Michael helped Harriet down the creek and ran with her across the lower quad to the Bear's Lair. He bought her a coffee and asked what had happened to her. Harriet said she'd been ill and nothing more. He was happy to see her.

"Will you march?" Michael asked.

"I don't see how not," she answered. "I'm a TA and I support the strike."

Brewing for Harriet was a story she could not tell alone. Medieval scholarship made her an expert in the ancient and enduring meanings of virtue. And Dante, of all poets, had said best what it meant to be present in the world. She could wait beyond Inferno's gate with flies in her eyes and follow misguided flags. Yet love was involved, and there was now a numinous meaning in this word. It suggested some deeper work that would have to be completed for a life to be worthwhile.

They sipped coffee for a long and silent minute.

"Ever thought of the Peace Corps?" Michael asked.

"The what…the Peace Corps?"

"I'm going to an orientation in an hour. Would you join me?"

Michael said he wanted to take some time away from the university and to leave the country. It would be a two-year commitment but he thought the work would be valuable and a lot more useful to the world than his getting drafted.

"We get so caught up in the academic drama," he said. "I love anthropology but I realize it's because I care about people, and about the current and miserable state of our species. The world is smaller,

Harriet. We can choose either to do well by one another or do great damage as we compete with each other. Look how frightened those cops are out there, smashing us with their clubs because we dare to speak out. I don't know if the Peace Corps is a way but it's the only thing I've found that seems committed to helping other humans on their own terms."

Harriet awoke again in Michael's bed, now more familiar to her in the light of another morning. While he slept, she searched her thoughts for the perimeters of this new life away from her parents.

The Peace Corps orientation had provoked a long conversation between them. Michael wanted to travel to east Africa and the Corps, while it would not guarantee any particular placement, had a need for volunteers there. The orientation had been enough to interest Harriet, and more than enough to raise serious questions about her other plans. For a crucial instant she imagined what Michael must have imagined: work that would make a material and lasting difference in the quality of human life at a risky precipice of its experience. A trip to Florence in the summer and all its organized and obscuring study, combined with another year or two in pursuit of yet another degree, seemed for Harriet too much and also no longer enough.

Her own life had been suspended perpetually in an orchestrated animation. Her crumbling goals appeared now as her father's selfish projections. She was under the influence of another man. She was also in his arms. And it also was not enough. She knew that. But it might become a passage that would lead eventually to a life she could call her own.

"I'm not going to Florence this summer," Harriet said to her father.

She sat in the professor's campus office where it was customary for him to review his daughter's career while he spoke the authoritative and imposing opinions with which she usually complied. But not today. The professor had begged his daughter for this meeting and it was Harriet who commanded the agenda.

"What will you do?" he asked. "That was going to be an important step for you, an essential step up the ladder toward…"

"I'm through climbing ladders," Harriet snapped.

"What does that mean? You're career depends on…"

"I'm looking at something else right now," Harriet cut him off.

"Look, if this is because of the thing, well, that foolishness with your friend…"

The professor's unfinished sentences were her father's effort to avoid nasty specifics though Harriet had no trouble completing them.

"That wasn't foolishness," said Harriet. "It wasn't just some *thing*. It was a disgusting betrayal and I will never forgive you for it."

The professor shrunk back in his tall, cushioned desk chair.

"Well, what then? What will you do?" he pleaded, ducking his daughter's accusation as if it were a tossed brick.

"The Peace Corps sounds interesting," Harriet said. "I've looked into it with my friend Michael. I have some money saved. The Corps doesn't pay much but the experience sounds like something with a lot of potential. I might be able to do some good in the world."

She had made two points. One, that she was finished following her father's plan for her and two, that another man was helping her to create a new one.

"Michael? Who is Michael?" the professor asked.

"None of your business, Daddy."

Harriet was surprised by the pleasure it gave her to say this.

"Where would you go?" her father asked again.

"Africa," said Harriet. "Michael has always wanted to go there. I may go with him. East Africa. Asmara. There's a rebellion going on there."

"My god!" the professor bellowed. "Have you lost your senses? I thought I was lucky not to have a son who would end up going to fight somewhere. And now my only child, my dear daughter, wants to leave a promising academic career and work in a war zone. Dammit, girl! Just come home. Just give this crap up and come home."

Harriet watched her father's frantic rant. She rarely saw him agitated and never within his sacred campus sanctum.

"No, Daddy. I've *come* to my senses. I'm not going home."

Harriet was calm and crisply emphatic.

"There aren't very many places in the world that aren't war

zones now. War zones are likely the places people need help. And that's what I want to do with my life now. I want to help."

Harriet surprised herself by speaking about things in her life that weren't yet real, and with the vehement conviction they were. She understood now how her abusive mother was also abused. Her father was Harriet's first strong prince and also her first dangerous friend. It was time to break with him now, to break and never again return.

Ginger told Harriet she imagined her perfect life as a cloud floating in a brilliant blue sky and as beautiful as it was unreachable. It was a dark winter morning and they were seated at the kitchen table.

"To grow my own food," Ginger said. "A house and land. Room to roam and time to do it."

Instead, she worked full days and longer for a law firm on Shattuck Avenue. It was a fifteen-minute walk from home that took her miles away from her heart's desire.

"How does Stan feel about it?" Harriet asked as they drank tea.

"He's an artist, of course," said Ginger. "He needs galleries and patrons, or thinks he does. We argue about this a lot."

"Where would you go?" asked Harriet.

"I picture a house in the woods. We have friends living near Mendocino on the coast. It's hard but they make it work. Stan doesn't need a city to do his art. But he thinks he needs a city to sell it."

Harriet listened to Ginger's lament.

"What can you do?" she asked Ginger.

"At some point I suppose I'd have to go it alone," Ginger said. "It's not as if we need Stan's income. He really doesn't produce any that matters. Not when you count the money spent on art classes and canvasses and paint. Every spring I start to feel this way, to want nature's bounty in my life. But…I don't know…I hope something happens before summer."

Harriet's turn outward had brought her a new friend in Ginger. In another turn later that week Harriet encountered Bronwyn, drawn to her as Harriet marched with other TAs at Sather Gate.

"Where have you been?" asked Bronwyn who carried a stack of fliers to pass out to students. "I was worried something happened.

Michael said you've been sick."

"That's all over," said Harriet.

She brushed away her illness as if it were an expired phantom though Harriet was taken by Bronwyn's interest in her and her spoken worry.

"I'm glad to be here, though who knows what will happen next."

Brownyn nodded and reached to give Harriet a hug she accepted generously as the silent assent of camaraderie.

"It's been a battle," Bronwyn replied. "The cops used mace last week. It's been nearly a month of busts and they've arrested nearly a hundred of us. It's evil and it's nowhere near to being over. Like it's been said, evil turns like spoiling milk, slowly and without mention until one morning it is clearly and irrevocably bad."

"You can't cry over spoiled milk," said Harriet.

Bronwyn smiled and left to distribute her fliers.

Each night Harriet stood alone in Stan and Ginger's kitchen, the refrigerator door open as she assessed the contents of her assigned shelf and the perishable food she bought and consumed. It was new for her to manage meals, to purchase their contents and to prepare them and then to sit down and to purposely, even pleasurably, eat them.

She realized it had been the food of others she refused, meals prepared for her that she would either not eat or, having eaten, vomit back up as soon as she could. One evening she prepared a meal for Michael, pesto pasta and a salad she spent days imagining and an entire afternoon preparing. He enjoyed it and Harriet enjoyed him enjoying it. She had given him the taste of an enveloping love that for the first time in her life included herself.

It was a Thursday that police first used tear gas on campus. Michael and Harriet were marching together, part of a snaking line of protesters that moved across the main plaza. Harriet held a sign that read *Don't Cross the Line* and that she shook to the rhythm of the claps and shouts of students who gathered for a rally to support the strike for Third World studies. Rallies had been banned by the administration for weeks but that did not stop protesters who arrived with megaphones and began to set up speakers on the steps of Sproul Hall.

Michael saw the first flock of cops emerge from behind the hall. They wore gas masks and in a few seconds Michael knew why as they threw canisters that landed at the feet of the marching strikers and exploded into stinging, blinding clouds that quickly smothered the plaza in a noxious, nauseating fog. Strikers dropped their signs and ran in all directions. Michael pulled a handkerchief from his coat pocket and covered his mouth and nose. With his other hand he grabbed Harriet's arm and pulled her back toward steps that led to the lower plaza behind the student union.

"This way!" Michael shouted and pulled Harriet down the steps and toward the campus bookstore.

He pushed against the door but it was locked. The quad was filled with surging groups of protesters, colliding and then splitting apart, everyone uncertain which way to go.

"We'll slip up to Bancroft and cross at Telegraph."

Michael pulled Harriet, who coughed uncontrollably, toward another flight of steps.

Emerging at the top, they were met by a posse of masked cops that pushed everyone against a wall. Michael and Harriet were handcuffed and led to a bus with others who were also arrested.

As the bus pulled away, Harriet looked out the window to see two police cars overturned, one of them on fire. She was leaving hell and, like the poet, on her way to a place of waiting where for whatever reason she would confront a moment of decisive consent to the discipline of time. She looked over at Michael, catching his profile in her thoughtful light. She was at one with some truthful goodness. Even with her wrists bound behind her, she had never before felt so free.

GINGER AND STAN

one

Ginger admired Stan.

No, really she feared him. She supported his art. No, she resented it. She loved him. No, she was addicted to him. She was a legal secretary for a downtown law firm. She was the family cash cow who worked too hard to be a decent mother. Stan was an artist on the threshold of discovery. No, he was a frustrated womanizer who depended on the kindness of strangers. He was a poet with paint. No, he was a fraud who couldn't draw.

He did flirt but never, to her knowledge, betrayed her. Most importantly, Stan loved her daughter Lila, loved her more than Lila's father who rarely phoned and never visited. And Stan loved Ginger and she knew Stan loved her. She was five years older than Stan with saggy boobs and a history of painful migraines that turned her unpredictably into a screaming maenad and still he loved her, held her, made deep and utterly exposed love to her and also fought with her, stayed engaged and battled late into any given evening and beyond and then awoke with her, took her in his arms to crush her under his tough, stringy body and poured over her all of his bereft and abandoned burdens.

They had worked together for many years to arrive at this reckless, impetuous intimacy. And still, it was not enough. Ginger wanted to have more in ways that would mean doing less. She was tired. Tired in her body and tired, also, of her designated place as the mirror of Stan's artistic image of himself. She wanted her own mirror, or a window through which she might see, if not herself, at least the trees and sky and blooms of a natural world.

"You might hear us fighting sometimes," said Ginger.

"I already have," said Harriet, which said to Ginger that Harriet also had heard them making love, which they did frequently and, like their fighting, never quietly.

"We're voluble people," said Ginger. "We're still finding our way."

"No explanation needed," said Harriet. "I think you're both really great and I'm so grateful to be living here."

Ginger made herself stand still and receive Harriet's kind words. Too often Ginger objectified her life as she might her dreams, by creating from herself a character that would act for her as she watched, that would live her real life while she did all the explaining and let the news decide what in any moment mattered most.

"Where is Stan tonight?" Harriet asked.

"A big show is taking shape," said Ginger. "Gallery in the city. Perhaps a make or break opportunity. He's trying to finish a painting."

Why was the show so important? It was hard to comprehend what was most important for Stan. Art was too large and general a thing for her to grasp though Ginger knew Stan cared deeply about his place in it. He wanted a solo show and there was no telling when that would ever happen.

"Cezanne was 55 before he had his first show," Stan said to Ginger.

"Wasn't Cezanne rich?" she responded.

Ginger knew some art history. She had taken a liberal arts degree at Sacramento State, which was more than Stan ever had done in school. A Boston native, Stan had come up through the trades and followed for many years in the footsteps of his Catholic father who also wielded paint brushes but whose canvasses were wood and drywall and who measured his achievements in thousands of square feet of covered surface and the multiplier of an hourly wage.

Stan's faith was gone but the roots of his childhood Catholicism held long enough for him to fall in love with Barnett Newman's abstract series of the Stations of the Cross.

"As if matter could actually exist independent of a human's awareness of it," Stan said, quoting D.H. Lawrence on Cezanne.

Ginger met Stan during his study at the college of arts and crafts in Oakland. Ultimately, he took an art degree that emboldened him to make a life as a painter. His good fortune was Ginger, who loved him enough to take him on, to gift him with her obsession for stability and refuge. She would work. He would paint. It seemed clear enough in the long view but not so easy in the day-to-day.

"What was it like to go to jail?" Ginger asked Harriet.

"Boring," said Harriet.

A week had worn away the shock of being handcuffed, photographed and strip-searched by a matron that forced Harriet to spread her butt cheeks and vulva before assigning her and the other women to cells.

"I was anxious," she told Ginger.

Harriet had been terrified. Once separated from Michael, her adventure of painless martyrdom, a journey into the poet's eternal map of hell, transmogrified quickly into a black stew of rue. She waited in a corner of the cell, gratefully too frightened to eat and unapproachable in her nearly catatonic state until a matron walked up to check on her.

"You high on drugs?" she asked.

Harriet shook her head.

It was more than a day before she was let out of jail. Michael waited outside.

"We were released on OR," Harriet told Ginger.

"Our date to appear is next week but our attorney says the charges will be dropped. The war is over. The faculty voted in favor of black studies and the administration is negotiating again."

"So you won?" said Ginger.

"For now," said Harriet.

"Are you in trouble at school?" Ginger asked.

"I don't know yet," said Harriet. "I met my class this week. No one has said anything to me about not teaching. The union seems to be handling it. My professor doesn't want any trouble. He's just trying to get through the semester. So are most of my students."

Harriet did not care if she were in trouble. She was in love, which was a far more interesting kind of mischief than anything offered in the university catalogue.

"You don't sound worried," said Ginger.

Harriet shook her head.

"What worries *you?*" asked Harriet.

The question surprised Ginger though she was the first to ask it.

"Money worries me," said Ginger.

"Money and food and living in a city."

Ginger grew up in the country. Her parents were what she described as "land rich and cash poor," ultimately losing the family farm outside of Marysville to a decade of debt. Thereafter, Ginger moved frequently with her parents from one cheap country rental to the next. Her father's knowledge of soil and animals won him occasional jobs as a foreman, plus a rent-free cottage or cabin on someone else's ranch.

When Ginger turned thirteen, her father took a job managing a vineyard. It was the steadiest work he had ever known and paid enough for Ginger to live in a home in Grass Valley and have her own bedroom all the way through high school.

"I can't say I'm settled," said Ginger. "I'd like to leave this place someday. But we still struggle. I don't understand money. Never have. All I know is that we don't ever have enough."

Harriet heard Ginger's deepening worry about her own life and could visualize her slicing physical chunks from herself first to feed Lila and then Stan and, at last, her own needs, though from what Ginger said there was never enough left over to alleviate her own hungers. Hunger was the issue and it was one Harriet understood even in the cells. For Harriet there had been too much of all kinds of food and for Ginger never enough.

"College ruined me," Ginger said.

She didn't mean it. It was just that after a liberal arts education she had no use for her parents or their gypsy life. She wanted and needed an anchor and renting in the city was in its way easier than buying in the country and she would never rent in the country where such an arrangement assured her a deep and disquieting dependency. Ginger wanted her own plot, her own garden, her own forest, her own animals and birds and sunrises.

And in Stan's dream, which Ginger had no choice but to share, there was no assurance of money or even food, not to mention the meeting of the very immediate demands of a growing child, measured in days and weeks as needs that could not wait.

"I walk to work and see all these teen runaways sitting in doorways and smoking dope," said Ginger. "Cars roll by, their drivers oblivious to the pain all around them, perhaps even to their own. It's the city and it frightens me to think Lila might grow up here, might have Telegraph as her main drag."

When Ginger was Lila's age she played in the fields, hid in the woods and cared for rabbits, goats and pigs. She watched a season arrive and waited for first signs of the next.

"My life was open and free in ways hers has never been," said Ginger. "It's hard because Stan loves energy and agitation. He thrives on the noise of a city. It stimulates ideas and feeds his art. It makes him feel real and alive. It gives him what he calls subject matter though I can never determine directly from his art just what that is."

Ginger was a countrywoman from the Shenandoah Valley east of Sacramento and what did she know?

"And he asks me that," said Ginger.

"He says 'What do you know?' like I just got off a bus from Lodi. Stan grew up with the Beats. He started in art when it was a funky business and spelled with a small "f." Now he's graduated to Funk with a capital "F," a Funk he's convinced has value and that collectors will buy. That's always the artist's question. Don't matter if the work is good. Who's going to pay for it? Sometimes I think he and his artist buddies are just a boy's club that collects arty junk instead of baseball cards."

Ginger could name only two women artists in the group.

"I met a third," she said.

"But she's not an artist. She likes Stan, though. What's her name? Inger? Met her at a show and she couldn't stay away from Stan who, of course, never minds the attention."

Harriet knew Inger.

"Inger?" asked Harriet. "I think I know her. She's gone. Went to

LA. That's what I heard."

"Really?" said Ginger.

Harriet could feel Ginger's relief and did not describe her own.

Lila awoke from her nap and entered the living room as if it were a new and interesting village. Her eyes wandered everywhere and past Harriet whose presence in her home was no longer a novelty.

"Looking for something, darlin'?" Ginger asked as the toddling child rubbed her eyes and, holding a small doll's blanket tight to her cheek, rushed to her seated mother whose arms swooped down like the wings of a large crane to gather Lila up and onto her lap. Lila burrowed into the cave formed from her mother's arms and breasts.

"I want Billy," said Lila. "Can't find Billy."

"Billy?" asked Harriet.

"Her special friend," said Ginger. "He's a yellow stuff and wears a cowboy hat. He gets lost a lot but always turns up. Right, Lila?"

Lila resisted the pressure to answer and, instead, tried to climb deeper into her mother's body though her mother, suddenly pinched and wobbly, resisted. Life was a one-way journey with no ticket back.

"Let's look for Billy," said Ginger. "First let's get something to eat."

Ginger cut apple slices and fed them to Lila as she sat in her booster seat at the kitchen table.

"Do you enjoy being a mother?" Harriet asked directly.

There was an uncomfortable pause.

"The answer is yes," Ginger said finally. "What I don't enjoy is battling for the time to do it. Lila always comes first but my job and Stan's art fight it out for second place and sometimes it's more trouble than there are hours in the day. Stan's a great stepdad during the work week but I don't know what's harder, being at work all day and wondering what I'm missing, or arriving home to hear Stanley tell me what I've missed."

Ginger was an engaged mother and Harriet could see how Ginger's parental love, even grown through the cracks of harried daily life, was better than her own mother's, which she remembered as given to her only after something went seriously wrong.

My stringbean,
how do you grow?
You grow this way.
You are too many to eat.

Ginger sang the words to her daughter in an improvised melody. And when Lila's face brightened in recognition, Ginger sang the words again.

"It's from a poem," said Ginger. "Anne Sexton writing about her daughter growing up. And here she is, little Miss Lila, my little string bean and growing up so fast."

Ginger pushed her face close to Lila's as they rubbed noses and together laughed at the common and silly pleasure they alone could conceive, as if fun itself were a blessed event unique to the conjoined lives of this mother and this daughter.

"Do you read poetry?" Ginger asked Harriet.

"It's about all I read," answered Harriet.

"But most was written before the 16th century and children and string beans are rarely mentioned."

"String beans remind me to ask you if you'd like to join a food conspiracy," said Ginger.

"A what conspiracy?" asked Harriet.

Ginger explained how she and Stan had joined with other households to pool their money to buy food in bulk from farmers and small wholesalers and to then distribute it cheaply among themselves.

"It's a kind of collective," said Ginger. "We take turns going to the Farmer's Markets and getting fresh food. It's cheaper than the supermarkets, even the Co-op. And it's fresh and better quality."

It would cost Harriet $10 a month to participate.

"I'll think about it," she said to Ginger, though the idea was attractive if only because it again brought forward the word *quality* as well as the assumption of values underpinning that quality. It was clear Ginger tried as best she could to live by the expression of values. It was a peculiar kind of integrity Harriet had not yet experienced and, if reliable, might become the glue of an abiding friendship.

two

"A lot of great enthusiasm just goes down the drain," Stan said to Mack.

"But don't quote me," he added. "There's plenty to go around, like space in the universe. It's limitless."

Stan had asked Mack to help him move his canvas into a truck waiting in the college studio's driveway. Framed on its wooden braces, the canvas was wider and taller than the two men together. It wasn't heavy, though Stan maneuvered it cautiously.

"Watch your end as we turn on the stairs," Stan said.

"Damn, it's harder to move these things than it is to paint them." Stan grunted.

"Not really. Don't quote me."

"What can I quote?" Mack asked. "This story has to say something. You aren't the only artist in the show."

"OK. Tell them it all started with the Beats. That abstract expressionism must move over for an art grown out of the modern quicksand of lived experience. It's the funk, man. We aren't alienated from culture like Pollack and Rothko. We are the culture, man. A rebellious, media-mad bunch of artists. Except, unlike the Beats, we've come up from underground. We dabble in beauties so obvious no one sees them until we paint, shape or reassemble them."

"And the show?" asked Mack.

"It's a big deal. A Geary Street gallery wants us, so I guess we've arrived. It's about time. Some of us have been working these ideas since the Fifties."

Stan was one of a dozen artists with at least one piece in the show, which was titled *"F" stands for Funk*. His painting, a canvas covered in an even, bright orange acrylic, was titled *Juicy*.

"You can say I'm honored to be included," Stan shouted as he climbed into the back of the truck while balancing his painting, wrapped broadly in a protective plastic sleeve.

"It's like Bob Dylan getting his first gig at The Gaslight."

Stan was more than honored. He was shocked. The invitation to have his work hang with that of artists like Harold Paris, Bruce Conner, Wallace Berman, and George Herms was unexpected and apparently the result of someone knowing someone who knew him. It was luck and barely enough. It was not an arrival but more than a break. Stan's art needed an audience and to hang for six weeks in a tony, downtown gallery would be unconditionally satisfying.

If the painting sold, Stan would earn $300. More importantly, his name and a color photo of *Juicy* appeared in the gallery catalogue that was distributed throughout the art world and would land on desks and coffee tables in Chicago and New York. And Mack was writing a story for the Chronicle. Stan felt awakened, his past life momentarily a dream.

Pauline's shack is made entirely of watermelon sugar.

This made no sense to Ginger who nevertheless had ingested more than thirty pages of a Richard Brautigan novel that, if obtuse, was at least easy to read. Her lunch hour in the downtown library was a holy respite from her work for a law firm that occupied most of the sixth floor of a nearby bank building. Freed each noon from confinement, Ginger opened her mind for a full fifty minutes in the city's non-denominational temple of words. The words were free and could be read while she sat or stood or snuck a bite of a sandwich in the stacks where students from the nearby high school lingered to make-out with their steadies, and a lanky, dull-faced security cop patrolled restlessly.

Words also could be borrowed and on this day she had returned Joan Didion's *Slouching Toward Bethlehem*, a best seller the previous year that had frightened Ginger straight with its lurid descriptions of a drug-encrusted Haight/Ashbury post-1967 Summer of Love. Didion's account of teen girls fucking older, toothless men who gave them acid and STP worried Ginger who could imagine herself easily as an absentee mother waiting like all mothers for the mean, lurid world to claim and ruin her precious child.

In her reading, Ginger had the choice of Brautigan's imaginary dystopia or Didion's real one. Didion mentioned a street Digger named Arthur, the leader of the leaderless, who stayed in the Haight after all the other Diggers left. Ginger knew a Digger, a sweet young man with hope in his eyes and an equally hopeful girlfriend. They had left the previous summer to join with others to create Black Bear

Ranch in the mountains west of Shasta. It was to be a loving and free community but Ginger had not heard again from her young friend and had only the unconfirmed rumor it had been a rough winter.

Ginger yearned to live far away, to escape farther and deeper into the woods than even her childhood home in the Sierra foothills. Her table at the library was a vicarious trailhead of infinite destinations within and beyond that she savored above the barely tolerable high school students. It was her luck to experience a natural urge in its least natural state.

It was too easy to watch the students and to imagine Lila as a sexual creature, a young woman in love, though not so easy to know what that would feel like. All of Ginger's Utopian visions were on a shoestring, which could be the title of a book she might write had she the time to write the way Stan had his time to paint. *Must tell him Cordell wrote,* Ginger said to herself.

Cordell was an old art school friend of Stan's who recently took a job as an adjunct professor at Humboldt State. He got the job during a phone call with the department's retiring chairman after submitting an impressive resume of exhibitions and reviews.

That he was a Negro did not come up because the chairman did not ask and Cordell had no reason to say he was black though Cordell knew when he arrived the chairman was surprised and at first thought there had been a mistake. There were maybe seven Negroes living in Arcata but the town was a liberal bastion in otherwise redneck redwood country. And Cordell had a two-year contract, taught a great class and got on well with everyone. The cops stopped him once, identified him and never bothered him again.

Cordell lived in an old farmhouse west of town on the Mad River and invited Stan, Ginger and Lila up for a long weekend. Stan would want to see Cordell again and it would lead Stan and Ginger into the coastal mountains and out again to the estuary of Humboldt Bay and its wild northern coast. Ginger thought she could make one more pitch to Stan, and not her last, but at least another for a life out of the city, a life for all of them in a way that could keep Stan painting while giving her what she wanted for herself and her daughter.

Her daughter. That sounded important. It was the separating factor because Lila was not Stan's daughter though he loved her. Ginger knew this, and he loved Ginger while also deeply and unrequitedly in love with his art. His painting was Stan's measure of himself and both a distraction and evasion from Ginger's frequently spoken fears. And more so now that he was a real artist in a real exhibition with recognition he had worked more than a decade to achieve. He was still the artist and Ginger was still his echo.

"It's the whole dream of a life!" Stan shouted.

"It's all I have to put between me and death. Can't you understand? Please don't make me choose between you and my destitution."

"Your what?" asked Ginger.

Again, and almost always when they fought, Stan rose above their argument to paint his masterpiece or, in this case, to resist a life without one. His words were dramatic and given without their meanings. Stan heard only his sounds while Ginger heard only his words. Both were bright, mercurial thinkers. Stan launched his words like burning kites toward the clouds. Ginger planted her words in the soil; their meanings left to root and grow.

"My life," he answered. "I hear you just at the moment of my success, I hear you pulling me down."

Ginger retreated to her strengthening ground.

"I'm trying to pull us together," she said. "I want you to succeed. I also want to live a good life. And Lila, I have a vision for her happiness that, frankly Stan, I can't imagine I will ever surrender."

It was Stan's turn to stop, to land on a perch and to wait. So much of their serious work as a couple bloomed in the places between land and sky. Ginger rose from the ground while Stan, eventually and always, fell like Icarus. Then Ginger would reach out and catch Stan and hold him up like a child and, without any loss of footing, show him another way to fly.

"Cordell wants to see you," said Ginger. "You have a lot to share with him. We can look around. That's all I'm asking."

"After the opening?" Stan asked.

His question landed comfortably.

"Of course," said Ginger. "I have a Monday off in two weeks. We'll make it a long weekend. Lila will love it."

Their sex after a fight took one of two paths for Ginger. There was the tender, long road that led through all their memorized places together, sweet remindful words and touches that accelerated toward a beautifully furious and usually mutual come. Or, from the distance formed from another reworking of old arguments into loving dead ends, there was the shortcut of a trick, a cultivated fantasy older than any lover that in the absence of comfort worked every time.

As he stood in the gallery to defend his art, Stan appeared tall and wispy; his thin body a vocalizing candle of ideas that illuminated an encircling press of friends and artists.

"Art cycles move forward in the name of life, fate, nature," Stan said to the quiet little crowd.

"Enjoy it now for what it is and not for what it will become. And certainly not for what it costs."

Ginger watched her husband from a steep remove, straddling the alcove separating one small gallery from three others and viewing Stan as she might a painting in the current show. He was handsome. In fact, he was beautiful, his high head above all others, a long, strong neck and a sharp nose that like his eyes penetrated deeply into any apprehended space. His black hair was washed and fell like a fluffy tar below his shoulders.

He was smart. He spoke with his hands and his voice. And it was his show, though as Ginger noticed, his painting hung in the smallest of the gallery's four rooms and far removed from the main attractions that, behind her, drew a much larger and better dressed crowd to a wall of untitled drawings by Bruce Connor. Suits and artists, thought Ginger. Separated by clothes and conversations.

A hand gripped Ginger's shoulder and she turned to see Mack.

"He seems in good form," Mack said as he gestured toward Stan.

"No offers yet, though," said Ginger.

"A little early," Mack replied.

"And who is this?" Mack said as he turned to look down the hall.

Harriet approached with Michael.

"You know each other?" Ginger asked Harriet.

"Mack was one of my dad's students. We used to see a lot of him." Harriet introduced Michael to Mack.

"How's your dad?" Mack asked.

"I don't see him much," Harriet answered coolly. "I moved out."

"Where are you living?" Mack asked.

"With us," said Ginger.

"You'll have to tell me about it sometime," said Mack.

"And what happened to Inger? Wasn't she living with you last year? I haven't seen her in, like, forever."

Ginger watched Harriet's face freeze in a look caught somewhere between fright and dismay.

"Gone south," said Ginger. "Right, Harriet?"

Harriet nodded weakly.

"Joined a commune in LA, or something."

The gallery's cluster of small crowds broke apart to continually reassemble at the wine table and as the wine ran the stories ran. Raj arrived with Yitzhak in tow, another difficult surprise for Harriet who remained cordial while Yitzhak barely acknowledged her.

"Fill my glass," Stan asked Ginger. "I need to stay here."

He stood by his painting like a sentry while Raj approached to express his good wishes, Yitzhak behind him.

"Hey, man," Raj shouted at Stan who grasped his fist in a brotherly shake. "What a crowd. You diggin' the vibe? Feels pretty cool."

"Hey there."

Stan greeted Yitzhak without knowing exactly what to call him. He knew him before as Raymond but understood from Ginger he went by another name.

"What you up to now, man?" Stan asked as he searched Yitzhak's eyes for a response.

"Yitzhak's working with the Provos, " said Raj. "He's volunteering while he hunts for a paying gig. Aren't you, Yitzhak?"

Raj emphasized his friend's new name.

"It's work for the people," said Yitzhak.

"Say, you ever thought of being a life model?" Stan asked Yitzhak.

The wine was talking now.

"A what?" asked Raj.

"A life model. You know, in an art studio. A man or a woman stands on a platform and artists draw or paint them. You're a big, strong guy with wonderfully chiseled features. You're perfect. And it pays well. Four dollars an hour. Six if you pose nude. The college is always looking for models. And there are some studios that offer classes. I have the phone numbers, if you're interested."

By this time, Stan realized he would get no visible response from behind Yitzhak's truculent expression.

A sudden tension was broken by the return of Ginger bussing Stan's second glass of wine. With her were Larry and Sylvia, who had just arrived. The couple stood together in the shadows made by the bright lights illuminating *Juicy*. Larry had his camera and asked Stan if he could photograph him with his painting. Stan was agreeable and followed Larry's directions to stand near, but not in front of, the canvass.

"This a big deal," Sylvia said to Ginger. "How many people can they crowd into this place?"

"A lot, apparently," said Ginger.

"Thanks for coming. It's huge for Stan to have friends here. Do you like art?"

"Yeah," said Sylvia. "I can dig this stuff. It's new and, like it says on the sign, it's funk. Reminds me of some of the works I saw last month in the Haight."

"At the Zoetrope?" Ginger asked.

"No," said Sylvia. "The Black Man's gallery. Been open about a year. Bill Thomas' place. In the ground floor of a small Victorian. All black artists. You never heard of it?"

Ginger hadn't.

"It's the black art experience. It's the black art experience in white art America and for the first time in this city it has a gallery."

"Well, how do you like this?" asked Ginger.

Sylvia looked around, her eyes resting at Stan's *Juicy* as she searched for words.

"Like the sign says, it's funk. But I have to say, it's a white man's funk. Very cold. Not a lot of soul but that's not what they seem to be going for. And, my goodness, the prices! Damned expensive funk, I'll tell you. Must be top grade funk. Black people do a different kind of funk. They started funk."

Ginger loved Sylvia's take down. She would never tell Stan.

"Honey, you got your picture?" Sylvia shouted at Larry, who nodded.

"How's Larry doing?" Ginger asked.

Larry had just started another construction job that would go until fall.

"Then we go to Chicago. The Panther breakfast program has been a big deal and Freddie out in Chicago wants us to help get it going there. Damn, since we started this breakfast thing at the church we've had a rush of Panther volunteers. And would you believe it? Most are women."

A small, older man wearing a tweed jacket and bright red tie entered the small gallery. Ginger noticed his grey-speckled red beard and thick, wavy hair as he approached Stan.

"Fitz!" Stan shouted. "What are you doing here?"

"What do you think?" said the older man as he was crushed quickly into Stan's impounding embrace.

"It's quite a show," said the man who was introduced by Stan as art professor James Fitz of Sacramento State University.

"No longer at State," said Fitz. "I teach at the Art Institute now."

Fitz had been one of Stan's first acquaintances in the art world. During a brief period at Laney College, Fitz taught a modern art survey course and showed a personal interest in Stan's work.

"Phone me," said Fitz as he moved past Stan to greet another visitor.

"And check out the Rauschenberg over the door in the foyer," he said to Stan. "It's humbling."

In a brief reflection, Ginger contemplated the nature of art and how irrationality and chance were so much its current and conditioning agents. She had been with Stan long enough to follow his art from the idea, to the brush, to the assemblage, and now into the gallery. She again explored the room as if it were just another kind of frame. And all the faces and bodies within were simply strokes on another kind of canvas.

three

Some things were temporary and for Ginger these commonly were her sudden, despairing moods and her fear of unanticipated danger. Each fed the other. Her moods aroused fear and her fear brought on the blues. Relief came usually in her parenting of Lila, brimful moments that left no time to fall into despair.

Her home was also a respite, an upstairs flat south of the campus with wide views of the hills through a panel of immense bay windows. The flat was warm and artfully furnished and where she cooked delicious meals, paraded at times nearly and comfortably naked, played with her daughter and loved her husband. The rent was not cheap but Harriet was helping now and whatever the cost, it was worth it to her to have a home in the city where she felt safe and free.

That is, until Ginger absorbed within days two direct disruptions of the continuities on which she so depended to manage her life. The first came in a call from Lila's preschool teacher, mortified to tell Ginger that Lila had been molested by another child, a boy that for whatever reason the teacher emphasized was a Negro and that action had been taken and the boy disciplined and sent home.

"God, what happened?" Ginger asked anxiously.

"He took her into the closet and pulled down her panties," said the teacher, her voice quavering softly. "He touched her…there."

"You mean her privates?"

"Her privates," said the teacher and then, recognizing a need to appear more professional, added "her vulva."

"What happened then?" Ginger asked calmly as her heart raced wildly.

"We found them," said the teacher.

"How is Lila?" asked Ginger. "Is my daughter OK?"

"We think this was a one-time thing," said the teacher. "Lila hasn't said anything about it. She seems fine."

"My god. How would you know if something's wrong?" asked Ginger.

"I don't know," said the teacher. "She might act out…I can't say."

"I'm coming to get her," said Ginger and hung up the phone.

There was no acting out. Lila said nothing and Ginger, who asked vaguely about her classmate Lonnie, could elicit no details from her daughter. Were it an assault, it was a quick one and one quickly terminated by the mortified preschool staff that overwhelmed the incident with their educated guesses and concerns. *They were playing doctor*, thought Ginger. The staff caught them.

That's what Ginger told Stan who agreed it was probably not a big deal and that the preschool staff was on top of it.

Which was fine until Ginger asked about Lonnie and learned the child had come to preschool with a bruise on his neck and red marks on his thighs and buttocks where he had been struck by an object, probably a serving spoon or the back of a brush.

"We phoned the police," said the preschool teacher.

Lonnie was examined by a social worker and an investigation was authorized.

"What happened?" Ginger asked the preschool teacher.

"Lonnie was punished," said the teacher. "We had to tell his mother about what happened. We didn't know she'd beat him."

"But why?" asked Ginger.

"You'll have to ask her," said the teacher. "But I don't recommend it."

Ginger found the mother's name and phone number in the preschool directory and phoned her.

"You don't get it, do you?" the mother said. "You not even mad. Must be 'cause you don't have to be mad. You white."

"Why does that matter?" asked Ginger.

"Because Lonnie gotta live in a white man's world. And if he messes up, he's at risk. Big risk. And messin' with a white girl…well, better he get a good whippin' now than get killed in the prime of his goddamned life."

"I wouldn't kill your son," said Ginger. "I don't hold him responsible. He's a child."

"That between Lonnie and the Lord," said the woman. "He gotta learn how to survive. And you ain't helpin'."

Lonnie's mother hung up.

A second incident further aggravated Ginger's urban apprehensions. Aware she had forgotten work papers at home, Ginger left the law office early for lunch so she could walk back to get them. Entering the flat's stairwell, she heard a scuffling along the upstairs floor.

"Harriet?" she called as she opened the flat's downstairs door and climbed the stairs to the living room.

There was no answer other than a furtive scratching sound and then the whoosh of the back door opening and a pounding shake of footsteps rushing down the back steps. Ginger ran to the kitchen and toward the open back door. Looking down, she saw the figure of a man hit the bottom step and then disappear down the driveway.

"A black jacket," she told the reporting officer. "Black jacket… maybe leather… and blue jeans. That's all I saw."

"Did you see his face?" the officer asked.

"No," said Ginger.

"And his skin color?"

"Oh, white…yeah, I saw his hands. And he wore a dark blue stocking cap. You know, like a sailor wears, and…."

"What's missing?" the officer cut her off.

"A transistor radio," said Ginger.

"Jewelry?" asked the officer. "Other small valuables?"

"Oh shit," shouted Ginger as she ran to the bedroom and opened the top drawer of her vanity where she kept her mother's pearl necklace and a cigar box containing a secret stash of family cash. Both were missing.

"Anyone you suspect?" asked the officer.

"No," said Ginger. "We have a roommate in the sun porch."

The officer walked to the porch door and opened it. The room was a confusion of disarray and debris, clothes thrown everywhere, the desk drawers pulled out onto the floor and rifled. A small closet had been emptied completely and everything within thrown onto the floor.

"You either have a messy roommate or your burglar started here first," said the officer.

"From what you've told me he was acting alone and only grabbed what he could carry. He's long gone now."

"This is awful," said Ginger. "How did he get in?"

"No forced entry that I can see," said the officer. "Someone left the door unlocked."

"But this is such a safe neighborhood…" Ginger said absently.

"This used to be a safe town," said the officer. "Ten years ago we had maybe a few hundred burglaries citywide. Last year we had more than seven thousand. We used to get less than a dozen reported rapes a year. Last year we had more than a hundred. And don't get me started on drugs. And all this crime doesn't include what's happening at the campus. You're lucky. At least no one got hurt."

"What do you mean?" asked Ginger.

"He heard you come in. He might have waited for you upstairs. You wouldn't have known what hit you."

In the evening, Harriet put Lila to bed and then joined Stan and Ginger at the kitchen table to share a mutual feeling of violation and to create a final assessment of the day's damage. The burglar had tossed large and breakable possessions in his search for smaller, portable ones. He seemed to want only trinkets and money and drugs, though there were no medications in the bathroom other than aspirin and neither the burglar nor the officer ever would have found Stan and Ginger's pot or acid. The thief had taken Ginger's spare cash, but not Harriet's which she hid in a book lodged on a shelf of her bookcase. He did take Harriet's favorite gold earrings as well as others not so valuable. In a spirit of collective regard, no one asked who left the back door unlocked. It could have been any of them though that morning Stan was the last to leave.

Leaving work early on Friday, Ginger still felt dazed from a week of crises. She did not notice the coming or going of anything as Stan packed their Plymouth Valiant and made a place for Lila to sleep on the back seat. The trunk was filled and Harriet possessed the house keys and instructions on bolting the new locks. They would return late on Monday. It was all that was known.

They crossed the San Rafael Bridge against the commute and slithered through the stoplights of San Rafael and Novato before at last joining the open road north. In the fading twilight they entered Ukiah and rolled through the last vast valley before the stoplights and stop signs of Willits gave way to Laytonville and the steep, forested foothills of the coastal mountains.

"I guess there is no way out of here…and there is no relief," said Stan as he tapped his foot to Bob Dylan's voice singing *All Long the Watchtower* as it poured from the tape player.

"I think it's the end of the world," said Stan. "It's Dylan the prophet. He's been gone for a year and a half. He's bringing something back we need to know."

They were listening to an eight-track of Dylan's new album, rummaging the poet's latest songs for their pure and intended meanings. Mercurial partners, Stan and Ginger shared a fascination with their era's most mercurial singer and songwriter. They spoke of him as if he were a wise uncle they saw often and who gifted them with a legacy and who for reasons that weren't entirely clear had been absent for a while.

"The businessmen drink all the wine and the earth gets plowed under and no one knows what it's worth," Stan added after another Dylan verse.

"It's a Scorpio song," said Ginger. "It's as if the world is going to sting itself to death. And why not? If a big war started, it could happen in minutes. Or the businessmen and plowmen will take everything and leave the rest of us to starve."

"There's a biblical reference," said Stan. "It's from Isiah, about preparing the table, and watching from the tower, for the Lord says 'Go set a watchman' to say what he sees; and the watchman sees a chariot and two horsemen who bring news that Babylon has fallen and all graven images of the city's gods are broken and on the ground."

"I'm ready," said Ginger. "I'm ready to leave the city behind, and its gods and businessmen and plowmen, too."

"I wish it were that easy," said Stan.

"It doesn't have to be hard," said Ginger.

"Where would I sell my paintings?" asked Stan.

"You don't sell many now."

Ginger's response was sharp and firm.

And it was the truth. Until now Ginger had been reluctant to say it though the truth quieted Stan whose sudden slump in the driver's seat telegraphed his sullen offense.

"We'd need jobs," he said. "I don't want a job. I'm an artist."

"Cordell is an artist," Ginger said. "He has a job."

It was a terrible dig and Ginger surprised herself by saying it. But she was suddenly angry and could not say why. Was it the burglary? Lila's preschool incident? The war in Berkeley?

"What's so great about where we live?" Ginger whined.

"We live three blocks from the campus. It's a perpetual war zone. Tear gas, pitched battles. We 've been through years of this. And the Avenue. It's getting scary. I think of Lila growing up in all this and I just can't. I can't."

Ginger began to cry.

"Do I have to choose?" asked Stan. "Right now. Do I have to choose between you and my art?"

It was his turn to be angry.

Ginger was silent for several miles.

"I think you'll have to decide," she said. "But not now. Let's get to Cordell's. Let's see what's he's done and what might be possible. I want you to be happy, Stan. I want to be happy, too."

That Ginger said his name told Stan the depth of her concern. She spoke his name to separate from him. Which suggested an abiding necessity too large for her to contain within the frangible reality of their life lived together. It worried him to hear this.

They were silent through Garberville as the wide road opened in the darkness to four lanes and they flowed with an urgent current toward the lowlands beyond the curtaining forest. City lights appeared on a bay and Lila awoke, screaming inconsolably.

"Pull over when you can," Ginger said. "Her panties are soaked."

Cordell welcomed them, his happy, gaunt and chocolate face illuminated only by the light behind his door. All the rest, the night and its wet, cold air, the rocky driveway and the steps to his porch, was invisible. It was late and Cordell showed Ginger to the guest bedroom where she sat to settle her restless Lila, freed at last from the confines of a vehicle.

Cordell and Stan disappeared into the kitchen to drink beers and to catch up on months apart. Stan had his show, but Cordell had his job and they weren't equal achievements though Cordell pretended they were.

"You got fame now," said Cordell.

"But you have a gig," said Stan. "How's that going?"

Ginger listened as the banter of the two men echoed down the hall of an old, creaky farmhouse somewhere under the stars. She didn't care where, only that she had arrived with her daughter at the edge of a verdant, starlit valley from which she could hear both the wind and the ocean. She also heard voices that were happy and occasionally prophetic, as when Cordell said that life is a trick being played by the mind and "then up you jump with love…" The last words she heard before falling asleep.

"How you diggin' Berkeley?" Cordell asked Ginger at breakfast.

"Not much," Stan answered for her.

"How do you like this place?" Ginger asked Cordell.

"Weather's not great," he said. "It rains a lot. The college is fine. But there are a lot of jocks here studying to be forest rangers. It's an ag school, and worse than Davis. The art department hangs on by a thread. The town is nice. There's one hip bar downtown. It's probably the only one in the county with folk music on Friday and Saturday nights. And a hippie poet who reads on Sundays. There's one decent bookstore off-campus. And beaches everywhere. Goddamned empty beaches. A few hippies. I see them in town on Saturdays. Most live out in the woods, though. And there are lots of woods. Big, giant redwoods everywhere."

"Sounds perfect," said Ginger as she bit into her toast and shoveled a spoonful of cornflakes toward Lila.

"At least it won't rain while you're here," said Cordell. "Thick fog, though. Sometimes all day. I'll drive into the mountains when it gets too bad. It can be fifty degrees here but a few miles into the hills and the sun is burnin'.""

By prior agreement, Stan and Cordell left in his Volkswagen van to explore the campus and tour the towns and beaches north of Arcata. Ginger stayed with Lila, free to walk the quarter mile to Mad River Beach or drive into town. Later she drove to a city park in the redwoods that had swings and picnic tables. Ginger sat on a bench while Lila played. The fog lifted and she drove them back to the beach where together they had a picnic in the dunes.

She bought a local paper and searched the classifieds. A handful of homes were offered as rentals for monthly rents that ranged around a hundred dollars. She found property for sale for a hundred an acre. There were few jobs of interest, however. Most of those offered were in retail or logging. Two lumber companies were hiring choker setters, whatever those were.

One listing caught Ginger's attention. A law firm in Fort Bragg needed an experienced office assistant and secretary.

Impossible, she thought. Might be a good job, and no doubt already taken. She would check the listings again on Sunday. She had no plan if the job were still listed, no plan other than to allow for more planning. She found a map in the glove compartment and located the town, a logging community on the coast just a few miles north of Mendocino. They had friends who had moved to Mendocino the previous fall, friends they still had not visited. With a detour at Leggett onto Highway One, they could stop to see them Monday on the way home.

Cordell roasted ribs and corn and they stayed outside until a sodden fog drove them back in where they continued to eat and drink and listen to music. Stan played his Dylan albums while Cordell alternated with selections from his extensive blues collection that included praise songs by African tribesmen, the yodeling dirt poor blues of Blind Willie McTell and Bukka White, the ballads of Robert Johnson, the hot steppin' of Lightning Hopkins and the blow-it-out Chicago sound of Elmore James. Ginger put Lila to bed and, after getting stoned with the men, waited patiently as they rambled through the arts and letters of their mutual experience. They pondered endlessly the cast and meanings of Dylan's *Desolation Row*, until Ginger announced she was slipping off to bed.

Ginger awoke before dawn and drove into town to find a newspaper. All the stores were closed so she walked quickly a half-block along a street of one-story bungalows, lifted a bagged paper from a driveway and ran to her car. Back at Cordell's house she searched the classifieds to find, again, the law firm's listing and a phone number. No one would answer on Sunday. She would phone tomorrow. She would tell Stan today. In the quiet morning twilight filling Cordell's kitchen she imagined how she would find the words to describe for Stan the concrete terms of a possible new life, and also to convince him to listen.

four

"What does it pay?"

She didn't know.

It was the first question Stan asked Ginger when at lunch, and with Cordell on a run to town for groceries, she told him about the classified ad.

"The job may be filled," she said. "But if it isn't, I want to stop on our way home tomorrow for an interview."

Ginger showed Stan the map and pointed to a detour to the coast that would put them in Fort Bragg by early afternoon.

"It's a long shot," Ginger said. "But what if …?"

Ginger didn't finish the question she hoped Stan would answer.

Instead, he hovered as he often did, caught in a draft and thrown through the air while Ginger blazed all earthly trails.

"Then what? We move to Fort Bragg?" asked Stan. "This just sounds so crazy, Ginger."

"One step at a time," Ginger said. "Even if I'm offered the job, I don't have to take it."

Stan knew better. Ginger was his anchor though life with her sometimes left him feeling the part of an unworthy acolyte. What she saw was a clearing in the forest. What he feared was the death of his art.

"You can still paint," Ginger assured him. "I'm still the wage-earner."

She knew immediately it was the wrong tack. Stan made virtually no income as a painter and why would that ever change? No one knew this better than Stan. It wasn't that moving to the north coast would end his career as an artist. It would isolate this career in an empty land where necessity might force an uncomfortable reckoning.

"Hardest thing about living in the country is finding a way to stay," said Cordell as he and Stan prepared dinner.

"These kids in my classes. They're supported by rich parents, most of 'em. Not a one that's homegrown that I can see. We're all immigrants. If my job goes, so do I. I'm outta here. Beautiful country but it's not utopia. We're all lookin' for that aren't we? A utopia. No, if I leave the college I'm leavin' Humboldt. I'm like one of five brothers in this county."

Ginger played Old Maid with Lila while she listened.

"But if Gin had a job, man, you might swing it," Cordell told Stan. "Two galleries in Mendocino. I know an artist there with a studio. He trucks his stuff to the City twice a year. It could happen, man. But you gotta like trees and fog and at least tolerate rednecks for neighbors. And don't get caught with dope. Sheriffs up here can make trouble. They got nothin' better to do."

Ginger's interview was at 2 p.m. at the law offices of Stuart and Hunter on Franklin Street. The job was still open and Ginger's city experience interested the partner who spoke with her.

"We're a small firm in a small town," said the attorney on the phone.

The salary was negotiable.

Stan drove south out of Humboldt Bay's thick coastal fog and into a bright spring sun filtered through miles of giant redwoods. Ginger watched the passing roadside and pointed out blooms of garnet and green to Lila who showed little interest. Stan felt locked into a form derived from old relational bonds operating at the edge of a new frontier. Escape was in the air. Who was the artist now?

My Back Pages ran through the speakers but Stan was the only one who heard the words. Was he also the victim of *abstract threats too noble to neglect?* Ginger rolled forward with him in a dream of infinitely wondrous and untested possibilities.

"Rents are cheap up here," she said.

"There's a reason for that," said Stan. "It can be a hard place to live."

Ginger did not argue and, as they turned off at Leggett and

snaked through the coastal mountains, she watched for the return of the cold grey fog that signaled their arrival at the ocean.

"Only a half-hour now," she said. "What time is it?"

Stan checked his watch. It was a little after one.

The ride south rolled and twisted along high fractal bluffs and dipped through pastures that straddled deep stretches of sandy dunes. Past Westport the fog thinned to reveal clouds of steam rising from Fort Bragg's one lumber mill.

Stan found the law office where he dropped Ginger.

"Here goes," she said as Lila awoke.

"Where mommy?" Lila shouted as Ginger opened the glass door of an old Victorian building and entered the lobby.

"She'll be back," Stan said.

He drove a block and parked near what looked like a local drive-in. He took Lila from the backseat, sat her on his shoulders and went looking for a bathroom. He walked two blocks through streets as grey and colorless as the fog that chilled him. He could feel the eyes of people assessing his long black hair. He passed three thrift stores and a Chinese restaurant before finding a grocery where a friendly older woman wearing false eyelashes and wrapped in an apron let Lila use the employee bathroom upstairs.

"Your first visit to Fort Bragg?" the woman asked.

Stan nodded. He tried to imagine shopping here, buying groceries and wine, rummaging through thrift stores and eating Chinese on special occasions. The idea frightened him.

"Most visitors don't get farther than Mendocino," she said to him. "We're not the usual destination, and beyond here there isn't much until you get back on 101."

"We're just passing through," said Stan. "It's pretty country."

"And pretty damned empty," the woman added with a self-effacing chuckle.

"Good. It was good," said Ginger cautiously as she climbed back into the car.

"What's good about it?" asked Stan.

"The pay is good. About $510 a month plus benefits. Hours are decent, and the town has a small justice court. That means for big cases I might need to travel to Ukiah."

"Do they want you?" asked Stan.

Ginger couldn't say.

"We got along well. The partner's name is Ted. Said the other partner would phone me this week. Ted knew one of my references. Old law school chum."

"Do you want it?" Stan asked.

Ginger fought an urge to answer in terms that she thought might annihilate her. Too often Stan's willful self-absorption ate her alive and forced her to curtail desires before she even knew what they were. She loved Stan in ways she should love herself and that too often trapped her between a resentful isolation and a desperate longing.

"Yes," she said firmly. "I want it. I want this new start. I want it."

They were quiet as they crossed a bridge over the city wharf and rolled through open country past the village of Mendocino and a river mouth lined with beaches and bluffs, the town's Victorian main street strung along its rocky peninsula in the late afternoon sun like the silhouette of a New England fishing village.

"We could stop in and see Johnny and Bev," Ginger said.

Stan shook his head.

"It's late. One way or another, we'll be back."

The words were vaguely reassuring to Ginger whose telepathy was on high alert. It was Stan's way of acknowledging the change between them, the shift of their respective limits and identities. They were married, as so many of their friends were not, and united in seasoned devotion to a deeply mutual dependency. They could have either an ecstatic oneness or a nameless dread. It was the paradox of loyalty that the greedy need of each should find its realization in the other's faithful recognition.

"Some didn't want the strike to end," said Harriet as she helped Ginger carry Lila and their bags up the back steps.

It was late and dark and Stan, still sullen and withdrawn, said nothing as he rummaged in the trunk for Lila's box of toys.

"Reagan had the National Guard ready," said Harriet. "But it's winding down. We've had a week without any trouble and the cops are gone from the campus. It's over at SF State, too. Everybody's talking."

"Thanks for looking after things," said Ginger before turning down the hall to put Lila to bed.

"Good trip?" Harriet asked Stan.

She worried there might be a problem since neither Stan nor Ginger had said anything to each other.

"In a strange way, yeah…" Stan answered vaguely. "My friend is doing well. It's beautiful, empty country. The redwoods. You ever been there?"

Stan threw the conversation back to Harriet.

"Once. With my parents. We spent a week in a cabin near a place called Weott. Swam in the river. It was nice. But I was thirteen and bored as hell. No TV or music. I've been a city girl most of my life. Big empty country scares me. Maybe, if I went with Michael…"

Stan lost interest and hoped Harriet couldn't tell.

"We're beat," he said to Harriet. "We'll see you in the morning."

Stan and Ginger fell asleep without words. When Stan awoke, Ginger was in the kitchen with Lila, both dressed for the day. News blared from the radio.

"John and Yoko got married," said Ginger. "They're having a honeymoon in Amsterdam. The press is invited."

"To the honeymoon?" asked Stan.

"To their bed," said Ginger. "It's a peace thing."

"Far out," said Stan as he reached for their first shared feeling since arriving home.

In other news, British troops had secured the island of Anguilla in the Caribbean, which had the temerity to declare its independence from colonial rule.

"Another victory for western democracy," Stan said sarcastically, drawing a smile from Ginger.

"And the campus strike is over," said Ginger. "Safe to walk the streets."

It was her turn to be sarcastic.

Days passed as they wandered through a dreary, work-a-day silence that kept them busy while holding them apart. Were Stan and

Ginger to touch the feeling they shared without words, and which they purposely avoided, it might electrocute them with its surge of unconsummated conjecture. So they fell back on the strength and virtuosity of their minds, continuing to chatter about everything but the miasma of sentiment forming within each of them.

They waited while the state of not knowing gave way to the state of not wanting to know. And when no call came by the end of Thursday, Ginger at last broke the silence of their forbidden secret.

"Looks like they've made their choice," said Ginger. "I guess that's that."

Stan's relief was obvious. He rushed to hug his wife, thinking to comfort her with a surfeit of inappropriate joy that Ginger greeted and then rejected as she pushed him away.

"It doesn't fix anything," she said to Stan. "I don't know what's next. But I can't continue the way we're going."

"We have some time," said Stan. "We can keep looking."

Like the art he made, the art of looking might take forever.

"I have no more time," said Ginger.

They were left without passage to a safe harbor and spent another inconsolable evening with Lila who laughed, cried, fussed and at last fell asleep in Stan's humbly extended arms while Ginger showered and went early to bed.

We are surprisingly alike, thought Ginger as she drifted in the darkness. *We even look alike though Stan has dark hair and I am blonde but our faces are wide and radiant. Our jaws strong and our eyes and their burning, bright azure everyone mentions. The similarities make people think we are related and Lila, she looks like neither of us and her outbursts of anger, affection and childish wit surprise everyone with their intensity. We are a family, even through the times I sometimes wish we weren't. Perhaps scientists will one day invent a microscope so powerful it will reveal the ultimate emptiness of all experience.*

A phone call came for Ginger, which surprised her because there were no calls she answered at work that were specifically for her. But the caller had asked for her and immediately Ginger worried about Lila.

"Law offices," Ginger responded as she always did when answering the phone.

"Is this Ginger Prentiss?" asked the voice on the phone.

"Yes. Who is this?"

"Jack Stuart from the law firm in Fort Bragg. You interviewed with Ted this week?"

Ginger steadied herself and covered the speaker with her hand as if to forge a pocket of privacy.

"Yes," she answered.

"Ted was impressed with you. Tell me, why do you want to move up here?"

It was the last question Ginger expected.

Ginger took a breath and grasped for her thoughts. Her reason for moving might be the unlocking key or the reason to reject her.

"I grew up in the country. I'm a gardener at heart who loves fresh food and fresh air. My husband and daughter and I were visiting last weekend when I saw your ad."

"Your husband. What does he do?"

"He's an artist," said Ginger. "His paintings are shown in galleries in San Francisco."

It was a stretch but Ginger felt the need to reach as far as she could.

"He's OK with living in the country?" asked Jack. "Some people, well, they aren't all that happy with our slow pace up here…I mean…"

"He can paint anywhere," said Ginger. "We've discussed it. It will work fine."

"And the salary?" Jack asked. "You OK with that?"

"It's fine," said Ginger. "It's plenty."

"So when can you start?" asked Jack.

Ginger held tightly to the receiver.

"Are you offering me the job?" she asked.

"Oh…sorry…yeah," said Jack. "You want it?"

Ginger recognized the terms of a country job offer which was often little more than a few words and a handshake, an informal protocol she watched her father perform many times to secure employment.

"Yes," Ginger said instantly. "I think we need a few weeks. When do you want me to start?"

"Can you come up this weekend to sign some papers?" asked Jack.

Yes, Ginger could drive up Saturday.

"Thank you," she said as she wrote down Jack's home phone number.

"Let's say one o'clock on Saturday, unless you call," said Jack. "Do you need a place to stay? We can put you up at a motel north of town, right on the water and…"

She thanked him.

"No," she said. "No, I don't."

It was a view of heaven, a view of things beautiful but also absent and not really there. Every hope Ginger expressed brought Stan back to every change he dreaded.

"I've phoned Bev," said Ginger. "I'll stay with them Saturday night. I'll leave early Sunday. I'll be home by noon."

"That's not the point," said Stan. "It's your life, Ginger. It's not our life anymore."

"Have I not been clear?" asked Ginger. "Why can't you see that I am offering something and not taking anything away? I still work. I still support you. You can still make art. Are you coming or not?"

"Sounds like I have no choice," said Stan as he stirred a pot of soup and Lila pounded the table with her fork.

Stan thought himself the tortured artist though Ginger was, in fact, the primal source on which his life depended. It was not true that the more he loved the more he understood. The only artful wisdom he could share, either with Ginger or the artist within, was that his opacity hid no special secrets. He was simply afraid. He knew and trusted Ginger more than he knew himself, which was not at all.

five

Stan's art was his omnipotent fantasy. But his first generally acknowledged triumph, the hanging of one of his paintings at a prestigious city gallery, was now suddenly cold and strange and intrinsically without value. For years Ginger had nourished his prolific vision, fed him through a mirror, made him feel invincible. But Ginger's truth, emerging now in her crystallizing desires, was that Stan's life—his art, his ego, his career at the frontier of creation— was negotiable.

Which was not to say Stan would no longer have his art. In her best efforts to be both anchor and partner, Ginger was the sentry of Stan's self-regard. And when Stan thought about it, which he did not like to do, he understood that Ginger was his salvation. This was hard for Stan to admit. Certainly he would be famous someday, would leave a legacy of beauty for the ages. For now, though, he could interpret their move to the vacant northwest coast as a hiatus, a pause many good artists take along the inconstant, fickle and wearying road to greatness. Indeed, he would have to. And perhaps one day he would thank her. But not now.

Ginger cried when Stan said he would go with her for the weekend and manage Lila while she met with the law partners and secured her employment.

"Least I can do," he said. "You're doing so much for us."

He didn't believe it. He didn't like what she was doing. But Stan acknowledged Ginger's willful certainty and would move out of her way.

"You'll want to cut your hair," said Johnny. "Looks great, man. But you don't want the attention."

Johnny and Bev lived in a small rental near the beach in Caspar, a small three-room cabin on a one-acre parcel owned by a retired couple from Sacramento. They had lived there a year and just signed their second lease. Johnny, tall and gaunt with sunken eyes and a large chest, worked for a fledgling vacation rental service in Mendocino cleaning cabins and homes. Bev, short, diminutive and shy, her hair brown and full, had found a job waiting tables at a seafood restaurant on the Ft. Bragg wharf. For six months she took any shift available, eventually securing a regular position as a lunch hostess. But she was now several months pregnant and soon would need to stop.

The couple met in the Haight during the Human Be-In, but left the city at the end of the year. Johnny wanted a country life though he had no idea where or how to find it. He was lured north by the rental, mentioned to him by his mother who was a friend of the owners.

"Yeah, cut your hair," Johnny said again. "You meetin' these lawyers tomorrow? Hell, let's cut it tonight. Go on. Smoke a doob. I got a razor and scissors. Bev can do it. She did mine."

Ginger's smile telegraphed her approval.

"Who's the wonderful man living under that big mop of hair?" she asked.

"You can always grow it back."

Stan asked for a few moments and went into the bathroom to look in the mirror. His eyes were all he saw. Gathering his hair into a ponytail made him look silly. He tried to imagine a look, but had never bothered to memorize one.

"OK," he said. "Let's just do it."

He knew short hair was a necessity if he hoped to live unmolested in this new land, though he hated the idea of it. He likely would need to work and during his previous visit he had felt the hard stares of the local world. He at last wished to disappear, to join collegially in some common and rural invisibility that would spare him an investigation.

Bev shaped Stan's thick black hair into a flat, layered look, leaving a couple of inches that fell neatly over his ears.

"Not too short," she said. "But enough."

"You look so cool," said Ginger, telegraphing with her eyes an unexpectedly intense attraction to his new appearance.

She had never seen Stan with short hair and that night, despite the cabin's thin walls and Lila sleeping at the foot of their mattress, Ginger forced herself on her husband, mounted him and fucked him like an impatient teen until she came and came again. Stan loved Ginger's unusually brash attention, even as he wondered whether her lust was for him or for his fresh appearance as someone else.

Ted and Jack were quiet men. Ted was tall and lanky and Jack was short and stout, giving them as a pair the strange likeness to film comedians Abbot and Costello, though tall Ted was the jocular one and short Jack not at all. Like the male country cousins they were, both men related strongly to Stan, which made him anxious, and not so much to Ginger and not at all to Lila who Stan held and rocked and carried outside the small law office on Franklin Street while Ginger signed papers and learned the ropes of her new job.

"April 21st," said Ginger as she left the office. "We have about a month to make the move. Oh, and it includes medical after 90 days. For all of us. No kidding."

Their plan for the afternoon was to look for a rental though driving south Ginger saw a For Sale sign and forced them away from the highway and west on to Ocean Avenue just south of the city limits. At the corner of Ocean and another street they found a wooded acre-plus with a small two-story house at its center. Behind the house was a detached garage. A sign on the property advertised it as a "two bedroom country bungalow with room to grow." Ginger wrote down the phone number.

"You think we can buy something?" Stan said skeptically.

"You never know," said Ginger. "We're not in Berkeley anymore."

She asked Stan to stop at the next gas station on the highway and she would phone the realtor. He could barely see Ginger's animated expressions through the dirty glass of the phone booth. Nearly a half-hour passed before she returned to the car.

"They want $9500," she said.

"Good luck with that," said Stan.

"No, wait. That's the sale price. They want at least $500 down but the rest we can finance. I've done the math. A thirty-year loan at eight percent. Stan, it would cost us less than $80 a month. And property taxes are one percent, which is less than $100 a year."

"Where do we get the down payment?" asked Stan. "And what the hell? The house may be falling apart."

"That's why we have a walk-through tomorrow morning," said Ginger. "The agent will meet us at ten."

Stan looked at Ginger as if she were the star in a movie that had not yet been made. She spoke like an actress that had memorized her lines for years in anticipation of the perfect role. And this was it. She had found her place in the country and the job to go with it. Why wouldn't she find also the home in which to live? And what more would she find here and make her own?

What had appeared to Stan as a mirage found everywhere its sudden and irrevocable roots. His confusion now was his last defense. He could resist only by professing bewilderment. He might slow her process but he would never stop it. Were he to threaten not to move, it would only sanction her quick and decisive departure.

"Every song he writes is a love song," said Stan as he pulled their Valiant into the shoreline traffic. Dylan's *Love Minus Zero/No Limit* thumped through the speaker.

"Even *Tom Thumb's Blues*. Lost in Juarez is like being lost in the dream of love—the pain, the addiction, the way you can't ever have enough but in the way that enough is always too much."

"Is that love for you?" Ginger asked. "Pain? Addiction?"

"Sometimes," he answered quietly.

"Like now?" Ginger asked again.

"No, babe," Stan answered directly. "Nothing wrong today. Loving you is what I was made to do."

His words satisfied Ginger who thought they sounded like a Dylan lyric.

Lila slept on the backseat as they slithered down the coast to the mouth of the Navarro River and then swerved along the redwood-curtained curves of Anderson Valley. At Cloverdale they joined a thick and velocious flow of cars and trucks on Highway 101, backed up for blocks at the town's single stoplight.

"Can you believe we've put in an offer on a house?" asked Ginger.

"I can't," said Stan. "Probably because we have a week to come up with another $400 that we don't have."

"My dad will help," said Ginger. "I know he will."

Their tour of the house on Ocean had been a surprise, though Stan's first response was to ask himself what was he doing there? He might have thought himself on acid until at one point, probably when they went upstairs and saw the two small bedrooms with a view toward the ocean, he began to sense something resembling a pride of ownership. He pictured Lila asleep in one bedroom while he and Ginger slept in the other. The detached garage, which from the outside appeared porous and weathered, suddenly assumed the potential for a perfect studio. Planter beds were already in place in the abandoned garden while intersecting rows of fir and eucalyptus created a privacy screen at the property lines but not too much shade. By the time the tour was completed, Stan was happy to consider himself the owner. That is, if they could swing a down payment plus fees and insurance and a home inspection revealed no problems.

They entered Berkeley during evening, rising east toward the hills on the slow incline of University Avenue, past the flashy lights of bars and liquor stores lining San Pablo and through blocks of closed retail businesses. They reached the west entrance of the university, then turned south before climbing again along Durant and crossing at Telegraph, its sidewalks choked with students. Driving past the Forum, Ginger saw Harriet sharing a table with a woman she didn't recognize. The bookstores and cafes were still open, giving Stan a charge of vitality he knew could not possibly exist in the country from which they had just returned.

He thought of North Beach, the music clubs downtown, the local galleries and museums, the artist friends who tripped with him in the hills. He thought of blues and rock 'n' roll and concerts in the park and performers that would never appear in Fort Bragg.

"I'm going to miss the Negroes," Stan said absently.

He meant he would miss the gravity and soul of city life, the vitality of diversity and its complex of irresolvable conflicts. Not all culture was black, but what was black fed every root that grew his art.

Ginger heard his words and was surprised.

"I'm going to miss our friends," she said, searching for agreement that would avoid lighting for Stan any fires of regret.

She knew she would miss nothing else: the panhandlers on street corners, the traffic, the anger spilling out of almost everyone. Berkeley was a small world at war within a brutalizing larger world and that for too long had infected her with a psychic claustrophobia.

Crime was increasing and she now felt a victim perpetually at risk in a way that left her waiting as the potential witness of some final destruction. She could feel, as if it were an incipient fetus, the promise of big trouble and wished to leave Berkeley before it was too late.

Ginger first told Harriet and asked her if she would take over the remainder of their lease on the flat, which would run through December. Harriet said yes immediately.

"The rent," Ginger said cautiously. "It's triple what you pay now."

"I'll probably get a roommate," said Harriet. "Anyway, daddy pays my rent. It will be worth it to him. He wants to know where I am. He knows I'm never coming home."

Ginger also told her employer, the senior partner of the law firm, who liked her and wished her well.

"If it doesn't work out," he said. "Just call me. We'll take you back."

At first he thought she was fleeing the city's plan to integrate its elementary schools.

"He assumed we were part of the city's white flight," Ginger told Stan. "I told him we were moving to Mendocino, not El Cerrito. He laughed. 'No Negroes up there,' he said. I told him you weren't happy about that."

There were other friends and communities to tell, including a fellow artist and his wife who arrived on Saturday to take acid with Stan and Ginger while Lila spent the night with a preschool friend. The day was spent touring the flat with meticulous and psychogenic awareness, Ginger laughing as she created a cosmic inventory of items to take or leave.

Stan, at first festive, fell into a deep and sullen sadness that he carried to the backyard and farther into the vortex of a death he hoped bore no recrimination. Would he ever again hang one of his paintings? Cradled by the drug's excruciating clarity, he wept until rescued by Ginger and their friends who swept him back to the calm and candlelight of the kitchen. The taste of fresh berries nourished his hope though at night he dreamt he was the image of a clown on canvass, blood pouring like paint in garnet brilliance from his empty hands.

"They've accepted our offer," Ginger whispered to Stan as she held and covered the receiver.

A week had passed since their return from the coast. The house on Ocean was theirs contingent on a hundred procedural details but none of them, according to the realtor named Joseph, of much concern. One contingency was the delivery of a down payment of $463.47 plus a few extraneous fees, including one for an inspection that showed no termite damage or major construction issues. A new floor would be needed eventually in the kitchen but all the plumbing worked, as did the gas heater and the fireplace. The roof was old but still secure. No leaks. The garage needed work but it was built on a solid cement pad and had electricity.

"The previous owner died suddenly," said the realtor. "The family hasn't been too eager to sell it. You got them at a good time. They're ready to move on."

Ginger's new employer vouched for her salary and her old employer for her character and dependability. It was enough to qualify for a loan from a local bank. The sale of property on this isolated coast was a big and welcome deal.

A wrinkle threatened to become a tsunami when Ginger's father declined to give her anything more than $100 toward the down. Infuriated, she threatened to sell the car or rob a bank. And then Stan received news his painting had been sold by the big city gallery. Between the $300 for his painting, and Ginger's larger than expected severance check, they had more than was needed.

Stan owed Ginger the beginning of a new life, to which he had been dragged resentfully and without will. He should have been grateful. In fact, Stan wanted change and thrived on it. What he could not abide was the idea that, as a man, he should have led this expedition.

Instead, when confronted with Ginger's creativity, he retreated. He was the passive, even womanly, recipient of the concrete products made from Ginger's earnest strength and vision. This, more than any fear of moving, was his most painful epiphany.

six

Stan drove to the gallery to pick up his check and say goodbye to his painting. Then he drove to North Beach to meet Professor Fitz for a drink at the Bohemian Cigar Store.

"Really? The redwoods?" asked Fitz. "Sounds like a trip. You excited?"

"OK, I guess," said Stan sullenly.

Another drink loosened his lips and shook free all of Stan's curdling resentments. He should have known better. All his worst fights started in bars.

"Yeah, the weather's not great," Fitz agreed. "And there probably isn't a cigar store."

Stan smiled cynically.

"It's more the way it all happened," Stan said. "Why so far away, goddammit? Arneson went to Davis and he lives in Benicia. Still in the Bay Area and an hour from Union Square."

"There's nothing intrinsically wrong with an artist living in the country," said Fitz.

He knew two that had moved to the coastal hills of Sonoma County. Fitz tried to fill a space Stan wished to vacate.

"Do they sell much art?" asked Stan.

"Some," said Fitz. "But the real question isn't what you will sell in the woods. It's whether you will continue to produce art without other artists around to talk to, without other art to look at."

Looking away, Stan saw a familiar woman enter the bar, her long, straight blonde hair swaying like a horse's tail as she laughed with a woman who entered behind her.

"Hold on a minute," Stan said to Fitz.

Stan bolted from his barstool and approached the woman.

"Inger," Stan said as he blocked her way.

"Stan," answered Inger. "Small damned world."

After a cluster of surprised hugs, Stan was introduced to Sheila.

"We share a place near here," said Inger.

"I heard you were in LA," Stan said.

"Yeah," Inger answered wistfully. "I tried it. I'm back now. Still trying to act, though. Right Sheila?"

Sheila nodded.

"Your hair's short," Inger said to Stan. "That's why I didn't see you."

Words were the bricks of a wall that hid both Stan and Inger from the pleasure each suspected might be the gift of the other. The crowd in the bar, the noise, the darkness, the décor, the lighted Coit Tower on Telegraph Hill outside the window, were the elements of an endearing unreality.

"Why don't you join us?" said Stan.

"Us. Who's us?" asked Inger.

"Over here," said Stan.

"Fitz. Jim Fitz. He was one of my art teachers."

Fitz sat with his back to the door and turned when he heard his name.

"Fitz, this is Inger and…Sheila, right?…her friend Sheila. Inger's an artist. She's just back from LA."

Fitz looked up to greet the women until, raising his eyes, he encountered a vaguely familiar face utterly out of context. Fitz appeared momentarily frozen. At first Stan thought his professor friend might be having a stroke, not seeing an ocean of unreality that stretched between Fitz and Inger like a long, wide beach.

"Mr. Fitz?"Inger asked ingenuously. "High school Mr. Fitz?"

There was a long pause as the professor searched for his words.

"I'm afraid so," Fitz confessed.

"You know each other?" asked Stan.

"You could say that," answered Inger. "At least we did once. He did, anyway."

Inger's words were crisp and cryptic and left both Stan and Sheila to stand outside of some burning filament forming between Inger and Fitz.

"It's been a long time," said Fitz.

"It's a small world," Stan interjected in a search for any available levity.

"Too small, if you ask me," said Inger as she looked directly at the professor who could not hold their shared gaze and turned toward Stan.

"It's best I go," Fitz said to Stan. "Phone me before you move."

Inger's face, red with either shock or anger, retreated with Sheila toward the door where she whispered something in her friend's ear that elicited first a furrowed brow of attempted comprehension followed by Sheila's expression of distraught surprise. Sheila looked again toward Fitz with some new understanding that completely eluded Stan.

"Is there a problem?" Stan asked Fitz.

"More than a problem," said Fitz. "A history."

The professor rose and walked toward the restrooms where he could leave through the only accessible exit not blocked by Inger. In his confusion, Stan looked back at Inger and followed the professor until he reached the exit.

"Fitz. Wait a minute. What th---?"

"No words will help right now," Fitz said without breaking stride. "I'll tell you sometime, but not here."

And he was gone.

From that moment forward Stan became the temporary property of Inger, drawn first by her mystery with Fitz and, eventually, into the attraction Inger always had on offer and that Stan found momentarily irresistible.

"Let's go to our place," Inger asserted.

Stan followed the two women up Vallejo Street to Leavenworth and entered the elevator to their third floor apartment. He checked his watch. It wasn't even six. Ginger knew he planned to spend a last evening with Fitz and would likely have dinner and a few drinks. He had at least a few hours to unravel the mystery of Inger and the professor, that is, if Inger were willing.

Sheila offered to prepare a snack while Inger opened a liquor cabinet and poured shots of bourbon for everyone.

"Nice place," said Stan, already a little drunk from his time at the Cigar Store. He noticed the walls were covered with Impressionist prints while a print of one of his favorite Paul Klee pieces, a 1928 painting of a man's perplexed face avoiding an arrow flying overhead and titled *Nearly Hit*, hung in the kitchen.

"Great location," he added.

"You're still in North Beach and not the Haight."

"We have to be here," said Sheila. "It's where we work."

"How was LA?" Stan asked.

"Weird," said Inger. She had gotten into a communal scene on an abandoned dude ranch in Topanga Canyon.

"Guy named Charlie ran the group. Mostly women. We were kind of a harem, which was OK at first but I got tired of him fast. When they started stealing cars, I decided I'd had enough. Had to sneak away, though. They didn't like the idea of people just up and leaving."

While Sheila cooked up a frittata, Inger took Stan out on the apartment's slender deck that offered a view of North Beach, Telegraph Hill and the Bay. It was a cool night and Inger snuggled into Stan's shoulder. He did not resist.

"So what are you doing now?" he asked her.

"Performing," Inger said at first, as if the word stood in for more than she might otherwise admit.

"OK. I won't lie to you. Sheila and I dance topless in the clubs. She works at Big Al's and I dance at the Condor. My tits aren't big enough for the weekend shows but I have a strong body and can really work it during the week. We make a ton in tips and we get the apartment for next to nothing because it's owned by, well…he's a principle in the trade."

"Trade?" asked Stan.

"It's a long story. Too long for tonight."

"And what was all that with Fitz?"

Inger's silence might have been enough. She had been ambushed by her past and did not need to revisit it. But now Stan was involved and she thought, bourbon in hand, there was no choice but to explain.

"Fitz was my English teacher in high school," she said. "He was also my first lover. I was sixteen. He spent time with me after school. I fell deeply in love in the only way you can at that age—completely."

"How? What happened?" asked Stan.

"He'd take me away after school. First, we just had coffee," said Inger.

"Then one afternoon we hiked together to a hill in Tilden Park. He brought his poetry and a blanket. It was improper and delicious.

And it was also illegal. He knew what to do better than I did."

"How long?" asked Stan.

"A month? I don't know," said Inger. "I wasn't thinking about that until, one week, it was over. He stopped seeing me. Even stopped speaking to me, or calling on me in class."

"That must have been awful," said Stan. "What was he thinking?"

"Yeah," said Inger. "I was pregnant."

The rest of the story followed, Stan attentive to what few details Inger thought useful to share, though she said enough for Stan to feel an urge to comfort her. That was all Inger wanted. She moved closer to him until there was no way either could avoid an embrace.

Stan awoke without immediately knowing how he had fallen asleep. Next to him in the bed and darkness was Inger, snoring softly. It was not a dream. He was naked and found his watch on the bedside table. It was 3:30 a.m. He sat up abruptly, his naked foot slapping something wet and sticky.

He looked down in the low light glowing from the hallway to see a shriveled condom. For a blazing few minutes he replayed the evening and its progress that at the time he thought he fully controlled. There was the pleasure of a novel kind of touching and some delicious food and more drinks and something saucy that led to something else and finally to the explicit and delicious loss of control over any outcome and Inger's precautions, though as he considered it now, was the condom for her protection or his?

He recalled flashing on Fitz and the continuity of his fucking the woman Fitz fucked first.

And what would he say to Ginger? And when? He staggered out of Inger's bedroom and found a phone in the kitchen.

"Where are you?" Ginger asked, her voice high above the pitch of worry.

"Got going with Fitz," Stan said through his hoarseness. "We lost track of time."

"Really?" said Ginger with uncharacteristic iciness. "Are you sure about that?"

"Yeah, of course," said Stan.

He was firm and well defended.

"I only ask," said Ginger, "because the professor phoned here at 10:30 looking for you. He said he'd left you in North Beach and wanted to explain something."

Ginger delivered her line as if she had rehearsed it, and probably had, for several hours.

"I have to find my car," Stan said. "I'll be home soon."

He realized again that he had said not enough and also too much. He could not say now that he had fallen asleep in the car. He would have to say something and it needed to be anything but the truth, though he tried out the truth.

Yes, we hooked up with Inger and her roommate and you won't believe this but Fitz fucked Inger when she was his high school student and she got pregnant and it was a big shock when we ran into her so I ended up at her place to hear the story and to sort of comfort her and ended up fucking her, too. Yeah, Inger. The woman you hate, remember? Well, I guess I just thought it would be a good thing to do before I left the City. You can understand, I'm sure....

No, there was no way he could tell Ginger anything resembling the truth. He would make up something and put himself somewhere anonymous and without identity. He would refer vaguely to a sad and impossible depression. He might even say he was suicidal and that he hadn't realized how much despair he felt about the move. But that now, after a night of roaming listlessly, he had seen the importance of this move and why it needed to happen.

And he wanted now, more than anything, to make it happen and to make it work. Ginger wouldn't believe him but it was only important if she believed he believed it.

"Sounds like you're in big trouble," said Inger.

She stood at the entrance to the kitchen in a peacock blue terrycloth bathrobe.

"Don't worry," she said before Stan could answer. "I'm not coming after you. I don't want trouble. But if *you* ever do, if you ever want to learn more about me, you know where I am."

Stan once again took in Inger's well-appointed apartment, its walls covered with art, expensive furniture in every room, closets full of clothes. *How does she pay for this?* he thought. *Or rather, who pays for this?* There is nothing she describes as her career other than topless dancing and acting and...something else or someone else stood behind Inger and Stan knew she would never say who or what it was.

Ginger did not believe Stan and at first ignored him when he returned home.

"Just drop it," she said as Stan sought again to offer a more elaborate version of his lie about the previous evening.

The more he spoke the less he was believed and while Ginger could let the whole messy issue go, at least enough to continue planning their move, she would not let it go away. Without corroboration, her lack of trust made Ginger a little crazy.

Is it just my imagination? she thought. *Am I being a suspicious bitch?*

Within a few days Ginger had talked herself back into a loving diminution. She was Stan's silent guardian and how, in the midst of her own tender trauma, could she expect him not to act out? Maybe he did just take a long walk in the City. She knew he struggled with their move north. How could she expect a strong and proud man not to feel a thunderous alienation and wander momentarily away to spend a dark night with his soul?

And just as it all began to make some peaceful if disjointed kind of sense, Ginger and Stan attended an art opening at the Black Man's gallery in the Haight. A photo show titled *Black and Proud* included seven of Larry's photographs of Oakland Panthers.

"You gettin' good," said Stan as he wandered among Larry's images, all 11x14 prints mounted in black, gold-trimmed frames. One was a tender view of a school-aged girl with hair in a short Afro accepting a plate of eggs and toast from a young, earnest beret-wearing Panther. The image was a tight portrait, two heads moving together in loving solidarity: man and child, the young Panther offering protection and sustenance to a new generation waiting to grow up black and proud.

Ginger left to use a bathroom and when she returned she saw Mack enter the gallery with Inger who rushed immediately toward Stan. Ginger watched Inger grab Stan fearlessly, watched her run her hands through his short hair and down his neck as Stan appeared reflexively to hold Inger at the base of her spine, barely resisting an obvious impulse to stroke her buttocks through the inviting texture of a short, silk skirt.

Her sighting of Inger and Stan together confirmed all of Ginger's lingering suspicions. Stan turned to see her and immediately took his hands off Inger and pushed her gently away. Ginger knew instantly what had happened that night in the City. And it didn't matter how.

"You need to tell me the truth," Ginger said at last from the silence of their drive home from the gallery.

"But babe, I…" Stan struggled again for the power to control his story.

"Stop it!" said Ginger. "I saw you. That night with Fitz…in all our time together we have never had such an unexplainable story between us. I don't believe you. I don't."

Stan began to cry.

"OK," he said, delivering an edited version of a true story in which his motives were not discussed, in which he argued desperately his case for mercy: that he was drunk, unclear, confused and not responsible and was easy prey.

"You?" Ginger said angrily. "Seduced? Please, Stan. Don't treat me like a fool. A woman ten years younger that flashes her ass at everything that moves—and you fuck her? The first chance you get you fuck her?!!!"

Stan stopped the car and pulled it into a parking lot just before the entrance to the Bay Bridge. He faced Ginger with all the new terror grown from his betrayal.

"I wouldn't blame you if you wanted to leave me," Stan said directly. "I've betrayed your trust. It doesn't matter what I felt. It was fucking wrong. I know that. So much is fucking wrong. You might be better off without me."

Ginger stared quietly out the window before turning to look directly into Stan's eyes.

"You know, I'm disappointed in your attraction to her," she said. "But I'm not really angry about that, or even that you fucked her. It's your lie that troubles me. It's the idea you would lie to me and then assume we'd go forward together without a hiccup. That's the hard part, Stan. That's what I have to deal with."

Ginger had always feared abandonment, and for many reasons other than those now provided by Stan. Acting from the source of his own fear of being caught, trapped and made vulnerable, Stan tried to hide his bad behavior behind an attitude that had usually worked for him: a theatrical and righteous arrogance that would curb anyone's questions.

He did not know Ginger had grown tired of a constant anticipation she would disappoint Stan, though Stan continued to believe this potential was still in play. He acted still from an old proposition that his art and his love were Ginger's priceless assets and that even a subtle threat of his withdrawal was enough to keep her contained.

Yet, like a naughty boy forced into obedience, he had followed her into the forest, facilitated the creation of a newly ventured nest, and seen—as much as he did not want to see—how useless his impoverished art was to the fulfillment of Ginger's pursuit of happiness.

So at the core of their conflict was a source of almost unbearable truth for both. Each needed to address the reflection of their worst fear in what they thought to be their truest strength. Ginger, who for most of her life was afraid to tell her deepest needs to anyone that might then turn and leave, was left with the power to herself leave, to herself disdain the attraction, and even the love, of an unwilling partner. Stan, who for most of his life disdained the gravity of cooperative living, who saw himself always and forever the fast, free artist first before he was an embedded link to anyone, grasped at last what real love was and what it required: to link without resistance to someone who was not his mirror but, in fact, an author who penetrated deeply to the core of his character and knew it and loved it better than he knew or loved himself.

"I'm sorry," said Stan. "I'm so, so sorry. I love you. I love Lila. I want all of this to work."

Ginger sat a while with Stan's sorrow.

"I think I can forgive you, Stan," said Ginger. "I want this to work, too."

She put her hand on Stan's shoulder and drew him to her so she could look firmly and deeply into his eyes.

"I forgive you. I forgive you this once. But never, ever again."

Ginger's last words, the proviso that clarified her limits, gave Stan a surprising relief. He knew her now. He knew her and respected her and loved her with a renewed and assuring gratitude.

"Now I have some news for you," said Ginger as she pulled back from Stan and sat straight up in her seat.

"I'm pregnant."

seven

Stan still worried that what he hoped to hold would not exist. He could not stop wondering how a nearly empty land would feed his art, would sustain a creative life. He wished to give Ginger everything he had available to make their home together and to make a place for the baby growing within her. He could do at least that. But what would that leave him? Who would he be?

"I know it's a long way to drive just to sign papers," Ginger said as they packed for another trip north.

"But it saves us more than a week, which means we can move in before the end of April."

The round-trip was a tedious 11 hours, made to feel longer by stops at a park near Philo where Lila played and Ginger bought produce at a roadside stand. The paper-signing took barely thirty minutes with time for lunch at Johnny and Bev's and then a weary drive back during which Lila thankfully napped until Cloverdale where she had an accident and, wet and bored, broke down in sobs until Ginger took her for a walk along the river. They arrived back in Berkeley after nine. But it was still Saturday. They could sleep in on Sunday and take the day to plan the next steps of their move north.

The closing date of the home sale was less than a week after Ginger's first scheduled day at the law office. Ginger herself would drive the Valiant to Fort Bragg to start work and stay with Johnny and Bev. Stan would care for Lila, supervise her preschool farewells, and bring her up the following weekend, furniture and belongings in tow thanks to Larry and his truck while Raj, Stan and Lila followed in Harriet's car. Move-in day was Saturday the 26th and Bev and Johnny agreed to host a party at the new house.

Sunday's tension was palpable as Stan and Ginger grappled with their need to pack. To move clothes, tables and beds, to sort and box dishes, appliances and objects, to review and edit their life together so that it might fit into a truck, caused them to shove and bump, at times roughly, against each other. It took one vote to keep an object and two to throw something out. But without a tiebreaker, except in the case of Lila's toys and dolls, there was much more to keep than to leave and by evening their discussions turned into arguments and, finally, a panic-inspired fight for personal survival.

At last they agreed to trade their losses, Ginger the first to throw out a box of unused canning jars while Stan then jettisoned several tubes of acrylic paint. And so the week went, Stan by day sorting his belongings into piles of valuables and trash while at night after work Ginger made hard decisions among the objects and appliances of her life.

At last, they agreed not to move several things they knew they could replace, which exempted all of Stan's 22 large paintings. These would be kept in the garage and moved later. Harriet, who at first offered to help pack, retreated after Stan and Ginger's loud Sunday fight and kept her focus on renting a room of the flat.

"I have an ad up on the department bulletin board," she told Ginger. "Don't worry. My dad's good for the rent through the end of the year."

Time didn't dull the edges of experience. Things did: things that left one trapped in trappings acquired to smooth edges grown like crystals from a life of self-earned inadequacies. And so it was that as Ginger prepared to leave the next Sunday morning, to drive one last time away from her home, she left behind her husband and her child and also most all of her non-living belongings.

She wondered if, after all her sorting and hard rejection of ordinary possessions once considered invaluable, she would ever again value any inanimate thing. She was free and also morose, sad most of all to leave Lila who could not understand why her mother needed to go away for longer than a day which, for Lila, might as well have been forever.

"We'll get pizza," Stan promised Lila as she sobbed and held tightly to Ginger's leg as her mother stood beside the car.

"We'll go to a movie."

"Mommy loves you," said Ginger. "I'll call you tonight when I get to our new home."

A new home had no meaning for Lila who had only known one and had no reason to think that wasn't all anyone ever needed.

"Mommy come back? Mommy coming back?" Lila shouted hopefully.

"No, mommy not coming back. Lila and Stanny are coming to mommy next Saturday."

It was too much for Lila to grasp, who heard only the word No and could not comprehend the ironic and eventual joy cleverly promised by her mother.

"We'll go to a movie," Stan said again to Lila. "Want to ride on my shoulders?"

"Give mommy a kiss," Ginger said firmly.

Lila let go of her mother's leg and turned away, her chest heaving in spasms of unmanageable grief. Stan picked her up and held her as she squirmed wildly.

Ginger climbed into the car.

"I'll phone at seven," she said to Stan. "Good luck."

The car pulled away, rolling down the street toward College Avenue as Lila stretched her arm out, grabbing in panic at its receding bumper, wanting to pull the car back until, as it turned the corner, Lila melted into Stan's chest to burn him with her tears.

Someone once told Stan that life was merely a series of little accidents. As he carried Lila down their street toward Telegraph he waited for the passing of one phase of his accidental life and the arrival of the next. He crossed College Avenue, Lila quieted by the loud engine of a passing bus while Stan lifted her to his shoulders. He would get her to Pepe's and order a pizza. He turned on Benvenue and wandered along the quiet street until turning at Haste he saw a large crowd gathered in the dirty vacant lot behind the Forum.

"This place is going to be a park?" he asked, incredulous. "Who says?"

"We do," said the shirtless hippie wielding a pickaxe, one of at least a hundred people gathered on the dusty, gullied square block it had taken the University a year to clear of its venerable homes and apartments. He handed Stan a flier that Stan scanned quickly.

Hear ye, hear ye. A park will be built this Sunday between Dwight and Haste. The land is owned by the University, which tore down a lot of beautiful houses in order to build a swamp.

On Sunday we will stop this shit…At one o'clock our rural reclamation project for Telegraph Ave. commences in the expectation of beauty…All artists should show up and make the park their magical possession…The University has no right to create ugliness as a way of life…We will show up Sunday to clear a third of the lot and do with it whatever our fantasy pleases…This summer we will not be fucked over by the pigs and their "move on" fascism, we will police our own park and not allow its occupation by imperial power.

Stan looked up again to take in the purposing chaos of a park under construction. A truck arrived with rolls of sod. Families and children from the neighborhood picked up bottles and cleared debris. A crew of carpenters set to work building a stage. A pole erected in the middle of the lot bore a sign that read *People's Park*.

"You can do this?" Stan asked a neighbor whose child went to Lila's preschool.

"We'll see," he answered. "But what else can we do? The city's not doing shit to give us a park. So we have to take it."

Stan remembered that the city council elections were held the previous week and that he and Ginger did not vote. It wouldn't have mattered, though Stan now felt a surge of righteous artistry. Why was he not on the barricades of this new revolution? Instead, he was running deeper into the forest. The thought made him envious. He could do so much as an artist to advance a beautiful park.

Lila, distracted by a ubiquitous and pleasurable commotion, struggled off Stan's shoulders and rushed toward a group of children waiting their turn on an improvised rope swing. Stan ran behind her, looking past her for a moment to see Inger at the opposite end of the lot near the back door of the Forum. She caught his glance and appeared to walk toward him until Stan lifted Lila again, smiled briefly at Inger, and retreated quickly behind a screen of people bent over to create a garden patch where corn would grow.

Through the following week, Stan made the park a daily destination for Lila. Each day something new was added: a play structure, swings, yet another vegetable garden, still more sod until by Friday the once and fearfully eternal square block of mud and garbage began to look seriously like a park. Occasionally the cops would drive by but they hassled no one. In the evenings, live music played from an improvised stage. Another community workday, advertised in the Berkeley Barb, was set for the following weekend when Stan and Lila would depart for the north coast.

On the evenings Ginger phoned, Stan tried to describe for her the scope and growth of the park. But his enthusiasm bounced off Ginger's new life far away.

"That sounds nice," she said without much heart before digging into the quotidian of her first days living in the country, her preoccupation with a new job, her search for a preschool for Lila, her hope of finding a midwife to help her birth her next baby.

The present was already the past for her and while listening to Stan's fervid, if brief, reattachment to the south campus community, Ginger felt oblivious to events she had every expectation would no longer matter.

"If we could just pack up our friends and bring them all with us," she said finally and not sincerely and in a way meant to placate Stan's ingenuous, if futile, enthusiasm.

Stan's arrival at the coast with Lila depended on the friends he would leave behind. Larry and his truck were indispensable for the transit of their beds, couch, children's toys, tables, bookcases and chairs. Harriet volunteered her car and Raj agreed to drive it up and back. By dawn on Saturday Stan had barely finished packing Harriet's Karmann Ghia with enough clothes to last a month. Later, he would return for the rest of their belongings, as well as his paintings.

"You excited?" Raj asked as Larry backed his truck down the driveway.

"It's either the smartest thing we've ever done, or the stupidest," answered Stan.

Either a brilliant escape or a dumb folly, he thought to himself.

"With that short haircut you'll fit right in," said Raj. "Put on a flannel shirt and big boots and no one will know you're a dope-smoking, tree-hugging hippie."

The joke was lost on Stan who left to feed and dress Lila and to lure her into Harriet's car with the promise that today she would at last see her mommy, which had less meaning for Lila than the upheaval of her room as Larry and Raj carried out her bed and books and dolls and stripped her drawings from the walls. Harriet entered the kitchen and comforted Lila while Stan directed the deconstruction of her once secure and comfortably known world.

"That's it," Larry said as he lifted the tailgate and snapped it shut.

"Let's go."

Raj and Stan huddled to conjure their route north, planning a stop in Cloverdale before tackling the meandrous curves and bends of the Anderson Valley. With stops, the trip to Fort Bragg would take at least three hours. Larry and Raj would stay over for the house warming party and return Sunday.

The small caravan rolled down the street to Telegraph, Raj in the lead with Stan beside him and Lila in the backseat. Larry followed in his truck, the contents of its open bed buckled down by tightly cinched canvass packing straps. Turning right on Telegraph, the vehicles passed Dwight Way where Stan caught a glimpse of another weekend crowd gathered at the site of the emerging park.

Different cultures present their different varieties of ignorance, which later explained why on the far side of the spacious Anderson Valley Larry and his truck were pulled over by a county sheriff's deputy. It was not in itself a need for concern, though Raj and Stan had fallen far behind Larry and by the time their car caught up, the deputy had Larry spread-eagled against the truck hood and was fastening handcuffs onto his back-stretched wrists.

"What's happening?" shouted Stan who jumped from the car to approach the deputy, a corpulent middle-aged man with a gut that fell like a scoop of khaki dough over his gun belt.

"He's moving my furniture to Fort Bragg. What's the problem?"

Stan's presence was a sudden complication. After attaching the cuffs, the deputy stood back and faced Stan.

"You know this man?" the deputy asked.

"He's my employee," Stan answered, thinking quickly.

The deputy had not expected company, much less a witness to what he must have thought to be the routine arrest of a subject suspected of burglary. There was a white, rural symmetry in the well-developed suspicion that a black man traveling alone on a country road with a truck full of property was likely up to no good.

"He just a dumb cracker," Larry muttered without looking up. "You tell him I'm not only a black motherfucker, I'm a Black Panther. "

The deputy's eyes flared. He grabbed Larry by his shoulders and pushed him to the ground.

"Return to your vehicle," the deputy said to Stan.

Stan walked back to the car while the deputy retreated to his cruiser. Several minutes passed until the deputy returned, passing Larry to approach Stan.

"License and registration?" the deputy asked.

Stan showed his license and searched the glove compartment to find Harriet's car registration.

"Not your car?" the deputy said as he examined the papers. "This is getting interesting. Who's the driver? And who's the little girl?"

Lila crawled into the front seat and climbed into Stan's lap.

Stan told his story and provided phone numbers and addresses, including that of his new home on Ocean Avenue, while the deputy walked to the driver's side and asked Raj for his ID.

"No pony tail in this picture," said the deputy as he examined the license. "Sure is cute, that ponytail."

Another sheriff's cruiser arrived. Two deputies emerged to strut audaciously toward Larry, still prone on the asphalt. One leaned down and muttered something to Larry who turned his head away. Then all three deputies convened at the far end of the pull-off for a prolonged discussion. Raj asked Stan if he had hidden his dope.

"Nowhere they wouldn't find it," said Stan.

There was nothing to do but wait, until the fat deputy who had stopped Larry again approached Stan.

"I pulled your employee over because he failed to slow down in Philo. The speed limit is thirty."

Stan watched as another deputy unlocked Larry's cuffs and helped him to his feet.

"How fast was he going?" asked Stan.

"Thirty-five," said the deputy. "Watch it next time. We're watching you."

The last words sounded to Stan like a menacing threat.

The deputies returned to their cruisers and left.

"Society is a network of lures," said Raj as he held court in Stan and Ginger's new kitchen. The sheriff stop made the caravan an hour late and it was nearly dark before the furniture and boxes were unloaded and set inside the house and garage.

"It doesn't take much to invite trouble."

"You'll get hassled," said Johnny. "Change is hard and some of the natives here are restless, not used to long hair and black people. But here we are."

Stan entered the kitchen with his arm around Ginger who balanced a smiling, wide-eyed Lila on her hip. A Tom Rush version of *Cocaine* sang from the speakers of the unboxed stereo. Ginger, the only one to know everyone's name, repeated a round of introductions: Johnny and Bev, Althea and Madge who had a farm in Albion, Gus who was Johnny's neighbor and worked at the market in Mendocino, Jenifer and her housemates Gina and Lois from Cleone who owned a small motel at Pudding Creek, and Gretchen and her husband Tomas who lived at the Table Mountain commune on Albion Ridge. Stan introduced Raj and Larry who filled paper cups from a gallon jug of Red Mountain.

Ginger organized a tour of the house and yard, finally leading everyone into the garage where Stan found the light switch and, within the humble glow of a single sixty-watt bulb dangling from a cord over the workbench, rolled two joints, lit them and started them around. A deep drag loosened Stan's tense grasp of the hard, long drive. This sudden ambit of new friends had emerged from the trees like a tribe of welcoming munchkins. He relaxed into their ingenuous curiosities, into their expressions of interest, into their cordial grace. He was finally held by the home he owned, whether or not it was where he lived.

eight

Stan's first week began in the new land. Raj and Larry left Sunday to return to Berkeley, leaving Stan to float like a bubble on an agitated sea. Ginger's head start left Stan far behind. A week to sink roots and make friends had surrounded Ginger with a surprisingly urgent system of support. She had visited Althea and Madge's farm on Albion Ridge, had even spent a night. She had gone with them to Table Mountain to search for a midwife.

"I think I've found one," said Ginger. "The women call her Mama Bear."

Stan poked at his toast and poached eggs as they sat together at the breakfast joint downtown, a classic greasy spoon with fogged windows and linoleum counters in an abandoned strip mall and the only restaurant open on Sunday. Lila sat in a highchair next to her mother while coloring the Disney characters printed on a single-page children's menu.

"So you're still liking the work?" Stan asked.

"Oh yeah," answered Ginger. "It's an easy job and they like me."

"Do they know you're pregnant?" Stan asked.

"No," Ginger answered. "In due time…"

Later they walked several blocks through their quiet new city, a patch of empty storefronts and closed-on-Sunday businesses that included a hardware retailer, the Chinese restaurant, three thrift stores, a modest-sized grocery and an old hotel. Returning to the highway in their car, they crossed the bridge over the town harbor before passing a nursery, a clinic, two gas stations, an automotive repair shop and two more thrift outlets that shared a parking lot where they took the turn-off to Ocean Avenue. Tall pines loomed in all directions, blocking any view of the mountains or the sea.

"We sure live in the boonies," Stan said.

If you miss the city, then drive to Mendocino," said Ginger. "It's where the tourists hang out."

415

He heard Ginger's contemptuous tone, immediate and quick and on him like a pouncing predator. It was so different from her affection the previous night, her aggressive lust after a week apart that both filled and emptied him. He sought the reassurance she almost always returned to him but all that returned now was his shadow.

"There's a lot to do," Ginger said while they unboxed their belongings and moved furniture into the empty spaces and corners of their new homestead. As Lila napped Ginger led Stan on a walking tour of their property. She pointed out the garage's leaky roof, the sticky, splintered window frames in the kitchen and living room, the water stains in the ceiling of the upstairs bathroom. She walked him into the weeded and overgrown half-acre that stretched out behind the house.

"We need a garden, Stan," she said directly. "I was hoping you could do this."

"Really? How?" he asked.

"I'm working, Stan," said Ginger. "I need you to figure that out."

"And my painting?" Stan asked.

The question sounded both supervisory and infantile, even to Stan. Where could the luxury of his art fit among the terms of immediate survival? For the first time he felt himself in retreat from Ginger, a woman that for years had been the supportive echo of his creation.

"Of course you can paint," said Ginger. "Sweetheart, I don't control you. But there is more now. There are the things we must do together to survive. And they have to come first."

Stan saw Ginger in all three of her dimensions: woman, mother and now custodial boss, all their voices joined in a declaration of fierce independence from a life left far behind.

After dinner Ginger put Lila to bed and returned with pen and lined binder, which she opened to a page featuring scribbled columns of words and numbers.

"These are our costs," she said as she pointed to a tally of expenses.

"And this is what we need," she said again.

Her salary was the only calculated income. It covered the basics. "We'll need more, though," she said.

"You want me to work, too?" Stan asked. "Who takes care of Lila?"

"I'm working on that," said Ginger.

"Lila starts school next year. I'm on to a day care situation that might work out."

"And me?" Stan asked.

"Part-time is enough. But we need something. Maybe Johnny can help you."

"Clean toilets at a motel?" Stan asked. "No fucking way."

Ginger projected a frustration she could barely tolerate.

"Stan, we are going to have a baby. In addition to my job at the law firm, my body is at work creating our child. It is physical labor only a female can do. And I am an older female nearing my mid-thirties. It is reproductive labor I am doing and it involves physically costly processes that include a full-term pregnancy, a possibly difficult birth and years of breastfeeding. I must acquire an additional sixty thousand calories just to produce a healthy baby. What my body must give after birth is incalculable. I need your willing help with all of this. I need you to step up."

It was clear Ginger had thought seriously and long about the challenges of their new life. She spoke to Stan firmly and with a clarity that quieted him. Now, though, she began to cry.

Stan waited, seeing in a flash too many things about himself that were not familiar, both urges and fears he had never before pondered. He recalled, also, his recent betrayal and Ginger's willing, if conditional, forgiveness. He saw in a moment how his arrival at this time and this place was the inevitable result of his first contact with Ginger, his first familiarity and ultimate infatuation.

It was the pull of gravity greater than his will. In a whirl of awareness he saw the difference between falling in love with beauty and loving someone beautiful.

"Sure, babe," Stan said.

He stood and leaned over the kitchen table, the same one they sat at in Berkeley and that now, like their searching, incomplete but splendid lives, sat with them in an old farmhouse in Fort Bragg.

"Yeah…sure," Stan said again before putting his hand on Ginger's shoulder. "Sure…"

"At least we got the garden in this year," Althea said to Ginger as she made tea over her woodstove. Outside Althea's farmhouse Ginger saw a man and woman working in a wide field, swinging hoes against a storm of high weeds sprouted across a rolling, distant hill.

"I give them about another two weeks," said Althea as she dropped the tea strainer in the sink and looked out the window.

"Young couples come up here all the time. Want the farm life and they take it all on with too little knowledge and not enough time. The men have big ideas but can't seem to execute. Expect their women to carry all the water and still cook their meals and wash their clothes.

"We let them stay as long as they work. There's a room in the barn where they can sleep but most live in town or shack up with friends. It's the men that stop first. And then they leave. We've had a dozen through here just since November. Which is nothing. Table Mountain up the ridge saw more than a hundred pass through last year. With spring just on us, we're expecting a deluge."

Althea was a tall woman and as she stood in the window light Ginger saw through her t-shirt the outline of strong shoulders and ample, braless breasts. Althea smiled through her electric blue eyes. Her strong chin and wide forehead gave her face the appearance of a beautifully chiseled moon.

"Madge says we should bar men at the gate," said Althea. "No men allowed. She's got a point but I'm not in a place yet where I can completely do without testosterone and upper body strength, especially when it comes to the heavy lifting. And there's lots of that."

Althea and Madge were lesbians and lifelong partners. They had been best friends and lovers in high school when Althea's parents were killed in a freak car accident and Althea went to live with Madge and her family. The girls ended up together at San Francisco State College and shared a dorm room. The insurance settlement paid for Althea's school and left her with enough for the down payment and some change on the forty-acre farm they now occupied at the lower end of Albion Ridge Road. A previous year spent on rented land in the Anderson Valley convinced them they could farm.

"We're a long way from being self-sufficient," Althea said as she cupped her hands under her teacup.

"I say three more years. The acid coastal soil isn't particularly friendly and needs lots of work. Madge wants a horse but right now we can barely support a goat and a few sheep. We need to dig a real well and irrigate, not to mention have enough heated water for a shower. That would be a luxury."

"What is working?" asked Ginger.

Althea smiled.

"I guess I make it sound pretty grim," she said. "It was our dream to have a small farm. We gave up teaching careers in the city to do this. We think about all the good movies we never see. All the art and music that we pass up because its mushroom season or shearing time or the apple trees bloom or the garden needs attention, which is every day between planting and harvest. What rewards us is that we are farmers and not farmers' wives. And in time we might be a magnet for other women like us, women who want to work together to live a full and natural life bonded to the earth."

Ginger knew Althea from her search for a midwife. As Albion's gateway farm to the ridge, Althea and Madge's land drew a lot of visitors, even those just asking directions, and Althea knew the comings and goings of nearly everyone. It was Althea who suggested Ginger contact Mama Bear, a regarded midwife who worked out of Boonville. Mama Bear was on good terms with two doctors in Ukiah who had hospital access.

"She's never needed them," said Althea. "But you never know."

"You've got an orchard of apple trees," asked Ginger. "What do you do with the fruit?"

"Drying, canning, applesauce. We have more than we can use," said Althea. "Much more. Sorry to say we were so busy last year we let a lot of it go."

"What about a food conspiracy?" asked Ginger. "Would you ever consider that?"

Ginger explained how the Berkeley conspiracy worked, how food arrived from several sources and was distributed at fair prices throughout a network of subscribers.

"We could get your apples to market," said Ginger. "They'd be a hit. They're organic."

Althea's eyes brightened as she considered an idea that was not her own and labor she neither had to cajole or hire.

"We make cheese, too," said Althea. "Sounds interesting."

"That's cool," said Ginger.

"Anyway, you and Madge come over for hot showers whenever you like. I'll make tea."

Ginger envied Althea's loving link to her land, an attachment Ginger imagined herself, bound like one of Althea's trees to a new earth. Ginger could hardly bear the pleasure of this beautiful place, made more majestic by the several women she knew and who, like her, were committed to staying.

Though it was not simply pleasure that made life authentic.

"I can't keep animals just for pleasure," said Althea. "I must do this well. I must do this in such a way that they pay for themselves and even more. I ask myself often, can I really do this?"

Can I really do this? Ginger also asked herself. Could she stand at the edge of the new land and decide once and for all to commit herself? It depended only on how much she wanted to be what she thought herself to be. Was she courageous? Or was she simply crazy?

Stan burrowed into the backyard, eyes constantly on the ground in reserve and introspection while he watched Lila play with her dolls and jump from the porch. He plunged his hands like Van Gogh. He thought of all the ways he might dig into the earth and make things grow. Dirty, boring work. Yet, a week of it had won him freedom from a certain kind of arrogance, had reddened his palms and severed several frivolous attachments, not the least of which was his link to the quickly distant world of his art.

He was still an artist, but one now in residence behind a shovel and a hoe. He was more the subject of a painting and much less its creator.

"Far out," said Johnny one afternoon after dropping by to visit the new house. He stood at the edge of the driveway and took in the flat, rolling dirt that once had been a vast field of weeds.

"You did all this without a backhoe?"

"A what?" asked Stan.

The rental place on Shoreline has a backhoe," said Johnny. "You can plow a half-acre in a few hours."

"How much?" asked Stan.

"Twenty-five for the day," said Johnny.

He had a friend who lived off the road to Willits and who rented it to clear land for his pot crop.

"Course, you don't have as much land," Johnny added, aware he had transgressed into Stan's unfiltered vision of the citizen farmer.

"Maybe next year," Stan answered tersely.

"Wanna smoke a doob?" Johnny asked as he reached into the pocket of his wrinkled Levis.

"I want a beer," answered Stan. "In the kitchen. Grab two from the six-pack on the top shelf and meet me in the garage."

Stan stayed in the yard, reminded of the times as a child he refused to leave home and instead hid in the garden from all the bad boys and mean men who threatened him with blows and tears.

"When's your baby due?" Stan asked as he and Johnny sat on empty packing boxes to drink their beers while he watched Lila who now sat beside him to experience the curious pleasure of a visitor.

"At least a couple of months. Maybe nine weeks. July sometime. Bev has a date but we really don't know," he answered.

"Everything cool?" asked Stan.

"Oh, yeah," said Johnny.

"We'll be OK. Not doin' a midwife, though. Some of the women aren't so happy about that but Bev wanted a doctor and we think we have a good one. Dr. Trencaro. He's in Ukiah near the hospital. Long drive but it's OK. There's no hospital here."

*Some of the women…*Stan reckoned with the critically formidable mass of women living in his midst. He first noticed those who visited with Ginger after work, arriving in twos or threes for potluck dinners during the week. Stan helped cook then left after dinner while the women talked deep into the evenings. He heard snatches and phrases while he bathed Lila and put her to bed. It was talk of living in the woods, of mothers and becoming mothers, of life with and without men, of work and weather, and survival.

There was gossip about people he did not yet know, most older and younger women who became subjects of catty cuts or gems of wisdom all spoken in the same breath, all discontinuous and not real. Good mothers were regarded and bad mothers blamed. Sex was beautiful or funny or lonely or nothing at all. And there was work, always work: whether slinging hash or milking goats.

In a week Ginger had organized a rotating playgroup with Bev agreeing to manage two afternoons a week from Stan and Ginger's living room. Stan would take Ginger's shift and two other mothers would also take turns supervising. On a Saturday morning, Althea and Madge dropped by for a shower and stayed for lunch. Stan had no specific role, other than as someone who opened doors, boiled water, served drinks and spent most of his active hours reclaiming the large yard for a garden. And he needed a job while Ginger already had one. He wondered if he would have to compete with the women in his midst for whatever work he could find.

"Ever heard of Mama Bear?" Stan asked Johnny.

"Oh yeah," he said.

"They say she's the best. Her name is Marty. Registered nurse for years before moving up here. Delivered at least a dozen babies the last couple years. She lives in Boonville but spends a lot of time at Table Mountain."

"Who's they?" asked Stan.

"The women. All those women. Who else?"

"Ginger wants Mama Bear to deliver the baby," said Stan.

"When's Ginger due?" asked Johnny.

"December. Could happen on Christmas."

That night Stan asked Ginger what the women said, what they did and why and who they were with. He asked about Mama Bear and for snatches of the stories whirring out of the chatter and laughter of the evenings. But Ginger fell asleep quickly as she often did during the workweek with its early mornings of nausea, then breakfast and Lila-care before Stan drove her to the law office at eight.

May Day arrived in a salt and pepper fog, moist and dark until its evaporation by an arcing, spring sun. Ginger awoke without nausea, that vague, inhibiting sickness had lifted at last like a large boulder off her suppressed libido. Stan was the surprised beneficiary though she hurried their sex before Lila awakened and found them.

They had lived in the new land together exactly ten days. On Saturday Stan drove them all to Table Mountain for a May Day party in the forest. A Maypole stood at the center of a large, open field. The property's old, broken farmhouse anchored a corner of the cleared land in the heart of what had once been an ancient redwood forest.

A few shacks had been built at some distance from the main house. Cars and old vans lined a graveled parking area. Several children played under the watchful eyes of young mothers, most of whom wore paisley-patterned granny dresses. Men in leather jackets and cowboy hats clustered near a picnic bench, sharing swigs from a gallon jug of something red, cloudy and homemade.

Ginger walked into a circle of warm welcomes offered by mothers and others while Stan found his way to the picnic bench to meet for the first time many men like himself, particularly those refugees and loners fleeing previous lives. Johnny was on hand to make introductions.

Stan met men who worked in the mill, who cut trees in the forest, who hid behind the evergreen curtains along the ridges and grew food and dope. The May Day party swelled until more than fifty adults held a perimeter containing at least a dozen children that danced and wrapped the Maypole. The afternoon then lapsed into the lacuna of a loosening party until a few men slipped behind the trees to smoke a joint, followed by other men and then a few women who were not mothers. By four o'clock the party began to dissolve.

"We're going to town," Johnny said to Stan. "Dinner at the Sea Gull."

Ginger drove them into Mendocino. At the mouth of the river the town's bluff appeared as a bright frontage of high grass and old, Victorian buildings, it's venerable profile strengthened against the horizon by long, amber shadows that raced above the incoming fog. Ginger parked near Mendosa's market. Lila bounded down Lansing Street ahead of everyone but by the time they arrived the restaurant was crowded with a long wait.

Won't work," said Ginger. "Lila's starving."

Bev agreed to take Lila back to Caspar in her car and fix dinner while the boys had a drink in the Cellar and joined them later.

Stan was restless. He drank a Brandy Alexander and then another. He probed the small Cellar bar for the women within, none of them apparently mothers. He ogled a slender blonde wearing a short-skirted shift and no bra. She saw him, winked at him, more aware than he of his own awareness.

This is the hang-out," Johnny said. "This is the party."

"I pity the poor immigrant," Stan said through an exhilarating inebriation as he observed that so many in attendance at the bar were young and rowdy like him and certainly and likely also fresh arrivals from somewhere else.

"Tell me Johnny. Is this new land your home?"

Johnny's face opened in puzzlement.

"For now," he answered finally. "No, it's more than that. I can't see us leaving."

Stan waited while a buzz whirled through his brain. He ordered another drink and bought another for Johnny.

"You can't go home again," he said to Johnny.

"It wasn't home," said Johnny. "Or we wouldn't have left."

nine

Stan wondered if he had entered a new dimension where silence was more valued than sensation. Increasingly, Stan and Ginger communicated through gestures and facial expressions, their actions speaking louder than their words. Ginger's nod could move Stan forward; the narrowing of her eyes could stop him.

That Stan followed these signed directions surprised him and he questioned why he was so willing to find his way as the bearer of his wife's water. Their sex now was initiated exclusively through touch and usually in bed and in darkness where sensations could be felt as thoroughly as possible in silence.

"Lila, my little Lila," Ginger sang one morning as Stan prepared

424

breakfast.

Ginger's morning sickness was all but gone and while breakfast was still her hardest meal, she now rose to the occasion.

Lila laughed. Stan heard her bumping about in the kitchen as he trotted downstairs.

"Should have the planter boxes finished this afternoon," he said as he walked to the kitchen counter and poured coffee into a fat ceramic cup, a housewarming gift from Bev.

"And the fence? Day care starts next week," said Ginger.

Ginger's cooperative day care was growing with Stan and Ginger's home its primary location. Six families agreed to participate and each pay $10 a week, which would support Bev and another woman named Marjorie to supervise and also cover lunch and snacks for the kids.

"I'll do it," said Stan who so far had never said he wouldn't.

Day care on Ocean Avenue began on the first Wednesday in May and Stan, who had built the backyard fence and strung a rope swing from a tree, had become a semi-permanent feature of the yard. Bev arrived after breakfast along with the stouter and older Marjorie who lived in Cleone and brought her two daughters, aged two and four.

Other women arrived, until by ten o'clock seven preschool children, three of them boys, ran and ambled into the yard under the supervision of Bev and Marjorie.

The boys charged the garden, thinking the planter boxes some kind of play structure. They dug their hands into the soil; turning up clogs of mud and exposing the white, fragile roots of newly planted seedlings.

"Whoa, stop!" shouted Stan as he ran toward the boys who, facing the urgent discomfort of an apparently angry man, jumped away.

"Stan, do you have a problem?" Marjorie shouted from the kitchen step. "The boys are just exploring."

"Maybe so," answered Stan. "They're also killing our garden."

"They don't know that," Marjorie said defiantly.

Stan heard a challenge intended to test his authority and to prove its error.

"Have you guys tried the rope swing?" Stan said, ignoring Marjorie.

Stan called to Lila who led the boys toward the swing, where Stan slipped one into the tire attached by a rope to the highest tree branch and gave him a gentle push. The boy smiled and held on tight. Marjorie stood, waited and then slipped back into the kitchen.

Ginger, given a ride home by one of the day care mothers, arrived after five. Others also arrived and gathered with Ginger, Bev and Marjorie in the kitchen. Stan watched as the several mothers sat at the kitchen table while Ginger made tea for herself and Bev and poured wine for the others.

Stan remained outside, aware it was the mother's hour as it one time might have been the artists' hour, or happy hour. He recalled city afternoons downing dollar margaritas on Washington Square before lurching toward the East Bay Terminal to catch the F bus home.

Fashionably artistic dissipation was turned now into the sobriety of wilderness survival though this was not a wilderness, however much it was a new land. It was a civilization built by rough, hardscrabble men though the corner he shared with Ginger was now very much a woman's world.

Stan entered the kitchen to begin fixing dinner. The women greeted him, all but Marjorie who ignored him. He caught the look of a younger mother he could see found him attractive.

"Your old man fixes dinner?" the woman said to Ginger. "Where do you find a man like that?"

The women laughed though Ginger didn't as she signaled the end of the kitchen table colloquy and saw everyone to the door. Lila scrambled down the hall after her mother while Stan pulled pasta from the cupboard and cheese from the fridge.

Ginger returned to make a salad amid the brief passing of news. Work was fine. Preschool was fine. Lila was fine. The world was not so fine.

"How's the job search coming?" Ginger asked Stan before taking a tentative bite of pasta.

"Tomorrow," he answered. "I start looking tomorrow."

The bodies of women were for Stan a source of artistic connection and experience and while Stan had spent his life admiring them, drawing them, painting them, he had no answer for them when like Ginger's they asserted their heart-driven needs. As a young man he thought he could mine a woman's body with his art and lift up for view some remarkably wonderful mystery. Increasingly he found his own response to be the most perplexing mystery of all.

He was confused by his own life now, which left him frequently feeling like the salt of some kind of earth and at other times a whimsical mirage. He needed a job and did not know what to do since as an artist he never really had one.

"I know the gallery on Geary," said Jason.

He had heard about Stan's show and was impressed that Stan had sold a painting.

"Funk meets Fluxus…or something like that," he said.

Jason owned a small art gallery on west Main in Mendocino where Stan had stopped to postpone his still stalled search for work. Jason's gallery bore his last name. It comprised two rooms of an old Victorian boarding house. Splashy, abstract watercolors hung everywhere, their stroked shapes barely suggestive of various local vistas and points of interest.

"Your work?" asked Stan.

"No, but good work," said Jason. "It sells."

"Would you look at my work?" asked Stan.

Jason was quiet in a way that suggested Stan's request was eerily familiar and likely unwelcome.

"Sure. But I don't think I can help," said Jason.

He knew Stan's story and did not need to ask further.

"People come here thinking it's an artists' colony," said Jason. "It isn't. It's a tourist colony. Art? What sells here probably isn't anything you'd describe as art."

"See these?" Jason asked.

He pulled from a wide drawer a selection of colorful greeting cards.

"Hand-painted. I charge two bucks. It's my biggest seller."

"I could do that," said Stan.

"Really?" asked Jason. "And not throw away your creative soul?"

"To throw it away, I'd first have to find it again," answered Stan.

Jason surrendered a knowing smile.

Ginger knew that motherhood was both a hindrance and a right. Madge had no use for motherhood or at least the specific biology that required men to insert themselves into vaginas. Althea, however, was not angry with mothers or uncomfortable with fathers. It was just not her thing to make a baby and certainly not wanting to insert a man into her vagina had something to do with it.

Bev, though, waited like a virgin for the gift of some powerful blessing that would consummate her body's fecund swelling and deliverance. Ginger's pregnancy with Lila had not been a happy one, created as it was by a man who quickly left her. But she enjoyed describing to Bev the rhythms of those past trimesters, the daily pleasure of an ever-rounder tummy, the increasing presence of pushes and kicks within, and a surprising assertion of sexual arousal that arrived spontaneously with no attachment to the rhythm of any particular month.

"Lila, my little Lila," Ginger sang to her daughter as she left her small bed to climb into the big one.

"A baby is coming, Lila. A new sister or brother for Lila, my little Lila…"

Stan could hear in Ginger's tired voice her certainty and uncertainty, her ascension and also her insecurity. He also heard old resentments that seemed increasingly woven into the mesh of Ginger's new life. Lila's father abandoned Ginger shortly after Lila's birth, leaving mother and daughter without support. Ginger had spent nearly half a decade accruing new powers, both of the purse and of creation.

"Lila, my little Lila…"

These words anchored terms of the new life growing for Ginger, growing within her but also growing in the kitchen, in the garden, in the law office on Franklin Street, in the orchards on Albion Ridge, in the company of purposed and empowered women that, like herself, had found this empty place to fill, as they were filled with a gritty, angry and ecstatic expectation. It did not surprise Stan that Ginger appeared to have lost sight of him, just as he had lost sight of himself and fallen into a preoccupation with the possibility of failure.

Stan waited, either for a brilliant source of hope or simply Ginger's new directions for him. He offered all he knew but beyond his self-exalted art there was not much more on offer than his arms and legs. Work would mean using them in some way not yet imagined. He knew about Johnny's cleaning job. And he knew men who worked at the mill. What would it take to bring his body, notably bereft of mystery, into relationship with the work of this drafty and barely settled land?

Stan wandered in the form he was and no other, which made it hard to imagine how he might hire himself out to do something other than his own work. But he would. He must. He could always mop floors, which Johnny did without concern, resigned as he was to the drudge of menial labor. But for Stan it made no sense to live in the country and spend his waking hours crawling around in dirty motel rooms, ocean views notwithstanding. There was the mill, but he had no experience and anyway it wasn't currently hiring. In the newspaper he found occasional ads for logging crews. It was outdoor work. He also understood that it could be dangerous. But he only needed part-time.

"You gotta know what you're doing," said Johnny. "Chokes and chain saws and the wind, not to mention slipping in the mud. Yeah, it pays…but it's hard work. It's fucking dangerous."

Stan said he would try to hold out for something else. But there was nothing else. He continued to check the few job listings that appeared.

"Harriet's coming up Friday," said Ginger as she sat down for dinner.

Stan was surprised.

"How's she doing?" he asked.

"Fine," said Ginger.

Harriet had phoned her at the law office.

"She's bringing her new roommate, Bronwyn. You know Bronwyn."

Stan liked Harriet. And he knew Bronwyn. He had met her once while having coffee with Mack.

"The student activist, right?" answered Stan. "Hangs out at the Forum?"

"She's not a student anymore," said Ginger. "Harriet says things are heating up in Berkeley. That park fight on Telegraph. Bronwyn's in the thick of it."

"Staying long?" Stan asked.

"Just for the weekend," Ginger answered.

"Bronwyn's living in our flat?" Stan asked again.

"Not our flat anymore, Stan," Ginger said smiling. "Bronwyn moved in last week. Harriet misses Lila."

Stan missed Berkeley. And more than Berkeley as a place he missed his place within that place. He missed his old life and friends, his usual habits that included painting and gallery openings and obsessive conversations with fellow artists who were mostly all men but who, like him, were profound and brilliant even if not fully appreciated since they were almost always broke.

In his new land he was a man among many women, what seemed like a tribe of women who through a widening network of competent, sober contacts had built among their several lives the sturdy bridges of connection and support. How it all happened so quickly was a mystery to him. Many evenings his kitchen was filled with their earnest voices, their children or their laughter while a few men hung with Stan at the edges or, with no other place to be, sat outside in the garage to smoke a joint or drink a beer.

Stan also was aware of how much more Ginger spoke with her women friends and how much less she spoke with him. He might as well have a job. Perhaps if he weren't around so much she might have more to say. Lila had become Stan's most constant companion through their lives lived daily in the large yard of their house. Certainly he spent more time with Lila than Ginger did though Ginger spent far more time absorbed in her pregnancy and in ways that held Stan transfixed by both fear and wonder. This was a new life. It was living and even as he struggled with a flood of stinging insecurities and resentments he knew somewhere it was the only way they could live together. There would be no return.

The arrival of Harriet and Bronwyn gave Ginger an audience from her recent history, women who could tell her, even with their eyes if they chose not to speak, could tell her what was actually happening. She prepared an itinerary to fill the weekend that included visits to the ridge; an afternoon with Althea and Madge, a meeting with Mama Bear and a Saturday potluck back at the house. Stan figured in her plans as a pillar of physical support, though she discouraged his attendance on the Ridge by what even she thought a selfish subterfuge.

"It's women's stuff," she told him. "Just the birth thing. Mama Bear and all…"

Stan took the hint. He said he would use the afternoon to get the house ready for dinner. He would take care of Lila, which was more than Ginger expected.

"You sure?" she asked him.

"Positive," he answered. "We're a team."

Ginger wondered if Stan's team included her or Lila.

Ginger was at the kitchen window when after sunset Harriet's Karmann Ghia rolled up the driveway and stopped outside. Ginger waved toward the women in the car whose bobbing heads searched tentatively until all eyes met in precise recognition. Ginger threw open the door to greet Harriet who, first out of the car, fell into her gripping embrace. Ginger noticed immediately how much heavier Harriet was. Her sylphlike shape was gone, replaced by a round, if still slender, solidity, especially in the hips and breasts.

"How the hell are you?" Harriet asked. "It feels like years."

"Welcome to the country," said Ginger as she looked beyond Harriet to see Bronwyn slip sluggishly out of the passenger seat, stand slowly and stretch while staring apprehensively into the trees.

"Is she OK?" Ginger asked.

Harriet turned toward Bronwyn.

"You OK, Hon?" Harriet shouted.

Bronwyn nodded.

"Just tired," said Harriet to Ginger. "It was a bumpy ride."

Dinner was easy. Harriet brought a bottle of wine and Stan grilled snapper steaks, which were served with brown rice and a tray of roasted Brussels sprouts. Ginger let Stan do everything including the dishes and he seemed, at least to Harriet, the family's tethered workhorse.

"Looks like Stan has settled in," Harriet said to Ginger while Stan put things away in the kitchen and she rolled a joint from a lid of Gold she'd brought as a housewarming gift from Mack.

"Yeah," Ginger answered. "He's planted our garden and he looks after Lila. But he still needs a job."

Ginger's reserve sent an unsteady message to Harriet who had noticed what little contact her hosts were having with each other. It was Lila who opened her heart to Harriet with her wild laughter. Lila's parents appeared otherwise occupied.

Bronwyn reported on the once and future Peoples' Park taking shape on a strip of barren land between Dwight and Haste east of Telegraph.

"It's something we can touch," she said. "It's land. Reagan says the university owns it. But we occupy it. Really, no one owns it. But we're going to fight for it."

"When?" asked Stan as he brought cups and a pot of tea to the table.

"No one knows," Bronwyn answered. "But the cops cruise at all hours and Reagan is bitching and moaning and the park is full every day with the people it belongs to. Damn, the park just keeps growing. Swings, a garden, a stage with music every night and weekend work parties. Must have a hundred people working to turn that place into a paradise."

In the morning Ginger awoke alone. Descending the stairs she found Harriet sitting on the couch and wrapped in a blanket.

"Where's Bronwyn?" Ginger asked.

"She took a walk. She'll be back. She's not herself right now."

"Something happen?" asked Ginger.

"Yeah. And No, " answered Harriet. "I mean she's coping with stuff. It's not my place to talk about it. But this trip is helping. She needed some time away."

"You seem pretty involved with her," said Ginger. "Is everything

OK?"

Harriet was still and silent, almost as if she were willing herself into a coma.

"It's better, Ginger," she answered. "That's all I can say."

Ginger walked into the backyard where Lila stood with Stan while he watered the garden.

"Ready for breakfast?" he asked.

Stan had become the weekend's shadow man. He rose early to water the garden and to find enough eggs to make an omelet. He was the busy host but never busy enough to compensate for his failure to earn income. It had become an issue in his life with Ginger in a way it never was in the city where his status as an art Brahmin obscured his material poverty. Embedded in this new opportunity to live on the land was a visceral vein of necessity to pull one's own weight. It flowed through his life with Ginger and forced him into urgent, unfavorable comparisons. Rather than loom large as the jobless husband, he felt better making himself small.

After breakfast, the three women left in Harriet's car to tour the region. Ginger first took them to Table Mountain where she found her midwife Mama Bear. She was meeting with another pregnant woman and had a book for Ginger.

"It's a woman's description of painless childbirth," said Mama Bear. "You'll want to read it."

She checked her progress and was pleased to learn Ginger's morning sickness had passed. Marty estimated her pregnancy at around twelve weeks and gave her a mimeographed page of dietary recommendations.

"No booze. No dope," she said as Ginger nodded agreeably.

Later at the big house a woman communard named Starlight sat by the wood stove to give a Tarot card reading for Harriet, finding in the placement of a reversed High Priestess with the Nine of Swords a notably difficult relationship that suggested subconscious fears and nightmares. Harriet handled the Priestess card.

"The goddess of your psyche," said Starlight. "The feminine mystery. Yours."

Harriet then examined the other card and its illustration of a woman awakening, her hands covering her eyes in fear or sadness against a cascade of nine falling swords.

"Something's gnawing at you," Starlight added. "There's a worry about the future and a difficult decision to make. Your psyche is vulnerably exposed so pay attention to your feelings. And despite your anxiety, there is no hurry."

A brilliant orange scarf bound Starlight's black straight hair and gave her the appearance of a confident oracle. Her words left Harriet visibly disturbed.

Starlight offered a reading to Bronwyn who declined.

"We have formed a women's group," Althea told Ginger and her friends as they sat on her porch to eat crackers and goat cheese.

"What for?" Ginger asked.

"Because we're women and there are a lot of us here now; because we need to share our stories; because we aren't men and something needs to change, is changing, for us. Because we can help each other."

"I'm in a group in the City," Bronwyn said quietly. "It meets at different women's homes."

"It's what's happening now," said Althea. "We have to do it. No men allowed?"

"Right," said Bronwyn. "No men. It's for me and not them."

"Men up here seem to lurk in the shadows and not be much of a factor and are actually more of a hindrance sometimes—at least when they're drunk or stoned or just trying to get laid," Madge said.

"I can live without them. We need a women's community here."

Ginger thought about how she and Stan had come north searching for community and Ginger thought they had found it, though the real community seemed to exist as an odd blend of older and newer communities, reflected back to her by the women she had met but also by what she addressed everyday from her office. There were traffic citations and drunk driving defenses and domestic squabbles and divorces and all the general mischief and mayhem of living anywhere and all certainly smaller in size and quantity than what she had encountered in the city but also magnified in importance by its confinement to a much smaller society.

A women's group? Why not? Madge had said something about how a group might raise women's awareness, raising them all up. Ginger worried only about succumbing to vertigo.

ten

"Mothers may be to blame for the bad men in our lives," said Madge as the women left the house to climb back into Harriet's car.

"I remember my mother saying she would never raise a son to be a bastard. And then my brother was born, a spoiled boy brat raised with ravenous adoration. He could do no wrong. He still can't, even though he does wrong all the time."

"Really? Are you sure?" asked Ginger. She was aware a son might now be growing in her womb.

"Naw," answered Madge. "I'm just pissed. It's a man's world and I have no use for them."

Ginger drove her guests into Mendocino where they walked a path at the south end of town to the river's wide, shallow beach. A massive grey fog bank hovered offshore and chilled the sunbaked sand. Bronwyn wandered away from Harriet and Ginger and found a small cove where she slumped below a shallow dune, curled up and self-protected as if to stay safe rather than warm.

"She seems sad," said Ginger.

"She is," said Harriet who waited a long, ponderous minute before speaking again.

"Sometime I'll tell you. She doesn't want to talk right now. And don't ask her. Please. I've already said too much. We took this trip to make it all go away."

Ginger suppressed her urge to probe further. A woman's trouble was women's trouble.

An evening potluck at Stan and Ginger's celebrated the arrival and imminent departure of Harriet and Bronwyn. The women from the ridge arrived, as they frequently did during the week, en masse and bearing food and drink. Bev and Johnny brought their barbecue

435

and Stan roasted ribs. Harriet enjoyed meeting Ginger's new friends and Bronwyn ate but said little until, apparently a little drunk and very dizzy, she collapsed in the upstairs bedroom. Harriet tended to Bronwyn and tucked her into bed while the party ended early and before Stan could tell Johnny about his new job.

In the morning, Bronwyn apologized to Ginger for rudely passing out, which Ginger was quick to accept and dismiss. After breakfast Bronwyn left with Harriet to return to Berkeley while Stan walked back into the yard to attend to his ongoing cultivations and waited in sullen silence for the right moment to tell Ginger he would start work on Monday.

Stan's large yard had become for him a new kind of wilderness where fertile abundance defined all that underpinned each day's practice of country living. He was born into a straight world that supported by default his manly primacy though the true terms of an intimate life, and certainly the one he shared with Ginger, were built on negotiation.

He held to his garage and garden as he might to a strong poker hand, believing the space an asset though, in fact, it left him isolated, except for Lila who loved to visit him and play with him. Ginger, however, stayed at the kitchen door and would not negotiate unless he returned to the house where the rooms and furnishings collectively amplified her terms and made her arguments before she needed even to open her mouth.

The truth in this left Stan with no other truth he needed to see. He had arrived at the conjunction of love and duty. He decided happily to surrender his devotion to the art of creation and exchange it for the act of living. Each day was enough. He had no more need to track either his past or his future.

"I have a job," he said as Ginger stirred a pot of meaty, red stew comprising remnants of Saturday's dinner. Ginger turned toward him, her face open and her eyes wide as if she were incredulous.

"What is it?" she asked.

"Logging," Stan answered. "It's a crew that works small timber holdings. I start Monday."

"What will you do?" she asked.

Stan knew his job description but wasn't certain what it entailed.

"I set chokes, or chokers, or something like that. They're what pull the logs up from the forest and onto a truck. I'll know a lot more in 24 hours."

"Is it safe?" Ginger asked. "Are you doing something really dangerous?"

"Does it matter?" asked Stan. "It's a job. And the only one I can find."

"Well, what does it pay?" asked Ginger.

"Two-fifty an hour to start," said Stan. "I begin at seven. Don't worry. I have a ride."

"That will really help, Stan," said Ginger. "But I want you to take care of yourself out there. I don't want anything to happen to you."

Ginger wiped her hands on her apron and walked toward Stan who welcomed her with his open arms.

Large trees swayed in the upper breeze as Stan rolled uphill in the back of a truck, crowded into the open cargo hold with three other men, all younger than he.

"You need boots, dude…and gloves," said Jeb, the young man who had picked him up at his house in the grey darkness of a false dawn.

"Go to the supplier on Franklin. Next to the hardware store. Really, man. You'll need 'em."

Stan had been given a metal hard hat but had no other idea what he needed to wear, which on his first day was a sweatshirt and jeans and a pair of low cut tennis shoes. His three crew companions wore overalls and large, cork-soled boots.

As the truck turned a corner of the mountain road Stan watched as a last curtain of embracing forest opened to a vast and empty cavern of plowed wasteland. Tall, old trees had been mowed down like the weeds in his yard, leaving acres of brown earth that sprouted nothing more than stumps and dead, broken branches. The truck stopped at the edge of an embankment.

"Everybody out," shouted the driver.

Stan followed his crew down through the garbage of dead and broken timber arriving finally at three long fir trunks resting together like old, fallen friends. Above, Stan heard the grinding of gears and watched as a large assembly rolled down a suspended cable and dropped more cables and their connectors to the men below.

"Here goes," yelled Jeb. "Let's get these bitches tied up."

He might have been an ant trying to move a branch but by the time the chokers were set and Stan had grasped the fundamentals of moving tree carcasses from their death to their service in death, he grasped also his new place in the world.

He worked all day to keep his heart from breaking until by quitting time, as early in the afternoon as starting time was in the morning, a cynical confidence took root. The men were rowdy, crude and funny and did not judge him. They assumed he was a vagabond and drifter and, as Jeb said over an after-work beer at the bowling alley, "no matter what you did down there no one up here cares."

As if he wouldn't come to this place unless he were a fugitive, unless there were nowhere else he could go. Perhaps there wasn't. Stan tried to fit himself into this new scheme. He was a worker who supported himself. He also was an enlistee in a tree-killing infantry that produced devastation for the profitable benefit of others.

By week's end Stan was marked by the dirty stain of life. His new overalls and boots were scraped and muddy, as was his once hopeful will. He hated his new work but the boys with whom he shared it were his newest and closest friends. Stan had relaxed into their pungent, graceless humor and foul-mouthed gamboling and endured their teasing with worldly, modulated cynicism. They liked his smart jokes, which Stan hurled during the first days to cover his incompetence.

"They should pay you guys my pay," Stan said to Jeb one morning when Stan's failure to secure a choker sent it hurtling at Pete and Butch who dove wildly to avoid it.

"No harm done, you motherfucker," Jeb shouted. "God, don't fucking ever do that again."

Beers after work were becoming a new routine and by Friday afternoon, Stan was accustomed to arriving home semi-drunk. Sometimes his weariness was all that suppressed a potential detonation, though it was clear that Ginger was happy to see him, and to see him all in one piece.

Though increasingly through the week Stan returned to a house full of women. Even when he arrived home before Ginger, the day care mothers already had gathered along with a few women from Albion Ridge who accepted Ginger's offer of free showers. Without Stan's proprietary presence in the large yard, they now lounged in his garden topless and nude, oblivious to him as the only male present and the one "spoken for" by Ginger.

His personal wilderness was taken from him just as he now labored to steal and destroy a larger one. It was too facile, even for him, to imagine that what he sowed he reaped. He stood in the kitchen and gazed at the women in the garden. He hovered quietly in an obscure corner and watched their naked bodies occupy his wilderness.

He indulged a delicious lechery, authorized by his time with the boys and their beers. He quietly assessed the women, their hips and breasts and hairy crotches, as they sat or strolled comfortably among themselves. He was delightfully invisible. And just as he was about to think to himself that this was the best sex he had had in weeks, Lila ran up to him and clasped her arms around his thigh.

He swept her up, her open eyes and warm breath all over his face as she hugged him and he felt in this single moment her entire childhood presence as an emerging woman, the nascent burst of her enthusiasm for love, for connection, for completeness in the trust of another.

"Daddy Stan, where do you go all day?" she asked.

She missed him. Just as in the first days when Ginger left for work, Lila now waited at the window for Stan who often beat Ginger home. The politics of love did not matter to Lila. She loved all the caring people in her life. She gave willingly and without any intervening thought her whole heart to everyone she loved. She wanted them all close to her and did not understand why they ever had to leave.

"How's the job?" Ginger asked as they climbed into bed.

"It's hard," said Stan. "

These were more words than they had spoken to each other all week about anything other than those concrete issues that occupied their shared quotidian of chores.

"It's risky work," Stan said. "But I understand something now I didn't before."

"What's that?" asked Ginger.

"What the first settlers needed to do to live here," said Stan. "Why they killed trees, just as they raised pigs and steers and chickens to kill; to freeze and store their carcasses so they could survive another hard, cold season."

"I like to think we're trying something different," said Ginger.

"Think all you want," said Stan. "From where I'm looking right now, not much has changed. At least, not here. What does Bobby say? *I pity the poor immigrant…alive as you or me.* Surviving anywhere means doing a lot of things you never think you'd do."

"Those immigrants weren't the first settlers," said Ginger. "There were others here before them. And the immigrants killed them and took their land."

"Which immigrants?" Stan asked sarcastically. "Oh…those immigrants. Thanks for clearing that up."

He rolled over and fell asleep.

Bad news arrived Saturday when Bev drove up and ran into the kitchen just as Ginger was preparing breakfast.

"Johnny's been busted!" she shouted. "He's in jail."

The news needed deciphering and Ginger calmed Bev enough to learn that Johnny was caught smoking a joint Friday night while he sat in his car after work. A motel guest thought he looked suspicious and, instead of going to the manager, called the police. Two cops arrived, arrested Johnny and searched the car.

"They found his stash," Bev said weakly. "More than an ounce. That's a fucking felony."

"Let's not jump ahead," said Ginger. "He has his rights. I hope he's kept his mouth shut."

"He's been so damn sloppy. Thinks everyone up here is a hippie. He should know better. Now he's sitting in a cell in Ukiah."

"Have they set bail?" asked Ginger. "It would mean finding a judge and this is the weekend so that might be a hassle. Let's go see him."

"He needs a goddamned lawyer. How are we going to afford that?" Bev was frantic.

"I know something about the law," said Ginger. "Let's just go see what we can do."

The women left in Bev's VW. Stan stayed with Lila and planned a day working in the yard.

Mid-afternoon Stan heard the choking sputter of the VW as it crawled up the driveway and parked. Johnny was driving. He stopped the car and climbed out along with Bev and Ginger.

"Well, this is pretty far out," said Stan as he approached Johnny and the men met in a buoyant embrace.

"Thought you were in for life," Stan joked.

"I made bail, man," said Johnny. "Thanks to your quick-thinking wife."

As Ginger explained it, the women arrived at the Ukiah jail and were told a judge was found Saturday morning and bail was set at $150 for possession of a controlled substance, a good omen since it meant Johnny likely was charged with a misdemeanor and not a felony. Ginger realized the car was worth more than the bail and she had Bev use the car registration to sign over the VW as collateral.

"Now all he needs is an attorney," said Ginger. "And I know a couple."

Johnny was still a man in jeopardy but Ginger had tempered the terms of his suffering.

More serious trouble arrived late Sunday when Johnny drove into the yard and knocked furiously on the kitchen door.

"Bev fell and is leaking water. I've called the doc and he needs her to come to the hospital in Ukiah!" he shouted. "We think her waters broke. She stood up from dinner and tripped on her chair. Fell straight to the floor. Then a lot of pain and wet all down her skirt. Would you guys follow us?"

Ginger ran to see Bev who sat crumpled in the front seat of Johnny's VW. She hugged Bev and ran back as Stan started the Valiant.

Stan followed Johnny's VW as it wound recklessly east through the dark hills of Highway 20. Ginger sat beside him and Lila slept in the backseat.

"Sounds bad," said Ginger. "She's past seven months, but still…"

She didn't finish her sentence and Stan had no response. He was alive to all the perils bought with pleasure.

Bev's doctor met her at the hospital and she and Johnny disappeared with him into the emergency room. After ten minutes Johnny emerged.

"She's on her way to Santa Rosa," said Johnny. "She's not having contractions but the doctor doesn't want to take any chances. They have an ICN there."

"Intensive care nursery," Ginger said to Johnny before turning back to the nurse.

"Wow. Are they going to deliver the baby?"

"Well, you never know," an emergency nurse said before thinking twice.

"Say, are you all family?"

It was clear immediately that Johnny would drive to Santa Rosa while Stan and Ginger would not. Johnny would phone when he had news. And if it were after eight a.m. he could contact Ginger at her law office. She wrote the number on a hospital brochure and handed it to Johnny.

Ginger's office phone rang late Monday morning and she picked up her extension fully expecting to hear Johnny's voice and not that of another man who asked if he were speaking to "Ginger, the wife of Stan Slinger?"

"Yes," answered Ginger.

"Who wants to know?"

"I'm with his crew, ma'am," the voice said.

"Jeb, ma'am. There's been an accident."

"He's not unconscious. Just sedated," the nurse said to Ginger before she entered a room of the small doctor's clinic in Fort Bragg.

"He's lost some blood."

Jeb had met Ginger at the clinic entrance but couldn't tell her much other than Stan had set a choker while "the crew boss Lowrie shouted 'go' and that was it, the cable caught a dead tree and pulled it up and sent the sucker flying and it hit Stan."

"Where is he hurt?" asked Ginger, suppressing a dizzying rush as she viewed Stan in bed, covered and bandaged heavily across his chest, which was all she could see over the covers.

"It's a serious injury," said the doctor. "But typical in this line of work. He has three cracked ribs and a deep wound to the thigh where a branch stabbed him and nearly went through. Didn't break his leg, though he bled pretty badly. For all of that, he's lucky. The crew threw him in the truck and had him here in 30 minutes. We've stopped the bleeding. He'll heal. It's going to take some time. Your insurance might cover some of his missed hours."

"Was their negligence?" asked Ginger.

"Not my department," said the doctor. "Talk to a lawyer."

Ginger asked when Stan could come home.

"He's going by ambulance to the hospital in Ukiah. End of the week, maybe," answered the doctor. "Infection is our enemy and we'll be watching that. If he gets a fever I want him to have it there. We lost a logger last year with a similar injury. He went home and within 24 hours was running a high temperature. No one contacted us until it was way too late to help."

Ginger returned to the office and told her bosses about her husband's accident.

"Was there negligence?" Ted asked.

He offered to help.

Ginger needed time more than money and asked for it.

"Sure. Take the week," Ted said. "Let us know what we can do."

It was comforting support, offered by the straight dudes that had hired Ginger and now valued her. She was a creature of value. Her new friends valued her. The women of the ridge valued her. She was a treasured gift to this forgotten coast and if she thought too much about it she was forced to address the extraordinary expectations she had for herself.

She might have ended the day a widow. Gratefully, she did not. She loved Stan but in ways he or she were unable to fully grasp just now. Their love needed attention and repair was something she appreciated but did not always know how to do. In any event, her husband was down and needed her strength, affection and support. There was no other choice. They had taken vows and, despite the meaningless of all other forms of faith, vows still meant something to Ginger. She thought he would live and expected to live with him, next to him, and in a constant and forgiving state of intimate relation. But if he died, she thought for a moment how easy it would be to let him go.

Johnny phoned as Ginger was preparing to leave the office.

"It's a boy," he said wistfully, alerting Ginger to ask if everything was OK.

"We're in the City now," he said. "At the UC hospital on the hill. Timothy Joseph was born just before noon. Everything's as OK as can be expected."

"How's the baby?" Ginger asked. "How's Bev?"

Ginger heard Johnny suck up a sigh.

"It's been crazy," he said. "He came in at three pounds seven ounces. All tiny skin and bones. He's OK now but no one can say yet how it will all turn out. He needs oxygen and his lungs aren't ready to take it. He's in an isolette in intensive care. Bev's asleep. She'll see him tomorrow."

Ginger imagined Bev and Johnny's descent through the increasingly hellish circles of their emergency, their fall from promise to crisis and all the stops along the way.

"It must be so hard," she said. "I'm sorry."

"Is Stan there?" asked Johnny. "Can he come to the phone?"

His question broke the seal of Ginger's already riven heart. She set the phone receiver on her desk and fell wailing into her chair.

For several days Ginger lived by herself, though she was not alone. Lila made her loud demands and the fetus within her its quiet ones. Ginger called on Marjorie to keep the day care going and carved out time between short trips to her office and long drives to the hospital to help out at home. By Wednesday, Stan was more alert and able to receive a visit from Ginger and Lila though he clearly had trouble remembering what had happened.

Johnny returned to Fort Bragg on Friday while Bev remained in the City to attend the post-natal hospitalization of their small, toiling son whose first hours and days of life were a precarious gantlet controlled largely by his risky discomfort outside a womb. As the parents of the still embryonic but also living Timothy, Johnny and Bev were now lovingly and adoringly indentured to him.

"We're moving back to Turlock," Johnny told Stan. "This is the $50,000 baby and we're going to need some help from my folks. I'll go to work in Dad's plumbing business. We'll live with him and mom for a while. A lot depends on what happens to Timmy."

Johnny's father also agreed to cover the cost of court and an attorney for Johnny's drug charge. Ginger phoned Ted who said he would take the case.

Johnny stayed through the weekend to help Stan leave the hospital and situate him at home. After a week of clinical convalescence Stan could use a crutch to rise from bed and go to the bathroom. His leg was heavily bandaged but he didn't need a cast. He was surprisingly mobile for the nature of his injury. The doctor thought Stan would need to use a crutch for at least a month and probably longer.

"Guess I've really done it this time," Stan said Saturday morning as Johnny helped him into the living room where Ginger had made their sofa into a bed for him.

"Don't blame yourself," said Johnny. "You didn't do a damned thing wrong."

Later Ginger pulled a chair up to the sofa and sat to hold Stan's hand as he slept and Lila watched him suspiciously.

"OK? Daddy OK?" Lila asked eagerly.

"Yes," answered Ginger. "We're all OK now. Daddy needs to rest. Let's fix him dinner."

At the kitchen window Ginger washed potatoes and stared out at the vast yard to see Stan's planter boxes bursting with color. Beyond she saw the cyclone fence that safely contained the children's play area. It was all Stan's work and in the throes of her engagement with some nobler idea of herself she had missed her husband's earnest endowments. Why had she insisted he take a job when his work on their behalf was always and plainly in front of her? She would phone Raj. She would ask him and Larry to retrieve the rest of Stan's paintings from the garage in Berkeley and drive them up to the house.

She saw new opportunities: a day care that could serve more than just the hippie families, a farmer's market for a community in which one did not exist, the export of food from farms and communes to food conspiracies in the city. A fall harvest was just a few months away. Her thoughts seemed potent and tough because they were now self-evident but like nothing she might have first imagined. Something wondrous still existed just beyond the immediate reach of her imagination. And it would require a different kind of venture. They had not moved to a new world simply to live by its old ways.

BRONWYN

one

She was drunk when the rapist appeared at the foot of her bed at 2:27 in the morning. Bronwyn later remembered looking to the luminous dial of her alarm clock for enough light to see who stood before her in the darkness and who in a deep, calm voice told her that if she yelled or resisted he would kill her.

The terms of this new and sudden relationship were immediately clear to Bronwyn and as she offered her frightened assent, she saw the rapist's flat, shadowed outline huge against the street-lit windows of her basement flat.

"You gonna be OK," he said. "Unless you scream. Unless you fuck up. You understand?"

Bronwyn heard his anger, pushed up from inside like a furious wind. She heard his attempt to tame it. She heard every microscopic shuffle as the rapist dropped his pants and knelt on her bed. She felt the point of a knife blade scrape across her thigh.

"You need to warm me up. Know what I mean?"

Bronwyn knew and groped the darkness for his penis, already erect and nearly in her face. She took it in her mouth, trying desperately to catalogue as many details as she could while making what she thought would be moves that would calm him.

"You done this before, haven't you bitch?" the rapist said, his voice smooth and apparently soothed by Bronwyn's attention.

The brackish taste of the cock assured her she wasn't dreaming.

"OK, OK," the rapist said. "I'm getting in the bed."

As he took off his pants Bronwyn asked him what was the matter. Why was he doing this?

He was bitter. He was pissed at bad bitches that treated him like shit. Bronwyn couldn't remember all his complaints though she tried to comfort him, knowing she could have been anyone. It only mattered that her rapist believed her. *Her rapist.* It felt slightly empowering to think herself as something more than an anonymous object.

"Why me?" she asked as her rapist stripped off her panties and pushed her legs apart.

"Been watchin' you," he said. "See you come home late at night. You should really be more careful."

He laughed.

She thought she felt him inside her but wasn't certain until his large, crushing body quickly convulsed and he fell out and away, the knife still in his hand.

A moment passed as he caught his breath and slouched down, apparently relieved and perhaps relaxed. Bronwyn remained still, quiet and now agonizingly alert. What was next?

The rapist began to give her advice, explaining calmly how careless she had been, how much noise she had made staggering around in front of her doorway. And how she had left her key in the lock after entering.

"You was shit-faced," he said. "You fuckin' advertised it. And the key in the lock…damn, bitch that was my invitation. Lot a bad people in this neighborhood. You need to watch out."

Bronwyn's rapist stood and, in his newly pensive mood, said he would let himself out. But if she told anyone what had happened he would kill her.

"Don't want to see no cops here," he said to her. "I'm watchin'."

The door opened and her rapist left without closing it. Bronwyn rose slowly. Her vulva felt scraped and achy. She waddled toward the door and, after yanking her key from the exterior lock, closed and bolted it. She pulled all her curtains closed before turning on the bedside lamp. She heard a dog howl as her rapist likely slipped through an adjacent yard. She waited, uncertain for what.

Two days passed and Bronwyn still waited. She slept in her clothes, though being dressed and ready to run did nothing to help her sleep. A nightmare woke her and repeated itself: he would come at her through the walls or drop by with friends as if he were there all the time. She awoke frequently, terrorized and out of control.

She pulled the phone across the room to have it next to her pillow. She did not leave her apartment though she wanted desperately to flee. She phoned Peter and Michael and said she would miss Sunday's Park strategy session.

On the third day she walked to the Seven Palms market and bought a bag of groceries, looking vigilantly behind her though she had no idea what her rapist looked like. He was big. That's all she knew and so every time she saw a big man she flinched and wondered.

And she blamed herself. What did she think? That she could live single like some man? That she could make the life she wanted for herself and the world would regard her and leave her alone? Now she faced the facts. She was nothing special. She offered her sexuality to so many men she met in the Movement and usually when she was drunk. Now she wanted to shut it down indefinitely for repairs.

But what would repair look like? She could not call the police. She was made fearful by her rapist's threat. But she knew also the police were no friends of hers and that most knew her as a radical and activist. It would feel worse than rape to have a reporting officer be someone who previously had arrested her: a man who like her rapist had stalked her and confronted her.

On Tuesday Bronwyn phoned Harriet.

"I don't know anyone else to call," Bronwyn said, her words spoken through a purging sob.

"I'm afraid, so damned afraid."

Harriet drove across campus and was at Bronwyn's door in ten minutes, admitted by the clack of a bolt into her claustrophobic basement studio that closed for days, smelled stuffy and rank. Harriet listened as Bronwyn hesitantly and painfully described her fear she was now watched and that she would be raped again. She was, in fact, under ceaseless attack by her own suspicions, fears and torments.

Harriet opened with questions Bronwyn could not answer.

"What did he look like?" she asked.

"I couldn't see him."

"Well, what color? Was he white? Black?" Harriet asked.

"I couldn't tell. He sounded black."

"Sounded black?" asked Harriet.

"You know…like a black man talks."

"How's that?" asked Harriet.

"I don't know—I don't know!" Bronwyn shouted.

"Why me? I work to help black people. Why me?"

It wasn't the point, but Harriet saved her words.

"You've been hurt. We need to get you to a doctor."

Harriet guided Bronwyn to her closet and asked her to dress while she phoned her physician for a referral.

"No! No!" said Bronwyn. "I don't want the cops involved!"

Bronwyn had a friend who worked at the Berkeley Free Clinic.

"Take me there," she said.

Bronwyn gazed out the window of Harriet's Karmann Ghia as it swerved down the switchback from the highway's last foggy coastal bluff and toward the gaping blue mouth of the Navarro River.

"Let's drive the coast home," Harriet said as she turned at the bridge to follow Highway One south to Point Arena and Gualala and farther through Sonoma County and then into Marin to San Rafael where they would cross a bridge to the East Bay.

"It's a couple more hours. We'll eat lunch in Bodega Bay."

"That sounds good," said Bronwyn who nursed yet another of her regular weekend hangovers, this from the previous evening's party at Ginger and Stan's house.

It had been two weeks since the rape and still she reeled from its effects as if it were yesterday, still felt ashamed and filthy and shaken but also angry and seized at random moments by a deep and unspeakable fury. Alcohol calmed this hurt and hate.

She was impatient to return to Berkeley and to her political work, the last unsullied experience in her life. All others, grown from her recent trauma into a new and horrific awareness of her countless failings, were seriously infected by an irresistibly sorrowful regret.

Infected. I'm infected.

Though not with a disease. The clinic tests were negative and she was due back at the beginning of the next month to confirm a final result.

Bronwyn continued to look out the passenger window as Harriet drove south, the fierce Pacific thrown at them in white, boiling waves that slapped rocks and bluffs.

"You're extra quiet this morning," she asked Brownyn. "What's up?"

"I like Ginger and Stan," said Bronwyn. "I'm sorry I got so drunk last night."

"I understand," said Harriet.

"Yeah, but do they?" Bronwyn responded.

"Probably not," said Harriet. "But why is that important? You did no harm."

"I wanted them to like me," said Bronwyn.

"They like you," said Harriet. "I like you. You don't have to worry."

But Bronwyn did worry, had always worried, had found her greatest satisfaction in the reliable arrival of worry she presumed protected her from harm. It was the worry she now shared with a therapist also recommended by Harriet who also gave Bronwyn the extra room in her flat, insisted that she take it and offered her two months rent-free.

The therapist, who went by the congenial name of Dr. Jeff, had helped Bronwyn to dig deeper into the persistent pain that preceded her rape, her life in politics, her scholarly achievements and also her drinking and her unmanageable promiscuity. Some of her current pain related directly to the history she owned as distinct from the assault she did not.

Her history began with a claustrophobic childhood–tight quarters, confining expectations, early limits unwisely unchallenged and lovers who were not friends and friends who did not love her. Her parents' tiny apartment in Queens set the economic and regional limits of her existence though her rough edges were not entirely contained.

Her mother, recognizing that her daughter at age 12 exhibited all the signs of a tom-boy-in-training, sent her to a womanly charm school where Bronwyn spent six weeks learning to walk, to speak, to dress and comport herself like a true "woman" which meant something entirely different to the daughter who had begun to masturbate long before puberty and felt solely and secretly at home with the lover she made of herself. At the charm school's graduation Bronwyn strolled graciously to the edge of the stage, tripped and fell off.

It was nearly the last of her mother's interventions though one remained when, at age 16, she convinced Bronwyn to have cosmetic surgery on her nose so that its prominent length and overhang, the nose shape Bronwyn knew from the faces of all her relatives, might be reformed into a small, perky ski jump of cuteness. Bronwyn consented, only to return to high school in the fall and to be teased and ridiculed for her "summer nose job." The surgery had done nothing to alter her short stature, to thicken her stringy, brown hair, to hide her bulging tummy or give an elongating shape to her compressed, bony legs.

At first these did not bother Bronwyn who excelled as the brainy class nerd, and a girl no less, whom everyone secretly regarded as a genius but that no one dated or invited to parties. When a small crowd of black-shirted seniors began to meet after class in the park across from the school, Bronwyn joined them to play bongos, smoke cigarettes and, later, to meet in a basement bedroom where they drank liquor stolen from their parents and listened to Charlie Parker.

She took her first drink and first lover in that basement room, both fervent imprints of unguarded joy—the first truly intoxicating high and the first touch of another more mysteriously endearing than her own. Neither lasted long enough, leaving her to spend years locked in an unacknowledged obsession to find in daily drinking and infrequent bedmates a route back to those magical first ecstasies. Now the search was over. Her rapist had seen to that. The search was over but the motions were not.

At the peak of another bluff Harriet left the river behind as another wide length of shoreline yawned ahead of them. Harriet hugged the ribbon of the two-lane highway and navigated what appeared the upper lip of a large mouth that barely held them away from the frenetic surges of a wild sea. At every sharp turn the waters rose as if to catch them, to swallow them whole. Bronwyn observed the symmetry of motions, a rhythm that incorporated the unsteady lurches and halts of Harriet's car with the syncopated surge of large waves that rose high in the ocean for miles down the coast.

"It's beautiful country," Bronwyn said weakly.

"It's a hard place to live, though," said Harriet. "You can see why. What can anyone do here?"

"The Indians made out OK," answered Bronwyn. "They lived here for thousands of years. They hunted. They must have been fat with game and maybe they planted food."

"White people didn't help much," said Harriet. "They knew how to make any patch of land into a private property. A lot of dirty work was involved: cutting down bushels of trees, overfishing the salmon, digging up dirt to burn and, of course, kicking Indians off their land even if it meant killing them."

"One thing you can say about Americans is that they know how to kill," said Bronwyn. "It's not that we have more guns, which we do. It's that we all seem more willing to kill each other if given half a chance."

"More than who?" asked Harriet.

Bronwyn did not answer. It was hard for her to separate what was true from how she felt. Facts alone had little meaning.

Another stretch of silence extended for several miles before Harriet asked Bronwyn about the People's Park.

"I've got my fingers crossed," said Bronwyn.

"The chancellor met with the park committee and an architect to create plans for a park."

"Really?" asked Harriet.

"Just like that. A park? What about Reagan? Will he go for it?"

Bronwyn couldn't say. The park had become Bronwyn's city on

a hill and the slow build toward a possible success was crucial. Years of protests were profoundly and also negligibly useful in assembling resistance that occasionally changed policies or opinions. Nothing permanent was secured but here was a chance to seize territory.

A park was real. It was an identifiable piece of valuable land that could secure a palpable and neighborly blessing to last for generations. To have helped create its existence gave Bronwyn enough of hope's warm fire to fend off an otherwise deep and personal depression.

Their drive south continued, rolling down the hill of Point Arena's quaint old main street before several more rises and falls pushed them through the larger town of Gualala and across a bridge and through the hills and bluffs of Sonoma County and another round of rigorous turns and dips until well past Salt Point they climbed the highway's longest and most treacherous ladder of hairpin turns before gliding down toward Bear Gulch and the broad mouth of the Russian River. In Bodega Bay they pulled into the wharf's parking lot and found a table at The Tides.

"Hitchcock filmed *The Birds* here," said Harriet.

Bronwyn hadn't seen it.

They ordered lunch and watched fishing boats make their orderly return through the bay's shallow, dredged channel.

"Thanks, Harriet," Bronwyn said. "Thanks for everything."

Harriet smiled and said nothing. There were no words for what Bronwyn wanted to say. She was grateful to live with her new friend though a change of residence had not stopped her nightmares nor was it always easy to share a space and her habits—and especially her drinking—under the perpetually refreshed scrutiny of a caring friend. At times Bronwyn heard Harriet and Michael make their sweet love, oblivious to its cuddlesome sounds, subsequent rumbles and sighs of laughter and relief.

It was a kind of sex Bronwyn had never experienced and that forced her to consider again what sex had been for her: raucous, masturbatory, infrequent and, ultimately, terrifying.

Men were not gods.

They were dogs and anger was all they understood.

"Get angry. Get real angry, and you're less likely to get bitten."

Bronwyn did not know the others in the room. The woman who spoke was small and wiry and wore blue jeans under a red shawl that draped around her neck and fell fluidly to frame her breasts. She slipped occasionally into Spanish and said her name was Rita and that she lived in the Mission. She had just broken up with her boyfriend.

"I'm damaged goods now," said Rita.

"I fucked him. I'm no more the virgin. *No puro mas.* My parents are old Puerto Rico. They don't understand the city. Since I'm not a virgin anymore I have no value to them. They can't marry me off to anyone respectable. So I can't go home."

Bronwyn sat in the small kitchen of a San Francisco apartment with seven other women, a self-described "consciousness-raising" group grown from the activities of *Sudsofloppen,* a new alliance of women in the City. The group was described as a free space for women and women only and was advertised in the alliance newsletter of the same name.

It was Bronwyn's turn to speak and she was a good speaker. For years she had articulated and synthesized the premises of insurgency, had argued incisively for revolution. Now she would try to describe her fear, her shame, and her heart's ulcerous wound she assumed apparent to anyone who met her. What words were safe to use in so personal a revelation? And would they matter? Why would others care about the rape and its consequences? Would she be judged for not taking precautions, for not phoning the police? She attempted to form with her lips some words to describe the depth of her torment. Tears flowed instead.

"You wanna open up, sister?" said Pam the moderator, a tall, lithe woman with short black hair who stood at the window.

"We're all here for you. You just take your time."

It was more than permission to speak. The moderator had foreshadowed the group's unconditional acceptance of whatever was coming. This was new for Bronwyn, who was accustomed to permitting without receiving, questioning without asking, and resenting without knowing who other than herself to resent.

Solidarity had been mentioned. Bronwyn was accustomed to using that word and she thought she understood, though in this group solidarity had an undefined depth she had never before experienced. Up until now all of Bronwyn's friendships had been alliances and within the Movement all alliances were political. Now something personal was included. She was out in the open not just for herself, but also for everyone. She was seen, and suddenly unafraid to be seen.

In the shocking power of this moment, Bronwyn told her story. She shuddered in the hurt of her violation and seethed with the anger of a feckless victim. At its core the hurt was not simply her own, but one that rippled more widely through the world, that ruined her trust in people and stole her hope for the efforts she devoted to improving the lives of others. She avoided people now, walked quickly past them even as she searched the face of every large man she encountered in a ceaseless, futile effort to find her tormentor.

"The meaning of my life has been defiled," she shouted at the end. "I am left with a constant, almost unbearable regret. I am nothing. I am no better than nothing."

A flat silence followed her last words until support arrived as the touch of many hands placed on her arms and shoulders. Women rose from their chairs to approach and shelter Bronwyn in a wave of candid regard and comfort offered with intimated understanding and without reservation.

"How many women here have been sexually assaulted by men?" asked Pam.

All hands shot up.

"How many of you have been raped?"

Four women raised their hands.

"And when you were children? Raped as children?"

Two hands stayed high in the air.

"You're not alone, Bronwyn," said the tall woman.

"We hear you. We all honor your truth. We're angry along with you. And we're sick and tired of this shit."

Bronwyn asked the sociology dean for a week off from her research assignments. She was paid from a grant to collate data for a department study on family income and its relationship to racial discrimination in housing. This and monthly draws from a small inheritance kept Bronwyn in graduate school while she did the work she loved as a political activist.

The Park Committee was to meet to develop a plan to present to the university. Bronwyn envisioned a permanent People's Park and was surprised by a feeling of relief, as if the burden of her assault was now born for her by others. Whether she had taken back some of her power, or grown new powers, it did not matter. She felt surprisingly buoyant and supported, and not hung over. She had gone two days without a drink. She was ready to get on with her Park work and ready, also, to speak her mind.

Bronwyn left Harriet's flat to walk to the campus. As she approached the park site she saw signs posted everywhere. She walked the perimeter. All the signs read *No Trespassing* and she counted more than fifty. People still lounged in the park while a few stood at the south corner and watched police cars make occasional passes along Haste Street and Dwight Way.

"Things are getting interesting," a Telegraph scavenger snarled as Bronwyn walked by. He flashed her a V with his fingers and asked for spare change.

"Bad news," said Michael. "The chancellor says he's going to fence off the park while the university decides what to do with it."

"Fence it off?" said Wendy. "What happened to our negotiations?"

"Good question," said Michael. "But don't try to ask him. He's in D.C. giving a speech and the vice-chancellor is in LA at the Regents meeting."

"What the fuck happened?" asked Raj. "We had a calendar. We were going to meet with the architect. I know the architect likes us."

Michael unfolded a release from the university press office.

"It's all here," he said.

"Chancellor Heyns says we failed to form a responsible committee. Well, fuck him."

"When does the fence go up?" asked Raj.

"Don't know," said Michael. "All I know is that we've got to get organized."

The committee agreed to use the next day to plan a march on the campus home of the chancellor.

"We'll give him a big welcome back," said Frank. "This is Reagan talking, not Heyns."

Bronwyn awoke and could not remember her dreams other than to note her agitation and the hollow feeling of a just-vanished ghost. The morning's foggy cool grey flooded the window with the light of a sky before sunrise. She ate a quick breakfast and passed Harriet in the hall, determined to score a hot coffee at the Forum before meeting Michael, Raj, Frank, Wendy and others at the campus to organize their march on the chancellor. Bronwyn strolled along College Avenue expecting to drop down the hill at Dwight Way before getting her coffee and walking up Telegraph to the campus.

At the corner she faced wooden street barriers and a dozen cops wearing helmets and holding batons. One waved her on and told her to stay on College. Looking past him down Dwight, Bronwyn saw the shiny steel of a chain link fence erected along a corner of People's Park. She hurried north to the campus and found her colleagues milling on the steps of Sproul Hall. The sun climbed in the sky, brilliant and increasingly torrid. High temperatures were predicted for the weekend.

"Rally at noon," shouted Michael.

The steps had been reserved for a rally celebrating Israel's independence but the student group sponsoring it agreed to give the podium to supporters of the park. Bronwyn saw Mack and ran over to him.

"You're covering this?" she asked.

"Yeah," Mack answered. "They have a team of reporters on this one. I'm getting union pay today."

"Did you see the cops?" asked Mack. "They came in at four this morning. They've taken over eight blocks and the park is completely fenced off. Threw everyone out. They have a staging area in the parking garage east of Telly. Must be a couple hundred there."

"We have support," said Bronwyn. She looked toward the crowd forming in the plaza.

"I'm guessing four thousand."

The campanile struck noon as speakers gathered at a microphone. Michael spoke first and described the history of the park. Wendy followed and told how negotiations had begun and now were apparently ended. Bronwyn was introduced.

"I'm Bronwyn DeGroot and until yesterday I believed the university would work with us to build a park. Now it is apparent it will not. Instead, the governor wants a fight. He wants to reward the voters who elected him by shutting down People's Park, an acre of muddy land that sat for a year as a garbage dump and parking lot and that in the past month has become a community park; turfed, planted and filled with flowers, swings, seesaws and benches.

"Why is our city now faced with a police occupation? Why are the resources of our city and state being used against us? Because we had the nerve to build a beautiful park? Because we were willing to create a green space for our community out of a barren, vacant lot? It is time to tell Chancellor Heyns we won't accept the destruction of the People's Park. We will protest, as we always have, against this unwarranted seizure. They think they will save our community by destroying it. We will save our community by building our park."

The last speaker was Dan Seigel, a law student and also the university's student body president. He admitted no one had yet "decided exactly what to do" about the park before telling everyone what needed to be done.

"Go down there and take the park!" he shouted before a police officer pulled the cord on his microphone.

These were the rally's last words as thousands turned together like the opaque water droplets of a smooth, moving cloud and rolled south toward Telegraph Avenue, its vanguard a phalanx of fury, kicking at the doors of the Avenue's Bank of America branch as it passed. Bronwyn followed, as did Mack who brought his camera and stopped every few feet to take pictures.

The moving crowd's edge reached Haste Street in time to meet a small squad of flack-jacketed sheriff's deputies marching down the block. They wore bright blue jumpsuits.

"Blue Meanies! Blue Meanies!" some in the crowd shouted.

A woman with a wrench opened a fire hydrant on the corner that showered nearby deputies in a hard stream of water.

Bronwyn ran ahead to assert some impossible containment, as if she alone could remind everyone this was a peaceful protest. She rushed to the front of the crowd that marched obliviously past her. Before she could speak, a series of explosions launched tear gas canisters that landed hard among the marchers and scattered them into two distinct rivulets, one running back up Telegraph as the other was pushed west of the Avenue and down Haste Street. Brownyn, swept up by the latter, found an alley where she went to cover her searing eyes and to vomit.

She could barely see but ran back to the street to find members of the crowd's greatly reduced vanguard charging the street barrier on Telegraph. Some in the crowd threw rocks. Others retrieved the tear gas canisters and lobbed them back at a handful of deputies attempting to close the opened fire hydrant. Deputies rushed out like licks of flame and tried to seize their closest antagonists, sometimes catching the shirt tails of one and dragging him into their web or, in futility, succumbing to a fusillade of rocks and bricks and retreating.

"Take the park!" a voice shouted as the crowd on Haste surged toward the park's new and shiny cyclone fences and forced the cops back up Haste until a second, larger army of helmeted deputies emerged from the parking garage and, behind a rolling jeep spraying tear gas, pushed the rioters back down Haste and away from the park.

The great crowd's second rivulet was forced to flow farther west down Haste. Bronwyn joined them, walking rapidly among hundreds who fled down the street's receding blocks, until gunshots rang out and several among her fell, grabbing at their legs and backs that now bled from clusters of small, hemic wounds.

"That's fucking buckshot!" someone shouted. "They're shooting to kill!"

Bronwyn helped to carry those wounded out of the street and into the foyer of a nearby student co-op. Police continued their methodical march west, rifles lifted and ready. A student left the building to enter an adjacent parking lot and without warning was shot in the chest. He was lifted by a friend and pulled back inside.

Bronwyn saw Mack run by with his camera. She followed him down Dana Street where he circled back up Dwight Way toward Telegraph. He stopped at the corner to photograph a burning police car three blocks to the south. On the roofs above them Bronwyn saw coveys of spectators perched like birds. Cops looked upward as if to locate their next attackers.

"Kill the pigs!" someone shouted and the epithet became a chant that spread across the rooftops.

"Kill the pigs! Kill the pigs! Kill the pigs!"

Above them on a commercial billboard the giant letters of the word *Showtime* framed the war in the streets as if it were a caption for the conflict in progress below.

Bronwyn counted more people on roofs than there were cops in the street. East on Dwight she saw Raj and Yitzhak pulling garbage cans from driveways and rolling them downhill toward the police. Hit by a can from behind, one cop stumbled and dropped his gun. Rocks hit the ground next to him while several deputies turned quickly and fired their rifles at the roof above Granma's Bookstore.

Bronwyn saw at least two people fall to the roof as they were grabbed and held by others. In a moment, a young man in a white shirt emerged from the bookstore and ran toward a cop.

"We need an ambulance. Now!" the man shouted.

The cop pointed his rifle at the man.

"You fucking pig. Are you going to shoot me?"

The cop backed away.

"An ambulance! He's badly hurt. You might have killed him!"

The cop retreated to the opposite corner, his rifle still pointed at the man now frantic in his helplessness.

"An ambulance! You fucking pig. An ambulance!"

A jeep arrived in the intersection to spray more teargas into the paths of protesters that now rushed toward the burning police car where a small crowd was attempting to push it over.

Bronwyn followed Mack who turned to see her.

"What started all this?" he asked her.

"You mean who started it?" she also asked. "Who called in all the cops? Who ordered the park fenced?"

"All these cops just to guard a park?" asked Mack.

"You think this is about a park?" Bronwyn asked again. "It's been waiting to happen. Years in the making. Maybe this is the revolution we've been waiting for."

"If so, you're badly outgunned," said Mack.

More gunshots exploded. Mack ran toward the police car. A single deputy stood with his rifle about thirty feet from the burning vehicle. As more cops arrived, protesters moved back. A young man carrying books passed by the deputy on the sidewalk and, seeing the deputy's gun, picked up his pace and began to run. Mack framed the deputy and car with his camera. As the young man entered Mack's viewfinder the deputy fired his gun and the young man fell.

"You shot him?" shouted a protester at the deputy.

"He's a student. You shot him? Why?"

The deputy backed off slowly before flipping his finger at the crowd. He turned and walked away.

Bronwyn rushed to the student who lay bleeding from an abdominal wound. Mack ran into a nearby market to call for help. He knew the police would not.

Bronwyn comforted the young man on the sidewalk and pressed her hand hard against his wound as if to hold him together. Blood seeped through the man's shirt and formed bright stains as it spread among Bronwyn's outstretched fingers. The ambulance arrived and without waiting for Mack, Brownyn fled the scene to walk briskly north toward Derby Street. A gassy, grey fog curtained off the campus beyond Telegraph from where she could still hear the sporadic pops of guns.

Bronwyn paused at a corner, feeling as if she were separated from all she experienced. She saw beyond her urgent fear the bestial nature of her life and all life, the bestial insistence of all things beastly to find their places and to hold them. Was this war in the streets anything other than a battle of beasts? Were her rapist's thrusts anything more than a panicked act of survival? Were her aberrant fantasies and drunken seductions, despite her lofty attributions of desire and affection, anything more than gluttonous abuses? Was her political work, or anyone's, a quest for justice or a hunger for control?

It was a mean world. It was a mean and mortal existence. Bronwyn reveled briefly in a cynical confidence she at last understood her meaningless life and all life until, staring hard at her hand covered in another person's blood, she grasped at an abiding hope and its coercive truth: that living was both fragile and tenacious. It was a contradiction that suggested only the bare outline of a deeper, more obscure and yet empowering secret, one larger than she could imagine and also smaller than she could see.

three

Bronwyn told herself provocative ghost stories throughout her cautious crawl east on Derby as she climbed through yards and hid behind parked cars to avoid patrolling sheriff's cruisers.

She could not yet imagine a life after wartime, a way to remember anything before the day's bloody fights in the streets. And when she tried, all that came up were the assorted and randomly disturbing details of her rape. Her rape. She was a woman in possession of a rape. A rape given to her by her rapist whose identity she still sought in the face of nearly every male stranger she encountered.

"Guns were going off everywhere," Harriet told Bronwyn as they sat in the kitchen.

"I saw three people hit near Sather Gate. When they weren't shooting, the cops were swinging clubs at anyone they could reach."

Harriet had missed the rally and did not encounter the police riot until mid-afternoon when she left her South Hall office. She walked outside and was immediately enveloped in a cloud of tear gas. At some point of potential confrontation, Harriet flashed her faculty parking pass at a charging sheriff's deputy who directed her away from the plaza. She ran east to Piedmont Avenue and circled cautiously through the hills above College before arriving home.

Harriet turned on the television and the two women relived the violent day on the evening news. Cops had shot at least sixty people. Several were hospitalized with serious wounds and at least three were gravely injured. A few cops were hurt, one stabbed by an attacker. The sheriff said he had authorized the use of birdshot because officers were vastly outnumbered.

However, a doctor at Herrick Hospital said he had removed actual, and much more harmful, buckshot from at least two shooting victims, neither of them protesters. The governor, using a state of emergency declared in February during the Third World Studies protests, announced he would send 2700 National Guard troops into the city. A curfew was declared between 6 p.m. and 10 a.m. and all gatherings or rallies were prohibited.

By dawn on Friday, a thousand National Guard troops lined Telegraph and the south perimeter of the campus, using as an outpost the fenced confines of the park. Cops forced an attempted rally to the center of the campus though three thousand protesters found their way downtown to gather in front of Berkeley City Hall. Friday night Bronwyn joined a meeting of the park committee held at Merritt College in Oakland to elude the Berkeley curfew. She was angry now, as was everyone else.

"We need to arm ourselves," declared Michael. "This is war."

It was an unpopular and short-lived idea. Mario, who had witnessed with Bronwyn the shooting of a fleeing student on Telegraph, urged the committee to return to non-violent resistance and to continue to seek negotiations.

"Reagan wants a war," said Frank. "Is anyone surprised? All this bloodshed is cool with his supporters."

"We still have the students and the faculty on our side," said Bronwyn. "And the city. Now more than ever, after what's just happened. If we keep this a local issue, if we focus only on the park, we can win. Those two men shot near Dwight. One was blinded and the other is near death. And neither was protesting. That might be OK in Bakersfield but it's not welcome here."

On Saturday, Bronwyn joined a march through downtown to protest the city's occupation. She watched Raj and Yitzhak and some of the Telegraph street people wander up to a corner occupied by a dozen guardsmen. A few young women strolled toward the soldiers, and two removed their blouses. They offered fruit and cookies to the flummoxed guardsmen that, surprisingly, they took and ate. Yitzhak and the women left quickly. An hour passed during which several guardsmen set down their rifles and began to laugh uncontrollably.

"It was the fucking oranges!" shouted a guardsman as an attending officer at last determined his soldiers had consumed healthy doses of LSD.

Later that day a hundred people showed up at a vacant lot on Hearst St. northwest of the campus and began laying sod and planting flowers for what they called the People's Park Annex. Throughout the weekend large numbers of protesters tried each day to march downtown but were dispersed by National Guard troops or arrested by cops.

On Monday an attempted rally on campus was cleared by the Guard marching in formation with bayonets pointed ahead of them. That night, Bloody Thursday's most grievously injured victim died of his wounds. James Rector had truly been in the wrong place at the wrong time. He had come that day from San Jose to visit friends and stepped on the rooftop of Granma Books just as rocks landed near sheriff's deputies on Telegraph. A deputy turned to fire randomly just as Rector turned away from the roof's edge. An autopsy revealed he had been shot three times, all in the back.

Bronwyn spent Tuesday helping to organize a memorial rally for the fallen Rector. It was an awkward effort, forcing her to use a phone tree to alert supporters, and complicated by the fact the victim had no connection to the park or the protesters.

A memorial rally for Rector was planned for Tuesday on Sproul Plaza and Bronwyn threw herself into the work of organizing it. Harriet helped her by fixing meals and making calls and Bronwyn attempted to contact Rector's family for details about his life. She could find no one who would speak with her.

Animals died to become food, she thought. Humans die and suffer the same pain but for what purpose? She wished to purpose the life of Bloody Thursday's single fatality, even as she knew it to be a random loss unattached to those fighting for a park.

The thousands who had gathered at the steps of Sproul Hall listened to subdued speeches and eulogies for the accidental hero of People's Park, for a life given by chance and not by choice and that could not encompass the breadth of their embattling fury.

When the rally ended, those leaving found themselves surrounded and trapped by long lines of National Guardsmen wearing gas masks. A helicopter appeared out of the east and began to spray teargas over the dispersing crowd. Driven by panic, the crowd moved urgently in a frantic wave, first one direction and then another until set upon by baton-swinging sheriff's deputies.

Standing at the top of Sproul Hall's steps, Bronwyn slipped along the side of the building and then north until she collapsed on a bench in the faculty glade near Kroeber Hall. The war of the park was nearly a week old and also nearly and completely lost. Bronwyn's chest heaved against the acrid, stinging gas filling her lungs and with each breath connected with another more enduring pain concealed deeply within. She succumbed completely to the fury of this new war now raging inside her and to the jeopardy and anger that were two sides of the same sad thing.

"There are so many unreported rapes. Why?"

The question floated above the collegial confines of another City kitchen, this one in a Victorian flat on Pierce Street between the Fillmore and the Haight. The women's group had grown by two and Bronwyn took her turn welcoming new members. One had also been raped and not reported it.

"Because women are kept helpless and society nurtures these criminals," said one woman.

"Because when we go to the cops they question our moral life and act like we wanted it," said another.

"Because they asked my friend if she was a virgin."

"Because I was supposed to be with a man. The cops figured since I didn't have a boyfriend I was fair game."

"Because they didn't like my attitude," said Rita.

"I was pissed. I wanted to cut the guy's dick off. And they knew who it was. They knew him from another rape. And they wouldn't arrest him."

Rita's outrage strengthened the angry timbre of the conversation though Bronwyn was the only one who didn't speak. The women's words became Bronwyn's words and she could go no farther with her confusions and resentments. It was enough that she looked into the faces of the speaking women and they into hers. It was enough for the women to see among themselves that in their mutual anger and support they were a singularity not different from any other oppressed people. Might this ripple of solidarity against rape, misogyny and oppression become a wave? Might it rush like an ocean over a world and its history of manly dominance so commanding as to be nearly invisible?

"At some point we have to realize that the only people who care enough about us to work for our freedom are, well…us," said Pam who again led the women's group.

"The politics of this experience—the work we do on behalf of any kind of change—will have to emerge from our identities. And guess what? We are women."

Bronwyn ascended into an altered state. All her knowledge of political resistance and social revolution curdled within the interior miasma of a very personal oppression given life by the irrepressible memory of her rape. She waited at an intersection of facts and fears and for some imaginary place in a line that in her fantasy climbed through a purgatory of real time. She needed an epiphany and an entitled blessing she fully expected to find but could not yet describe.

"The boys in the movement aren't any help," said Rita.

"They talk revolution but you try to talk to them about *our* revolution. They look at you bug-eyed. 'Yes,' you say, 'our revolution in many ways involves you. You bastards don't know shit about what a woman faces in this mean and manly world.' And they just look at you, like, are you fucking crazy? You're a woman. You're a vessel of life. We respect you as long as you aren't bitching at us about something. We don't want you to trouble yourselves. Trust us. We'll handle it. We'll handle everything. We'll handle you.' You know what Stokely said about the place of women in the Movement? He said the place of women in the Movement is prone. And it got a big laugh."

Later Rita bought a drink for Bronwyn at a bar on the quieter end of Polk Street.

"It was jut one long and unhappy life," Bronwyn said through another tearful exposure. But Rita was someone she could cry with, someone who knew more than she did about herself.

"You've had a bad time, darlin'," said Rita. "How does anyone grow up a woman in this world without that deathly, broken feeling you got to bear so much witness, got to meet a man's demands and expect nothing in return?”

That was true, thought Bronwyn. But there was more. There was a presumption, implanted by her parents no less, that she was not beautiful and therefore cursed with a critical handicap in the pursuit of what they thought to be happiness: a boyfriend, a husband, a home…and children, beautiful children that were her own.

If she could have her children, strong healthy children and at least one boy, then nothing else mattered. She would, by the definition of every ancient culture, be richer than Croesus.

Instead, she found she could at least be smart in ways that would translate her assumed homeliness into a sharp-witted and asexual power. She won debates. She told uncomfortable truths like Cassandra to which no one paid any attention.

“Telling the truth meant not being invited to parties,” Bronwyn told Rita.

“I told the truth and a lot of good it did me. I still wanted a man to hold me, to tell me he loved me and then to lovingly fuck me.”

When she discovered alcohol she enjoyed drinking too much of it, partly for the oblivion it produced in her but also for the oblivion it produced in others. She learned that a drunken man, and especially at a late hour, might find her attractive. She became a sexual aggressor in ways that some men liked but that most did not.

“I never expected to be loved,” Bronwyn continued. “Though that’s really all I wanted, even more than sex. But sex was what I offered and so why should I be surprised I was raped?”

“Wait a minute, woman,” said Rita. “There’s nothing wrong with you wanting sex. You didn’t ask to get raped because you like sex. You got raped because you left your door open to a mean ass predator. One day we women won’t have to lock our doors and pull the curtains. But we ‘re not there yet. Hear me? You did nothing wrong.”

“I guess I’ve always mistaken a screw for power,” said Bronwyn before ordering another drink.

“I’ve always loved sex. Even if it leaves me disappointed. I draw men to me who won’t challenge me intellectually and so are vulnerable to the one squeaky form of intimidation I can throw at them. The sad truth is that my brains, as much as my lumpy body, are a turn-off that at some point in time usually pushes men away.”

"So you went into the revolution business?" asked Rita. "You did Civil Rights and then the Peace movement and now the Park?"

Rita knew the Bay Area activist scene. She had attended the Free Huey rally in San Francisco on the first day of May. She was there with members of the Third World Liberation Front, part of a wider coalition that included the Black Panthers, the Red Guard Party, as well as Asian and Latino groups.

"And Free Speech," said Bronwyn. "I started in '64 with Mario and the FSM. I was an undergrad then."

"I'm working for Los Siete now," said Rita. "I was at the Huey rally when I heard a police motorcycle's radio. It said an officer had just been shot in Noe Valley and it named the suspects. One of them, Ralph, was standing right beside me! He couldn't have possibly done it. Anyway, you know the officer died and the seven, Los Siete, and including Ralph, are now on trial for their lives. Those pigs are all over, aren't they? Really tryin' to mess us up."

Rita praised the Panthers.

"They give us space in their newspaper. They pass out our leaflets. They've invited us into their breakfast program. We had seven thousand people at that Huey rally. Maybe this is the uprising we all need to get a change started. Maybe your park fight is that kind of thing. The cops sure shot up the place, though. Dozens hit with buckshot? Killed a kid? That happened out a Hunter's Point in '66. Boy was 17 and running from the cops. Shot in the back. There was a three-day riot."

Rita recalled a woman at the Huey rally who spoke for women's freedom.

"She said women needed to arm themselves and you could hear the hush, men saying 'hey, that's not cool, we can't have no women running around with guns.' And I thought: Why not? Women of all colors are oppressed by this capitalist system and we certainly don't hate men. But a lot of men continue to oppress us."

Rita said she met Eldridge before he fled the country.

"He asked me if I would kill to free women. I wasn't sure. I said there were other struggles—like Black power or Chicano power—where killing might be necessary. And you know what he said? He said when you fight for your own liberation you fight on all fronts."

"And so?" asked Bronwyn. "Are you saying we should get guns to fight off our abusers?"

"I'm learning karate now," said Rita. "I'll fight any oppressor. I don't care what class, what color or what sex. Power to the people. Power to the god damned people."

Rita dropped Bronwyn at the East Bay terminal where she would catch her bus back to Berkeley.

"Love you sister," said Rita. "See you next week."

The bus bounced calmly as it crossed the Bay Bridge, city lights swimming and blinking their silver and gold behind it. Bronwyn stared into the starry darkness ringing the Bay.

The liberation of women was not a civil rights struggle. It wasn't fighting for equality or jobs. Bronwyn didn't want to do a man's work in a corporation and she certainly didn't want to be a pilot that dropped napalm on the Vietnamese. She was fighting for her reality as a woman, for its place in the world, and for her psychic survival. And the male-dominated Left, where for years Bronwyn had nested to fight what she perceived to be capitalist oppression, turned out to be the belly of the beast.

"The whole thing stinks of male supremacy," Rita had said to her.

Bronwyn could not imagine even faintly what revolutionary role a white and heterosexual male could fulfill on behalf of a woman's push for her own freedom. Would they do the shit work women had done for generations? For women to triumph would it be necessary for men not to exist? No, she didn't mean that. On second thought and in a new sort of way, yes, maybe she did.

four

Bronwyn fell asleep in space formed from a silence so primal and quiet she could hear the sound of her own hearing. In a dream she fell into a loud and crashing world conjured entirely from nothing.

Morning's headlines alerted Bronwyn to what she had missed by visiting her Thursday women's group. Some five hundred people were arrested in downtown Berkeley: swept up in a clumsy dragnet that took without discrimination protesters and hippies, but also news reporters and shoppers and a few high school students returning late from their lunch break. All were taken to Santa Rita Jail and lodged in its old barracks in Dublin that were originally an army base. By morning most had been released on bail, with men describing hours handcuffed and lying prone on the ground while guards kicked them and called them Viet Cong.

"Payback," wrote Mack in a story he filed for the Chronicle's late morning extra. He had left his press pass at home and was swept up in the bust.

We were told not to move, he wrote.

Guards wouldn't let us get up. We were kicked while down and a few beaten with clubs. And all of this occurred before we were processed or charged. Fifty dollars bail for the crime of blocking a sidewalk. A few with rocks in their pants were charged with felony conspiracy to commit assault. A professor writing a check in a health food store was grabbed out of line and arrested.

At the Park Committee's afternoon meeting, Bronwyn learned that Raj also was arrested and would not be released.

"He's on probation for a drug charge," said Michael. "Raj is a no-bail prisoner at least until his hearing. If he's convicted, he's going to jail for awhile."

Talks between the Park Committee and the University started again and were not going well. The chancellor, once amenable to a university architecture department plan to assist in the development of a public park, was now adamantly opposed to public use.

"The chancellor once called me a soul brother," said the university architect.

"Now, I don't think so."

The Park Committee acquired a city parade permit for Memorial Day the following Friday that would begin with a rally at a vacant lot on Grant Street where a new park was rising and then proceed north and east on Hearst to the campus and then to People's Park.

Guerilla parks were going up all over Berkeley as park supporters broke curfew to sneak out at night and slip into vacant lots to plant flowers and signs announcing the bloom of several new outlaw open spaces.

The Memorial Day march offered resistance but nothing close to revolution. If Bronwyn thought too hard about it, she heard an emptiness hearing its own emptiness, much as she did in her silence before sleep. It seemed hardly real and, in the presence of cops and soldiers and men throwing rocks, another war fought on lethal terms created almost exclusively by men. She found herself hoping the march might be a turning point by which everyone, even children, might see and feel an agreeable and peaceful emptiness at the core of every atom or galaxy.

It was the first time she had ever imagined such an outcome from an act of political defiance and she wondered what was happening to her. For half her life politics gave Bronwyn the key to what she confidently thought was the accurate view of herself in the world. What she had not faced until now was the tender and liable world within.

"I'm a Blue Meanie now."

Raj tried to make light of his situation. Clothed in blue prisoner overalls he sat across from Bronwyn in the visitor's room of Santa Rita jail.

"A Beatle Blue Meanie or a cop Blue Meanie?" Bronwyn asked.

"What's the difference?" asked Raj. "They're all bad. Just like me. I'm bad. So bad. Look at me now."

"Did they hurt you?" asked Bronwyn.

"They hurt all of us. One kid—they pushed his face against a pole on the fence around the yard and then hammered the pole with a club until his nose started to bleed."

Bronwyn had driven to Dublin to check on the status of her dear and arrested friend and to determine how she might help him.

"What did the attorney say?" asked Bronwyn.

"That I'm essentially fucked," answered Raj. "I'm stuck here because my arrest violated parole, even though I didn't do anything but walk downtown. I'm here at least until a hearing, which is maybe a couple weeks away. If I'm convicted, I'm looking at hard time based on my drug bust. No one knows how long but it could be more than a year."

"Will they make a deal?" asked Bronwyn.

"D.A. isn't in the mood, from what I understand. Reagan wants to set an example. Get tough. Fuck the protesters. Fuck the park."

Brownyn heard Raj's hollow grief.

"I was supposed to be gone. In Shasta with Sonia. I was going to say goodbye and not come back. My last day. I walked downtown like a denizen kissing his old town goodbye. Like, not very smart."

"You were going to move to Mt. Shasta?" Bronwyn asked.

"And never come back," answered Raj. "Sonia has friends at Black Bear Ranch. We were going to go up to help with harvest and repairs. Tough winter last year but they made it through. It's way back in the mountains. A commune on the site of an old miner's village. We'd live there. But not now, I guess."

"It's not over," said Bronwyn.

She heard Raj's alternative vision of his life and wondered if it weren't simply an embroidered illusion to pass his time in jail. The turns in Bronwyn's life left her to wonder if the sweetest and only assured vision was no vision at all.

"How can I help you?" she asked. "Can I bring you anything?"

"Just keep the lawyer working," Raj answered.

"Oh, and if you'd send a message to Sonia…"

Raj dictated a description of his predicament and asked Sonia to write to him. He would write more as events evolved.

"You can give her your address," said Raj. "Bring me anything she sends back."

"I will," said Bronwyn.

"And don't lose hope," she added.

"Hope? What's that?"

Raj flashed a cynical smile.

Bronwyn transcribed and mailed Raj's dictated letter to Sonia. She addressed it to a post office box in Mt. Shasta and for this reason Bronwyn assumed it would be more than a week before anything would come back from Sonia. So she was surprised when 70 hours later she answered a knock at the door to encounter a tall woman with long hair the color of dusk.

"Yes?" Bronwyn said coolly.

The woman's face was boyish and beautiful and also dirty. She had the smell of foul water though she appeared ingenuous and pure. She wore grease-stained jeans and a faded green sweatshirt and looked directly at Bronwyn through clear, piercing eyes. Her honey brown tan gave the look of a surfer girl who had migrated to the mountains. She set a rucksack down on the steps.

"I'm Sonia," the woman answered directly.

"Where's Raj?"

Bronwyn invited Sonia in and offered her food or tea, both of which she declined.

"Took all day," Sonia said about her trip south. "Got your letter yesterday and left last night."

Sonia had hitchhiked.

"Would have been here sooner but couldn't get out of Sacramento until this afternoon. Long wait for a ride I could trust."

How trust was created between a driver and a woman hitchhiker intrigued Bronwyn but she did not ask. Instead, she offered Sonia the sun porch.

"We can visit Raj tomorrow," said Bronwyn. "He'll want to see you."

"He was supposed to be in Shasta now," said Sonia. "We had a plan. What happened? How did he get busted?"

Sonia might have been a womanly version of Orpheus, descending into an underworld to rescue the other half of her perfected love.

"I'm here to take him back," she said.

Bronwyn grappled with her first impressions of Sonia. She was a woman of the wild drawn into the city like a doe to a garden. She might be at risk and need protection. Sonia conveyed a rough-edged innocence that was not entirely innocent and Bronwyn sensed a woman different from others and happy to be different and who had left the forest to experience this difference without it being reflected back to her in altering and denying ways.

"I hope I don't have to stay here long," said Sonia.

"You can stay with us as long as you like," Bronwyn said.

"I only have a little cash…"

Sonia let her confession melt away.

"Your money's no good here," said Bronwyn. "This is woman

helping woman."

Later, Bronwyn would prepare for Sonia a dinner of poached eggs and toast which she ate ravenously and washed down with a cup of Earl Grey tea before retiring to the sun porch. Sonia seemed grateful but still reserved, like a feral cat on the first night in its rescuer's home.

Bronwyn fell asleep assessing Sonia the beautiful and wild that, untamed and capable, was also unself-conscious and apparently ignorant of her face and body's classic features. Bronwyn saw why Raj loved her: a woman without the mask of a woman and who shared with Raj a broad, if not yet commonly defined, vision of freedom.

Bronwyn realized this was why Sonia did not send a letter. She sent herself. There would be no intermediary between them. All was direct and fiercely alive in an attraction held like electrons in some strong orbit of magnetic exchange.

"So it's a ranch?" asked Bronwyn as she drove Sonia to the Santa Rita jail.

"No. No cattle, if that's what you mean. It was a mining town way back when. It's a commune now. About twenty people. They had a rough first winter. My friend Nattie made it through and told us to come on up. We'd like to live in the woods all year and there's a lodge at Black Bear. Some are building cabins for next winter."

"And where is it again?" asked Bronwyn.

"Marble Mountain Wilderness. About eight miles over the Summit from Sawyer's Bar."

"Whose bar?" asked Bronwyn.

Sonia smiled.

"Never mind. It's way out there. A few hours west from Highway Five. The road in wasn't passable for a while last year. Freaked everyone out."

"And this year?"

"We'll take our chances," said Sonia. "It's free. Just like the mountain."

It was free. What anymore was free?

Raj wasn't free and as Bronwyn sat at the back of the visitor's hall at Santa Rita she watched Raj and Sonia talk and gesture excitedly as if there were no bars, no partitions, and no limit to their visit. Truly they were together in their own world and, whatever the circumstances, would not be interrupted.

Until they were. A guard finally ended the visit and while Raj was led back to his cell Sonia held her place until he vanished behind heavy metal doors.

"He doesn't think he's getting out soon," Sonia told Bronwyn on the ride back to Berkeley.

"I know the attorney who's working on it," said Bronwyn. "He's not discouraged. If charges are dismissed, they have to let him go. When's his hearing?"

"Last week in June," said Sonia.

"That's nearly a month. Listen, why don't you stay with us? I can drive you to see Raj."

Sonia turned toward Bronwyn. Her expression transmitted a message of detached, even suspicious, gratitude.

"You want something from me?" asked Sonia directly.

Bronwyn heard in Sonia's question the hint of a story, maybe a dozen stories, that informed the roots of a cautionary suspicion.

"No. Oh, no," answered Bronwyn. "You could help us with our protest against the pigs trying to take our park. You could do the dishes from time to time. But, no, I don't want anything. "

Sonia appeared unmoved so Bronwyn tried a different tack.

"If I came to you, and my lover was in jail and I needed to be near him while he fought the law, would you help me?"

Sonia did not answer.

Bronwyn walked with Sonia to Moe's Books to explain Raj's situation to his employer and asked if Raj could keep his job.

"Hell, I'll pay his goddamned bail. Is that the problem?" asked Moe.

"I wish it were," said Bronwyn and explained the complication created by Raj's previous arrest.

"Tell him, no problem," said Moe. "I've been busted. I've got his ass covered. It's cool."

Moe reached into a drawer below the register and pulled out a check.

"His pay for last week. He might need it."

He offered it to Bronwyn who told him to give it to Sonia.

"You his old lady?" asked Moe.

As he stared at Sonia, his eyes brightened.

Sonia, freshly scrubbed and shampooed, wore an olive Moroccan one-piece dress that fell lightly over the flexuous angles of her slender body.

"Why do men always look at a woman's tits first?" Sonia said later as they left the bookstore.

"Maybe because I don't wear a bra?"

"It wouldn't matter if you wore a bra," said Bronwyn.

"It makes me feel weird," said Sonia.

"I'm afraid Moe doesn't really care how you feel," Bronwyn added. "Does any man?"

"Raj does," said Sonia.

Sonia's words were not a rebuke.

To address the issue of Sonia's breasts Bronwyn first had to address the fact of Sonia's attractiveness and also the reality that Sonia was in love. For Bronwyn, who by her own assessment possessed neither attractiveness nor love, Sonia's capacity to draw a man's stare was both hateful and enviable. Hateful in the way it brought forward the leering stares that Bronwyn now thought the first inclinations toward a sexual assault. Enviable in the way it brought Sonia adoration and the luxury of choosing for herself one good man from the many that desired her.

The rape had estranged Bronwyn from her vision of a humanity of authentic caring and hope. As she recalled her loveless life she encountered first her twisted *modus amore* by which she chose her sexual partners. Wading into the deep weeds she would find a man as vulnerable as her and drink him under the table until, every resistance smothered but his irrepressible libido, she would take him home and fuck him.

Few called again and none became lovers, which forced Bronwyn to stare regularly and soberly in a mirror and to contemplate with dour disappointment her stringy hair, her shallow forehead and small chin, eyes too close together and a short neck set atop a stocky, barrel frame and small breasts, uneven in size and shape, their nipples sprouting from tiny tracks of wiry black fringe. She joked to herself at times that her calves were larger than her thighs and while this wasn't true, it was sometimes the effect when she tried to wear pantyhose with a short skirt.

"When we first look inside ourselves, we find a total shambles," said Pam.

"Our bodies are half-dead, our vulvas completely separated from our hearts and our hearts completely cut-off from our heads."

The women's group had agreed to meet twice a week and Bronwyn now took Tuesdays as well as Thursdays to attend. What Pam said aligned precisely with what Bronwyn thought. These moments of shared clarity, of descriptions by women of themselves that mirrored her own experience, were why Bronwyn continued to come.

"Seems to me that a man is like a creature cut off from both his mind and his body," said Carol.

By the third session Bronwyn knew everyone's name and they hers.

"I mean, why are we still interested in men? Why are some of us still attracted to them?"

Bronwyn recognized the woman speaking. She had been a leader of the Third World Studies strike at the state college.

"I'm sick and tired of our so-called brothers in the Movement," she said.

"They have co-opted our revolution and continue to stink of male supremacy."

The woman's anger caught Bronwyn's attention. She could not recall a single action or strike or protest or fight for freedom that had not been dominated by men. From Civil Rights to People's Park, men marched ahead of everyone, led the chants and cheers, threw the rocks and bottles, and negotiated all the outcomes. Yet why, and as a politically aware, even intelligent, woman, why had Bronwyn spent so much of her young career fighting for other people's liberation?

"None of this shit is invisible to a Latina woman," said Rita to

Bronwyn as they sat again in the Polk Street Bar. It was Bronwyn's turn to buy.

"My name is short for Clarita and from my Quinceañera on I was subjected to pressures to be a good girl. I am my father's only daughter and he was counting on me to produce a litter of grandchildren to carry his proud seed forward. I loved the birthday dress and for a year I tried. I really tried. Felt guilty when I had sex with Roberto while we were in high school. Now I don't care anymore. My father called me a cheap whore. And yet I'm the first of my family to graduate from college. They all know that means something big. Bigger than they want to admit."

Bronwyn heard in Rita's anger a dynamic binary larger than any one culture and well beyond the clash of dominance with subordination. Those subdued would always struggle against those who dominated. Those with power would work ceaselessly to hold it away from those who were bereft. What was ever possible in struggles for liberation when, for an eternity, the only choice was either to assert authority or to serve it? Bronwyn envisioned a world rid of gender that, while it might wipe away the historic dominance of men over women, would still not resolve a larger discontinuity, one she suspected to be older than all human suffering.

five

In shadows thrown by the battles on Telegraph, the guerilla annex park on Hearst Street north of the campus had become a small patch of green sod and a few clusters of contraband flowers. Planted at night by revolutionary gardeners, hundreds bloomed without notice under a week of warm suns.

It was the Thursday night before the Memorial Day protest and by dusk hundreds of park supporters had gathered at the Annex for a barbecue and party. As the crowd grew through the evening, the county sheriff, his hands shaking, announced at a press conference in Oakland that his deputies were again being issued guns and buckshot for Friday's march through Berkeley. There would be no backing down if marchers again attempted to take the park.

But if a curfew still existed, no one was enforcing it. The Berkeley faculty had voted overwhelmingly not to teach classes until the Guard left town. More than 14,000 students had voted in a referendum to support the People's Park. And several guardsmen still on duty had talked with protesters. A few no longer supported the police action. One guardsman stripped off his gasmask, threw down his gun and walked away. He made it a block before a commander intervened and held him for arrest.

All this Bronwyn followed attentively. The battle of People's Park would not be won in the streets, though she hoped a march would fill them to choking, would pave the roads with so many people the whole world would once again be watching.

The battle for the park was fought now on two fronts. The first and least important was the war declared by a governor who preferred a bloodbath to colloquy, who wished to spank an entire city and demonstrate his muscular capacity to burn the roots of a cultural and political resistance. The second and most important was, as Bronwyn knew from her years of activism, that all politics were local. Were the park issue to be acquired by the city, were the university to surrender the land, described formally on property maps as Lot 1875-2, and allow the city of Berkeley to acquire it, then a park would be built.

And who would ultimately own the park? As Michael and Frank had argued at the beginning, the park had been left a vacant pit and a doctrine of user's rights, one used by European explorers to claim all of North America from its original residents, allowed a claimant to take land if the claimant showed it would use the land more productively and more wisely than the prior owner. This was the core claim of colonialism and nothing more delighted the supporters of the park than the idea this Western rationale for barbarous conquest might be turned back against the conquerors.

Bronwyn arrived at the Annex after sunset. Sonia was with her because Bronwyn said she would not again go out at night alone. Bronwyn wandered among the young hippies and street people filling paper cups from a jug of Red Mountain. She saw the tall, muscular Yitzhak sharing a joint with his Telegraph brothers. She stood in front of a small bonfire at the center of the lot.

"I'm looking for march monitors," Bronwyn shouted at no one in particular.

"What's a fuckin' monitor?" yelled someone in the darkness.

"You keep the march moving. You give directions. You help people. You wear an armband and maybe carry a walkie-talkie. See?"

She pointed to Sonia who modeled an armband and held up a radio.

"We want to keep everyone safe. Who wants to help us?"

In fact, Bronwyn had all the help she needed. Hundreds had turned out for a monitor training the previous week. But it was Bronwyn's idea that those most likely to react violently along the march were those most alienated from its process. To enlist even a few of them as monitors, and to give them a job, was a preventive strategy.

"Sure," said Yitzhak. "We work for the people."

His loud assertion pulled others in who agreed to stand dutifully at designated intersections to direct Friday's marchers along a city-approved route that began from the Annex, climbed the modest incline of Hearst Street to Oxford and then moved along Oxford to enter the south campus and pass the Haste Street side of Lot 1875-2.

Marchers then would turn to cross the UC campus and descend Hearst back to the Annex where the march would end, assuming all went peacefully. It was a nearly four-mile route and Bronwyn hoped for peace but understood the terms of this war in the streets were still being established and nothing that might happen would surprise her. Though if fights and shooting broke out again, the battle would be lost. More martyrs would have no meaning to a resistance effectively and violently contained.

"How many are marching?" asked a wiry street hippie toking with Yitzhak.

"Maybe 15,000," shouted Bronwyn.

She thought it would be closer to 10,000.

"Cool," said the hippie. "I'll do it, sister."

Within a half-hour Bronwyn had a couple dozen monitors assigned to their posts along the route. While she passed out armbands more people arrived for what appeared to be the beginning of an all night party. It was the Telegraph street scene relocated to the scarred earth of the Annex, a patch of ruined ground bulldozed for the construction of rail transit and now propped into existence as an alternative park for the people.

Creation was a wonderful apparition and as Bronwyn arrived at the Annex on Friday morning she was surprised to see thousands already gathered for the march on People's Park. She enjoyed a flash of elation for she had as much as anyone authored this gathering, organized its constituencies and put into place the enforceable terms of a peaceful protest. She had fought for an end to the rough talk of some of her male colleagues who wanted revenge against the pigs and a fight to the death, which most likely would have been their own.

By mid-morning on Friday the crowd of marchers had swelled to fill several blocks of Hearst Street.

"Twenty-five thousand easy," said Mack.

"How do you get that number?" asked Bronwyn.

"Pick a block, count those in the crowd, then calculate from there," answered Mack.

"I bet I'm right."

"Who will ever know?" asked Bronwyn.

"It's not what anyone knows," said Mack. "It's what they believe."

After preliminary remarks by park advocates from a makeshift stage and a blessing from Berkeley Free Church pastor Rev. Richard York, the march began a lumbering trudge east along Hearst. An hour passed as the vanguard reached the western edge of the university. Thousands still waited at the park Annex to begin the two-mile trek to the fenced People's Park site south of the campus. Those that marched noticed immediately that all side streets were blocked by concertina wire and rifle-toting guardsmen while Sheriff's deputies and local cops straddled rooftops and pointed guns and cameras at the marchers.

"It's beautiful," said Harriet to Bronwyn as they hitched a ride on a truck loaded with protesters waving signs and banners.

"Yes, I suppose it is," said Bronwyn. "But will it get us the park?"

"The park is big news," said Harriet. "My dad went to a faculty senate meeting for the first time in five years just to vote for a strike. That's pretty far out."

"But will it get us the park?" Bronwyn asked again.

As the first marchers reached their destination, they pushed against the park fence's steel mesh while guardsmen stood behind it in formation. At the annex Quakers had distributed thousands of daisies to marchers who along the route had given them to guardsmen or tucked them into the helmets of patrolling cops. Now a flurry of daisies poured over the park fence. Several women danced topless, shaking their breasts at the amused soldiers. A small truck arrived and dropped rolls of sod on the pavement that were quickly unrolled and spread like a carpet across Haste Street.

Hours passed as the thousands marching arrived at the park and strolled past while shouting and raising their clenched fists. At Telegraph they made a slow turn to walk the final leg of their route that would lead them across campus and back down Hearst. They would disperse at the Annex after snaking through Berkeley streets as if in a Ghost Dance of defeated acceptance. Many would leave the march well before its conclusion.

Bronwyn returned to the Annex in the late afternoon to find another party in progress, this one louder and wilder than the previous evening. As a rock group blasted its music from an improvised stage a blonde woman wearing only a pair of shorts writhed wildly in front. People cheered and, again, Bronwyn watched the emergence of gallon jugs of wine while a crowd of returning marchers huddled to light and share joints. Several people stripped off their clothes and as another hot evening turned to dusk, they danced madly to the sybaritic whoops of those assembled around the stage.

Once any threshold of violence was crossed, violence controlled the outcome. And in this case the supporters of a park, defeated in battle, had only what was permitted: a large and noisy parade watched over by an army of soldiers and cops dressed and ready to kill.

"I think sometimes that the Movement has hit a wall," Bronwyn said later when she saw Mack arrive at the Annex.

"It's something more than that," said Mack. "It's easy to make demands. It's much harder to gain compliance, especially when you've already lost the war. You know what the Panthers say: that power emerges from the barrel of a gun. Well, if that's the case, then more power emerges from more guns."

"At least no one was hurt," said Bronwyn. "We had a lot of children out there today."

"That's probably why," said Mack. "No one, not even a cop, wants trouble with children."

"You wanna get a drink?" she asked Mack.

She heard herself clearly, heard the words that in a previous time she would have used to launch one of her subversive seductions. She thought the words exposed her, that Mack might guess instantly her characteristic plan to take him home. Though it wasn't what she wanted, wasn't what she intended at all. She waited for his rebuke.

"Sure," said Mack. "This place is starting to look like the Avenue after midnight. Let's get outta here."

Mack knew a dive bar on University where he met frequently with reporters from other papers. Brownyn climbed into the passenger seat of a pea green pre-1960 Volkswagen sedan. Mack started the engine, which sputtered and belched until a reliable rumble set in and Mack put the car in gear.

"It's old, but it's a bug," said Mack. "They never die."

"You still fighting for justice?" asked Mack.

Bronwyn shrugged.

They had taken a small table against a wall of velvet paintings, one featuring Elvis with Jesus and another showing a card table at which dogs of various breeds played poker.

"Oh, yeah," she answered. "Justice. Precious little of that around here. How about martial law? We're fighting martial law. Pretty weird that we have to do that now."

"And you aren't even fighting," said Mack. "That was not a fight today. It was Berkeley's Memorial Day parade. Tell me, is there anyone who hasn't been arrested yet?"

"I haven't," said Bronwyn. "But Raj is in a jam. Have you seen him?"

Mack had visited Raj twice at Santa Rita and wanted to do a story about him. But Raj vetoed it.

"He's worried he'll have to do hard time," answered Mack.

"He's promised that if he gets out of jail, even for a minute, he's going somewhere no one will find him."

Bronwyn told Mack about Sonia.

"She's young and pretty. She doesn't say much but she's a great guest. Keeps the house clean and does our dishes. She sees Raj every day. They visit and talk. They have plans to live on a commune way up north."

"And you?" asked Mack. "Are you still up for the fight after all this warfare?"

A second drink arrived while Bronwyn weighed whether to tell Mack about her rape.

"I'm into women's issues now," said Bronwyn. "I'm in a women's group in the city."

"What goes on there?" asked Mack.

"It's politics but with a different focus. It's about power and inequity and how they affect women."

"Do you mean like sex?" said Mack. "Do the women have a problem with men?"

"How about rape?" responded Brownyn, suppressing an angry urge to shout.

"How about women as victims of violence, as sexual objects, as underpaid workers, as a social class confined by society to the constraints of patriarchal control?"

"You sound like a Marxist," said Mack. "Only it's women who are getting fucked and not just the proletariat. Is that what you're saying?"

"Women aren't the proletariat," answered Bronwyn emphatically. "Most of their work–raising children, caring for the family, and cleaning house–pays nothing and when they do work outside the home, no union will have them."

"You're pissed, girl," answered Mack.

"Don't call me girl," said Bronwyn.

Mack retreated. He drew inward to register, not just the words he had heard but also the deep hostility they bore. Accustomed to Bronwyn's thoughtful arguments for progressive outcomes, even revolution, he was ambushed by her personal passion for what seemed to him an amorphous pool of womanly complaints. Where did they start? Where did they end? He was afraid to ask.

"You have something I can read?" asked Mack.

"I'll find something," said Bronwyn.

There followed a moment of dry silence.

"And you?" Bronwyn asked.

"I'm cool," said Mack. "This park business is killing me, though. Why can't they build a fucking park? My editor at the paper knows my sympathies but he keeps me on because I'm the only hip contact he has, the only one who can talk candidly with you guys, the organizers and the activists. I know he's stretching the union contract to keep me on part-time. And I have to work or I'll get drafted. Hell, I might get drafted, anyway."

"You…drafted?" asked Bronwyn.

"Yeah," said Mack. "It's something you oppressed women don't have to worry about."

He couldn't help himself.

"If women had their way, there would be no more war," said Bronwyn.

"I can't wait for that but right now it's the draft that's a problem," said Mack, attempting recovery.

"Last year the whole world was watching. This year the whole world is fighting. They're even fighting at Harvard… and there's a man with a gun over there…"

Bronwyn laughed at the song reference.

"Give me a ride home," she said. "There's a memorial for Rector tomorrow in Tilden."

"There are four kinds of men," said Rita at the next meeting of the women's group.

"Husbands, Fools, Beaus and Brothers."

In was a peculiar taxonomy, one she had drawn from a collection of feminist essays entitled *No More Fun and Games* and published by a women's collective in Cambridge, Massachusetts. Rita said husbands were keepers of appearances, the righteous men whose anger projected onto a woman an internal and eternal blame. Work was a husband's love and he was punctual. Love and sex were subordinate to his work and he was as insensitive as he was uncomfortable. In arguments it was, tirelessly, his way or the highway.

Fools were attractive because they were emotional. Though their emotions were a construct or a trick that concealed jealousies and insecurities. And these could not be seen until a woman had the courage to pull back the curtain, at which time the Fool's real goals were revealed: to slip luckily into power, to escape a bad debt, to gain reassurance from a woman's failure. They would readily go down on a woman but pushed against the wall, an exposed Fool could call his lover a cunt.

Beaus made more than half an effort because they wanted desperately to be liked, even as they struggled to like themselves. They argued rationally but without conviction because they didn't care about winning. They claimed to admire honesty. But didn't care if they were honest. Loyalty was negotiable but that went two ways. If a woman cheated on a beau, the beau usually was more curious than disappointed.

Brothers weren't perfect but they were usually passionate and present. Their touch was authentic and their sex directed toward orgasms, separate or simultaneous. They were receptive and existential and wished to learn. They were reliable and not afraid of intimate exposure of themselves or others. In the throes of an argument their worst insult might be to call a woman "unkind."

"It's not that any man has to be any one thing," said Rita. "A man could be a brother with us in life and in bed, channel the beau with his friends, play the fool at work, and act the husband to fight with an enemy."

"And rapists?" asked an angry voice at the back of the room. "Where are rapists on your chart?"

Bronwyn turned to see who was asking.

"They're off the chart, sister," shouted Rita. "Some men exist for any number of twisted reasons to hurt us. We won't let them. Ever. See this?"

Rita pulled a yellow handled object from her pocket and pressed a button to release a shiny, serrated blade.

"I'm ready, sisters," she shouted. "You get ready. We aren't helpless bitches. You hear me?"

As Bronwyn listened to this exchange, she thought both of her rapist and also the feckless strategies that for years she employed to have sex with men. The two experiences were married in some weird and unspeakable way. She could not have the memories of one without the blending memories of the other.

She tried to sort the sex she sought from the sex that was forced on her until her own life appeared to her as a both magical and monstrous apparition. She was held like a fly in a web between essence and irrelevance. She was a woman on a shifting verge and where she would fall could not be known.

six

"You're pregnant," said the physician at the clinic. Bronwyn had missed her period, which at first wasn't unusual until the varying days of her cycle's arrival turned into a week and then nearly two. A test was scheduled but only to confirm the obvious. Sore, darkening nipples, surges of morning nausea, and tears—so many useless and unexplained tears. She could not concentrate. She was dizzy with an unwanted potential that, quietly alive within her, still demanded her thorough and perpetual attention.

When she thought of this affliction as a baby, as a life in the making, she felt herself as her rapist's vessel. It was another of his terrible and lasting inflictions on her, as if she were the repository of all his hate and also his hope: that his seed would through Bronwyn assure his immortality and also hers.

And what was she now to do?

Reject this roll, of course, and kill a baby.

"It's not a baby," she said to herself.

"No. No. No. Not a baby."

And how?

Abortion was illegal. She would face great risk and threat to reclaim her own life from the life of the fetus within her, the life that threatened to take hers away. And it was the fetus within. It was not her fetus. She said that over and over through her first wakeful night of sleepless and somber reckoning.

487

And then she weighed its life against its imminent death, seeking refuge in a rational brightness that would illuminate the good reasons for her decision, that might help her to view it clearly as anything but the taking of a life. Should a fetus die simply because it was not the life Bronwyn might choose to birth or to raise?

She imagined the baby's color, its hair, its eyes. She visualized its infancy, its childhood, its adolescence. She imagined herself an old woman attended by a middle-aged man to whom she had given birth. Or a woman. Or a daughter. This was worse.

She detested these thoughts even as she indulged all their richly mortifying suggestions. In the end, and usually every morning at some time just before dawn, she arrived at the same conclusion. The life inside her was unwelcome while her own was still unanchored. It had—as an agent of her rapist—invaded her without permission and with no purpose other than to threaten her freedom.

"How far along?" asked Rita.

"Maybe seven weeks," said Bronwyn.

"Pushing two months," said Rita.

"We need to move. You want to end the pregnancy?"

"Yes," said Bronwyn. "Of course."

"Really? You sure?"

"Yes, god dammit, Yes!" shouted Bronwyn.

"OK. OK." said Rita.

"Just want to be sure. Once it's gone, it's gone."

"Can you help me?" asked Bronwyn.

"Help you?" said Rita. "Sister, I've got you covered. Can you come up with $150?"

"Yes, of course," said Bronwyn.

"This time next week you're flying to El Paso and crossing at the border into Juarez. The money covers your plane ticket and a visit to the clinic of a very good Mexican doctor. And I'm going with you."

Rita had done this before. For herself and for others. And the doctor, a mild mannered Mexican gynecologist named Davalos, had a clinic in Juarez that provided a needed service for women: a procedure known as dilation and curettage by which a woman's cervix was opened to allow a gentle scraping of the uterine walls, medically to remove unwanted tissue deposits but more generally to remove an implanted fetus in the early stages of pregnancy. His service was legal, but its use as an abortion illegal in both Mexico and the United States.

"We'll fly to El Paso," said Rita. "Cross the border into Juarez. Bring your driver's license. We'll spend a night and fly back the next day."

"You make it sound so easy," said Bronwyn as she tried to sort regret from her feelings of relief.

"It should be easy," said Rita. "It should always be easy. When can you leave?"

The rest was waiting. Bronwyn waited for her abortion but Harriet also waited. Within weeks she would learn her fall Peace Corps assignment and that of her boyfriend Michael. And Sonia waited impatiently for Raj's release from jail. The waiting women shared a household though Bronwyn's wait was a secret she told no one but Rita. Rita was a sister and, as yet, Harriet and Sonia were not sisters. Sisters were new women making history, women publically committed to revealing that the invisibility of women was an optical illusion.

Waiting was one of the old ways. Bronwyn thought herself Athena, the goddess of the embracing mind. Harriet was Aphrodite, the goddess of the embrace. And Sonia was Artemis, the defiant wood nymph bathing at a stream. All waited for the next breath of their lives and what new air they each might breathe. All waited first for the beginning of journeys that would take each of them away while Bronwyn likely would be the only one to return.

"It's Africa," said Harriet. "Michael and I applied together though there is no guarantee we'll be treated as a team. We aren't married. I don't have to take it."

"Why wouldn't you?" asked Bronwyn.

"Scared, I guess. I haven't traveled much. My dad and mom are adamantly opposed. And it's two years or bust. And it's Africa, either Uganda or Swaziland. But another semester of Dante will kill me."

Harriet paused to hold herself together. Otherwise she might cry.

"And you'll get the flat," Harriet told Bronwyn. "The owners like continuity and you're perfect."

Harriet planned to introduce Bronwyn to them the following week. Bronwyn waited to tell Harriet she had made other plans. She would be gone for a few days visiting friends.

"This has been my long, tired and uncomfortable home for too many years," Harriet said. "I have to leave."

Sonia also had to leave. But she would not leave without Raj. She had little need for a city that would fight a war over an open space the size of a small campground on the slopes of Mt. Shasta. She also had no need of money, accustomed as she was to trading work for services and time for goods. And the city was a money hole. She constantly needed it here.

Bronwyn arranged to get Sonia cash for her help with the march. Forty dollars. And Bronwyn shared her meals and arranged with Harriet for Sonia's free lodging while she waited for Raj. But even as she accepted it, money was one of Sonia's unwelcome considerations. People here lived in the streets and survived on the usually coerced kindness of strangers. People in the mountains lived in the woods and simply survived.

With time on her hands, Sonia found Telegraph Avenue where the street scene, which she had neither the interest nor capacity to judge, enveloped her. She had met Yitzhak during a visit with Raj and he welcomed Sonia to the enlarged patch of sidewalk outside Cody's Books where a clan of street pals and gals congregated regularly to smoke and panhandle. Many arrived daily before noon and within an hour most were high on something. Yitzhak became Sonia's escort through the street kingdom west of the fenced-off park.

Sonia avoided drugs but not the people who used them and who reminded her of Shasta hippies at home on their mountain. And though these people were more like grifters than hippies, their craziness was not foreign to Sonia who had consorted with mountain people convinced that aliens lived inside Mt. Shasta and who emerged from time to time to take the form of humans so as to speak their profound truths.

Acid flashes and speed-fueled raps did not surprise her and Yitzhak stayed close, silent and protective as she sat among the street's salty earthlings and occasionally hustled for spare change. As crazy as they were, these were the outlaws Sonia identified as closest to her in their spirit of freedom, if not their experience of it.

One evening Bronwyn returned home to find Sonia entertaining Yitzhak and a woman Bronwyn previously had seen hustling on Telegraph. The three sat together at the living room's bay windows. Surprised, Bronwyn at first said nothing before choking out a wobbly "hello."

Bronwyn knew Yitzhak and had her own concerns about his seemingly loosened mind and tripped-out existence. He was big and strong and hugged the sofa like a fixture. The woman, who appeared no older than 17, rambled wildly as if she were thoroughly stoned on speed.

"Smoking in the park and I got busted. Can you believe that? And I was thirteen. I tell you the pigs out here got nothin' on the pigs in Missouri. And I was such a bitch then. The worst little bitch. My daddy held me up to my sisters and said 'Don't you ever turn out like this goddamned cunt. She's such a fucking cunt. She's not even my daughter. Your mother fucked someone else to have her. That's gotta be it.' And then he came after me which is why I ran away and met Don at the bus station and we got to Denver. Hip dudes in Denver, and lots of good dope. Man, I got so high and then we decided to come West—warm, fucking warm California. And look, motherfuckers, here we are! And the living is easy, we're…"

"What's your name?" Bronwyn interrupted.

The woman stared sharply at Bronwyn, her eyes narrowing to slender slits.

"Who wants to know? You a cop?"

Bronwyn froze as several dead seconds passed.

"Ha! Gotcha!" said the woman.

"I'm Joanie."

Bronwyn sat down in a chair opposite the windows. Sonia looked at Bronwyn, yielding and acquiescent as she might appear to a returning parent. Yitzhak was impervious and said nothing.

"Missouri? Were you born there?" Bronwyn asked Joanie.

"Hell if I know. No one has ever told me where I was born. I'm a bastard. A bitch and a bastard…How about that?...my mother, God that fucking asshole, my mother…"

Joanie began another of her high-speed monologues. It was apparent to Bronwyn and Sonia and, likely, even Yitzhak that Joanie was spinning wildly out of her orbit, that she was in a true and unauthorized trance, her words arriving in streams poured from a fractious state of mind.

"He was getting into junk…you know I smoke dope and get into some heavy downers…always looking for a place to crash…with a dude I can usually panhandle and score some acid…I'm happy? Hell no, unless I'm high and then I'm on…everything is just so far out…and this fucking park and your pigs…well, I'd rather fuck up here where my daddy won't ever find out…Unless I get busted but I'm pretty careful about that now…"

Joanie's incessant motion moved passing time closer to the home's informal dinner hour. For a week Harriet, Bronwyn and Sonia had shared one common meal, making from it a surprisingly private and guarded ritual that kept them all connected and informed, even if Sonia at times had little to say. Bronwyn wondered resentfully if it were Sonia's intention to invite Yitzhak and Joanie to dinner?

Bronwyn looked closely into Joanie's face to see the lines and scars of her warped and incomprehensible suffering: a 17-year-old woman possessed by too many embracing demons. Joanie was short, perhaps crucially undernourished, with one entrancing feature: her brilliant green eyes that shimmered with a fierce and angry energy.

The door opened below and Harriet bounded up the stairs into the flat and entered the living room.

"Oh…" Harriet said, before walking quickly to the back of the flat.

Joanie, who had not stopped talking, continued with a story impossible to follow.

"I got a lot of head hassles, and I'm not really happy…got a lot of problems with dope, you know…and it's not my fault…."

Harriet returned to the living room and asked Bronwyn to join her in the kitchen.

"What are they doing here?" Harriet demanded.

"I don't know," said Bronwyn. "They were here when I came home. Sonia must have…"

"I want them gone…out. Now."

Harriet's voice surged with a ferocity Bronwyn had never before heard.

"But I think Sonia…"

"Fuck Sonia," Harriet sneered.

"I want that guy out of here and that woman—is she a druggie?

"Damn, Harriet. Why are you freaking out?"

Harriet paused and paced the kitchen nervously.

"Long story. Not now. Just get them out. This is my flat. Get them out."

Harriet left the kitchen, walked into her room and closed the door.

Bronwyn had never heard Harriet declare her territorial imperative or make such an urgent demand. She returned to the living room.

Joanie rolled on, her voice rising into her higher registers as a kind of panic set in and she spoke almost without breathing, as if to stop would end her presence in the world.

"It's our dinner time…" Bronwyn said.

"Cool," said Joanie. "What are we having?"

Bronwyn looked toward Sonia who appeared to look helplessly back. Joanie's words were a trick, a well-honed attempt at survival. Bronwyn opened her mouth irritably and jumped out into the world.

"I don't know what you're having," said Bronwyn. "Yitzhak, you and Joanie need to leave."

"You kicking us out?" screamed Joanie. "You kicking out the people? We're the people, you snotty fuckin' bitch. We're the real deal…"

Joanie began a monologue without restraint. Every psychosis brought with her from the Midwest was sprayed around the living room like the pee of a fiercely angry and territorial cat. Joanie expected this. Everyone treats her like shit. Privileged fucks never give her a chance.

"You are all just rich motherfuckers. You don't know what it's like…what…"

Yitzhak at last stood up and positioned himself between Joanie and Bronwyn.

"Why can't they stay?" Sonia at last spoke up, responsive to Joanie's framing of herself as "the people. "

"I'll share my food…" Sonia began.

Bronwyn shook her head, knowing that Sonia's food was actually Bronwyn's and Harriet's food and that while it was sometimes given without reservation, it was not free. It was not a right. And time with Yitzhak and Joanie was something Harriet surely did not desire.

And so this is who we are? thought Bronwyn. Harriet is the rich bitch, the daughter of privilege who can afford to leverage all her needs. And I am the political advocate with such a broad and comprehensive view of the struggles of an underclass but also unwilling to share, to open a space in my private life for an intimate link with people who appear either catatonic or crazy no matter their states of need. And who am I that I'm so deserving of security and comfort? A woman sloppily impregnated by a rapist, an activist that has lost her confidence, who am I to tell anyone what to do?

Yet here she was speaking directly to Yitzhak at Harriet's behest, as if Harriet by virtue of her gift of housing was Bronwyn's boss and able to order her to expel Yitzhak's comatose ass and that of his psychotic lady friend out of Harriet's house. Joanie was a woman. Women were sisters and Bronwyn was throwing out a sister? Though it was obvious Joanie had no idea she was a sister.

Climbing down the stairs behind the screaming Joanie, Bronwyn grabbed her hand and pulled it close. She reached into her pocket and extracted a five-dollar bill and pushed it into Joanie's palm.

"Get dinner at Robbie's," she said calmly. "My treat."

Joanie looked at the bill and again at Bronwyn who saw the young woman's psychosis briefly revealed as something separate from Joanie. Joanie's eyes opened as they might have when, as a child, she was given something wonderful and unconditional. It was a view of love long lost and then, as Joanie's eyes narrowed again, Brownyn saw the return of the grifter obsessed with the bird in her hand, quickly cooperative and agreeable to leaving without further trouble, to take the small thing she could get that never in her life would substitute for a persistent, painful and ravenous need.

After the departure of Yitzhak and Joanie, the house became an abode of cooling, quiet and separated women. Sonia disappeared onto her sun porch. Bronwyn went into the kitchen to open a can of beans and steam some rice. Harriet remained in her room. Hunger, which had been a new and welcome friend for many months, had suddenly abandoned her.

Bronwyn waited through a lonely meal, at one point knocking on the sun porch door but getting no response from Sonia whose actions spoke more than what few words she could ever say. In this instance, Bronwyn could not extinguish the feeling that an injustice had occurred though what expectations were involved and whose rights were violated? It no longer worked to assess the most needy as the most deserving. Needs alone justified nothing.

seven

Bronwyn tried to think calmly of all her friends and some of her enemies. She did not yet know where to place Sonia, only that sometime during the night she grabbed her rucksack and ran. Morning knocks at the sun porch door produced no response, until Bronwyn at last entered to find the room empty, the bed haphazardly made and the window blinds half-drawn. There was no note, as if one were needed. She would have to accept Sonia's lurching, secret departure.

"It appears our guest has left," Bronwyn said to Harriet who had slipped silently into the kitchen.

Harriet shrugged her shoulders.

"Don't you have anything to say?" Bronwyn asked.

"What would I say?" Harriet asked coyly.

"That maybe you're sorry," said Bronwyn.

"Sorry for what?" asked Harriet.

"For chasing her off, Harriet. God Damn, don't you have any feelings about what happened? You threw her friends out of the house."

"No, you did," Harriet countered.

This was too much for Bronwyn who drew inward to assess the flashing chimes of anger ringing in her ears. She had experience with anger, had needed constantly as an activist to manage her response to both her own feelings of outrage and to those others outside her who inspired it. In this instance, the outrage was intimate though no less a fire of perceived injustice.

"I did what you asked," Bronwyn said. "Now I wish I hadn't."

"Why do you care?" Harriet asked again, attempting to sound ingenuous, as if some obvious truth were at hand that Bronwyn would not accept.

"Anyway, they're street people. Avenue druggies. I don't want them here. Nothing but trouble."

Bronwyn heard the sonorous dismissal of privilege. Harriet, the scion of wealthy ideas, had no use for an underclass. And it seemed odd coming from someone who was joining the Peace Corps, who thought she might travel halfway around the world to live in service to the poorest of the earth.

The contradiction intrigued Bronwyn who used the paradox to free herself from her anger knowing any expression of her own anger would do nothing to change Harriet's point of view. Harriet was either utterly malicious, in which case nothing would ever be gained from engaging her, or she was in error, which meant her seeming disdain for suffering might be transient and passing.

"You sound angry with Sonia," Bronwyn said calmly. "Is there something about Yitzhak and that woman—Joanie—that's...well... really the problem?"

Bronwyn's query was met with silence, though Harriet's clinched fists loosened and she ceased banging cups and bowls on the counter, stopped all her furious, clamoring breakfast preparations to sit wearily at the table.

"It's a long story," said Harriet. "I can't talk about it, other than to say I have a past with Yitzhak and I hated to see him. It's painful to remember."

Bronwyn had no more questions. Invariably when she confronted anger with patience, Bronwyn uncovered another's pain. It was a lesson learned well in the trenches of the revolution where every step forward could induce fierce and angry resistance.

June days arrived indecisively, the first week's early mornings shrouded in cool fog. The smell of teargas was gone as were the soldiers. A fence still surrounded the park and Bronwyn saw Sonia nearby, hanging close to Yitzhak and his accruing band of street folks. Bronwyn saw her but did not attract her attention.

Bronwyn had been thankful for Sonia and her crazy life and for a distraction from herself and her own body, bursting with aches and nausea and an illimitable flood of hormones and anxiety. Were she a woman who wished to be a mother…though she never completed the thought because she wasn't and didn't. Why would she ever wish to nurture a repugnant fertilization? She had never before thought of a human life as a parasite and still could not fully accept that her impregnated uterus carried a flourishing implant that she, the unwilling and repulsed host, wished destroyed.

And yet there was more to consider, more which involved the weighing of life and death. She took comfort from the thought that death was by far the more common and lasting condition and life something temporary and exceedingly brief. This life inside her, if she dared to think of it as a life, would not be known and therefore not be missed.

Bronwyn was surprised to walk into Moe's and see Raj behind the register.

"What are you doing here?"

"What does it look like?" Raj answered. "I'm working. Surprised?"

"Yeah, I mean…you know…the jail…"

Bronwyn had no coherent words.

Raj gave the register to another employee and took Bronwyn aside.

"My attorney made bail. Moe fronted $40 for a bond. My hearing is in two weeks. I've been out since Monday."

"Listen, about Sonia…"

Bronwyn opened her mouth only to realize how much and also how little there was to say.

"She's fine," said Raj. "She's staying with me now. I would have thrown her the key to my flat but the jail had all my clothes and shit.

I'm glad you gave her a place to stay. She tells me some heavy stuff went down at the end. But tell me, did you really throw her out?"

"No, of course not," answered Bronwyn. "She left."

"She wasn't welcome?" asked Raj.

Bronwyn embraced the many shadows that now shaped a proliferation of infinite realities.

"Everyone believes what they want to believe," Bronwyn answered. "I don't know what Sonia believes because she never spoke to me. But she left. That's true."

Raj stepped back as if to ruminate on Bronwyn's answer while she wondered what Sonia had actually told him. Was there a truth? There were more versions of the truth than there were galaxies and which version prevailed depended entirely on what or who was attached to it.

"I won't lie to you," Bronwyn said again. "Harriet wasn't expecting guests and Sonia invited her friends over for dinner. It could have been handled better. But I was sorry to find her gone in the morning. I really hoped we could have talked about it."

"Yeah…." Raj answered vaguely.

Having just escaped jail he appeared reluctant to enter into another conflict.

"Anyway, we're leaving," he said. "Going to Shasta. Got a lead on a commune where we'd be welcome."

"Black Bear?" asked Bronwyn.

"You know," said Raj.

Raj said he would wait through the hearing because his attorney assured him he would either be freed outright or given credit for time served.

"And once that happens, we're gone," he said again. "Real gone."

Bronwyn left Moe's and considered what was not said, all the values that went undeclared or unchallenged and how those values imprisoned people and forced them to create unspoken stereotypes that fixed all their lasting impressions. She thought this a kind of personal mystification and that it was a characteristic of capitalism's tightly engineered labyrinth of fear and suspicion. How was her anger related to revolutionary struggle? Where was her pain in relation to poverty?

"I can't say what I would do without Rita," Bronwyn told the assembled women in yet another City woman's flat, this one off Fillmore near the park.

Four more women had joined, forcing the women's group into a living room for what Pat called "C-R," letters that stood in for the words *consciousness raising.*

"We be sisters!" Rita shouted to a mild teeter of laughter from the women, though most were quiet. Bronwyn's abortion was serious business and every woman in the room understood this.

"I've never felt so relieved," said Bronwyn. "I've never felt so guilty."

And was she a sister? Bronwyn wondered for a moment what distinguished a sister from just another woman. C-R obviously had something to do with it. A test was that she could tell Rita about her pregnancy. She could tell the women in the group. And she could not tell Harriet.

"And yes, Rita, we need more sisters," Bronwyn added to a subdued cheer from the group.

Bronwyn described her fear, her loneliness, the false and real alarms of the first and second weeks after missing her period and the guilt, humiliation, shame and ridicule she inflicted on herself.

"And I'm denied the right to rid my own body of an invader, even as I still struggle with the fact that invader is also part me: my genes, my flesh, my eyes, my mind, perhaps even a woman—a sister."

It was too much and Bronwyn collapsed into a reckless, angry sob.

"And I'm running out of time. There is no more time."

Again, the women of the group gathered around her, touched her shoulders and arms and hair, let her lean into them as she shook uncontrollably.

"It's the honesty," Rita said later as she and Bronwyn again shared drinks on Polk Street.

"You can tell the truth to these women and they hear it. We all want the truth. If we want any real change, we'll have to start with the truth. And it sure ain't pretty. Feels sometimes that women are the last to understand all the bad shit that has been done to us. And that's because we let ourselves get isolated, get cut off from what is happening and what each of us is thinking and feeling about it. Who else before tonight did you tell about your pregnancy?"

"Just you," said Bronwyn. "Because I knew you wouldn't judge me."

Before leaving the meeting, Pat had asked Bronwyn if she would write up her experience for an article in the group's newsletter.

"It would be a big help for other women," said Rita. "Not a lot of new literature out there. Unless you count Valerie Solanas and her *SCUM Manifesto*, and I don't."

"Didn't she shoot…the artist?" asked Bronwyn.

"Warhol. We have our issues with men but I don't want to kill them."

"Well, not all of them," said Bronwyn.

The problem of being a woman was for Bronwyn becoming a problem of language. She had grown up with messages of how to be a "natural" woman defined by breasts and periods and some culturally enforced forms of appearance and sexual attraction that offered only optional roles as a temptress, wife or matron.

It made no sense, however, when she looked in the mirror to see how unlike any temptress she appeared, or to grasp how much more interested she was in history and politics than make-up or homecoming. It wasn't until leaving high school that Bronwyn understood that the term "natural" woman referred to some kind of inherent female sexuality that was perceived by the society—and the men who ran it—as something both delicious and dangerous in ways that required intimidating management and control.

But women were going mad under the control of men; women's sexuality and its natural expression managed through the physical and financial power they held over a naturally "weaker" sex. For years, Bronwyn huddled shamefully in shadows so as to hide her lack of presumed physical beauty until a man was drunk enough or horny enough to engage with her own assertive desires. What was "natural" was a muddle and for Bronwyn in her new state of fertile terror, the term was categorically useless. She was not society's version of natural. She was her own unique kind of natural.

Rita phoned Bronwyn and gave her the itinerary for their trip to Juarez. They would leave on a Wednesday, which meant Bronwyn would miss an important park strategy session days before a meeting of the university regents in Berkeley. She would return with Rita on Thursday too late for Bronwyn to do anything but go back to Harriet's flat and rest quietly through the weekend.

"And remember. No food after midnight," said Rita.

At the next C-R session, the group was joined by a woman from New York associated with the *Redstockings*, a group of radical feminists who had organized demonstrations and protests for women's liberation.

She spoke about the history of the women's movement.

"I remind you that the same media that rationalize the war in Vietnam will distort our history as women. We demand a new form of history, one tailored to the lives we actually live as women."

Bronwyn got the speakers phone number and the mailing address of the Redstockings.

"Bring pajamas," Rita said to Bronwyn after the meeting. "And a dozen pads. The doctor will give you some but you can't have too many."

Mack met Bronwyn at the Forum, opened again after the park riots. He wanted news, of course. Was the park committee seeking to negotiate with the regents or was the plan to push the city council into buying the park's fenced lot from the regents?

"No chance of that," Bronwyn confessed. "Not now anyway. Not after our long march last month. No one wants another fight in the streets. I think the revolution has hit a wall or, rather, a fence. Most park activity has moved to the annex and it's staying peaceful which will keep the cops from fencing it off."

It was land the university did not own so Bronwyn thought there was a chance to keep it open.

"I have something for you," said Bronwyn as she handed Mack her edition of *No More Fun and Games*.

Mack thumbed through it.

"More than a hundred pages and mimeographed…that takes dedication. And it's pretty dog-eared. Been read a lot. What is it?"

he asked.

"History," answered Bronwyn.

"The beginning of it anyway. A women's history," she said. "Promise me you'll read it."

"As much as I can," said Mack. "That's a small type face… someone sat for hours at a typewriter, that's obvious."

"It's all we have right now," said Bronwyn.

"We…" asked Mack. "You speak for women now?"

"I am one. Why not?" answered Bronwyn.

"Women's Lib, right?" said Mack. "Like burn your bras?"

"Come on, Mack," shouted Bronwyn. "Don't. I'm asking you to do some critical thinking. OK?"

"Yeah, OK," said Mack. "Want to see a movie?"

Mack was planning to walk down Haste to the Cinema Guild on Shattuck to see a screening of Bergman's *Persona*.

Bronwyn declined. She had bought the Who's *Tommy* album and wanted to walk home to listen to it.

"You know Raj is getting ready to go back to Shasta," said Mack. "And Larry–there's a going away party in a few weeks for him and Sylvia. They're moving to Chicago to work for Freddie Hampton's Panthers."

"Breaking up that old gang of ours," said Bronwyn. "There goes the revolution."

Mack laughed.

"It's a great film," he said. "You sure?"

Bronwyn smiled. Mack was just a friend but it flattered her to be asked out.

"Seen it," said Bronwyn. "It's Bergman. The end is strange but it's not a surprise."

"No, but it's women," Mack said.

He thought Bronwyn would be interested.

"It's a man's view of women," said Bronwyn. "And a neurotic man at that."

"Neurosis is the zeitgeist of our time," answered Mack.

"Very good," said Bronwyn. "You should apply to graduate school."

"What does it pay?" he asked and then stood to leave.

eight

As the plane lifted off the tarmac Bronwyn heard a thump in the floor below her.

"A wheel just fell off," she said to Rita.

Another thump followed.

"That's OK," said Rita. "There goes the other one. Does flying scare you?"

"I don't fly much," said Bronwyn. "It's supposed to be safe. It just doesn't feel natural to be so far off the ground."

Bronwyn looked out the window and surveyed the shrinking world below that appeared as an endlessly coiling spread of debris. The plane lifted above the eastern hills of the South Bay until Bronwyn's view opened on the vast green and brown patches of central valley farmland spread like a monstrous and crazy quilt reaching toward the puffy white-capped pillows of the distant Sierras.

For a moment she imagined herself an angel and her fetus an incipient cherub like those painted by Rubens, together flying naked high above a world of human hysteria and hunger. Bronwyn's atheism prevented her from imagining the existence of a soul though this did not stop her wondering just for a moment if what grew inside her might possess a soul, might exist even now as something or some person distinct and independent of her.

It was a difficult thought and Bronwyn dismissed it long enough to watch the plane sink from the sky and slip over rising rooftops and swimming pools to land with a thump in Los Angeles.

Rita managed Bronwyn's carry-on bag and led her across the terminal to the American Airlines flight to El Paso.

"I'm tired," said Bronwyn as she fell into a seat at the gate.

"And hungry, too," said Rita. "Won't be long. This will all be over soon. And dinner is on me. Room service included."

The flight to El Paso bounced for two hours through the turbulent air currents flowing over the high sands of the southwest deserts. But Bronwyn was too tired and nauseated to care. Rita held her hand until exhaustion took over and Bronwyn at last fell asleep, not awakening until the plane was on the ground and rolling to its gate.

"Enjoy your stay in Juarez, or wherever you're going," said the stewardess to Rita and Bronwyn as they left the plane.

"She knows, doesn't she?" said Bronwyn.

"Think of her as a sister," said Rita. "Maybe she's made the same trip."

Rita hailed a cab at the curb of El Paso's miniature airport and gave the driver the address of a hotel in Juarez.

"You have your IDs?" asked the driver.

Rita fumbled for her driver's license and helped Bronwyn find hers in her purse.

The cab, a late Fifties model Chevrolet, rolled through the prim residential streets of El Paso before entering a lane that led to a border crossing where uniformed guards stopped the cab, had the driver open his trunk and then asked the women for their IDs.

"And how long are you planning to visit Mexico?" an armed guard asked Rita.

"A few days," she said.

"And the purpose of your visit?" the guard asked again.

"Tourism," said Rita. "We've never been to Mexico."

The guard eyed them suspiciously before returning their licenses and waving the cab forward toward the long bridge stretching across the Rio Grande.

"Avenida Hermanos Escobar," said Rita to the driver.

She then gave him the name of a hotel. The cab entered the swell and turmoil of Ciudad Juarez, a city of infinite and incomplete streets through which traffic ran frantically and without regard for signals or stop signs.

"There!" shouted Rita as she pointed toward a flashing neon marquee that read *Hotel Vista*.

The cab pulled up in front. Rita grabbed the carry on bags, paid the driver and guided Bronwyn through the hotel's narrow street entrance and into a spacious, dark lobby. A woman at a desk seemed to recognize Rita who stepped over, reached into her purse and handed the woman several bills.

"Let's get settled in our room," Rita said to Bronwyn. "We'll meet with the doctor's assistant at five. He'll take you to the clinic and return you after the procedure."

Bronwyn appeared frightened.

"You aren't coming with me?" she asked Rita.

"I can't," said Rita. "Trust me. It's OK."

At five Rita and Bronwyn entered a small meeting room behind the hotel counter occupied by a handful of other women of various ages, all of them Americans, and some like Bronwyn accompanied by others. One was a young girl who could not have been much older than thirteen and who waited with an older couple, likely her parents. The girl wore a floral dress, a white sweater and saddle shoes, appearing as if she might have been pulled from her classroom that morning. Her face showed no feeling though Bronwyn saw the redness of recent tears under her eyes. Her father, stout and wearing slacks and a khaki work shirt stared straight ahead and made no eye contact with anyone while the mother paced nervously.

A woman in her mid-thirties appeared. She was alone. A college-aged woman sat in a corner with an apparent boyfriend who crowded close and stroked her back in a way that seemed to irritate her. An older woman, which Bronwyn judged to be approaching menopause if not already underway, arrived with an older teenage girl dressed in jeans and a torn sweatshirt and palpably defiant.

A small, tan man arrived and asked everyone to sit down. He wore a shiny blue suit and a black string tie. He stood in severely polished leather loafers as he made eye contact with everyone in the room. His sharp nose and moist, thick black hair gave him the look of a young entrepreneur with something on offer.

"I am Dr. Davalos' associate," he said. "The doctor's clinic is near here. What we will be doing for you is the D and C."

The assistant put a long stress on the letters, making them sound like a cheer, *Dee an Seee…*

"The procedure is very safe and clean and will take only a few minutes. You will get a sedative and won't feel any pain. After the procedure you will wait at the clinic while the doctor checks that you are OK to leave and gives you some pills."

Bronwyn noted the assistant did not give his name nor did he say anyone was receiving an abortion.

"We will transport you to the clinic in our van. And we will return you in the van to the hotel. We will leave in fifteen minutes and everyone will be returned no later than 9 p.m. Those who are paying for this procedure need to meet with me briefly at the back of the room. As we said when you phoned, this payment must be in cash."

Rita went first. Bronwyn watched her hand five twenties to the assistant who then checked a name on a list on a clipboard. The young girl's father went next, followed by the older woman, the co-ed's boyfriend and the menopausal mother.

"Those of you receiving the procedure, please come with me now," he said after collecting payments and slipping them into the vest pocket of his jacket.

"Everybody been fasting?" he asked.

Each woman nodded as the group stood and crowded forward to the room's rear exit and outside where a van waited in the alley.

The van windows were covered with black shades. The assistant turned on the passenger light to illuminate the cabin.

"It's a ten-minute ride," he said.

"Well, it's the god damned last time I'm putting anything up there," said the older woman, eliciting a chuckle from both Bronwyn and the co-ed.

Sitting next to the youngest girl, Bronwyn saw her shoulders shaking through her sweater.

"You OK darlin'?" she asked.

"No…no…," the girl answered and began to cry. "I'm scared. Daddy says I could go to hell for this. He said if I die tonight it's what I deserve."

"You aren't going to die," Bronwyn said. "You certainly don't deserve to die. None of us do. But none of us want to have a baby right now for all kinds of reasons. Do you?"

"No…" said the girl.

"It's Tommy Morton's fault. He made me…"

"I know what that feels like," said Bronwyn. "What's your name?"

"Ginny," said the girl.

"Listen, you hold my hand until we get there," said Bronwyn. "This is a good doctor. He has helped lots of women like us. And you aren't going to hell. If your dad could get pregnant he'd understand this. He'll get over it. This isn't about his life. You are all that matters right now."

Ginny went first and then a half-hour later, Bronwyn was called. Two nurses helped her onto an examination table and placed her feet in its extended stirrups. She was covered in a sheet and given a sedative that left her woozy but still conscious. She remembered the smiling face of an older white-coated Mexican woman with grey hair looking into her eyes.

"OK?" she asked. "Everything is fine."

She felt some pressure from the insertion of a speculum and some brief cramping. And then she was lying in bed, slowly awakening. Ginny was in the bed next to her, already awake and drinking from a plastic cup. Over the next two hours the other women were wheeled past Bronwyn and lifted onto nearby beds.

An hour passed as the women all began to stir and awaken, sit up and sip water from paper cups. A nurse arrived and spoke to them.

"Everything went good," said the nurse. "Everyone is fine. No problems. You will bleed for a few days. Maybe some cramps. But nothing to worry about. Not as much as a period. There is a bathroom at the end of the hall. Go there to change back into your clothes. More pads there. Once you're all dressed you will go back to the hotel."

Vacuo," she added. *"No mas la molesta, no mas el dolor."*

Rita was waiting when Bronwyn walked back through the meeting room and into the hotel's large, dark lobby.

"You OK?" asked Rita.

"Sure. Still dizzy but not bad."

"Any pain?" asked Rita again.

"Not much," said Bronwyn.

"Well, I've done that now," she added after a moment.

"Yes you have," said Rita. "You're a brave woman. Let's get upstairs. I have something for you."

Rita opened the door to the hotel room, a squat rectangular box with a single window on the noisy avenue and one other door that led into a tiny bathroom with a shower. Two double beds filled nearly the entire room except for a space at the foot of the beds where a table and two chairs hugged one of the room's sickly green walls. A framed photograph of the Rio Grande bridge was bolted above the beds.

On the table was a meal of tacos and burritos spread on a section of a newspaper that shouted its headlines in 42-point Spanish. Next to the food were two bottles of Corona and a stack of small paper napkins.

"Damn, I'm starving," said Bronwyn.

She sat in a chair and picked up a plastic cup of salsa and poured it over a taco.

"Chicken," said Rita. "Are you cool with that?"

"I'm cool with eating until I burst," said Bronwyn as she cradled the taco and positioned it for her first purposeful, exuberant bite.

"Slow down, honey," said Rita.

Bronwyn finished her first taco in a moment and after a whimsical toast proposed by Rita, swigged half her bottle of beer.

"Thirsty," said Rita, who watched Bronwyn sit back in her chair.

After a few quiet minutes her eyes began to flutter and she set the bottle on the table before sliding down in her chair.

"And tired," said Bronwyn.

Her eyes were nearly closed.

"C'mon babe," said Rita, as she helped Bronwyn to one of the beds, removed her skirt, pulled back the covers and slid her into the bed as she might a letter into an envelope.

Later Bronwyn would recall the way Rita climbed quietly onto the bed and settled beside her, slipping an arm under her neck to enclose her in a protective embrace. As she fell into her deep sleep Bronwyn heard Rita's whispering voice and felt her breath at her ear.

"La noche larga de vida…el deseo ignorante…criatura…creacion…es nada…es solamente nada…"

Sailing the night sea, Bronwyn woke in the safe harbor of Rita's arms. Rita was behind and pushed up against her under the covers with a hand on her hair and the other at her shoulder. It was a tender and friendly spoon that reminded Bronwyn of childhood spend-the-nights with special friends, some silly and a few also naughty in important and exploring ways that could be thrilling without being dangerous.

Bronwyn had to pee and, hearing Rita's sleepy sighs, she slithered and slumped carefully until her feet were on the floor and she could stagger into the bathroom. As she peed, Bronwyn examined her pad, noting the modest remains of a dried, dark pool of blood. Not much, she thought. Like the nurse said. Her heart beat calmly for the first time in weeks. She was relieved to be sitting on a toilet without the need to comprehend every excretion, push or pain as a reminder she was not empty. She *was* empty. She would feel fullness again but it would abide a familiar cycle and not shake her either with improbable threat or impossible guilt.

At the El Paso airport, Rita unloaded their bags and with two hours before their flight, guided Bronwyn into the airport's spacious café to order them breakfast. An old movie played on the large television at the end of the counter. It was a black and white musical, probably from the Thirties, and as Rita asked for menus, Bronwyn watched the screen. A party in a nightclub faded into dark black, from which out of the distance the small face—and only the face—of a singing brunette grew slowly as she belted out a tune to the honky tonk strains of a 1930s studio orchestra.

> *Come on along and listen to*
> *The lullaby of Broadway*
> *The hip hooray and ballyhoo*
> *The lullaby of Broadway…*

The lyrics described the rumble of subway trains and the rattle of taxis, dinner at restaurants like Angelo's and Maxi's. It celebrated "Broadway babes" that only say goodnight in the early morning and don't fall sleep before dawn. *"Good night, baby,"* sang the woman whose eyes grew larger as she sang. *"Good night, the milkman's on his way…Sleep tight, let's call it a day…"*

Bronwyn stared transfixed as the woman's face at last filled the screen and then as the face turned, its outline dissolved into a city tableau. A sequence began that featured a young woman returning at dawn from a wild party and to her apartment where a kitty waited at her door. The woman opened the milkman's delivered bottle and poured milk for the kitty into a dish before picking up her newspaper and falling into bed.

As the orchestra pounded out the song's riveting melody the story leaped forward with the woman waking again lazily at the dinner hour, climbing out of bed to dress and to go out again to a club with a flashy boyfriend who in the next shot opened a wine bottle and poured champagne. A couple tangoed across a large stage. A hundred other dancers joined the couple, men and women who imitated the tango-like steps of the primary performers and, at last, reached for the woman and her boyfriend to pull them up to the dance floor.

Bronwyn watched the woman run through the crowd and in some coy escape flee to a balcony where she hid behind closed windows as her partner and the dancers crowded around and, pushing the windows open, sent her tumbling over the ledge.

The remaining shots panned the woman's empty, dark bedroom and its fully made bed, ending at last at her front door where the frantic kitty waited beside an empty dish, an unopened bottle of milk and the morning's unread newspaper. As the camera returned to the view of the city, it's outline again became the face of the singing woman shrinking back into the darkness as she sang the song's last lines.

> *Sleep tight, baby*
> *Sleep tight, let's call it a day*
> *Listen to the lullaby of ol' Broadway.*

Bronwyn felt tears forming in her eyes but could not have anticipated the convulsing cries that followed. She became a notable attraction at the breakfast bar, more notable than the television which few people were watching but that for Bronwyn had become the vehicle for a powerful parable, one she knew that by its timing and accessibility was meant only for her.

"Honey," Rita asked urgently. "You OK?"

It was more than Bronwyn could explain: the small face growing from the darkness became her fetus growing in her dark womb; the song its cry for the terms of its new life, for its share of life's hooray and ballyhoo and who would not, could not, sleep tight until the dawn. The woman in the story was Bronwyn, seeking incessantly for the kindness of a lover who would enjoy her without her having to conjure or initiate the terms of pleasure, and then only to be abandoned for having the temerity to do so. And the alcohol, the pouring wine a reminder how oblivious Bronwyn needed to be to open herself to the dance of loving which was, in fact, just another way to control the flow of her incessant sorrow.

And the dance–the syncopation of a hundred men and women modeled, it seemed intentionally, to remind Bronwyn she could not dance, that she was not able to move with the grace and beauty she had for all her childhood imagined as the most wonderful and desirable capacity of a truly "natural" woman. And then at the bitter end there was the kitty waiting helplessly without its milk and none ever again to be poured. This and a singing face that at the end faded into oblivion, wounded Bronwyn with its portrayed allegory of all her life's difficult choices, even those that were not hers to choose.

nine

Bronwyn hadn't noticed the color of Rita's Corvair. It was an early model and the sky blue paint was faded. Rita inherited the car from a brother who gave it up for a new Ford Mustang. Rita drove Bronwyn home from the airport.

"It's like a great distraction…and it's gone," she said to Rita.

"You left it in Juarez," said Rita.

Not exactly, thought Bronwyn. It wasn't something one left anywhere. It was a living thing now dead and gone the way the dead were gone and in the way the dead always left something behind. Bronwyn's grandmother died three years before, and not unexpectedly. Still, her mother felt deep grief and spent a year mourning the loss of her mom, pouring over old photos and scrapbooks and telling and retelling embellished stories of their entwined lives. Bronwyn had no story yet to tell about her aborted fetus. It had been present to her in a most intimate way but without a voice, a face or anything but its fiercely determined attachment to

511

the wall of her womb. As such, it was a loss and there was no other way Bronwyn could think about it, even if its death was sought and welcomed.

In the week that followed, Bronwyn also noticed how she avoided being alone with men. Raj and Mack were the exceptions but she no longer felt comfortable sitting at committee meetings unless at least one other woman, and usually Wendy, was also present. She needed the voices of other women to amplify her own. Otherwise she would not speak, knowing that men very often did not listen.

At first Bronwyn thought she had lost her nerve and that the abortion had drained her will. In fact, it was the rape that had most affected her, had exposed her vulnerability as a victimized woman. In Rita's view, the abortion was a sacrament, a responsible and maternal decision to protect the gift of life by ending an unwanted and unplanned pregnancy. And it was her right, even if priests and judges still refused to honor it.

"This new women's thing didn't just pop out of the blue," said Rita. "Black Power opened our eyes to oppression. Hippies opened our hearts. Students showed us how to protest. As women we now face our oppression and the economic and cultural deprivation we share with all exploited minorities, and especially and unfortunately from the men within the movement. At least for awhile, and until we prevail as women, some of our friends may also be our foes."

Bronwyn admired Rita's assertive style. Their conversations were never tentative, never punctuated with tag questions or non-committal queries. Bronwyn had not before had a woman friend that so easily told her the truth. Now on the nights she went to her C-R group, she had a whole room full of women who spoke their minds. Rita called it blobbing.

"You don't blab, you blob your voice right out there and let it land for all to hear. You fucking own it, sister. It's—what can I say—*blobvious.*"

Bronwyn smiled.

Rita described a germinal women's movement as something grown from the "politics of experience."

"All our feelings now must start from the source of our own alienation. As women we were born into a world in which alienation was here waiting for us. Each knows it in our own way. The personal is fused entirely with the political."

It occurred to Bronwyn that throughout her life she had always felt deeply. But feelings could not be freely experienced in isolation. She used sex and alcohol to access these feelings in the company of certain men but never succeeded in making a satisfying connection.

She now saw her rape as the inevitable outcome of a sloppy disrespect for her own feelings. Bronwyn now wished she could take all of it back, all her disturbed and disturbing urges to lead exclusively from the head and not the heart while trying to hold her own as one of the boys. What she had once wanted most appeared now as something with no location, something false and also fantastic.

"My God are you OK?" Harriet asked.

Bronwyn had not intended to tell anyone about her abortion so she was surprised to hear herself spilling every detail to Harriet within minutes of returning to the flat. Harriet sat in the kitchen and had asked Bronwyn where she had been for two days and Bronwyn simply told her. After the shock of her first words, the rest was easy. Harriet expressed concern but not with the understanding of those in Bronwyn's women's group.

Harriet asked Bronwyn why she decided to end her pregnancy and Bronwyn knew no real sister would ever ask her why.

"Because I could," answered Bronwyn. "It's not an easy thing to talk about. I can't believe I'm telling you."

"Can I help you?" asked Harriet.

"Just accept it," answered Bronwyn. "It was my choice. Right now I need to rest. I could sleep for days."

Harriet stood and began to putter helplessly; perhaps aware she had asked the wrong question.

"Can I fix you something, can…?"

"Not now," answered Bronwyn as she waved Harriet off and left the kitchen, sorry now she had said anything.

Later, Harriet knocked on the door of Bronwyn's room and offered to fix her a dinner, which Bronwyn accepted.

"Listen," Harriet began she as she served pasta from a deep, orange bowl.

"I'm going north again for a few days. Stan was in an accident and Ginger needs a little help. Would you like to come with me?"

"Stan OK?" Bronwyn asked as she stuffed her mouth with noodles. She was famished.

"Yeah. Hurt his leg in a logging accident a couple of weeks ago. He's walking but it's slow going. Anyway, I'd like to take you again. Nothing heavy. Just thinking you might like to get away for a rest or a walk on the beach."

Bronwyn hesitated to answer, thinking first and only of her embarrassing drunk that ended her last visit but then realizing a repeat appearance offered a chance at redemption and also relief from the increasingly tedious and stagnant battle for a people's park.

"Althea and Madge, that their names? The women with the farm?" asked Bronwyn. "Would be nice to see them again. And I remember, they have a women's group, don't they?"

Harriet couldn't recall.

"Woodcutting was the biggest test," Althea told Bronwyn.

"We thought we needed a chainsaw to have enough wood to burn. After blowing a wad on a chainsaw and hating the roar it made all day, we learned about the two-person saw. Cut as much wood and without the rattle or noise. Always, we had a problem taking on too much without knowing enough or not having enough time to learn."

Bronwyn followed Althea out of her barn, its wide door propped up against a wall of rotting boards. She and Madge had owned their farm for nearly two years and the barn still needed repair but not before they fixed the house's broken windows and leaky roof.

"First things first," said Althea. "But what do you do first? Half our work is deciding what to do first."

Harriet had dropped Bronwyn at Althea's farm before taking Ginger farther up the ridge to see her midwife Mamma Bear at Tabletop Mountain. Bronwyn was told a women's group would be meeting but Althea told her it had been canceled.

"No one phones in the country," said Althea. "They just show up…or they don't."

She offered to show Bronwyn the farm.

"It must feel good to raise your own food, to be self-sufficient," Brownyn said.

She watched Althea slip her feet into fat, rubber waders and plunge to her ankles in the mud of the pigpen.

"We aren't self-sufficient yet," Althea shouted. "Madge is in town buying groceries. And self-reliant? That's our goal. But our hope it would happen by this year was based on some wishful thinking."

"Like what?" asked Bronwyn.

"Depending on other people, for one," said Althea. "We had three couples come to live with us, but it didn't work out. The women weren't into heavy lifting and the men were bossy and lazy. They were gone before the rains. We were pissed about it. Had to cut back on what we thought we could do. We just got the new well and pump in this spring. Still, we have our good times. We ride our horses, pick our fruit, explore the forest. We still have the dream, whether or not we're ever able to break even. But we've agreed if we open the farm up again it won't be to men. Goddamned women only."

Bronwyn waited as Althea fed the pigs and then followed her to the garden where she turned soil, pulled weeds and filled a basket with cherry tomatoes.

"It comes down to this," said Althea as they trudged back to the house. "We are the first women here for ourselves. Here to become farmers and not farmers' wives."

The air was cool and clouds of coastal overcast hung at the farm's western boundary. Bronwyn had trouble imagining how everything here got done, accustomed as she was to a city's vast system of expensive and labor-supported products. The construction of a breakfast on Althea's farm was the pinnacle of hours, perhaps days of preparation. In the city, it was ordered over a counter and ready in minutes without any further investment than a few bills from her wallet and no personal attachment at all to the servers.

"Another life," Bronwyn said to Harriet and Ginger when they picked her up and asked her for her impressions of Althea's farm.

It oozed with mud and smells and the plunge of red fingers into all kinds of earth. It was also and undeniably a kind of natural woman's work to build protective structures like barns and sheds, to measure the seasonal arc of the sun before locating the patch of a garden, to husband animal life even as it was prepared to become food for others, to be awash in a lovely pulsing fecundity, season after season and year after year.

It was not a surprise. When Bronwyn and Harriet arrived the previous afternoon at Ginger's they had encountered a half dozen women clustered to pick up their children while Ginger, at last showing her pregnancy, waddled lightly among them, trailed by her daughter Lila while Stan, balanced on his crutches, peeled potatoes in the kitchen. Ginger hugged moms and their children as she fulfilled an orbit of filial and maternal regard. These were mothers and, at some other time, Bronwyn might have dismissed them as housewives. And it had been easy at first to think of Ginger as such a woman, one who had babies and supported them, and also a husband, to a fault.

Except this was not the case and the closer Bronwyn looked, the more she saw in Ginger a strong leader among the women in her midst, the kind of leader Bronwyn could envy, one that inspired strong emotional loyalty and not simply agreement with the arguments for revolution. The kind of power Ginger asserted was emotional power on behalf of children, people, and justice. And how did she do it? Bronwyn was both impressed and puzzled by a sturdy feminine preeminence seemingly without an ideology but still devoted to the consistent and irresistible assertion of a woman's sensibility on the course of experience.

If Bronwyn thought too much about these women, she could become sick with the grief of her empty displacement from the fruitful heart of all this maternal abundance. It was hard not to feel like a fuck-up, like a lame excuse for a woman as Bronwyn wrestled with what now loomed as perhaps too much time supporting revolution and not enough time given back to herself. Did she have life backwards? Any revolution needed to support women. Did hers? Did the park? The condition of a woman was the defining oppression, and one that reached across and through all classes, castes and races.

By visit's end, Bronwyn had connected with Ginger and a few of the mothers and not had a single sip of wine. She had been a model guest to the point that Ginger invited her back anytime and Althea offered her a room at the farm "if you ever think this life up here would work for you."

It didn't and wouldn't.

"I'm not a country girl," Bronwyn announced summarily on the ride back with Harriet. "Though I have to hand it to those country women. They've got something going for them and being mommies seems to be part of it."

"I'm with you," said Harriet. "I couldn't do it. I'm still figuring out my own life. How could I take care of another's? And I'd miss the city."

"You would?" asked Bronwyn. "Then why are you going to Africa? Why did you join the Peace Corps?"

The question quieted Harriet.

"It was Michael's idea," she at last answered. "He wanted to go and he wanted me to go with him."

Bronwyn settled back into her seat and gazed at the passing shoreline. She had no response and knew Harriet, if she even understood Bronwyn's imagined questions, would likely become unsettled and defensive.

"So Stan the artist is homebound," Mack said. "Would you like another beer?"

"Yes…and no," Bronwyn answered while she watched Mack give their menus to a passing waiter.

"Yes, Stan has been laid up after a bad run-in with logging. But he's done a lot: put in a garden, repaired and painted the garage for a studio, fenced a yard for Ginger's day care. And no, I don't want another beer. I've hardly touched this one."

Mack used his question as it was intended, and ordered another beer for himself. It was a Wednesday night at Spenger's Fish Grotto and the service was unreasonably slow, which didn't bother Bronwyn who had been surprised by Mack's offer to take her out to dinner. At first she thought he wanted to source her for another story on the park. He said no, he wasn't thinking about the park, so Bronwyn wondered if this were a date.

"Doesn't sound like Stan's doing much painting," said Mack. "I thought that might happen."

"It's not because he doesn't want to," said Bronwyn. "But there's a lot to do."

"Sounds like the women run things," Mack offered.

"Whether or not the women run things," said Bronwyn, "well… they should."

Mack gave Bronwyn a beady-eyed double take.

"Women's rights?" he asked. "We're still doing that?"

"I am," answered Bronwyn. "Did you read the piece I gave you?"

He had.

"A lot of anger," he said. "Especially towards men. The idea that women should meet in small groups and not invite men seems kind of backward. Don't women need men to help them with this liberation thing? And these small groups—are they like revolutionary cells? Are women going to run the revolution by themselves? Sounds very Marxist. Except women are described as a special and unique class. The chapter *What Do Women Want?* reads like Lenin's *What Must Be Done?* It seems pretty god damned extreme. Don't women like us anymore?"

Mack meant the last comment as a joke but Bronwyn wasn't biting. Date or not, she was no longer in the mood to humor a man.

"The oppression women suffer they endure together," said Bronwyn. "The struggle of each woman, her own retreat into a role as sex object, as unpaid housewife, as vessel of childbirth, and ultimately useless and unattractive old hag, is an experience entirely her own."

"Really?" asked Mack. "Women don't want to be mothers? Come on…"

"Whether she wants to or not, it should really be her choice," said Bronwyn.

"And she needs to know the truth of other women who also have a context for her experience. Men do not. In fact, men usually don't care about or understand a woman's experiences. Most men have a big interest in keeping women in their place."

"So these groups…they're supposed to…what? Uplift women?" asked Mack.

"Seems like these small groups just keep women apart."

"Except the women in all these different groups are saying the same things," said Bronwyn.

"Like the Chinese peasants who met in small groups before the revolution and found that talking about their violent oppression and their poverty was a way to begin thinking their way out of their struggles. They described the activity as *talking bitterness*, talking among themselves about the state of their common and individual suffering. It is what women in the movement call consciousness raising. One person's experience of injustice brings it to mind in the lives of everyone in the group. It is speaking the unspoken."

"And are you in a group? Are there a lot of them?" asked Mack.

"Yeah. I've been in a group in the City for about a month and a half," said Bronwyn.

"About ten of us, but we keep growing. And yes, there are hundreds of these groups. Probably thousands. The women's group is probably the single biggest force in this growing movement. A woman might bring up a difficult secret. Maybe she's been raped. Maybe she's had an abortion. Other women listen and add their own experiences until an act or a problem otherwise consigned to the oblivion of a woman's shame or privacy, can be examined as a condition of the world. And it *is* a condition of the world. Women easily assume they are totally accountable for the grief in their lives. But they aren't because they are not responsible for the social and economic conditions that produce it."

It gave Bronwyn strength to refer, however obliquely, to her rape and abortion.

"But what about men who want to help?" asked Mack.

"What about men who sympathize with women? Why shut them out? The civil rights movement didn't shut out women. The SDS didn't shut out women. The anti-war movement hasn't shut out women."

Bronwyn sighed and tried to restrain her impatience.

"The men who led these movements expected women to fall into line, to do the chores men don't want to do, like cleaning, preparing meals, typing up meeting notes, answering phones, fucking them. Remember Stokely saying to a SNCC crowd that a woman's place in the movement is prone? Got a big laugh, I remember, at least from the men. And when women stood up a couple of years ago at an SDS meeting to request endorsement of a women's rights platform, they were hooted off the stage by the male delegates."

There followed a pause and an awkward silence that Bronwyn at last broke.

"Do you sympathize with women, Mack? What are your expectations of a woman? Is she a wife? A mother? Will she cook your meals? Wash your clothes? Clean your house? What if she wants to be a reporter like you? What if she wants your job? Will you clean *her* house? Will you cook *her* meals?"

"So this is what groups do?" Mack asked, avoiding Bronwyn's pointed question. "Bring women together to discuss how they suffer. I wonder, though. Women seem to have it so easy. Really, what is so hard about taking care of a home and not having to work and…"

"Mack, who are you to say what a woman should want? Would you want to spend your life working without pay for a partner who is gone for most all your waking hours and one day, after you've passed a certain prime, decides she would like a younger, more attractive model?"

"OK, OK…" Mack conceded. "I guess I haven't thought that much about it."

"Exactly my point," said Bronwyn. "And the point of the article I gave you. *Men haven't thought that much about it*. But women have. And if more women don't start thinking and talking about these things, it's unlikely any man will. Many women today want a different kind of world. We aren't necessarily anti-men. We certainly aren't anti-child. We aren't really anti-family though some big changes are needed to make marriage something that doesn't cost women their lives."

Mack waited, seemingly unresponsive, until Bronwyn finished. Then he nodded.

"I have to say I've never looked at a woman's life in that way," he said almost plaintively. "I can see, though, that women have a reason to think about all this from the challenges of their own experience. I'd like to keep the paper and read it again. Would that be OK?"

Bronwyn was surprised. In her experience with such dialogues, and especially with men, ignorance usually took the initiative. She expected Mack to be offended, to argue a man's truth in a man's way, furiously and defensively. Instead, he opened to her, to her ideas and to her resentments. He was not afraid. These thoughts aroused Bronwyn. She wanted Mack immediately. She wanted to revel in his willingness to hear her, to reward his apparent comprehension with her own wordless lust.

As he drove her home, Bronwyn harbored irresistible fantasies of Mack's touch, even as she tried to manage an assessment of her heart's desire. *I am a woman. I do not need a man. I am myself enough.*

"These thoughts you describe," he said to her. "I need to read more about them. Women…this is really an important change. I want to understand it."

Bronwyn imagined now the pleasure possible with a thoughtful, accepting man. Instead of thinking of her own life she was drawn deeper down into her dreams of something wonderful, something she had never dared to permit herself to desire, much less have. A life with a man she could see clearly and who also saw her. Mack stopped his car in front of Harriet's flat.

"Would you like to come up for a drink?"

Bronwyn asked the question she had rehearsed for the entire drive home.

"Thanks, Bronwyn," said Mack. "I've got an early day tomorrow. But let's do this again. OK?"

He reached to give her an affiliating hug, which Bronwyn searched for any shred of passion. Mack was kind, generous, intellectually connecting and he genuinely liked Bronwyn. But he was not attracted and that could not be more obvious to her, which threatened to become another one of Bronwyn's heartaches until she recognized the lengths she went to protect herself from such pain. And it was Mack's right, as much as hers, to choose whatever he desired. Her affection was unrequited but for the first time ever it did not frighten her or force her into compulsive self-loathing. Without freely acknowledging such affection how might she ever know what her heart really wanted?

ten

Bronwyn could no longer see the results of her own labors. The park business was at a crawl as the city tried desperately to take some role. The University Regents, responding to a cue from their firebrand governor, sought to quell any and all academic rebellion. There were muffled threats of violence on both sides.

At one committee meeting Bronwyn heard Michael propose again that park supporters arm themselves. Though a few men were supportive, cooler heads prevailed and the idea went nowhere. For their part, the Regents said the National Guard would be called back to quell any riots. But neither side wanted a repeat of Bloody Thursday and so negotiations drifted on into June without resolution.

Bronwyn's distracted involvement was noticeable and at mid-month she formally left the park committee. She was attending three C-R meetings a week and had become a section organizer for several East Bay sisters who wanted to create a support group. During its first week, the women helped a member file divorce papers against a violent husband and went with another woman to the police station in San Leandro to stand with her while she reported a sexual assault.

It was the closest she had come to living a life of unselfish and helpful kindness and by leaving the park committee she anticipated that all contact with Mack would stop, since she was no longer a reliable news source. But he phoned one afternoon and asked her to join him again for dinner.

"Going to a gallery opening at CCAC. Student art but it's usually pretty good. Thought we could get dinner somewhere on College. Would you join me?"

"I'm not on the park committee anymore, Mack," Bronwyn announced ruefully. "Don't know what I can help you with."

"No. No," said Mack. "I don't care about that. It's *No More Fun and Games*. I read it again and I have a shitload of questions. What do you say?"

"Your call, Mack," answered Bronwyn. "Sure. Where and when?"

Bronwyn suppressed a wave of excitement, clear about her official position as a woman on the verge of liberation. But what

Mack proposed sounded very much like a date and in a way that might not align with the terms she thought should describe or even define a feminine politics. However she looked at it, she could not view Mack as an enemy.

"Thursday. I'll come get you around six. Cool?"

"Oh yes. Very cool."

Bronwyn tried to sound blasé.

"See you then...oh, what should I wear?"

The question sounded lame and frivolous, like a sophomore asking how she should dress for the prom. It caught Mack off guard.

"Clothes," he said at last to break the tension.

"Do you ever worry about being raped?" Bronwyn asked Mack as they again waited for menus.

"No...." he answered. "Why would I? I worry about being mugged sometimes."

"Do you stay inside and cancel an evening out if you don't have a ride?"

"No...put I think I see your point," answered Mack.

"So that's one issue for women. Men's privilege over our bodies. Their assumption they can hoot at us, call us cute or ugly, or grab us, or fuck us when they wish. They assume this, of course, because they've been able to control just about everything about us. Last year I needed my dad's signature to get a charge card. I'm a fucking 24-year-old woman, Mack."

Mack didn't argue.

"What else?" he asked.

"My god...everything. Marriage, parenting, careers, wages, the arts—how many famous women artists can you name?"

"Not many," said Mack. "A couple, Frida Kahlo and Joan Mitchell and Jackson Pollock's lover, what's her name ... Lee Krasner...but women writers..."

"Well, like Virgina Woolf said—women write because pens and paper are cheap and they can do it at home," said Bronwyn.

"But what you gave me to read—a woman wrote 'as long as a man is in power he will never admit the necessity of his demise.' That seems pretty severe. Do women who want this liberation thing, do they hate men?"

Bronwyn waited.

"I don't hate men. But I don't like anymore a lot of the things men do. It would be interesting if overnight the roles were switched and men could get pregnant and women made war. I wonder what would change? I'm reminded of a line from an Anne Sexton poem… *Live or die but don't poison everything…*"

Mack had more questions and Bronwyn tried to answer them, even as her mind wandered back to dwell on how she was dressed, how Mack looked at her, how she had looked at herself in the mirror before he arrived for her, her hair longer now and no more hidden in a protective, stringy bun. She imagined that Mack saw her differently, and if not as a beautiful woman at least as a woman fully present and self-possessed.

As she looked at her menu Bronwyn reviewed their last hour in the college gallery, Mack comfortably next to her and speaking with one of the student artists. She sensed a linkage with him that continued to feel kind and present and visible. He appeared thoughtful and respectful and, as he said when he phoned her, he valued her, her thoughts, her experience in the movement and, she imagined at the core of it all, her womanliness.

His curiosity about women appeared limitless and his attention to the writings of women's liberation Bronwyn found vulnerably arousing. Mack might be the anti-rapist whose generous, respectful hugs lifted her up and allowed her, if only for moments at a time, to forget that it had been barely two months since her life was toppled by a violent assault. Mack had no idea he played such a role, which increased Bronwyn's regard for his sincerity and affiliation.

Bronwyn also pondered a peculiar interaction with Inger, a woman acquaintance of Mack's who had a painting in the show and who, slightly drunk, rushed Mack when he entered, oblivious to Bronwyn. Inger's aggressive, intimate embrace of Mack convinced Bronwyn that Inger had screwed him, though Mack made a quick effort to push her off, agreeing to follow her to where her canvass hung. Bronwyn also followed.

"This is interesting," Mack said as he viewed Inger's work, a basically abstract pastiche of bright, dreamy magenta, cerulean blue, brash orange and shadows of light brown and minty green. The colors washed over a concealed aggregate of lines that pushed forward from beneath the paint the shapes of long, womanly legs and torsos that accrued in a curious and sensual relation. The colors were bright and Inger's ink drawings bold and skillfully rendered. It was as if she had amplified with her loud colors the emotions of some particularly sensual human contact.

"You still live in the commune?" Mack asked her.

Inger nodded.

"That has always struck me as extraordinary," Mack responded. "A sexual commune…how many partners in your groups? Does this painting, I mean…"

A tall male approached Mack from behind and pulled him back toward a cluster of people gathered at the bar. Mack swung around.

"Now? OK. Excuse me a moment…"

Mack walked away, leaving Inger and Bronwyn together.

"What's a sexual commune?" Bronwyn asked Inger directly.

She had seen Inger before at the Forum and had made some unflattering assumptions. A sex commune didn't surprise her.

"What it sounds like, I guess," answered Inger.

She was not shy.

"We live in small groups and share our beds with each other. It's called Kanda…the Kanda House."

"Does that cause any problems?" asked Bronwyn.

"No," said Inger. "We all want to please each other. That's the point of sex. At least our sex."

"Really?" Bronwyn asked, taken by surprise by Inger's frankness. She had nothing more to say.

"How long have you known Mack?" asked Inger.

"Awhile. We met during the student strikes. He's turned out to be a good friend."

"He's one sexy man," responded Inger, leaving Bronwyn to feel like a ghost fumbling for footing in the wrong world, though later it would make sense that Inger's sexual life and Bronwyn's feminist vigor would find in Mack an object for both. The comment built for each a sudden feeling of animosity and also alliance.

Mack returned to hear Inger describe wantonly her future plans.

She was trying to get into a new women's art program that she heard was forming at Fresno State College. Inger had submitted a portfolio.

"Fresno? Wish you luck," said Mack as he led Bronwyn away.

"Let's get dinner," he said. "I've seen enough."

After dinner Mack drove Bronwyn home, his rush of questions about women giving way to an interest in Bronwyn's life as an activist, a student, and a child. Her responses floated out of her in a rush of careless intimacy, leaving her again powerfully aroused by Mack's ingenuous interest in her. And again, as he walked her to the door and hugged her sweetly and swiftly before turning to leave, Bronwyn waited to dissolve into a sullen place where nothing either changed or disappeared.

Bronwyn hadn't read *The Second Sex* though she knew its author's name well enough to throw her name into selected party conversations where, depending on how drunk everyone was, it would land like a bomb or not at all. Much depended on the crowd. She was stunned it was published in 1953 and something her mother might have read—or at least should have.

"She understood everything," Bronwyn said to Rita as they followed a C-R session with another drink on Polk.

"Simone de Beauvior wrote that women have always been oppressed and that its basis is as biological as it is historical. Women have never held power over men, so forget the idea of some grand matriarchal time when women ruled. That's bullshit."

Rita listened closely before responding.

"I coulda told you that," she said coolly.

"And though she's a communist, she acknowledges socialism has done damned little to improve the lives of women," Bronwyn continued. "But with the destruction of economic classes women at least stand a chance."

"How?" asked Rita. "Women occupy all classes. There are women who hate us for wanting to be free. You get that, sister? There are rich women who do not want freedom—for themselves or anyone—if gaining freedom will cost them their privilege."

"I just think this book is the best, most comprehensive and radical analysis I've ever read about a woman's life," said Bronwyn. "I'm not saying it's the last word but it's a great place to start."

"You ain't seen nothin' yet, sister," said Rita. "It's on us. We're the ones who will write the next chapter. Hell, we're writing it now."

Rita's assertion brought Bronwyn back to what was really on her mind.

"I'm thinking about going back to New York," she said.

"Why?" asked Rita. "What's back there?

"Well, home for one thing," said Bronwyn. "A fresh start. I could use that."

"What's fresh about goin' home?" Rita asked. "Seems like the wrong direction to me."

"No. You don't understand," said Bronwyn. "The Redstockings are in New York. And they're just one of at least a dozen New York women's groups. How many women groups here? Sudsofloppen? And what is that? No, New York is where the women's movement began and where it's most interesting work is happening. And I know that place. I grew up there."

Bronwyn was prepared to explain her still developing plan: how she would spend the summer with her parents in Queens, find work on Manhattan and enroll in graduate school at NYU while volunteering with the Red Stockings.

"You called your parents yet?" asked Rita.

"No…" Bronwyn hesitated. "I'm still thinking about it…"

"Would you take me with you?" asked Rita.

Surprised, Bronwyn looked deeply into Rita's eyes.

"You're serious, aren't you?" Bronwyn responded.

Rita looked down, as if her confessed desire were a wrongful presumption, though Bronwyn saw nothing between them but an empty, clearing space. At that moment Bronwyn held her pivotal place as object and potential and also as the hospice of her dear friend's heart.

"So here's my question," Mack said. "Is it really necessary that for feminism to succeed, women must dispense with men completely? Or is there room for men in a women's movement?"

Bronwyn considered Mack's question as they sat at the Forum. Mack again had called her, had asked to meet with her after still another reading of *No More Fun and Games.*

"That's all in who you ask," said Bronwyn. "Some women have serious issues with men and see them as an enemy, see the whole male energy as the planet's biggest problem. They blame war, poverty, family violence–you name it–on men. So they want nothing to do with them. Other women…well, they still want to be with men, still want children and want fathers for them. Some women had loving dads and don't see men as the enemy, as such. It's a big challenge. There are radical feminists and, I guess, you might call them liberal feminists–or maybe movement feminists, who see feminism as something separate from the war of the sexes."

"What do you mean separate?" asked Mack.

"Well, maybe something we call the feminine isn't something women alone possess but is something more like a cultural force. That is, something historically womanly but not inherently womanly. Nothing says men can't raise children, can't have real feelings, can't march for peace, can't work for human rights. Some already do."

Mack was quiet, as he usually was after Bronwyn spoke. It was a sign he listened to her and considered seriously what she said, which did nothing to dampen her obstinate attraction to him.

"It does seem odd for women to protest their wrongful exclusion from power by invoking the very differences they want to eliminate. Which raises the question, again, can men be feminists?"

"Can men be women?" Bronwyn asked, she thought rhetorically.

"Can women be men?" Mack asked with a sudden syncopation.

"We're getting far afield," said Bronwyn.

"Maybe not," said Mack. "We're talking gender now and it's another question when you consider that there are men who wish they were women, and women who wish they were men."

"Not so fast," said Bronwyn. "We're getting pretty far away from abortion rights, free birth control, poor wages, limited career choices, child abuse, family violence…women have real grievances, Mack. Deep and abiding and heartfelt grievances."

Black Panther Brother David approached the head of the table with a sheaf of notes, which he threw on the floor as he began to speak.

"I had some things to say about Larry," David said to those

crowded around him in Panther Headquarters.

"Some great things," he said again as the crowd—some fifty people–rippled with "right-ons" and "teach-it-Davids" and other hoots of approval and celebration. Though it was not a celebration.

Larry was leaving the Oakland Chapter of the Black Panther Party to travel with his fiancée Sylvia to Chicago where they would recreate the Oakland Panther's successful Free Breakfasts for Children program on the city's Southside.

"But now I'm thinkin' the FBI is in on this," David sneered.

Boos filled the headquarters.

"The FBI is in on just about everything these days," David said. "Wouldn't surprise me if they got some undercover agent workin' to get Larry outta here. 'Cause Larry and Sylvia have been incredible. And I don't know what we're gonna do without 'em."

A cheer went up from the crowd, an enthusiastic aggregate of beret-wearing Panthers, college radicals, community organizers, and parents, including Sylvia's mother and father and Larry's dad. Larry's mom, opposed to her son's departure, did not attend.

Bronwyn and Mack stood in the front row, pushed up against the table by the press of the crowd. Mack scribbled notes for a news story.

"So here's to you, Larry and Sylvia," David said as he gave the crowd a Panther salute. "Freddie Hampton be one lucky Panther to have you workin' for him in Chicago."

Larry appeared with Sylvia to say a few words, though it was Sylvia who held the floor with a passionate call to the crowd to continue its support of the Free Breakfast Program and also a West Oakland voter registration drive the party was organizing. It was well known to most everyone present that in less than a year Sylvia had become one of the party's essential dynamos, credited with a significant increase in party membership, especially among women.

"She's OK," Bronwyn later heard Larry say to Mack. "Mom lost one son and don't want to lose another."

"So when you leaving?" Bronwyn asked Larry.

"We're outta here Saturday," he said. "Driving. We'll be in Chicago mid-week. Freddie has a place we can stay."

"Gonna be hot," said Bronwyn.

"And in three months it gonna be cold," answered Larry. "That's Chicago. But it's where we can do the most for our people."

Later Mack walked with Bronwyn through the poorly lit and unfamiliar blocks of West Oakland south of the Panther headquarters as they searched for Mack's car.

"It's here, I know it is," Mack said plaintively.

"There it is!" he shouted as he ran ahead of Bronwyn.

Behind her, Bronwyn heard voices, deep male voices but one in particular she knew she'd heard before. Was it Brother David? She turned and saw two large men bouncing toward her. Seemingly unaware of her presence, one collided with her as she tried to move out of the way.

"Sorry, ma'am," said the man who turned to look at her, his face shadowed by the bright street light above him which caused Bronwyn to squint. The large man had grabbed Bronwyn at the shoulders and waist to keep her from falling.

In a long moment Bronwyn and the man each experienced the full range of imaginary human life until the man, aware of something before the same something occurred to Bronwyn, released her, pushed his friend forward and scurried away.

"We outta here," he said as his touch, his voice, his size and the shape of his silhouetted face congealed into the irrevocable truth of Bronwyn's own imaginary life: that the man she had just encountered was the rapist. Her rapist.

MACK

It was on the morning the Viet Cong took back Hamburger Hill that Mack Bellis confronted his personal exposure to war. A letter from Local Draft Board No. 46, Alameda County California, informed Mack his student draft deferment status of II-S had been revoked and he was now classified 1-A. He had lived on borrowed time. He had known for a year since graduating that such a letter might arrive and at any time. Now it had.

His editor was no help. A full-time reporting job, even if one were available, would not qualify as work critical enough to keep Mack out of the Army. Now he weighed what he thought were his only two choices. One was to enlist, which would limit his time of service. He then might land a job as a scribe, a cook, a bugler, anything that would keep him away from combat.

There was no guarantee. A college friend of a friend, caught in the draft during a semester break from school, enlisted and ended up at Fort Leonard Wood in Missouri where he fell through a recruitment funnel and into the infantry. Six months later he was shot dead during a reconnaissance patrol south of Saigon.

The other choice was to run. Mack knew this was a last choice. He might have to leave the U.S. and never return. And there was no assurance he would find life as an exile acceptable or that another country would want him.

"You must a pissed somebody off," Larry said to Mack as they spoke after Larry's farewell party.

"Maybe," said Mack. "It's more likely I'm just caught up in a faceless, mindless system like all the other dumb fucks who hang around with expired deferments. I should have moved on this last year."

"Not too late," said Larry. "You can go to Canada. Wish my brother had. Hell, I wished he'd thrown his rifle down and gone to jail. There was a Black Brothers Union in the army, a Black Liberation Movement of the Armed Forces. There were black prison riots in the military jails in Long Binh and Da Nang the week Sam was killed. He'd be lookin' at hard time. But he'd still be alive."

"Yeah," replied Mack gravely.

Nothing could make up for the death of Larry's brother, which Mack knew to be an unbearable family loss. To die was not nearly the pain one's dying caused for others.

"I'm sorry," Mack said, wishing he knew another way to say what he always said to Larry when the subject of his brother entered a conversation.

Larry nodded this time and said nothing, leaving Mack to realize that Larry, too, was tired of repeating their ritual exchange of grief and sympathy.

Mack phoned his mother

"God, don't enlist!" his mother shouted at her son. "Stay as far away as possible from that goddamned war."

"I might have to leave the country, mom," Mack said.

"Don't tell your dad that," she answered. "He would never forgive you for running away. I won't forgive you if you don't."

Mack thought only mothers should be sent to Paris to negotiate peace.

"Dad's not my concern," said Mack. "Nothing he can do to me now. I worry more about what that will leave you. What he'll do if…"

"Your father and I have our differences," said his mother. "And this damned war is one. Listen, he's not a bad man."

His mother's voice became whiny and pleading.

"He's a good provider. He sent you to college, didn't he? He just doesn't understand or if he does he just doesn't want to think too hard about it. And he voted for Nixon. And he knows I didn't. His first choice isn't to see you in the Army. And he doesn't want you killed, for God's sake. But he's a patriot. You know that."

"Yeah. I love ya, mom," Mack said, his voice trailing off. "I'll be OK. Tell dad I'm fine but don't mention the draft thing."

"Our secret," said his mother. "Write the board. See if you can get it changed. Maybe a Berkeley shrink would write you a letter. Must be a lot up of them up there against the war. He could say you're a nut case or something like that. I've heard that might work."

"I've heard it doesn't," answered Mack. "I'm a little weird mom, but I'm not a nut case."

Mack hung up the phone.

It was the start of another news week, which for Mack began with a tributary of story assignments that gathered downhill momentum and flowed into a foamy river as his deadlines mingled with those of other writers and reporters. By midweek enough stories accrued to fill several additional newsprint pages supported by Wednesday grocery ads and inserts. By the weekend the river of news copy would form pools of special sections, culminating in a fat Sunday paper packed with news, features and promotions. Readers were to be informed though Mack knew it was more important to the paper's circulation that readers be entertained.

Leaving his second story studio on Addison Street, Mack walked to Palmer's Drugs in time for the weekly restocking of newsstand periodicals. He would pick up *Time, Newsweek,* and a copy of *U.S. News and World Report* and devour them over breakfast as he did the evening news over dinner, televised at six each night by the nation's three commercial television networks. Later he would check Moe's for the latest copy of *The Realist.*

Mack's search of the news shelves was halted by a new edition of *Life* magazine, its tabloid-sized cover a haunting, tightly-cropped black and white close-up of the face of a young man, his piercing eyes pushed attentively outward under a brief printed tease line that read *The Faces of The American Dead in Vietnam* and, in smaller block letters, *One Week's Toll*.

Thumbing past ads for sunscreen, cigarettes and cameras, Mack found a featured article that spread over several pages and consisted almost entirely of headshots of young American soldiers who during a single week had been killed in Vietnam.

Mack scanned the pages of photos as he might those of a high school year book, caught first by the varied expressions of the young men that, as in most mug shots, were poses in progress while the flustered subjects tried in a split second to formulate an immortal appearance. Could any have thought at the time this might be their last photographic pose, the last version of themselves to be viewed and held in memory by anyone?

Some smiled awkwardly, some projected stern determination, some stared out of the frame as if directed by a photographer seeking a more natural look. Most were in uniform but some appeared in graduation gowns and caps or suits and ties, suggesting the experience of grieving parents who, contacted by the magazine, must have undertaken a stumbling, heartbreaking search for the most recent photograph of their dead son.

As Mack continued to stare into the faces of so many recently dead boys, he searched their names and homes, printed with their rank in three lines under each photo. Mack found a dead soldier from his southern California hometown of Lakewood but he didn't recognize the soldier's name and his age was given as 18, nearly six years younger than Mack. He would not have known the soldier or seen him in any school he attended.

Mack counted more than a dozen whose hometowns were in California, the nearest in Alameda. Mack considered phoning the family to see if anyone would consent to an interview. It was a journalist's instinct but a terrible idea, even as he rationalized how eager the family might be to tell more of their son's life story, to read his short, shriveled life into some accruing and official record.

The names, 242 of them, were released by the Pentagon for the week May 28 through June 3, read a brief story under a headline that read *One Week's Dead*. It was described as *a span of no special significance except that it included Memorial Day. The number of the dead is average for any seven-day period during this stage of the war.*

Mack turned the tables and wondered how one week's toll of Vietnamese war dead might read. Based on American estimates there wouldn't be a magazine large enough to contain the photos and names of the thousands of Vietnamese allegedly killed each week. Did anyone believe these body counts? The Pentagon's reported killing ratios suggested as many as ten enemy combatants perished for every dead American. This was no longer believable.

Meanwhile dead Americans were perpetually accumulating in the jungles and rice paddies of Vietnam. Mack pictured a wounded Marine limping frantically back into camp, holding in his hands the intestines leaking from his exploded abdomen as he begged someone with a gun to shoot him. It was an image of a dying soldier Mack received in an interview with a veteran of the battle of Khe Sanh the previous year.

However they died this week, each soldier would be listed the following Monday as among that week's American war dead, their names and ranks to be released like the latest edition of a regular newsletter and as the informing and irresistible truth of what everyone, from the president to the sad parents of the war dead to the Vietnamese and the Viet Cong, what all understood was an unwinnable war. Mack would never fight in such a war though he worried his escape from a role in its combat might end up being itself unwinnable.

The farewell of Raj was improvised in a way that suggested to Mack his old friend really did not want to take the time to say goodbye. Raj phoned Mack in the newsroom and invited him for a beer at Kip's before he left Berkeley.

"When?" asked Mack.

"Tonight," said Raj. "We're splittin'."

"You have a car now?" asked Mack.

"We have a ride," said Raj. "It leaves at six. Sonia and I are going back to Shasta."

Raj and Sonia were riding in a caravan of local hippies bound for Black Bear Ranch, several miles and two mountain ranges west of Shasta.

"The hippie commune in the Siskiyous?" asked Mack. "Didn't it nearly fall apart last year?"

"It's doing fine," Raj said defensively as he sipped beer from his schooner and offered Sonia a swig which she declined.

Kips was full of people drinking and ordering food and it was hard to hear over the noise.

"They got about thirty people," Raj yelled. "Crops are in. We're going with four others. We've all been invited."

Raj emphasized the word *invited*. It would not do, even for Raj, to be seen as a hobo looking for a free place to crash.

"Three couples. We're ready to work."

It did seem to matter that Raj was bringing a partner.

"Well, that sounds pretty cool," said Mack. "Can I visit some time?"

"Any god damned time you want," answered Raj. "It's beautiful country."

Mack walked with Raj and Sonia down to the block in front of Raj's rooming house on Haste. A rusting Volkswagen microbus and an older Ford Fairlane idled at the curb while Raj and Sonia carried a duffle and two backpacks from Raj's empty room and shoved them into the Fairlane's nearly full trunk. Sonia climbed into the back seat of the Ford while Raj took shotgun in the Volkswagen.

"We're the ones who know where we're going," Raj said as he slipped into his seat.

The voice of Van Morrison rose from a dashboard tape player, singing about slipstreams and dreams, and cracking, immobile steel rims, and an easy silence that would "lay me down...to be born again..."

Mack cared about Raj. In fact, he loved him. Mack considered the many losses and departures in his life and felt thankful his friend was born toward a chosen destination. For a moment Mack loved everything and thought it possible because everything must end. He loved all that stood and all that would fall. His death was simply his own perception of death and suddenly and obviously nothing to fear.

two

Arguing with his editor was like pouring water into the sea. Mack would talk and talk and nothing would change until, in one gesture Joel Cuthbert stood, his squeaky voice landing like a loud wave that clears a beach.

"It's got nothing to do with that goddamned dead bitch Judy," he shouted at Mack. "Not all homosexuals are a bunch of prancing queens who cry when they hear *Over the Rainbow*. And it wasn't a bunch of queens who rioted at the Stonewall last night."

"I guess you'd know," Mack said with a bite.

Cuthbert was gay and though everyone in the Chronicle's East Bay bureau knew this, the editor still presumed no one could tell. Joel Cuthbert wore khaki slacks, a short sleeve dress shirt with a navy blue string tie cinched at his throat, and black loafers, no doubt thinking boring men's clothing was enough to conceal anything suspiciously effete. He was wrong. He spoke with willowy waving arms and pronounced each syllable of every word with a clear, considered precision.

He was short and wiry like a boy, shorter than Mack who was not tall. Mack sneered when he heard others call him short. Cuthbert barely noticed when the same description was applied to him. A man's body proved only that birth makes bodies. It proved nothing about the man. But Cuthbert's body raised suspicions his voice and gestures only heightened.

"Leather Boys," said Cuthbert. "Big strong boys. Not fags, goddammit. They'll kick your ass. No blowing up their skirts. Just you try."

"So you think Garland's funeral on the same day as the riot at a famous New York gay bar is just a coincidence?" Mack asked his editor.

"The cops started the riot," said Cuthbert. "It could have happened anytime and anywhere. Often does. It's not safe to be, well…different."

"Then you think the riot was justified?" asked Mack. "Like a student protest?"

Mack knew Cuthbert hated student protests. In fact, he hated both students and protests. To say Cuthbert was conservative was to understate the obvious. Fluent in Spanish, Mack's editor had spent three years covering the capitals of Latin America. He saw protests and riots that had brought down governments and killed thousands. Revolutions were dangerous in ways that confirmed for Mack's editor Mao's premise that political power grows out of the barrel of a gun.

And Cuthbert was on the gun's side, certain—as he often said—that the wars and revolutions of the 20th century were all orchestrated to support the ascension of a world government controlled by the ancestors of the Illuminati, an 18th century cabal of European thinkers determined to take over the world.

"Fags in the streets rioting," said Mack's editor. "That's all we need, goddammit. Won't be safe for anyone. They'll all just become scapegoats. Won't be safe anywhere."

"For you?" asked Mack.

"For anyone," said Cuthbert.

Mack listened as his editor started again on his theories of world conspiracy and its founders, the Illuminati.

"Russian and American governments," said Cuthbert. "Run by the same thugs seeking the destruction of democracy and the creation of a world state. Those dumb college kids, if they knew what pawns they are, how they are being used to create disorder that will bring down on all of us a socialist dictatorship. If it weren't for the cops...."

"Wait," said Mack. "Aren't the cops...like...well aren't they the instruments of totalitarian rule? What do you call the martial law this city was under last month?"

"Those park hoodlums are lucky the cops were only using buckshot," said Cuthbert. "Look at what happened last year to the students protesting in Mexico City. The army had it its own ideas. Four hundred killed? Will we ever know? And Mexico still held the god damned Olympics."

"Funny," said Mack. "I thought the troops in Vietnam were cannon fodder. And why a socialist dictatorship? Why not a fascist dictatorship?"

Cuthbert shrugged.

"Would you have gone to fight in Vietnam?" asked Mack.

Cuthbert fielded the question indifferently. He was a male in his late thirties who, for reasons known and also unspoken, had never faced the choice.

"It's a lousy war," he said. "But it has to be fought, if for no other reason than to tie up the resources of communism."

"How do you explain that the communists in Southeast Asia seem to have so many more resources?" asked Mack.

"It's rigged," said Cuthbert.

"So would you have gone to fight?" asked Mack.

"Yeah," said Cuthbert contemptuously. "I'd fight, get my medals and then come home and run for Congress."

"Bullshit," said Mack.

"You can say that again," said Cuthbert. "Bellis…listen to me. It's all bullshit."

Leaving the newsroom Mack tried to picture his editor at home in his own life. Unknown to Cuthbert, he had been seen by another staffer cruising through Buena Vista park one Saturday in a rented Buick Skylark. At an intersection, it was said Cuthbert whistled toward a young, muscular boy, no older than sixteen, modeling shirtless on the lawn.

The boy seemed to recognize the editor and ran toward the car as Cuthbert threw open the passenger door and welcomed him in. Man-Boy love was the most dangerous. It must have been thrilling, thought Mack. It must be the thrill of potential annihilation, the kind of excitement that forces a burglar to pee as soon as he secures entry to an unoccupied home.

Mack was sleeping with Inger again. She stopped by his apartment and caught him at home. She was quickly affectionate and Mack couldn't help responding. If Inger wanted him, then he was usually available.

"What about Kanda?" he asked her after rolling away from her strong, sweaty body.

"It's OK…and it isn't," Inger answered. "It works for some things but not for others."

"Can you be more specific?" asked Mack.

He lit a joint and passed it over to Inger. She took a deep drag,

the kind a veteran tobacco smoker could manage and Mack could
not.

"Think of a group of friends, like you're at a party," said Inger.

"OK," said Mack.

"How many of them do you like?" she asked.

"Easy," said Mack. "They're my friends. I probably like all of
them."

"How many of them do you want to ball?" Inger asked.

Mack considered the question.

"Seriously?"

Inger nodded.

"One or two…if that," answered Mack. "I probably brought a
date to the party so when it comes to sex I'm not even thinking about
my friends."

"That's the problem with Kanda," said Inger. "Too many
friends."

"Conscientious objector is out," said the older graduate student
named Jeff at the Resistance table outside Sather Gate.

"You don't have a religious affiliation. You can object anyway,
but you'll go to jail. Until '65 you could avoid the draft by getting
married. But now you need a kid. Do you have a kid?"

"Not married or a father," said Mack. "Not even close."

"You can smoke inky cigarettes a week before induction to stain
your lungs for the x-ray," said Jeff.

"When you get there you can say you're a homosexual. All kinds
of things guys try at the induction. Some work and some don't. The
sergeants have seen it all. It's a crapshoot to wait for the physical at
the induction center. Lotta pressure there. You say you don't want to
fight; they'll turn you over to the FBI on the spot. You'll be held for
interrogation and that's no fun. You're looking at 10 years in prison
and huge fines."

"What about graduate school?" Mack asked.

"Are you studying to be a doctor?" asked Jeff.

"No. Journalism," said Mack.

Jeff laughed.

"Not a career that will keep you out of the Army. Depending on what you write they may love to get you out of circulation, if you'll excuse the pun."

Jeff was silent for a moment.

"Some guys enlist. I'm guessing that's not what you want to do because you're here at the Resistance table."

"I hate this fucking war," said Mack. "What about Canada?"

"Yeah…though it's a little tricky," said Jeff. "Go to Canada after you're called up and it's draft evasion, pure and simple. You won't be able to come back without facing arrest. If you can secure landed immigrant status, then you can cross the border and establish residency in Canada, but if you're drafted, technically you have an obligation as a U.S. citizen to serve. Though Canada won't kick you out if they've accepted you as a permanent resident. Canada isn't kicking anyone out right now. Even army deserters appear to be welcome. How old are you?"

"I'll be 24 in November," said Mack.

"You're draft eligibility ends at age 26. That's more than two years for you," said the Resistance guy.

"Long time to wait. Odds are likely you'll be called or you'll go crazy waiting. Ever been to Canada?"

Mack shook his head.

"I can put you in touch with a Resistance group in Seattle," said Jeff. "They can tell you more about it. They have links with American ex-pats living in Vancouver."

He pulled out a notebook and copied a paragraph of names and addresses onto a sheet of notepaper. He handed it to Mack.

"Good luck," Jeff said as Mack turned to leave and Jeff flashed him a V with his fingers.

Mack read once that a plant proved only that planting made plants. In such a way his thoughts of war—obsessive, scary, and now personally threatening—proved only that thinking made thoughts. He tried to turn his thoughts away, crawling out of bed at three a.m. to sit again by his window and to imagine how he might save his life from the vast national gravity tugging him toward a sickening slide. He would not go to war. He knew that. He would not.

He knew the stories: had interviewed veterans who had watched young Vietnam girls raped by GIs who then shot them and left them to die, who had seen fellow soldiers step on improvised booby traps and lose everything below their bladders. War was cruel and this one especially as Americans appeared to be devastating a society they were allegedly determined to save from what? Communism? Though the enemy, perhaps driven by its defense of a homeland, was even more ruthless, inflicting limitless death and torture as it climbed over a mountain of its own people's corpses to kill every American and South Vietnamese soldier within reach.

It was in this sweet darkness before another dawn that Mack conceived the plan for a road trip north, one he would chart through the spacious northwest and that would take him before fall into British Columbia and into contact with others like himself who had considered immigration as a way out. The thought eased Mack's urgency but also fed every one of his encroaching fears. A clock was ticking and he had no way to tell the time.

Mack awoke on the Fourth of July momentarily relieved of his difficult thoughts by two news stories. The first described a break-in by resisters at the New York City draft board in Rockefeller Center where they destroyed 6500 draft files. Another was an announcement by President Nixon that 15,000 troops were being withdrawn from Vietnam, the first step in what Nixon described as the *Vietnamization* of the war. It was convenient for Mack to see the first story as firmly linked to the second and to hear in the president's oddly coined noun an admission the war eventually would have to end.

The Fourth was not a holiday for Mack, whose editor had loaned him to the city desk for an assignment in San Francisco. With the People's Park issue locked up in fitful negotiations and meetings, Mack was told to attend the opening of the O'Farrell Theater, a new venue showing skin flicks that were testing the limits of decency with racy depictions of nudity and simulated sex that pushed the envelope of presumed community standards.

It was one of nearly two-dozen such theaters in the Bay Area and it seemed only a matter of time before one or more were busted by the cops for violations of municipal codes that prohibited the showing of explicit pornography. Customers, too, might be cited.

The O'Farrell could be busted and Mack was to be on hand to interview the owners, the cops, any patrons who would talk, and to write a story.

In the early afternoon Mack entered the theater, a refurbished industrial building at the corner of O'Farrell and Polk Streets. He bought a ticket for $4, was offered a free coffee and then directed toward a dark passage and into a modest viewing room illuminated by a screen across which young women walked, stretched, undressed and prominently displayed their breasts and bottoms. The collection of six film sequences, which Mack later would learn were called loops, lasted about 80 minutes. In one loop a woman turned to reveal a brief view of her vulva's pubic hair before turning away. No men appeared in the film. Mack searched the room, which featured a dozen rows of movie seats, about eight in a row and divided by an aisle. Mack counted about twenty patrons, all adult men of varying ages.

The only skin flick Mack had ever watched was a Forties-era black and white stag film shown at a fraternity party he attended in his freshman year. It was illegally explicit, but grainy, scratched and of remarkably poor quality as it told the minimal story of a masturbating nun interrupted by a young male voyeur who enters her bedroom to have sex with her.

What Mack noticed about the O'Farrell film was its crisp detail and brilliant color. The performers' bodies filled the room's modest sized screen and the action of the women, filmed from several angles, created the impression Mack was sitting in the room with them. The visual effect was stunning and Mack became fully absorbed in the action before realizing there was no soundtrack other than a medley of current pop tunes coming through the speakers. The women moved around or stretched out on a bed or couch and occasionally, their hands and crotches out of view, simulated a sexual climax before fading from the screen. The film quality surprised Mack who could not help feeling aroused.

"You really worried about getting busted for this?" Mack asked one of the two brothers who together owned the O'Farrell.

The owner went by the name of Big Bob. In his mid-twenties, Big Bob was a film student at San Francisco State College. He said his brother was Little Bob and together they had been producing loops for a couple of years.

"This is good quality film," said Mack. "But how is it different from topless dancing in North Beach or the nudies shown at the Roxie on Mission? No one gets busted for that now. Why don't you think you can do this?"

"It's not what we *can* do," said Big Bob as he lingered in the lobby with Mack. "It's what we want to do."

"What do you mean?" asked Mack.

"Visit the Screening Room tomorrow," answered Big Bob. "They're pushing the envelope, man. More nudity, some beaver-shots, and one feature that has two women touching each other. Two dozen skin flick theaters in this region and eventually someone is going to show the real thing. It's all moving that way."

"What way?" asked Mack.

"Toward full-on sex, that's what way," said Big Bob. "An audience should be able to watch explicit sexual films without being hassled by cops. Especially in this town."

Mack scribbled notes.

"Mind if I quote you?" asked Mack.

"I have something to show you," said Big Bob.

Mack followed Big Bob down a hall and into a smaller room with a blackboard-sized screen on a wall and a 16mm-film projector positioned on a card table. A back wall was lined with shelves that each held dozens of film canisters.

"Our latest loop," Big Bob said and turned out the lights.

It featured a young woman seen nude from the back as she looked out a window while brushing her long, reddish blonde hair. A tan, slender man entered the scene and approached her, placing his hands on her bare shoulders while pulling her up for a smothering kiss. The next view showed the woman's bare legs outstretched on a bed as her lover, now undressed, settled tenderly between them and placed his lips just below her belly button and began a series of downward directed nuzzles and kisses.

The camera then panned slowly up the woman's body, past her small breasts held firmly in the hands of her lover and toward her neck, her lips and her eyes that blinked with conspicuous pleasure at the presumed contact of her lover's lips with her vulva.

The panning camera then pulled away from the woman and showed her face, following her expressions for several minutes as they aligned into a look of tense, eager and greedy desire. Until at last she came and the camera widened to reveal her heaving body's prolonged orgasmic spasm. Mack sat motionless as if in a trance. He knew the woman in the film. It was Inger.

three

"So you got a story or what?" Cuthbert asked Mack when he returned to the newsroom.

"Not much yet," Mack answered. "No bust. But they expect one. Other theaters have been hassled by the cops. I spoke with the owners. It's a big deal. There's a story here. Yeah, and they make the movies themselves."

"Really? They shoot them?" asked Mack's editor. "Damn, that's a story. How? Where? Who acts in them?"

"Mostly young women. Local ladies. Students. Hippies. The footage I saw was very professional."

"Think you could get a woman to talk about why she does it?" asked the editor.

"I don't know," said Mack evasively.

"Sex sells papers. Stay with it," said the editor. "Talk to other owners. Find out how they make these movies and hire the talent. Human interest, you know."

"Yeah," said Mack. "Sex is definitely a human interest."

Although Team members observed no brutality, they noted the fearful reaction of the inmates whenever prison officials appeared. All prisoners are oppressed by conditions of overcrowding. Sometimes many prisoners are stuffed into small cells which do not allow for lying down or sometimes not even sitting: and this, when it is steam-hot, when excrement accumulates, and when the prisoners are seldom released for exercise, is torture indeed. Beating is the most common form of abuse. Several ex-prisoners testified that it is not unusual to torture family members,

Mack marked these paragraphs with a pencil as the F bus bounced into a turn off the Bay Bridge and rolled along the Embarcadero freeway toward the Mission Street exit. The abridged article in *I.F. Stone's Weekly* quoted a report by the U.S. Study Team on Religious and Political Freedom in Vietnam. The team comprising prominent American religious leaders and educators had spent weeks traveling through South Vietnam. An anti-war congressman had recently read the report into the Congressional Record where Stone uncovered it.

Mack admired Stone as a mighty David whose one-man news service consistently uncovered powerful and uncomfortable truths about the monstrous Goliath that was the U.S. government. Mack didn't know what he could do with the marked quote. Maybe save it to throw at Cuthbert the next time his editor defended the war. It didn't matter. The study team's description of the quality of "freedom" U.S. soldiers were defending in Vietnam, if not a surprise, at least further affirmed why Mack could never serve in the Army, not to mention fight in the war.

Mack left the bus to walk toward the Tenderloin. He had an appointment with the owner of the Screening Room, a skin flick cinema that for two years had shown "nudies" despite occasional harassment from the cops. Mack took a seat in the theater, another small room of about sixty seats occupied by less than a dozen men each alone in his separate row.

A young woman on the screen wandered across a beach at sunset. She wore a white silk robe that caught the wind like a billowing sail until, reaching a copse of large rocks, she dropped the robe to the sand leaving her fully naked. A series of cuts showed her as she improvised a dance among the rocks, until arriving at a small gulch where she fell back against the sand and closed her eyes. A long view showed her moving a hand to the tip of her brushy mons before panning up her body toward her breasts and face. The view held while the motion of her shoulders and the tightening lineaments around her eyes suggested certain arousal. Teasing shots at times dipped down to the wrist of her active hand, occasionally showing the upper dark fringe of her pubes. It was skillful and sexy and, as he learned later from the owner, still safe to show.

Much as they had at the O'Farrell, six more sequences followed, all of young women smiling, disrobing, and then engaging in some kind of sexual activity, mostly masturbation, that produced visible signs of arousal and release. In the final sequence a woman and man together embraced before the woman backed away while her partner began filming her, occasionally reaching in to touch her or to show her how he would like her to touch herself. It was a clever way to introduce a man into soft-core relation to a naked, sexually aroused woman.

"No erections," said Alan, the Screening Room's owner, a tall, slender man in his early thirties with a black Fu Manchu moustache. "At least not yet."

He wore a white cardigan sweater and grey wool slacks and tennis shoes. He tapped his desk nervously as he spoke to Mack in a small office behind the theater.

"No, we can't show hard core films yet. But I say *yet*. It's a matter of time, though it's going to become more difficult before it gets easier."

"Why difficult?" asked Mack.

"There's a new sheriff in town," said Alan. "That's the word, anyway. And one of the county supervisors, a woman, says this is just dirty smut and should be banned. And she's a Democrat! The women in the films don't think it's smut, do they?"

"Well, do they?" asked Mack. "Who are those women? Where do you find them?"

"Second question first," said Alan. "The women answer our ads for models and actresses, the ads you see in the underground papers. They're mostly hippie chicks from the Haight or students at the colleges. Though a few come to us from the suburbs. All have to be eighteen or older. We check IDs.

"As for your first question, there's nothing phony here. These women—all of them—enjoy what they're doing or we don't film them. If there's a problem, we stop the shoot. Our films are different because the pleasure isn't fake. One day we'll show couples balling and all that goes with it. Those movies are being made now in living color and sound. They've always been made, since the beginning of film. They always will be. And you know what? It's art. A pure erotic art. And it should be an adult's free choice to see it."

"What do you pay?" asked Mack.

"Fifty to a hundred…it's negotiable," said Alan.

"That's for the loops. Longer films…well that's different."

Mack asked if Alan or anyone was making a feature film.

"Can't say, but I'm going to show hard core no later than next year. And I'm going to do it legally."

"How?" asked Mack.

Alan described his plan to attend a porn film festival in Copenhagen and make a documentary that would include explicit footage from Danish hard-core films. He would add commentary and cut together a feature that, because it was a documentary, would be nearly impossible to ban in the U.S.

"And once the door is open…" he added without finishing his sentence.

"Would any of your actors talk to a reporter?" Mack asked at last.

The owner pondered the request.

"Maybe. I'd have to ask. We promise not to release any information about them. It's not just theaters that risk arrest. But it's too much of a hassle, at least so far, for the cops to try to find our actors. We want to keep it that way. What I worry, though, is they might start busting our patrons."

Every time someone loses something, it is because they have something to lose. Mack pondered the investments represented by the theater owners, built from the attractive assets of actors on offer with the most renewable resource there was: their own pleasure. Why did this plentiful and widespread asset have such value when it cost all who had sexual pleasure absolutely nothing to reenact? Or was it without cost? There was an exposure involved, one that could change any subject's relationship with place and time and even pleasure.

Was being filmed in sexual thrall truly victimless and without cost? Still, it seemed ironic to Mack that the vast profits accruing to the theater owners were grown from other people's sex. Notably, the willing and apparently enjoyable display by women of their bodies and its furtive, secret and private indulgence by sullen, isolated males huddled in dark theaters.

Mack thought he might be sleeping too much. He awoke late one morning to the news Apollo 11 had left the earth. A successful launch sent four humans hurtling toward the moon with the goal of landing two on its surface. It was the news and today the only news that like many headlines absorbed him more than himself.

News painted Mack into the corners and crevices of his life because he so strongly identified with the broad, rich trouble fomented out of human commerce. And as a journalist, he thought himself a privileged midwife of events that were scattered like seeds of a living history. Apollo 11 was such a seed; its historical relevance guaranteed whatever happened. Either success or disaster, the mission was his species' boldest assertion of its unique and reflective consciousness. Though in reading the news, it often appeared to Mack that ignorance made the world which intelligence explained.

Mack shaved in the bathroom, the mirror reflecting an Esquire magazine cover from the previous year pinned to the wall and featuring Muhammad Ali posed as St. Sebastian and pierced with arrows as he stood in his white Everlast boxing shorts seemingly bound in a passionate, painful torture. He had refused induction into the Army and, in addition to facing prosecution, was stripped of his heavyweight title and prohibited from fighting again professionally. Mack admired Ali, applauded his resistance to war and his argument that he wouldn't fight in Vietnam because no Vietnamese ever did anything to hurt him. The cover reminded Mack that he, too, was approaching a confrontation with resistance. He wanted to run from the draft and wished he had another identity he could trade for the one that was now classified 1-A. He wondered what he might look like with a beard.

"She's gone. She didn't tell you?" said Harriet.

"Bronwyn and her friend Rita left Sunday to drive to New York."

"Is Bronwyn coming back?" asked Mack.

Rummaging in his apartment, Mack had come across Bronwyn's copy of *No More Fun and Games*. It had been at least two weeks since he had seen her. He stopped by Harriet's flat to return her copy and to invite Bronwyn to see a movie with him.

"I have to think so. She paid July's rent. But she hinted she was looking for a change. I know she's close with Rita. Part of her women's circle, or whatever they call it."

"Consciousness raising group," said Mack. "It's a women's movement deal. We've talked about it."

"Yeah, well I know Bronwyn is planning to visit her parents in Queens. She left me the address. Want it?"

Mack nodded.

"Still going to Africa?" Mack asked Harriet.

Harriet had gained some more weight, which Mack thought looked good on her. He noticed also that Harriet wore a tight-fitting top that highlighted her more substantial breasts.

"I don't know…." Harriet said after a long pause. "Michael left for his training and I'm set to go in September. But I'm getting cold feet. It looks like we're going to end up with assignments in different places. The whole point of this commitment was for us to work together. But we're not married so the Peace Corps has no obligation to field us together. Now…well…like I said, I don't know."

"What would you do if you didn't go?" asked Mack.

"I can't say yet," she answered. "Michael is still real, even if I have my doubts. He seems to love me and I love him. But something, there's something I can't name…"

An hour passed in the kitchen of Harriet's flat as she spoke to Mack about her worries. Michael had formulated a grand plan that would carry them through the next two years and leave him after their Peace Corps assignment with a path either into a prestigious faculty placement or politics.

"He figures we'll be married by then and that I'll be a perfect partner in a way aligned with his career goals. But he's never asked about mine. My god, before he left for his training he told me where we'd get married. On Cape Cod at his uncle's family compound. He didn't even ask me."

"Does he know how you feel?" asked Mack.

"I've been afraid to tell him. I thought I could get used to this after he left for his training. But now that he's gone, I'm realizing I don't want to do this. He has planned everything for me. Just like my father did."

Mack told Harriet about the change in his draft status.

"What will you do?" she asked.

"I'm not going to war," Mack said. "I may have to leave the country."

"You sound determined," said Harriet.

Mack was determined not to fight largely because he was determined not to die. Was he afraid to die? Or did he just cling desperately to something that was going to die anyway? The fear of death wasn't a fear he would lose consciousness forever. His fear of death embraced the consciousness of its pain, the awareness that a grievous, excruciating blow would be his last known experience.

Inger staggered behind Mack up the steps to his apartment. She wasn't drunk but tipsy enough to spend the night. Mack drank his share in the city's only downtown bar at the old and venerable Hotel Shattuck and couldn't drive her home. His place was a walk from the theater where they had seen *Easy Rider* before spending an hour drinking gin and tonics.

Inger had found the movie's story depressing, especially the ending in which the traveling motorcycle druggies Wyatt and Billy are shot dead by rednecks on a rural Louisiana highway.

"It's a man's film," Inger said when they went for drinks. "Lots of violence, a little sex. Very few words. Men are people of few words, I guess."

Mack loved the movie. He listened patiently to Inger before strongly disagreeing.

"These men are trapped in a journey," he said. "Their lives, especially Wyatt's, are still works in progress. Mardi Gras in New Orleans becomes the goal of a twisted odyssey, I grant you. But it's a test that undoes Wyatt's certainties even if it has little effect on Billy.

Men are thrown into these tests of survival constantly. Little wonder a journey is almost always a male metaphor for experience."

"It might be easier for men if they could talk about it," said Inger. "They might understand more and also be able to ask for more. That might make these kinds of journeys unnecessary."

"When they stop asking men to go to war," Mack answered bitterly. "When they stop asking men to die for what some bully decides is right?"

"Tell me about this draft thing," Inger asked Mack. "What are you going to do?"

"Take a journey. Go to Canada," he said with subdued sarcasm, though as he said it he knew he meant it.

As they entered Mack's apartment Inger threw her jacket onto a chair and wandered off to the bathroom. She knew his home like she knew her own and Mack considered all the time he spent with her. In bed they continued a conversation about art and Inger's plans to join a women's art class at Fresno State in the spring. She was warm, tender and aroused and seemed to cherish Mack's intellectual respect for her as an artist, which she told him she did not experience with most men.

Their touches began in a familiar way though Mack surprised Inger by slipping slowly and teasingly down her body as he left a trail of nibbles and kisses before softly testing her mons and labia with his tongue. She was instantly responsive and threw open her legs, much as Mack remembered from her O'Farrell loop. He probed and teased her with consciously applied licks that, following an urgent tension which filled less than a minute, brought Inger to a thrashing, convulsive come.

"What's happened to you?" Inger asked later, after she pulled Mack up to enter her and in a fury of quick, short thrusts he also came.

"Just thought it would be fun," Mack said disingenuously.

"You're right about that," said Inger. "Wish more men had your adventuring spirit."

"Hard to know what women want," said Mack self-consciously.

Watching porn loops for a week had further confused Mack about the sexuality of women. Those he watched on the screen, several his age and many younger, appeared shameless in their pleasure with both sex and themselves. It was as if each's sex was a personal power, the sharing of which was also a power and one the women, perhaps unknowingly, held over a dark room of shy and suppliant men.

"Why don't men ask women what they want?"

Inger's directness flustered Mack. He had fucked Inger for more than a year and never asked her what she wanted. He had asked her what she liked in art, spent hours conversing with her about films and shows and her aspirations as a painter, but had not spoken with her about their sex.

"Yeah…" Mack answered weakly. "I guess we're afraid."

Mack was surprised to hear himself speak for all men.

"Afraid of what?" asked Inger.

"Afraid of being put down," Mack at last answered. "Afraid we can't do what a woman asks."

"Women worry about that a lot with men," said Inger. "Welcome to the club."

Mack was silent for a long minute.

"Tell me," he said finally. "Tell me what you think of me as a lover."

"You're attractive, Mack," said Inger. "And you share my interests, which is a big turn on. And you like me. Really like me like a friend. That makes me feel secure."

"But in bed…" Mack asked again.

"You're affectionate and funny. But like most men you're quick. Too quick, frankly. Except tonight. God, what got into you? Anyway, there are times after we fuck that you fall asleep and I get down, y'know. Take care of myself. It's cool. Don't feel bad. I like the closeness. And I like you."

Mack at first retreated from Inger's intimate critique, even as he knew he had asked for it. Inger was a handsome, horny woman that men found attractive, though Mack knew Inger herself found certain men attractive and had no trouble making the first move. Sexual variety excited her. Love, however, was never discussed and as they spoke, Mack opened to the fact Inger would never love him nor would he love Inger. It was not a question of whether in her libido-driven life Inger could ever settle down and love only one man. It was whether Mack could, or would, ever love any one woman.

four

As a student of human history Mack accepted membership in a species constantly carried away in fits of madness. With the right words and thoughts he too could be drawn into delusion.

The draft board that two weeks before had notified Mack he was now eligible for induction in the army was located a block from the campus. Mack wondered why he did not just go down to the board, stand at the counter and beg obsequiously for a change in his draft status. He passed the board's office almost every day on his way to Telegraph Avenue. One afternoon he saw a mob of draft protesters out front while two young men set fire to their draft cards and held them high in the wind.

Mack willfully resisted a restless temptation to react, to respond without thought from his puerile place of fear and likely run headlong into the jaws of death. Fortunately, he could see the jaws coming. He knew the predator and how it satisfied its appetite, though this knowledge still allowed no easy choices. He imagined himself running out of time to act or places to hide before ending up trapped in a tree.

As Mack prepared coffee in his kitchen, Inger phoned.

She had left before he awoke to catch a bus back to the City.

"Good morning," Mack said warmly.

He welcomed the sound of her voice. The evening had been sweet and Mack regarded Inger as a close and honest friend.

"Listen, I have to tell you something," Inger said.

Mack heard the tension in her voice.

"Yeah…?" said Mack.

"I've got a pretty good case of crabs. I should have told you last night. I don't know why I didn't."

Mack stood frozen as her words sunk in.

"Damn, Inger. Why didn't…?"

Mack did not finish his question.

"I'm sorry," Inger interrupted in a way that telegraphed her vast experience with apology.

554

"You'll want to check yourself and your clothes. You'll want to wash the…"

"I know what do," Mack answered curtly.

"Damn, Inger," Mack said again. "What were you thinking?"

"I wasn't thinking," Inger answered. "I was having fun. I was drunk. You asked me to stay over."

"That would have been a good time to tell me," Mack replied.

"Yeah. I know. I'm really sorry I didn't."

Inger's humble insouciance might have been well rehearsed but Mack didn't feel manipulated. Inger was simply thoughtless about much of anything or anyone beyond herself. The philosopher Norman O. Brown was Inger's guiding star, the author of *Life Against Death* who seemed to give Inger personal permission to open herself to sexual adventures simply because they were what she wanted.

She needed no justification to explore intimacy beyond the pleasure it aroused in her and the responsibility she took for her own body and its satisfaction. It was the Inger version of polymorphous perversity. It felt to Mack more like *caveat emptor.*

"Goodbye, Inger."

Mack hung up the phone.

News swung on the pivot of chaos and for Mack any day's headlines were evidence of the million ways expectations were tested by the irresistible influence of discord. On Sunday he waited to see if men would walk on the moon. Having overcome earth's strong gravity enough to be captured by that of another heavenly body, would the Apollo 11 astronauts succeed in strolling its surface? Would they then be able to escape the gravity of another world? No human had ever done either. The event was planned for the evening, as if punctuality were important for a momentous step into space never before attempted.

Mack would arrive in front of a television in time to watch it, though this morning his attention was diverted by a headline that read *Ted Kennedy Escapes; Woman Drowns.*

Leaving a Martha's Vineyard party for campaign workers the previous Friday night, Senator Kennedy drove away with a young woman aide, and then plunged his car off a rail-less bridge leading to

Chappaquiddick Island. Facts were fuzzy but those that were known had Kennedy escaping the sinking car, leaving the woman aide behind to drown, and not reporting the accident to authorities until mid-morning Saturday, presumably long after a blood test might reveal the presence of alcohol in his system.

Sunday's photos showed the senator's car being pulled from the shallows at a far end of the Chappaquiddick bridge. Touted as a likely Democratic nominee for president, the youngest brother of two famously murdered Kennedys was suspected of being both a drinker and a womanizer. And in addressing the chaos grown from this incident, it was impossible for Mack—or anyone —not to conclude that a drunken Teddy had panicked and run. No amount of reason could divert the events of the night away from the presumption of the senator's moral ataxia, one ruinously self-inflicted and that now pivoted disastrously and tragically toward disorder.

That evening men walked on the moon and Mack watched until his phone rang. It was his editor.

"You got a few minutes?" Cuthbert asked.

"You have some news?" asked Mack. "Thinking of a Kennedy story?"

"No…no more stories," said Cuthbert.

There was silence.

"Listen, Bellis. I hate doing this. But the union finally got to management over the hiring of stringers. And I've been busted. I have to let you go."

"Gee, it's been two years…" Mack responded weakly. "I mean, how does anyone…"

"You know I'd hire you if I had a reporter's job."

"Do I?" asked Mack as he succumbed to a cynical musing.

"Seems with things settling down on campus you don't need my contacts anymore."

"C'mon, Mack! That's not fair," Cuthbert countered. "I've been sticking my goddamned neck out to…"

"Save it," shouted Mack. "When am I finished?"

"Now," said Cuthbert. "They don't give me any wiggle room with this."

"Well, that's one fucking blue-ribbon quality bummer," snipped Mack.

"Yeah," said his editor. "Yeah, it is that. Listen, I can give you a letter. A recommendation. Whatever you need. I have nothing but great shit to say, nothing but the best…"

"OK. Enough," Mack cut Cuthbert off. "I wouldn't expect anything less."

"My stuff at the office," said Mack. "Notes, some books. My Strunk & White."

"Come in anytime," said Cuthbert. "Maybe you'd let me buy you a drink."

"Thanks anyway," said Mack. "But I'm going out to do my drinking now. Goodbye."

Cuthbert's words continued but Mack wasn't listening.

Mack walked toward Telegraph where he found Yitzhak sitting at a table in the Forum. The moon landing had emptied the café. The Forum had no television. As Yitzhak sat he wrote in an open, leather-bound journal.

Yitzhak had a notably different appearance. He wore a brown flannel shirt and black jeans. Gone were his red head bandanna and his white, puffy sleeved gypsy shirt along with the leather vest that covered it. His sideburns were shaved and his dark, exposed hair was cut back into a curly, manageable crew. Instead of his signature Caribbean black boots, Yitzhak wore suede blue loafers. The once cultivated look of an acid street pirate was gone and, if Mack didn't know him, might have taken Yitzhak to be just another student studying for a summer mid-term.

"What's with you?" asked Mack ingenuously.

Yitzhak looked up, seemingly puzzled by Mack's question.

"The clothes…" Mack said. "They're new."

"They're old," said Yitzhak. "Been in my closet. You like 'em?"

"Make you look like a student," Mack answered.

"I am," said Yitzhak. "Taking a class."

"What are you writing?" asked Mack.

"Words," Yitzhak announced without looking up.

Mack grabbed a chair.

"May I join you?" he asked.

Yitzhak nodded and continued to write.

"Am I interrupting you?" Mack asked.

Yitzhak at last looked up and shook his head.

"It's a huge head trip, man. Give me a minute. I need this."

Mack waited until Yitzhak finished writing and closed his journal.

"It's for my class," said Yitzhak.

"What class are you taking?" Mack asked incredulously.

"It's Monday nights in the City," said Yitzhak. "An SF State class."

"On what?"

"Current affairs," Yitzhak said with a truculent wink.

Mack knew the look but wasn't always certain if it meant anything.

"I need a drink," Mack said. "Let me buy you a beer."

Kips Upstairs was full, a crowd of mostly summer session students gathered at the bar and turned away from the grainy black and white TV images of astronauts in bulky white spacesuits bumping across the moon's opaque surface. The video quality was poor and, after absorbing abstractly the miracle that what they were viewing was being televised from the surface of the moon, interest in the mission widely ceased.

"Turn on the ballgame!" someone yelled from the hall.

"Quality is so bad, you have to wonder if they're even ON the moon," the bartender said as he served pint schooners to Mack and Yitzhak.

"Could be televised from a TV studio in Burbank for all we know."

"Maybe for all you know," said Mack, resistant to any idiosyncratic suggestion that such an obviously public and noble scientific breakthrough could be so stupidly dismissed.

Mack looked at Yitzhak who appeared sullen.

"He's got a point…" Yitzhak began before Mack waved him off.

Mack took a few swigs from his schooner while Yitzhak watched the television.

"What have you done about the draft?" Mack at last asked Yitzhak.

"Nothing," said Yitzhak.

"Nothing? What? What's your classification? They haven't come after you?" asked Mack frantically.

"4-F," said Yitzhak succinctly.

"Since when?" said Mack.

"Since years ago. Probably because I'm collecting disability."

As he explained it, Yitzhak had tried to enlist at some time he could not now recall. For reasons he could not explain he was rejected after an interview with an Army psychologist.

"A lot was going on then. Doing a lot of acid, y'know. Really trippin'. Anyway, I told my mom and together we applied for disability. Been getting it ever since."

"How much is it?" asked Mack.

"About $140-somethin' a month. Mom deposits it. What about you? What do you do about the draft?"

The question surprised Mack who wasn't accustomed to Yitzhak's interest in much beyond a seemingly gossamer fog that appeared always to veil his mind.

"Well, I better do something…and soon," said Mack.

Mack described the loss of his II-S deferment and the immediate loss of his job. He railed for a moment about the iniquitous evils of war, the army, labor unions and Republicans. He described a rejected plan to change his name and address and go underground.

"Mack Bellis c/o 1969 HellKnow Lane, San Narsisco CA."

He picked the city from a Thomas Pynchon novel he'd read the previous year.

"Really, I want to go to Canada. If my car would make it, I'd leave."

"I'll take you," Yitzhak said without hesitation. "When you wanna go?"

Mack thought of his friend's Chevy bomber that belched black smoke and barely made it across town.

"Nice try. But no fucking way, not in your Chevy," said Mack.

"I have a new car," said Yitzhak. "No fucking sweat."

"New car?" asked Mack.

An uncle had died and inexplicably left his 1965 Chevelle with barely 21,000 miles to his favorite and only nephew, Raymond "Yitzhak" Jaffe.

"Mom helped me register it last week. It's cool," said Yitzhak. "Never been to Canada. A road trip, man. Maybe we could stop at Black Bear and see Raj."

Mack held his breath. Yitzhak's enthusiasm sounded remarkably coherent, though Mack couldn't be certain. What Mack knew was that his '57 Bug, its transmission slipping badly, would likely die before he reached Oregon. And a new car was out of the question.

"And you're serious?" Mack asked. "What about your class?"

Yitzhak gazed toward the bar's television, his eyes aligned as if he were entranced, a state familiar to Mack who attributed the look to one of his friend's many acid flashbacks. In most instances Yitzhak's gazes appeared to be directed into a void and rarely did they return him with relevance for the current conversation.

"Yeah," Yitzhak said, his eyes drawn back to Mack's with a surprisingly focused clarity.

"The class will be there when I get back. It's been going for a year."

Mack could not imagine such a class. But decided not to ask.

"Ever driven a Chevelle?" asked Yitzhak.

"Is it a stick?" asked Mack.

"Yeah," answered Yitzhak.

"Cool," said Mack.

"You don't sound like you've thought this through," Mack's mother shouted into the phone.

Mack could hear water running and assumed his father was doing the dishes, which meant his mother was in the kitchen.

"Please don't tell Dad anything about Canada," Mack pleaded.

"No sweat, son," said his mom. "Pa's done. Aren't you Pa? He's leaving to watch Laugh-In. Go on, dear. Get outta here. I'm talkin' to your boy…OK…your dad says hi."

"Hi back," said Mack.

A silence followed.

"He's gone. So tell me again, how long have you been serious about Canada? You know anything about it?"

"I will soon," Mack answered defensively. "I have some money saved. I have a ride. And I just lost my news job."

Mack described the sudden disappearance of his employment and listened to his mother's railing anger with his editor.

"I've done it already," said Mack. "Time to move on and, in my case, time to move out. I think that's a military term."

His mother didn't laugh.

"So what am I supposed to tell your father? That you've lost your job and have decided to look for work in…Canada? What the hell is in Canada?"

"I'll tell you when I get there," said Mack. He could be as sarcastic as his mother. He credited her with the trait.

"I thought you'd be happy I wasn't hanging around to be drafted."

Mack tried to project an outraged tone.

"I thought you'd do more to figure things out. Not just up and go," said his mom.

"It's my next phone call. To a draft resistance group in Seattle. A local tells me they send a half-dozen Americans into Canada every week and get them all the papers they need. Mom…even if it's not something I want to do at least it's something I *can* do."

"So what do I tell your dad?" his mom asked.

"Nothing. Not now. Just say I'm doing fine. Tell him I'm on assignment or something. I'll stay in touch and send him a letter when things are settled and I know what I'm actually doing."

"I hate this damned war…"

His mother could not complete her thought before Mack heard her voice break and go silent.

"We love you," she said finally. "Don't forget."

Mack knew his mother loved him but wasn't certain about his father. So much a man loved in a son seemed to Mack based in what a father saw reflected back of himself. And in this Mack had been a persistent failure. A college degree from a prestigious university was a pinnacle and something so beyond his father's reach that he had to marvel at a son who could achieve it. Beyond that, there was little to share or for either to applaud in the other.

"You won't tell them you want to leave the United States," said the voice from Seattle.

"You need to tell Canadian Immigration why you want to live in Canada. It's easier now. But it's no cakewalk across the border. Do you have a job lined up?"

"No," said Mack.

"You know what city you want to live in?"

"No," Mack said again. "Maybe Vancouver?"

"You going to marry a Canadian woman?"

"No…I don't know one," said Mack.

"What's your line of work?" asked the voice from Seattle.

"Journalist. Reporter," said Mack.

"Well, that's one point for your entry interview. You need fifty."

Mack was growing weary of the discouraging words of Jasper, a volunteer for Draft Resistance-Seattle, a University of Washington group that for four years had assisted draftees who did not want to serve in the Army.

"You're not very encouraging," said Mack.

"Doesn't mean I won't help. Just want to be realistic. When are you coming to Seattle?" Jasper asked.

"Three, four weeks," said Mack.

"And you're 1-A but haven't been called yet?"

"Right," said Mack.

"We probably have some time, then. Would be better if you could cross the border before you receive your induction letter. Immigration officers aren't supposed to ask about your draft status anymore, but it's better for you if it's not an issue."

Jasper gave Mack the group's Seattle address.

"On Madison, east of Capitol Hill. And read up on Canada, for chris' sakes. Know something about the country you may live in the rest of your life."

Yitzhak's mother sailed on a sea of suffering. It was immediately apparent to Mack who made a point of visiting Yitzhak in his home, to assure himself the Chevelle existed, that it was Yitzhak's car to drive and that his mother—who seemed to continue in an ill-defined role as her son's guardian—approved the trip.

Mack entered Yitzhak's house, a classic if marginally rundown Berkeley craftsmen likely built in the Forties. It was located at the narrowing end of The Alameda and snugly tucked into the first gentle, rocky foothills of the old Thousand Oaks subdivision.

In the living room sat Yitzhak's father, strapped into a wheelchair. His square head bobbed as he tried vainly to maneuver a stick taped to his forehead that danced across a tray of qwerty-arranged letters. A young girl, perhaps twenty, sat next to him and offered assistance.

"He's learning how to spell again," said Yitzhak. "That's my sister."

Yitzhak waved at her.

"Hannah?" he shouted. "This is Mack."

Hannah looked up.

"You the guy who's taking a trip with Raymond?" she asked.

Mack nodded.

"Mom!" Hannah shouted. "Mom! He's here!"

A small, wiry woman stepped out of the kitchen and strolled steadily down a short hall and into the living room. She had black hair streaked with irregular shocks of grey. It was curly and roughly combed back, its burgeoning length wrapped into a loose bun. She wiped her hands on an embroidered cotton apron that covered a solid beige dress.

"I'm Mrs. Jaffe," she said to Mack. "Raymond says you write for the newspaper."

"I did," said Mack. "Now I'm looking for other work."

"Is that why you're traveling to Canada?" she asked.

"I'm looking for a new start," said Mack. "I've known your son for a few years and he expressed an interest in traveling. I'm not certain about Canada but I'm interested in the Northwest. He seems interested, too."

Mack said nothing about the draft.

"Raymond says you're paying for gas," said Mrs. Jaffe.

"That's right," said Mack. "I'm covering lodging, too. Though I expect we'll do some camping. And we're visiting some friends. It's beautiful country."

"Raymond says you'll be gone a few weeks?" Mrs. Jaffe asked, phrasing it as a question but one Mack would need to answer successfully.

Mack looked toward Yitzhak, aware that like a hopeful child, he deferred entirely to his mother's questions as if the quality of answers would determine whether he would receive permission to go.

"Not any longer," said Mack. "I'll be sure your boy gets home safely."

Mrs. Jaffe searched Mack's eyes for a truth she knew he could not tell her.

"It's nice Raymond has such a good friend," she said.

Mack sensed her unexpressed joy that her troubled son had a friend, and one that appeared capable and competent. The proposed journey had worried her, but Mack's words were reassuring.

"It's been a rough couple of years," she said bluntly. "We've had some loss, as you probably know. It's taken a great toll."

Mack felt immediate compassion for the wearying truth of Mrs. Jaffe's labors and tasks and all the unexpected worry that engaged her but was not of her direct making.

"I guess I worry about everything now."

Mack heard in Mrs. Jaffe's vague reference a specific worry about her son. She had not given up on him though the untimely and unfortunate emergence of his mental illness was sadly coincidental with his sudden and obsessive use of psychedelic drugs.

"Your son is one of my best friends," Mack said to Mrs. Jaffe. "I'll take good care of him."

Mack had said too much. Yitzhak needed supervision but no one in the room wanted to acknowledge that now. He had been so recently a bright and ambitious young man and now was something frightfully in progress, growing like a virus from an incalculable quantity of permutations and changes that now brought Mack, Yitzhak, his mother and his father into the bend of a common orbit.

As Mack left the house, he felt charged with a responsibility for his friend, a charge given wordlessly by a mother who, like his own, worried that her dear, vulnerable child might fall off the earth.

five

*A*rbitrary was taken from the Latin word *arbiter* that translated as *judge* but in other languages had meanings extending from *determinative* to *tyrant*. It was a word Mack tried to use to describe the conditions affecting him, all driven by a momentum larger and more powerful than his own and that were inflicted historically and without invitation. He was currently an object of these arbitrary forces that, while they had no emotional or personal connection with him, could determine in this Anno Domini 1969 whether he lived or died.

His preparations to leave thereby became the strategies for a campaign against this arbiter that would take over his life and possibly throw it irrevocably away. It was a war within a war. Mack's War. *Mack's Vietnam War*, as if he were a franchise of the larger struggle, a small owner trying to assert his option to withdraw from a nasty contract imposed by the time and place of his birth.

Mack determined he would need two weeks to prepare for his departure. He calculated his savings at around $1300, kept in a bank downtown. He had one more check coming from the Chronicle. He thought it would be about $100 and would arrive at the end of the month. He needed to find a renter for his studio and unload his VW. Jeff had told him what documents he would need to bring to apply for permanent residency in Canada.

Vaguely, Mack estimated a departure around the end of the first week in August and no later than the 10th. He wanted to be in Seattle ten days later. He imagined sending Yitzhak home and crossing into Canada well before Labor Day.

The journey would feature farewell visits. Yitzhak had mentioned his desire to see Raj at Black Bear. Mack wanted to stop on the coast and visit Stan and Ginger one last time. He budgeted a week and some change for the trip north. He would need to pare down his belongings and gratefully owned no furniture since his studio was furnished. He had books he would first offer to Harriet before trucking them in boxes to Moe's. And he would have his mail forwarded to his parents' house. He did not want his father to be the first to receive his induction notice but he knew his mother would be the first to the mailbox.

565

"Glad you could come around," Cuthbert said to Mack as they sat in a Mission Street dive bar.

"Thanks for the letter," said Mack. "And the drink."

"And I'm sorry. Again. I know it must…" Cuthbert struggled for words.

"Fuck it," interrupted Mack. "I have to leave anyway."

"It's a bad war," said Cuthbert. "But no worse than the people protesting it."

"I'm protesting it," answered Mack. "What are you talking about?"

It was the opening for Cuthbert to rail again on his common, driving theme of world conspiracy. The Communists were behind all the agitation for civil rights and against the war. It was their way to weaken America and destroy its basic freedoms.

"Civil rights?" asked Mack. "What's subversive about that?"

"Equalitarianism," answered Cuthbert. "It's a conspiracy to destroy competitiveness and to lower IQs through the mixing of races. It's no secret that Negroes score consistently lower on IQ tests. You have a UC psychology professor and a Nobel Prize winning scientist saying as much. Jensen and Shockley. You must know their work."

"Yeah," said Mack. "It's pretty controversial. It's eugenics. The idea you can manipulate the intelligence of the species through selective breeding. But it boils down to the idea that white Europeans are smart and all other so-called races aren't."

"And your point?" asked Cuthbert.

"That race doesn't exist as a definition of anything. It's just another way to divide humans up into tribes. And we sure as hell don't need any more tribes. We need more human rights."

"Let the jigaboos run wild…" Cuthbert couldn't help himself.

"Or the homos," countered Mack.

"You're a homo, Joel. Aren't you?"

Cuthbert was silent.

"You like to think no one knows. But you know I do. We all know you're gay. You should really be defending the rights of minorities and not condemning them. You're a member of a minority and as

I recall the last big European tribe to nearly rule the world wanted all of your kind killed. Kind of like what Negroes have been dealing with on this continent for more than three hundred years. Why don't you stop all this bullshit? Make a donation today to the Committee for Homosexual Freedom. Leo and Gale would really appreciate it."

Cuthbert's blush was enough to satisfy Mack's thirst for blood.

"Those fucking flamers," snorted Cuthbert. "Want to ruin the party for everyone. Bring us all out of the closet. Get us all fired and jailed. This country will never accept homosexuals. It's a goddamned death sentence to be marching around downtown."

"You mean like Selma?" shouted Mack. "You mean risking your life to stand up for your rights? Well, that doesn't sound very smart to me. Maybe you're right. Making waves might be a pretty stupid thing to do, after all. And no, you can't have your letter back."

Cuthbert managed a weak smile.

Later Mack would ask himself why his ex-editor couldn't see himself victimized by the system he seemed to revere. Why couldn't he sign on for liberation? Could he not imagine himself openly gay, or the freedom that acceptance might create for him? Perhaps not having his freedom was part of the thrill. Perhaps not having his freedom gave him permission to take it from others.

Mack was sorry for hanging up on Inger.

"I don't have crabs," he told her on the phone.

"I don't either," she answered. "At least not anymore."

"This might sound crazy," said Mack. "I need to give up my studio next month and I wonder if you'd like to rent it? I've paid August's rent and the lease ends the end of October and you could collect the last month's deposit, so it would be virtually rent free for you and…"

"Wow," Inger interrupted Mack. "Are you kidding? This is like so cosmically groovy I can't stand it."

Inger's crabs were the last straw at the Kanda commune and Inger wanted out as quickly as possible.

Mack liked Inger. And he liked fucking her. But he liked more watching her in the loop at the O'Farrell. The watching was more obsessively involving in ways that confirmed his participation in observance, an experience of two opposites that fed the same desire. He found himself unreasonably curious about his visual engagement with her, as if he held a secret that, of course, was not a secret and was never meant to be one. Though while Inger might have imagined any number of men watching her on film, she probably did not think it would be a man who knew her and who had screwed her.

Women were an awkward curiosity for Mack. He appreciated their friendship and had loved one once. Really loved her, a high school girl who had transferred in her junior year from the Valley and who immediately attracted Mack's wanton attention. She was bright and shy, beautiful and repressed. She hid from him all her secrets. She was furious the afternoon he surprised her at home and she was lounging braless in sweats and a t-shirt. She menstruated secretly and gave him no information about her body or its desire until, very late in their relationship when she opened briefly to a deeper probing that pushed her ultimately into a shamed withdrawal.

She left for college immediately after graduation and Mack never saw her again, nor had he again regarded or loved another woman as he did his first sweetheart. He had dated, had even gone steady a couple of times in college. But nothing lasted. Instead, Mack turned his passion outward to the world. He was attracted to the worldly stories of a worldly species and all its news and secrets.

It was as if he were infatuated with all people everywhere but in a way that kept him an observer and safely withdrawn from their passions. Though he could not deny the visceral arousal he derived from examining these passions in candid detail, and in writing about them. He loved the role of viewer and the newsworthy exposure he might compose and actualize, though his greatest fear was being himself personally exposed, found out, seen and identified.

He wondered at times if all journalists were simply eremitic voyeurs and all historians just scopophilic archivists. Certainly the best of both were intensely nosy and intrusive, though journalists generally spied on the living and historians shadowed the dead. Whatever it was, whatever his urge and need, it would only occupy the dread that existed between birth and death. It was dread, ultimately, that informed all he experienced with the fibrillations of a beautifully intense anxiety.

"Are you free?" Harriet asked.

The sound of her voice surprised Mack. He had given Harriet his number but had not expected her ever to phone him.

"Now?" he asked.

"Yes," she answered. "I know it's late."

"Not that late," said Mack who checked his watch.

"I need to talk with someone," she said, her voice quavering.

It appeared Mack was the chosen, or at least most readily available, someone.

It didn't matter. He liked Harriet and was happy to be counted among her someones. He knew he liked her much more than he could admit. He said he would be right over.

"It's just a god damned mess," she said when she answered the door.

Mack waited. The details would follow.

"I've broken up with Michael."

Harriet released the words quickly so as to make way for the aching sobs that followed. Mack reached to hold her. She fell against him, her chest convulsing against his as he continued to wait.

"Broke up?" asked Mack. "How? When?"

Harriet stood back to recover her composure.

Michael had phoned Harriet an hour earlier from Virginia where he was enrolled in his Peace Corps training. Harriet knew something was wrong. Michael's voice was distant, his comments filtered through an uncharacteristic monotone.

"He said we wouldn't be living together in Africa. He knew that would be hard for us. For me, anyway. And he wanted to give me a chance to back out of our commitment."

Mack waited as Harriet gained her composure.

"And…?" Mack asked.

"I accepted," answered Harriet. "I don't know what I was thinking. I heard his tone, his controlled tone as if this were a crucial formality for him, a way to test my love and commitment to him."

"What did you say?" asked Mack.

"I heard myself say—OK, if that's how you feel—and then I heard the panic in his voice, his fear this was really happening in a way he did not expect."

"Sounds like he might have been having the same doubts you had," Mack said.

Harriet took a tissue from a box she was carrying in tow. She wiped her eyes.

"I suppose," she said. "I can't deny that. But when we heard together what popped out of my mouth, he tried to take it back. He tried to say he was just feeling insecure. I sympathized and said I was feeling that way, too. And I couldn't say why, but what he said sounded reasonable and I…"

Harriet again began to cry.

"And then he just went off. He started calling me names. He said I was a frigid intellectual twit and he'd never really liked me that much. He went off like a cannon. I started to cry and he hung up. I still can't believe what happened."

Mack waited while Harriet took another tissue.

"Sounds like you got off easy," he said.

"What?" Harriet asked warily.

"I'm sorry for the pain," said Mack. "But it's nothing like the pain you'd have if you went with him. That might have lasted the rest of your life. Besides, you're a beautiful, brilliant woman and no man has any right to treat you like shit. I wonder what you really meant to him. From what you've told me, he managed you like some kind of accessory."

Harriet sat quietly for several minutes. Mack resisted an urge to fill the silence.

"He was so kind at first," said Harriet. "He was the first man I thought I might actually love. And now he's gone."

Mack nodded.

"First love is rarely the last love," he said and while Mack could boast the wisdom of his words he had not lived their proof. After his first love there had been no other.

"So what will you do now?" Mack asked.

"Take the fall off. Apply to some schools, I guess," said Harriet. "I need the doctorate. I've put so much time into…"

"You're already enrolled here…" said Mack.

"Not Berkeley," shouted Harriet. "Not ever. It took me 24 years to leave my father's house. Now I want to leave his school…and his goddamned town. It's time."

"Yeah," said Mack. "It's definitely time to leave."

Later Mack thought how he might have used his last moments with Harriet to describe his own crucible of departure. His evening with Harriet felt like a strange and gawky state of reckoning with a deeper connection doomed by separate trajectories that appeared to grow irresistibly in opposing directions. He felt both his affection for Harriet and hers for him and also the pain of its certain disappearance within the congested traffic leading toward different harbors.

The day after the Apollo XI moon walkers splashed down in the Pacific, Ted Kennedy pleaded guilty to a charge of leaving the scene of an accident. He received a one month suspended jail sentence three days after attending the funeral of his doomed young passenger.

"He'll never be president," Mack said to Inger, who had stopped by to get a copied key to Mack's studio.

"He shouldn't be," said Inger. "Who could ever trust him? What woman, anyway?"

Mack described his plans to go north with Yitzhak.

"Really? You trust him?" asked Inger. "Kind of an acidhead, if I recall."

"He's changed," said Mack. "Not doing acid anymore. No hanging out on the street, at least I don't see him there. And he's taking classes, or at least a class."

"Where?" asked Inger.

"San Francisco. Monday nights. But not for credit."

"Is that the Monday Night Class? Stephen Gaskin?" asked Inger. "I've gone to that. It's pretty far out."

"Must be a big class. How many are enrolled?" asked Mack.

"About 1500, but no one enrolls. You just show up and Stephen talks about whatever is happening. Held at the old Edgewater Ballroom near Playland on the Great Highway. Family Dog uses the place for weekend concerts now."

"So Yitzhak's not in school…"said Mack.

Mack backed off, aware how futile it was at times to fight for possession of a moment.

"You sound disappointed," said Inger. "Stephen is very cool. He's an instructor at State. He covers a lot of ground: psychedelics, spiritual living, relationships, power and the people...you should go sometime. From what I've heard he has a lot more to say than most professors. Anyway, he packs them in. Say, are you growing a beard?"

Inger reached to touch Mack's chin.

"Trying," Mack answered.

"Explains the rough face. For a sandy blonde, though, those are awfully red whiskers."

"We'll see," said Mack. "I'd like a new look since I'm clearly on the verge of a new life."

Later Mack phoned Yitzhak and got him at home. Yitzhak had received his disability check and cashed it. His mother was giving him another hundred dollars for the trip.

"Two weeks from today," said Mack. "Let's talk Monday and, say, can I park my Volkswagen in your driveway if I can't sell it? Your sister could drive it or sell it or…"

"Sorry, man. No way," said Yitzhak unequivocally. "It's a German car. And we're Jews."

"I thought you were Irish," said Mack.

"We are. And we're Jews. No fucking way. My mother would never go for it."

Mack backed off. If the car didn't sell, he'd give it away. Put a sign on it that read "Free Car" and list his phone number. Could he even get a hundred for it?

The following Monday a letter arrived from Bronwyn, penned in neat swirls that had the look of an incipient calligraphy.

Mack,

Sorry to have left without saying goodbye. Came with Rita and we're in New York now. Stayed at my parents for a week but now have a studio in SoHo. Tight quarters but affordable and close to NYU where I've been accepted for the fall. Graduate work, of course, in political science (what else?).

Big news is I'm working with Red Stockings on women's stuff. Rita's involved, too. I'm feeling like I've finally found something truly liberating. Harriet told me you wanted to return No More Fun and Games but don't worry about it. Copies everywhere. Appears to be required reading here (Haha).

> *Really, I've found work that brings all my issues into focus. There were times I was like a stone. Couldn't speak. There was an important part of me that was dead and not there at all. I would wake up sometimes and say to myself should I make breakfast or go jump off a bridge? Thank god for Sudsofloppen and C-R*
>
> *Hope you are....*

A gentle salutation followed and Mack dropped Bronwyn's letter on the kitchen table. Something seemed unsaid and he did not know what it was. He worried he had put Bronwyn off. Had he missed something important? Had he seen her? Really seen what she was about or really heard what she said to him during those last weeks together? It made sense he might not fully see Bronwyn during a time he could barely see himself.

six

The cause of sorrow began in the division of all things. Mack divided himself into the two Macks: the one who sought an honorable and frightening sanctuary from the war of all his wars and also the Mack who would not hesitate to use his wounded friend Yitzhak to make an escape. Mack admitted to himself he had encouraged Yitzhak's fantasy of a road trip to hitch his own ride north to Canada.

A poignant visit to Yitzhak's miserable family brought home the suffering all had endured as the result of his father's physical failure and Yitzhak's mental collapse. The father and son of the house were crippled dependents, held up however provisionally by the women. Mother and daughter, drawn out of their respective pursuits of happiness by deep duty to the unrelieved suffering of father, brother, son. Mack knew many families were unhappy ones and that they failed most those who believed such intimate relations to be the solemnly regarded key to happiness. Children, especially, bore the tortures of unfulfilled hopes though like Yitzhak, many children could themselves become the provocateurs of family dysfunction.

Mack remembered as a child witnessing fights between his parents: loud, intemperate, ruthless in their accusations. One night he heard his mother wail her regret she had ever given birth. Mack lived for years angry he was born and now, even as his mother over a lifetime of enduring care had restored their closeness, he refused to share his destabilizing frights, convinced she then would take him back inside her and dissolve and extinguish him in the womb that had grown his place in the world.

Mack could not speak for Yitzhak, or so he pretended. On one hand, Yitzhak had exercised a free will; had suggested the trip north and offered to drive. On the other, it was reasonable to wonder if Yitzhak knew anything of what was involved. Mack had been direct. He told Yitzhak he would cross into Canada and leave his friend behind though how much that registered wasn't clear.

Without Mack, how would Yitzhak find his way home? Weakly, Mack had promised Yitzhak's weary mother he would assure her disabled son's safe return. Like Wyatt, Mack thought he might be leading a senseless Billy on a quixotic journey that would kill them both. Mack mentally subtracted $200 from his savings. *I can always put him on a plane*, Mack thought to himself. *I can call his mother and she'll meet him.* It was enough. Saturday Mack sorted through his belongings and spent the day reducing his possessions to the contents of a single backpack and one suitcase. He was another animal among animals, all running around and separated from each other.

Sorting through his belongings, Mack was struck with the idea that all these things, so discriminately his own, had no essential reality. Perhaps it was because they were things. His stereo, his books, his clothes, his broken down VW, his phone service and heating bill, his news clippings, even his body and its stubbly beard, were transient possessions. The morning he had this thought he considered he might be tripping. He might be crazy, as crazy as Yitzhak, to think he could run away. He lived like a flame that existed only because it could be extinguished.

Inger phoned him and asked if she could move in a week early.

"I told everyone at Kanda and they're pissed," she said.

Mack told her she would have to sleep on the couch. And that he preferred she did not smoke in the apartment. His departure was set for the weekend of the ninth.

"Good. I'm trying to quit anyway," said Inger.

"You're always trying to quit," Mack snipped.

"We'll make it work," said Inger, ignoring Mack's cut. "I'll fix dinners."

Mack said OK.

It felt that a large part of him was already gone.

The urgency Mack felt to leave reminded him he was running. The previous spring three soldiers imprisoned in the Presidio brig escaped and disappeared. They were members of the so-called Presidio 27; a group of incarcerated soldiers that, following the fatal shooting of a 17-year-old fellow prisoner the previous year by a trigger-happy guard, formed a circle in the brig's recreation yard and refused to move.

As a result of their action, the protesting soldiers faced charges of mutiny that potentially carried the death penalty. Despite demonstrations by thousands who marched to the gates of the Presidio, the first three prisoners were found guilty in the spring and sentenced to up to 16 years of hard labor. Though the charges were eventually reduced to insubordination and the sentences cut to a few months, Mack knew he could not endure a personal battle with the U.S. Army.

"It's as if your draft card is some kind of deed of ownership," said David Harris, the student activist and partner to folksinger Joan Baez recently arrested for refusing to appear for his induction.

"It's issued to you by the government and it says the life of the bearer belongs to the United States of America, which can do with it whatever it wants."

Mack had heard Harris speak in Berkeley during the spring. Both Harris and his wife urged young men to burn their draft cards or to send them back to their draft boards. If enough young draft-eligible men refused induction and were willing to face jail, it would destroy the Selective Service System. Or so they theorized.

The problem was that among all young men eligible for the draft, very few were willing to risk years in prison simply to make a point.

That Harris and Baez thought otherwise, thought it was a draftee's duty to resist and face arrest, seemed to Mack unrealistically naïve. Already nearly half the men being drafted were not showing up for their physicals and this appeared to be no drag at all on either army enlistment or the arrest and persecution of draft resisters.

So Mack would run. He would move deliberately toward the exit like a smart thief leaving a busy market. He would move slowly so as not to draw attention or raise suspicions. But when he reached the door, or in this case the border, Mack would dash away as fast as he could and not look back.

The last items Mack packed were his camera and a dog-eared travel guide to western Canada he had purchased at Moe's. The camera and seven rolls of film were intended to bolster his credentials as a journalist but he had no clear idea how he would use them on the trip north. Mack hoped the travel guide would give him all he needed to know, or to say he knew, about his presumed new country. Mack could appear at his immigration interview as a knowledgeable and working journalist. The camera alone might be worth an interview point.

Monday morning Mack was awakened by Yitzhak's knock on his studio door.

"You're early," Mack said.

"Yeah, but I'm here," answered Yitzhak, as if he sensed Mack's concern about his reliability.

"What did you do with your VW?"

"Gave it to Inger," said Mack. "She'll sell it for me. I don't care what she gets. I just want to be rid of it."

Yitzhak lifted Mack's case while Mack slipped his right arm through a strap of his backpack. They stood together in the hall of Mack's building, Yitzhak towering over the diminutive Mack while he held his small friend's suitcase high in his arms.

"Guess this is it," said Mack.

He looked momentarily at Inger sleeping soundly on his couch. Mack closed the door. He would not miss her snoring.

Yitzhak hurled Mack's suitcase into the back of the Chevelle and next to a fatigues-green army duffle that Mack assumed contained his friend's clothes and articles. Mack shoved his backpack into the back seat. It held his documents and valuables, including his camera, and he wanted it always in sight.

"I need a paper," said Mack as Yitzhak started the engine. Mack raced down to the corner and pushed a dime into a news rack. Yitzhak cruised down to meet him.

Yitzhak drove the Chevelle north on Shattuck, leading Mack to ask where he was going.

"The freeway's down University," said Mack.

"It's also down Solano," said Yitzhak. "Less traffic and fewer lights."

Mack didn't argue. He watched the passing storefronts, examining their surfaces and facades as they simultaneously came and went. In moments Yitzhak drove onto the freeway and after crawling through the streets of downtown Richmond they crossed the bridge to San Rafael. Flying over the bay beneath him gave Mack a feeling of magic liberation from all previous causes and conditions. He was momentarily a cosmic passenger lifted beatifically out of all he had previously known.

And Yitzhak was his angelic pilot, sturdy and strong and evidently in charge. All these places he passed Mack might never see again. It was at first a great exhilaration to imagine himself free as a bird though no bird is at all free from its place in the flock or in the sky. A bird's every journey serves something other and larger than itself, which reminded Mack he was not soaring. He was fleeing. He was a refugee and his and every creature's urge to survive provided the most essential reason to run.

"Another bad murder in L.A."

Mack announced the news as he read the paper's leading headline. The bodies of five people, including the very pregnant film star Sharon Tate, had been found Saturday in an exclusive home north of Beverly Hills. All had been stabbed and whoever killed them wrote the word "pigs" on the walls in the blood of the victims. Sunday a husband and wife had been found murdered in their home in the Los Feliz hills, a wealthy couple that owned a local supermarket chain.

"The same M.O." said Mack. "Stabbed to death and 'pigs'

written in blood on the walls."

"Weird," said Yitzhak.

"Yeah," said Mack. "Someone's pretty crazy or pretty pissed off or both. There appears to be no connection between the two groups of victims. But it sure as hell sounds like the same killer."

"Or killers," said Yitzhak.

Mack rolled up the newspaper and dropped it on the floor behind his seat.

An hour passed in silence as the Chevelle rolled north on Highway 101 at the speed limit while passing slow, packed lanes of commuters heading south toward the Bay Area. The busy road opened past Santa Rosa and through the area's reputed and lushly verdant vineyards. It wasn't yet 10 a.m. and August's heat already was evident in the valleys.

"Hope you like this," said Mack.

The Chevelle had a tape player and Mack popped in a cassette. The pounding opening of *Born to be Wild* by Steppenwolf blasted through the speakers. Mack tapped his foot and Yitzhak joined in, rocking the car's brakes in contrapuntal syncopation with the keyboard and drums.

"Whoa…" shouted Mack. "We turn here."

Yitzhak pulled off the road, seemingly thrown into a trance by the raging beat of the music.

"Let me drive," said Mack. "It's about another hour to Fort Bragg. I know the way to Ginger and Stan's."

Yitzhak moved over.

Mack shut off the player and drove over the bumpy, forested ranges that walled off the last valleys before the coast. He passed through the flash of a town named Boonville and into the tall, shading groves of redwood trees aligned with the shallow summer run of the Navarro River. At the river's mouth the road climbed to the steep bluffs above the ocean and glided north through a fog as thick as wet cotton and that forced Mack to turn on the wipers. Yitzhak slept.

Past the restored Victorian buildings of the Mendocino headlands, Mack began searching for the turn-off to Ginger and Stan's. He needed two passes before he found it, arriving in their driveway to see Stan in a raincoat stacking logs under a canopy of dripping tree branches. Mack sat for a moment in the shade of the fog and the silence of Yitzhak's sleep.

Stan embraced Mack who felt the strength in his old friend's warm, calloused hands, no longer like those of an artist but now with fingers that had been worked hard against harsh, sharp surfaces; the manual hands of a vigorous and daily manual labor.

"Quite a beard," said Stan who fingered Mack's chin. "Looks red…"

Yitzhak passed them carrying Mack's suitcase.

"My friend Yitzhak," Mack announced.

"You need some help?" asked Stan.

Yitzhak turned and smiled.

"Where does this go?" Yitzhak asked.

"Put it on the porch for now," said Stan. "And welcome to the farm."

"You still painting?" Mack later asked Stan as they shared dinner with Ginger and Lila.

Yitzhak sat at the far end of the table and drew Lila's obsessive attention as she watched securely from her mother's lap, propped against the protruding womb that grew her sibling-to-be.

"He's a big man," Lila said as Yitzhak turned toward her and smiled.

Lila looked away to bury her head between her mother's newly ponderous breasts.

"When I can, I paint," Stan answered. "I need to squeeze it in."

Stan's words sounded to Mack like a tactful retreat.

"Say, Yitzhak," Stan shouted. "Did you ever look into live modeling?"

Yitzhak appeared embarrassed. He shook his head without speaking.

"Still a good idea," Stan said. "You have an intriguing face and a great physique."

Yitzhak gave Stan a perplexed look.

"In fact, while you're hear could I sketch you?" asked Stan. "Just a portrait. You have a strong jaw and deeply chiseled features. What do you say? Wouldn't take long."

"When?" Yitzhak at last asked.

"In the morning," said Stan. "In the studio."

Yitzhak gave Stan a brief, affirmative nod.

Stan thanked him and the dinner continued with the patter and banter of old and new news. Ginger's baby was due in nine weeks. Stan's leg was healing though he still limped noticeably.

"I'm a seeing a specialist in the City next month," he said, looking over to Ginger who nodded.

"I can't run. Maybe never again. But, hell, I never did much running."

Ginger rose from the table to put Lila to bed.

Stan began clearing dishes and stood with Mack and Yitzhak in the kitchen as Yitzhak washed and Mack rinsed. He asked Mack about Canada.

"Long story," said Mack. "But I don't have a choice. Can't support this war and I sure as hell won't end up dying in it."

"Too bad you can't stay and live here," said Stan. "Gin's the queen. The attorneys love her. She's organized a food conspiracy with the local hippies and sponsors a women's group here on Thursday nights. And the day care co-op is a hit. Some of the moms are working again and the kids are really cool. Lila has more friends than most people have relatives."

Ginger appeared later and poured all the men small glasses of sherry.

"Anyone want to get stoned?" asked Stan.

Mack declined and was surprised when Yitzhak also shook his head.

"I'll pass, too," said Stan. "No fun getting stoned alone."

Mack found Yitzhak the next morning in Stan's studio. As agreed, he sat as Stan sketched his face with a charcoal pencil, a flush of lines and smudges on paper that began to emerge as the essential features of Yitzhak's face. Stan had drawn the jaw wide and large to emphasize his subject's long, broad presence. The eyes were just taking shape.

Lila ran into the studio. She asked Stan for a ladder.

"Why?" he asked.

"I want to climb into the clouds and open a hole for the sun," she said. "I want to find it and kill it and give it to mommy to cook in a pie."

Mack laughed.

"Can I help?" Mack asked.

Lila's reticence surrendered to the reality an adult was willing to help her.

"Let me show you," she said and took Mack's arm to drag him out into the yard. For an hour thereafter Mack held a long pole that Lila directed he poke into the swirling fog to find the sun.

"Is this it?" asked Mack many times.

It never was. The game for Lila was in the search and not the recovery. When other children began to arrive for day care, Lila tired of her search for the sun and ran from Mack to greet her friends. Mack watched her run off. He was helplessly charmed. Would he ever father children? What would that involve and with whom? He thought of Harriet, though dismissed his urge as a greed for something he never had and might not really want.

As day care mothers arrived, Ginger prepared to leave for work. She spoke with the two mothers who would supervise for the day and said she would be home for lunch. Truly, she was a local queen. Mack met a few of the women and listened as they spoke of the Tate and LaBianca murders in Los Angeles and of the young Sharon Tate whose grisly murder was particularly fascinating.

"Nine months pregnant?" asked one incredulous young mother.

"Stabbed repeatedly in the belly while hanging from her wrists," said another.

Several mothers gasped. Mack watched them choke through their eager and unfiltered curiosity to comprehend the horror of such a death. One mother began to cry and was comforted by others. However repulsive, Mack listened as the women eagerly shared and absorbed every known and bloody detail. Their interest was unfiltered and it fed a weird empathy that Mack immediately recognized was rooted in the voyeurism that sold newspapers.

The mood changed when Yitzhak entered the house to use the bathroom and sauntered wordlessly through the kitchen.

"Who's that?" asked one of the women with eyebrows raised in a pose of faux arousal.

"One groovy old man," said another after Yitzhak left the kitchen. "Whose?"

The women laughed together from within a common and also suppressed carnality.

"Your friend?" asked one mother. "How do we meet him?"

"We're leaving tomorrow," said Mack. "Going to Canada."

The women sighed a collective "Awwww" before bursting into lusty laughter.

Dear Harriet,
On the road right now. Visiting Stan and Ginger for a couple of days.

I didn't have time to tell you before I left, but I'm going to Canada. Have a ride to the border and I'm applying for landed immigrant status so I can stay there. I'm eligible for the draft and can't fight in this awful war. Of all the options left for me, this appears to be the best.

I won't have an address for a few weeks but I'll write again when I've landed.

Hope your plans are shaping up the way you need them to. I hope sometime to see you again.
Mack

Mack put the letter in an envelope, sealed it, addressed it and asked Ginger to mail it for him. It was barely enough and its few words were completely out of proportion to the vast well of feeling from which they were drawn. Mack realized he was out of the orbit of human contact and that all future communications with family and friends would be through letters or from a phone booth or not at all.

Another day was needed to finish Yitzhak's portrait, which Stan found exhilarating to draw and which Mack acknowledged as an extraordinary image that oscillated within a surprisingly controlled thatch of streaks and lines to reveal, in ways Mack could not say, so much of Yitzhak's intemperate, non-linear and incomprehensible mystique. Was it genius or madness? Somewhere along his carefully and also wildly applied lines, Stan had caught something of his subject's concealed essence.

"I didn't know you could draw so well," said Mack. "It's better than a photo."

"Something new," replied Stan. "Something old and also new."

Stan said he hoped to see Mack again.

"Would you come north?" asked Mack. "Ever?"

"Maybe," said Stan in a way Mack knew meant no, not ever. The trappings of a country life had trapped Stan and Ginger, had saddled them with the necessity of a common and eternal devotion to a one and only place.

This reality left Mack with both fear and also sadness significant of a far deeper loss than he previously imagined. He might never again see his friends. Every mile of flight was now a mile likely lost and left behind. His life might be simply some kind of reiterated stupidity to which he continued to return for a futile search for something fresh.

"What will happen?" Ginger asked at last.

Mack didn't know. Life was driven by a conditional avarice and he had no choice but to go on grabbing for every available experience.

seven

Yitzhak drove up the coastal highway while Mack searched a map for landmarks. The men were free which was itself a consequence of their separation from the anchor of what had just been and their flight toward what not yet had occurred. They were outside in the world but not outside themselves and the flat, straight highway lured Yitzhak into a strangely loquacious mood.

"Hot in the valley today," he said. "Once we leave the coast, it's gonna bake us."

"Too late to make Black Bear tonight," Mack responded as he traced with his fingers a route on the map.

"We'll be lucky to get to Shasta. Let's check the radiator in town."

Yitzhak was no longer getting stoned and Mack felt more

secure, especially after a clear evening when Yitzhak dazzled Stan and Ginger by finding and naming the planets and several stars. Yitzhak might be insane but he appeared determined to experience his madness responsibly. *Perhaps he is a savant*, Mack thought. *A secret, unheralded savant.*

Or perhaps Yitzhak had simply abandoned the fog of hallucination to plunge deeper into the pleasure of his neurosis. There was such a thin membrane between derangement and dharma. But the evening's calm and the morning's earnest start eased Mack's worries about the trip while also alerting him to a chafing potential for trouble.

One such potential arrived at the gas station in Fort Bragg. As Mack checked the water in the radiator, he watched a small woman approach Yitzhak at the restrooms. She appeared young with curly brown hair and wore a puffy sleeved, sky blue peasant blouse and a long brown leather skirt that reached to her ankles. Beside her was a colorful, bulging cloth bag that rippled with rich tie-dyed reds and greens.

"Dolan," said the woman after Mack walked over to meet her. "Maeve Dolan. Where you dudes going?"

"Canada," said Yitzhak.

"Damn, I'm not going that far," the small woman said as she laughed. Her eyes twinkled and Mack wondered how she could make that happen.

"We need to be in Shasta before dark," Mack said firmly. He hoped to discourage the addition of another passenger.

"Sounds like you're going up 299 from Arcata," she said.

"You got that," said Yitzhak before Mack could stop him.

"You'll pass through Willow Creek," said Maeve.

"It's where I live. Give me a ride and I'll make you dinner."

As Yitzhak drove, Mack studied Maeve from his angular access to the rearview mirror. Was she thirty? *No, older,* thought Mack. She was quiet and propped herself against the armrest behind the driver's seat.

"What do you do in Willow Creek?" asked Mack.

"Live the good life," said Maeve. "Have some acreage and a cabin. Left to me by my grandfather who was a logger. Real land.

Not one of those phony mining claims."

Maeve had been in Fort Bragg visiting her uncle. She said she lived off the land, but Mack suspected she also lived off others, including Mack whose anxiety about another passenger eased as Maeve opened up with an apparent, but likely well-rehearsed candor.

They arrived in Eureka around two and Maeve, who said she liked to be called by her last name, knew a good place for lunch.

"Great sandwiches, Dolan," said Mack who sat on a bench at the wharf as all ate ravenously. Mack had warmed both to the woman and her journey.

"You make this trip often?"

Dolan shook her head.

"It's a trip, man. Family. Still see family when I can. But I stay at home as much as possible. My land is on the river. I leave only to shop or catch an occasional ride to the coast. Hester, she's my housemate, she takes care of the animals."

"Where you from?" asked Mack.

"Originally?" she asked.

Mack nodded.

"I have no idea. But my earliest memories are of my mom and dad living in King Salmon. He was a fisherman until he drowned. I was five. Gramps took care of us and loved me like a queen. Then he died, too. Too much whiskey, probably. Anyway, I was in college when I got the news he left me his land. Five years ago. Been there ever since."

Were freedom a secretion, the Maeve who wished to be called Dolan would drip of it. Mack took over the driving and pushed the Chevelle up the mountain on 299, winding along the road's perilous switchbacks before entering Willow Creek where he waited for the Dolan woman to point out where she lived.

"A little farther," she said.

An hour later, after turning off at Hawkins Bar and driving the Denny Road north to its intersection with Hoboken, Mack steered down a one-lane dirt road for another twenty minutes before Dolan yelled.

"Here! Pull in here!"

Mack rolled the Chevelle under a canopy of firs and down a

one-lane gravel road to arrive in a grassy meadow fronting the porch of a small, languishing log cabin. A Volkswagen older than Mack's was parked nearby.

"Your car?" Mack asked.

"Hester's," said Dolan. "It doesn't go far but it gets us to town."

Hester appeared. She was short and shy and apparently and painfully surprised by Dolan's guests. She wore a green t-shirt and Bermuda shorts that gave her the rounded appearance of a Russian nesting doll on vacation in Puerto Vallarta. Hester had short dark hair and Mack noticed her thick, perhaps cultivated, black moustache. She smiled during introductions but said nothing and left to finish the preparation of a meal Dolan was clearly expecting to be ready for her and that now was to be more than doubled for her guests.

Dinner appeared as promised, a strange green stew with the flavor of basil that was supplemented with slices of homemade bread.

"You dudes are welcome to stay for a while," said Dolan. "If you're not in a hurry."

Mack was in a hurry, but Yitzhak was not and as the driver and owner of the vehicle his opinion mattered.

Later, the men were shown to a sleeping platform on a sandy river beach. A polyurethane border surrounded it and provided about a foot's height of privacy.

"I sleep here a lot," said Dolan.

"Nights like this the temperature doesn't drop below 80 degrees. I can spread out all day. Get myself off if I want to. You guys make yourselves at home."

Mack wanted to leave in the morning while Yitzhak wanted to stay a week. Mack engineered a compromise that included two more nights with Dolan. Mack, at the very least, could not expect on this trip to exist wholly for himself. It was a situation he might not have chosen, though nevertheless his situation.

The time passed quickly, Mack arising the first morning to hike a short north ridge above Dolan's property. It was mid-morning and as he looked back he caught a view of the river platform and Dolan, naked, vigorous and sweaty, on top of Yitzhak and thrusting hard against him. At last her wild wail bounced up to the ridge and she collapsed onto Yitzhak's chest.

Later, Mack sat on the cabin's porch to peruse a stack of anti-draft literature. He read in the Veterans Stars and Stripes for Peace an account of the escape of three of the Presidio 27.

Paulowski and Mather, as well as defendant Linden Blake have all escaped from the Presidio while awaiting trial and made it to Canada…VS&SP readers are urged to raise the demand for freeing all 27 men, trying those guilty of violating Army regulations in operating the Presidio stockade, and launching a Congressional investigation.

"You been called for your physical?" the draft counselor in Berkeley had asked.

Mack recalled the afternoon. The counselor was an ex-Marine who had served in Vietnam and was determined to keep anyone else from going there to fight. He occupied a small office across from the high school. It was staffed by volunteers aligned with the Movement for a Democratic Military, war resisters and GI veterans committed to disrupting the draft and keeping boys out of the Army.

"No," answered Mack.

"Been arrested?" the counselor asked.

"No," said Mack.

"Then you aren't a draft dodger or an army deserter? Shit, get your ass to Canada and they'll take you, if that's what you want. Of course, you could stay here, decline induction and go to jail…you could…"

"Does anyone really do that?" asked Mack. "I mean, David Harris and Tom Hayden are all over telling boys to go to jail to protest the draft. But look what happened to the Presidio 27."

The counselor nodded and then told Mack to get his ass to Canada as fast as he could.

"You'll be accepted," he said. "Canada will like you…but will you like Canada?"

One last day on the river included a drive to Willow Creek for food and gas all paid for by Mack, including a half-gallon bottle of red Ripple that Dolan threw into the cart at the last minute.

"For dinner," she said with an amused look, her eyes wide like a manipulating child in a way that melted Mack's stern glance. That afternoon Dolan balled Yitzhak again at the river and at this rate Mack wondered if they would ever leave.

"We're going tomorrow," Mack said as Yitzhak fell on their mattress to sleep.

"I was going to ask, you know…" Yitzhak stalled.

"Raj is expecting us. Remember our friend Raj?" said Mack.

It was a lie but Mack didn't care.

"You can stop in and see Dolan on your drive back."

"But what if I don't come back?" asked Yitzhak.

It was an answer that alarmed Mack who had to think fast.

"That's up to you, man," said Mack. "Not me."

Mack told Yitzhak they would leave before daybreak and probably not say goodbye. The visit with Dolan and Hester had cost a half tank of gas, $18 dollars in groceries and had thrown Mack three days off his schedule.

Mack awoke to see the morning stars appear like a snowy fire in the sky. As he understood it, the universe was both the strangest and most utterly common reality imaginable and, if he forgot about the factor of time, as empty and also as full as his own life. He packed the car before waking Yitzhak and when his friend stood, Mack pushed him forcefully toward the Chevelle. Mack also took the wheel and as he started the engine and drove up the gravel lane he saw a light go on in the cabin. He could make out Hester's egg-shaped shadow at the window as she watched the car turn away and disappear into the dark forest.

Morning broke in Weaverville and Mack found a café open for breakfast. Mack wolfed poached eggs and home fries while Yitzhak devoured a cheese omelet and sourdough toast. While they ate a longhaired male, perhaps in his late twenties, approached them. He carried a red knapsack and his wrinkled clothes smelled of sweat and campfires.

"You guys going east?" he asked.

Mack was suspicious and said nothing.

"Yeah man," answered Yitzhak. "Need a ride?"

"Name's Luke. I live on a commune outside of Hayfork," said the traveler who lounged in the backseat while Yitzhak drove and munched on his leftover home fries.

"Say, instead of dropping me in Douglas City why don't you take a trip down to Hayfork? Just over the mountains. Nice people. Nice women."

Yitzhak's eyes brightened.

"Where do you live?" asked Yitzhak.

Mack asked Yitzhak to stop.

"I need something from the trunk," said Mack.

He turned to their new passenger and asked him to get out and help.

Alone at the rear of the car, Mack grabbed the fellow traveler named Luke by his shirt and pulled him close.

"You motherfucker, we aren't going to Hayfork. You get it? Say it again and we're pulling over and I'm putting you out on the road. In this heat, good luck even getting to Douglas City."

The suddenly compliant rider did not speak again until pointing out the junction in Douglas where he would stand for his next ride. Shortly after noon Yitzhak drove into Redding where Mack filled the tank for their last leg to Black Bear Ranch.

The big snows of the eastern mountains drifted in and out of sight as they drove north on the big highway. Emerging on the down of a monstrous grade the great mountains grew larger until they filled the entire eastern horizon. Beyond countless lakes formed from the mountains' run-off, the Chevelle moved west into a valley of low foothills.

Mack took the turn-off to Yreka and after passing through the modest seat of Siskiyou County he drove toward the even smaller town of Etna where at a last gas station Mack stopped to ask directions to Black Bear Ranch.

"The hippie ranch? Well, see them mountains?" said the station attendant.

He pointed toward the foothills of the Marble Mountains that rose west of the town and by three in the afternoon already were casting fat, dark shadows over Etna.

"You got to get through them and over two summits. About forty miles. Maybe two hours if you don't get lost. Dirt road all the way. Stay on Sawyer's Bar to Eddy Gulch Road. And when you get to the summit be sure to get onto Black Bear Road. Easy to miss. The other roads take you miles out of your way."

Mack topped off the tank and bought a quart of oil to store in the trunk. The drive was easy at first until the first mountain range twisted the nearly narrow road into a series of steep, pretzel-like switchbacks. At the Summit Mack stopped for a view of a wrinkled washboard of hills and peaks that stretched endlessly in all directions.

Mack then plunged down toward a river gorge, sliding through another patch of sheer switchbacks, his foot perpetually on the brake until the smell of burning rubber forced him into first gear. Along the North Fork of the Salmon River, Mack searched for Eddy Gulch Road until stopping at a market in Sawyer's Bar where a helpful clerk told him he had missed it.

Eddy Gulch climbed steadily until it reached the summit of Black Bear Mountain where Mack stopped for another view of the geologically upheaved and steep washboard of mountains through which they had passed. He searched three spur roads for the one to Black Bear before settling on the track with the freshest tire ruts. Another slow, winding descent over potholes and rocks brought him at last to the entrance of a long, green valley. At the road's end, he arrived in front of a sizable, vintage wooden ranch house and a crowd of residents who had heard him coming.

"Not the truck," a naked man with a ponytail yelled.

"New arrivals?" shouted a woman. "Don't need anymore of those. And not men. Shit. More fucking mouths to feed. Did they bring any groceries?"

Mack bounded out of the driver's seat.

"We're looking for Raj," said Mack. "We're friends."

"Over here, Mack."

The familiar voice belonged to Raj who emerged from the crowd to greet him.

Yitzhak climbed out of the passenger seat and grabbed Raj around the waist. Mack also embraced him. Raj was thinner than Mack remembered.

"In time for dinner," said Raj. "Have anything you can contribute?"

Mack pulled a shopping bag from the back seat. It contained

two bags of potato chips, a tub of cheese dip, a can of cashews and eight apples.

"Where's Sonia?" Mack asked as he walked with Raj and carried the shopping bag into the ranch house.

"She's here," answered Raj. "But we're not together anymore."

Mack gave Raj a double take.

"It's cool," said Raj. "You'll see."

Dinner was a greasy, brown stew and slices of two-day old flatbread. Everyone gathered at the ranch house table. Mack counted about three-dozen people: 12 women, 18 men and the rest were children.

"Still eating the pig," said Raj. "At last we're down to the innards so it's soup and I can pretend I don't know what I'm eating. Joey shot it a week ago. He was busted for killing a deer out of season. And then the sheriff's deputies busted him for having pot. He and his old lady Sue were carted off to jail where it was learned they both had hepatitis. So we fixed the shitter on the hill. Fitted with big oil drums. You can sit and have a great view.

"Anyway, Joey shot one of the ranch's pigs that kept wandering up to his sleeping platform near the beehives where he slept with his gun so he could chase off a pesky bear. But he pissed off everyone. Not his right to decide to kill a ranch pig. We had to ask him to leave. We never ask people to stay. That's up to them. But we do ask people to leave."

After dinner Raj walked Mack around the ranch in the clement evening twilight and along a shallow creek to a clearing where a campfire burned as people leaving dinner approached to sit nearby. Mack saw Sonia strolling forward with another man.

"That's Jake," said Raj. "We have a different way of thinking about ourselves here. We're all one family and in all ways imaginable."

As night fell those warmed by the fire retired together to the ranch house. Yitzhak, who had found himself welcomed by the women, walked inside with everyone. Mack told Raj he would sleep in the Chevelle.

Dawn shook Mack out of his uncomfortable sleep and he made his way to the house where coffee and tea brewed and Yitzhak sat with others to discuss how the Chevelle might be used to go get more food.

"For the people!" Yitzhak shouted.

Mack looked away as Yitzhak then nodded to everyone agreeably. There was no more time for Mack to serve the people but Yitzhak owned the Chevelle.

"You can drive to Yreka," said a man named Melvin who appeared to be one of the ranch leaders.

"We can pay. If the food truck doesn't arrive by tomorrow we're fucked."

After breakfast the rumbling sound of a truck engine swept down from the mountain and everyone ran outside to welcome it. The truck pulled up in front of the house but it was not the food truck from the San Francisco vegetable market. It was the drug boys in their Ford who brought a regular supply of acid and pot in exchange for a few nights of fun and partying at the ranch.

On the second night Sonia took Yitzhak away to fuck him, which was cool with Raj and Sonia's newest old man, Jake. A busty woman in a sack dress named Laurel approached Mack who declined her invitation and returned to the Chevelle. He fell asleep marveling at the amount of labor required to make a ranch work, knowing only how often men used work as their protection from another, inner life.

"The women stopped sleeping with the men last winter," Raj told Mack. "No more sex until we went out into the snow drifts to chop wood. Now it's summer and three babies are on the way."

eight

Mack wished he could catch everything, everything he ever knew and did not know, even those things he never knew but also knew too well. He would catch them like he clutched at the flies swarming at the ranch. He would catch them and hold them up to the rising sun and know them all as he never had or as he needed to again.

It was bath day and in the morning ranchers and their lovers and children lined up along the shallows of Bear Creek to dip into the cool, slender stream. Some brought cups from the kitchen to use as ladles for dipping and pouring. On a hot summer morning no one wanted to fire up the big house stove to heat water.

Mid-morning a familiar and unmistakable rumble filled the valley and everyone ran to the ranch house to eventually and heartily welcome the Black Bear food truck, loaded with produce, grains, cheeses and meats from the old Farmer's Market in the City. No one was happier than Mack to see the diesel-smoking flatbed arrive. He would not have to drive with Yitzhak to Yreka for more food. It was alarming to imagine how long a community of some forty men, women and children might go without eating.

"Truck broke down this side of Red Bluff," said the driver named Joel as he reported to Martin, one of the first ranchers to approach.

The drivers hid their dope in the trees and it was a good thing. Cops started arriving and it was a few minutes before they realized the cops were circling to block the truck so they could search it.

"Didn't find squat, man. Not even a roach," said Joel.

Joel hitched into town and found a mechanic who uncovered a problem in the fuel line.

"Took a day," said Joel. "Sorry we're late."

Mack watched Yitzhak climb into the truck bed to push boxes to men waiting on the ground. He stood tall and purposive, his long black beard and bare chest giving him the appearance of a jolly, warm Samson in the service of his people. Yitzhak was one of those people Mack thought he knew but wished he really knew. For someone certifiably crazy, Yitzhak appeared remarkably liberated from his self-absorbing psychosis to a point where his attention was now focused directly and enthusiastically on the needs of others. Was it possible? Had Black Bear done this to him? Was it sex with Sonia? Something had aroused Yitzhak's hipness, the friendly version of his delirium that rode a wave of uncertain size and speed.

In the kitchen Martin and Diane with the help of two women named Joy and Brenda inventoried the food, separated it all into bins and buckets, pushed boxes onto shelves and found cool places to store perishables. They calculated it was enough food to last Black Bear for another two weeks. A garden of vegetables and herbs grew in the sunniest outreach of the meadow, but it would never be enough to feed everyone. This remote and hidden hippie Shangri La still depended on the big distant city for its survival to the point that Diane continued to pay rent on a Victorian in the Haight where ranchers could crash on their returns to town.

The day of Black Bear's provisioning was momentous and purposeful. Residents clustered like hornets around the truck as if it were the seasonal delivery system for their essential sugars. Joel had also secured several bottles of cheap wine for "virtually nothing" from a vegetable market wholesaler who was giving up booze. The wine was opened before dinner and by sunset the day's tension, which had united everyone in useful work, petty politics, good and bad vibes and had both advanced and smothered infinite joys and resentments, found its ultimate and familiar discharge in the night's sexual common ground.

No anxiety grown during daylight appeared resistant to the pairing off and fair exchange of evening sex. Raj had told Mack that the understood rule at Black Bear was that one slept no more than two consecutive nights with the same person, which still left Mack to wonder how a fair exchange took place when by his calculation several men each night would have to do without. Later he learned a few women were fine sleeping with more than one man. And at least two men were fine sleeping with each other.

Mack watched couples near the evening fire crawl into their spooning embraces and, in the heat left from the vanishing day, get naked and make love. Mack had his camera and photographed what he could in the diminished light. Again, the woman named Laurel approached him and again he declined her invitation to sleep with her.

And, again, Yitzhak was popular and swept away by a woman other than Sonia as if word had spread that he was a special and perhaps fleeting pleasure, though Mack wondered why Sonia had not exercised her option on Yitzhak for a second night. Mack learned later from Yitzhak that the second woman also had attended the city's Monday Night Class, as had two others who were drawn through Yitzhak's attachment to the words of Stephen, its teacher. That Yitzhak could remember these words and repeat them was, for the women, an apparently additional turn-on.

Ignorance was a mistake at the heart of life and by morning Mack fumbled with a dull headache, feeling foolish and hung over from too much cheap wine, his throat wretched and scratchy from too many tokes. He staggered down to the stream to wash his face from where he could see a half-dozen ranchers, several naked including Yitzhak, heave together as they pushed the frame of a wooden shed into a carved out flank on an adjacent hillside. Again, Mack pondered the ease with which his presumably crazy companion could navigate, with apparent success, the dynamics of this complex, emotional and vigorously survivalist tribe. Either Yitzhak was now suddenly and inexplicably sane, or all Black Bear's residents were themselves crazy.

"You think you'll stay in Canada?" Raj asked Mack as he strolled with him around the ranch. Mack took pictures while he considered Raj's question.

"May not have a choice," answered Mack. "I'm sure as hell not going to fight in that war."

"An exile?" asked Raj.

"No. An immigrant," answered Mack. "If I'm called up, I won't come back. I'm not going to Vietnam. And I'm sure as hell not going to jail."

For the workers on the hill, the ranch was subdued after its night of feasting and fucking. Raj showed Mack the new latrine with its innovative seats set on bottomless oil drums. He walked him into a small neighborhood in the forest that contained sleeping platforms, lean-tos and sheds.

"These are fine for late spring and summer," said Raj. "But when winter comes, we'll all be back in the big house. Black Bear was a gold mine forty years ago. Lot of hobos came up here during the depression to stake claims under the liberal terms of the Mining Law of 1872. Now it's the hippies and the BLM hates it."

The hot day passed in a buzz of chatter and desultory work. Few had energy and those that did, including the morning work crew that enlisted Yitzhak, were done by noon. A lunch was created from leftovers and in a post-prandial daze Mack found a small clearing above the meadow and stretched out on the grass. It was the rare window of leisure at Black Bear where any dream of freedom could be sustained only by an exhausting, wakeful labor.

One percent free. The poster hung in the big house, large on the side of one wall with the words printed under a silk-screened image of two Chinese Tongs smoking cigarettes in San Francisco's Chinatown days after the city's 1906 earthquake. No one entirely understood it. *One Percent* was printed on a patch worn by the Hell's Angels motorcycle gang to identify them as among the "only one percent" of bikers that an article in a motorcycle magazine described as troublemakers. Perhaps to be in trouble in America was by definition to be free. Yitzhak, Raj, the Black Bear ranchers, were all troublemakers. And now Mack was on the verge of making his own trouble. It was time. There was never change without trouble. There was no worthwhile history that was not forced into existence by troublemakers.

"We got to go tomorrow," Mack said when he found Yitzhak at the big house.

Yitzhak gave him a sour look.

"These are the people," said Yitzhak. "These are my people."

Mack sensed a flash of his friend's frantic madness and felt oddly and momentarily relieved.

"You can come back," said Mack. "But I'm late, man. I need to get my ass to Seattle."

Yitzhak's eyes beaded with his suppression of difficult thoughts until the sound of an angry, shouting woman caught their attention. Ranchers ran past them while Mack and Yitzhak fell in behind to arrive with everyone in front of the big house where a young woman with long black hair yelled furiously at a flummoxed, silent man.

"You fucking asshole!" the woman shouted. "I don't want your baby. I want to die."

The woman, obviously pregnant, began beating her fists against her protruding belly, slugging hard against it and leaving fresh red bruises as three women rushed toward her and restrained her.

"Sarah!" shouted one of the women. "Stop, goddamnit. Stop! You'll hurt the…"

"I want to kill it," screamed Sarah as she stared furiously again at the quiet, perhaps frightened, man standing before her.

"You motherfucker. I wish I'd never fucked you. I hate you. I hate you! I hate this baby…"

The three women pulled the struggling Sarah away and surrounded her as they each grabbed her clinched fists and pulled them behind her. Together they walked her away and back toward the house.

The growing crowd of ranchers turned toward the man, who squinted painfully, his wizened face appearing to Mack as a tablet of a life lived in considerable and lasting pain. He wore an embroidered peasant-style shirt, one likely made for him and probably by the woman named Sarah.

"You OK, Nick?" asked one of the men.

Nick shook his head.

"It's time, Art," said Nick. "I'm bailing. This is all too fucking much."

Nick picked up a knapsack at his feet and began strolling toward the entrance to Black Bear road.

"C'mon, Nick," shouted Art. "We can try to…."

Nick kept walking as Raj approached Art.

"Let him go," said Raj. "He's right. It's time. He should have left long ago."

"But its ten miles to Sawyer's Bar and he's walking out," said Art.

"And he walked in. Remember?" answered Raj. "Let him go."

By nightfall Mack was determined to leave Black Bear and worried how in the morning he would sway his driver to start the car and go. For the fourth night Yitzhak was pulled into bed by yet another woman as if this tall, dark and masculine creature was an imported novelty. It was not love, not even hippie love, the kind more evident in the tension between Sarah and Nick. For all their communal devotion to kindness, the Black Bear ranchers seemed caught in a blind exchange of aches and agonies. For all their talk of tenderness, there was not much evidence of intimate duty.

Mack found Yitzhak in the morning as he approached the big house. He had spent the night with Laurel in her shed in the woods.

"We got to go today, man," said Mack. "I'm already late, I'm…"

"Yeah, we're going," said Yitzhak directly. "For the people!"

"For what?" asked Mack, relieved to have Yitzhak's agreement to leave the ranch.

"That woman who's having a baby," said Yitzhak. "We're giving her a ride home."

Mack winced.

And where's that?" asked Mack.

Yitzhak didn't know.

"North," said Raj at breakfast. "A family outside of Florence. Anyway, that's what they call themselves. True Art Family. Have a house on a creek east of town. You'll go west from Eugene, maybe an hour and half, then cut over to Highway One and catch the road to Portland."

"It's really cool of your friend do this," Raj added. "Sarah is hurtin' and she needs her people. We can't handle it anymore."

Mack hated to take a detour but was grateful at last to be moving again. Once they dropped Sarah, Mack would take the wheel and get back on course without the fuddling distractions of the Ranch, its women or *the people*.

It was mid-morning before the Chevelle was packed and Sarah ready to leave. She walked down from the house with three women, one of them Sonia, and dropped a bulging backpack embroidered with rainbows, which Yitzhak shoved into the trunk. She hugged the women, looked grimly at Mack and squeezed into the back seat. The Chevelle climbed Black Bear road and dropped slowly down the other side as Yitzhak rode the brakes over potholes and ruts.

It was an hour before they entered the logging road from Sawyers Bar to Etna. Yitzhak drove two miles before they saw Nick hitch-hiking. Mack told Yitzhak to speed up and Sarah turned away from the familiar face that appeared to Mack now as a weak, empty mask and that returned Mack's stare with eyes of sagging resignation before a cloud of road dust swallowed him whole.

In Etna, Yitzhak stopped for gas while Sarah peed and then walked across the street to enter a phone booth. Her waving hand told Mack she had made contact with someone. After several minutes, she left to return to the car.

"At least they're expecting me," she said to Mack, her first words of the trip.

"Who?" asked Mack.

"My family," she said. "Actually, The Family. We're a bunch of artists who live together in a big country house. Haven't seen any of them since January. What a goddamned fuck. That man sure took me for a ride. And look at me."

Sarah folded her hands under her protruding belly.

"I'm a ruined woman," she sighed.

And then she laughed.

She was feeling better. Mack asked her what happened.

Sarah said she met Nick the previous year at a local country festival. He moved in with her at the Family retreat where she created fiber art and painted while working as a teacher's aid in a local school. She had a teaching certificate from Oregon State where she studied art. Nick was charming and the Family was at first accepting, until his drinking got out of hand and the Family, comprising seven other artists, asked Nick to leave. Furious, Sarah left with him and they found their way to Black Bear in time for the spring thaw when all hands were needed to survive.

"Nick can survive," said Sarah. "Not much else, but he can survive. And we were welcome to survive along with everyone else at Black Bear. Survival is hard work and we could do it."

"Nick—what about, y'know…" Mack pointed at Sarah's belly.

Sarah said she would spend the rest of her life trying to understand her attraction to Nick.

"I think I just wanted Nick's wanting me," said Sarah. "He wanted my wanting him. It was a perfect contract. And guaranteed to fail. And now I'm going to have his baby. At least, I think it's his. Damn, I've already said too much."

Sarah turned to look out the window, immediately absorbed in the views of amber grasses in a narrow canyon that opened to the wider valley and the big snows to the east. They climbed in silence over the long green ridges leading north into Oregon. They were in Eugene at two and after a gas stop Yitzhak drove west on Highway 126.

"Not far now," said Sarah and it wasn't. Crossing the Suislaw River into Mapleton Yitzhak was directed through a small residential neighborhood and up a forested western hillside to a driveway and, beyond, to a large, two-story farmhouse surrounded by sheds and outbuildings.

"Wait here," said Sarah as she exited the car.

In the twilight cast through an encroaching coastal fog, Sarah approached the porch, climbed the steps and knocked vigorously on the door.

A tall woman answered and reached immediately to clasp Sarah in a deep hug. She was joined by another, shorter woman and then a man, older with grey hair whose large arms surrounded all the women as they stood in a strong, gathering embrace. Mack could see others bobbing in the lighted room behind the door.

Sarah turned and pointed toward the Chevelle. The large man squinted to see and then waved vigorously to Mack and Yitzhak while shouting something that sounded like a welcome.

"You eat like this every night?" asked Mack as he sliced into a salmon steak served up from a full kitchen where four people had scurried to prepare dinner.

The house's large dining room was clean and appointed. Paintings hung from the walls and a polished wood floor flowed throughout the home's interior like a shiny lake.

"We try to eat well," said Victor, the large man with grey hair who sat at the head of the dinner table. "We live in a place where good food is plentiful and not expensive."

The gentility of the Art Family was mind-blowing and a severe contrast to the wild, feral ways of Black Bear. Mack and Yitzhak had been invited to stay the night in a guest cabin behind the farmhouse.

"Victor is the founder of this artists' feast," said Sarah as she took another bite of potatoes.

"These people work hard but they have a lot to show for it."

Mack wondered how anyone could work harder to survive than the penniless ranchers of Black Bear.

Yitzhak appeared confused but said nothing, even as two women stared at him.

"Has anyone asked to sketch your face?" one asked. "You have remarkable features."

"Sarah says you're going to Seattle," said Victor.

Yitzhak nodded.

"There's a music festival in Olympia this weekend, just south of there. Virgil, one of our artists and, incidentally, my nephew, wants to film it. Could you give him a lift?"

Yitzhak nodded vigorously while Mack again was sunk into the likelihood of another, uncontestable delay.

nine

Mack wondered why anyone who suffered so many kinds of pain should want to suffer any new kinds. Mack wished to understand Yitzhak better and still felt guilty dragging his presumably sick friend into the Northwest simply to get his own ass into Canada. But in doing so, Mack had succumbed without any negotiation to an obstacle course of Yitzhak's creation.

Because they traveled in Yitzhak's Chevelle, it was Yitzhak who decided where and when they would go. Now Mack was done with it. He awoke on Tuesday morning prepared to confront his friend and to demand they drive straight to Seattle without another stop, other than to drop Virgil in Olympia.

He was surprised to see Yitzhak gone and, when he walked outside, to see his friend helping Virgil load two cases of film equipment into the Chevelle's trunk. Their conversation appeared animated though it quieted as Mack approached.

"What time are we leaving?" Mack asked.

Mack hoped to learn some details of their conversation but Yitzhak looked at him quizzically and then looked to Virgil who said he didn't know and that around ten sounded good.

"It's about a five hour drive," said Virgil.

Emerging from the big house after breakfast, Mack was again surprised to see Yitzhak at the wheel of the Chevelle with the engine running. Virgil sat beside him in the shotgun seat usually occupied by Mack, who now climbed into the back seat as the delegated passenger on his own trip north. Virgil and Yitzhak, who had been chattering as Mack approached, again stopped talking when Mack opened the car door.

"When do you want me to take the wheel?" Mack asked Yitzhak.

"I'm cool," said Yitzhak who gave Virgil a wink. "I even know the way."

It was the last Thursday in August and when Mack planned this trip he imagined that by now he would have been in Canada for more than a week. He looked ahead to arriving in Seattle by evening. He could be in Vancouver on Sunday.

The drive north along the coast was marked by its silence. Neither Virgil nor Yitzhak spoke while Mack watched wide, sandy beaches slide past under a deliquescing fog. By noon the ocean had changed under a bright summer sun from a pale green to a crisp blue just as the road left Lincoln City and veered toward the highway leading east to Portland. Coastal hills gave way to valleys of fruity vineyards and then subdivisions and then the bridges and tall buildings of a large city bordering a very large river.

"Beautiful country," Mack said in an attempt to start a conversation.

Virgil nodded and Yitzhak said nothing.

In Portland, Mack bought a paper, his first in more than a week, and read about the Woodstock Music and Art Fair. The so-called rock festival had been held a week before in a pouring rain on a farm in the New York Catskills. It drew nearly a half-million and clogged the roads. Mack read accounts of naked hippies dancing wildly to the music of some of rock's most popular performers. For reasons not immediately clear, it was being described as a signature moment in the history of a blooming counterculture.

"Sky River's next. What do you think?" Virgil said whimsically when Mack mentioned Woodstock.

Mack couldn't think. His mind was on Seattle and as Yitzhak slowed at the Olympia exit, he asked where they would stop to let Virgil out.

"I want to see this scene," said Yitzhak. "We'll let Virgil out where Virgil wants to get out."

Mack wasn't used to taking orders from Yitzhak.

"But to get to Seattle, we have to…" Mack tried to redirect the conversation.

"I may want to stay for a while," said Yitzhak. "These are the people and they are gathering. That's important."

Mack sank back in his seat while Yitzhak cruised off the highway and towards the town of Tenino, passing a small sign for the Sky River Festival and Lighter than Air Fair #2. Following a caravan of trucks and vans, Yitzhak arrived at the entrance to a large ranch near a river. Vehicles lined up at a gate where they were checked and admitted.

"We'll park first. Then we can set up camp," said Virgil who passed Yitzhak a piece of paper to give to the security guard at the gate. The guard took the paper and read it.

"Paid!" he shouted to the gate manager and the Chevelle was waved on through.

Virgil directed Yitzhak toward a meadow where he parked the Chevelle.

"Wait here. Need to find my troops," said Virgil before he leapt from the car.

"Look, man…" Mack said to Yitzhak. "I need to get to Seattle. Remember? Remember what this trip is about?"

Yitzhak turned and pushed his big, full-bearded jaw and muscular shoulders deep into the back of the car's shallow cabin. His nose was inches from Mack's face.

"This trip isn't your trip," shouted Yitzhak. "It never was. It's about me getting my freedom back, getting away from my crazy bitch mother and my sick family; getting control of my life and my money—my goddamned checks that I can cash myself now. It's me, Mack. Me and the people. I care about the people. They are all that matters. And where the people go, well, that's where I go from now on."

Mack sat silently, both dazzled and frightened by Yitzhak's coherent and reasonably articulate words. They were direct in a way Mack had never before heard. It was a revelation that Yitzhak had real thoughts and that this one was spoken with such uncharacteristic conviction.

Mack forgot about Seattle and for a moment could wonder

only if Yitzhak's madness was ever real. Or had it always been an act, a way to move subversively through his life without detection. Before this trip Mack had considered Yitzhak one of life's eternal hitchhikers and not a driver, though all hitchhikers have their own visions of the beauty waiting at the end of their roads.

Virgil returned to the car. His friends from Oregon had set up a small camp in the shade of several oak trees at the far side of an otherwise grassy, bumpy field. Among Virgil's equipment was a 9x12 cabin tent which Yitzhak and Mack carted to the campsite.

"Good we got here early," said Virgil. "Gonna get real hot this weekend."

Mack felt himself pressed into unwilling service and after sorting through the particulars of his new situation decided not to resist. He pulled his suitcase and backpack from the car and threw them into the tent with Virgil's bags and Yitzhak's duffle. He had a blanket in the suitcase he could wrap around himself to sleep. His backpack, which he kept always in sight, would serve as his pillow.

I'll make some photos, Mack told himself. *I'll hang out. I'm close. I will never again worry about Yitzhak. I'll leave him if I have to.*

Evening came and Virgil's friends, some of them college students from Eugene, organized a chicken barbecue and started a small fire. Jugs of a cheap red wine were passed around and by nightfall Mack was comfortably drunk enough to sleep until he awoke at dawn to the sound of loud and multiple hammerings. He looked outside the tent to see a large crew illuminated under a row of car headlights while its members scrambled like ants to construct from large pieces of plywood the foundation for a music stage. Mack thought of condemned prisoners awakened during a final night of sleep by the sound of their gallows under construction. He lay back down but could not close his eyes and went outside with his camera.

Mack walked the property and was unimpressed by its small, potentially restricting size. A Woodstock half-million would never fit within the barbed wired confines of this ranch. He wondered if it could hold even thirty thousand. He checked a billboard for the Festival and read the names of those scheduled to perform. Few he recognized, though those he did included Country Joe and the

Fish, the New Lost City Ramblers, Fred McDowell, the Steve Miller Blues Band, Dan Hicks and his Hot Licks, Sons of Champlin and the Youngbloods who were rising on the radio charts with their big hit *Get Together*. Groups he'd never heard of included Black Snake, Frumious Bandersnatch, Collectors, and the Cleanliness & Godliness Skiffle Band. No, this would not be another Woodstock.

When Mack returned to the tent, Virgil and his friends were cooking breakfast on two Coleman Stoves. Mack was offered a pancake and sausage that he accepted. Friday was a workday and after breakfast Virgil and his friends met to discuss the festival and, Mack presumed, how it would be filmed. Yitzhak was included in the discussion, which at first surprised Mack until it became apparent that Yitzhak had befriended Virgil who, at least up until now, had not befriended Mack.

The rest of the morning was taken up with stage sound checks featuring countless replays of the Rolling Stones singing *Honky Tonk Women*. By noon a crowd had arrived at the gates. Musicians in vans, large buses and motor homes came first and parked in a roped off area behind the stage. The Seattle Free Clinic erected two large tents for a first aid station. Mack learned from a stagehand that a Thurston County judge that morning had denied the Tenino Chamber of Commerce's attempt to stop the festival and by three in the afternoon cars lined the highway for nearly a half-mile outside the gate to the ranch.

Tents sprouted slowly throughout the field, growing into subdivisions organized as if by the intervention of some natural law of urban planning. Near the stage a tightly crowded assembly of tarps and pup tents asserted the congestion of the festival's downtown where, lined up at tables along each side of the stage, vendors sold everything from coffee to cocaine. Farther from the stage a sizable suburbia formed where tents were separated by enough space to assure some privacy and where groups established tight perimeters to keep out strangers. At the back of the field, and near the oak trees, a few compounds grew. These were the equivalent of gated communities and one, especially large, belonged to a gang of bikers from Tacoma. It was not far from where Virgil and his friends had created their camp.

As evening approached, Virgil's friends again fired up the barbecue and began roasting ribs and potatoes. Several women arrived together from Eugene and helped with the food. Instead of wine, Virgil passed around fifths of bourbon and offered joints and mushrooms. Mack held back but noticed that Yitzhak was toking and also drinking. The day had been hot and the heat lingered into the evening while Mack roamed with his camera.

Mack approached the river where several new arrivals were swimming naked. At one end of a shallow beach a man and woman bounced lewdly behind a picnic table. Mack photographed the scene from the shadows of the oaks. Back at the campsite Yitzhak was sitting at the fire, his arm around one of the Eugene women. Mack found his place in the dirt and took a seat. He had nothing to do before he was born. He had nothing he could do now.

Mack awoke Saturday in the back seat of the Chevelle. He had tried at first to sleep in the tent but Virgil and his friends had dropped acid and were up and high all night. Yitzhak had bounded away with the woman next to him, leaving Mack to fend for himself in a cool, silently hostile atmosphere. For some reason, and one only Virgil seemed to know, Yitzhak was hip and Mack was square.

Mack hiked back to the tent to find Virgil and Yitzhak asleep inside. He was offered a sweet roll and a hard boiled egg by one of Virgil's friends whose turn it was to fix breakfast. Mack thanked him and left with his camera and backpack to visit the stage where he could hear the first performers warming up. Mack wandered the perimeter of a fast-growing crowd as he searched for photo ops. A long American flag hung vertically from the light rafters above the stage. Another flag flanked the larger stars and stripes and featured the image of Che Guevara in military fatigues and wearing a beret.

Mack paid little attention to the names of the first groups that played, recognizing none though he photographed all. He also photographed the assembling crowd and, after studying the situation, saw he could get a better angle from a corner of the stage. An experienced newsman, Mack flashed his California Highway Patrol press pass at a kid working security and walked confidently past him. From the lower stairs leading to the stage Mack was elevated above the crowd and had wide vistas into the audience along with intimate views of the musicians.

By early afternoon several of those at the front of the crowd began dancing and taking off their clothes. More men and women got up off the ground and joined them in a sketchy burlesque of the nude audience at Woodstock. Behind the stage in a corner out of the crowd's view a couple was balling hard, the woman astride the man as she rode his cock with the pumping stroke of a piston. Mack leaned farther forward to capture the action until he felt himself slip and fall forward on the stairs. He grabbed for a nonexistent bannister and continued forward as his camera hit the ground and his head hit the camera.

"My camera…" Mack fretted as he sat up in the grass and checked its focus, its light meter and clicked off a few test frames.

"Not your camera, man," said a stagehand that ran over to assist him.

"It's your head."

Mack had opened a large gash over his eye that was bleeding liberally.

The stagehand led Mack to the clinic where he sat with an ice compress and waited to receive treatment next to a cot on which a long-haired, shirtless teenager wriggled and spoke angrily to himself.

At last on the table, Mack heard a physician laugh about Mack's "bad trip," a joke picked up by the two nurses assisting the doctor. After receiving six stitches, Mack was bandaged and given a small bottle of Valium. He was told to take two pills. He took three.

His injury and medication left a shiver in Mack's chest. He walked away from the clinic. He felt woozy and was still behind the stage. Beyond, he could see the dancing bodies in front of him and thousands more that rolled off behind and toward an infinite horizon of faces, all laughing and waving at him. Something lurked and it was not comfortable. Mack sensed a subtle threat growing out of the apparently pleasurable chaos of Sky River. He succumbed to an existential dysphoria, imagining himself dead and yet still present to witness what he could no longer influence or ever again enjoy.

Behind a copse of distant, leaping bodies, Mack thought he saw Yitzhak, a familiar checkered bandanna covering his head. He appeared to be making an exchange with a tall, shirtless male. A flash of green suggested money had changed hands. Was Yitzhak selling something, and what? Mack walked out from behind the stage and pushed through a mob of cavorting nude bodies toward the crowd's perimeter.

He saw Yitzhak move farther away and tried to follow until Mack lost sight of him. He decided to return to the camp under the oaks and wait for Yitzhak to return. When Mack arrived, the big tent door was zipped shut and he could hear inside Virgil's voice as it fired off rapidly delivered but barely audible instructions.

"Yitzhak here, he'll bring it to you and…," said Virgil.

Mack unzipped the tent and entered. Inside, Virgil and Yitzhak sat together facing two members of the Tacoma bikers' gang. Open on a blanket between them were two of Virgil's film cannisters. One was filled with small red pills. The other was packed tight with a white powder. Several wrapped plastic baggies stuffed with weed were stacked to the side.

"What the fuck are you doing here?" Virgil shouted at Mack.

Yitzhak jumped up to push Mack through the door of the tent. Outside, Yitzhak zipped the tent closed and led Mack toward the other side of the oak trees.

"You selling dope?" asked Mack.

"Virgil's dealing," said Yitzhak. "I'm just helping."

"What's he selling?" asked Mack.

"Grass, reds, a lot of acid, a lot of mescaline, some skag but not much. People are buyin' so he's sellin'.

"So Virgil's not a filmmaker? He's a dealer?"

Yitzhak's mouth broke into a slow, wicked grin.

"No. He's a filmmaker. Victor, his uncle, is the dealer. How do you think their family can afford that cool, good life in the country? Virgil is…well, he's like a rep, man. An agent for the boss."

"What do you get out this?" Mack asked.

"I get a cut. I get enough swag to buy my freedom. I get a hustle. And it's my fucking hustle, Mack. If you try to screw it up, I swear I will…"

Mack backed away from Yitzhak, recognizing in his driver's eyes the dangerous fury that bore every quality of a briefly dormant madness suddenly reignited in a burst of white, hot sparks. If Mack were to live in a world of violent men, he would have to arm himself or run.

"Why would I do that?" Mac asked and turned to leave.

At the river Mack joined a circle of campers preparing their dinner. One asked about his bandage. Mack rambled on about his photos, his fall backstage, his day of wandering and that he hadn't eaten since breakfast. A woman offered him half her cheese sandwich and Mack devoured it.

"Thank you," Mack mumbled as he chewed. "I'm a little out of it."

"Got just the thing," said a tall, slender bare-chested man wearing jeans and moccasins.

He handed Mack half of a small grey pill.

"Organic mescaline. No sweat. It won't hurt you. Think of it as refreshment for the soul."

Mack didn't argue. He took the small tab and swallowed it.

Within a half-hour Mack stood at the property's barbed wire fence, his camera focused on a herd of cows that approached him from a pasture on the other side. These were his new friends and they recognized him, engaged him, really saw him as others could not. Mack photographed the cows, lingering with his telephoto lens on each of them, gathering in the details of their knowledgeable expressions so evidently and perfectly presented to him. Mack shot three rolls of film; more than a hundred images of a unique engagement with the only sentient creatures that truly regarded him, perhaps even and ever loved him. Mack knew he loved the cows and when they wandered away in the twilight Mack took his leave to search the parking lot for Yitzhak's Chevelle.

He climbed into the back seat, found his blanket and wrapped it around him. His head fell on the backpack and he closed his eyes. The sound of the Youngbloods soothed him as did the crowd's exuberant and distant cheer that rolled against the car like the roar of a friendly ocean. He pictured himself a bug in the grass lost in a forest of desires.

It was another morning and Mack waited in darkness outside the Seattle Draft Resistance Office on Madison. He was early. The office did not open until nine.

The previous morning Mack had awakened in Yitzhak's Chevelle and hiked back to their Sky River campsite to straighten things out with his suddenly surly companion. The tent was gone. Yitzhak and Virgil were gone. Mack's suitcase lay in the dirt, opened and rifled, his clothes strewn everywhere.

Mack gathered what belongings he could find and shoved them back into his case. He walked down to the stage to search near the concession tables and check the clinic's infirmary. Not finding Yitzhak, Mack walked toward the biker compound to search for him there. As Mack approached, a fight broke out between members of the biker gang and a mob of hippies who had arrived to complain that the Tacoma riders had stolen purses and dope and raped two women.

Pops that sounded like gunshots scattered the hippies who fled toward the meadow, Mack lumbering to stay ahead of them. When he arrived at the road, Mack saw the Chevelle was gone. He followed those fleeing toward the highway and against a phalanx of cops charging onto the ranch. Mack stood in front of a truck and won a ride by agreeing to get out of the way. He bounced around in the cargo bed all the way to Seattle.

How had this journey become Yitzhak's? How had Mack lost control of a trip he had planned and carefully manipulated? He realized Yitzhak was quite adept with the madness he proffered, and perhaps always employed as a mask through which to assert uncertainty and unease. And it was just enough so that, even as he believed he was ultimately and fully in control, Mack would end up doing Yitzhak's bidding. His driver's madness was a ruse and as Mack totaled his losses he also counted his blessings. He was at last in Seattle and in possession of all his valuables and most of his clothing. And even if the truth stinks, he thought, the truth was still the truth.

"It's an unsteady but reliable trip to the grave," said Ernie, the counselor who unlocked the door of the Draft Resistance Office to admit Mack, his backpack and suitcase.

"How you get there matters and too many American boys are taking shortcuts through Vietnam."

Ernie was tall and stocky and wore a tweed jacket over a green t-shirt and black corduroy slacks. He was older than Mack, his face pale but strong as if someone had chiseled his features out of a block of granite.

Mack sat down at Ernie's desk at the back of a large room of desks and stared at the anti-war posters that lined the walls.

"You don't look like a deserter," Ernie said as he eyed Mack, who knew he looked dirty and disheveled from days in the Tenino dust and a night without sleep.

"For one thing, you don't have a crew cut and you're sporting quite a beard. Looks red. Is it red?"

Mack nodded. He wasn't a deserter and his beard, in the right light, was definitely red.

"Must be a draft dodger," Ernie said. "When were you ordered to report?"

Mack said he had not yet received any orders. More than a month had passed since he lost his student deferment and was reclassified 1-A.

"Not a dodger or a deserter?" asked Ernie.

"Not a dodger yet," said Mack. "I never want to be a deserter."

"Yeah…" said Ernie in quiet agreement.

"What about you?" asked Mack.

He wanted to change the subject.

"Big Bad Marine," answered Ernie. "Infantry for my three years of service. The last year was the worst. We were killing civilians for the hell of it. Inflating body counts. And then Tet happened. And we were toast. Search and destroy became search and avoid. I couldn't support the war anymore and I said so. But then I had to watch my back. Other soldiers were pissed, too, and some deserted. I didn't. Soldiers that grumbled too much could find themselves taking a shot from the rear, courtesy of a patriotic sharpshooter. No one would believe it but I can tell you a lot of mothers got their dead sons home with a government-issue bullet in the back of their head."

Ernie gave Mack the address of a home on Capitol Hill where he could spend a couple of nights before making the trip to Canada.

"Take the bus to Vancouver. It lets you off in Chinatown, a block from the office of the Vancouver Committee to Aid American War Objectors. On Georgia Street."

Ernie pulled out a notepad and wrote it down.

"Can't miss it. If you decide to stay in Canada, they'll help you. At least 60,000 American exiles there now. You'll fit right in."

The bus arrived as Ernie had described and Mack thought there was nothing now that could hurt or kill him, nothing but his own mind and its vault of imbedded insecurities. Passing into Canada was like crossing from California into Oregon. He wasn't even asked if he were carrying fruits or vegetables. He was presumed a tourist, though both the U.S. border patrol and the Canadian Mounties must have suspected otherwise.

"Dodgers come from middle class backgrounds. They're college bound or college educated, like you," said the Committee counselor named Andrew.

"Deserters are usually poor. Barely finished high school and the most likely to have enlisted. The army is fine taking for its infantry anyone with a tenth grade education. The U.S. Army has been a magnet for poor people. Three meals a day. You could learn a trade. But up here it's a little different. The poor deserters will do the jobs no one else wants to do. And you can't stay here if you aren't working. Apply for welfare as an immigrant and they'll throw you out of the country."

Mack gave Andrew his letter of recommendation from Cuthbert.

"We don't need any more journalists," he said. "What else can you do?"

"I can type," said Mack.

"That's cool. How fast?"

Andrew's charitable assignment was to settle Mack in a new country and to try to find for him a way to survive.

"Frankly, you aren't our most urgent case," Andrew told Mack. "You haven't been called up yet so you aren't a fugitive. And you have a wad of cash. I've got Army deserters who came home on leave just to run, and they're broke and they're facing 15 years in prison if they have to go home."

Andrew made a phone call and got Mack into a shared room in

a boarding house in Kitsilano, a section of Vancouver that wasn't mentioned in Mack's travel guide.

"A block south from Fourth Avenue," said Andrew. "Five Canadian a night."

He gave Mack directions on public transit.

The bus crossed a bridge to a part of town that faced a long beach and that was not far from the university. The boarding house was near a theater and a coffee bar, and in a working class neighborhood that appeared to be turning hip, much as in the early days of the Haight-Ashbury. He passed businesses with the names Positively Fourth Street, the Psychedelic Shop, a music venue called the Afterthought and a vegetarian restaurant with a heavy cloth awning that read Naam.

Men his age filled the hostel, managed by an avuncular ex-GI named Larry who worked for the Committee. Mack's roommate was named Dirk. He was an army deserter, as were most of the men staying in the old Victorian just off Love Street.

"A guy in my platoon saw a grenade in the road and we told him not to touch it," said Dirk. "He picked it up anyway and it blew his hand and forearm completely off. Within three weeks we'd lost five men to booby traps. That was enough for me. After a few months of combat, enlistees were offered a month's leave back in the states if they signed up for another two years. I took it. It was the fastest way to get home...and to get up here."

Dirk invited Mack to join him and some other deserters for dinner. They met in the downstairs hallway and walked down Love Street to a joint called the Bistro that Mack might have found on Haight Street. The men lined up in front while women in Afghan dresses and paisley blouses strolled passed with longhaired boys wearing high-heeled leather boots.

"Feels like home, doesn't it?" said Dirk who grew up in Oakland.

Mack hardly tasted his pasta while listening to the deserters share their new stories and, after a couple of beers, their old ones. The big news grew from their refugee status and their search for work, two conditions crucially intertwined.

"No work, no room at the inn," said Dirk's friend Jack.

It was sometimes enough to have a job offer. But a real job was better.

A third round of beers opened the floodgates. As much as they might have wished otherwise, there was no avoiding the war after Mack asked what drove them to desert.

Jack said he had escaped three times from MPs trying to capture him when he "ran for it" during his court martial trial.

"They'd just gotten me back into a police car to take me to Fort Ord when I pushed open the door on the other side and took off. They fired shots that went over my head."

He escaped to a beach near Monterey and phoned his girlfriend who picked him up and hid him in Berkeley for a week before driving him to Vancouver.

Harvey was leaving his tent at a base camp near Hue when a rain of human body parts smattered him on the way to the latrine. A suicidal soldier had carried a grenade to breakfast, pulled the pin and rolled it under the table where he sat with six others.

Another deserter named Franklin described the systematic murder of civilians in villages burned to the ground.

"In a free-fire zone you can fire on anything that moves. Two snipers shot at us and we were ordered to mow down the entire village. Men, women and children. *Stars and stripes* wrote it up as a fight between 300 Viet Cong and an American company with one US wounded and 300 enemy dead. It was sickening."

"Kept the body counts up," said another. "It was all the lieutenant cared about."

Though lieutenants didn't always fare so well.

"We fragged 'em. Well, someone fragged 'em," said a deserter named Clement, who told how unpopular commanding officers sometimes died in their sleep without an enemy soldier anywhere nearby.

"You should talk to Lin," said Dirk.

"He's got a hell of a story. One of the Presidio gang in San Francisco. He and a buddy sawed their way out of the brig and escaped naked. Planned the whole thing for a month. Roomed with a prisoner so they could get his hepatitis and then were transferred to a lower security cell in the basement of a hospital. Think he's still in town, unless he's gone to the valley. Lot of exiles are heading inland or up the Strait and settling in the country."

Mack heard more than their stories. He heard a history that

no one was writing. He asked his dinner companions if he could interview each of them and if they knew other deserters willing to talk about the real war in Vietnam. Mack knew he could do this. He could tell this story and break it open for the world to read. It wasn't a paying job, but it was work, real work.

One week passed. And then another. Kitsilano was enough like home to keep Mack safely withheld from desperate regret. Interviewing the men at the hostel kept him busy. The spacious city beach was a few blocks away and gave Mack a place for long, restorative walks. By the end of the second week he had established his address, mailed a letter to Harriet and also to his mother and had tried again to reach Inger by phone.

If no one responded, he was willing to accept his own full resignation from his previous American life. He lived in another country but one so much like his own he sometimes thought he had been remade into a new version of a previous existence.

Vancouver's September afternoons were still warm, if not balmy, and its very northern latitude extended daylight later into the cool evenings that he now spent at coffee houses and pubs. By the end of a third week, Mack had a scheduled interview with an immigration officer in Victoria for later in the month.

"We need a port of entry," said Andrew. "We'd do it here but the calendar is jammed and, besides, the Vancouver mayor hates American deserters and I don't want to send you back to the border at Blaine."

It was mid-month when Mack at last heard from home. A large envelope arrived from his mother. It contained a letter from her along with several pieces of junk mail, a gas and electric bill for his apartment, and a final paycheck from the Chronicle for $83.25. There was nothing from Selective Service. Mack was still not a draft dodger. He skimmed his mother's letter.

Your father is getting a little nervous not knowing what's up…can you write and tell him something? Anything? And you can always call. Hope you are safe in Vancouver and that it's working out for you. No draft stuff has arrived, as you can see. Guess no news is good news. Does this mean you can come home?

Mack did not want to call. He did not want to talk with his parents. He wanted to be as far as possible from their judgment and advice. He was living on a different planet now and did not want to hear their unhelpful and useless voices. The next day a letter arrived from Harriet.

Canada? How do you like it? Seems weird but I'm enrolled in graduate lit studies at the University of Washington beginning in January that will get me the doctorate next fall. Have a TA job, too. Seattle. I'm moving up there in December. Never been there but I believe that's not far from you. Any chance we could meet sometime?

There was always a chance of something and while reading her letter Mack thought of nothing else but a chance again to see Harriet. He had been a celibate exile, drawn down like any soldier who wanted nothing more than to survive. Harriet's letter put him on leave and gave him permission to dream, to feel a deep attraction and to masturbate.

On the Saturday of his immigration interview Mack sat on a ferry from Tsawwassen to Swartz Bay and read in the *Herald-Tribune* that Nixon was asking for 50,000 fewer army draftees. The war, even if the US was retreating, was far from over. Mack would need a good reason to retrace his steps and undo his tedious, impertinent odyssey. Short of failing his interview, he could think of nothing that would induce his return to the States.

A bus ride south on Highway 17 brought him to the provincial capital. Inside a stately building fronted with marble pillars he waited to meet an immigration officer who appeared at the doorway with a red beard. Mack smiled and the officer named James laughed. Within ten minutes Mack's paperwork was reviewed and found in order. In another twenty minutes he was passed on the comprehensive ranking tool. With Andrew's permission Mack was able to report he had been offered a job with the Committee as a communications consultant. James then completed Mack's paperwork, gave it back to him and directed him to a clinic for the mandatory chest x-ray after which he would receive his permanent resident card in the mail.

It was that easy, thought Mack as he rode the ferry back to Vancouver. It was something I wanted and it was so easy. Something I wanted and probably never needed. But now it is still something I want. Something I want more than anything else.

Mack wrote Harriet and said yes he would like to see her and to stay in touch. He explained he was now a permanent resident of Canada. He thought she would like Vancouver.

He continued with his deserter interviews. Referrals brought him dozens eager to talk about their war experiences.

As for why this happens, shooting down defenseless civilians, torturing those taken prisoner, well I've tried to figure it out with psychology and also socially and spiritually. But all I can come up with is that there is something about holding a weapon, about a man holding a weapon over someone smaller and taking that person's life in his own hands. Is it a human quality? I don't know. Is it because America is a violent society? I don't know that either. But there is without a doubt some satisfaction that comes from killing somebody. Shit, everyone knows that. In Vietnam every gook is responsible for you being there and you hate each of them for it, each of them except maybe the whores you are fucking in Saigon. The war, it is entirely their fault. What men love about war is contained in the power of life and death held over some faceless person labeled the enemy.

By the end of the month, Mack had written a 2,000-word article featuring the highlights of his interviews. Andrew sent it to the AMEX magazine in Toronto, the newspaper that served American exiles in Canada. Peter the editor ran the story on Page One and sent Mack a check for $150 Canadian.

September turned into October and cool afternoons became cooler evenings. A northern darkness closed over Mack like an aperture that shut out light but that also lengthened his focus and opened him to a wider view.

Headlines from Mack's old country passed by him on the back pages of the Canadian press. The Chicago Eight trial began at the end of September while October opened with a failed riot by the Weathermen in Chicago called *The Days of Rage* but that did nothing but break a few windows downtown and get a hundred people arrested. And the once lowly New York Mets won the World Series.

The October 10th issue of Life Magazine contained a prominent article on the military abuse of soldiers who resisted the war. The article featured drawings of the torture of GI prisoners in the Fort Pendleton Marine Brig, many hamstrung for hours or confined for days in black boxes with barely room to move.

As a member and chronicler of the resistance, Mack connected naturally with the life plans of his old country's exiles. Two deserters and their women partners had purchased land fifty miles north along the Sunshine Coast in a place called Desolation Bay. They invited Mack to join them.

"It's the next level," said Carol, the wife of one of the buyers. "Jarrod and I think we can make it up there. We don't need much but the land."

It sounded to Mack like the pipedream of sanctuary he had encountered at Black Bear. But it was time to withdraw, to work quietly and not to raise his profile. He thought he should give it a try. He wired for another $400 he thought could get him through the winter. There was a house on the land that overlooked the bay.

"You won't freeze to death," said Carol. "And you can write about it. We could be rich for a season and then broke ever after. But even if we're broke we won't be poor."

Time would slow, perhaps more slowly than he needed. If he had trouble surviving, he could work. Fishing paid. Logging paid. Light retail paid. Even tourism paid and it would not be crazy for Mack again to apply journalism to the making of a new life.

Mack sat in the rear seat of a van, his suitcase and backpack shoved behind him as a thumping Caribbean soul beat played through Jarrod's speakers.

"Reggae," said Carol. "Ever heard it? Jarrod's into this new Jamaican sound."

"Cool," said Mack. "Who's the artist?"

"Jimmy Cliff," said Jarrod as he turned up the sound.

The music rolled over Mack like the syncopated hoofs of a grazing bull. The words were clearly spoken: *Vietnam, Vietnam, Vietnam, Vietnam, Vietnam, Vietnam, Vietnam.*

Cliff sang the story of a mistress Brown who lived in the USA and who received a telegram that said, *mistress Brown your son is dead. And it came from "Vietnam, Vietnam, Vietnam, Vietnam…."*

Mack watched his new driver rock to the song's gripping reggae beat. He did not know what to anticipate in a land named for its desolation. But he thought it would make for him a story that on some distant and inevitable day he would want and need to remember.

YITZHAK

one

Yitzhak was an imaginary traveling phantasm. He hurtled south in his Chevelle on Highway Five, Virgil beside him and counting out cash.

"What will you do with your money?" he asked Yitzhak.

Yitzhak was momentarily liberated from an identity. It was often the case that the intensified sensations produced from a drug's enveloping high would inspire within him a host of novel characters, each with its own persona and all with their peculiar relationships with each other. As the voice of this tribe, Yitzhak had long ago learned not to speak about them until a consensus was reached. Yitzhak offered Virgil a weak smile to conceal the vigorous colloquy within.

"Don't know," Yitzhak answered before turning his eyes back to the road.

"What happened to your friend?" Virgil asked.

"Don't know," said Yitzhak again.

"Don't know what happened. We're finished, though. He's going to Canada."

"What a fuckin' square," said Virgil. "How'd you hook up with him?"

"Long story," said Yitzhak who had few words left to share.

"What happens to her?" Virgil also asked, pointing to a woman asleep in the back seat of the Chevelle. Her long black hair poked out from under a puffy white comforter that covered all of her but

620

two bare and dirty feet.

"Black Bear," said Yitzhak, now weary of giving answers. "Goin' back to the ranch. She lives there. That's what she says."

"Who is she?" asked Virgil again.

"Cayenne," said Yitzhak. "Like the pepper."

"You sure have a way with women," Virgil sighed, at last aware he was intruding on Yitzhak's psychic space.

"They were all over you in Tenino."

Yitzhak flashed another weak grin before turning back to stare intently at the endless ribbon of asphalt that vanished constantly beneath them.

Before noon, Yitzhak took the exit to Eugene and found a café near the university where he left Virgil and his bags to await a ride back to Mapleton.

"We got the job done," said Virgil as he chuckled. "And you're several hundred to the good."

Yeah, thought Yitzhak, but nothing to the thousands Virgil was taking home to his Art Family. Virgil's filmmaking was a ruse for the transport and sale of drugs at Sky River. And his ride with Yitzhak reduced Virgil's exposure for which Yitzhak, unknown to Mack, received a cut of the take.

"Here," said Virgil. "It will keep you awake."

Virgil handed Yitzhak a half-dozen Benzedrine tablets.

Cayenne stirred in the backseat.

"Where are we?" her voice called.

"Back in Oregon," Yitzhak said without turning to look.

"Damn, that's the last time I mess with those Mexican reds," sighed Cayenne whose thin face, brightened by two brilliant green eyes but otherwise drawn and pale, appeared momentarily in the rear view mirror.

"I'm starving," she announced as she sat up and tugged to straighten the sleeves of a wrinkled purple turtleneck.

"And I have to pee."

She found a brush and ran it through a knot in her matted black hair.

There were many versions of an inexhaustible pleasure but all were vulnerable to their inevitable endings. *Without grief, without gloom, without death*…Yitzhak had spent days in a hallucinogenic trance and free of an identity that, heatedly and disturbingly, returned now to demand its authentic and unwelcome due.

Cayenne stretched her aching limbs and pushed open the rear passenger door of the Chevelle. She crawled out of the backseat, wrinkled, groggy and uncertain where she was or how much she wished to be there. She was a small woman and Yitzhak examined her tiny, stringy limbs as if he had never before seen her.

"You hungry?" she asked Yitzhak, who gave her a diffident nod.

"What do you want to do about it?" Yitzhak asked.

Cayenne volunteered to liberate food from a nearby market. She reached into the backseat and pulled out a large shoulder bag.

"Bet they have a bathroom. Be right back," she said and walked toward the store.

Yitzhak generally found it useful to wait on the decisions of others. If he did, he was frequently rewarded with the benefits of someone else's risk. In this instance, he might be the recipient of a stolen meal and without any danger to himself. Unspoken was Cayenne's obligation to Yitzhak for a free ride to Black Bear. They were at the halfway point and, as Yitzhak thought, it was Cayenne's weakest position. Yitzhak would not leave her here, that is, unless she was arrested or flipped out or disappeared or was otherwise detained. But she could not be sure of that. A free ride was anything but.

"An old trick," said Cayenne as she pulled from her bag two pre-wrapped sandwiches and two cans of beer and set them on the sand of a shallow river beach at the end of a one-lane road just south of town. Yitzhak had followed a sign pointing the direction to a nearby county park. Once there, they hiked a short distance to their secluded beach.

Cayenne described how she entered the store and bumped into a display case of canned goods and sent them rolling across the floor. After an obsequious apology, she left the flustered and preoccupied store attendants to find the bathroom while along the way filling her bag with food and drinks. Leaving the store, she purchased a bag of potato chips, again apologizing for the trouble she caused.

Yitzhak smiled. It was clever, even if risky. Most thieves hide in the shadows. Cayenne, however, drew all the attention to herself in a way that left her alone and unobserved.

"Cool," said Yitzhak and nothing else.

He was still not certain who within could speak for him.

Food and alcohol mixed with a warm valley sun to arouse Cayenne's connate lust.

"Let's smoke a doob and ball," she said to Yitzhak.

His eyes widened. Anything free made Cayenne happy and sex was the freest thing of all. Yitzhak's habitual calm, the strategy of his life, engendered all of Cayenne's attention. He was sexy in his silence, accessible and tender and anything else Cayenne wished to believe about him. After smoking some dope, Cayenne removed her skirt and panties and pulled down Yitzhak's jeans to pop out his fat, substantial cock, still not fully erect but more than her small palm could grasp at its base. She wrapped it in both hands and then took the tip into her voracious mouth.

Yitzhak was accustomed to the attention. His long legs, broad shoulders and full beard advertised perpetually the promise of his body. Women curious about it were rarely disappointed with its ultimate presentation. He was big. He knew that. Women told him that but moving naked in the world made it clear to him. And at times he knew he was nothing more than a curiosity but one that, even in a passing and transgressing moment, could be memorably pleasurable.

"You are so goddamned hard," Cayenne asserted breathlessly as she squatted over Yitzhak, her buttocks thrusting vigorously against him until she gave up one long, sonorous gasp that Yitzhak punctuated with his own quick, throaty yelp.

The afternoon's sky turned a darker shade of rose while the highway stretched out before him. Yitzhak watched shadows fold like amber cellophane over the asphalt, the mountains, and the tedious valleys of southern Oregon until, sliding hard down a long mountain he landed low and hard in California. No vegetables. No fruits. And he was free to move about the state. Cayenne slept in the front seat, her head thrown back and her mouth open while she snored.

Would he stay in Black Bear? Yitzhak remembered Stephen's words at the Monday Night class, that to work out one's karma was to work out God's karma. Two people could find it by getting together and vibrating together. That wild, honey sweet feeling, it runs up the backbone, said Stephen. But Yitzhak didn't have it. Not with Cayenne. She did not answer the call of his mystery though he had to admit her body was too entangling to reject even as his was too entangled to grasp.

There was a place in Yitzhak's life where he would need to stop being a fish and instead become a mammal. Stephen talked about the need for evolution, for becoming heavy enough to make a difference, to stop digging on Mom and to get out there in the cold world and to make your own heat. *Sharing out the karma.* That's what Stephen said. You're supposed to change your destiny. That's what we do. It would require becoming a magician and Yitzhak still wondered how. When would he know the magic? He had taken two of Virgil's Benzedrines and now reached in his pocket for another. He was in the mood for speed. The long shadows pushed him forward.

"Where are we now?" Cayenne asked groggily when Yitzhak stopped in Yreka.

"Close," answered Yitzhak. "Two mountains. You know the way."

If she did, Cayenne wasn't telling.

"OK," she said. "I'm thirsty."

She grabbed her shoulder bag and walked across the street to a small market near the gas station. She returned with a bottle of Coke.

"Want me to drive?" she asked Yitzhak.

"No way," he answered.

They were silent the rest of the trip, rolling over Black Bear mountain at sunset and arriving in front of the big house in the blue shadows of nautical twilight.

Raj stood with others at the road and was the first to greet Yitzhak who left the car to hug his old friend and bro.

"Back so soon?" asked Raj before looking inside the car to see Cayenne.

Raj then pushed Yitzhak away from the car and the crowd.

"Where did you find *her*?" Raj asked somberly.

"Sky River," answered Yitzhak. "Up near Olympia. She wanted a ride back to Black Bear."

"Shit," said Raj. "We thought we were rid of her."

There was a story and one too long for Raj to tell.

Cayenne stepped from the car as the crowd cleared away.

"Where's Misty staying now?" she asked.

No one answered.

"Guess I'll have to find her myself," Cayenne stated coldly. "Doesn't look like too much has changed."

Again, no one answered. Cayenne grabbed her bag and comforter and walked toward the house.

Yitzhak could not have known of Cayenne's tumultuous contribution to Black Bear's brief history. She had arrived the previous spring on the back of a Hell's Angel motorcycle and fallen instantly in love with a hippie dude named Happy Pete. In the spirit of the place and season, she fucked Pete's brains out, despite the furious jealousy of her hard ass Angel who responded by chasing after Pete with a bowie knife. It was the first time, and everyone hoped the last, that Black Bear would have to go get the sheriff. Pete hid in the woods for three days until the sheriff arrived, took the Angel aside, read him his rights and gave him a half-hour to get out of the county. Thereafter, everyone shunned Cayenne until, despite the pleas of her one friend and housemate Misty, Cayenne gave up on Black Bear and hitched a ride north.

"Bad karma," Raj said to Yitzhak.

Karma was something Yitzhak thought he understood. There was good karma and bad karma and Cayenne was clearly bad karma, something Yitzhak might have suspected but that was now confirmed.

"What the fuck do you want me to do now?" Yitzhak asked as he tried to fend off a surge of paranoia.

"Help us build a fence," said Raj.

Yitzhak slept in the Chevelle and awoke in the cool morning air of a new fall season at Black Bear. September's first week was a prelude to the Equinox and now the experience of living on the ranch moved away from summer's feast of pleasure toward fall's harvest and the newly essential preparations for winter. One full year of foolishness had been enough and those who remained at Black Bear were determined not to freeze again, not to run out of food, not to die into darkness and/or again fearfully flee.

After breakfast Yitzhak joined a work crew building a fence around the garden in the meadow, one formidable enough in size and height to protect the ripening produce from a suddenly attentive and fully present variety of nocturnal predators. In a sense it was busy work because Black Bear still depended desperately on the twice-a-month arrival of the city food truck. But the garden was an important gesture of self-sufficiency and expressed the ranch's unspoken hope that a day might arrive when a vast and lovely garden would feed everyone and forever.

Yitzhak worked two days sawing wood, digging and setting posts, and nailing boards. The exhausting labor lasted most of the daylight hours, leaving all who worked—and it was mostly the men—too exhausted to drink wine or get stoned. The women retreated after dinner and the ranch's casual sexuality appeared notably attenuated. Cayenne stayed in Misty's cabin and waited for a proper and welcoming moment to make an appearance. No other women approached Yitzhak who during his previous visit had grown accustomed to invitations to join ranchers in their beds. He slept again in the Chevelle, and—after another day of fence building—again slept alone.

"We can't let our guard down," Raj said to Yitzhak. "Not this year. We don't make it through this winter, we're fucked."

Yitzhak heard the hard words of a new farmer. The land spoke and there was no way to wish away its truth. There were lessons in the earth that perhaps even Stephen did not grasp and Yitzhak had no place within where he could hear or learn them. His life rode a wild horse he could barely dream of breaking.

As Raj spoke, Yitzhak absorbed the end of his fantasy of a life on the ranch. It had lasted two days which was longer than most of his dreams lasted, longer than he could remember caring about anything. Memory was a problem, of course. And drugs assisted Yitzhak enormously in forgetting that memory was a factor in the confusion that sometimes flowed from his sporadic assertions of an incomplete will.

Yitzhak was gone before dawn and filling his gas tank in Yreka as the sun rising above the big mountain forced him to shut his eyes and for a silent moment feel the heat he could not see. Life was a dream of appearing and disappearing and within these parameters Yitzhak accepted there was no place like home.

Before leaving the mountains, Yitzhak took another Benzedrine and as a result his mind raced faster than he could drive. He was going back to Berkeley, back to the people he knew and the streets where he lived. As his mind raced forward he remembered again what Stephen had said about vibrations and the body. The *eros* vibration could not lie but the *logos* was capable of communication and therefore *could* lie. Running on logos juice was dangerous but sometimes necessary to put you in a place where you could be detached.

Yitzhak hummed with energy. He felt the juice. He surged excitedly, as the Chevelle seemed to drive itself home. He waited for his body and mind to do their thing together. He observed in a flash the mental hang-ups that had stolen Mack away and that now suggested other potential anchors.

He was going home but not to his mamma. He was going back to Mack's studio. He knew Inger was staying there and perhaps she would let him in. He had money now and would offer to buy her dinner and, if she let him stay, he would offer her rent. He needed a story about Mack that wouldn't be hard to remember. The prick abandoned him or didn't show up at a specified time or stole something from him. He couldn't call Mack a prick to Inger. His story had to be believable and even in his current agitation, Yitzhak could not even begin to fabricate a credible lie. Why not say simply that Mack had crossed into Canada? That was cool enough and Yitzhak would not be expected to know anything else.

But Yitzhak didn't know if Mack was in Canada. In fact, he couldn't know if Mack already had communicated with Inger and given his presumably resentful if believable version of the truth. In which case, Yitzhak would be busted and again caught in his lie.

Instead, Yitzhak told himself to stay cool, though reassurance was not his strength. Numerous scenarios of easily imagined deceit were presented to Yitzhak and he had at last no way to discern truthful descriptions from what was untrue. There was much he did not know and so he would not say it. I don't know. Don't ask *me*. I don't know. I know and you know I don't *know*.

It was after six when Yitzhak parked on Addison Street in a vacated parking space. He walked up the indoor stairs of Mack's building and knocked on the door of his second floor flat. The door opened and Inger stared at Yitzhak, surprised and perhaps even alarmed.

"You?" Inger said in guileless shock.

"Mack asked me to let you know he's fine," Yitzhak lied. "Haven't seen him since he left me in Seattle. But he wanted you to know he's OK."

There was no response from Inger.

"That's nice," she said, relaxing into the moment occupied by news of Mack.

"Say, would you like to get some dinner?" asked Yitzhak. "My treat."

Inger looked deeply into Yitzhak's attentive eyes as if to weigh a pound of potential outcomes. It took a moment for her to decide if she could abide any of them.

She told Yitzhak to come in while she changed her clothes and grabbed her coat. Yitzhak remained quiet and attentive; aware he had won an opening where a moment before there was no hope of entry.

two

By the time the soup arrived, Yitzhak had found someone inside himself who could at last speak. He was quiet during the three-block walk to the Italian restaurant on Shattuck near Hearst. It was Inger's choice for dinner. Words were tools but Yitzhak had no secure idea how always to use them.

"How's the art going?" asked Yitzhak.

Whoever finally spoke from within reminded Yitzhak that Inger was an artist. It was a good question that bought him time as Inger

628

easily discussed the latest developments in her creative life. She hoped to go to Fresno State in the spring to study art with a group of women. A bright woman artist was leading the program and only women were invited to apply. Inger had made a kind of semi-final cut and was driving to Fresno for an interview at the end of the month.

"You think it's hard for women in the work world?" Inger asked. "A woman artist doesn't count for shit in this country. A lot of men artists won't exhibit with a woman unless she's married to one of their male friends or she's screwed them."

Yitzhak offered affirmative nods as he listened, his large beard fluttering with every nod like a fat black bird.

"It's been a rough year," said Inger. "Berkeley was my home once. But it isn't now. I need a change."

Berkeley also had been Yitzhak's home. And it still was a home though he did not want to return to his family, did not wish to see anytime soon the wailing mother that had ruled his life or the broken and nearly dead father who beat him as a child and now in full paralytic incompetence, could lift nothing to his lips, could not speak without a stick held precariously in his teeth which he used to poke at letters that spelled out on a game board the rough headlines of his newly desperate needs and intentions.

"How *is* Mack?" asked Inger.

Were he listening to anything but his own voices, Yitzhak would have known this question was coming. Inger liked Mack and had inherited from him the studio where she was now living.

"I can't tell you," Yitzhak said without guile. "We were hanging out at a big rock concert outside Seattle. And then we weren't. Guess he needed to get to Canada and I couldn't help him."

"Is he in Canada now?" Inger asked.

"Can't say," Yitzhak answered. "He doesn't write to me. And you haven't heard from him?"

Yitzhak knew the answer but still phrased the question.

A bottle of wine arrived with the main course and the waiter offered both Yitzhak and Inger a generous pour. Within a half-hour Inger was drunk and Yitzhak was quoting Stephen from the Monday Night Class.

"You go too, don't you?" asked Inger.

Yitzhak again nodded.

"Want to go with me next week?"

"Sure," said Yitzhak.

Yitzhak still enjoyed the freedom of someone on the road. He paid for dinner with a fifty-dollar bill, which was not lost on Inger. After a quiet walk back to Mack's flat, she invited Yitzhak in to smoke a joint. Yitzhak again asked about Inger's art and sat quietly as she spread out on the floor an edited portfolio of canvasses and drawings. He liked her work and another one of his voices arose from within to tell her. She heard it and opened to more than his words.

Inferiority is not a conceived idea. It is a lived and felt experience. Inger was profoundly and intimately insecure about her art. It fed her nothing and cost so much in time and money. She earned a living in ways she knew would shame most people and certainly embarrass her family. Yitzhak had little to say but what words he used were clear and supportive and suggested stunningly that he understood what, with her strong lines and washes of brilliant color, she was trying to do.

"It's kinda like you see me," said Inger as she offered Yitzhak another toke from her joint.

"Yeah," answered Yitzhak. "I see you."

Those were the last words either said for the next hour and for several more hours thereafter. It was morning before Inger again uttered a complete sentence, waking to find herself half-crushed within the broad, hard and encircling arms of a new overnight guest.

"I need to get up," she whispered as she gave her new bedmate a push.

Yitzhak rolled like a groggy pet toward the edge of Inger's bed, which he knew just weeks before had been Mack's bed. The thought was arousing and incestuous. Yitzhak felt a frisson of intimate conquest. He was briefly wrapped inside a place of pleasure once taken by his estranged friend and fellow traveler. He also had found somewhere in Berkeley other than his mother's house where he might hope to spend a night.

Inger told Yitzhak to return the next evening and she would fix him dinner. She was frank. He could spend another night but she would need to be alone for the weekend.

Yitzhak shrugged. He was used to receiving the dregs of freedom. They were all he needed. He lived with the continual secretion of his nothingness. At least, that's what Stephen said he lived with, that if you feel uptight, man, and like you're on a high, well; you gotta take care of the homework on the material plane. If you get loose from the bottom you are just flapping in the breeze. And Yitzhak was a Pisces. He was the fish and he could swim anywhere.

It had been nearly a month since Yitzhak had made the scene. He drove his Chevelle toward the campus and parked above College Avenue where there were no meters. He walked down Channing Way to Telegraph and passed the new cyclone fences that enclosed a vacant and useless People's Park. It was early but he found Crazy Pete hustling for change in front of Cody's Books.

"Hey, there," Pete yelled. "The rabbi is back."

Yitzhak hated Pete's name for him, one meant to either honor or warmly ridicule Yitzhak's Jewish roots. But he was happy to see Pete, a short, yellow-bearded hobo pushing forty and one of the Avenue's older denizens. Pete waved from the sidewalk and Yitzhak crossed the street to join him.

"What's happenin'?" Pete asked. "Where you been? Thought you'd taken acid and checked out of the cosmos. But here you are."

It was still morning and Pete was already high, the smell of whiskey on his breath, his pupils wide and dilated from something, probably some strong pot he scored from Biggie.

Drugs weren't Pete's hustle. But he would never collect enough spare change to support himself. Disability checks kept him alive for years and a condemned house at the Oakland border became his latest crash pad. He lived many places where for a while he contributed what he could until his irascible nature and a predictably bummer dope trip pushed him back onto the street. Eventually he found someone else briefly willing to adopt him.

Pete modeled himself after the R. Crumb character *Mr. Natural*, who he thought was a real person and whose history, once scribbled in loving, calligraphic detail in one of Crumb's comics, merged over time with the details of Pete's own autobiography.

Yitzhak had a loyalty to the people on the street, people who addressed him kindly, who stoned him, who bought him a coffee when it was cold and shared their joints and roaches. He loved Telegraph's crazy energy and its noisy, barbaric edge. He was home and offered to buy Pete breakfast at the Med.

"That's cool," said Pete. "Sounds like you got some new money."

"I'm fresh," said Yitzhak. "I'm diggin' it."

Yitzhak guided Pete to a table at the rear of the Café Med. He had Pete to himself for a while until Pete, as he often did, drew a crowd. Joanie was the first to find him, followed by Dutch, Tom, Michael and Annie, all street people who knew Yitzhak and who crowded around the café's small table with the thought someone else would pay. And because Yitzhak was a man of the people he offered breakfast to everyone.

"You one great brother," Dutch said to Yitzhak, one of the street's younger vagrants who had arrived the previous spring from Omaha. He lived at the condemned house with Pete.

Joanie was her crazy self and Michael and Annie weren't happy when she pushed to the front of the Med's breakfast buffet. A fight nearly broke out when Michael called Joanie a bitch and Pete had to jump up to settle everyone down.

"Who's paying?" said the annoyed cashier to Pete's grubby friends.

"I am!" Yitzhak shouted from the table.

After breakfast, Yitzhak let Joanie lead him and his people to a cluttered apartment off Parker where Joanie lived with three other women. The women were gone so everyone sat on the unit's slender cement balcony and passed a joint provided by Dutch.

Yitzhak sat among his people that, for the afternoon at least, revered his power to be present and to provide. A few tokes into his high, Yitzhak embraced his role as the street king for a day.

"You must a done some good somewhere," said Crazy Pete.

He thanked Yitzhak for breakfast.

"You made our god damned day."

"The day isn't over yet," Yitzhak said. "Every new reality is a new horizon."

It was the wisdom of a street king.

"Fuckin' heavy," said Joanie.

She wanted to ball Yitzhak then and there and would if she thought it wouldn't start another fight with Michael.

An hour passed. And another. Joanie made a pitcher of lemonade and put out a platter of stale potato chips. The dope kicked in and united everyone in the absurd humor emerging from a neighboring yard where a dachshund puppy tethered to a clothesline ran frantically back and forth to protect the weedy lawn from an assault of worm-searching robins.

"He's one busy little guy," said Pete. "Workin' so hard and just for nothin'."

"Why does anyone work when it's all for nothin'?" asked Michael.

"Heavy," said Dutch.

Yitzhak closed his eyes. He loved his people but was now tired of them. A few hours were enough, especially while stoned. At some point in his high the walls of the experience closed around him and created the sensation of intense claustrophobia.

"Gotta split," he said as he stood.

"See you tomorrow?" asked Pete.

"Can you get me a meeting with Biggie?" Yitzhak asked.

"When?" asked Pete again.

"Tomorrow," answered Yitzhak. "I'll find you. Just check it out."

"Cool," said Pete.

Yitzhak stood, knuckle-banged everyone but Joanie whom he hugged closely, and left.

It was only infatuation that occupied existence. It was something Yitzhak remembered someone saying but not who or when. A rabbi? A teacher? A poet?

Now Stephen said it to a hall filled with at least eight hundred people that hung in silence on his every word.

If you're talking to straight people and they won't cop, what do you do? Jesus, when he was giving the instructions to the apostles, told 'em when you go into a house, feel the house, and let your peace descend on the house, and if the house accepts your peace then you're cool. But if not, leave the house, and don't bother arguing with somebody that don't want to know...

"He doesn't sound like Jesus," said Yitzhak.

"No, but he looks like Jesus," said Inger.

"You met Jesus?" Yitzhak asked.

Inger probed Yitzhak's deadpan expression before at last laughing.

"He looks like pictures I've seen of Jesus," said Inger. "That's all."

"What pictures are you talking about?" asked Yitzhak. "There are no photos."

Inger sighed.

"No big fucking deal," she said. "I guess I could say he speaks the words of Jesus but you'll say we don't even know that and I don't want to get started again."

Yitzhak had made his point. He felt empowered, having stoned Inger before the drive over to The Family Dog to attend another of Stephen's Monday Night classes. The dope Yitzhak bought from Biggie was good shit. He had fronted Biggie a $100 for half a kilo and 20 tabs of acid. Biggie, a large black man who drove an MG and made infrequent visits to the Avenue, had met Yitzhak at the Forum. The terms were cash only and Yitzhak decided to put it all out there. He could turn a five-fold profit if the shit was good. And it was.

Now he and Inger were righteously stoned and digging the words of a master. And Yitzhak's stash was safely stored in a backpack he now kept in the closet of Mack's flat. He was down to $85 but a disability check waited at his family home, when and if he wished to retrieve it. He didn't. Not yet.

Yitzhak thought every horny woman's passion was an expression of empathy with his heroic struggle for the people. He was the revolution's unknown rock star and women who asked him into their beds were his sisters in struggle. This was true also for Inger who rewarded Yitzhak's attention with just enough of her own to send him off to sleep. When he woke, Inger was gone. Yitzhak found a note in the kitchen.

Have a day at the studio. Back late afternoon. Fix us dinner.

She left him a key to the flat.

Inger's note and the key suggested Yitzhak was welcome for

another night, which pleased him and put off a decision to go home and to see his mother. He thought dinner might be a test and that if he prepared a good one he might win more nights in Inger's studio.

Yitzhak washed Inger's breakfast dishes, made her bed, showered and left for the streets. It was his first day on the job.

"So this is Dick," said Crazy Pete as Yitzhak approached Pete's table at the Forum.

"He goes to Cal. A resident at Barrington."

Dick was a junior majoring in English Literature. He lived in a residence hall on Dwight Way.

"He and his friends want to buy some grass," said Pete.

Dick nodded. Yitzhak leaned in close.

"How much?" asked Yitzhak.

Dick didn't know.

"A lid," he answered, attempting to sound drug savvy and cool.

"An ounce?" said Yitzhak.

"Sure," said Dick after a flummoxed moment.

He was inexperienced and clearly had drawn the short straw among his roommates.

"How much does it cost?" asked Dick.

"For you, since you're a friend of Pete here, for you its $50."

Pete sat back and, out of sight of the student, rolled his eyes.

It was a lot to ask but Yitzhak sensed this was a purchase by committee and no one would complain.

Dick looked doubtful.

"Good shit. Michoacán," Yitzhak said encouragingly.

Dick reached into a pocket for his wallet.

"Not here!" sneered Yitzhak.

"I need to bring it to you. Meet me in the faculty grove in an hour. I'll be sitting on a bench. We need to be cool."

Sales like these would keep Yitzhak free and when Inger returned from the art studio Yitzhak was cutting onions and tomatoes for a spaghetti sauce. He poured her a glass of a Napa red.

"You have a good day?" Yitzhak asked from the kitchen.

He knew domestic rituals. His mother built her life around the quotidian of simple questions that offered love and asked for news.

"Yeah," said Inger. "I'm finishing a painting I need to take with me to Fresno. I…"

And it was from that point forward all about Inger, through dinner, through a second glass of wine, through her warm exhaustion and sleepy tenderness. Yitzhak knew like the Eskimos that the best place to store a surplus was in another person's belly.

He did the dishes and later climbed into bed with Inger, who was already asleep. He had no need for her now. Not of her body, anyway. No need for anything but the roof over their heads and the domestic tools employed to create something slightly more than survival. He was grateful, but wondered what she did on the weekend. Yitzhak had spent a desperate Saturday night bunking with Joanie and a Sunday fighting with her roommates who finally threw him out. He crashed at Pete's but did not again wish to sleep on a hard floor. The only thing worse than that was to go home.

"And let them come to you," said Crazy Pete to Yitzhak as they drank coffee together at the Forum.

"Never let them know where you live."

It was drug-dealing 101: be available but not too available. Have the dope nearby but not on you. Cash first and then you hand over the bag or the pills or whatever you are selling. Count the cash slowly, said Pete. Take your time. After a long wait they'll be desperate for the product. Every minute you delay giving them their dope doubles their high.

"Consider it a public service," said Pete as he laughed.

Two days had brought Yitzhak three sales. Already he had more than made back his $100 investment and still had plenty of stash to sell. Dick returned, obviously happy with his first purchase. He bought another lid and spent an extra ten dollars for three tabs of acid. A taste of the hustle had hooked Yitzhak on the prospect of easy money.

It was capitalism but not anything life-threatening. It did not support the war. It did not do the harm of alcohol or tobacco. It did nothing but make people silly and ultimately happy. What he sold created happiness so healthy it could get Yitzhak a felony conviction and five years in San Quentin.

It was that larger society Yitzhak knew as the enemy of the

people. It wasn't capitalism. It was capitalists. It wasn't soldiers. It was generals. It wasn't the poor. It was the rich. All Yitzhak did to secure his survival was a means to an end. And the end Yitzhak most desired was the triumph of his people, those like him who carried very little and owned even less.

three

Drug sales were Yitzhak's complicated form of begging. He identified with the street people of Telegraph and their wearying and destabilizing leisure. Like them, he was haplessly unemployed though unlike most he owned a hustle. And what he had on offer was little more than what was offered to him. He nearly always paid for drugs, both for those he used and those he sold.

He took the bait, but with a plan to sell it back to the smaller, leaner fish that would not, could not, fight there way upstream. Drugs made all pain into the music of the spheres; made every miserable soul the most important creature of creation.

"What do you do all day?" Inger asked Yitzhak one evening over dinner.

"I'm cool. I visit my friends. I look for work."

The last statement was a lie, since Yitzhak already was working but he did not tell Inger he was dealing, did not share with her any details of his merchant life, though he did share with her his drugs. And she enjoyed them.

"Want to get stoned?" he asked.

Inger had no reason to refuse and after sharing a joint she and Yitzhak fell into a laughing fit in the kitchen as he tried to pass her dishes and she attempted to wash them. She fell into bed before him and also fell asleep before he could summon the interest to caress her.

"You'll have to be gone again this weekend," Inger said as she slipped off. "Come back Monday night and I'll take you to dinner."

Yitzhak did not argue. He would not. He was a guest in Inger's apparently comfortable life and nights he could spend in her apartment were times he did not have to roam.

637

Inger's daily routine began with a shower during which she listened to news and music on the radio. Yitzhak heard through the bathroom door the loud broadcast of a station that announced itself continually as "Jive 95" between cuts from an eclectic playlist of rock tunes and headlines read by a voluble newsman named Scoop.

It was how Yitzhak learned that the president was reducing the year's military draft by 50,000 as he pursued a policy no one in his party would acknowledge was the beginning of the withdrawal from Vietnam. Yitzhak wondered if Mack would hear the news and come home, return to Berkeley and take back his apartment. It seemed far-fetched but something Yitzhak could worry about. After any drug high, anxiety fell over Yitzhak like a smothering shawl.

"Where do you go?" Yitzhak asked Inger.

"When?" Inger replied as she toasted two slices from a loaf of French bread.

"Weekends," answered Yitzhak.

"Weekends I don't go anywhere," said Inger. "I just need time alone. I need the time because I'm going to leave. Want to leave, anyway. I work on art, get my portfolios together."

She told Yitzhak she would travel at the end of the following week for her interview at Fresno State and would be gone six days. Would Yitzhak housesit the apartment?

"I have the place through November," she said. "I'll give you a key. You can pick up my mail for me."

She would leave on a Thursday and return the following Wednesday.

Space and time appeared before Yitzhak like an optical illusion. He would have a home and bed through the end of the month. He would have it all to himself. Heaven above had intervened to grace him with an uncanny anchor. And heaven above was heaven within where everything he wanted could and should be his.

Yitzhak and Inger attended another Monday night class where Stephen said that everyone was perfect.

Even if you draw a circle and it isn't perfect, what you draw isn't a perfect circle but it is a perfect whatever it is. That's true for each of us. We are perfect whatever we are. Everyone is beautiful if they got the juice turned on inside.

Yitzhak and Inger were stoned and the perfection of their lives was suddenly so fully and crushingly evident that they saw it in each other's eyes and broke into a loud and inappropriate laugh that stopped Stephen for a moment.

Everyone is beautiful…if they are lit up, because that's what beauty is, it is being lit up. And anything that gets lit up that way is beautiful.

It was too heavy to ignore and Yitzhak watched Inger closely, watched for the revelation of her beauty and the mirroring back of his own beauty. He searched her eyes until she could no longer tolerate his search and turned away to look at Stephen. Yitzhak waited for a new signal but none arrived. He waited for her eyes to return but they avoided his. He felt it. He knew it. She was not beautiful. She could not tolerate his beauty. He resisted telling her this new and volatile truth. He drove silently home and, as if she grasped this secret, a secret he had not hidden well enough from her, she said nothing.

Yitzhak ended up on the couch while Inger went to bed. It was all done without anyone speaking, this separation into two beautiful and perfect people who had uncovered the fact they were not really beautiful. They were not really perfect. They were not useful mirrors for each other.

Yitzhak waited at a back table of the Forum until Crazy Pete arrived, again with another student in tow.

"Friend of Dick's," said Pete.

"Wonders if you deal."

"Deal what?" asked Yitzhak.

Yitzhak honored his paranoia. He first encountered it clinically and as an assessment of his personality during the troubling season that followed his second year in college. He was afraid of nearly anything that crossed his path without clarity and that in any way confused him. At least, that was what he was told. He did not argue with his fear. It was a larger truth than perfection and one Stephen never discussed at his classes. Yitzhak respected his fear with the fealty of an errant knight.

The issue was drugs and once Pete vouched for the student, Yitzhak opened to the possibilities. The student wanted two ounces and, on the information provided by Dick, offered $100. Yitzhak set up an exchange in the campus redwood grove near Strawberry Creek and within an hour the deal was done. Dealing drugs was the most control Yitzhak could remember ever having over his life. He used the money as a gauge of time and looked ahead to the ways it might be saved or spent.

He took a night away from Inger to drop acid with Crazy Pete, Michael and Annie. It was a warm afternoon and they had climbed to Tightwad Hill above the campus football stadium. Yitzhak had selected the destination. As a child he roamed the campus from the outpost of his father's faculty office. The hill's clusters of shading Eucalyptus and its vast network of trails drew him in, took him far from the unreality of his life as a family object of scornful imperfection.

One afternoon the campus police searched for the child in the hills and Yitzhak hid from them until, at last, he was found and returned to his father. And then punished severely.

He never blamed the hill for his troubles and as the acid kicked in he visualized the hilltop forest as a kingdom and his friends as long, lost siblings of some deep and mysterious origin. They did not cooperate. Pete began one of his endless, indecipherable monologues about "all the cosmic bullshit that fucks us up." Michael went catatonic to the point Yitzhak had to check his pulse. Annie argued with Pete until Yitzhak intervened at which point Annie began arguing with Yitzhak over the meaning of his remarks, his karma, his incarnation, and his miraculous and irritating presence on the planet.

"We all were *born*," said Annie, with a throaty inflection intended to project powerful and inescapable truth.

"Yeah," said Michael. "Heavy."

Before sunset an onshore flow pushed a heavy fog into the hills, chilling Yitzhak and his acid rangers who were notably ill prepared for the drop in temperature. They made a human chain and crawled cautiously down the hill, past the stadium and through the campus, arriving at Telegraph just as their tripping peaked. Annie was quickly out of her depth and Yitzhak wondered if her acid had been laced with speed. Twilight was gone and the Avenue was too bright for Annie who said she was disappearing into the spectral and existential dysphoria of the universe.

"The fucking what?" asked Yitzhak as Annie's eyes rolled back into her head and she wobbled weakly until Yitzhak grabbed her and held her up and walked everyone forward into the Avenue's blazing night. The Forum was too bright for anyone to handle so Yitzhak took his tribe across the street to a small reading space on the basement floor of Moe's Books. Each took their seat in a stuffed chair and waited while Yitzhak held a finger to his mouth to signal aggressively that all were to be silent.

His instruction was useless. Annie asked Michael if her face was melting and Michael tried to stifle an irresistible laugh. His helpless snorting drew the attention of bookstore browsers, which heightened Yitzhak's enveloping fear. He pulled his friends back together and led them out. He was annoyed now, the acid inducing an anger that roiled up until it became an ecstatic sadness that pushed him out the door and back up the street, leaving his fellow trippers behind.

"Hey man, where you goin'?" shouted Pete.

"Where's he going?" asked Annie.

"He's going…" said Michael.

"He's on a bummer, man," said Pete.

"Leave him alone. He's flashing bright. He's really freakin' out."

A sad, brown twilight shadowed Yitzhak at the noisy corner of Bancroft and Telegraph. The streetlights hurt his eyes. He waited for a signal and crossed furtively into the campus. His mind was deployed to its rare regions and there were too many voices to which he might listen. It was a familiar dilemma and, if he could describe it adequately, also something of a trauma.

He wished he were in a desert wandering along a slender arroyo or at the ocean alone with its violent rhythms. He was one of many beings divided into many selves. And he carried all of them forward out of the lights and the noise and into the gentle, hilly campus and deeper into a black, dark grove of eucalyptus trees fed by the quiet bubbling of a creek. The light was gone though he could hear the traffic, hear the noise of cars and occasional footsteps. He found a soft bank by the stream and fell to the ground. He was one with this place, this comfortable shell of dark, humid calm within his clattery and clamorous city.

Yitzhak had a relative existence with the world so he wasn't immediately concerned to be awakened by two campus cops who through a blur asked him who he was and what he was doing. It was morning. Yitzhak could see the tops of the trees and the heads of the talking cops, or something within him could at least register an ambient reality. He did not feel called upon to answer.

"This is vagrancy," said one cop, the smaller of the two who wore the hat of his uniform like a pentagon balanced over his ears.

"We need to ask you to leave the campus."

"What is vagrancy?" asked Yitzhak. "This land belongs to the people."

"Yeah, but you can't sleep here," said the taller, heavier cop.

He stood over the prone and drowsy Yitzhak like a triumphant gladiator.

"The people," Yitzhak repeated from some place between innocence and attachment.

"I am the people."

"You OK? Are you high?" asked the tall cop.

Yitzhak felt his face smile. Felt a laugh coming. Felt the hands and arms of the cops lift him off the ground.

"5150," one of them said into a microphone. "We're taking him to Herrick."

Yitzhak sat handcuffed in a waiting area of the hospital's psychiatric ward. A woman sitting nearby winked at him. She had long, dark hair and lively brown eyes and wore a blue cotton Mumu over a small, squat body.

"What are you in for?" she asked.

The light was still too bright but Yitzhak summoned a consensus within.

"Vagrancy…or some fucking thing," he answered.

"It's bullshit," said the woman. "You speak to someone in the wrong tone of voice in this town and you're suddenly a psycho. You on hold?"

Yitzhak remembered an admitting nurse saying he would be

held for 48 hours.

"Yeah," said Yitzhak.

"I'm Ramona," said the woman. "I'm on my way out and I have to wonder why I keep getting myself busted into this place. I'm a little crazy, but the people who run these joints are crazier. We don't need hospitals. We need freak-out centers where we can talk with people like ourselves, people with hang-ups who treat us with sincerity and respect. The whole world is hung-up. We're crazy? Hell, we're the only sane people on the planet."

Yitzhak tried to follow Ramona, tried to quiet the voices within, which made the constantly present noise that prevented him from hearing.

"These mental commitments are crap," said Ramona. "We need an end to this so-called science of psychiatry. We're called mad by a world that is mad. And if we complain, we're called paranoid and sent to a shrink. Say what's your name?"

"Yitzhak."

"Jewish?" asked Ramona. "Sounds Jewish."

"Jewish and Irish," said Yitzhak.

"That's sexy," Ramona announced loudly. "When you get out of here, phone me. We can get coffee."

Ramona stood and walked to a counter where an orderly in green scrubs held a pen and wrote what Ramona dictated.

Ramona returned with the page from a notepad and gave it to Yitzhak.

"Stay dry," she said buoyantly. "And call me."

"You've been here before," said Dr. Solomon.

He sat next to Yitzhak who lay on a bed in an otherwise empty room of the hospital ward.

"Once last year and twice before that."

Yitzhak had no response. He continued to lie on his back and gaze at the ceiling.

"What's up this time?" asked the doctor. "Is it drugs?"

"It's never drugs," Yitzhak answered. "I'm clean. I'm fucking clean. Ask those cops. None of you have anything on me."

"OK," said the doctor. "We have you for a couple of days. I'll come back later."

In an hour the doctor returned with another announcement.

"You have a visitor," he said.

Yitzhak turned toward the doorway to see his mother. She stood just outside the room as if waiting for a cue to enter. She wore a familiar sweater and a flannel black skirt that fell just below her knees. She wore a brown and green scarf that Yitzhak knew she had wrapped quickly over her greasy, unwashed hair.

"Mom's here and she wants to take you home," said Dr. Solomon.

"Home?" Yitzhak shouted. "I don't have a fucking home."

"You go with her now or stay with us until we let you go," said the doctor. "That could be days. You know how it goes. Your choice."

Years of psychiatric emergencies had toughened Dr. Solomon. He knew when to listen, when to negotiate, and when to threaten. Existence never answered anyone's questions but that did not prevent the doctor from telling patients what they could and could not do.

"What got you committed this time, Raymond?" his mother asked wearily on the ride home. "And when did you get back? Where have you been?"

It was a curious truth that the person who was Yitzhak everywhere else in the world was, within the parameters of his family, still the feckless, disobedient and inconsiderate son known as Raymond. In truth, Yitzhak was many people and it was difficult in the melancholy of this dispiriting journey to remember his choices. There were characters he loved but would never show, never betray to his mother. If she knew, if she had any idea of the army of identities available to Yitzhak, she would shrink in terror. But as small as she was she was too large for Yitzhak to engage. She was his mother and always would be.

"You never tell me the truth," his mother said. "And where is your uncle's car?"

"It's not uncle's car. It's mine," answered Yitzhak.

His mother looked at him, her wide brown pupils magnified by her pink-rimmed glasses.

"Your sister will get it. Just tell her where it's parked."

Yitzhak turned away.

"You never tell me the truth," his mother said again. "And your father? Do you know what this does to your father?"

"Not enough," Yitzhak snorted.

"Oh, that's right. Your father, he hasn't suffered enough already?"

No, he hasn't, Yitzhak thought to himself.

He would never say this, not because it wasn't true but because he wanted no more of his mother's reliable incriminations. These were all he had known; all he could remember and he did not wish again to be back in their grip. He decided to plan an escape. But he was hungry and would wait until he ate.

four

October's first weekend was the hottest of the year. And for Yitzhak the soporific heat was a blessing. Among other things the heat required that his mother turn on the air conditioner, its fan loud enough to mask any noise Yitzhak made the morning he escaped. When his sister returned from retrieving his car she mistakenly gave him back the keys to the Chevelle.

On Monday, Yitzhak arose quietly at 4 a.m. and left. He had his disability check and had promised his sister $10 for each subsequent check she could intercept in the mail and deliver to him. Time ran only one way and Yitzhak wanted his freedom before time ran out.

He drove toward town, the campus campanile beckoning like a lighthouse as he swerved onto Addison and parked his car. He waited for the bank to open and cashed his check. He returned to the apartment and knocked on the door. He heard Inger in the bathroom and the mumble of Jive 95's morning headlines. Yitzhak turned the door handle and Mack's apartment opened to him. He waited by the studio's one bay window for Inger to emerge from her shower.

"God damn, you scared me," Inger said when she saw Yitzhak.

"Didn't think I'd see you until evening. How did you get in?"

Yitzhak said he opened the door. It was unlocked.

"Well, that's pretty fucked," said Inger. "That means it's been unlocked all night."

Inger returned to the bathroom, a burgundy towel wrapped

around her torso while her wet hair dripped a trail of water drops along the apartment's bare, linoleum floor.

Later she reappeared in a terry cloth robe the color of faded sage.

"You want breakfast?" she shouted after entering the studio's tiny kitchen.

"I have some eggs but I'm out of bread."

Yitzhak wasn't hungry.

"No, thanks," he answered before asking Inger what she was doing with her day.

"Studio…have to pull my work together and just hope it fits in the back of the Opel. That and start packing."

She ate her eggs while Yitzhak found his jacket in the closet and checked that his stash was still in its pockets, acid tabs on one side and a paper bag half-filled with pot on the other. Inger did not ask Yitzhak about his weekend and said nothing specific when he asked about hers.

"The usual," she said. "It's work time for me. I have to pull my shit together."

It was a vague answer that concealed something. Yitzhak was certain about this but he could not guess what. She often went away during the week but said nothing about a job.

"Do you work?" he asked. "How do you make your money?"

Inger stopped eating, her eyes immediately fierce and piercing as she stared at Yitzhak who took two nervous steps back.

"I'm fine," she said with a hard, annoyed emphasis. "A student loan and a free place to live. I don't need that much."

"How the hell do you make *your* money?" she asked Yitzhak.

Yitzhak offered a weak smile and nothing else. He had been played by his own game. Inger knew. And now he knew she knew. He excused himself and walked to the door.

"Come back tonight and I'll fix you that dinner I promised," said Inger.

Yitzhak ambled across the campus toward the Avenue, stopping at the grove and stream where days before he had been taken into custody. The shade cooled him. He had thought to throw some clean clothes into the back of the Chevelle, which remained parked on Addison and to which he would have to return and move before noon.

He felt the onset of a "tic," the term used by one of his first therapists to describe a peculiar kind of vision drawn suddenly and vividly from Yitzhak's memory. Which was peculiar because Yitzhak had trouble remembering anything. But the tic brought to life either the pleasures or disturbances of a time past and served them back to him in the endless present where his awareness was at its best. As the tic came into focus it took on the apparition of a woman, one lovely to behold and easy to touch until the woman grew roots that wrapped him and bound him down in a malevolent attachment. The lovely woman, her legs spread like those of a *sheela na gig*, then took on the face of his mother, holding him for several minutes above any promise of pleasure before rubbing his face in the fearful, depriving facts of his miserable and entrapping youth.

It was an ecstasy of horror and one that, even in its grim and nearly complete influence, he could still put somewhere outside. And though he could see clearly just for a moment, it was long enough to identify the source of his experience and to watch himself depart from this hallucination and to see at last that his place of origin was no longer his destination.

I will not go home again, he said to himself. Nor would he return to the psychiatric ward; that padded, imprisoning lounge which served as his clinical home away from home and the malevolent *in loco parentis* of his bridled adulthood. In a flash of psychedelic awareness, Yitzhak arrived at a vulnerable junction with the reckoning course of his life. And just as burglars leave a traceable criminal record, so the insane like Yitzhak leave a historical trail of troubling illusions. No, he would not go home again. He would not return anywhere where he could smell the oldest rot or feel again the earliest and thereby most persistent pain.

Yitzhak reached the Avenue and crossed Channing Way to push through an approaching mob of Hare Krishnas dancing and chanting, two at the front beating drums while three at the rear held out cups to collect donations. Yitzhak waved them off and walked toward the corner of Haste where Pete occupied his place in front of Moe's and held up a hand-lettered sign that read *Spare Change, Anything Helps.*

"You survived!" Pete shouted when he saw Yitzhak.

"We thought you were a goner, for sure," said Pete who recalled Friday's acid trip with uncharacteristic clarity.

"Either you'd drown in a creek or the cops would get you."

The cops did get him and Yitzhak told Pete what he remembered. He offered to get his street buddy a cup of coffee at the Forum.

"I need another meeting with Biggie," Yitzhak said after they sat together at a table.

"I have cash."

Pete gazed reflectively out the Forum's window as the Hare Krishnas made a return trip past the café.

"That's what we need," said Pete, ignoring for a moment Yitzhak's query.

He pointed toward the Krishnas.

"Showmanship…and some critical mass. We old panhandlers need to perform. At the very least we need a union."

Pete laughed.

"Why do you beg?" Yitzhak asked. "You get a government check. You're a vet. What else do you need?"

Pete reached to scratch his scalp, running his fingers through greasy strands of gray hair.

"It's leisure," said Pete. "I don't need to work at all and I get paid just for standing around on a warm, sunny day. I watch the world passing me by. I see the ladies and their cute asses. Kind of like a tribe of Indians—excuse me, Natives—I read about their lives in New Mexico. They don't work. They are the poorest people on the continent but they have the most leisure time of anyone. There's something to be said for that."

"But Biggie…" asked Yitzhak.

"It's complicated," said Pete after a pause. "Biggie doesn't sell to just anyone. He's got a security issue. And he should. I'm amazed he still talks to me."

"Doesn't *money* talk anymore?" asked Yitzhak.

At that moment, two Berkeley police officers entered the Forum and, after looking around at the assembled patrons, walked toward Yitzhak's table.

"You have an ID?" one of the cops asked Yitzhak.

Yitzhak, appearing flummoxed and anxious, removed his wallet and with shaky fingers drew out his driver's license. The cop took the license and stared at it while everyone in the Forum watched.

"So Raymond, we got a call from your mother," said the cop. "She asked us to check on your welfare. Are you OK?"

Yitzhak felt himself blaze illimitably within. An angry fire burned in his throat and warmed his cheeks.

"I'm fine," he said.

"And where are you staying now?" asked the cop.

"With friends," answered Yitzhak. "I'm fine."

"Could I ask you to stand for a minute?" asked the cop.

Yitzhak gauged the terms of his relationship with authority. He could not make a choice but his legs moved anyway and lifted him. The cop drew his flashlight out and shined it quickly into Yitzhak's eyes, which closed instantly as Yitzhak turned away.

"OK," said the cop. "We'll tell her you're OK. Right?"

Yitzhak nodded and sat back down as the two cops sauntered demonstratively out of the Forum, as if to state their absolute right and duty to go anywhere on behalf of law and order.

"Well, that's kinda what I mean," Pete said as the cops exited the café.

"Biggie sure don't want anything like the attention you just got."

Were she nearby, Yitzhak would kill his mother. For a flash he thought he could strangle her just to watch her die. Whether he stayed or left, his mother seemed always to be seeking revenge for his birth and for the way his life burdened hers. Now it was his turn for revenge and, as angry as he was, he knew after a moment of hating her that he had no stomach for the death of anyone but himself.

Yitzhak's mind was home to invisible guests. He at times, and more frequently of late, turned over his decisions to a brood of voices abiding within. He once listened to all of them. But now he heard only the loudest. They told him his anger was useless, that his only hope forward was to accept a minor restraint before it became a major one. In this case, it was the need to become small, to hide himself within the folds of the street if he had any hope of meeting Biggie again and to again earn money by selling drugs.

Inger was in the kitchen and fixing dinner as she had promised when Yitzhak showed up, his voice quiet in a way that amplified the strength and beauty of his long, solid and potent body.

"You have a good day?" she asked him without looking up from a pan where with a large fork and spoon she stirred the blood red sauce intended for their meal of pasta and asparagus.

Inger knew nothing about Yitzhak's weekend nor did she particularly care. Her mind was on leaving for her interview in Fresno and, if that went well, leaving Berkeley for a very long time.

Yitzhak was crazy, but he was also cool. He could mask his madness, even if he could not escape it. He offered to stone Inger and, after sipping for a half-hour from the bottle of cheap red she had used to make the sauce, Inger was easy and willing.

A few tokes aroused Inger's chatter just as they enclosed and silenced Yitzhak.

He tried to hear her voice over those of his mind's perpetual guests and to remember all she told him.

"You'll hold down the fort," she said. "Lock the doors, of course. Keep it quiet on weeknights. The neighbors downstairs are cool but they get up early. Cute young couple. He's a grad student and she's a receptionist. I'll call and give you my phone number when I land at the motel. I'll be back a week from Wednesday. Afternoon, sometime, depending on how the interview goes. It's such a shot. This woman professor—she's a hell of an artist. Women, you know, trying to be a woman artist is, well it's not easy…say…are you listening to me?"

Inger stopped talking to see Yitzhak nod slowly. He was listening, he did listen or someone within did, but what was heard wasn't always clear.

"OK…" Inger turned back to the sauce and spoke again without looking at Yitzhak.

"So there's food in the fridge…and the lease to the place is up December 15th. If I get this, I'm leaving early December and the place is yours after that unless Mack comes back. That is, if you want it and the landlord goes for it. Is that cool or what?"

Inger grasped Yitzhak's fragility and, for all his beauty as a male creature, she remained alert to his apparently uncertain grasp of the world, but only enough to anticipate his common human needs and not those that reached out like tendrils to his ocean of people and that stormed so mightily below his stoic and silent exterior.

Yitzhak told Ramona to come by his new apartment on Addison, expecting a few friends to join her but not the entire *where's the party* crowd that haunted Telegraph each evening in search of soirees and crash pads and involuntary hospitalities that might include free dope or booze. Yitzhak told Ramona and Crazy Pete about his housesitting gig but by the dinner hour he was opening the door to Mack's apartment cum Inger's pad to too many people he did not know.

"It's cool," said Crazy Pete as he rolled another joint and began passing it around.

"But we need food. Someone should go get pizza."

He waved at Michael.

"Pass the hat, man," said Pete before turning to the nearly filled room.

"Let's go, you motherfuckers," he said to the crowd. "Spare change for dinner. Put it out there. We're the people and this is a people's party."

The words reminded Yitzhak he was hosting the salt of his earth, the denizens that owned the street and that kept him high and that, since his transformation into a street citizen, had given him unconditional love. Ramona stood close by him, welcoming those who knocked and allowing those she knew to enter. Yitzhak, stoked on several tokes of an aromatic gold, allowed the frenetic, excitable woman to run the show. She knew the people of the Avenue, knew who could be welcomed and who should not.

Within a half-hour two large, boxed pizzas arrived along with two men carrying three six-packs of beer and a jug of Red Mountain. The people of the street were now the people of the apartment and, numbering nearly two dozen, barely left anywhere to sit. At this critical mass, Ramona shut out new arrivals until the people of the street stopped coming and the party rolled on.

Joanie found Mack's records and turned on the stereo. The Jefferson Airplane's "White Rabbit" blasted from the speakers, it's Bolero-like eastern flamenco beat pounding out an Andalusian rhythm that set Yitzhak in motion. He moved with the tune's ascending half-step and danced away from Ramona into the center of the room where his boots crashed against the floor to tap out a gypsy beat, one as old as the Moors and aligned with the peasant ethos of *gitanismo*. His strong, long legs rose and fell. He held the mysterious half-step beat in a way that, if not authentic, still appeared skillful. Others clapped in rhythm, pushing Yitzhak into a series of fervent twists and stomps. He was now the gypsy king, the true man of the people able to express in the rooting dance of the ancient peasant class a revived spirit of rebellion.

"Ándale!" shouted Ramona as Yitzhak slashed through the crowded room, his wild stomps pushing people out of his path.

"Ándale!" shouted everyone until the song ended in a surge of loud chords and, in the ensuing silence, a louder, persistent knock heard at the door. Ramona went to answer it.

"Damn! What is going on up here?" shouted a stocky man in a robe and pajamas.

"Where's Inger?"

"Gone," said Ramona bitterly. "Who are you?"

"Jack. From downstairs. It's after ten."

He was groggy and sounded resentful as if he'd been awakened from a deep sleep.

"Do you have permission to be here?" he asked accusingly.

Ramona pulled Yitzhak to the door.

"Housesitting," he told the man who said again he was a neighbor. His name was Lou and he had seen Yitzhak with Inger.

"She'll be home next week."

The man at the door surveyed the crowd behind Yitzhak that now stared silently at him as if he were the irritating curiosity of the moment.

"My wife and I are trying to sleep," he announced plaintively. "Early day tomorrow. Can you please keep it down?"

Yitzhak nodded and closed the door.

"Time to get out," said Ramona. "All of you."

Within fifteen minutes everyone had left but Ramona and Pete who stayed to help Yitzhak clean up.

"That wasn't hard," said Ramona. "Some of these street folk need a shove to leave but not tonight."

Yitzhak found two broken beer bottles behind the couch and a drawer rifled in the bathroom by someone likely searching for meds. After Pete left, Ramona asked Yitzhak to sit with her. Her wide eyes made room for all of him though she searched first his face for any sign of attraction to her and finding no obvious signal, opened her own face to express her attraction to him. It was enough. Yitzhak was accustomed to being an object and Ramona most comfortable acting on her desire. It was a perfect match.

Later, lying in bed, Yitzhak and Ramona were first naked and then quiet, and then noisy and then quiet again before Ramona recovered enough to express a thought.

"I completely grock you, man," she said to Yitzhak from her wet place beside him.

"You are like a warm rain and I have my face right up in you. I could stand all day in such a rain."

Her poetry passed Yitzhak by. He experienced the sensation of pleasure but could not easily comprehend its words. There were others within who might speak differently but for now he had no need of another imaginary dialogue. Those within, like those at the party, were gone and he was alone in Ramona's arms.

On Saturday Yitzhak at last remembered to check the mailbox and found it stuffed with letters and advertisements. Stacking it all on the counter, he found a letter to Inger from Mack. The envelope bore a Canadian stamp. Yitzhak opened it and scanned the typed page folded up inside. He found immediately a paragraph that mentioned him by name.

I'm concerned about Yitzhak. He ditched me outside Olympia. He's dealing drugs now. I don't know if he's coming back. He is a friend but I can't say I even know him anymore. If you see him, be careful. He seems to slip in and out of a certain quality of awareness and it appears he's dealing pretty heavily so it might not be safe. I'm worried.

Yitzhak wadded up the letter and envelope and stuffed them in the front pocket of his jeans where they formed an ugly bulge. He would throw them away later. He would walk quietly east. He would see the moon rise. He would see clouds. And not hear a sound.

five

Paul was dead and Michael was inconsolable.

The mop-haired Beatle and songwriter Paul McCartney actually died in an auto accident in 1966. After an angry fight with his fellow Beatles, Paul drove away in his Aston-Martin and was decapitated in the crash. Secretly, the remaining Beatles held a Paul look-alike contest and selected a model to appear on the group's album covers.

Now the secret was out. It was a story denied by the prevailing arbiters of reality, those conspiratorial masters of news and media who decided what everyone should know or believe.

"I know that this world is run by a committee," said Michael who also knew himself to be particularly and uniquely enlightened.

"They only tell us what they think we should know. But Paul is dead. Isn't it obvious?"

Yitzhak listened as Michael listed the incontrovertible facts: that the words *turn me on dead man* could be heard when *Revolution 9* on the White Album was played backwards; that a quiet line at the end of *Strawberry Fields Forever* whispered the words *I buried Paul*; that when *I'm So Tired* was played backwards, you could hear the words *Paul is dead now, miss him, miss him, miss him*; that reversing a part of *I Am the Walrus* revealed the lyric *Paul is dead, ha ha.*

"The word walrus is the Greek word for corpse," said Michael. "It's been written up, the whole plot to keep Paul's death a secret. You can see someone has been trying for a long time to tell us, even though they don't want us to know."

"Who's trying to tell us?" Yitzhak asked.

"Must be the Beatles," said Michael. "They must be in trouble and they're sending a message. We need to help them."

Yitzhak doubted Michael's alleged facts, though he did not doubt all trouble in the world was caused by a conspiracy against the people. And because he was the people's advocate, Yitzhak, too, needed to worry he might be targeted, might become a victim of manipulated injustice. He wondered if his mother was in on the plot, if her efforts to suppress him were driven by the orders of someone above her to whom she was slavishly and methodically loyal. It would make sense to Yitzhak in a world where nothing else did.

Yitzhak turned on the radio in Inger's bathroom and climbed into the shower. As he soaped himself he heard reports of Bobby Seale freaking out at the trial of the Chicago Eight. The judge had ordered Seale bound and gagged as a response to Seale's outbursts in the courtroom. Despite this, Seale continued to shout, continued to physically and verbally protest.

Yitzhak thought this was really cool and wished he could be there, could join Bobby Seale in his struggle for the people. Yitzhak thought himself to be very much like Bobby Seale and wondered how best to throw himself onto the gears and levers of the manipulating machinery that vigorously sought to control his life. He thought this would be fun until he realized he could not become a highly visible warrior like Bobby Seale and also sell drugs.

The concept of empty space was for Yitzhak an exuberant truth, a thought with which he could consider a wide range of eternities and also understand why his grasp of them lasted only moments. He was empty space. His father the scholarly mathematician had pointed this out repeatedly to him, had explained the implications of reality's underlying physics.

And his father had the formulae to prove them. Yitzhak learned early never to argue with his father and so, early on, accepted the fact of his nothingness. And when his father beat him, because Yitzhak was made of nothing he felt nothing. Under the blows of his father's fury, Yitzhak found refuge in the idea the boy enduring such punishment actually did not exist.

There were three ounces of pot left and seven tabs of acid. Yitzhak considered how best to expand his sales. He was a businessman now, an entrepreneur for the people. Were his father not now a vegetable, and if he could move beyond the criminality of drugs, such a father would salute his son as an innovator, as a bright, successful light. Yitzhak decided to ask Pete to tell Biggie that he could meet Biggie in Oakland. Yitzhak had cash. He had more money than before and wanted to buy more drugs.

"So-called sane people are as crazy as the rest of us," said Ramona. "They just hate people who appear strange and act differently. That's why we end up going to hospitals for observation and they don't. And observation, what is that crap? What do they think they're going to see? Someone wants to watch me, well, I'll show 'em."

Ramona had been released again from a two-day hold. Mid-week she had boarded a bus to the City and when it arrived at the East Bay terminal two cops were waiting for her. She had disputed the fare, a disagreement with the driver that grew into a verbal attack on his character, his intelligence and, finally, his ethnicity. It was a line of argument she would not drop.

"Power to the people, you nigger mother fucker…" were her last words as she was dragged from the bus and put into the back seat of a patrol car.

"Paranoid reaction, my ass. Being paranoid in this world is being a sane human being. Twenty minutes away from nuclear annihilation. All of us. And they say we're crazy for being afraid? We're in the streets where it's happening. We're for real. The people, Yitzhak. Like you say: *the people*. We need a crazy people's march for justice."

Ramona began rattling off the planks of a crazy people's platform: an end to the existence of mental institutions and the freeing of all those imprisoned; the creation of neighborhood "freak-out" centers, entirely controlled by the so-called "crazies" that would use them; an end to the practice of psychiatry based on assumptions that individuals have problems that are really caused by the society; an end to the "bigotry of the sane" and the intolerance of people who appeared strange or acted differently; and an end to the capitalistic system with its repression and anti-human values.

Yitzhak was crazy and, until Ramona's arrival, assumed he would keep his madness a secret and survive among the shadows.

The tribe within him argued without end like the characters in one of R. Crumb's Big Ass Comics stories and it was all he could do to manage their incessant conflict. But now he was a god to Ramona's angel. He was a tower of delirious strength, a potential leader who might rally street people as a separate class, a minority persecuted because, like other minorities, it could not easily acquire jobs or money or food or housing.

"We could do this," said Ramona. "I'm angry and you're strong and we're both insane."

It is possible to have an unplanned astral trip. It is possible but you don't usually do it. It's awfully hard to get out of your body when you're uptight because all that clenching and stuff messes up your astral bod, it messes up the electrical fields. Sometimes you can slip out of your bod just by being relaxed, or when you're going to sleep. Weird stuff happens when you're astral body finds its way out of your physical body. Because there's one thing about energy: you can't store it. You have to let it out. We're not batteries.

Yitzhak wondered if Stephen's reference to the unplanned departure of the astral body meant he might unexpectedly and without warning lose the quorum of inner voices that informed many of his choices. It was one thing to wonder if he might lose his mind. It was infinitely more worrisome to think his mind might choose to escape.

"This is heavy shit," said Ramona, who came with Yitzhak to the Monday Night class.

"This dude is really saying something."

Yitzhak drove the Chevelle back to Berkeley, Ramona talking all the way.

"You're a man of the street," she said to Yitzhak. "You could lead. You could do for all of us crazies what Stephen does for the stoners. You could make us real. Make the world see us and dig our energy."

Her flattery moved something within Yitzhak, gave him a feeling that power was possible, that his energy—like Stephen said—could serve the people, whom he now identified specifically as those on the street, those who wandered like naked sadhus and lived at the corners of their lives, as he also lived.

Yitzhak drove Ramona back to Mack's apartment. Inger was not returning until Wednesday so Ramona could spend another night, maybe two. She had lost her place in the apartment she shared with three women and was on a list for new lodging kept by the Berkeley Switchboard.

"And there's always Harold's House," she said. "But I'd rather not. I'd have to share a room. Never know who you'll end up with. And if you stay too long, Harold tries to fuck you."

Ramona continued to push her vision of Yitzhak the leader of the street people. She suggested a people's march to city hall. Her rabid and rapid assertions of power and control infected Yitzhak's mind and all its inhabitants with an epidemic of fever. He could not grasp enough of what she was saying to fully understand his proposed role but enough to feel a calling. It was Ramona's skill that she could tell a lie and enforce its appearance as truth by telling another.

"You aren't alone. You suffer like the people," said Ramona. "And you speak for all of us."

Yitzhak heard her. Ramona's talk was her rent and as long as Yitzhak listened, she had a place to sleep and a ride across town.

Biggie waited in a deep, darkened diner on Adeline. It was after two and the joint was nearly empty. Yitzhak arrived late. He had trouble finding a place to park.

"So you want more of my shit?" Biggie said as Yitzhak sat and waved off the waitress.

"I have cash," said Yitzhak.

"You honkies all got cash," said Biggie. "Just don't always know what to do with it."

"What can I get?" asked Yitzhak.

Business was a hard language for his confederated mind to process. Interpretation needed to be kept to a minimum.

"You can get what you want…and what you can pay for," said Biggie.

"Let's hurry. Don't have all day."

"More grass…a whole key…and ten more tabs of acid," said Yitzhak.

"Three hundred," said Biggie.

"Up front."

Yitzhak scanned the restaurant before counting out his bills and handing them to Biggie.

"Where you parked?" Biggie asked.

Yitzhak pointed toward the corner.

"Get in your car. I'll be there in five minutes."

"Is it good dope?" asked Yitzhak.

"Best available," said Biggie. "Have I ever fucked with you?"

Yitzhak waited nervously in his driver's seat until he saw Biggie turn a corner and approach the car. Biggie pulled open the passenger side door and slipped into the Chevelle. He pulled a package wrapped in newsprint from inside his jacket and wrestled a plastic bag of white tabs from the pocket of his jeans.

"Here," he said. "You set now. Go forth and stone the honkies."

Biggie laughed at his own joke, then jumped from the car and walked quickly away.

Yitzhak tore at a corner of the package to take a deep smell of his purchase. The aroma had a sweet and fungal pungency. The leaf he could see was dark green and crumbly. He shoved the package under his seat and placed the bag of acid tabs in his glove compartment. He multiplied the number of ounces in a kilo by 25. The math his father taught him confirmed Yitzhak would more than triple what he spent.

It was capitalism. It was market capitalism with the price of a product rising significantly every time it changed hands. He was happy to let dope pass quickly through his fingers, happy to be the middleman of an exchange vital to the people and their need to get high. It was the people's sacrament of truth and pleasure and Yitzhak was its worthy and loyal suppliant.

Yitzhak was a brother with all others in the same life and death. He believed Ramona when she said that insanity was a perfectly rational adjustment to an insane world. The voices that spoke to Yitzhak did not have faces that allowed him to assess their expressions or talk back to them. He thought himself occupied by an experience that was not hallucinatory though he knew fantasy could often have the look and feel of perception and that his voices spoke many things and in many ways.

He spent more time sorting out their words than trying to comprehend how they made him feel. But these voices were not ghosts. They were not demons like the *dybbuk* or the *yetzer hara* his mother said possessed him. *The devils have taken my son!* she shouted and always shouted. The devils. No, he was not a container of devils. He was the people. He was a voice for all people, including those that lived within and spoke to him in ways he could not speak to himself. He did not ask why. He recalled that why was why and that was all why was.

Ramona awoke with Yitzhak in the apartment. It was Wednesday and the day Inger said she would return. Ramona needed to sleep somewhere else and probably not with him. Yitzhak had helped her move into a commune forming on Parker Street. She would be fine. Whatever the voices that spoke to her, they never complained to him.

"Vietnam Moratorium," said Ramona. "There's a rally on campus or we can march in the City."

The march was a distraction of the larger world but one aligned with Ramona's embedded anger that today was directed at the war.

"It's the people," Ramona said. "And we are the people."

They were the words Yitzhak heard best and Ramona spoke them with modulated passion, loud enough to sound convincing but also soft enough to be heard.

Madness might not always produce a breakdown. It might also spark a breakthrough and Yitzhak trusted Ramona to illuminate its uses for him. Today their passionate madness was to be applied to a collective and cathartic protest against the War in Vietnam. The Moratorium was a surprisingly logical and appropriate container. They hiked to Sproul Plaza through a pouring rain in time for a rally attended by thousands. Speakers railed against the government, against Nixon and the raging never-ending war. Veterans and professors regaled the crowd with the war's atrocities and bragged about a Moratorium march that was drawing millions of protesters into the streets of more than a hundred cities.

And it was true, as they learned later when they sought shelter from the pelting rain and ended up in front of a television monitor in the Student Union. It was true that the Moratorium had created a widespread and national action against the war. Yitzhak basked in the idiosyncratic limelight of his decision to be present, and felt gratitude for Ramona's urging that they march today.

He thought himself an infinitesimal part of the protest but heard no argument from the voices within that his time marching might have been foolish or wasteful. The campus rally was followed by classroom teach-ins that Yitzhak and Ramona skipped.

Instead, Yitzhak drove Ramona to her new commune and escorted her to her small bedroom on the second floor. Previously it had been one of the large Victorian's windowed walk-in closets and was barely spacious enough to contain a double mattress and a table.

Ramona told Yitzhak to drop her bags on the floor.

"That's the thing about living in a closet," said Ramona. "Who expects a closet to have a closet?"

On the way back to the apartment, Yitzhak parked on College and walked down to the Avenue. He found Michael and Dutch drinking from a paper bag behind the Med.

"Got some good grass," Yitzhak said to them. "Want to try some?"

Michael and Dutch nodded and Yitzhak ducked behind a car to roll a joint.

"A little harsh," said Dutch as he sucked in a drag.

Michael waited his turn and nearly choked as he inhaled.

"What's in this?" he said. "There's some shit in this. I can taste it."

Yitzhak took the last drag and caught the sniff of a sweet, chemical odor.

"What the fuck?" he blurted.

Yitzhak left his friends to search for Crazy Pete, who he found in his usual spot, wearing a raincoat and huddled under the eaves in front of Cody's.

"I think it's the stuff from the cans," said Pete after slipping with Yitzhak down an alley behind the bookstore where he held a small baggie of Yitzhak's latest dope score to his nose and took a deep breath.

"Bunch of shit came in from Mexico in cans…some say it was

spiked with STP but no one really knows. Does it get you high?"

Yitzhak didn't know but also didn't care.

It was shitty dope.

"I bought it from Biggie," said Yitzhak. "Why would he….?"

"To tell you something, probably," Pete finished his sentence. "That he doesn't want to sell to you."

"He sold me *this* shit," said Yitzhak.

"Yeah," said Pete. "Why not? You asked for it. Why wouldn't he use the chance to take you one last time? Damn, we've been taking his people for 400 years."

"What do I do now?" asked Yitzhak.

"Eat it," said Pete. "You don't want to mess with Biggie. Or try the co-op. Students don't know from shit and they might buy it if you sell it cheap. Looks like pot. Just get far away before they smoke it."

Yitzhak heard Pete and also the voices within, together a chorus of unbearable recrimination. Yitzhak was a fool, a stupid mark waiting to be taken. He was imminently reachable by the voices he could not identify or touch. His interior multitude was intrusive, condemning, abusive and unforgiving. The voices were aimed at him and singled him out and drove him out of the alley and up the street toward his car.

"Hey, man!"

Yitzhak heard the words shouted from somewhere outside himself and turned to see Michael running toward him

"Yitzhak. I have to tell you…"

Michael paused to catch his breath.

"Paul isn't dead."

six

Yitzhak returned to Mack's apartment and unpacked his wounded hustle. He was tempted to flush a useless kilo of bad pot down the toilet but his voices thought better and talked him out of it. One in particular rose above the others, a voice he named Marlo for reasons he could not explain. Marlo spoke with a woman's voice and Yitzhak knew it best when he was aroused or having sex.

Marlo urged him on, hummed to him and whispered fantasies that fed his circulation and arousal. He thought Marlo an ally, unlike others that he suspected might be spies. It was unusual for one of his voices to offer assistance. They weren't friends. And whatever they were, Yitzhak would be foolish to trust them.

He did not know when Inger would return. Yitzhak changed the sheets and made the bed. He swept the floor and emptied the garbage. He washed dishes and scrubbed away the stains of spilled wine left from his party. He cleared the bathroom of the evidence of Ramona's feminine hygiene. He thought about fixing a dinner but did not know what time Inger would arrive.

He waited. He would simply wait for as long as his mind and body could be still, which he knew was not long.

In a moment he heard a jiggle in the lock as the door opened, Inger pushing it wide as she shoved her suitcase into the apartment and turned back to get another bag. She wore a clear plastic raincoat, her long, red hair stuffed under a blue stocking cap.

"It's miserable out there," she said without looking up. "Traffic was totally fucked up. Took two hours to get through Stockton."

Yitzhak leaped to help her but he was too late. She had managed fully her entrance and return.

"I'm starved," she declared. "Let's go somewhere to eat."

They walked four blocks to Vito's Pizzeria just south of the United Artists Theater. It was crowded for a Wednesday and likely filled with Moratorium marchers. Inger and Yitzhak waited for a table.

"Well, I got in," Inger said somberly.

She appeared frustrated that Yitzhak had shown no curiosity.

"The program leads to an MFA and all the artists are women. I start in January. But I'm leaving in six weeks. Have a lead on a housing share with another student. A class for women artists is in the works for the spring. Sculpture. A woman artist from LA is interested in teaching. She calls herself Chicago. Judy Chicago."

"That's a funny name," said Yitzhak.

"Not for an artist," replied Inger. "Anyway, something cool seems to be happening in Fresno, if you can believe that."

A waitress guided them to an empty table. Inger ordered a glass of red and Yitzhak a coke. They were handed menus, searched them together, and agreed on an artichoke-anchovy pizza with pepperoni.

"And a salad," said Inger.

She gulped her glass of wine and ordered another.

"Sure you don't want anything to drink?" she asked Yitzhak.

He shook his head.

"You're real quiet. But I guess that isn't a surprise. You're always quiet. How was your week?"

Yitzhak considered telling the truth but knew it would not make him free.

"Cool," he said. "I've been looking for work."

It was a lie and he knew Inger knew it was a lie. But she wouldn't challenge him. Would not ruin a happy evening for herself. She was on the threshold of a new life and wanted desperately to celebrate.

"Were there any phone calls?" Inger asked.

"None," Yitzhak also lied.

The phone rang daily and Yitzak did not answer it. Enough voices spoke to him. He refused to hear any more.

They returned to the apartment where Inger undressed, showered and invited Yitzhak into bed with her. He obliged, and did not seek a quorum from within. The sex was natural and his arousal something Inger took for granted. She fucked him vigorously while touching herself. Beyond his hard cock, slim waist and strong shoulders, Yitzhak had nothing else to offer.

"I'm leaving Berkeley," Inger said before falling asleep. "You want the place, it's yours. I haven't heard from Mack so we have to assume he's not coming back."

A golden smoke filled Yitzhak's mind. He could not tell the difference anymore between boredom and well being. Living and dying things would come and go without duration or substance.

Inger told Yitzhak he could stay at the apartment through the weekend.

"But I'll be on my period so I won't be fucking you," she said. "Heavy flow days and cramps so forget about it."

Yitzhak nodded. He had no need of anything more than a

place to stay where he could sleep and do his laundry. He could visit Ramona but her closet would not hold both of them and anyway the Parker Street commune had voted to permit only its designated members to live in the big house. Yitzhak was a guest and, while he might occasionally spend a night with Ramona, he could not call her closet home.

Nor could he know how long Ramona might last at Parker Street, might be able to participate, do her chores and obey house rules before losing it entirely as she often did, and earn for herself yet another psychiatric hold. There was a time long ago when being crazy actually meant something important. Now everyone was crazy.

Yitzhak helped Inger unload paintings and sketches from the trunk of her Opel. Her larger canvasses she left in Fresno to be stored with a woman artist she met during her interviews.

"They liked my work," she said cheerfully.

Yitzhak wondered if the "they" of Inger's experience was anything like the "they" of his own, a mob of voices that argued over the direction of his life, the range of his choices, and the meaning, if any, his life might ever embody.

"It leaves me breathless," said Inger as Yitzhak dropped her last drawings on the apartment's glass coffee table.

"I'm an artist. And it's true. You really aren't an artist, no matter what you think, until someone else calls you one."

Yitzhak wondered what Inger meant since he was called nothing. He danced, of course, but what else did he do? He dealt dope, but very poorly. He listened to his voices and realized he walked fecklessly and without pretense through a world of profound and ponderous mendacity.

For a week Yitzhak left Inger alone, departing in the early mornings to search the Avenue for his people, with an eye out for Biggie though he had no idea what he would ever say or do if he saw him. Inger spent her days at the CCAC studio where she had impressed an instructor with her acceptance to the Fresno art program. Of course, she already had fucked him so the teacher's support was fundamentally and completely assured. He had written a letter on her behalf and Inger said he was happy to learn it had been helpful.

On Sunday, Yitzhak found Ramona begging for spare change at the corner of Haste and Telegraph.

"You OK?" he asked, afraid she had fallen again from the grace of a rented residence. "You still at Parker Street?"

Ramona laughed.

"Oh, fuck yeah," she said. "It's just that the deposit took my entire disability check and, well, once that's gone I'm on my own."

Her next check was due at the end of the week.

"Here," said Yitzhak.

He pushed a ten-dollar bill at her. He did not need a quorum of his voices to assert kindness. The voices within were drawn only to his anger or despair.

"You can do this?" asked Ramona as if surprised by Yitzhak's charity and also by the tender feelings it brought up in her.

"You are far fucking out," she said through an awkward and ill-fitting grace.

"You come see me. Come see me soon."

Yitzhak smiled.

"Yeah," he answered. "We have work to do for the people."

"It's just that life feels sometimes like a god damned surgery," Ramona confessed. "But it hurts so good. I want the intensity. I don't want it to stop. Until I finally need the pain-killers, the alcohol and drugs, in order to prop myself back up."

Yitzhak nodded. He understood and also wished he didn't and he waited for a wave of delicious sadness to roll on through him, to leave him before tears arrived and he faced the riveting wonder of his dangerous proximity to a feeling his voices would have to acknowledge and accept as love.

Jack Kerouac died on Tuesday, which surprised Crazy Pete who also knew the writer's death was no surprise to Kerouac. *You can't have birth without existence and you can't have death without birth…*Pete thought he had read every line Kerouac wrote and this was his favorite.

"He was 47…his silence now is his loudest sound."

Pete was drunk. Yitzhak had taken him to Kip's and bought him two beers as a way to improvise a wake for the author Pete credited with insight, truth and the spiritual rationalization of his vagrancy.

"What killed him?" asked Yitzhak.

"Booze, man. Booze and lots of it. He was drunk all the time. He was an angel of desolation, a wild man and poet who erupted out of a zeitgeist of conformity and grey flannel suits to point the direction of the artist. It cost him dearly to be the spiritual savior for the rest of us who have found the beat. We who hear again the rhythm of the spheres, and bend like monks toward an everlasting and soulful truth."

Yitzhak thought that was so heavy and that Crazy Pete wasn't so crazy even if the alcohol did most of his talking, even if he would likely live not much longer than Kerouac.

"Another life's seal produced my stamp," Pete said as if drawing at last the truth of Jack's fervid life and early death. And that was it. Yitzhak offered to buy another beer but Pete declined.

"I need to go home," said Pete. "That is, if I can ever find it."

Yitzhak returned to Inger and waited for another weekend to arrive. He had spent the previous weekend with her as she menstruated, as she wallowed in moody bleeding and on Saturday gifted him with a profoundly exquisite blowjob presumably in gratitude for his attendance to her physical needs. He had cleaned the apartment, fixed a few meals and found enough attention span to buy groceries at the U-Save market while Inger lounged, ate and read *Portnoy's Complaint*.

But another weekend was approaching and for whatever her reasons, Inger warned Yitzhak he would have to be gone, have to find another place to stay from Friday morning through Sunday afternoon.

"It's not personal," she said. "I just need my space."

Though he did not understand, Yitzhak did not argue. He was welcomed by Ramona who also touched him the way he wanted to be touched, also made his body happy and complemented his estranging sorrow with her own version of loving kindness. And she cared about the people. She was one of them. Yitzhak found this an important quality few others he knew shared with him. The people. Ramona's salty earth was becoming for him the bedrock of solidarity. He began to imagine himself at the head of a long line of people seeking justice, people without allies or advocates, people like Ramona and himself that the social order considered outliers at best and more likely outcasts.

"Yeah, you can crash here," said Ramona. "We'll make it work."

And she did. She brought him rolls from the breakfast table in the mornings and shared her coffee. She left with him when he needed to make himself scarce from the commune. She smuggled him into her closet room after midnight when all her communard brothers and sisters were asleep. Yitzhak was accustomed to the attention of women though among most it did not last. If he spoke, if he danced, if he so much as rolled his eyes, the mood could change instantly. Only Inger and Ramona welcomed him and only Ramona unconditionally. He knew this and did not need the affirmation of a quorum to take his place in their lives.

Yitzhak had not been successful acting out his power. As a self-appointed spokesman for the people he had enough judgment, if barely, to know he had failed horribly on their behalf. He needed to sell his bad dope and struggled with how to unload it without stealing from the poor street fools who were most likely to buy it. Selling his ideas to the people was easier while he was also selling them good dope. Bad dope would sell nothing of value. He was crazy but not crazy enough to sell out, or so he thought.

He wanted to hurt Biggie for hurting him. But it was complicated to hate Biggie who was black and as much a victim as anyone. Now Yitzhak was also a victim and felt a peculiar solidarity with his most recent tormentor.

"Sell it to one of those ratso fraternities on Piedmont," said Pete. "Rich mothers, all of them. And a bunch of assholes."

"How?" Yitzhak asked.

Standing still for hours on his corner Crazy Pete saw the world differently. While Yitzhak wandered through it, Pete watched it all wander through him. He knew when the fraternity boys made their infrequent appearances on the Avenue to search for a connection.

"I see them," said Pete. "I know what they want. I'll take the middle and you'll be the seller. You'll see. Stay in touch. How much you want?"

Yitzhak wanted full restoration, wanted to blot out his foolishness and cover his losses. In fact, he would settle for enough to barely break even.

"Oh, charge 'em top dollar," said Pete. "They won't buy if they don't think it's worth spending a load for. Take them all the way. I'll set it up."

Yitzhak grasped that Pete had difficult feelings about Biggie's rip-off and wanted to make amends. Telegraph was a long way from Lexington Avenue but it was the same kind of magnet. White boys in search of dope would invariably find their way uptown.

"You should have taken the money first, man," Pete said to Yitzhak as he sat disconsolately at a table in the Forum.

"Damn, always get the money before handing over the dope."

Crazy Pete saw them coming, three frat boys in loafers, corduroy pants and patterned surfer shirts that buttoned at the collars, clothes that gave them the look of baby Beach Boys.

"Lookin' for weed?" Pete muttered as they passed.

They heard Pete and turned around and the rest was a negotiation. Pete told them to return in an hour during which he went to Yitzhak and told him to be ready for an exchange behind the Forum.

The boys arrived with cash and Yitzhak waved them over. He pulled from his jacket a black plastic bag containing his kilo. One of the frat boys asked to see the dope. Yitzhak handed it over. Another looked at it and smelled it while another pulled a wad of bills out of his pocket.

"Wait, Jasper. This shit smells funny."

And that was that. The bills disappeared back into the frat boy's pocket and the plastic bag was returned to Yitzhak.

"Not today," said one of the boys. "Nice try, hippie scum."

Yitzhak stood frozen as the boys quickly departed.

"Almost…" said Pete. "We can try again…"

Yitzhak shook his head. He accepted his failure as a lesson, a punishment for straying from his love for the people and for his cultivation of tremendously bad vibes. He could not have success offering something to others he did not himself believe in. In a vow of profoundly uninformed celibacy he told Pete he was finished selling dope.

Yitzhak sat in his Chevelle and waited. It was a rainy Friday night and he had parked near the corner of Addison and Oxford from where he could view the third floor window of Mack's studio flat, illuminated by a single lamp near the couch. Through two hours in a pouring rain he had seen no shadows moving inside though Inger's Opel remained parked on the street. At midnight he was ready to give up and drive to Ramona's to sneak into her closet when he saw a sporty, black MG swing around the corner and take an empty space at the end of the block.

An older man emerged from the driver's seat and raced around in the rain to hold up an umbrella as he opened the passenger door. Out stepped Inger, wearing a burgundy overcoat that flew open as she stood up to reveal herself dressed in a short light-colored cocktail dress. She grabbed the man's arm as he extended the umbrella and they raced clumsily up the street and toward the entrance to Mack's building. The man wore a suit and tie and looked like a banker who had just left his office. When they reached the door Inger laughed and the man scooped her up to kiss her hard before they entered.

The rest of the story was told in shadows that, through the apartment's window, Yitzhak could see rolling across the walls and ceiling as Inger and the man entered, embraced again, sat at the window and then fell below it. The shadows continued moving irregularly, allowing Yitzhak to imagine anything until nearly a half-hour later Inger stood briefly and naked at the window and turned out the light.

The peculiar scene enlivened Yitzhak's rumbling dysphoria. He considered himself Inger's lover and more than her friend, even as he worked to serve the people. Now he felt displaced and pushed down into a tightening ball of helpless fuck. It was too easy for him to think he might not survive. His sense of self was so fragile and now he was close to being out of friends and also out of money. The voices within returned to taunt him. He was a bum, a tramp, a failure. Yitzhak tried to confront them but they were voices and not persons. He could not know them the way they knew him. Yitzhak wanted them gone and they would not leave.

He could always die. There was nothing to hold him here and he thought seriously how he might die. It would have to be painless because there was no point in ending a painful life by engaging even more unbearable pain. *If it's only a matter of time before I'm buried in my grave, then I'm already buried in my grave.* It was another one of Pete's favorite Kerouac quotes. And it described for Yitzhak the epiphany of the moment, the hour, the week, the month, the year, and the rest of his life however measured or remembered.

seven

Whatever his failure, Yitzhak knew he was not personally responsible. A family of failures stood behind him and made him what he was. A family of failure also lived within and held him frequently in a dismal rapture. November opened among the eucalyptus trees of a small grove under Grizzly Peak where he had gone to take a tab of Biggie's acid. It was good shit.

Yitzhak wandered in flashes among the white-trunked and sturdy trees, the prickly resins of their leaves almost too pungent in his nostrils. He was a tree, a walking tree, a tree that wanted to sneeze and couldn't. It was mid-afternoon and as the acid peaked Yitzhak comforted himself with a swig from a big bottle of Coke.

He had prepared for his trip, stopped at the U-Save and purchased a soda and a box of crackers. He knew he would not be hungry but also at some time would need to eat. The air was warm though there were few hours of sunlight. Eventually the sun drifted away from him and he waved goodbye as the little world he occupied swung him into another night's cool, darkening shadows.

In this sliver between night and day and for a moment coincident with a final, enchanting acid flash, Yitzhak found pleasure in indifference until he did not and the rapidly cooling night air threatened his presumed existence. He was not afraid to die or so the acid told him. But he did not want to die unless his death made it possible for others to live. He would die for the people and nothing else.

In some way and with no memory how, Yitzhak arrived at the front door of Mack's flat and punched the buzzer.

671

"What?"

Yitzhak heard Inger's somnolent confusion. She was still half-asleep.

"It's me," said Yitzhak.

"Fuck," said Inger after a pause. "Do you know what time it is?"

"No," answered Yitzhak. "Do you?"

Yitzhak awoke in his clothes on Inger's bed, the sound of her shower muffled by the loud broadcast of news headlines from the bathroom radio. Bobby Seale was sentenced to four years in prison for contempt of court. A journalist had exposed the army cover-up of a 1968 massacre of Vietnam civilians in the village of My Lai. It was just one of many carried out by US troops.

The shower stopped and Inger emerged from the bathroom wrapped in a towel, her blonde hair stringy, dark and wet.

"You still stoned?" she asked.

Yitzhak waited a moment before shaking his head.

"Then we need to go get your car. It was towed. That's why you couldn't find it. And it's a good thing. You were in no shape to drive."

Yitzhak sat in Inger's Opel while she drove them into south Berkeley. He had returned from the mountain to find his car missing from the trailhead parking lot. Yitzhak climbed down the hill and hiked back through the college's botanical garden before crossing the campus to Mack's apartment where at sometime around 4 a.m. he aroused Inger. After eight she phoned the regional parks office and was told how to reclaim Yitzhak's Chevelle. He could get his car back by showing his license and paying the fee of $35.

"I've got it," Inger said as she pushed in front of Yitzhak at the towing yard.

She shoved a wad of bills at the attendant while Yitzhak displayed his driver's license.

"What are you doing?" Yitzhak asked.

"Covering your ass," Inger said. "You'd do the same for me. The people, right?"

Yitzhak nodded weakly, still not certain what had happened or what was happening. He did not remember his nocturnal trek to Inger though he must have been able to describe it. How else would she know?

"You going to be OK?" Inger asked as they walked to the Chevelle and Yitzhak opened the driver's door.

"You have your keys?"

Yitzhak reached into the pocket of his pants and felt a familiar bulge of chain and steel.

"I'm cool," he said. "Thanks."

"Come by later," said Inger. "I'll fix you dinner."

She turned and left while Yitzhak sat in his car and wondered what of him could actually exist. Existence was insanity. There was no world, nothing that was Yitzhak and nothing that ever happened. He lived an insolent, sepulchral and unwilling life.

Yitzhak found Pete inside Moe's shifting on his feet as he stood to read the latest edition of Snatch comics. He was midway through Number 3, stuck at a page on which Horney Dwarves frolicked with the Trollops from Town, another orgiastic centerfold drawn by the comic master Robert Crumb.

"How does he fuckin' do it?" asked Pete. "How does he get away with it?"

The clerk at the counter appeared impatient so Yitzhak fronted Pete fifty cents to buy the comic.

"Cool," said Pete. "And I got somethin' for you."

Back at the forum Pete passed Yitzhak a matchbox stuffed with the flakey shake of a Michoacán.

It's good shit," said Pete. "For the beers the other night. It's cool."

Yitzhak didn't argue. Instead, he reached in his pocket and pulled out a small piece of folded aluminum foil.

"At least Biggie sold me good acid," said Yitzhak. "I'm here to tell you. Here are three tabs."

It was Pete's turn to blush with gratitude.

"We are truly hip," said Pete. "This is the life. Friends trading dope in the street. The people's high. It's a gas, man, and we be trippin'. We are the flower children, right?"

Yitzhak nodded, though from the penumbra of his acid trip he thought himself more a flower, an ethereal explosion of tissue and color that could not last but that before vanishing might at least leave some seed somewhere that would grow more.

"We are the people," Yitzhak said firmly.

"The real thing," responded Pete. "The goddamned real and true thing. We are still fighting, aren't we?"

Yitzhak could think only that there were reasons for wars and wars for reasons but that in the end the same earth covered all who died.

Yitzhak left Pete and the Avenue aware he had nothing to which he could return. He had no home, no hearth and no heart for another evening with Inger despite her offer of dinner. He was everyone's guest and barely welcome even among the voices that spoke from within. What silence he first imagined was slowly filled with their recriminations and complaints. They said he should go home but what they intended was not what he desired.

Yitzhak counted his wealth. He possessed forty-three dollars, three tabs of acid, a matchbox of Michoacán, two pounds of bad dope and a half-tank of gas. It was early afternoon and he wanted to see the ocean. He drove toward the Berkeley flats, found the highway and accelerated through Richmond to the San Rafael Bridge. He crossed the bay into Marin County and drove past San Quentin prison to Sir Francis Drake Boulevard which wound him west through a cluster of wealthy, congested cities, into the funky town of Fairfax and then over its hills into the valley of San Geronimo.

Another half-hour brought him to the village of Olema and the coastal highway that ran through it. He stopped at a small market and bought a coke and a sandwich. From there he turned into the Point Reyes Seashore and in another twenty minutes parked behind the broad and limitless dunes of Limantour Beach.

He grabbed a blanket from the trunk of the Chevelle and hiked a slender trail behind the dunes until he found passage into a copse of withering pines clustered near the shore. There he spread the blanket and ate his meal before rolling a doob from Pete's good pot which he smoked as the sun fell out of the sky and into the sea.

Once again the planet dragged him and his trees away from the light and into a vast and interminable darkness. He wrapped the blanket around him and fell back into the sand, upheld by the rhapsodic swish of crashing waves. At last the voices were silent and it was the perfect sound. He was truly alone and not concerned that something might happen to him. Rather, he worried nothing would.

"God damn, Hannah," Yitzhak shouted into the phone's receiver.

"I need that check now. Can you meet me on Solano?"

Yes, she could. Where?

"In front of the wine shop," he said. "At noon. And I have your ten bucks.'

He did not forget to thank her.

The ruse Yitzhak invented to collect his disability checks under his mother's nose had one fatal flaw. His sister could intercept his check in the mail but she could not deliver it if she could not find him. It was the liability Yitzhak did not consider until he phoned his home from a gas station in the town of Point Reyes Station. Luckily for him, Hannah answered.

"Are you ever going to have an address?" Hannah asked him when Yitzhak found her standing near the Park and Shop on Solano Avenue.

She was short with her black hair cropped in a pageboy that made her face look like a fat moon. And though she was not fat, the grey cotton dress she wore did give her the look of a short, stocky version of his mother.

"I can't get your check to you if ..."

Yitzhak nodded.

"I'm working on it," he said. "Would you like some ice cream?"

He walked her to a creamery at the corner of Colusa where he bought her a coffee fudge sundae and gave her ten dollars.

"How's dad doing?" Yitzhak thought to ask.

"Shitty," said Hannah between slushy bites. "But mom's worse. She really needs help, Raymond. Are you ever going to come back? Will we see you at Thanksgiving?"

Yitzhak had no will to weigh his sister's question. It went to the heart of his experience, exposed unsettling memories and pushed him away. Whether he endured emptiness or solitude, either was preferable to living again among the sticky and resinous delusions that had formed him.

Society appeared to Yitzhak an organized form of cruelty. He was a problematic member that for a few days attempted to accept solitude by walking the streets in the sun and hiding in his Chevelle in the dark until one night, and another, and then another, he was awakened after midnight by the cops. Each time they stood together in a bath of flashing blue lights while one approached, knocked on his car window with a flashlight, and asked what he was doing.

"Sleeping," he always said. "Is it a crime to be sleeping?"

Yitzhak was informed it was, if one slept on the public street. He needed to leave and the cops at first didn't care where he went though on the second night they searched his car, which reminded Yitzhak it was a week since he had been to Mack's apartment where he had left in Inger's closet his jacket, acid and kilo of ersatz grass. The third night he was written a ticket and told the next time he would be jailed. The ticket was for vagrancy and if he did not contest the citation he could pay the $20 fine by mail.

Of course, you're supposed to change destiny, that's what we do, we're all in agreement here, we have a mind-level agreement, but we agree about sharing out the karma. Like most of the people who come here on one level or another say okay, I'll buy in behind all fair systems of karma-sharing rather than having to go to the trouble of becoming one of those kind of magicians who's going to like try to get better karma than what he's got coming...

"Yeah, right on," said Ramona when Stephen stopped talking. "We gotta share the karma, the people's karma."

She looked to Yitzhak for affirmation but his eyes were on Stephen and he seemed lost in a trance.

The hundreds in the hall appeared to shuffle uneasily until hands shot up and Stephen called on a tall man who asked about reincarnation.

Stephen repeated the question and began talking again. Ramona last heard Stephen say the words *astrological imprint...*

Yitzhak turned to look at her.

"I need to get out of here," he said.

"Are you bored?" Ramona asked.

"No. I just don't understand. I am a magician and I don't understand."

On the drive back to Berkeley Ramona tried to quiz Yitzhak on what of Stephen's talk he had taken to heart.

"You seem a little fucked up," she said. "Something wrong?"

There was a lot wrong but Yitzhak could not say what it was. There were too many voices again vying for his attention and the once dominant woman's voice that for months had soothed him was gone. In its place was a petulant, wailing child with an insisting and insatiable need for attention.

"I'm a little crazy tonight," Yitzhak said.

"Is that all?" answered Ramona. "I can cope. You couldn't be any crazier than I am."

It was true, but Yitzhak took no encouragement from Ramona who was now attending outpatient rap sessions at the new Berkeley Free Clinic and, perhaps as a result, seemed uncommonly calmed and stabilized. She was also dosed regularly now with thorazine. But speaking with other crazies seemed always to relax her. Though there was nothing calm about the noise growing inside Yitzhak's mind. He thought himself a magician because he *saw* what others did not. Now he began to think if his magic were real, he might *do* what others could not.

"You still thinking about that march of the people?" he asked her.

"You mean the crazy march? Hell, yeah. We could do it. I know a dozen people who'd do it in a second. We could have a rally. We could…"

Yitzhak listened to Ramona in a way that calmed the voices within and that soothed even his newly present angry child. Yitzhak imagined himself again at the head of a long line of the misplaced and mistreated. He saw himself holding up his vagrancy citation and lighting it with a match. He imagined standing with the people and against all the lonesome sadness of the world.

There was purity in his wakefulness as Yitzhak sat in the Chevelle. He was parked again at the Oxford end of Addison where he could watch, also again, the lighted window of Mack's apartment. It was again a Friday night and Yitzhak didn't worry about the cops. He was legally parked and he wasn't sleeping.

Near midnight a car swept around the corner and found a parking space. An older man, who was not the man Yitzhak saw the week before, emerged from the car, which was a Mercedes and not an MG, and walked to the passenger's side where he opened the door. Inger emerged, shrouded in the same burgundy coat, which did not open as she stepped out and which remained buttoned as she and the older man strolled arm in arm to her building. They entered and Yitzhak watched as the shadows inside Mack's apartment again danced in response to their entry and movements until again Inger at last appeared briefly at the window, a towel wrapped around her bare body as she turned off the light.

Yitzhak came back the next night to park and wait. Around midnight he saw yet another car, a Cadillac sedan, sweep around the corner. But it did not stop and no other car arrived. Yitzhak noticed Inger's Opel was gone. He left and drove deep into the hills of Tilden Park. He found a forested cul de sac on the Orinda side and parked far from two homes near the highway. He slept until dawn, when he awoke and drove back to Berkeley. It was Sunday morning. He parked on Telegraph and waited for the Forum to open. He ordered coffee and toast. He needed to understand what he had taken the time to see.

"It's my life," Inger told Yitzhak Sunday night. "Certainly not yours."

"What do you do?" asked Yitzhak. "How many boyfriends do you have?"

"Only one at a time," said Inger. "But that doesn't include my real friends. And I thought you were one."

Yitzhak shushed his voices and tried to hear Inger.

"I am. I am your friend," said Yitzhak. "But you never told me."

"What would I tell you? That I work weekends as an escort?" answered Inger.

"That I am provided to wealthy visitors by an agency that offers me as a benefit? That it pays me enough to fund my whole first year at Fresno State? That it is safer than streetwalking or whoring in bars? That I'm attractive enough and smart enough to do this? Are you worried about getting the clap? You shouldn't be. I get a free check-up every week."

Yitzhak didn't care about the clap. He wasn't certain what he cared about or why he ever would expect Inger to solve for him a mystery that wasn't his to comprehend. He wanted at some deeper place to protect her. But why would he protect a woman—or anyone—who never asked for protection? Rising within him was an uncomfortable and fearful compassion, something that set his voices screaming in delirious debate over the future of his own humanity and also that of the people.

eight

Yitzak awoke in his clothes, again outside the covers of Inger's bed. He was the perfect man and had a strange and delirious urge to phone his mother. He was going to save the world even though there was so little time left. Above the sound of Inger's shower he heard the radio headlines announce that more than 50,000 people were marching past the White House, each bearing the name of a US soldier killed in Vietnam. He imagined himself sweeping up every crazy person he could find and holding each in his arms. He riffed on Ramona's idea of a march for insanity that would inaugurate an advocacy for all people labeled insane by the gatekeepers of an insane world. Yitzhak was one of those people and the desire to phone his mother, even as it subsided behind his knowledge she would not understand, was evidence of his belief in the people. He jumped to his feet and when Inger emerged from the bathroom she saw Yitzhak pacing furiously.

"Are you OK?" she asked.

"I'm ready," Yitzhak said.

"For what?" asked Inger.

"For another revolution. It's time the real people threw off their chains."

"And who are they? What's a real person?" asked Inger.

"You're looking at one," said Yitzhak as he glared at Inger and she stepped cautiously back into the bathroom.

"Let's get breakfast at the Egg Shop," Inger shouted from behind the door. "My treat."

679

They walked six blocks to the corner of Walnut and Vine, Inger feeling safer with Yitzhak outside her apartment.

"What's this revolution that's coming?" she asked. "Aren't we having one already?"

"It's mine," said Yitzhak. "My turn. Do you think I'm crazy?'

The question surprised Inger.

"You're…eccentric," Inger answered after a thoughtful pause through which she searched for any word that might soften her real opinion.

"Yeah, I'm crazy," said Yitzhak and smirked. "There's a lot of us."

"Well, the world is a pretty crazy place," Inger said, attempting to express empathy.

"That's the point," said Yitzhak. "Who's really crazy? Me? You? Nixon? The Russians? J. Edgar Hoover? The Blue Meanies?"

"Depends on your definition," Inger said as they turned to climb the short flight of stairs to the Egg Shop.

They found their place in a line that slithered among a few tables on the porch. They were stopped in front of a seated woman reading a book while she finished her coffee. The woman looked up at Inger. It was Harriet. Her face registered immediately with Inger who looked and looked again. Yitzhak, thrown off by Harriet's shorter hair and fuller body, took longer to recognize her.

"Been awhile," said Harriet to Inger. "How have you been?"

Harriet at first ignored Yitzhak.

Inger's surprise embarrassed her. She recalled with a feeble defense her last exchange with Harriet who was a dear friend before Inger's desperate betrayal of her. Inger had no words, even to describe herself.

"I'm fine, Harriet, " she said at last. "And you?"

"And you, Yitzhak?" Harriet asked at last, ignoring Inger's response. "How are you?"

Yitzhak placed the experience of Harriet but not her name. Harriet was a woman he had balled, a woman whose intimate, hidden body he could conjure quickly but without a reliable context.

"I'm cool," he said. "Are you cool?"

"Oh, I'm more than cool," Harriet said with the confidence of a seated woman that, like a queen, deigned to address a couple of trapped, standing courtiers.

"I'm leaving in a week to move to Seattle," she said. "Finally getting my PhD at the University of Washington. Expect to see Mack when I get up there. He's in Canada now but I guess you know that."

"Do you hear from him?" asked Inger.

"Just last week," answered Harriet. "He's way up north on a farm. Someplace called Desolation Bay. He sounds happy. Has permanent resident status now. Doesn't think he'll ever come back to the States. And you?"

Harriet looked deeply into Inger's eyes as if searching for a vulnerable exposure she might take hold of and shake at her. Harriet again ignored Yitzhak.

"I start at Fresno State next month. A women's art program. Finally going to get my MFA."

Inger was grateful she had a comeback and from Harriet's expression it was not the one Inger's old friend expected.

"Well…congratulations," said Harriet, finally able to respond.

The line of customers waiting for breakfast trudged forward and a waitress handed menus to Inger and Yitzhak.

"Goodbye," said Harriet as the courtiers moved off and away.

"Has Mack written to you?" Inger asked Yitzhak while they sat at a table and waited to be served.

Yitzhak shook his head.

"I'm living in his apartment. You think he'd…"

Inger appeared confused, perhaps even shaken.

"What did you guys do on the trip? Did he say anything about me?"

"Mack's a no good fuck," said Yitzhak. "He bailed on me, too. Forget about it."

"It has to start somewhere," said Ramona as she and Yitzhak watched the Parker House TV while Saturday's second Vietnam War Moratorium march was televised across the nation.

"That could be us in a year. It has to be done. Why not here?"

Yitzhak resisted the urge to succumb to a rueful vacuum. The work of the people was at times daunting and he could not know when or why.

"Listen to me," said Ramona. "The majority of mad people, the so-called mad people, are women. It's the natural result of our oppression in a field of medicine controlled almost exclusively by male shrinks. Our march for the mad people could become another kind of women's march. And we need to make that clear to everyone."

"Where do we march?" asked Yitzhak. "Where do the people march?"

Ramona had read the Rolling Stones were going to hold a free concert the following month in Golden Gate Park.

"That's big. We can march to the stage. A parade of so-called crazies arrive at the altar of the noisiest and angriest male rock group in history. We really show up. We will be seen. Signs held high. They'll say something like *I'm Mad*. Really seen. And you, Yitzhak, big crazy man of the known world, you will be our leader. You'll push us forward through the crowd and help us make our stand."

"And who marches with us?" asked Yitzhak.

"The clinic group is eighty percent women," said Ramona. "Each crazy woman tells another. We have sisters who support us, even if they aren't classified as crazy. Though we know they are crazy. Everyone is crazy in his or her own way. And crazy is a class issue. The poor are always crazier than the rich and get into a lot more trouble. And, come on, man, it's the Stones. Who doesn't want to see the Stones? Though we women know what's up. Ideally, we'd hit the stage when those bastards start singing *Under My Thumb*. Someone in my group said that life is a sexually transmitted disease with a mortality rate of one hundred percent. What the hell do we have to lose?"

The human body suffered like the bodies of all creatures. This much was clear to Yitzhak. It was natural and Nature, as scientists like his father enjoyed saying, was a woman and something that like a woman men could examine, strip and do with what they wished. It was what Ramona railed against in her treatment, the rigors of science applied to her very unscientific willfulness and behaviors.

People, even and especially street people and those labeled crazy or insane, were entitled to their markings, their colors, and their eccentric behaviors that defied any conventional or logical understanding. They would survive or they would not. But the choice should always remain theirs because that was their right as Nature's chosen children.

So Ramona's idea was to march as the Mad People, to march as the people who were mad because they refused to be defined, refused to be described as ordinary or unusual or as dreams or visions or memories, or to have their behavior categorized as strange, bizarre, weird or psychotic, or even as familiar or sane. Whatever they were was natural and Nature did not exist on any recognized or factual foundation.

Yitzhak continued to visit with Inger but no longer stayed with her. Their conversations were friendly and she found the emotional distance relieving to a point where she enjoyed fixing him meals, even if he did not, would not, sleep with her or fuck her. Ramona's energy tapped all that Yitzhak had on offer. The Stones free concert was less than three weeks away and Ramona had created an organizational meeting at the free clinic that drew more than forty clients and their friends. Several volunteered to spread the word and Ramona phoned Stephen—and spoke with him—getting his assurance he would mention the Stones concert Mad March at a Monday night class.

Yitzhak was in awe of Ramona's energy. She was both crazy and medicated and the combination appeared to produce a chemical reaction that exploded into both a woman's power and a revolutionary power.

"Did you see that the Indians took Alcatraz?" Ramona asked Yitzhak.

It was Friday and Yitzhak, who never read the newspaper, had no idea. A Native-American student at SF State named Richard Oakes had led nearly a hundred supporters in a predawn boat ride to the old prison's island in the middle of the Bay. When their boats arrived at Alcatraz, Oakes jumped out and swam to the island.

"He says he's exercising the right of Indians to take back land abandoned by the federal government," said Ramona.

"And he's doing it with less than a hundred supporters. We can do that. Our march can do that, too. We aren't many but we represent the many. If we speak up, those who are told they're insane and who are alone in the streets, they'll speak up, too."

It was the power to rise up as one and, in so doing, represent and draw in the many, which characterized Ramona's hope as a revolutionary. Certainly the thorazine helped, but to remain so focused on the Mad March and its larger objective of legitimizing the lives of those defined as crazy, Ramona needed to draw on deeper reserves. These fascinated Yitzhak who now assigned to Ramona the attributes of a goddess, one who railed righteously against the patriarchy that was science and, specifically, the scientific application of psychiatry on to those who might be described, even by themselves, as powerless and incomplete.

Yitzhak went home for Thanksgiving. His home was the source of all he had become and he wanted to make his peace with it. It was the first place from which he tried to determine how he got *here*, what he was doing *here* and also why he was here with so many other people. Yitzhak was welcomed back as he knew he would be welcomed, and as the perpetually prodigal son he was.

He could not manage the resources of experience in a fashion that would keep him away and so for him a return home was a personal failure, though for his mother and sister and other members of his family who worried and cared about him, it was a dream come true. His return brought always the hope that a fully capable and functioning male would assert his control of the home, would take up the commanding role abandoned unwillingly by his desperately sick father.

But Yitzhak had only to spend one night in his old bedroom to know he would never want to become his father. He fingered the spines of books on his shelf that he once read voraciously and that now meant nothing, the words of which were gone from his memory and replaced by a much more ample and important instruction: he was a fool and as much as he pushed against a door that felt bolted against him, his foolishness was perhaps his best feature.

Ultimately, Yitzhak's father tried to tell him the facts of life, to describe the pleasure of sex and also admonish Yitzhak that such pleasure was forbidden, which seemed ironic coming from a man who beat him regularly with a belt from the ages of three to fourteen. When his father, assigned by his mother, tried to tell Yitzhak the so-called facts of his life, Yitzhak pretended to know them already. And this was a great relief to his father who could not know that Yitzhak was instinctively terrified to hear the terms of human physical pleasure and their meaning from a man who so devotedly and enthusiastically inflicted tortuously painful punishments on him.

His father would not stop beating him until Yitzhak's screams at some point shattered the trance that held his abuser in thrall. At a juncture of sorrow and suffering the father would sometimes recognize his blows were falling on his own flesh, his own creation and that, like the Christian God, the father was sacrificing his son to free the world of sin. Such a metaphor was an anathema to an Irish Jew and his father stopped though he never asked forgiveness.

Now his father could not speak, could not strike out, could do nothing but laboriously telegraph with a pointer the simplest words for his most basic needs. And while he was at home, it fell to Yitzhak to interpret these needs and to find some way to meet them when in his heart Yitzhak had all he could do to resist an urge to break his father's pointer into two pieces and to use each to fiercely pummel him.

Yitzhak's aunt Rebecca and her husband drove over from their home in Tracy to spend the day with Rebecca's horribly stricken brother. Their visit leavened the preparations of a Thanksgiving dinner and cheered Yitzhak's father into a tiring alternation of squeaks, wails and guttural cries.

Rebecca embraced him and sat with him through dinner, a kind gesture that reliably calmed Yitzhak's father and permitted the fulfillment of a traditional holiday meal. The warm sharing of food and family news lasted almost an hour until a fecal smell alerted first Yitzhak and then his mother to a small crisis in the making. The face of Yitzhak's father melted into the helpless grunting look of a two-year-old in trouble while Yitzhak's sister leaped from the table to wheel her burbling father away.

"He wants to tell us so much," said Yitzhak's mother. "He tries so hard to say what he needs. And he can't. I wonder how he must struggle to express his brilliant insights and theories. He is—he was—

one of the world's regarded and gifted mathematicians. It must be so discouraging. It breaks my heart."

Yitzhak's mother began to cry. Yitzhak did not rise to comfort her. That was left at last to Hannah who stood and walked to hold the mother in her arms, forming a pietá of womanly support while she looked quizzically at Yitzhak as if to ask *Where are you? What are you thinking? This is your mother and she is suffering.*

"I don't care," Yitzhak announced coldly, as if anticipating Hannah's question.

"And why should I care? Give me one reason why I should care about their misery. They aren't the people. They aren't the poor and suffering. Their suffering is nothing compared to the suffering of the people."

Yitzhak pushed his chair away from the table; aware he had smashed Thanksgiving into irreparable and hurtful chaos. He left the table and locked himself in his room, an old strategy of youth that kept everyone out of his life no matter how hard they knocked or how loud they yelled.

Except today no one knocked and no one yelled, leading Yitzhak to go to the door and press his ear to it. He heard the sonorous and sympathetic voices of Aunt Rebecca and her husband but could not make out their words or the sharper words of his mother.

"Raymond's just crazy, that's all," Hannah shouted loudly as if she intended Yitzhak to hear.

"He's a drug addict. He's no help. And if he won't help I wish he'd just go away and leave us alone."

Yitzhak heard his mother mumble something. He also heard again the kind and sonorous voices of his aunt and uncle that seemed to fade into the distance and then vanish through the opening and closing of the front door. And then it was quiet. He heard the sounds of someone clearing the table and more noise in the kitchen including the seemingly interminable running of water until an hour passed and then another and there were no more noises or voices.

Things came and went forever and nothing happened. Yitzhak waited until after midnight to slip out of his family home and to drive back into town determined never to return. He went to Mack's apartment and knocked but no one answered. He waited in his car at the corner until shortly after 10 o'clock Inger's Opel turned the corner and slithered between two large cars into a shortened parking space. Yitzhak met her at the building entrance and walked upstairs with her.

Yitzhak asked if he could spend the night and he could. Inger had no qualms and asked Yitzhak if he wanted Mack's apartment for himself.

"We need to get moving," said Inger. "We have about ten days left. Do you want the place? I need to tell the landlord by Monday."

Yitzhak knew he could not afford to rent Mack's apartment. But he said nothing. The occupation of his own body seemed a provisional residency and one that could end quickly with dissolution, dispersal and the destruction of what felt increasingly like an incoherent collection of cells. There was no lease on anything, including his life that Yitzhak ever would sign.

nine

If Yitzhak had a choice about his conception he might have given no as his answer. He had reasons to believe his parents did not want his birth and that therefore his life was not a welcome intrusion into theirs. His sister had been welcomed. He was a young and loving member of the welcoming that embraced her six years after his own birth. And she was never beaten. She was never told how noisome or loud or obnoxious she was.

She was loved deeply and particularly by the father that so consistently disparaged the presence of his son. The empty space Yitzhak occupied inside his mind was emptiness without end. It was his great reality.

Monday was the first day of December and the Indians still held Alcatraz. They had occupied the island for nearly a dozen days and the white man's government, from which Richard Oakes and his supporters were taking back the abandoned land of their fathers and mothers, appeared incapable of acting.

"He doesn't want to start another war now," Ramona said

referring to the President.

"Nixon is a shark, of course. He's probably just biding his time."

If resistance were ultimately futile, it didn't matter to Ramona, who saw in the Alcatraz rebellion the origin of every previous and momentous outbreak of human resistance to conquest.

"Ours is a simpler fight," said Ramona. "And one with greater width. There are a lot of people who are told they are crazy just for feeling a righteous anger. Our march will speak to them. And they will speak back."

Yitzhak wasn't so certain. In his world it was not possible to pick a flower without disturbing the stars. His madness was his dearest possession, since he had no others. And his madness spoke truthfully. He was sucked in, drawn down and pulled and dragged in countless directions. He also was kept out and distant from experience in ways that might cause him to perish from exhaustion. He was frantic, impotent and helpless. As a result he rode on the back of Ramona's pure vision but worried persistently it could not last.

Though her plan was simple and might work. She had won the commitment of nearly a hundred Berkeley street people and their friends to board trans-bay buses early on Saturday and arrive together downtown where they would take public transit to Golden Gate Park and meet in a grove at the park's northwestern quadrant near Haight Street. Stephen had announced the march's meeting place at his Monday Night class, which Ramona thought would assure a large and angry crowd for the Mad March.

"We'll have more than the tribe that took Alcatraz," said Ramona. "We're gonna make some noise."

Yitzhak tried to discard all his imaginary judgments. It might work. Ramona's might be an effort worth making though it still felt estranging to put himself in the role of bragging about his madness and the madness of others. As Ramona said, each was mad in his or her own way. And he had taken comfort from a vaguely successful mastery of his madness that kept hidden any evidence of its vast and deep power over him.

There was no such thing as harmless evil. And Yitzhak weighed his complicity with trouble against the mission of the Mad March. He was not a good person and did not expect anyone to think he was. He had no pretension of excellence. His parents saw to that. But his goal now was to grow in some fecund place where the despair of his childhood would disappear as a memory buried under the flourishing of a new bloom. He knew drugs were essential to keeping him focused on the one mission left and the one that might redeem him: his place at the head of a mad march for the people.

Ramona did not care that Yitzhak spent nights sleeping on the floor of Inger's apartment. She liked to screw him but never expected him to be her exclusive partner anymore than she would try to be his. There was fluidity to life on the streets by which each moment and its intersection with each individual was unique and exceptional. Ramona had her lovers at the Parker House and Yitzhak did not care anymore than she did that others shared her body with him. It was cool, man. It was hip to be cool. In fact, it was critical to be cool because there was ultimately nothing that could secure for him an enduring attachment.

Though Yitzhak did imagine Ramona to be his friend. She spent two afternoons helping Yitzhak get a post office box and to switch the mailing of his disability check from his parents' home. While waiting at the social security office, they planned more Mad March logistics. The biggest challenge was to be certain everyone took the right buses, knew where to get off and where to meet in the park. Ramona had some help from Free Clinic staff that allowed her to use a mimeograph machine to print out flyers with routes and instructions for marchers.

It was a great plan until it wasn't. On Wednesday the city of San Francisco announced it would not issue a permit for the Stones' free concert. Officials were worried the concert would interfere with a scheduled football game between the 49ers and the Chicago Bears to be held the same day at the park's Kezar Stadium. The next choice was a car racetrack in Sonoma County but the owners wanted $300,000 in advance and all the movie rights to the concert. Ramona and Yitzhak awoke Friday morning to learn Saturday's free concert would be held at the Altamont Speedway near Livermore, well east of Oakland and inaccessible by public transit.

"Are we fucked or what?" Yitzhak shouted at Ramona as they watched the TV news at Parker Street.

"How can we get everyone to this concert if they can't take the bus?"

"How many people does your car hold?" asked Ramona.

"Five, I guess," said Yitzhak.

"We could get seven or eight in it. And what if we made two or even three trips? Picked up people the night before? We could sleep out at Altamont if we had to. It's a racetrack. Is there a gate? We could wait outside the gate. Anyway, three car trips and we've got maybe 20 people. Three or four cars and with the whole night to bring people out we could get a hundred out there, no sweat. We just need a few more cars and a place for everyone to meet. Damn. It will be easier than taking a bus. Free rides to the Stones concert for those joining the Mad March. Is that cool?"

The proof was always in the pudding and Yitzhak, while he remained skeptical, knew better than to doubt Ramona's confidence in any plan. She left the living room to make phone calls from the kitchen. After an hour she returned with a short list of four drivers that would be willing to make one or two trips from Berkeley to Altamont. Dutch had a friend with a Volkswagen bus that could hold 8-10 easy. She had a list of people signed up for the march and said she would contact all of them to change the meeting place from a downtown bus stop to the curb at Bancroft and Telegraph. And she would have to give up on those coming from the City though it occurred to her that a sign at the concert might be enough to attract more marchers.

And she was stoned. Yitzhak felt her speedy energy and sensed all the symptoms of a meth high. He encouraged her to move fast. He knew that once her high was spent she would become petulant, erosive and splenetic.

Yitzhak had his doubts but on Friday night he gave Ramona his car keys and let her drop him and a few marchers off at the end of the long road above the Altamont speedway. It was nearly dusk and already the road was lined with parked cars, vans and trucks. A makeshift campground had formed on a naked hill leading into the raceway where cars pulled off the road to park. Yitzhak staked his claim to a circle of earth blooming with grassy green stubble and posted a sign that read *Mad March.*

In the distance below him he saw through a cyclone fence the speedway's tapered hill that fell gently toward a giant stage at the lowest point of a narrow, flat valley. Dutch and Michael rolled out their sleeping bags and Joanie and Annie put up a pup tent. Joanie had brought a bag of food she said was donated by the Garden Spot market on Telegraph.

"Where do we pee?" asked Joanie.

Yitzhak pointed toward a short row of portable potties lined up at the road though he knew people were pissing and shitting wherever they could. Yitzhak asked Michael to watch his backpack while he wandered the campsite where a few thousand had already arrived for the concert.

Yitzhak had broken his kilo into ounces and bagged them for quick sale. He planned to dump his inferior dope for cost and basically break even. His experience at the Tenino festival convinced him he could pass off his bad dope to strangers without having to worry about payback. He made several quick sales before returning to the Mad March campsite where another group had been dropped by Ramona and three other drivers. He counted nearly twenty new arrivals and it wasn't yet dark.

Dutch brought some whiskey and sat up to drink with Yitzhak as they watched the parade of shadows formed by those arriving for the concert. After midnight, Yitzhak rolled onto his sleeping bag and fell asleep. At dawn Ramona staggered into the camp with seven additional marchers.

"We're three miles down the road," she said as she looked around at the gathering crowd.

"It's bizarre out there, man. Never seen so many heads in one place."

Yitzhak looked up to see waves of people arriving over the short hill separating their disorderly camp from the road. A roar of motorcycle engines announced the arrival of a gang. More than a dozen riders in single file chugged their bikes slowly like a river of black treacle streaming toward the speedway gate, down the hill and toward the stage.

"Hell's Angels. Shit," said Dutch. "What are they doin' here?

Where are the cops?"

"They *are* the cops," said Ramona. "The Stones hired them."

The line of bikers rolled forward, the rider at the front blinded by the low morning sun while he pushed his tire against anyone who stood in the way. They flowed forward and plunged into the deeper densities of people gathering at the gate, which was opened for them by someone inside. They rolled down the hill and toward the stage.

Ramona and Yitzhak counted thirty-seven marchers gathered with them at their camp. Ramona had brought a half-dozen signs stapled to thin, light wooden planks. The signs read *I'm Mad!* with the sub-line *Don't call me crazy*. Ramona and Yitzhak each kept one and gave the others to Michael, Dutch, Joanie and Annie. Like Joanie, Ramona had brought food but no water.

As the sun climbed in the sky the temperatures warmed and their friends, sitting on the grass as crowds of people surged pass them, said they were thirsty. Yitzhak walked out to find water and confronted a group in front of a trailer with several plastic water jugs stacked outside.

"We'll sell ya' water," said the hippie in charge.

"What'll you pay?"

Yitzhak offered one of his ounces.

"Cool, man. You're a brother, for sure."

Yitzhak carried two five-gallon jugs back to the Mad March encampment that by now had been swallowed up in a pack of people growing like a cellular cancer out from the speedway.

"What the fuck do we do now?" Yitzhak asked Ramona. "We can barely move and we're a long way from…"

He pointed towards two giant speakers mounted to towers on either side of the stage and that immediately exploded with the sounds of rock 'n' roll, even though no band appeared. The tune and lyrics were familiar, a ranting ballad about "folks born made to wave the flag but It ain't me, ain't me…I'm no Senator's son, I'm no fortunate one…"

"Creedence," said Dutch. "Fortunate Son…Creedence isn't here today. The Stones are trying to warm us up or cool us down. This is a pretty insane crowd."

"Then it's just right for us," said Ramona. "Though we probably aren't the craziest people here."

By noon the sun was past its zenith and the still-growing crowd was restless. At once, the gate was opened and thousands began to pour through, a mass of bodies that like boundless hot lava oozed toward the stage. Most everyone who entered became trapped in the shallow bowl of the speedway where they passed the time by getting stoned or getting angry, and so did the Mad Marchers. This left Yitzhak and Ramona to hold the marchers together while they each tried to defend their space among the tens of thousands crushing in around them.

Early afternoon arrived, the winter sun already low at the western horizon of the valley's coastal hills. A woman walked by passing out flyers for the Panther Defense Fund and holding out a can for donations.

"On Thursday the cops killed Freddie Hampton in Chicago! It's a god damned murder!" she shouted, her eyes brimming with tears.

Yitzhak knew from Mack that Larry had gone back to Chicago to work with Freddie and the Panthers. Yitzhak gave her a dollar.

Santana climbed onto the stage and began to play. As the concert opened, a roar spread like a slow motion sound wave from the front of the crowd to the back. A fight broke out in front of the short stage and three Hell's Angels jumped into the crowd to beat people back.

The Jefferson Airplane followed Santana to the stage and another motorcycle club, gathered at the top of a hill and waving a Nazi flag, made its move, riding like the Angels single file through the crowd and toward the stage.

"Get in behind them!" Ramona shouted to the mad marchers who could still hear her.

"We're going. Now!"

If Yitzhak thought about it, he could envision himself entrapped in a social reality so ugly it could not possibly be worth celebrating. Beauty, to be possible in this instant of time, would have to be a lie. He passed a couple fucking in the trampled grass, the man on top as with one free hand he held the leash of a confused Doberman. Yitzhak decided to approach the stage in a spirit of innocence, truth and love as if it were possible and even likely it would make no difference.

He held up his sign and led the people forward behind the bikers. How many followed he could not say. He never knew. He marched with his sign, pushing through an ever more tightly packed crowd as they approached the stage, stopping frequently to reassemble and wait for others. It seemed to take hours. At some point it was nearly evening and December's quickly fading sunlight dissolved into darkness just as the Stones appeared.

By the time he arrived near the stage, Yitzhak could no longer see anyone behind him. He focused, instead, on Mick who danced and strutted wildly as he sang *Street Fighting Man*. Yitzhak searched momentarily for Ramona as if she might be able to tell him anything. He could not find her. He could not find anyone. He saw only a fat, naked woman make an effort to climb the stage.

He followed her; his eyes on Mick who he knew had made contact with him. A Hell's Angel appeared and furiously pushed the woman back off the stage. As she fell, Yitzhak braced to catch her. He would catch anyone who needed catching. He was a man of the people. From the corner of his peripheral vision he saw a black man in a lime green suit rush forward. The man was set upon and a knife slashed the air. Yitzhak turned to watch before experiencing the sensation of lightning striking him and then a dizzying slashing sensation of deep, sorrowing pain. He tried to stand with the people and, instead, fell forward. He tasted dirt and heard nothing.

Yitzhak had been acted upon, much as he had been by his family: coerced, blackmailed, made guilty and left scarred and in pain. The *we* of the people was simply himself now, the *we* abandoned by the people. It also was the *we* of his mind again telling him that there was no *we* that could be trusted and no *I* he could grasp as his own.

"You took a hit," said the man wearing a white shirt and pants. He said he was a nurse.

Yitzhak's eyes were open and he knew enough to realize he was in a hospital or a clinic, bright lights everywhere and with someone in charge of him sitting at his bedside.

"You're going to be OK, but you'll need some rest. We phoned your mom."

It was not what Yitzhak wanted to hear.

"Where am I?" he asked. "What happened?"

"Smashed with a pool cue, I think," said the man in white. "Not alone. We've had more than forty tonight from Altamont. We got you an hour ago in an ambulance. Good thing. You were bleeding and really out of it. A few stitches but a lot of blood. You'll need to see your doctor next week or come back here so we can change the bandage and check the wound."

"What now?" asked Yitzhak.

"We'll release you to your mom. Found her through your driver's license. You're in Livermore right now. She'll be here in about a half hour and she'll take you home. Want to get dressed?"

Yitzhak nodded and the nurse helped him up.

"Where's Ramona?" asked Yitzhak.

"Who?" asked the man in white.

"The people. Where are they?" Yitzhak asked again.

"No one followed you," said the nurse. "If that's what you mean. Just you and me, kid."

The man in white was trying to be funny which suggested to Yitzhak his injury wasn't serious.

Yitzhak was helped into a bathroom where he dressed in his clothes, including his long-sleeved shirt now speckled with dried bloodstains.

"I'll wait with you," said the nurse as he handed Yitzhak his wallet.

He escorted Yitzhak to a waiting area outside the emergency room of what appeared to be either a large clinic or a small hospital.

"I'll get your papers," he said. "Your mother will need to sign you out."

The nurse stood with his back to Yitzhak and walked toward the nurses' station. Yitzhak also stood and, as a woman passed pushing a man in a wheelchair, Yitzhak joined in behind them, walking at their slow, labored pace toward the exit. Once there, Yitzhak ran. He did not look back. In a few minutes he was blocks away. It was dark and the night, as it had been for many years of his life, was his guardian, a safe and bottomless scape again open to igneous dreams of all possible things.

Yitzhak did not know nor did know the truth. He waited for the morning like a fugitive awaits arrest. He was cold, his head bandaged with white gauze taped and bound over two-thirds of his scalp. It felt like a hat but he worried it appeared more like the badge that identified him as a wounded victim and at risk of exploding.

He had his wallet but had left his jacket in the hospital waiting room. He wanted his car and knew he would need to find Ramona to reclaim it. And he was in Livermore. If anyone were looking for him now, he would not be hard to find.

Yitzhak hid behind a building near a bus stop. When the bus arrived, Yitzhak ran to board it. He asked the driver for directions to Oakland and was rewarded with a printed schedule and the promise he would be dropped at the appropriate stop to make his connection.

It was mid-morning when Yitzhak stepped off the 51 bus in Berkeley. He had left at least a half-pound of dope in his jacket at the hospital, assuming the dope made it even that far. If it had, he would need to lay low. The cops would be looking for him. He thought Ramona could hide him for a day. He would shower and lick his wounds at the Parker Street house. He would get his car back and start his life fresh. It was what he always did and what he thought he always would do, even now as the range of his free movement seemed increasingly restricted to the time of dark nights and the space of small rooms.

He arrived at the Parker Street house to see his Chevelle parked in the driveway. He knocked on the door and was admitted to the kitchen where he surprised Ramona.

"Where have you been?" Ramona asked Yitzhak.

Yitzhak could have asked her the same question. Instead he asked her what had happened.

"You were there and then you weren't," he said.

"We followed you," said Ramona. "But they told us there wasn't anything we could do. So we came home."

Ramona was lying. No one followed Yitzhak anywhere. No one appeared to see him or to identify him or to help him.

"That's bullshit," said Yitzhak. "I want my car keys."

Ramona was high again. It was ten in the morning and she was wound up on meth like a tight spring. Her eyes fluttered in the way Yitzhak knew telegraphed a festering hostility that would soon enough pour out and all over him. He braced himself.

"I was hoping you'd let me use your car this week," said Ramona. "I'll give it back on Saturday. I promise."

"What for?" he asked.

"March stuff," said Ramona, weak and incapable of manufacturing a lie for someone who would not ever again believe her.

"The march was all fucked up," said Yitzhak. "No…I need my car. I need it right now."

Ramona already had dismissed from her memory every betrayal and every endangering experience of the past week. She was on this new day after Altamont in a new state of mind and saw nothing in the past, not even herself. She did not understand, from her anxious and speedy high, that Yitzhak could see clearly through her attempt to claim his car.

Yitzhak wondered if the entire march idea was a ruse to endanger him and to steal from him. The specifics did not corroborate with a plot but that never stopped his vigilance from seizing on the terror of any uncomfortable experience.

"Give me my keys!" Yitzhak shouted at Ramona.

His loud voice attracted the attention of others in the house. They turned to see what was happening and Ramona recognized that Yitzhak's demand had put her suddenly under scrutiny. What would she do? Everyone was watching.

"Just a minute," Ramona said.

She went upstairs and vanished for several minutes while Yitzhak waited nervously under the immobile, quiet stares of Ramona's roommates. Finally, she appeared at the top of the stairwell and hurled a bob of keys down at Yitzhak who stumbled in an effort to catch them.

"Take your fucking car!" shouted Ramona. "Take your car and get out of here!"

Yitzhak picked up the keys, realizing that Ramona was gone now. There was no point at which she would turn back. There was not a next-time-I'll-be-better, or a next year, or next life. This was really it. And Ramona was high enough to risk losing even this little thing, this home where she at last lived.

"Thanks," said Yitzhak, hoping to dampen any worries of her fellow Parker Street tenants.

"You take care of yourself, Ramona. It's cool. It's all cool."

Yitzhak's calm departure quelled Ramona's anger and seemed to soothe the other residents who resumed their respective movements through various doors and rooms. Whatever anyone feared might happen did not happen, so all worries could at last be lost and forgotten.

Yitzhak drove by Mack's apartment but Inger's Opel was gone and though it was Sunday night, he decided to wait until Monday to see her. He drove back to Tilden Park and found a dark pull-out on a public street that straddled the forest. He fell asleep under the stars and also under the soporific influence of a sleepless weekend, as well as the hospital's strong meds.

He was unprotected and could not hide behind high fences like the rich and successful. The richest were the farthest away from any type of threat and Yitzhak felt the closest. He could not keep harm away but still slept fearlessly. He was injured and too exhausted to nurse any of his deep wounds. It was time to wait. Time to hide like a hunted animal until another turn of the world illuminated a path back to safety. He knew he was sick. He knew that both his body and his mind were damaged. But healers were no help with their salves and diagnoses that only allowed him to feel afflicted in new ways, though he knew he was not yet annihilated. He was simply empty.

Yitzhak awoke in his car, constrained by thoughts of both his past and his future. Within the slender envelope that was the present, he drove again to Mack's apartment and saw that Inger's Opel was parked at the corner. He would get a jacket and some clean clothes he had left in her closet. He would shower and trim his beard. He would deal with his wound and likely rest and spend the night and worry about his next steps later. He walked into the building and without knocking opened the apartment's unlocked door.

He saw Mack sitting at the kitchen table with Inger. Both

appeared surprised to see him.

"What are you doing here?" Inger asked.

Yitzhak looked again at Mack.

"Are you talking to me?" Yitzhak asked Inger. "Where did he come from?"

Yitzhak heard himself refer to Mack in the third person, as if he were a ghost or shadow not really present in the room, a person, perhaps, but not a reality.

"Passing through, Yitzhak," said Mack. "On my way south to see my parents for Christmas. Probably for the last time. I live in Canada now. Got a low number in the draft lottery last week so there's no chance I'll return until this damned war is over. "

"What happened to your head?" Inger asked Yitzhak.

Yitzhak reached to touch the bandage; something he no longer felt was different from any other part of his body.

"Altamont," said Yitzhak. "A bad trip."

"Yours or someone else's?" asked Mack.

"Hell's Angels," Yitzhak said. "They beat the crap out of people. The people. I got in the way."

"We've been reading about Altamont," said Mack, holding up a copy of the morning Chronicle.

"More than a hundred got beaten. Four were killed and three babies were born? Who goes to a rock festival so pregnant they have their baby there? Must have been a busy night for the medics and the hospitals."

Yitzhak nodded.

"And this guy Manson, Charles Manson and his family in LA… arrested for the Tate-LaBianca murders. Inger knows him."

"Mack…come on," Inger demurred, turning away.

She did not wish to talk about it. She did not want to admit that the man named Charlie that Harriet had connected her with at her friend's apartment in the city, that this Charlie she traveled to see in LA with Sadie and with whom she lived for a month and with whom she shared her body, was this same Charles that allegedly orchestrated the violent deaths of seven strangers, including a very pregnant movie star. These were bloody, grisly murders involving knives and torture and it was still a developing shock for Inger to confront what felt to her like a peripheral complicity.

"It's awful, Mack," she said. "Please, just drop it. Just stop."

Inger turned again to look at Yitzhak.

"That looks like a bad wound," she said pointing to his head. "Still oozing…?"

She stood to touch his bandage but Yitzhak bobbed and danced away.

"It's fine. I'm fine," he said.

"Let me get you a hat," said Inger.

She went to the hall closet and pulled out a blue ski cap.

"Here," she said. "I'm leaving Thursday."

Yitzhak took the cap from her and held it as if it were an awkward token of her concern for him.

"You know, the place has been rented," Inger added. "You never let me know and the landlord couldn't wait any longer."

Yitzhak nodded vaguely. He understood.

"And one other thing," Inger said, looking directly into Yitzhak's eyes. "Mack says he wrote me a letter. Did you ever see a letter from him while you were staying here?"

"I need some clothes," said Yitzhak, ignoring her question.

He hurried to the bedroom closet where he grabbed a sweatshirt, ripped two shirts from their hangars and found a clean pair of socks. He would not answer Inger. He knew lies were involved but could not remember which ones.

Yitzhak trotted to the door and Mack followed.

"Hey man, we need to talk. Where you going?"

Yitzhak did not look back. He opened the door, stepped outside and closed it quickly. He bounced down two flights of stairs and ran to his car.

"I'll call you, man!" Mack shouted.

Yitzhak ignored him. There were many ways by which things were emptied and those he no longer could see or hear were the emptiest of all.

Fear was the operative street response to the terror of existence. Each new day Yitzhak lived on the streets was a new beginning. But whatever began was subject to breakdown and had little chance of completion. Yitzhak wore Inger's stocking cap as if it were a clever disguise. He at first feared he was the object of a police search but a cop car passed him on the Avenue and did not stop. Still, Yitzhak wanted to run. He had his car and could drive anywhere. He imagined a destination where he would never be found.

Yitzhak approached Crazy Pete in front of Cody's.

"You want to go to Big Sur with me?" Yitzhak asked him.

"You crazy, man?" Pete said as he held out his palm to catch imaginary raindrops.

"Storm is coming in tomorrow. Bad weather for a camping trip. No fucking way."

Pete noticed that Yitzhak looked tired and that his face was pale.

"You OK, man?" Pete asked.

"I'm cool," said Yitzhak.

"I took a hit at Altamont last Saturday."

He tilted back his cap to show Pete a corner of his head bandage.

"Ouch," said Pete. "Don't look so good. You seen a doctor?"

"A doctor bandaged me," said Yitzhak. "I'm fine."

"Whatever you say," said Pete. "But you might want to let that heal before going to Big Sur in December."

Yitzhak thanked Pete and entered the Forum where he ate a last breakfast in Berkeley. After finishing his coffee Yitzhak walked to the Garden Spot and bought a jug of water, a six-pack of beer and some groceries. By noon he was south of San Jose and by mid-afternoon he passed Point Lobos south of Carmel and wound along Highway One toward Lucia. Just as the sun set, Yitzhak parked near the Pacific Valley trailhead and hiked along a creek that dropped from a steep ridge and down to the old stone house by the sea. It was empty but someone had been there recently and left a pile of sawed up plywood remnants that he could use for a fire.

Yitzhak put his food bag on a shelf and struggled back to his car in the fading twilight to retrieve his bottle of water and a blanket he stored in the trunk. He was tired and felt dizzy as he slid cautiously back down the trail. He managed to start a fire that warmed him as he ate a dinner of potato chips and cheese. He opened a beer and hoped it would both quench his thirst and relieve a throbbing headache. He climbed onto the cabin's sleeping platform and wrapped himself in his blanket. He heard first the lenient ping of raindrops against the house's tin roof until they grew heavier and faster and became a torrent of splashing fury. A wind whistled through the roof slats above him. He could hear the branches of pine trees moving in the mist.

Dawn's cool dampness stirred Yitzhak to poke the last dying coals of his fire and to throw more scraps of wood on it. He could not say how long he would stay here. He might die here and though the idea at first frightened him he realized he was a fragile identity and not a thing. Identities held their ground for a moment while things lasted forever.

And this place and this moment were all he wanted now. His headache was gone though he shook with a chill and thought no number of blankets would ever again warm him. But by mid-morning the storm had passed and the sun felt hot enough on his face to draw him to a perch just outside the house where, wrapped in his blanket, he could watch walls of high waves smash against the rocks.

Later he found the foil he kept in his pocket and withdrew it. It contained the last two hits of Biggie's acid. Yitzhak did not hesitate. He swallowed one and set the other in a small crevice inside the door of the stone house. His body and mind opened in the way he had expected and, while he still felt enormous pain behind his eyes, after an hour it no longer seemed important. Slowly he lost all sensation of hot or cold and realized he had been emptied of everything including any conception of emptiness. There was no present moment and there was no eternity. He was comfortable in a cool, dark space and sailing forward on a sea of joy far from the usual gnashing and thrashing of his mind.

He felt as if hypnotized and thought momentarily he might have stopped breathing. As the sun fell into the ocean Yitzhak retreated again to the house and, still wrapped in his blanket, felt too tired to start a fire. He shivered in the darkness but was not worried. Another day was coming and indeed dawn broke and the sun again warmed his face though he could not rise, could not move from his prone, safe place.

He waited this day out, passed it entirely as the fallen man he was. He reached for his grocery bag and tried chewing on another piece of cheese. Its rancid flavor and texture of coagulated cream revolted him and he spit it out. He crawled over to the water bottle and tipped its mouth into his. He drank deeply before falling backward in ecstatic exhaustion. He decided to wait and could not think for what.

Yitzhak's thoughts were like the dirt on the floor of his stone house. Wherever he moved they smudged and irritated him. He was filthy with thoughts and in the vacant foggy glow of another morning he realized he was no longer hungry. He peeled another beer out of the six-pack and drank half of it instantly. He then reached for the foil in the crevice and swallowed his last tab of acid.

His eyes swept the horizon for an ancient vision but continually he was redirected within where a host of cheerless impressions chewed on his bones and made every part of him ache to the core. He reached all the way out of himself but there was nothing to hold. He laughed. He wasn't anxious anymore. He was perhaps at the end of his assignment to a life not happily begun. He waited for a hard wind that might make the pines talk again.

"Yitzhak, Yitzhak," the familiar voice shouted.

"Hold on, brother. I got ya'."

Yitzhak heard the words and heard the voice. It was familiar. It was Mack or the hallucination of Mack. Yitzhak looked up to see his onetime friend's blinking, frantic eyes over him and staring deep into him. He perceived his friend was worried about something, and the seriousness of this concern at first frightened Yitzhak.

"Hold on, hold on," Mack kept muttering. "Your mom is looking for you. Pete told me you'd gone to Big Sur. I thought I'd find you here. Damn…"

Before finishing his thought Mack pulled the ski cap back from Yitzhak's head. Yitzhak watched as Mack's eyes bulged in fearful terror. Mack fell over Yitzhak and hugged him hard. Mack began to cry.

"Don't move," he said through a shaky sob. "I'll be back. We need help."

And then again there was a voiceless silence held indelibly above the building rhythm of winter's crashing waves. Mack was gone. Everyone was gone. Yitzhak was now the person who existed before he was born. But Yitzhak was not alone. He welcomed a brief and unexpected expression of the deep and abiding love that would outlive him. The entire ocean was a cool, inviting blue. He waited now and watched for the clouds to pass finally away.

Acknowledgements

This is a story drawn from the lives of people I knew and regarded during an era with a notable and controversial history. I am grateful to all of them for the experiences we shared and for all the ways we shared them. The years 1968 and 1969 marked a watershed in the life of an American Counterculture, with the San Francisco Bay Area a crucial locus of its creation as well as a key port of departure during its diaspora. It is the latter that drives the heart of this novel. I am also grateful to my dear wife and loving partner Claire Marie Beery, who unknown to me resided nearby in Berkeley during the time this novel is set and whose thorough and thoughtful editing has been a priceless contribution to both its clarity and verisimilitude. And as always I am indebted to the creative book design of A. Cort Sinnes and his beautiful cover that amplifies the novel's themes with my own photography from the era. A brilliant writer and artist, Cort specializes in creating and formatting the presentation of literature in stunningly elegant ways.